AN OPHELIA LEGACY NOVEL

OPHELIA

DEMONS & MONEY

SPENCER STONER

INDIGO

Livonia, Michigan

ALSO BY SPENCER STONER

THE OPHELIA LEGACY

BOOK 1
OPHELIA & LYAN ARE DEAD MEAT

BOOK 2
THE THIRD LIFE OF OPHELIA

MULTI-AUTHOR COLLECTIONS

IN CREEPS THE NIGHT
CONTAINS THE STORY "ON THE WAY HOME"

For my family.
They put up with a lot to make this happen.

Karen, Malia, and Pete, thank you for
reminding me that one question
can have three different answers!

DRAMATIS PERSONAE

IN THE TIME BEFORE...

Ophelia – A mercenary hired by the Romefeller Guild to escort the party back to the organization's headquarters in Emerald City. A heavy drinker and puncher.

Havarti – Sometimes Ophelia's conscience, sometimes her weapon. Okay, in all honesty, always her weapon since he is a living, sentient bastard sword.

Harbenigyr – A cleric of the Order of Kuan Yin. Probably the kindest elf you would ever meet, considering he was raised by dwarves.

Saya Kushrenada – An "Intelligence Officer" of the Romefeller Guild. An albino underground elf of a noble line. She knows it and you better treat her as such, too.

Folken Kizoku – One of the highest leaders of the Romefeller Guild. He knows more than he tells, sometimes telling people so that they know how foolish they truly are.

Josie Swithchild – A half-elf ranger hired as a guide for Folken. She's a dead-eye shot at shooting.

Lyan Yo Bunpy – A proud warrior of the Yo Bunpy tribe of Bunny Barbarians. More muscular than a typical woman and a vast majority of men.

Hero Von Yuy – A bard from the prestigious Edge School. She's hiding something unpleasant.

"Lily Cat" Lilicaitcydia – A wizard that specializes in horticultural magicks. She is also a lightweight in the drinking category.

Raiko de Junamend – A man who fights in sword duels for money. A bracer wrapped around his arm bonds him to Harbenigyr. If he dies, the cleric dies as well.

TWO DECADES LATER...

Appelonia – The daughter of the cleric Harbenigyr. The proverbial "Apple" of his eye. She inherited her looks from her mother, along with her impeccable aim with a bow and arrow.

Phinegann – A half-ogre, retired prison guard hired to accompany Appelonia. He's ready to move on from his past but his past isn't quite done with him.

Jonas the Shepherd – A human paladin of the Order of Stewart. He has a well developed sense of justice and a nicely shaped jaw.

Illyria Warflower – A gnome who likes to invent things. She wants to have a good look at some of the magic items for ideas to create new technology.

Jin Vega – A monk. What more do you want to know? He's bald and has a bushy beard?

Bronwyn La Rue – A thief who likes stuff and the group has a lot of it.

Genevieve – She joins the group later on, although her motivations are completely different from everyone else. Her hair stands straight up.

CHAPTER ONE

"I never said that I was proud about how all this started," Oph-elia said, "I mean, I know you wanted to hear everyone's side of the story but you're writing everything as if you were there observing. You weren't, were you?"

I assured her that I was not physically there. It was simply easier to write a report from a neutral point of view. I also assured Ophelia that I was not here to accuse her or anyone of any wrongdoing but sim-ply gather all the facts.

The subject then paced back and forth across the room several times before returning to face me. After a minute or so of silence, she decided to tell how she how the incident began...

OPHELIA HAD NOT been this drunk in a long time. As she downed yet another shot of the wood tinged, sweet tasting amber liquid she had to wonder: why was she still wearing pants?

The woman sat across the table from a man with silver hair that was trimmed short, just above the stubble stage on his head. He looked much younger than the impression his hair color gave. No matter his age, he was built from solid muscle. That was why Ophelia approached him to begin with.

The sleeves of his white shirt were rolled up, showing of his well defined forearms. His hands hovered on either side of the stack of shot glasses in front of him. They stretched up to his broad shoulders from the surface of the table that had at some point in its life been polished.

His hazel eyes stared in disbelief as Ophelia placed her now empty glass on the top of her own tower of glasses. The top reached just up to her chin.

At least, when she had been sitting up straight. The woman was decidedly not able to do that anymore. The main thing holding her upright at all was the elbow of her right sleeve, the leather was wedged between the flat slats as it rested on corner of the wooden table in front of her.

"Issn– isn't that a peach, Horta?" Ophelia snickered.

The woman pointed at her competitor and grinned triumphantly, giving a playful wink in his general direction. There seemed to be more than one of him now but Ophelia knew that was just an illusion caused by the liquor. At least she was pretty sure.

Speaking of people who could create illusions, Lily was sitting to Ophelia's left. The young wizard was already laying face down on the surface of the table. Her tightly curled hair shot out in every direction, obscuring the rest of her head from view and burying Lily's pitiful stack of three shot glasses in the unkempt nest.

She only joined in the drinking contest as a favor to Ophelia. Lily went up against Horta's buddy. His name was Andor, Ophelia was pretty sure. He was sitting across from the plump magic user earlier.

The only reminder that he had been there at all were the two shot glasses that rolled back and forth on their sides on the right half of the table. Andor was sleeping off his two shots of Ogre Hickory whiskey under the table, all but forgotten.

"Do you have a hollow tit or sumptin'?" Horta smirked back as he lifted the second to last glass on the table between unsure fingers.

"Nothing holl– hollow about them," Ophelia fell more than leaned back in her wooden chair, the tall back keeping her from toppling to the floor.

She pulled the red leather of her long coat apart so that Horta could get a good look at her chest. The green half-shirt that covered her upper torso was loosely laced up, giving the man an only partially obscured view of her cleavage.

"You wanna feel?" Ophelia invited him, a sudden hiccup making her entire body bounce.

She was hoping that the drinking contest was finally over and they could move on to the celebration. Honestly, who needed to drink so much to get someone into bed?

The vague control Horta had over his fingers faltered and the shot glass fell to the table, dumping its golden colored contents onto the flat surface. The liquid quickly spread across the wood, enough getting through Lily's hair to seep up the young woman's nose and cause her to jerk back into the land of the living.

"Tansy cakes!" Lily blurted out as she was suddenly upright and stiff as a tree trunk.

Just the mention of food made Ophelia's stomach threaten to let the whiskey she'd forced down make a return trip up. It made the mercenary second guess the wisdom of taking up this game that was supposed to be mere foreplay down in the bar to the, well, foreplay up in the room. Then the full on play. Finishing up with trying to get out of bed, dressed, and out of the room without waking Horta up in the morning.

The young wizard with the thick torso looked back and forth from the man to Ophelia at the table with her sheepishly. Her plump cheeks, already pink from the more-than-she-was-used-to amount of alcohol she drank, seemed to actually start to glow.

"Excuse me," Lily said slowly, being very careful to enunciate every syllable properly, "I think I will go up to my room now."

Ophelia and Horta both nodded in agreement as the wizard rose. Lily adjusted her black cloth corset over her tan cotton dress as she rose to her bare feet with utmost caution.

"Please, let me help," the man offered, starting to stand himself.

His calloused hands rose to wrap around the arm of the much shorter woman. Unfortunately, he had forgotten about the teetering tower of upended shot glasses and they tumbled over like a brittle, transparent tree.

The topmost glass shattered against the wood of the table. The rest rolled around like wandering drunkards, unable to figure out where they were going but not letting anything stop them from getting there. One shot glass reached the edge of the table and dived off. It hit Horta's boot, just avoiding a crushing fate.

It continued its travels under Lily's bare feet, making her lose her already precarious balance. The drunk man tried to wrap his arms around her, one getting around her bare arm and his other hand getting tangled in the soil hued curls of the woman's hair.

It was no use. Both of them were too fettered by booze to steady themselves, let alone another person, and they tumbled to the floor.

Ophelia caught herself laughing, biting her lower lip to stop herself. Pulling the braids that draped down either side of her face out of her line of sight, the mercenary slipped her head under the table to check on the two laid out drunkards.

"You okay down– down there?" She blinked her pale blue eyes, trying to get them to focus properly.

"Nothing hurt butmypride." Lily muttered, losing the elocution she tried so hard to maintain as she lifted herself to a sitting position.

It was more difficult than she thought it would be. Not because of her intoxicated state, but because Horta's calloused fingers were tangled within her hair.

With some quiet cursing and digit wiggling, his hand finally came free. But not without taking some wavy strands, soaked and sticky with alcohol, with it.

"Sorry," Horta mumbled.

Then he lifted himself to his feet with more dexterity than Ophelia thought he was capable of at the moment. Not to say that it was a perfect lift. He had the edge of the table in a vice grip with the hand not covered with Lily's hair.

He was back on his feet and steady. Despite that, he didn't try his luck with coming to the shorter woman's aid again.

"Perhaps, agerni– ajornin– Perhaps adjourning to our respective rooms for the night would be fer the best," Horta nodded at his own suggestion.

Ophelia bumped her head on the bottom of the table once before she was able to successfully straighten up in her seat. She was lucky that her own stack of glasses only ended up leaning precariously rather than follow the lead of the other shot glasses that fell before them. She grinned at the man as she carefully lifted herself up. Their heights were almost exactly the same.

"I thought you'd never get around to that love– lovely suggestion," she wiggled a finger at Horta in a way that she figured would be beckoning, if it was moving right.

"Oh yeah," his mouth spread into a wide grin that exposed his pristine teeth, "I did need to check for hollow parts, din't I?"

Horta made his way around the table. He wrapped his clean hand, unmarred by spilled liquor and sticky hair, to cradle Ophelia's cheek.

The woman's hands wrapped around his taut waist then slowly made their way up to his broad chest, "Well, there is at least one hollow spot that you might be able to–"

A piercing scream suddenly echoed through the entire tavern. Ophelia's attention snapped over to Lily, who was bent over and clutching the back of her chair. She looked back at Ophelia, equally clueless as to the source of the shriek.

Again the screeching cry filled every empty space within the building. It was coming from upstairs. After going through thick wood walls and floors, it should have sounded muffled but the scream was as clear as if the source was standing just beside Ophelia, Horta and Lily.

As the third screech started, Ophelia's drink addled brain recognized the voice. The shorter wizard came to the same conclusion and the women looked at each other in horror.

"Harbenigyr!" They both yelled.

Ophelia turned on her heel, her hand finding the edge of the table just beside theirs, to keep her balance. She hurried straight for the stairs that went up to the second floor and the rooms the tavern rented out. The mercenary didn't bother weave around the tables in her path. Ophelia simply shoved them aside, toppling drinks and making other patrons scramble out of her way.

Lily was right behind her. Usually, she would beg excuse from the displaced civilians unlucky enough to be in the way, but the worry that was so clearly etched on her face made her forget her proper demeanor.

Horta stared after them, a few stray strands of Ophelia's hair resting between the fingers of his formerly clean hand. Instead of going after the women, he kicked under the table.

The motion was answered with a burp that came from a very relaxed throat. A man dressed much like Horta emerged, finding his feet easier than the larger man had been able.

"I don't like the sound of that, Andor." Horta frowned at the other gray haired man before motioning to the door that led out to the street.

OPHELIA REACHED THE room she shared with the cleric and shoved the door open. Saya was already inside. Crouched over Harbenigyr, she was struggling to keep the thin elf still.

"Harby! Harby, can you tell me what's wrong?" Saya yelled once the other elf's latest wail subsided.

Her right hand, covered with a black leather glove that was buckled closed around her wrist, made the sheer opalescence that was the woman's albino skin stand out against even the white sheets that were crumpled under the woman and the cleric. The muscles in Saya's right arm strained with effort against the thrashing elf. Her left hand, however, held Harbenigyr's right shoulder against the worn planks without any sign of strain.

Unlike the right glove, the one on Saya's left arm covered most of her pale limb. It ended at the woman's shoulder with thin pink scars emerging from the black leather, looking out of place against the snow white skin. Ophelia wondered why she had never noticed them before.

The only answer to Saya's question that Harbenigyr could give was another pained scream. The spindly elf's back arched and Ophelia saw that the cleric wasn't clothed.

The only thing on his body to protect his modesty was a simple loin cloth. That and the pewter cuff wrapped around his left arm. It was enchanted in a way that made it so he could never take it off.

Harby's eyes, usually radiating with kindness, were shut so tightly that it seemed the lids were crushing the wet spheres under them. His shoulder length black hair was strewn all around, sweat making it stick to his face as Harby cried out.

Saya was about acknowledge the other women who just arrived when she glanced back down and let out a surprised shriek of her own. Blood was suddenly welling out of what looked like a burn on his chest.

"Lily! What's happening to him?" her tone had only a touch of the usual regal demeanor with which she usually ordered others in the party.

At the mention of her name, the short wizard dashed around Ophelia and dropped to her knees on the opposite side of the cleric. Lily leaned her own weight onto the cleric, helping pin him to the floor as she squinted down at the oozing wounds forming on Harby's torso.

She reached into one the the many pouches on the belt around her stocky waist, pulling out a fibrous root and lifting it to her mouth. After three quick chews, Lily had to stop herself from retching.

Pulling the now paste-like root from her mouth, saliva stretched from the mass to the woman's lips. Lily blew a raspberry to clear the strings of spittle and tumbled sideways onto her rear end.

"I'm sorry. I never partook of whiskey before." She mumbled before she pressed the mound of moist plant matter against the first wound to open on Harby's chest.

"You're drunk, Lily?" Saya's violet eyes turned stern, "Now?"

"I was not aware that I would be treating wounds tonight, my Lady," the horticultural wizard stared down at the wound she was attempting to mend, her face a mask of guilt.

"It's my fault," Ophelia confessed, wrapping a hand around the doorjamb to steady herself, "A guy I was trying to pick up had a friend."

"I don't care!" Saya snapped, "You both had better get your wits together enough to figure out how to help him!"

The albino svartalfar, a species of elf from underground, motioned back down to Harbenigyr. The blood from the wound treated with Lily's root thickened up and stopped after only a few seconds but the wounds were opening faster than the woman was able to clot them.

"Where's Raiko?" a familiar voice popped into Ophelia's head, "At this time of night, he should have been with Lady Kushrenada but she came to Harby's aid alone."

A bastard sword leaned against the wall just beside the small set of drawers that served as the end table beside the lone bed in the room. The red jewel in the hilt shimmered, the light refracting from the surface differently every time a word was spoken, or rather thought, to Ophelia.

That's right. The mercenary had asked Harbenigyr to look after him while she drank that evening.

Ophelia stepped over to the sword and pulled it away from the wall, "That's a good question, Havarti. We should ask her," the woman thought the answer back to her bastard sword.

And she did just so to Saya. The albino woman looked confused but only a moment as her purple eyes moved toward the cuff on Harbenigyr's arm.

"He is celebrating his advancement to the semifinals in the tournament. He should be downstairs. Did you not see him?" Saya quirked a platinum eyebrow at the woman in the long red coat.

Ophelia shook her head. She had an idea of where he was, though. The mercenary made her way back downstairs.

The innkeeper was rushing up the stairs as the woman was marching downward. She grabbed the half-elf's arm to keep him from rushing up to Harbenigyr's room. He wouldn't be any help.

"Is the party in your back room still going on?" It came out more as a statement than a question.

"Y-yes, but I hardly see what that has to do with– yelp!"

Ophelia shoved him so that he spun around in place and stumbled back down the stairs. The only thing that saved him was the fact that he was sober and able to catch himself.

The woman actually lost her own footing and slid down two steps to end up beside the innkeeper. She quickly straightened herself up and again glared at the old man.

"Take me there," she ordered.

"Madam, that celebration is for an elite clientele–"

"Unless you want to join the death rattle chorus," she motioned back up the stairs before raising her arm and pointing downward, "you will get me in there. Now!"

The innkeeper nodded and quickly trotted down to the first floor. They had already straightened up most of the toppled furniture that Ophelia had left in her wake rushing to the cleric's aid.

Instead of a repeat performance, the woman wrapped a hand around the back of the half-elf's collar and used him for support as they made their way between the tables. Then they walked along the length of the bar until they reached the open portion that led to where the bartender served his drinks.

It was also where the door to the back room resided. It had a man who was as tall as the entryway standing in front of the curtain that obscured whatever was happening behind it. When the innkeeper and Ophelia neared, he straightened up and crossed his bulging arms over his steel encased chest.

His armor was immaculately polished. His skin was dark brown, like the chocolate cakes that Ophelia had found herself enjoying that were baked by the wife of the tavern owner. If she had seen this guard first, she might have tried to bed him instead of Horta. Unfortunately, he'd lost his chance when Ophelia went from being tipsy to an angry drunk.

"This is a private game," a voice that had a thick Wildevalean accent came from his mouth, "Piss off."

"This is an emergency." The old half-elf pointed back over his shoulder at the displeased looking woman in the long coat behind him.

"I need to speak to Raiko." Ophelia said simply.

"Don't know who this Raiko is and I don't care," the guard answered. "No one goes in."

The thing about armor is that it was designed to protect the wearer from attacks coming from the most common angles with the most common weapons. It couldn't protect everything from every direction without severely hindering the movement the fighting man or woman inside it.

While Ophelia's boot would generally be useless as a weapon, the codpiece of a suit of armor was designed to stop attacks from the front. Unfortunately for the guard with the sexy accent, her foot came and struck his testicles from below, actually sandwiching them between the stiff leather of her footwear and the unforgiving metal of his armor.

He fell to the ground in a heap, weeping in a language that didn't sound so sexy anymore. The innkeeper whimpered as a renewed fear of the woman swept over him. Ophelia let go of his collar and stepped over the armored man struggling to simply breathe.

The mercenary looked back over her shoulder as she pulled the curtain aside, "You heard him. Piss off," she said before stepping through the doorway.

Ophelia found herself in a narrow hallway. Keeping one hand on the wall to steady herself, she started walking. The first room was the restroom with holes sawed out of a long bench big enough for about a half dozen people to sit and do their business but not fall through.

Except for gnomes. Gnomes, being half the size of a typical human or elf, would have an unpleasant surprise if they tried to sit up there.

The next room was the innkeeper's personal sleeping quarters. His wife was already dead asleep and didn't even notice when the mercenary peeked in.

There was only one more door. Ophelia pushed it open and stepped inside.

Raiko de Junamend was there. He was sitting at the lone round table left in the middle of the room. All the others that usually filled this private banquet hall were on their sides, leaning against the far wall.

The duelist was shirtless, his long silver hair pinned between his bare, muscular back (which was facing Ophelia) and the wooden slats that made up the back of his chair. He wasn't alone. There were five other men around the circular table.

None of them wore shirts and Ophelia thought that a couple of them really should. On the table, well, not exactly on as much as floating several inches above the center was a black rock that was just barely small enough for a man to hold in one hand.

Raiko claimed to value it more than anything. He called it "Meteorend".

Of the three men Ophelia could see from the front, two of them had sores like the ones that were forming on Harbenigyr. But hey weren't as severe as the ones welling on the cleric's chest.

As the woman stepped closer, the one man whose flabby chest was completely smooth and uninjured jumped in surprise when he noticed her. That caused Raiko to turn and look back over his shoulder.

"What are *you* doing here?" he practically snarled.

"I was going to ask you the same thing, de Junamend," Ophelia answered. "I'm sure you could hear Harby screaming even in here."

The woman closed the remaining distance and was able to finally see the front of Raiko's body. He was as bloody as the cleric! Even the cuff that was wrapped around his right forearm was covered with his blood.

"No, I can honestly say that I haven't heard a sound muttered from that pathetic wood sucker." Raiko snapped back.

"Over your own screaming, you mean," the flabby man across the table chuckled.

Raiko's hazel eyes turned to stare him down, "That reminds me, Tybalt. Isn't it your bet?" he sneered.

"Ah, yes." Apprehension suddenly washed over the man, "With the lovely lady's arrival, perhaps we should call the game off?"

"She's no lady," Raiko scoffed as he shook his head, "and Meteorend can't be called off. You either bet or it broils you alive."

"You've been using your rock to play svartalfar roulette?" Ophelia ground her teeth at the realization.

"My rock. My money," the silver haired man answered, "My life."

"Not just yours, you ogre's ass!" the woman in red roared back. "That stupid bracer bonds you with Harby now, remember? He's trusting you to keep both of you safe and alive!"

Raiko nodded to Tybalt, "Bet or die."

Ophelia snapped a finger up to point at the fat man across the table, "Don't you dare!"

"But I don't want to die!" Tybalt protested, "This game started with six players. Vlad tried to run and Meteorend charred his bones!"

"I don't care. If you're bet causes the cleric this man is bonded to to die, you'll wish the rock had–"

"Triangle!" Tybalt blurted out before the mercenary could finish her threat.

The entire room filled with the smell of molten metal as Meteorend turned from obsidian black to casting an orange glow throughout the whole room. Tybalt unfolded the piece of paper he'd been holding in his palm and held it up.

"Blank, oh thank you merciful Juna!" he laughed with relief, "I'm safe!"

The man to the jubilant Tybalt's right unfolded his piece of paper, "Circle." He didn't look as relieved as the fat man before him. Then he turned his attention to the next contestant on his right.

The well built man, save for his entire right pectoral muscle being practically skinned unfolded the piece of parchment he held, "Blank." He held it up to show everyone else at the table before his body collapsed into a relaxed slump against the back of his seat.

The one with the circle piece of paper mirrored his reaction. All their attention turned to Raiko.

Ophelia hadn't even noticed the piece of parchment in his hand. She was still not quite able to stand steadily while Raiko stared into her pale blue eyes, as still as a mountain. Not even glancing down at the paper as he pulled it open, he held it up so that everyone else at the table could see it. Except Ophelia. The already quiet room fell into an unnatural hush.

"It's a triangle," Tybalt announced, then tension becoming too much for him.

Sparks flew from Meteorend toward Raiko. Ophelia dived to tackle the man and into the path of the burning projectiles.

Just as the first shard of metal started to singe the red leather of her coat, the mercenary suddenly found herself at the opposite end of the table, just beside Tybalt. She had blinked.

The magical defense mechanism Doctor Efreeti had imbued her body with jumped into action to save her, teleporting her out of the path of the threat Meteorend represented with its attack.

The molten sparks didn't hit Raiko either. Ophelia successfully knocked him over just before she disappeared. Harby was safe, at least for now.

"You are so lucky that I didn't bet square," the corpulent man said to the woman. "That outcome doesn't allow outside interference. You and Raiko would have both been killed."

"You're right," Ophelia nodded. "But I told you not to bet, didn't I?"

All the color drained from Tybalt's face. "Yes, but then *I* would have been killed. And Raiko didn't get hit so your cleric friend is safe, isn't he?"

The woman agreed, the nausea that should have come from nodding didn't happen. "You didn't know I was going to interfere."

Before the fat bastard could utter another word, Ophelia pulled Havarti free and chopped Tybalt's head from his slumped shoulders. As it hit the floor with a hollow sounding thunk, the black rock called Meteorend dropped onto the table and went still.

"I guess that means the game is over, boys," she announced, moving with a grace she was incapable of only moments before. "You don't have to go home but you can't stay here."

Ophelia again lifted Havarti, the blade slowly moving to point from one man at the table to the next. None of them were in the room before the tip of the bastard sword's blade made it to their position at the table. When it was only she and Raiko left in the wide room, she strode over to where he was still lying on the floor.

"You promised Saya that you wouldn't pull crap like this until we figured out how to get that damn thing off." She kicked the pewter cuff on his arm.

"My life is my own to do with as I please," Raiko groaned as he lifted himself to his feet, "I do not live my life at Saya's whim."

"Maybe not. But anything that happens to you happens to Harby," Ophelia frowned, "Not to mention that blinking makes me completely sober. So you made me waste an entire night of drinking *and* kept me from getting laid."

The man scowled back, "I'll take the relieved looks from all the men I pass on the way back to my room as thanks enough for sparing them your foul embrace."

"You're not going to have that bracer forever, Raiko." Ophelia slipped Havarti, who had already shaken Tybalt's blood from his surface, back into his scabbard hidden in the back of her long coat,

"When that comes off, you and I are going to cross blades and I guarantee that you will not walk away from it."

"You trust in that blinking trick too much, woman," Raiko answered, "I have no such weakness. I do not trust others, nor do I expect them to trust me, and I surely do not trust in something not of my own hand."

"That explains all the lonely nights you had before you met Saya," Ophelia sneered, "But you promised her that you would keep from doing anything that could harm Harby outside of your tournaments. What do you think she'll do when I tell her about this?"

"Saya will not do anything," he responded, "She knows that trust is for fools."

OPHELIA INTERROGATION NOTES

"Okay, from here it's going to get a little complicated. If you want to understand everything, I have to jump ahead a bit."

"To what end?" I inquired.

"Appelonia was privy to everything that led up to us being here," Ophelia said.

"Are you sure that you can keep two divergent trains of thought coordinated?" I was personally skeptical but I did not say so vocally.

"I'm confident it will all make sense by the end," Ophelia assured me, albeit with an uncertain grin on her face, "But what Raiko said made me remember who was referring to with his remark..."

Two decades (and a lot of change) later...

Harbenigyr, the Grand Cleric of the Order of Kuan Yin, said, "Now remember, Phinegann, I am trusting you with that which is most precious to me, my daughter. Specifically, with her safety."

The man addressed as Phinegann stood stiffly in front of the two chairs that made up the focal point of the keep's meeting hall. He had heard the stories, that Dianmeyer keep used to be a place of opulence. The former owner showed of their wealth in every facet of the castle from the walls down to the décor.

These chairs were not part of that aesthetic. They were well made, but simple, seats. In fact, any gold or jewels that had been anywhere in the keep were long since replaced with wooden sculptures or, if stone pieces just had to replace stone pieces, jade. There was no hint of the decadence that used to fill this place.

Phinegann was a heavily muscled orc, more commonly known as 'orcs', complete with the underbite and tusks common with that species. His tusks were short, one only reaching the top of his upper lip, while the other had been broken years ago and barely peeked out from inside his frowning mouth.

It was unclear whether his bald head was due to age, an argument that the deep lines on his face supported, or by choice of style. That possibility was backed by the thick chops of black hair on his cheeks that would have been a beard if his smooth cleft chin had had even a hint of fuzz. It did not.

The man was dressed in the red uniform and black, polished armor of the guards from the prisons run under the command of the Romefeller Guilds, although he had recently... retired from that service. As such, he had taken some liberties regarding the upkeep of the clothing.

Specifically, he removed the sleeves from his shirt, exposing his bronze skin. His hue was only partially from continued exposure to the heat of the sun.

Also, the former guard's left arm was different from his right. It was completely made of steel and polished to the sheen of a freshly oiled sword. In shape, though, it matched his natural arm with massive biceps perfectly.

Almost everything about the man radiated an air of military-like discipline. Except for the red streaks dyed into the chops of hair on his face. Were they a hint of rebellion? Some kind of family or clan custom? No one in the entirety of Dianmeyer keep dared to approach him and ask.

After Harby finished speaking, the silence hung heavy in the wide open room. Finally, Phinegann's only response to the Grand Cleric's words was a nod.

While there were two chairs in the immediate vicinity, neither man sat in one. Neither did the young woman who stood beside Harbenigyr. She was the one he described as his 'most cherished', his daughter, Appelonia. She had a frown on her face almost as deep as the one the orc wore.

She leaned in close to her father's long, pointed ear, "Does he really have to go with me?" she whispered the question.

Harbenigyr quirked an dark eyebrow at the girl who had only just reached an age that could be considered womanhood, "What's the issue, Apple? He came recommended by Folken himself. Do you really think anyone would think to hurt you with him around?"

The Grand Cleric motioned to the orc man who towered over both members of the Order of Kuan Yin. Phinegann didn't move.

Appelonia let out a heaving sigh, followed by blowing her ruby colored hair out of her eyes when her shoulders dropped back down to their natural position. Folken sent him. She should have known just by seeing the metal arm. It was almost the sorcerer's trademark.

Chewing on her lower lip, she nodded to herself and stepped between the two simple cherrywood chairs that had replaced what had previously been thrones. As she approached the massive orc, "Mr. Phinegann, sir, do you *want* to accompany me on my pilgrimage?"

The bronze skinned man's head tilted to the side, the only sign that he had even heard her question until he actually spoke a long count of seconds later, "I didn't volunteer."

The young woman tugged at the bottom of her white tunic. Embroidered swirls of pale green ran along the length of her loose sleeves. The only real splash of color in her uniform along with the jade toggles that held it closed. Long white tails drifted down to the back of her knees while the front was much shorter, ending just above her navel.

"Why are you here, then?" she asked.

"A job's a job," he shrugged.

"Surely a man as experienced as you could find another, better paying job than gallivanting around Honua with some neophyte like me," her emerald eyes narrowed, "Couldn't you?"

"Apple, really," the Grand Cleric shook his head at Phinegann apologetically. "Asking questions is one thing but you're teetering awfully close to rude."

The confidence the young woman had been radiating didn't falter, although if it had been armor it would have shown a few chinks that could be exploited. Appelonia's hands wrapped around the leather belt on her waist, toward the sides where the white material of her pants had been trimmed away from her round hips, as her attention turned back to the orc.

He didn't say anything. Phinegann stood as if he were a statue made of the same metal as his prosthetic arm. Again, silence dominated the room. It lingered so long that Harbenigyr started to wonder if the retired prison guard did indeed have a choice whether to be there or not.

Just as the orc opened his mouth to speak, a cacophony of bells rang through the halls of the castle. It took the Grand Cleric only a couple of seconds to recognize what the sound symbolized.

"Someone is breaking into the vault!" He rushed for the double doors that served as the room's main entrance for visitors.

Appelonia was barely a step behind her father. Phinegann was a step and a half behind her at most. Even as the ran through the halls to the source of the alarm, the young woman felt as if she were being smothered just by the half-ogre's mere presence.

Emerging from a set of stairs that deposited the trio onto the floor just above the main hall, a man covered in plate armor from his high collared neck to the steel molded tips of his boots was already standing to the side of the fortified door that served as the keep's vault.

It didn't hold much in the way of valuables. The Order of Kuan Yin didn't keep stores of money as a matter of principle. No, this vault held enchanted items and weapons created by the castle's former occupant, a sadistic woman who took pleasure in the pain of others.

In order to keep her 'toys' from doing such terrible things again, Harby had them shut away. Folken, along with the assistance of some of the Order's most talented evokers, created locks, wards, alarms and deterrents to keep the devices from ever seeing the light of day again.

It was strange that the alarms went off without any of the defenses being activated. The fact that the hall wasn't scorched with carbon and filled with ash was a testament to their lack of use.

"Cleric Harbenigyr" the human in the full suit of heavy armor gave the elf a short, quick bow.

"What's the situation, Jonas?" the Grand Cleric asked.

Appelonia's jaw went slack when she saw the man. His black hair was trimmed short on his head but it was a look that suited him. This Jonas had a solid, squared jaw, a fine, straight nose that showed no signs of ever being broken, full lips... Appelonia shook her head to focus back on the job at hand.

His armor let out only the slightest creak as Jonas raised his arm to point at the door. "There's no sign of forced entry but I can hear some rustling around in there," he reported.

The fact that Jonas was in full armor and carrying a claymore sword made it obvious that he was not of the Order of Kuan Yin. Appelonia would have surely seen him before. Repeatedly.

The red lightning bolt painted along the left side of his breastplate and over the pauldron covering his shoulder (that Appelonia was sure was broad and well muscled), showed that he was a paladin of the Order of Stewart. They were a religious order that aided migrants in their travels whether it be a single wanderer or a displaced village seeking refuge. They made sure those in their charge found a place of solace. Because of that charge they were often referred to as 'Shepherds'.

Had the paladin come here because he somehow heard that Appelonia was about to leave on her pilgrimage? She felt her cheeks become very, very warm at the idea.

The father of the young woman rested a hand on the door. "How could they have gotten in there?" he asked, his brow furrowing as his black eyes snapped back over to his daughter.

Appelonia noticed the look on her father's face and she couldn't help but fidget. Refocusing herself, the cleric reached for the leather case that hung off her belt at the small of her back, stretching down well below her knees to make it look almost as if she had a stiff tail.

Flipping the top open, she pulled two sticks of jade free, each just about as long as her arm. Holding one in each hand, she nodded back at her father to signal that she was ready to follow him into the vault.

"Jonas, Phinegann, follow me inside when I open the door," the Grand Cleric spoke with an air of authority as he slid his finger over the surface of the door to disengage the system of locks and defenses. "Apple, you guard the entrance and keep anything that might get past us from escaping."

The frown that Appelonia had in the main hall came back. She wanted to be the first to go in with her father. But she also knew better than to argue with him. With the alarm still going on, and whoever was in there having a literal roomful of weapons to use against them, time was critical.

"One, two," Harbenigyr counted, his voice barely audible, "Three!"

And the elf pulled the door open. He disappeared so fast that Apple thought for a moment that he might have teleported. The heavy man in black armor rushed in next. Then Jonas, in his mirror like armor, charged inside. He left an afterimage of his silhouette in the young woman's vision, the metal was so bright.

Then Appelonia crowded the doorway as much as her diminutive frame could. She held her fighting sticks out in front of her to ward off any possible attack.

What she saw inside the vault was confusing to say the least. Not only was her father not fighting, he was standing with his hands on his hips and a flabbergasted look on his face. The girl knew it well, having seen it many times growing up. Mostly after she'd been caught doing something she should not have been.

Both Phinegann and Jonas looked equally befuddled as they stood behind the Grand Cleric. The tip of the paladin's sword was even resting against the floor, not a position that denoted readiness to defend himself.

Then Appelonia shifted to look where all three men were focusing their attention. To the right, along the wall, was a small... Apple was hesitant to call her a "woman" since she only came up to the cleric's waist in height. On her back was what looked like butterfly wings made of stained glass.

Her chin length hair was a shade of purple that was unnaturally bright and her face, which looked cheerful, was full of freckles. No, they were too organized. They were a curved, horizontal line and another vertical line of black dots tattooed along top and middle her cheeks. She had what Harbenigyr called a 'soul orb' in her hands (it could have been held easily in one hand of anyone else in the room), one of the few things in the fortified room that was not a weapon.

"Young lady, what are you doing in here?" the Grand Cleric tried to make his voice sound stern but confusion was still able to find its way in.

"Hmm?" the winged midget blinked as if she was just noticing that she wasn't alone for the first time, "Oh, hello. I presume you're the residents of this castle?"

"Yes," Harbenigyr nodded. "And this is a highly dangerous area, sealed off to keep anyone from entering."

"Really?" the excessively little woman pursed her blue painted lips, "The guy I followed in didn't seem to have any trouble."

"Guy you followed?" Jonas repeated, looking around the room, "Where is he?"

The tiny intruder pointed to the furthest corner, "He's looking for something over there."

The paladin's sword rose from the floor to point in the direction the half-sized woman indicated. A bronze ball, attached to a chain made of brass hung from Phinegann's metal hand. An odd weapon but the ball was covered in spikes so it definitely looked deadly.

"That won't be necessary," an unfamiliar voice came from the behind the shelf that obscured that corner.

A man in white robes, much like those worn by the clerics of the Order of Kuan Yin, stepped into view, holding his empty hands out to his sides. He had hair as black as the Grand Cleric's, only his seemed to stand straight up as if he were being held upside down.

"Who are you?" Jonas asked, gripping the handle of his claymore tightly in both hands.

"I am Abernathy," the newly revealed man smiled politely, the tuft of black hair on his chin spreading along the bottom of his face. "I regret the inconvenience. I found myself in here by mistake and was unable to leave. I was merely seeking something to use to get me out."

The paladin seemed to relax, if only slightly, as he looked toward the Grand Cleric. Harbenigyr turned to the nearest shelf just off to his left. His black eyes scanned from one end to the other, looking for something specific.

"I know every cleric under my charge, Abernathy," the elf said, picking up a thin rod that looked to be made of a mixture of silver and lead swirled together, "You aren't of Kuan Yin. In fact, I hate to sound rude but you... reek of demonic essence."

"Reek *is* a strong word," the false cleric furrowed his brow as he let out a dejected sigh. "I wanted to do this quietly. Get in, retrieve what belongs to my people and get out without any mortal all the wiser."

A light, identical to embers igniting, lit up in Abernathy's hazel eyes. He didn't move but his entire body seemed to take up more and more space in the vault as the "mortals" around him tensed, feeling a battle was about to begin.

"But no, this frustrative room pulled me in and wouldn't let me go," his voice had an unearthly growl under it, "I should thank you. Without you tripping that alarm, there is no telling how long I would have been trapped in here."

His glowing eyes turned toward the minuscule woman with glass wings. She chuckled uneasily, her gaze moving back and forth from the false cleric, to the true Grand Cleric and the rest of his party.

"So this area is off limits? That make this… awkward." She put the soul orb back on the second lowest shelf with the other half dozen that rested on a thin cushion of satin and a large black rock, "I will just let you all clear up this misunderstanding while I head to the main hall and wait to get proper permissions to be here."

The stained glass on her back fluttered as she moved quickly, just short of running, for the exit. Appelonia dropped one of her jade sticks between the little woman and the doorway.

"What's done is done, miss. Please stay here until this is all sorted out," the young cleric ordered.

Jonas spared a look back toward Appelonia as she stopped the small intruder from leaving. The young woman had to stop a self-conscious giggle from escaping her lips when she saw him shoot a pleased smile in her direction.

"What is here that you believe to be your property?" Harbenigyr asked the false cleric, who stood over a head taller than the elf, "If there is merit to your claim, we can keep this situation from turning unpleasant."

"Oh, it is too late for that, leg licker." Abernathy answered.

Leg licker? The depiction of the goddess Kuan Yin on the tabard worn by the Grand Cleric had her carrying a container of water with one leg emerging from her long robes. Was Abernathy mocking—wait were those horns growing out of his forehead?

"The fact that you took what was ours to begin with marked you our enemy." his voice sounded even more like that of a monster as the false cleric's teeth turned sharp and pointed as he spoke, "I was always going to come back and pass the judgment of the efreeti upon you, now I will just do it sooner rather than later."

Harbenigyr frowned, "I am sorry to hear that. And also if this causes you pain."

The Grand Cleric pointed the silver and lead rod at Abernathy. A narrow stream of metal shot from the end of the magic item. About every foot or so, the stick would jump in the elf's hand and a barbed piece of metal would launch out with the stream.

Abernathy let out a surprised yelp when the first barb dug into his shoulder. Blood immediately stained the white cloth of the robes that were now tightly wrapped around his body. The stream of metal wrapped around him as if it had a mind of its own, pinning the false cleric's arms to his sides and continuing downward.

"But I cannot let you harm innocent people just because you think they *might* have something belonging to you," Harbeningyr pulled the wand back and the stream of metal stopped.

With even his ankles tied together, Abernathy found it difficult (but not impossible) to remain standing. His entire body started to grow, only making the metal barbs dig deeper into his limbs.

"This is the understanding of Kuan Yin, eh?" Smoke started pouring from Abernathy's nostrils, "You go about forcing your will upon others and taking whatever you wish?"

Fire suddenly flashed to life all around the man. It only lasted a moment and caused everyone in the room to have to shield their eyes. When it stopped, what stood there was no longer a man but some kind of monster. Nor did it have the barbed metal wrapped around it anymore. The restraint laid in smatterings of molten metal on the stone floor all around the creature.

This was the most monstrous thing that Appelonia had seen in her short life. It was a vision that would stay with her as long as she lived. However brief that may be.

———◆··• •··◆———

CHAPTER TWO

"Okay, now we go back to the past, back at the bar when Raiko almost killed Harby with his stupid game. You already spoke to Saya about this," Ophelia pointed at another piece of parchment, "You can see how angry she was..."

The report from Saya Kushrenada follows:

Two decades before...

"YOU CAN'T JUST go around like your will is the only thing in this world of import, Raiko!" Saya's words bit into the man as she continued, "Until that bracer is removed from your arm, you have Harbenigyr's life to consider. Even if you didn't, why would you wager your life? Am I truly that unimportant to you?"

His teeth ground so hard that they could be heard by the woman, "In this case, my feelings toward you were irrelevant. I couldn't let you influence my decision one way or the other."

Saya's violet eyes narrowed as she crossed her arms over her chest, "So there was an ultimate goal here? It wasn't just some insipid game to prove your machismo?"

"There was an ultimate goal," Raiko unbuckled his long brown leather coat to reveal his blood caked torso. "I endured this to work and gain the allegiance of that politician Tybalt and Ophelia turned the entire effort into an exercise in futility!"

"And how was she supposed to know this?" Saya snapped back, "You never told me that you were seeking any politician's fealty. Why not? I know you are aware of my family's influence. If you had just told me I could have..."

The woman's words trailed off as a realization hit her. Saya's hands slipped down to cradle her flat stomach. For a moment, the albino svartalfar looked as if she was going to be ill.

"I was another means to an end for you. You wanted access to the information that the Romefeller Guilds share with me to gather intelligence," she said, more to herself than anyone, "You are building separate cells of influence, completely ignorant of each other in each city we pass through. To what end, Raiko? And why keep it hidden from me?"

Everything about Saya, from her voice to the way she held her body, radiated accusation. She was not a woman to be used. She was not a plaything, not a pawn in some nobody's play to obtain some form of social stature.

A quiet groan escaped from Raiko as he buckled his coat back together, "I needed what you had. I did not intend to fall in love with you, Saya. When I realized that I had I- I had to protect you from what needed to be done."

"And what needs to be done?" the woman looked unmoved by his confession. "You can either tell me or I will set every resource I have available to find out. And we both know they are ample."

Raiko stood silently for a long moment but finally nodded, "You know that when I left my people, I took the heirloom of my family with me, yes?"

"You mean Meteorend?" Saya said.

He nodded again, "It is not just a mere inheritance. It is what my people are."

"What do you mean?" she again folded her arms over her chest, her gloved left hand sliding up to Saya's chin as she listened.

"It is... complicated," Raiko looked as if he were lost, trying to figure out what to do next. "How your people are all svartalfar but you are of Tribe Kizoku. Your people also have other tribes, the Lytyl, the Xaviour, the Sauntaran, and so forth."

Saya nodded.

"My... family, my tribe, my clan, whatever you want to call them, they are all the same. My people make no such distinction."

"I am waiting for the point here, Raiko," Saya scowled.

"When I say that I took the heirloom of my family, I took that which was most important to the entirety of my people, Saya. All of them."

"All of this is to hide from the de Junamend?" She rolled her eyes, "Or were you planning on some kind of assault to take them out of your misery?"

"No! I am doing all this to *save* them!" Raiko blared, slamming his fist against the wall, "But they would not let me take Meteorend beyond the safety of our borders."

"So you took matters into your own hands," Saya shook her head, her platinum white hair spilling over her shoulders, "You seem to have a habit of that."

Before Raiko could reply, a knock came at the door to the couple's room. The svartalfar noblewoman granted the visitor permission to enter.

Lily stepped into the room, "My Lady, Lord Folken has arrived."

Saya's eyes grew to the point that they looked as if they were about to fall out of her head, "Folken is here?" her voice couldn't get above a whisper.

"Yes, my Lady," the horticultural wizard answered, "He is in Harbenigyr's room with the cleric and Ophelia."

"You left him alone with Ophelia?" Raiko scoffed, "We had all best hope that she isn't contagious after having lain with so many men."

"Shut up," Saya ordered before marching out into the hall.

The pale woman headed straight for the cleric's room. As she turned the corner, Saya almost ran straight into another woman with red hair so long that it reached her hips, which were exposed by the odd style of pants she was wearing.

Right where the curve was deepest the green fabric had been cut away, leaving only skin visible. It was an unusual fashion, considering that the rest of the garment fit her loosely and covered her legs all the way down the floor so that only the toes of her boots peeked out.

She also wore an aqua colored half shirt with no sleeves to hide her tanned arms. It occurred to Saya that the woman's choice in attire was much like Ophelia's, albeit not as tight.

Regardless of her tastes, she stood right in front of the door to Harbenigyr's room, leaning up against it in fact. After both woman got over the initial surprise of seeing each other, the one with ruby colored hair spoke.

"You must be Lady Saya." she said, patting her chest as she quickly calmed down, "Folken is waiting for you."

With that, the woman pulled herself away from the entrance and stepped to the side. After pushing the door open for Saya, she motioned toward Raiko and Lily, who were just behind the svartalfar.

"They can't come in yet," she said, "Folken's orders."

Lily nodded as if she expected that, although she looked confused at seeing the red haired woman at the door. The newcomer was almost the same exact height as Saya, making her well taller than the stocky wizard but Lily still walked up to her with confidence.

Saya stepped through the doorway and into the room. As she closed the door, she only caught the beginning of the conversation the shorter wizard began.

"Who are you?" she demanded, "You weren't here before."

"My name is Josie, and yes I was," the stranger answered.

"No you weren't, I stepped out of that room less than a minute ago and you weren't here."

"I was. You just weren't looking for me," Josie responded.

Raiko interrupted, his voice gruff and tone annoyed, "I don't care if you were here or not. Why must I stay out here?"

"Because that's what Folken said and he's the one paying my bill," Josie answered, "So you stay put. I'm sure that–"

Saya's worry of Raiko making a scene was greatly diminished by this Josie and her shutting him down so easily. The svartalfar woman had already lingered with the door open for too long.

Judging from the look on Folken's face, he agreed with her. Like Saya, the man had purple eyes but instead of platinum white hair like his cousin, Folken had hair as green as a field of grass after a rainstorm.

He returned his attention to the wounded cleric that Saya and Ophelia had returned to the bed. The sheets only covered the thin elf up to his waist. Neither woman wanted to risk the sheets getting stuck against the still drying wounds on Harbenigyr's chest when he was finally able to lie still.

"This is a result of the bond this man shares via that metal cuff your previous correspondence mentioned?" with his bass heavy voice, the question from Folken sounded more like a statement of fact.

Saya nodded, "Apparently, Raiko was attempting to garner the favor of some local politician with a penchant for games of chance."

Folken wrapped a gloved right hand around the metal on Harbenigyr's left arm and lifted it for a closer look. "Ophelia here mentioned that this... *Raiko* was playing a variation of Svartalfar roulette."

"He was," the pale woman confirmed.

"She also mentioned that he appeared to be losing," he squinted where the circle and lines etched into the surface of the metal intersected, finding that area to be of particular interest, "Badly."

"I'm not going to defend him, Folken," Saya sighed as she stepped up to the side of the bed and beside her cousin, "He may have been my *beau* but he lost my favor some time ago. The only reason I have kept him around was for Harbenigyr's sake."

Folken switched his grip on the metal bracer to his bare left hand. A thin claw, no wider than a needle, popped from the glove covered tip of his right forefinger. He scratched some symbols into the pewter that the woman didn't recognize, although she did see that none of them broke the lines already carved into the cuff.

Only after he was done with that did Folken look back up at his cousin, "This Harbenigyr has been enough of a resource to warrant this much of a headache?"

Ophelia spoke up from the foot of the bed, "I wouldn't be standing here now without him. He brought me back from being turned to stone."

Folken was a man not easy to impress. Saya was well aware of this. When her cousin's right eyebrow lifted up to a sharp angle, only she knew that meant he found the feat outstanding.

"And how did he accomplish this?" the svartalfar asked as he placed Harby's arm back onto the bed.

"With some concoction given to us by a man during our travels," his cousin answered.

"He did not create this *concoction*?" Again, it did not sound like a question coming from his mouth.

Saya shook her head.

"Nevertheless, this recipe would not have been enough to bring a..." Folken's violet eyes turned to scan up and down Ophelia's well curved frame, "fully grown woman like you back to life, fair Ophelia. This cleric must have some knowledge of the body's workings that are hardly commonplace."

"So you are saying that you can save him from the bond that thing has with Raiko?" Saya felt some figurative weight lift from her chest.

The man let out a quiet grunt, "Not without getting him and... Raiko back to Emerald City. The enchantment is too intricate, too closely bonded to both their life forces to wrench them apart in these decidedly less than ideal conditions," Folken looked around as if the room were covered in filth.

"But it can be done?" Ophelia asked, leaning against the footrest of the bed.

The man nodded to the mercenary, "I have added several runes that will dampen the pain bearing signals from this... Raiko if he decides to indulge in some other extra curricular activity."

"Then Harby has nothing to worry about anymore?" Ophelia asked.

"That, I did not say." Folken scowled, "Their life forces are still bound together. While the cleric will not feel an equally proportionate amount of pain, he would still die if and when this... Raiko is struck down. He is hardly out of danger."

"So we need to keep Raiko from doing something else stupid." Ophelia straightened up and started for the door, "Maybe between Saya and you telling him to stop being an idiot, something might actually sink in."

The mercenary pulled the door open and was greeted with the sight of Josie and Lily. The crimson haired woman with pointed ears was standing with her back to the door, dutifully guarding the entryway as she had been ordered. Although she had shifted off to one side to make room for Lily beside her. The plump wizard was caught with her ear right where the door had been only moments before.

The only person not there was Raiko. That made Ophelia uneasy. When he wasn't around she was sure the man was doing something foolhardy. Up until now she didn't have getting killed in the list of his potential acts of stupidity.

Ophelia looked down at the horticultural wizard, "Where is he?"

"The tournament caller came and collected him. His next match is about to begin," Lily reported.

"Why didn't you tell us before?" Ophelia snapped, stomping past the shorter woman.

"Master Folken left explicit orders not to be disturbed," she said to the back of the mercenary.

Ophelia looked over her shoulder in Lily's direction as she reached the top of the stairway, "I'm sure he didn't ask to be eavesdropped on, either!"

The wizard's round cheeks turned bright pink. Then a familiar feeling came over her, like when a bank of clouds rushed in front of the sun and stole away the warmth that had been beating down on her. Lily didn't even have to turn around to know the source. Folken was standing right behind her.

He ushered the stout woman into the room. Only after she endured a long session of direct eye contact did the sorcerer speak.

"It would behoove us to make our way to the tournament grounds to prevent this... Raiko from getting himself killed," the order to leave wasn't explicit but it was understood, at least to Josie. "You will watch after the cleric," Folken said over his shoulder to the platinum haired woman and the shorter wizard before closing the door.

OPHELIA INTERROGATION NOTES

"You know, I didn't tell you what happened to Harbenigyr and his daughter after that explosion in the vault," Ophelia realized.

"No need," I had to rifle through my papers until I found until the one I was looking for surfaced, "She shared her version of events right here."

Said report continues here:

Two decades later...

Appelonia coughed as the cloud of dust slowly dissipated. She still couldn't see anything in detail but the room seemed brighter than it was before.

Her suspicion was confirmed when a breeze wafted through the room and cleared the fog of dirt and debris. There was a hole in the stone wall so big that the young woman could look down to the first floor as well as the story above if she wanted.

But her first instinct was to make sure that nobody was injured. Especially Jonas, no, her father! And Harbenigyr was the first one that Appelonia found. He had just found his feet when she ran up to him.

"Are you hurt, Dad?" the younger cleric asked, patting at the sleeves of his tunic to check for injuries as much as clear the white material of dust.

He gave his daughter a soft smile, "I think that's my line. Are you hurt, Apple?"

Appelonia shook her head, "Where did that thing go?"

Harbenigyr looked in the direction of the hole in the wall, "Out there. Phinegann and Jonas are already giving chase."

"I should probably join them," the young woman said, "They could need some spiritual back up."

"That's why you should go back downstairs and tell the others what happened," her father said, starting toward the hole.

"No, Dad," Appelonia grabbed his sleeve, "You're too important to the Order. Besides, unlike you, I can attack from a distance. You know, out of harm's way."

As if to punctuate her point, she pulled a mechanism made of steel and inlaid with silver. It had two hollow cylinders, one on each side, that doubled as handles. They were separated by a span of smooth metal that stretched back and away from the cylinders. A likeness of the goddess was etched into the surface with the lines filled in with silver.

Appelonia slipped a jade stick into one cylinder and the second into the other. The sticks, while they were indeed coated with polished jade, had flexible wood cores. This allowed them to bend and perform double duty as not only close range weapons but also as components of her custom made bow.

Apple pulled up a wound up mass of line from another pouch. A silver cap was tied to one end that slipped over the far end of one stick and then a cap on the other end of the line popped over the opposite side of the other stick.

Then, reaching again into the long pouch from which she took the sticks to begin with, she pulled out an arrow and nocked the feathered back end against the string. Unlike a normal arrow, the head of this one was a blunt, rounded disk of metal.

The flat edge could bludgeon and potentially knock the target unconscious rather than kill. That would violate the tenets of Kuan Yin that Appelonia swore to uphold.

"Nice try, Apple," Harby smirked at back at her, "Little miss, could you go find another cleric and tell them that we are chasing the monster that broke into the vault?"

The exceptionally short woman stepped out from behind one of the still standing shelves, her wings folded over her head like a glass umbrella to protect her from falling debris, "Me? I don't want to be involved in any trouble."

"Then this will keep you out of it, Miss..." Harbenigyr blinked, "I'm sorry, I never got a chance to ask you your name."

"Ilyria. Illyria Warflower," she said with a curtsy, a habit with introductions the cleric figured. "An inventor from the Gnomelands to the west."

"Do this for me please, Illyria." the Grand Cleric said, "Then you can stay in the safety of the castle until Appelonia or I return to sound the all clear."

"Well, when you put it that way..." the wings on the short woman's back spread behind her back and, with a heavy flap, launched her toward the now unguarded door, "You'll have back up post haste!"

And she disappeared into the halls of the castle. Appelonia turned back to her father, her face a mask of worry.

"Are you sure we can trust her, father?" she asked.

Harby shrugged, "She seems nice enough for someone who moused her way into Dianmeyer. We don't really have time to debate it though, do we?"

Apple couldn't help but agree. Both she and her father turned for the hole in the wall and started after Jonas and Phinegann, who were surely deep in battle already.

OPHELIA INTERROGATION NOTES

"Ophelia, I understand that these events are ultimately connected," I said, "But what I am unclear about is back at the tourna-

ment. Raiko had slipped away from you. Surely you would not let such a slight pass."

The subject shook her head, "Of course not. If not for his connection to Harby, I would have killed him right then. Folken and Josie had just met him and I think they were trying to figure out a way to murder his pasty as-, er, hide. But first we had to find him..."

Two decades before...

Ophelia, flanked by Folken and Josie, weaved her way through the crowd assembled to watch the contest of violence. Raiko was going to be in the middle of it but finding him was going to be the easy part.

Ophelia could count the number of young people with silver hair she had met on one hand. Saya's hair had the slightest hint of gold when in direct sunlight, so the mercenary debated raising a finger to count her. If she did, and added Raiko as well, meeting Horta and Andor brought that total to four.

That made the five silver haired people wandering among the crowd stand out to the mercenary. One of them was Horta. She recognized him from behind with little difficulty. That meant that Andor was likely another one of the silver topped figures. That made three new ones with a very distinctive color among the non-elderly. Ophelia was starting to think that this was not a coincidence.

She recalled that Raiko had run away from his people. Had they hunted him down? If they had, was it to bring him home or to kill him for abandoning them?

The first option was troublesome enough. They likely didn't know that Harbenigyr and Raiko couldn't be too far away from each other without dying because of the cursed cuffs. The second option, while Ophelia wouldn't mind Raiko becoming permanently horizontal, still had the same collateral damage of a dead cleric of the Order of Kuan Yin.

A woman with silver hair pulled back into a tight ponytail slipped between two other random citizens in the crowd. Ophelia didn't recognize her and pretended to not even notice her as they passed each other.

Josie let out a pained groan and quickly spun around, "That witch just pulled my hair!" she snapped, her hand darting to the short sword hanging from her belt.

Folken placed the hand with the long black glove on the woman's shoulder. "Focus on the immediate task," he ordered.

His left hand, pale against the violet and gold of the cuff of his elaborately stitched doublet, idly ran through his own grass colored hair. He didn't look as if he were in pain but rather like he'd been given a particularly difficult riddle to solve.

"Continue on, Ophelia," the svartalfar man issued another order, "We must get to Raiko before the match starts. From this round on, lethal force is commonly used in this competition."

Great. No pressure.

The woman became less gentle as she shoved her way through the teeming audience. After a half dozen complaints of her rudeness, Ophelia spotted the familiar, flowing silver hair of the duelist she had come to so loathe.

"Raiko!" she shouted as the men she pulled apart to get by tumbled to the dirt, "Raiko, you–"

Ophelia suddenly found her face inches away from a familiar, broad chest. It was Horta who, judging from his smile, was very happy to see the woman again.

"I've been looking all over for you!" he had to raise his voice to be heard over the crowd hooting cheers and yelling last minute bets. "You disappeared so suddenly last night that I thought you had alcohol poisoning!"

Gods, his timing couldn't have been worse! Ophelia motioned for Folken and Josie to go around her as she tried to figure out a quick, efficient way of getting him to back off that didn't completely destroy the possibility meeting again later.

"No, a friend of mine was in trouble," she peered over his shoulder to see Josie's way blocked by another man with silver hair that was almost as big as Horta. "He still isn't out of the woods, to be honest."

"Oh?" the man with short silver hair sounded concerned, "That's terrible. Is there anything I can do for your friend?"

"First, I need to get this next match stopped before it starts." Ophelia tried to step around Horta only to run into his heavily muscled arm.

The woman who pulled Josie's hair stood in front of Folken with her back to the man. No matter which way he tried to step, she found some excuse to block his path. First she 'dropped' her bet ticket, then she 'mistakenly' thought that the man beside her had asked her a question.

Before the svartalfar man could just pick her up and toss her aside, the tournament herald stepped out into the middle of the circle that was the only place devoid of people in the immediate area. He spun around as he spoke, projecting his voice so that even those at the back of the crowd could hear him speak.

"Ladies and gentlemen, as well as those who are neither!" that quip elicited a couple of chuckles from the surrounding audience, "Our next match will pit the skilled hand of this man, Raiko de Junamend..."

Raiko stepped out from the edge of the throng of people to stand beside the herald at the mention of his name. As Horta placed his large hands on Ophelia's hips, she realized that this was no accident, coincidence, or anything else that could be considered innocent.

This man and the other silver haired people wanted this match to happen. This was part of some plan, some kind of trap for Raiko, and she was powerless to stop it from happening.

"He will be facing the fearsome ax of the Cardasian!" the herald motioned to a man that was surprisingly small for wielding something as cumbersome as pole ax.

The Cardasian only came up to Raiko's chin as they stood side by side. His weapon, though, stretched well above either of their heads.

A bronze helmet, with an eerily average looking human face sculpted into the front of it, covered the man's entire head but Ophelia had a suspicion of at least his hair color beneath. His armor was of the same style, sculpted to look like the chiseled, muscular torso of a man. Judging from the size of his arms, it may not have been inaccurate.

From the waist down he was armor free, wearing a baggy pair of pants that were a well worn taupe color. And a pair of sandals. That was weird. Sandals didn't strike Ophelia as combat garb.

Speaking of things that confused Ophelia, she looked up into Horta's gray eyes, "Why are you doing this?" she asked him.

"What do you mean?" he cocked his head to the side. "Offering to help your friend?"

Ophelia sighed, "No, making sure we couldn't stop the match. What are you going to do with Raiko?"

Horta turned to look back to the silver haired duelist as he and Cardasian raised their weapons and readied to fight. Then he returned his attention to Ophelia and shrugged.

"Why do you care? From what I gathered, you don't really give two mounds of ogre droppings for him."

"I don't," she agreed, "But you see that metal cuff on his arm?"

Horta let his arms slip from Ophelia's sides to face the fighters as the match officially started. The Cardasian was immediately on the defensive, avoiding the flashing movements of Raiko's rapier. One would think that having a heavy pewter cuff wrapped around his arm would slow down the man's stabbing but if it did, Ophelia couldn't tell.

"We were counting on that to give Cardasian the edge against him," the man rested his hands on his own narrow hips.

"That bonds his life force to the friend that is still in trouble," Ophelia explained, "If Raiko dies, that person dies, and that I do care about."

Horta let out a long, soft sigh, "I am sorry about that. If we can do what needs to be done without killing him we will but we can't let one life stop us from doing what needs to be done."

"What *does* need to be done?" Folken asked.

The svartalfar man walked up to the mercenary and her road block. The woman who had delayed Folken followed after him now, unable to get ahead of the green haired man and likely not sure if she should at this point.

"It is a private matter. Raiko is of us and we would rather it stayed between us," Horta frowned at other, thinner man.

"You lost that privilege when you got in our way," Josie said as she stepped between the two closest audience members, "and leaving another man's life in jeopardy."

The silver haired man that had stood in her way limped up beside her. Once his body was visible, Ophelia and the others saw an arrow sticking out of his knee. Oddly enough, he didn't seem to be upset that the woman ranger had done to him. If anything, he seemed impressed.

Horta scanned over all the people assembled around him, those three sharing allegiance with him and the three who did not, and shook his head. He opened his mouth to respond but was interrupted by the voice of the herald from the ring.

"And the winner is Raiko de Junamend, ladies and gents!"

All of them turned to face the scene of the fight that had just started and, apparently, just ended as well. The herald wasn't mistaken. The Cardasian was laying prone on the ground with six holes punched into sculpted left pectoral muscle of his bronze armor.

"That... wasn't supposed to happen," Horta's voice radiated the disbelief he must have felt at the turn of events, "Card was specifically trained to be able to counter any of his techniques."

The herald raised Raiko's cuffed arm up into the air to physically show his declaration of victory. The duelist glared in the direction where Ophelia, Folken, and Josie stood with the three silver haired people hunting for him. Raiko patted the front of his long coat, just above the belt line.

The herald spoke up again, "Don't go anywhere, my friends. The other match finished even faster than this one, meaning that we can have the second semifinal contest as soon as the contestant makes their way from that ring to this one here!"

"No! The next match wasn't supposed to be until this afternoon!" the silver haired woman beside Folken spoke up. "We have no time to get it back now!"

The albino svartalfar cocked an emerald eyebrow, "I presume this *it* to be Meteorend? What is so important about this stone that you would go through such subversive means to retrieve it?"

Horta spat a curse from his lips before turning back to the face Folken, "Meteorend is our salvation when it is in possession of our people. Without it, that *stone* will lead destruction to each and every one of us!"

The man with the arrow in his knee spoke up, "If Raiko dies without one of us there to retrieve it, Meteorend could be lost forever!"

"The barbarian is here, ladies and gentlemen!" the herald hollered into the crowd, "The next round is about to begin! The piercing rapier of Raiko de Junamend will be up against the equally penetrating spear of the newest record holder for fastest lethal victory, Lyan Yo Bunpy!"

"Even faster than Raiko's match just now?" Ophelia's brow furrowed, "Just what kind of monster will Raiko be facing?"

OPHELIA INTERROGATION NOTES

At this point, I accidentally scattered my notes all over the floor. The subject aided in gathering up the now unorganized witness statements.

She happened upon the testimony of Jonas the Shepherd, paladin of the Order of Stewart, "What is this doing here?"

"I told you that we are being as thorough as possible," I answered.

"What did he tell you happened?" Ophelia started reading the report while simultaneously rebuffing my efforts to retrieve it from her.

In the interests of full disclosure, this is the recollections of said paladin regarding his encounter with the Efreeti demon, Abernathy:

Two decades later...

Abernathy's unnaturally wide mouth snapped shut where Jonas the Shepherd's head was just the moment before. The paladin swiped his claymore back at the face of the beast.

The blade entangled with one of the crooked antlers growing out of Abernathy's forehead. The horns stretched away from his head, looking like lightning frozen mid-strike and the sword was caught up in one of the holes.

Abernathy jerked his head back and pulled the claymore out of the hands of the paladin. Then the beast's hand reached out to grab him. His fingers completely encircled the man's gauntlet.

Jonas jerked his arm free, the metal encasing the limb feeling warm enough that if he touched it with bare flesh it would have burned. Still, the monster's actions made the paladin stumble forward a couple of steps. That brought him right back into the reach of the monster's jaws.

And the mouth of the beast was met by a ball covered in spikes. The chain attached to it led to the steel arm of the former prison guard, Phinegann. The orc jerked back on the chain and the ball flew back toward him.

With a whipping motion from the massive man in black armor, the ball changed course in mid-air to dive back at Abernathy. The beast leaped back and out of the weapon's path. The brass ball left a crater twice as large as the metal sphere when it connected with the soil.

Abernathy's back was met by the fist of Jonas the Shepherd. Then another punch and another.

The creature wailed in pain and drove its elbow back. The appendage had a horn much like the ones that grew out of its head, only smaller and even sharper. When the paladin dropped his arm to block it, the force drove him even closer to the trees at the edge of the clearing.

Abernathy was driving them right where he wanted to go. His chance at subterfuge was gone and, despite his tough talk back in the castle, the monster's every action was to get him further and further away from the men chasing him down. If he could reach the trees, with his now immense size of at least ten feet tall, he could reach the tree tops and just launch and swing himself away faster than the men could run.

Again, the sphere and chain interfered with Abernathy being able to press his advantage on the paladin. The brass chain wrapped around the beast's neck and started pulling him back toward the middle of the clearing.

Jonas spotted his sword next to a bush with… oddly organized branches. They stretched straight up and down about five feet, the leaves tucked between the lengths rather than hanging from them. Whatever. Jonas needed his weapon more than his curiosity needed satisfaction at the moment.

A quick dash later and the claymore was back in his hands. He turned to see Abernathy charging at him, Phinegann being pulled along in the dirt behind him.

Jonas dived out of the path of the beast, who careened into the too organized bush. Sticks and leaves scattered everywhere, revealing a thin bald man sitting where the makeshift shelter had been.

The stranger had a thick black beard and almost as dark cloak wrapped around his torso. Oddly, he stayed sitting with his legs crossed with his eyes closed and not seeming to notice the commotion now only inches from his back.

Abernathy dropped a gargantuan fist, intent on killing the newcomer before he could become a new threat. An arrow struck the monster right in his now curved, pointed ear.

The arrow didn't stay embedded in the beast. It fell to the dirt and Jonas was able to see why. Instead of a sharpened arrowhead, the tip of the shaft had a flat circle set on it edgewise. The arrow would still fly straight but the blunt edge couldn't pierce the surface of it's target. Jonas was willing to bet that getting hit by it would sting like the dickens, though.

He was right. Abernathy raised his hand to the side of his head rather than down to crush the stranger. Both he and Jonas looked back in the direction from which the arrow came.

The Grand Cleric Harbenigyr, along with another cleric he called "Apple", were rushing toward the fighting. The young, red haired woman was holding a strange looking bow that looked to be made of jade. She already had another one of those unique arrows nocked on the string.

Abernathy turned to Jonas. His plan must have been to take the paladin down before the two clerics could get within arm's reach. Instead of his hands balling up into fists, the fingers of the monster stretched and curved, obsidian claws emerged from the tips. Every one of the monster's swipes and strikes were aimed at Jonas' head.

Blade and claws sparked when they connected but they wouldn't be cut short by the claymore's sharpened edge. Another arrow shot at Abernathy, who ducked to avoid it this time. Jonas took the opening to drop his blade on the creature's head.

Abernathy was quick. He pulled himself forward with his hands and feet all at once, closing the distance almost instantly and again biting for the paladin's face.

Jonas dropped back, kicking his feet up to meet Abernathy's hairy jaw. Then the paladin's breath was knocked from his chest as he landed flat on his back.

Phinegann stepped in, swinging the ball and chain around like a flail without its handle. The monster jumped behind the orc when Phinegann launched the spiked ball at him.

Abernathy slashed for the bald head of the man in black armor. Phinegann ducked down and the monster thought it was to avoid his claws until the spiked ball stuck Abernathy in the shoulder, the former guard had pulled the weapon back to reverse its path. It tangled with all the fur that had grown to replace the white cloth of Abernathy's disguise.

Blood pouring from the new wounds in the shoulder of the beast made gripping the bronze ball more than difficult. When another of those blunt arrows struck Abernathy in the eye, it became impossible.

The efreeti howled in anguish, although if it was the anger or the pain that was more dominant in his scream was anyone's guess. He charged straight at Phinegann, using the length of chain as a guide.

Abernathy slammed the metal ball still stuck in his massive shoulder square into the man's midsection. He could hear metal scraping against metal and the orc gasp for breath as he tumbled back into the ground.

Phinegann laid on the dirt, motionless, with the now freed bronze ball between his arms. The paladin thought for a moment that the retired guard was dead, until his metal arm slapped the ball away as if it were an annoying pet.

Abernathy's eyes still watered but his vision was returning. As evidenced by his face turning in the direction of Appelonia, who was readying another arrow, and the Grand Cleric. The elf's hands were glowing jade green as he prayed to his goddess for some kind of power.

Jonas wasn't familiar enough with the the Order of Kuan Yin to know what spiritual blessing would come, of attack or defense, healing or weakening, What he did know, though, was that the monster wasn't facing him anymore. When a strange hand suddenly appeared in front of him, he couldn't hide his surprise.

"You need some help." A gruff voice said.

It was the bald stranger in the dark cloak. He was thin but, when Jonas took his offered hand and was assisted back up to his feet, the man didn't even strain with any effort.

"I'm not one to turn away a helping hand," Jonas replied, "You have any ideas?"

With an inhuman roar, Abernathy rushed at Harbenigyr and Apple. The Grand Cleric stretched out his hands and the jade light poured away from him and toward the beast like rapid currents of water.

And the beast found himself slowed down, as if he were fighting against the flow of an actual river. The young woman cleric loosed another arrow that seemed, if it were affected by the light at all, to only became faster.

Regardless, Abernathy swatted it out of the air. The monster forced himself to continue toward the clerics as Phinegann stepped up to Jonas and the stranger.

"Who is this?" the orc pointed at the man in the charcoal colored cloak.

"Jin Vega but details can wait. Now it's time for action," the stranger motioned toward Abernathy and the clerics.

"He considers them the biggest threat now," Jonas observed. "He wants them down and out before he has to deal with us again."

"His shortsightedness is what's going to take *him* down," Vega replied and then pointed at Phinegann. "Ogre, pull him out of the Current of Reflections toward me. I will pin him down and you," he pointed at Jonas, "will strike him down with your blade."

The paladin shrugged at the retired guard. He, personally, didn't have any better of a plan. A faint growl grew at the back of Phinegann's throat but he started spinning the bloodstained ball around as he made his way to Abernathy.

"You will be able to hold him, right?" Jonas readying his grip on the long handle of the claymore.

"Damn straight," the bearded man nodded and started walking after the orc.

With that, the spiked ball sailed into the current of green light, unnoticed by the monster. It rocked to and fro as it made its way though the turbulent spiritual energy and caught up to Abernathy. Without being able to see it coming, like the cleric's arrow, even in slow motion the ball whipped in front of the creature's face before he realized it was there.

The chain wrapped around his neck and the ball made another orbit, this time connecting with the back Abernathy's head. The retired guard wrenched the dazed beast off his feet and out of the green light.

Jin Vega was waiting. "Kum Geit Sohm!" He screamed.

It was called a 'word of power'. They were used by many sects of monks, experts in hand to hand combat. While Jonas didn't know which sect of monks this man belonged, they all used certain words to focus their power, their energy into one move. It supposedly made them even more deadly in hand to hand combat.

Before Abernathy could collapse to the ground, his bloodied shoulder was met by the foot of the thin man and a fresh spurt of blood erupted from its skin. Then Vega pulled a long staff, at least as tall as he was, from… somewhere.

"Biet Chein!" One end slammed into the side of the monster's neck and only then did Abernathy find the dirt.

The other end of the staff in Vega's hands had some kind of round ornament mounted on it. Four prongs came to a point where they met in the center of the circle, though never quite became one.

The bearded man spun the staff around, slipped one of Abernathy's claws between the prongs and wrenched back, pulling the creature's hand back to a painful looking angle. The scream from the thing's mouth confirmed it.

"Now!" Vega yelled.

Jonas hoisted his massive sword over his head as he charged at Abernathy. The efreeti struggled to control the pain radiating down his arm and found enough focus to see the paladin coming for him.

His unnaturally wide maw opened so far that it looked like it fell out of joint.

Abernathy's tongue, long and squirming between his sharpened teeth, glowed red like fresh coals from a campfire. It was sheer luck that Jonas noticed and let the weight of the claymore pull him back and out of the path of the plume of flame that erupted from the monster's face.

"He can breathe fire?" the paladin had to take several steps to right himself. "Did anyone know he could do that? I wish he'd let us know about any other tricks before we try this again!"

A glint appeared in the slit pupils of Abernathy's eyes and, as smoke still spilled from between his teeth, his mouth stretched into a delighted smile, "Wish granted," he said.

And then he disappeared but only for the briefest of moments. Abernathy appeared behind Vega and slammed both of his massive fists into either side of the bearded man's head.

Vega's unconscious body had not even reached the ground when the monster rushed toward Phinegann with such speed that flames where his feet touched the ground burned the grass and undergrowth.

He shoved the orc down onto his back, then the efreeti lunged down to take a bite out of the bronze skinned man. Phinegann was just able to get his metal arm up in defense.

The man's arm was too big for the beast to get a good grip with his teeth at Phinegann's elbow so his mouth moved down to the guard's wrist and chomped down hard. Like a dog playing tug of war, Abernathy whipped his head back and forth, finally sending Phinegann flying back toward Dianmeyer keep.

Again, jade hued light encircled the monster. It floated all around Abernathy, working to take on some solid shape.

"Not this time, cleric," it growled.

Abernathy straightened his back, his barrel chest expanding as he sucked in as much air as he could hold. Again, his tongue started to glow and he bellowed a stinking stream of orange flame that overwhelmed the green light and made it dissipate into nothingness.

The light itself must have been connected to Harbenigyr somehow because when the jade light disappeared, he collapsed to his knees. The pot of water that the depiction of his goddess carried on her head was barely visible just under his waist.

"Daddy!" Apple hollered as she bent down over him.

Jonas hadn't realized that she was his daughter. He probably should have. They both had the same black eyes that, under normal circumstances, reminded one of a calm summer's night. But the look on the face of the young woman was anything but calm.

She quickly nocked another arrow and let it loose at the beast, then another and another at a speed that defied any kind of expectation. Abernathy was able to duck out of the way of the first, but it was as if the cleric had predicted his reaction and the second arrow struck him right in between his yellow eyes.

The next hit him in the throat and Abernathy doubled over. As the next flew for him, he slammed his fists into the dirt and fire completely enveloped the monster and incinerated the arrow before it could strike.

When the flash of flame subsided, Abernathy had again disappeared. Jonas saw the efreeti slinking behind Apple, who was still facing where he had been only moments before.

"No! Apple, watch out!" Jonas was already charging.

The cleric looked at him quizzically. That is, until she felt the heat of the flames that engulfed the claws that were capable of removing her head from her shoulders with a single swipe. Her hands slipped onto the jade sticks that made up the two ends of her bow and the silver piece in the middle fell away. She started to raise the weapons but there was no way Apple could strike Abernathy before he could reach her.

Somehow, Jonas started this with his comment that the monster interpreted as a 'wish'. Something about what the paladin said made Abernathy able to mow through everyone who had been giving him so much trouble up to that point.

No more. The patron deity of the Order of Stewart as his witness, Jonas would not let Abernathy harm one more soul.

The paladin charged past the young woman, holding his heavy sword upside down. He swung the blade upwards, meeting the flesh of the beast right between his legs.

Letting out a howl that encompassed his frustration, the entirety of his sense of justice, every hint of anger that boiled inside him, all the righteous fury that Jonas felt in that moment gave his strike more power than he alone was capable of wielding.

Abernathy froze when the claymore dug through the patch of fur that hang between his thick thighs. The slit pupils of his eyes widened round as the blade continued upward.

The sword of the Shepherd met the bone of the efreeti's rib cage. It did not stop. Bone after bone snapped around the sharpened steel, giving way to the claymore. It sliced through the length of Abernathy's throat. His jawbone couldn't stop the vicious, blessed cut from continuing.

His sharp teeth split against the metal onslaught of the long blade. Finally, the sword slipped past the base of the creature's antler and reemerged into the cool late morning air.

One part of Abernathy fell to the left of the paladin, the other to the right. Jonas gasped for breath as he the realization of what just happened rushed through him. The tip of the claymore's blade finally finished its arc and met the dirt, only steps away from Apple, who looked dumbfounded.

She stared at him and Jonas stared at her. It was as if time stopped. His worry about whether or not the woman had been injured subsided when he saw her cheeks ever so slowly turn a bright shade of pink.

Then worry for her father made time move again. She bent down over the elf that, to Jonas anyway, looked too young to have a daughter Apple's age. But he was hardly an expert when it came to the life span of elves.

The young woman helped the Grand Cleric back up to his feet. They each fussed over the other, making sure neither was hurt before they both made their way to where Jin Vega was stretched out on the ground.

Harbeningyr muttered a prayer that made the same jade light that attacked Abernathy wrap around the bearded, bald man. Almost immediately, his eyes opened, followed by the twinge of a sharp pain that was interrupted by the relief the energy from the prayer provided.

Phinegann marched toward Jonas, waving his metal arm in circles to make sure that everything still worked properly. His eyes, of which is right appeared to be permanently bloodshot, narrowed when he saw the carcass that had been Abernathy.

The orc strode over to the dead efreeti, wrapping a steel hand around one of the antlers that looked like lightning frozen in place.

With a snap that sounded like a tree being felled by hurricane force wind, the horn was separated from its former owner.

Phinegann placed the antler in the hands of the paladin. "To remember this," he declared.

Jonas doubted that he needed anything to remind him of what happened here. Still, he nodded back at Phinegann and tucked the dulled end that used to be the base of the horn into his belt to be packed properly later.

"Who is this man?" Harbenigyr looked up at the two other men still standing, even as he maintained the healing glow around the stranger.

"He called himself Jin Vega," Jonas answered, "That's all that we know at the moment."

Vega was able to sit up after only a few more short minutes in the green glow. By that time, a group of seven clerics of Kuan Yin had marched out, each carrying staves or maces that had varying degrees of combat readiness to the looks of them.

All except for one. He had no weapon. He was easily the biggest of all the clerics (including the Grand Cleric and Appelonia) and wore leather gloves over his massive hands. His tunic had no sleeves to obscure the view of his equally immense arms.

His salt and pepper hair was tied back into a tight ponytail, his full beard showing the same smattering of gray throughout. Jonas recognized him immediately as the Order's herald, Samson. He had met with the paladin when he arrived at the keep, introducing him to the Grand Cleric and his wife, Josie.

He couldn't hide an obvious look of surprise when he saw Vega and Harbenigyr sitting beside each other, "Jin, what are you still doing here?"

The Grand Cleric's black eyes darted back and forth from his herald, to the newcomer, and back, "You two know each other? How is it that I don't, Samson?"

The heavily muscled cleric sighed, "I fear, sir, that this will take some time to explain..."

OPHELIA INTERROGATION NOTES

After retrieving the parchment containing the testimony from Jonas, I insisted that the subject continue her tale about Raiko's next match in the tournament:

Two decades before…

Ophelia blinked in surprise when she saw Raiko's opponent, "He's fighting her?"

Horta had a confused look on his face as he turned back to the woman in the long red coat, "As a woman, I would think that you'd be cheering her on rather than assuming she was going to lose just because she looks silly."

"Who said anything about her losing?" Ophelia's pale eyes floated back and forth between this Lyan Yo Bunpy and Raiko before returning to Horta, "She's going to tear him apart."

Raiko was not a short man. He was a couple of inches taller than Ophelia, who stood about six feet even. Lyan Yo Bunpy, though, was the same height as him. Unless you counted the rabbit ears on top of her helmet, then she was even taller.

The right ear stretched tall and proud over a foot above her head. The left ear was folded in half but still stood stiffly. Two long teeth, or horns, Ophelia wasn't sure to be honest, stretched from the front of the woman's fuzzy headgear. They were right between her brown eyes and reached down to below her chin.

She didn't wear much in the way of armor. Some pastel blue fur covered her chest, which was carved out of muscle. But this Lyan also had breasts larger than Ophelia's, which weren't small by any measure.

The muscles on the abdomen of the challenger were so well defined that most of the men in the audience were surely envious, let alone the women. Her narrow hips were wrapped in the same soft blue fur. She even had a large, white cotton tail protruding from the back to support the rabbit theme of her wardrobe.

Boots reached up to the middle of the woman's muscular thighs, made of the same fur. The feet looked to be the front paws of an immense rabbit, complete with the claws.

Lyan Yo Bunpy's arms could very well have been larger than Raiko's. Her left arm was permanently scorched black, unlike the rest of her skin that was colored much like the contents of a mug of hot chocolate. The fur covered gauntlets she wore on her forearms ended in what looked like stylized rabbit head with the protruding teeth sharpened and extending past her calloused knuckles.

Ophelia personally thought that she had taken the rabbit theme a little too far. Surely it was some kind of psychological ploy to throw off her opponents at competitions such as this, making them treat her lightly.

That would have only worked for maybe a round or two. This close to the finals of the tournament, the mercenary doubted that it would have had any effect anymore. So if this woman *had* been counting on that before, the musclebound barbarian would have changed into something different, more combat ready, before her matches today.

The spear she held had a blade that was also in the shape of a sharp-toothed rabbit head. The sharpened buck teeth made up the tip of the blade with a tuft of blue fur hanging from between the ears where it attached to the staff. It had been hurriedly cleaned but the weapon's blade still smeared with traces blood. Some of the fur on the head was clumped together with bits of dried viscera.

"She's using a spear," Josie frowned as she folded her arms across her chest, "Doesn't that mean that he'll be able to just repeat what he did to kill that Cardasian guy?"

Raiko, for his part, didn't appear concerned. Perhaps the same thought was going through his head that the ranger had just stated. Many fighters that used weapons like staves, battle axes and spears did so to keep their distance from their opponent. The thinking was simple: an opponent using a sword, particularly one with a shorter blade like a rapier, could not reach them while they were able to hack their victim to pieces.

Raiko countered that strategy by simply closing the distance between himself and his previous opponent before the Cardasian could get the heavy blade of his battle ax down between them. Then, the only thing the ax was good for was using the long handle to block and there was no way it could match the speed of a light, thin piece of metal like a rapier.

But the blade of the spear was a lot smaller than the head of a pole ax. It was meant for stabbing, making it closer to the rapier than the pole ax strategically. Also, the staff of the weapon didn't seem to move... right. Ophelia wasn't sure how to describe it. It seemed as if the stick *wiggled* more than it should have. That meant that it wouldn't move like any other traditional weapon used in these types of competitions.

The herald stepped out from between the two combatants. Lyan Yo Bunpy and Raiko then turned to face each other. The duelist raised his cuff wrapped arm until the hilt of his rapier was near his face in a traditional salute.

The woman simply nodded back. Then she planted the butt of her spear into the dusty ground between her and Raiko. It was almost the exact position that the silver haired duelist had trapped and killed the Cardasian. Raiko's mouth stretched into an amused smirk.

"Ready!" the Herald called.

Raiko raised his blade into the space between himself and the barbarian. His knees were bent, ready to spring him forward in a lethal lunge.

Lyan Yo Bunpy stood up straight and she waited. She pressed a thumb against one of her nostrils and let out a hard puff of air, sending a spray of mucus to the ground.

"Begin!" the Herald called and jumped back into the crowd that lined the edge of the ring.

Raiko showed no hesitation. His thin blade shot forward.

The barbarian stepped off to the side. She leaned her spear so that the man's sword shot past the far side, keeping the shaft between her and the rapier.

Then Lyan Yo Bunpy threw a punch. Not at Raiko but at her own weapon.

Her fist slammed into the polished wood of the shaft and, just like Ophelia thought, the spear bent as if it were made of rubber. The sharp teeth of her gauntlet slipped around either side of the duelist's blade even as the rapier was knocked off target so badly that the tip of the blade was pointed right at the suddenly panicked looking Herald.

Lyan Yo Bunpy's fist twisted and the blade was wrenched from the overconfident hand of Raiko. The rapier kicked up a cloud of dust as it tumbled toward the watching crowd. Then the woman's blackened elbow struck the side of the man's head and he stumbled back.

"I told you," Ophelia couldn't stifle the grin on her face, "He's completely outclassed."

"No!" Horta looked as panicked as the Herald had only moments before, "If she kills him now, all is lost!"

"She isn't looking to kill," Ophelia said matter-of-factly.

"What do you mean?" Horta didn't even try to hide his worry, "Killing is how you win!"

"That's only one of the ways." The mercenary explained, "Raiko is free to yield now that he is disarmed, or she could knock him out, or make him tap for mercy if it degrades to a wrestling match."

"What?" Horta looked overwhelmed.

"The barbarian wishes to test herself," Folken clarified, "As a warrior, she will not kill a competitor weaker than her unless he gives her no other choice. It is rare to see such a specimen these days."

"What will happen to Harbenigyr with those other options?" Josie chimed in.

"The runes *should* insulate him from the worst of the effects," There was only the slightest hint of doubt in the svartalfar's voice.

Both competitors in the ring paused for a moment. The voice of Lyan Yo Bunpy carried over the audience as she addressed the unarmed duelist.

"As you are unarmed, you may yield without loss of honor, Raiko de Junamend," She offered.

Raiko rolled his eyes, "I won't surrender in the face of a cheap trick using a spear that isn't an actual weapon."

"Even if Raiko decides to get himself killed?" Josie groaned when she heard his retort.

Lyan Yo Bunpy tilted her head to the side, "You speak from ignorance. Did you not hear the Herald announce my record of fastest victory? It was with this *actual weapon.*"

"Fine," Raiko snarled, "Then face me without it. Hand to hand."

Horta and his allies, as well as Ophelia, Folken and Josie either groaned, slapped their own faces in disbelief, or rolled their eyes. Ophelia was sure a welt was going to raise on her forehead as she watched the stupidity of the duelist reach new depths. This had to end.

The mercenary grabbed Horta by the collar and pulled his face toward hers, "What's Meteorend worth to you?"

"As you refuse to yield, I will even the terms of the engagement," Lyan Yo Bunpy tossed her spear aside and it landed beside Raiko's rapier.

She started to unfasten the buckles holding the bladed gauntlets on her wrists. They found their way to the ground beside the weapons.

The barbarian strode toward Raiko, who raised his hands in a very stylized fighting posture. The back of his fists were toward the barbarian, his cuffed right arm pointed upward while his left was down just below his waist.

Lyan Yo Bunpy, on the other hand, strode toward the duelist as if he were an old friend and they were about to have a completely nonviolent conversation. Despite her size, she did not stomp. In fact, her feet did not even kick up dust.

"Why in the world is he doing this?" Josie didn't bother to hide her exasperation, "She's already won if you go by the strict rules of this thing."

"Perhaps he is trying to save face." Folken suggested. "He was disarmed with embarrassing ease."

Judging from the look on Raiko's face, Ophelia didn't think that Folken was right about this one. Raiko was not only looking for a way to win, but also hurting the barbarian as much as possible along the way.

Horta looked back and forth to his two compatriots. The way they acted, it was as if they were having a conversation but without moving their lips or making any sounds with their mouths.

"Suppose they're telepathic?" Ophelia thought to Havarti in just that fashion.

"So you are checking to see if they can hear our own personal Tête-à-tête?" the bastard sword replied, "It would appear not."

She nodded in agreement.

Horta seemed to think her reaction was directed at him. He pulled away from the other two de Junamend and bent down close enough to Ophelia's ear that he could whisper.

"We would not only physically stop the authorities from arresting you, but we can pay you a handsome bounty. Also, if you insist, have me for as long as you like."

"A little frosting on the cake there, eh?" she smirked back at him, "I hope you aren't too fond of those pants because you're not going to be seeing them for awhile."

As Ophelia stepped around the man and made her way to the ring, the full ferocity of the match was unobstructed from her view. Ophelia let out a curse that was only partially drowned out by the roaring of the crowd around her.

Fists flew back and forth between the combatants so quickly, it was hard to see what strikes were connecting. Neither the barbarian nor Raiko reeled back so it seemed as if neither felt any of the blows.

When a pause finally did come to the action, it was Lyan Yo Bunpy gripping two of the duelist's fingers and stretching them to a painful looking angle, "Yield!" she commanded.

In response, Raiko tried to pull his hand away from her. Fot his effort, the man's digits were crumpled into to crooked, broken and useless members.

As he doubled over, clutching his hand to his chest, Lyan stepped forward. He turned his back to the woman and threw a kick for her midsection of hardened muscle. She caught his foot in both hands and twisted. His ankle broke with a stomach turning snap that everyone around the ring could hear.

"For the last time! Yield!" Lyan screamed, "It is a waste for this to carry on any longer!"

Dragging his useless, boot wrapped foot behind him, Raiko worked to create at least a little distance between himself and the woman who sorely outmatched him. He flicked a hand at her, the silhouette of a dagger only visible for the briefest of moments between his fingers before it was thrown.

Lyan ducked off to the side, the blade sailing over her broad, scarred shoulder harmlessly, "You have no honor! Death is your only accomplishment this day!"

Snatching the dagger out of the air, about one pace in front of an audience member that didn't even realize they were about to be skewered, Ophelia cursed again. Looking down at the weapon, she recognized it as one of Saya's daggers. Why did Raiko have it? Where had he been hiding it?

It didn't matter. This had to end now, before Lyan Yo Bunpy unwittingly killed an innocent elf cleric along with the mound of excrement that was more than deserving at this point.

Ophelia rushed over to the herald, who was conveniently halfway between her and the two fighters. "Declare her the winner. By the rules he's already lost because of that dagger. Do it now!" she didn't wait for a reply before charging toward the furry blue barbarian.

"Lyan Yo Bunpy is the winner by disqualification! Raiko de Junamend used an illegally hidden weapon in a sneak attack!" the herald announced to the crowd.

"I trust my services will not be necessary in this case?" Havarti's voice was ironically calm in Ophelia's head as she ran with everything she had to stop the fray before it was too late.

Ophelia didn't answer as she leaped, wrapping her hands around the shoulders of the barbarian to pull herself up even higher until she was able to wrap her long legs around Lyan Yo Bunpy's head. "I'm sorry about this," Ophelia muttered before crossing her ankles and throwing herself backwards.

Both women tumbled to the dusty earth. The mercenary in the long red coat released her grip and skid in one direction while Lyan Yo Bunpy rolled in another.

"Now comes the even less easy part," Havarti said.

Ophelia silently agreed as she dug her fists into the dirt. She pushed herself back up to her feet and started toward Raiko, her pale eyes locked on the waist of his long jacket. Right where he kept Meteorend. Right from where he was pulling the black rock.

"Your minion will not save you, coward!" the barbarian slapped dust from the fur on her massive chest as she lifted herself onto one knee.

The duelist, his eyes glowing like fresh embers, pointed the rock at the ground between him and the two other women. A stream of magma spilled out from Meteorend as if a hole had been poked into it and the rock was bleeding.

When the burning liquid hit the dusty flatness of the ring, the ground shook and cracks opened in the dirt. They spread like the earth's answer to lightning, shooting straight at the two women in the ring with Raiko to swallow them whole.

"By the gray hells." Lyan Yo Bunpy spat as she started throw herself out of the path of the parting earth.

Ophelia did exactly the same thing, only faster, and slammed her leather covered shoulder into the bare one of the barbarian. The dark skinned woman had a confused look on her face as she spoke to the mercenary for the first time.

"If you are not with him, why stop me from killing him?"

"*It's complicated* seems so inadequate," Ophelia answered as the women helped each other up (who was assistance to whom was debatable), "Short version is that, if you kill him an innocent cleric will die. And I need that rock that he's using to kill us but it will disappear when he dies."

The cracks that Raiko made continued past where Ophelia and Lyan had been. The audience trampled each other to get away from the growing chasms when an arrow struck the ground at the feet of the Herald, who was about to be swallowed up.

A shunt of blue light engulfed the arrow and the crack was frozen in its tracks. The other crack had been stopped in the same manner, with another glowing arrow in its path.

While it was Josie who shot the arrows, it was Folken who provided whatever energy was stopping Raiko's magickal attack. The entire right arm of the svartalfar sorcerer glowed with the same blue light, making what appeared to be the bones of his arm visible. Only the bones looked too symmetrical, as if they were smithed by a metal worker and then put together.

Folken's fingers looked more like talons as they rolled closed into a fist. The azure light shot back and forth between the arrows and the wooden shafts jumped down the length of the cracks as if they were being picked up by some unseen, giant seamstress. The light continued bouncing back and forth between the fissures. They became narrower and narrower until they were *sewn up* by whatever spell Folken concocted. Then the arrows toppled over into dust that quickly mixed with what already covered the earth.

"I am suddenly relieved that he is on our side," Havarti quipped.

"So what is your plan to retrieve that rock you so desire without killing the panicking dust bunny?" Lyan snatched her spear from the ground.

"Plan is an awfully strong word," the mercenary replied, "I'll head over there, hope punching him in the face doesn't do any permanent damage to my friend, and relieve him of it."

"But he is mine to kill!" the barbarian protested.

Ophelia started marching toward the now floating Raiko, "Not while he's wearing that bracer, he's not!" she pointed at the man's right arm.

Lyan frowned, only looking more confused as Folken, Josie, Horta, and his partners stepped up to her. Josie gave the barbarian a quick nod of a greeting while Folken inspected the now sealed fissures, though his attention did not seem away from the duelist who still loomed as a threat to not only him but the fleeing crowds. Horta and the other silver haired ones stood and waited.

"I know it may bring Harbenigyr to harm but perhaps it is time I make an appearance," Havarti's voice was filled with resignation in Ophelia's head.

Her pale blue eyes locked on the man in the long brown coat floating five feet in the air, the mercenary reached over her left shoulder and pulled the bastard sword free from his hidden scabbard. Raiko's glowing eyes turned in her direction and the woman knew this was not going to end well. The only question now was for whom.

"We'll hope those protections that Folken guy put on him hold," She telepathically answered.

A massive version of those sparks that scorched Raiko's chest the night before leaped from Meteorend and right for Ophelia. The woman dived forward in hopes of avoiding it but the human sized glob of light landed right on top of her.

An explosion rocked what was left of the makeshift ring, the flash blinding Lyan Yo Bunpy and the others. Stepping out of a purple shadow behind the fit throwing duelist, Ophelia stumbled away from where the enormous spark would have hit the mercenary squarely and incinerated her. Once again, blinking had saved her life.

Raiko hadn't noticed yet and Ophelia didn't want to waste the opportunity to close the distance. The man was floating high enough that his broken foot was hanging at an awkward angle at the same level as her shoulders.

"Time to stop your tantrum and get down here, boy!" Flipping Havarti around in her hand, so that his blade faced downward and his hilt up, Ophelia slapped the handle of the sword across the man's broken foot.

The unexpected splash of pain caused Raiko to lose his concentration. He tumbled to the ground, just barely staying on his feet, er, foot, as he turned to glare at Ophelia.

"You heard her," the duelist rasped, "She was going to kill me!"

"Only after you broke the rules and tried to kill her with an illegal weapon," the woman responded, adding a word that described his family lineage as... wanting, "You brought *all of this* on yourself."

"How is it you think you have earned the right to be *this* self righteous?" Raiko growled, Meteorend still radiating orange light in his hand, "You, who will lay with anything with a pulse except when it comes to my aid?"

"*That* is why you're so upset with me?" Ophelia ran her tongue along the inside of her cheek, "The kid couldn't even grow a beard yet, Raiko!"

"But he was the heir of a powerful clan," he growled, "You sleeping with him would have assured his loyalty to me and *my people!*"

Her thick eyebrows pressed together, "*Your* people. You mean like them? Over there?"

She pointed where the smoke from the explosion was just clearing behind her. The barbarian was shocked to see Ophelia alive. Folken was apparently the one responsible for the flames dying out, judging by this once again glowing arm. Josie was nowhere to be seen.

Horta and his consorts aided several lingering bystanders up from the ground so that they could continue their flight from the battle. When Ophelia motioned in their direction, it was as if all three silver haired people looked back on cue.

Now it was Raiko's turn to curse, "They're fools if they think I will stop now."

"You've pretty much stopped yourself at this point," Ophelia said, "If you give them back that rock, they may even let you leave again."

The mercenary reached out to take Meteorend from the man with her empty right hand. As her fingers wrapped around the stone, the flesh on Ophelia's hand immediately boiled, the bubbles of what had been her skin popping to release scorching liquid to drip into the dirt.

As she reeled back in pain, cradling her skinned hand to her chest, Raiko couldn't help but laugh. "I told you that you were too dependent on your blinking to protect you, Ophelia," pulling his long coat open, the duelist slipped Meteorend back inside.

When he closed the brown leather, there wasn't even a lump to hint where the rock rested. He turned to square up to Ophelia, his eyes still glowing. Somehow, Meteorend was still feeding him power.

It took every ounce of control left in the woman to keep from lashing out with Havarti and chopping Raiko into little pieces. Small, tiny, minuscule to the point that the stray animals wandering the town would not find any chunk a satisfying meal pieces.

But that meant the same thing would happen to Harby. The cleric brought her back to life from being petrified by a gorgon. How could she repay him by letting him die in proxy with this (Really, Havarti? You feel it inappropriate to curse now? Fine.) loomwaffle?

Her body wasn't sure how it should react to her new injury. Ophelia was shivering as if she was caught in a snowstorm while, at the same time, sweating as if she were standing in the middle of a desert on a cloudless midday.

Still, her grip on her bastard sword remained as firm in her left hand as her breathing was ragged. Spittle ran down her chin as she gasped for air, her pale eyes locked on Raiko. There was only one person she ever hated more than this man, at this very moment.

"You cannot take Meteorend from me," the man limped toward Ophelia, "But I was able to take this while you were busy melting."

Raiko held up Saya's dagger. As he waved it back and forth in the air between himself and the woman, the blade started to steam and gleam with orange light, as if it were freshly pulled from a blacksmith's forge.

"How many times do you think you can blink before I land a blow that will finally take?" he smirked.

She *was* going to have to kill him. "I'm sorry, Harby," Ophelia whispered, regret filling every word.

The two figures charged at each other. Before Raiko could reach Ophelia with the sweltering dagger, even before the woman could reach the duelist with the much longer blade of her bastard sword, Raiko was suddenly jerked to the side.

Landing on his shoulder, Ophelia heard the joint snap even as Raiko skid to a halt in the dirt. Lyan Yo Bunpy's spear stabbed through the middle of the man, the blue fur now caked in the duelist's blood. Any of the red liquid that didn't immediately pour from the wound in his stomach *and* back came out of his mouth as the coughed out his last breath.

Raiko de Junamend was no more. Only the meat that made up his body remained, and even then it was no longer complete.

Ophelia slipped Havarti back into his scabbard and then made her way to Raiko's corpse. Pulling his brown jacket open, much easier now that the silver buckles were completely severed from the leather, she reached inside to take Meteorend.

It wasn't there.

She patted at his side with her good hand. Ophelia felt along the interior of his long coat. Meteorend was nowhere to be found.

The woman looked along the ground all around them, looking further and further away with each turn of her head. There was nowhere the rock could lay hidden, even being struck by as powerful of a blow as the spear delivered. If Meteorend had fallen out of Raiko's coat it should have been visible.

Folken stepped up to the other side of Raiko, careful to avoid the puddle of ichor that was forming in the dirt behind the body of the duelist. Gathering his long black cape up, he knelt down. His gloved hand pulled away the coat just as Ophelia had moments ago.

He only grasped the blood soaked material with a thumb and forefinger. His grass hued eyebrow arched for a moment before he let go and stood back up.

Horta and his compatriots were only moments behind. They all hurriedly muttered back and forth in a language that Ophelia didn't recognize before Horta looked down at Ophelia expectantly.

"Please tell me that you found Meteorend," he practically begged, "Tell me you got to him before he breathed his last!"

"Sorry," Ophelia shrugged, motioning down the the spear still resting within the body, "That wound killed him in seconds."

Lyan Yo Bunpy was the last to rejoin the group. As she walked up the barbarian didn't have a look of satisfaction on her face, which Ophelia expected for some reason, but a hard expression that was struggling to stave off remorse.

"You!" Horta turned and pointed an accusing finger at Lyan, "You did this! You doomed all my people!"

While the turn of events didn't appear to please the heavily muscled woman, it didn't stop anger from twisting her face in reaction to the man with the short silver hair's accusation. Her entire body stiffened as she straightened up to her full height, which as actually taller than Horta.

"I saved her life," she motioned to Ophelia, "at the expense of not only his," Lyan pointed at Raiko's body, "which was just, but also the life of their friend. If anyone should have a grievance against me, it should be Ophelia and her magician partner. I do not see how *you* have been wronged!"

Aghast, Horta looked down at the corpse of Raiko, then to Ophelia, to Folken, and finally back to Lyan Yo Bunpy. "Bah, you are not worth our effort," he said dismissively.

It wasn't only his words that were dismissive. Without another sound, Horta and the other two de Junamend marched off. They were met by the remaining two silver haired people who had been wandering in the crowd earlier. Only now, they carried the body of the Cardasian between them on a stretcher.

When all five (six if you included the corpse) disappeared between a couple of buildings, Ophelia turned her attention back down to Raiko. It was then that she noticed something different.

"The buckler is open," she reached down and pulled the now loose, metal cuff away from the arm of the dead man and into the air.

Folken nodded, "It was his life force that powered the enchantment. That ceased the moment his body fell dead, so the cuff halted its purpose."

"The same thing probably happened to Harbenigyr, right?" Ophelia bit down on her lower lip as she looked up at the svartalfar.

"It is likely," he answered.

"Make that definite," Saya said as she stepped out from between the same buildings that Horta and his party disappeared between.

Behind her came Lily along with Josie, who was deeply crouched to match her height with the shorter horticultural wizard. In between was–

"Harby!" Ophelia and Havarti both gasped with relief and shock.

The still living, if groggy cleric was practically being carried between the woman with crimson, and the other with wild and curly, hair. He was dressed in his long white tunic, although Ophelia did notice that he was lacking in pants.

Ophelia lifted herself to her feet, brushing dust from her knees with her good hand as Saya and the others closed the distance. As surprised as the mercenary was, Folken looked anything but.

"I did not say to bring him," the man motioned to Harbenigyr as he addressed his cousin.

"He insisted," Saya replied, "He wanted to see if there was anything he could do to aid Raiko."

"I'm afraid there is little more you can do for him save pray to your goddess, Cleric Harbenigyr," Folken's brow furrowed into a tight wall of lines.

"Then why am I still alive?" the elf's voice came hoarse out of his mouth.

Ophelia stepped up to the cleric and shooed Lily away from under his arm before taking up the same position. Josie looked thankful as she was able to straighten up to her full height, which was just under Ophelia's own.

"Do you think those symbols you scratched into his cuff could have had anything to do with it?" Saya directed the question at Folken even as her violet eyes fell on the furry barbarian.

The green haired man let out only a short grunt in response. That was when the authorities finally arrived and he turned his attention to them, his hand already starting to drift toward his coin purse.

The barbarian stepped up to Ophelia, the cleric, and Josie, her mocha face a mix between worry and confusion, "This is your friend whose life was bonded to that of Raiko?" She poked his chest as if to check if Harbenigyr were real.

He flinched. She must have pressed against one of the wounds from last night. But he still smiled kindly back at the barbarian.

Ophelia nodded, "Still alive somehow," her pale blue eyes darted back toward the hilt of her sword for a brief instant. "Thank Kuan Yin or whoever."

"Then I did not kill two to save your life," Lyan's shoulders seemed to loosen at the realization.

"Nope," the mercenary agreed, "And don't think I don't appreciate the save but I didn't really need it."

"Oh?" the taller woman reached up and pressed a mere pinky onto the other woman's seared right hand.

Ophelia loosed a string of profanity as she stomped at the ground again and again, fresh pain washing through her. She hadn't forgotten her injury but she had been successfully ignoring it since she saw Harbenigyr still among the living.

Once she was finished with an overly detailed description of avian genitalia, Ophelia settled into a few, deep gasps for breath before answering Lyan, "Yes, even with that."

Harbenigyr's cheeks burned bright with embarrassment to witness such a display of vulgarity. Still, he remained silent, not wanting whatever he said to be taken as judgmental.

The barbarian, on the other hand, had a frown that curved deep down her chin. As the mercenary readjusted her grip under the arm of the cleric, she grinned back at Lyan.

"Don't get angry. It's nothing you could have known about and is kind of a long story anyway," Ophelia explained, or rather, didn't, "Anyway, it all turned out okay in the end."

"So have we picked up a new traveler to augment our suddenly reduced ranks?" Saya turned away from observing Folken's negotiations to face Lyan, Ophelia and the others.

Lyan Yo Bunpy shook her head, "If the remainder of the tournament has not been canceled, I must remain for the finals. Besides, I must travel alone. The why of it is," she glanced back at Ophelia, "a long story."

The platinum haired woman nodded, though she still stepped up to the larger barbarian woman, "If you decide that you wish to change that, please come to Emerald City. It is to the northeast of Valen Court. You need only ask for Folken Kizoku or Saya Khushrenada."

Lyan's response was to bend down and pull her spear free of the corpse of her opponent. A fresh set of protests came from the city guards to whom Folken was speaking. When his gloved hand passed over theirs, yet again, they suddenly became far more agreeable.

CHAPTER THREE

OPHELIA INTERROGATION NOTES

The following events were taking place during the events of the tournament. The subject has not been made aware of the existence of this report:

Elsewhere...

THE WINDS HOWLED outside the tent. The heavy cloth that made up the makeshift walls of the structure kept the worst of the cold air out but Horta, however, still felt a chill.

Most of it wasn't from the weather. It was the ashen gray eyes of Vulcan, staring him down from the metal seat that was welded together specifically for him. With the wide fire pit in the middle of the space, it made every doubtful line in the face of the Elder of the de Junamend look that much deeper.

"So what you are saying, essentially, is that after all this time, effort, and gold spent, you could not get Meteorend back?" Vulcan's unkempt silver hair spilled over the back of his chair, brushing the carpet laid out over the hard ground as he grumbled.

"Raiko defeated Cardy with little trouble," Horta crossed his arms over his broad chest in an effort to fight off the cold as much as to appear defiant, "So the training was lacking. Then Raiko picked an unregulated fight with a Yo Bunpy warrior. They were no more than ambivalent toward us in the past. He has single hand-edly poisoned the well of possibly opening negotiations with them. There was nothing we could have done to stop that."

The old man frowned, "But you did let those he traveled with reach his body first. They must have taken Meteorend before you finally decided to approach."

"You and I both know that it was pointless," Horta frowned, his hands moving down to rest on his narrow hips, "Ophelia fought to retrieve Meteorend *for* us but the Yo Bunpy spear was too effective. You know that Meteorend dissipates if the wielder dies with it in their possession."

"You and I both know, we all know..." the old man leaned forward in his seat, "that Meteorend still exists. What about this Folken? He reached Raiko before you as well, yes?"

Horta reluctantly nodded, "But he didn't have it when we came up."

"That you noticed," the old man snapped.

Rising from his seat, he motioned for the larger, younger man to come along. Vulcan didn't bother with the fur lined cloak offered by a valet as he pushed the flaps of the entrance open and stepped out into the wind. Horta dutifully followed.

The wind ripped the heat from the body of the younger man. If it bothered Vulcan, he didn't give any indication.

Thankfully, the walk was short. The old man guided Horta into a cave that had lines of lit torches lining the walls and making it almost as bright as day within the dank tunnels. After several turns, a line of heavily armored guards cut off the path to get any deeper.

"Out of the way, ruffians!" the old man continued forward and the men wrapped in metal scrambled to get out of his path.

Only a few paces behind where the guards stood was a wooden wall that was cut to fit into the area of the tunnel perfectly. A set of double doors, just big enough for Horta and Vulcan to be able to walk through them side by side, sat right in the middle.

As each door was pulled open by those same guards who rushed to get out of Vulcan's way, Horta stayed behind him. Once both silver haired men were through the doors were quickly closed behind them, Horta still so close that he felt the wood hit the heel on his boot.

"It is important to maintain a controlled environment down here," Vulcan explained, "We are going to your secondary stratagem, Horta. I suppose, in hindsight, it should have been our first."

"You are actually using my doppelganger plan now?" Horta looked at the back of the old man questioningly, "To what end?"

"Raiko's former companions are the only lead we have on Meteorend," the old man answered as they continued walking, "It is likely that one of them is in possession of it. We need it back."

They rounded one last bend to enter an antechamber where the albino svartalfar woman, Saya, stood silently. She was a perfect imitation of the other, thanks to the hairs that Horta was able to retrieve.

"This one was tricky," Vulcan pointed at the woman with platinum hair, "She had a prosthetic arm that our alchemists could not clone via your sample. Fortunately, the mechanism was simple and our machinists were able to duplicate it."

Beside her stood a severely displeased looking Folken Kizoku. The entirety of his right arm was missing.

"I presume this one had a false arm as well?" Horta motioned to the empty space within the doppelganger's black cloak, "Are the machinists recreating it, too?"

"Unfortunately, his appears to have been far more... complex in its design," the old man shook his head, "The best we can do for our Folken is a cosmetic duplicate. When it is his turn to infiltrate, we will have to hope that he will not be called upon to use whatever functions the appendage performs."

The cleric, Harbenigyr, yawned as the two men stepped up to him. His was the most difficult sample to acquire since he was not one to drink, like Ophelia was, and was always close to Raiko. When he discovered that the young woman they called Lily had snipped some of his black hair for samples of her own, it was truly a boon for Horta (though the job of actually stealing them fell to Andora, who succeeded shortly before passing out).

"And what, pray tell, are you looking at in such a hungry-like-the-wolf manner?" the thin elf smirked at the much larger man, "I don't think I'm your type. I don't just bend over for anybody, you know."

"Hungry-like-the... bend over?" Horta mumbled in confusion, "Are we sure this one isn't defective in some way? The true Harbenigyr never spoke like this."

"Without souls, none of them will have the same personality as the hosts, Horta," Vulcan sighed, "But the process of reading the structural energies of their entire body from a sample of a single part is brilliant magick, truly. The detail in even being able to rebuild their memories is nigh-miraculous. They will be able to pass when the time comes."

After an obscene gesture from the copy of the cleric, Horta and Vulcan continued their inspection. Next came the crimson haired woman that accompanied Folken Kizoku to rendezvous with his cousin. If memory served, her name was Josie. He never heard her clan name.

The polished elm bow that she held in her hands was an exact copy of the one the ranger carried. Horta doubted that the real Josie handled it in much the same manner, though.

The woman stroked the end of the hard wood, rolling her thumb around the tip, just beyond where the taut line of tendon was stringed. When she saw Horta approach, she gave him a wide, flirtatious smile.

"Will *you* be coming with us on this mission?" she asked, her round, bare hips swaying from side to side.

Horta shook his head… and then cleared his throat, "All of them can recognize me, I'm afraid."

"Pity," she grinned in response before turning her back on walking back to the waiting chairs and beds only steps away.

The muscular man scanned up and down the length of the line of people who looked exactly like the party that accompanied Raiko before his untimely demise, "Where are the doppelgangers of Lily and Ophelia?"

Vulcan again wagged a finger in a silent command to follow, "The one you called Lily will be the next in the process. They are recreating Ophelia at the moment. In fact, she should be nearing completion."

They both walked toward the back of the cavern. All the almost daytime bright light that was in the antechamber disappeared.

Horta looked around. The torches were still burning but whatever light they were putting off just wasn't radiating out. Then he remembered.

It was the Krialope' Crystal. The source of the de Junamend's ability to create the doppelgangers in the first place. Second only to Meteorend in sanctity to Horta's people.

After a short walk through the darkness, a white light became brighter and brighter with each step the men took. After only a few steps, the brightness started to hurt the larger man's eyes.

Raising his hand as a shield, Horta squinted at the source. The four feet tall, six-sided, nearly infinitely faceted crystal slowly spun in front of them. The fact that it was not touching the ground meant that it was performing the magickal rites for which it had been created so many centuries ago.

The Kiralope' Crystal took literally centuries to grow to this size and power. At first, it's purpose was to create more tools to aid in the building of the first village of the de Junamend. As the crystal's surface area increased, it was discovered that it could copy anything with a small sampling rather than having to be in the presence of the original.

The ability to duplicate living things came in a time of desperation for the ancestors of the de Junamend. A terrible famine had caused the once fertile land to turn to dust. In a bid for survival, the old ones tried copying an ear of corn. Upon that success, they copied the few remaining farm animals again and again for meat. The de Junamend not only survived but thrived after that.

It wasn't until the Clan Wars a decade ago that the de Junamend dared copy a person. It was Horta's father who suggested such a course of action. It was thought that if they had a doppelganger of the enemy, they could somehow convince him to become a spy.

They did not need worry about providing incentive to the copy of the soldiers they duplicated. They were more than willing to take the place of their source material, turn on their brethren, and aid their creators in destroying them.

The de Junamend came to realize this was for one simple reason: the Kiralope' Crystal could not copy the soul. Even with only a single hair as the source material, the subject's entire body, their memories, even the clothing they last wore were perfectly duplicated.

But they were not the same person. They had different personalities, often a more primal, unrestrained version of the source, and their own motivations for why they continued to exist. But as the Kiralope' Crystal was subject to the will of the de Junamend, so were the doppelgangers.

Not due to any threat or other controls via the enchanted device. It was just the way it was. How it had always been.

Horta's reflections were interrupted when the light from the crystal ceased and the responsibility for lighting the antechamber returned to the torches. The first thing Horta could see was the long red coat wrapped around a body that was curled into a tight ball.

Ophelia's doppelganger had her arms wrapped around her folded legs, her face tucked into the little gap between her chest and knees. The newly created woman tumbled from the crystal and to the ground. She landed on her side, her long auburn hair draped over her face, obscuring it from view.

Horta suddenly found himself wondering if this version would be as attracted to him as the original seemed to be. And those thoughts evolved into others that wondered if there was anyplace the two of them could have some privacy before the doppelgangers left on their mission.

"Ophelia," Horta stepped up beside the deathly still woman, "Ophelia?"

The process of creating the duplicates was fairly quick, only taking several hours. The only variable would be how large the original subject was.

The time it took for the doppelganger to become active, though, should have only been seconds. No more than it took for a person to wake up from a refreshing nap. This Ophelia, though, she was completely motionless.

"Odd," Vulcan muttered, wrapping his hands behind his hunched back, "Some kind of error in the duplication process?"

"It never would have reached this stage if there had been. The failed duplicate would have been absorbed back into the crystal and restarted," Horta answered as he knelt down beside the woman, resting a hand on her red leather covered shoulder.

At his touch, Ophelia's head snapped up to face him. What stared back at Horta, though, was not Ophelia but some reptilian monster!

Her skin was green and covered in moist scales, from the front of her neck down her chest looked like the underbelly of a snake. The rest of Ophelia had copied perfectly from the braids in her hair to the leather coat to her black boots. What caused her to turn out so wrong?

"Lover!" it hissed excitedly before lunging at the man.

The creature sank its needle-like teeth into the man's neck. The Not-Ophelia chewed loudly, not letting the man go as she moaned happily.

After only seconds Horta's head fell away from his body, a look of shock and horror frozen on his now permanently still face. That look was mirrored in the face of Vulcan, who stumbled away from the unprecedented show of violence.

Not-Ophelia slurped at the warm crimson liquid that still streamed from the man's neck for a few moments before it became too cool for her tastes. Dropping his remains like a spent apple core, her jade eyes darted toward the old man. The thin slits of her pupils widened as they discerned their next target.

"Harbenigyr, Saya, Josie, Folken, defend me!" he shrieked back at the successfully created doppelgangers as Not-Ophelia rose to her feet.

She did not lunge for the old man instantly. This... thing was not brainless, it would seem. A long, tendril-like tongue lapped at the ichor that coated her face from brow to her neck as she watched the party that looked like those of her original's friends gather to attack her.

"You are a de Junamend," Not-Ophelia smiled a smile that stretched from once edge of her jaw to the other, "You tried to recreate his prize with your little trinket?"

The reptilian woman motioned to the massive Kiralope' Crystal that now rested on its side in the dirt. She started to pull her long coat off her shoulders, keeping an eye on the duplicates of the party that the real Ophelia knew.

"I trust you recognize the signature?" Not-Ophelia chuckled as she turned her back toward Vulcan, her head not changing direction at all as her body faced the opposite direction, "You should not have interfered in his work."

The violet runes that ran from between the monster woman's shoulder blade and down to the small of her back, there being the only human looking skin on the entire creature, started to crackle with growing energy.

What little color there was in the old man's face disappeared as recognition of the symbols came to him. His legs lost the ability to hold him up and he tumbled to the ground. He felt his hip snap apart as he landed in a heap. Vulcan could only hope that the end would come quickly.

Not-Ophelia turned her body back toward the doppelganger party, "Now isn't this a grouping of beautiful people?"

She couldn't help but laugh as her eyes scanned each party member. They stood ready to fight. Her attention finally landed squarely on Folken's duplicate, followed shortly by her clawed finger pointing in his direction, "Except you. Without that arm, you'd be useless to me, I think. Unless..."

In a flash of violet light, Not-Ophelia disappeared. Another flash of purple and she mounted Folken's back.

Her clawed hands scratched deep into doublet wrapped around his chest as he spun around, trying to throw her off. The pale doppelganger reached back with his one hand and Not-Ophelia kept slapping his palm away with her own again and again in a grim mockery of applause at his effort.

"Atta boy!" She giggled, her long legs wrapping around his waist to keep her firmly in place. "I like men with spirit!"

The claws of her other hand shredded the black material and gold buckles of his jacket, leaving his firm chest bare. Then they pierced his pale flesh, her fingers digging deeper and deeper into his chest. In short order, she was was able to curl her fingers around one of his ribs and twist, snapping it completely free from his skeleton.

The intense surge of pain caused Folken to topple over. He had enough sense to try and land on top of her, to at least try and stun her so he could get away. The rough landing only seemed to amuse the monster more.

Saya dived after them. Wrapping her hands around the arm causing so much damage to her cousin, she desperately tried to pull it away. Not-Ophelia slapped Folken's hand away yet again and grabbed the albino woman's throat with the same hand.

"You wait your turn," Not-Ophelia hissed, then slammed her scale coated forehead into Saya's face.

With another push of her hand, the monster's hand sank into the chest cavity of the green haired svartalfar up just past her wrist. Folken's breathing froze as shock washed through his entire body.

Not-Ophelia's arm moved from side to side, her buried hand searching for something unseen. "Move this lung to the side..."

A squeak escaped Folken's mouth that would have been comical in just about any other situation. Another squeak, this time followed by a gurgle as the monster woman finally pulled her hand free of the man's chest.

Folken's heart left his body with Not-Ophelia's hand. It didn't beat anymore and the formerly life giving crimson liquid drained from the ripped apart valves.

Not-Ophelia kicked the albino corpse away. As she sat up, an arrow launched at the monster. Not-Ophelia bent down, raising her hands in a defensive reflex. When she realized she wasn't dead, and not even feeling any painful wound, the monster opened her jade eyes.

A chuckle escaped her scaled lips when she saw the shaft of the arrow protruding from the limp organ in her hand, "I know we just met, Josie, but there is some deeper meaning to this. Don't you think?"

Not-Ophelia held the pierced heart up as she lifted herself to a standing position. She scanned the few pockets of shadow for the other woman. With bright red hair and such a brightly lit area should have been easy to spot. She wasn't. Josie was good.

The monster raised her chin, addressing the ranger even if she couldn't see her, "You can get through this alive, Josie. I'm not after you. This old *t'zzrid* meddled where he ought not to and now he has to pay. You, Harby, and Saya... when she wakes up, can go about your lives free of any de Junamend commands or controls."

Not-Ophelia turned toward the massive crystal. Bending down, she rested Folken's still, bloodsoaked heart on the glassy surface. Staying still for a long moment, the serpentine woman expected to feel an unpleasant piercing sensation from behind. She was pleasantly surprised when it didn't come.

Not-Ophelia rested a hand on top of the dead organ that rested atop the Kiralope' Crystal. "tigeLe em Oitatum." she muttered.

Harbenigyr suddenly rose up from the other side of the massive jewel. Resting a hand on the Kiralope' Crystal, he leaned in closer to the monster woman with a wide grin on his face.

"Is that svart-speak I hear?" the cleric asked, "You know that the de Junamend have a tacit alliance with the Xaviour Tribe, don't you?"

"Not my concern, tiny cutie," Ophelia smirked back, "After I finish this ritual, I'm not headed back that way anyway."

"Vulcan, the old man, knows. Doesn't he?" Harbenigyr motioned back to the owner of the name laying prone on the ground behind him, "Did the Xaviours send you?"

"He knows who sent me," Not-Ophelia smirked.

The cleric of a deity who was not Kuan Yin chewed on his lower lip thoughtfully for a moment, "Then I guess we're just about done here."

"I could take you with me when I leave," the monster offered, her long tongue flicking from between her scaly lips.

"Like you said, I don't think we're going to the same place," Harbenigyr pointed a finger behind Not-Ophelia.

The reptilian woman turned to see Saya standing less than a foot away. The albino svartalfar's face was an iron mask of hatred as her violet eyes stared into the monster's emerald ones.

"You do not kill a member of the Kizoku Tribe without consequences," the platinum haired woman declared.

Saya pulled a dagger from the wrist of her long glove and buried it into Not-Ophelia's chest, just under her solar plexus and upward into her heart. The monster let out a gasp of surprise, but then her mouth stretched into a wide, predatory grin that made the pale woman take a step back.

Without turning her body, Not-Ophelia looked back over her shoulder at the copy of Harbenigyr, still smiling. "I guess we're not. I hope you weren't planning on more company."

The purple runes etched all over the monster's back arced with overflowing energy, finally shooting violet lightning into Folken's dead heart which, in turn, drained the destructive force into the Kiralope' Crystal.

"Get back!" Harbenigyr yelled, following his own advice.

Not-Ophelia let out a loud laugh that echoed through the antechamber, "I'm going home, Harby! Too bad I couldn't introduce you to my father!"

Everything turned blindingly white. A rush of heat washed over the the doppelganger of Harbenigyr as he huddled behind an outcropping of rock.

It wasn't over quickly, like after an explosion. At least then, the damage may have been traumatic but it was done and over. No, whatever destructive force was happening here and now, it took its time to finish its work thoroughly.

The target of the destructive force, apparently, wasn't Harby or anyone else in the cave. When all seemed calm and the cleric poked his head out, he saw what was: the Kiralope' Crystal itself.

It was little more than a pile of sparkling ash. It's days of copying anything and anyone were done.

Harbenigyr walked over to the remains of the very thing that created him, keeping an eye out for the remains of Not-Ophelia. There were none. The ritual must have used the whole body of the monster as fuel while Folken's heart, a creation of the crystal, was made into a catalyst that let the destructive force in.

Clever.

A breathy groan caught the elf's attention. It was Vulcan, still alive.

Harby made his way to the old man, who was struggling to breathe through the pain of his broken hip. The cleric could tell from the angle of the de Junamend's leg that it was a severe fracture. He crouched down next to Vulcan, brushing the man's silver hair out of his face.

"You're still with us," the cleric said, "You survived the Xaviour Tribe's plot to assassinate you."

Vulcan blinked through the overflowing water from his eyes that his pain was causing him, "She was not sent by those svartalfar," he gasped, "Her creator was… something worse."

"Something worse?" Harbenigyr quirked an eyebrow as a sudden understanding overtook him, "You mean the thing that you want Meteorend back so badly to defend against."

Vulcan nodded, his entire body twitching with the effort.

"Okay, weathered rock. We'll get your little toy back for you from our doppelgangers." The cleric moved his hand down to the old man's disjointed leg, faint wisps of green light trailing from his fingers. "After we're done, me and my lovely ladies go our way with a healthy stipend from your coffers. I mean *enough to keep us in alcohol and whores for the rest of our days* healthy."

The elder of the de Junamend let out a quiet sigh of relief as the light from the hand of the cleric started dulling the pain from his hip. But when Harbenigyr stated the terms of his service…

"It should be your pleasure to serve my people. We have never had need to pay your kind before."

"My kind?" Harby grabbed Vulcan's hip and roughly squeezed, "I'm afraid I'm a little confused about that. I'm an elf that was raised by dwarves on a chain of islands an ocean away. Which kind are you referring to again?"

"Created. B-by. Our. Crystal!" Vulcan struggled to get each word out as the pain returned tenfold due to the cleric's ministrations.

"Oh, that," Harbenigyr chuckled, "That's gone. Your boogeyman was able to get to it before we were able to get her. But we did what you said. We defended you, right? You're being alive is a testament to that."

The cleric returned to again pouring pain numbing green light into Vulcan's leg. Any real treatment would need healing salves and splints, in addition to the healing power of whatever deity the elf was channeling.

With no more doppelgangers able to be made, the doppelgangers of Harbenigyr, Josie, and Saya were the best, and perhaps only, chance for the de Junamend to get Meteorend back. Harby knew that Vulcan had no choice but to agree.

And agree he did. A pleased cleric of a deity that was not Kuan Yin raised his other hand, rested it on Vulcan's forehead and placed him into a healing sleep. Then he stood up and slapped his hands together as if he were trying to wipe away a layer of filth.

"It's safe to come out now, Saya," he called out and then turned to look in the direction of the entrance. "You can let the guards in now, Josie. We need to tell them all the good news. We're going to be their saviors!"

OPHELIA INTERROGATION NOTES

"What about this... Diomedes?" I asked the subject, having to refer to my notes to make sure I had the name correct.

"What about her?" Ophelia replied.

"Are you aware of her meeting with the Order of Kuan Yin to recruit their aid?" My inquiry elicited a surprised expression from the subject, "Then I should read this to you..."

Two decades later...

APPELONIA TAPPED HER father on the shoulder, pointing toward the treeline to the north, "What about him, Dad? Do we know him or will he need an explanation, too?"

A man stepped out of the trees, immediately turning to walk toward the group gathered around the fresh carcass of the efreeti demon that attacked them. As he closed the distance, more details became noticeable.

First, he was carrying a backpack that looked too large for him yet he didn't show any sign of strain or fatigue. What appeared to be black hair was actually a helmet that covered the whole top half of his face. His pants were the same color, although he had a steel codpiece that glinted in the late morning sun.

Upon closer inspection, his helmet and pants were both made of black fur. It became obvious to what group this man belonged, at least to Appelonia. While he was thin, the new arrival had very defined muscles, and scarring along his shoulders and upper arms from what looked like old, long healed acid burns.

When the front of the helmet turned out to be that of a slain saber-toothed rabbit, complete with the yellowed, sharp teeth that stretched down to just past his collarbone. Not to mention the cod-piece in the shape of a stylized rabbit head, and lingering doubt Appelonia may have had was gone. This man was a warrior of the Yo Bunpy tribe of Bunny Barbarians.

When he was still about twenty paces away, Samson called out, "Please identify yourself! We were just attacked and do not wish further violence."

The Bunny Barbarian stopped without taking another step. His head shook from side to side, the flopping ears slapping one shoulder and then the other. "I can't believe this! You could not have started the battle an hour later? Or even kept it going a little longer?"

The man groaned as he paced around in a circle and pointed at the remains of Abernathy. *"That* was what you fought? I came here to find glory. That thing would have surely fit the bill and I miss it by only a few minutes?" he groaned in frustration.

Looking back at the Grand Cleric, it was clear to his daughter that whoever this was, he was expected. Appelonia suddenly felt as if she'd been set up for something unpleasant.

With no further sign of danger, the paladin, Jonas the Shep-herd, turned away to busy himself with cleaning his sword. Appe-lonia would much rather sit and watch him do that than deal with this... ruffian who had just arrived.

Phinegann gathered up the chain connected to the spiked ball and wound it back into his metal arm. Appelonia didn't get a chance to see where the ball itself went.

The Grand Cleric rose and, after pacifying a worried looking Samson, strode over to the Bunny Barbarian. Appelonia dutifully walked up beside her father, not at all pleased if this had to do with what she thought.

"You missed this one, Tokki, but you will have more chances in the days to come," Harbenigyr raised the first two fingers of his right hand, motioned them around in a circle before giving the man who was even smaller than him a short bow. "I asked your cleric Rayflintr for a champion to accompany my daughter on her pilgrimage and he sent me you. It is an honor for both our peoples.

This... Tokki Yo Bunpy returned the traditional blessing gesture of the Great Chromatic Rabbit and bowed, "I shall endeavor to be worthy of this right. First, by not being late for the call of duty again."

"That would be a good start," Harbenigyr chuckled.

Illyria separated herself from Samson's band of clerics to join the group surrounding Appelonia and her father. While Samson was also returning to the keep with them, the group that came out with him were remaining behind to figure out how to prepare the body... halves for proper burial.

As Appelonia turned to start back for the keep, she almost ran into a woman that no one had noticed before. With her bright, magenta coat with its unusually long long sleeves, her bright, lime green pants and her head tilted at an odd angle, it was hard to believe that anyone could have been missed seeing her at this point.

Her hair was an even brighter shade of red than Apple's, a shade that the cleric wasn't sure she had ever actually seen in nature. The smile of the stranger was wide and kind but also seemed... off like when someone is smiling at something funnier that they are thinking about rather than what is happening around them.

But it wasn't until Appelonia looked into the woman's eyes that she really started to feel disturbed? Worried? Confused? Amused? Saddened? Nauseous? The young woman couldn't center in on any one feeling and had to look away. The stranger's eyes didn't have any one specific color as much as all of them.

The cleric hadn't realized that she had screamed until she found herself looking into the worried eyes of her father. He held her firmly by the shoulders as Jonas stepped around to direct his heavy blade at the newly arrived woman.

"Sorry. I have that effect on people?" the woman shrugged in response, "I would have shown up earlier but no one said that the explanation would be complicated."

Jin Vega stepped between the Grand Cleric with his daughter and the stranger before he motioned over to Samson, who towered over all of them, "He said that no more than a minute ago."

"You did?" the woman, looked over at the gigantic cleric and let out a breath of air that made her lips bounce up and down for a brief moment, "I guess that means I missed my cue."

"Who are you?" Harbenigyr spoke up.

"My name is Diomedes," she said, "I'm a cleric, like you. Surely you remember me."

The Grand Cleric of the Order of Kuan Yin and his daughter looked equally confused.

"We have not met, Lady Diomedes," Harbenigyr answered, "I have a feeling I would have remembered if we had."

The strange woman pursed her lips thoughtfully. "Oh, that's right! We didn't meet for the first time for another three months."

"That... doesn't make any sense," Harby replied.

"No wonder you seemed so knowledgeable before," the strange woman muttered to herself before speaking again to the Grand Cleric, "Perhaps if I told you, again, that I am a cleric of Ferekane?"

The elf's dark eyebrows pressed together for a moment. When recognition of the name came to him, Harby's head dipped down and a resigned sigh escaped his mouth.

"What kind of deity is Ferekane?" Jonas asked.

The paladin moved to stand between Appelonia and Diomedes protectively. The young cleric tried to remember that it was his job but she still truly appreciated it at the moment. Not so much for the defense posture as much as that he was standing closer to her.

"Ferekane isn't any kind of deity," Apple's father answered, "Ferekane is the word people on the Silver Herald Isles used to describe a force of nature. Something you can't stop but have to live through from time to time. Like a storm or earthquake."

"Forces of nature can have clerics?" Appelonia could only ponder the implications.

Harbenigyr shook his head, "Not in the strictest sense, no. If we're using my childhood home as a reference, I'd say the word Lady Diomedes is looking for is *avatar*. A personification of the idea."

"Oh no, no no." Diomedes lifted a hand and wiggled a finger from side to side (at least that's what Apple thought she did. Her long sleeve kept it hidden for the most part). "I told you that the a-word had some negative connotations involving blue people so I wouldn't use it. Then you said *cleric* would work well enough."

"Three months from now, right?" the Grand Cleric frowned.

"What's three months from now?" Diomedes tilted her head in the opposite direction to the point that it looked painful.

Samson groaned, "Sir, this is a waste of time. I recommend we take this... disturbed individual inside and let one of our mind healers look after her."

"Inside!" Diomedes jumped up and down, clapping her sleeves together excitedly, "Yes, we should discuss this all inside before you all have to go outside again."

Appelonia blinked and when her eyes opened she, along with everyone else, was in the meeting hall within the walls of Dianmeyer. Her father, Jonas, Phinegann, Tokki Yo Bunpy, all looked as confused as her to be standing in the middle of the room.

Apple had almost forgotten the other new arrivals, Illyria Warflower and Jin Vega. They were there, too. The room was filling up quickly.

Unlike everyone else, who looked simply disoriented, Phinegann looked as if he could not decide if he needed to vomit or rip someone limb from limb. It took several long seconds, while everyone else was conversing, for him to decide.

The half-ogre stomped straight for the much smaller Diomedes. He bent down until his face was only inches from hers. "You will not expose me to magicks without my permission!"

Even as flecks of his spittle hit the smaller human's face, she only grinned back, "If I were you, I would get used to it, fuzzy."

Diomedes reached up and patted Phinegann's metal shoulder. In response, his elbow shot up and snapped her arm like a dry tree branch.

Which is exactly what he held in his hand, a broken tree branch, as the woman turned back to Harbenigyr and Appelonia. The former guard started after her again, only to be stopped by Jonas stepping in his path. A conversation of whispers concluded with the orc stuffing his hands in his pockets and turning his wide back to the avatar (cleric!) of Ferekane.

"Now, we probably should do first things first," Diomedes continued as if she hadn't even encountered Phinegann, "Samson should probably explain who Jin Vega is so that I can get through my part uninterrupted. I mean, I do have a lot of exposition to lay out for you and your pallies."

When Diomedes skipped off to the nearest wall and leaned in to get a close look at all the detail in the stone, it was apparent she wasn't going to talk anymore. Judging by Phinegann's lack of success at getting physical, there didn't seem to be any way to make her until she was ready.

"Very well," Harbenigyr said with a shrug, "Samson, would you care to introduce me to your friend and explain why he was hiding behind the keep?"

Being such a large, strong man, Samson was not easy to intimidate. Nor was he a man who was short of words when the situation called for them. Both admirable traits in a Herald.

Now, though, Samson Jhericord rubbed at the back of his thick neck as nothing came out of his mouth. Finally, Jin Vega himself stepped up beside the larger man.

"I am known as Jin Vega. I am a monk of the Mekun Ekud Temple to the south," he rolled one hand into a fist then covered it with his other, open hand in salute, "I visited Dianmeyer with my Teacher before, back when she was," the bald thin man motioned over to Appelonia, who started to fidget where she stood, "about ten years old. I was not much older myself, having just taken the oaths to train within the temple as an acolyte. I don't blame you for not recognizing me."

He ran his fingers over his bushy back beard, which, if his numbers were correct, he would not have been able to grow then. Despite his taking over the conversation, Samson did not seem relieved.

"I came out here in search of some artifacts that are valued by my Temple," Jin continued, "So I found Samson and Organa, asked them or a quiet corner of land and to not trouble you or anyone else. I can take care of myself."

"But why not tell my father?" Appelonia shrugged at the monk, "From what you're saying, it's not like he would have objected or anything. Right?" the last question was directed at the Grand Cleric.

"Not if everything you have said is accurate," he agreed with his daughter before turning his attention to the Herald. "Why *didn't* you tell me, Samson?"

It took several false starts before the massive man was able to get words past his lips, "Do you remember when Organa and I took the matrimonial bonds, sir?"

Harby nodded.

"The only reason I found the courage to do so was because of Jin's, um, *interference* to make me see how foolish letting her go would be," he shrugged his immense, bare shoulders, "I felt like I owed him."

"That explains why *you're* here," Harbenigyr turned from Jin Vega to face in the direction of Diomedes, who didn't budge from beside the wall. "So now the question is why she wants you with us now."

"And me," a feminine voice came from about waist level, "I didn't mean to stumble into... whatever this is."

Illyria Warflower stepped out from the assemblage of people, stretching out her stained glass wings when there was finally enough space. She turned back to face the Grand Cleric, Appelonia and the monk in the long gray cloak.

"I'm not one for fighting. I came here to study the soul orbs in your vault," the tiny woman said, "But, knowingly or not, I did break your rules. The gnome way would be to help you in another task, to apologize for the wrong doing."

"And hopefully be given the access you want afterward," Appelonia smirked down at the smaller woman.

Illyria's purple hair fell in front of her eyes when she nodded her agreement. The grin on her face didn't even try to have the guile to hide that goal.

"I appreciate the offer, Lady Warflower–" Harbenigyr started.

"–But it is going a while before you are going to be back." Diomedes finished.

The cleric in the magenta coat was sitting cross legged in front of the gnome, who jumped in surprise at her appearance. No one saw her move away from the wall.

"Maestro Vega should probably join Appelonia's party for the same reason. Don't you think, chief?" Diomedes looked up at Harbenigyr with a wide smile and presumptuous look on her face.

The elf's eyes narrowed as he looked back at the sitting woman, "He didn't mean or do any harm. I don't see why–"

As the leader of the Kuan Yin was speaking, Diomedes turned her head (a little more than she should have been able) to look back toward Jin Vega. The presumptuous look on her face wasn't meant for Harbenigyr, but for the monk.

No words were expressed between them but, to Jin, volumes were spoken, "I'll go. My teachings state that helping others can lead to the very help you need yourself," He knew that she knew.

"Go where?" Harbenigyr and his daughter both asked at the same time.

"I presume Phinegann and Jonas came to accompany her on her pilgrimage?" Jin pointed at Appelonia, "Oh, and the rabbit man, too."

Tokki Yo Bunpy, who had been quiet to that point, riled at the monk's crack about his attire, "Shall we have a duel to see who lives to make the trip?" he growled.

Appelonia had had enough. She stomped away from her father and slammed a boot covered foot to the floor, "No one is fighting! No one is going with me on my pilgrimage! No one, not even my father, is going to change that!"

Apple's black colored eyes snapped back to stare down at her father. He didn't look angry, like she'd expected. The Grand Cleric looked... hurt and the young woman felt her resolve waiver.

"What if he isn't your father?" Diomedes asked, still sitting on the floor just to Appelonia's left.

"What?" the idea was so foreign to the cleric's mind that she though that this crazy woman just challenged her to a fight of their own.

"Well, he is your father," Diomedes stood up, grabbing Apple's hand and pulling her back to stand across from her father, "I mean you both have black eyes, right? That means that you both probably have efreeti lineage in you. You know that, right?"

"Impossible," Harbenigyr shook his head. "My parents were both elves, born and raised in the Jaded Woods."

"What about their parents?" the cleric in the lime green pants inquired.

The elf's brow furrowed but no answer came.

"Not that it really matters where your efreeti line is," Diomedes turned back to Appelonia, "Any efreeti, no matter who the physical parent is, is a child of the original efreeti. They all sprang from one."

"That doesn't make any sense," Appelonia said, her entire demeanor betraying how stunned she felt at this.

"Really?" the cleric of Ferekane blinked, her eyes turning from emerald green and amber to sapphire blue and puce, "I thought it was pretty straightforward for me. The first efreeti has learned that there is an efreeti child on this plane of existence. To his mind, she has been taken from his presence and he wants her back. Crazy, right?"

"Daddy, do you think she–?" Apple's eyes practically pleaded on their own for him to argue with her.

And he did, "You said that the efreeti were looking for a child. Look at *my daughter*, Diomedes. She's no child anymore. She is a woman in control of her own fate."

That was the first time he had said anything like that. Apple couldn't think of anything to say back.

Which was why the other woman cleric was able to respond. "Time works differently in different dimensions. One is faster than the other. In some, time even works backwards from this one, but that has neither hide nor hair to do with this conversation. Let's stick to the faster and slower time zones right now, shall we? And don't get me started on the ones with daylight savings. I always confuse those with the one that have, um, er, eh…

"To the original efreeti, his child has only been missing a matter of days," she pointed a long sleeve at Appelonia, "When Abernathy doesn't come back, he's going to keep sending demons here to retrieve her."

OPHELIA INTERROGATION NOTES

"This doesn't make any sense," Ophelia shook her head.

"I was surprised myself, considering the criminal history of the Order's Grand Cleric." I said.

The subject used a vulgar expression of disbelief, followed by a graphically detailed threat upon my person. I attribute the reaction to shock rather than genuine malevolence.

"You forget how thorough we can be, Ophelia," I told the subject, "Perhaps this will refresh your memory…"

Two decades before...

SHORTLY AFTER MORNING made its presence felt and breakfast had been eaten, Harbenigyr guided his steed along the road out of the town of Dracoleaf. That steed was a wingless griffin he named Triton, whose falcon shaped head stood proudly from his lion-like body, though that still made him and, by extension his rider, shorter than the rest of the party, who were mostly mounted upon horses.

Lily was the other exception. She rode what the stable hand referred to as a 'war chicken'. Apparently, they were a popular means of transportation on a continent beyond even the islands Harby had called home growing up. It was the same height as a horse but about half the length, even counting the long tail feathers.

Whatever everyone else was riding, Harbenigyr trailed just behind Folken, Saya, Ophelia, Lily, and Josie. That was not, however, due to Triton's lack of speed as much as the cleric's desire to be alone with his own thoughts for a while.

Among other things, Harbenigyr realized that he had not been formally introduced himself to the newly arrived, ruby haired woman yet. At least if you didn't count him being dragged out to the town square to try (and fail) and keep Raiko from dying.

Somehow, the cleric didn't pass away when the duelist did. The enchantment on the bracers around both their arms should have made them share the same fate, as they had for several months. Thanks to the symbols that the man introduced to him as Saya's cousin etched into the cuff, he'd felt where the spear that killed Raiko hit but not to the painful degree the duelist surely had before succumbing.

Perhaps, that was why he was still alive? Because he couldn't feel the damage Raiko brought on himself as intensely? It was a theory, he supposed, but it may be one of those questions that never actually get a satisfactory answer.

They reached a crossroads, the first outside of Dracoleaf, that was recovering from the eventful semi-final round of the fighting tournament. Folken turned his massive, obsidian furred horse around to face the rest of the party. He leaned forward, resting his pale hand on the pommel of the saddle as the rest of the group stopped just in front of him.

"Lilicaitcydia, you will take these to Emerald City," his gloved hand pulled the leather satchel that carried the metal cuffs free of his saddlebags and handed them to the wizard, "Give them to The Judge, have her give them thorough inspection and study. It is a far stronger magic than some stray hamlet should have had in their possession. I want to know all there is to be learned about them by the time we return home."

Lily nodded at her master, bid quick farewells to Saya, Ophelia, and Harby before starting down the path to the east. Saya gave the shorter, rotund woman a kind smile and pat on the shoulder while Ophelia was digesting the information that that "Lily" was actually short for something else. The elf had some trouble understanding what was happening.

"Pardon me, Sir Kizoku," Harby spoke up even as Lily continued on her way, "I thought we were all going to Emerald City. Why is she leaving?"

"Please, call me Folken, Harbenigyr. My Tribal name is not something I wish to broadcast over the surface world," the sorcerer replied, "As to our destination, Saya informed me that before you and this... Raiko, were forced together that *your* destination was altogether different."

Harby turned to look at Saya, who nodded back.

"You mentioned that you wished to visit the Jaded Woods," she said, "As I understand it, that was where you were born. You were hoping to learn more of the family that you were forced to leave behind, yes?"

The cleric hadn't realized that anyone was truly listening when he had told all these things to them. Raiko surely didn't and, eventually, Harbenigyr gave up trying to influence where they went next.

The elf felt his chest get tight and he had to gulp a lump down before he could speak up again, "Yes. Yes, I would like that very much."

"Then that is our next destination," Folken declared, directing his steed for the trail heading to the north, "Far be it from me to keep one from learning of their own history. As a svartalfar in general, and a Kizoku in particular, I understand how *connecting* such knowledge can feel."

"Besides," Saya added with a smirk, "It would be a shame to waste the retainer that Folken paid to hire Josie."

"You mean she isn't a," Harby suddenly realized his breach in etiquette and turned his attention from Saya to the ranger on the brown pony with turquoise spots, "You aren't a member of the Romefeller Guilds, Lady Josie?"

The woman shook her head, her hair spilling over her bare shoulders, "Being an alphan, I've made it a point to be as independent as possible. It's hard enough for someone like me to get hired. I'd hate to add another complication and not be able to be guide someone just because they disagree with some group I happened across one day."

"Noble. Although that was why I joined with the Order of Kuan Yin," the cleric mentioned, "To help people. I wouldn't be able to do much of what I can without their training and support."

"Don't take this the wrong way, Harbenigyr," Josie said back, "But I haven't seen you do anything. You needed everyone's help just to survive yesterday."

"But please, don't take being called a burden an insult," Ophelia chimed in before turning her back on the ranger and starting after Folken, "I mean it's not like he healed anyone's wounds or brought anyone back from the dead before."

The mercenary held her bandaged right hand up with a single finger lifted in a salute meant solely for the ranger. When she was sure the red haired woman got the message, Ophelia quickened the pace of her caramel colored horse.

"Brought someone back from the dead?" Josie eyed Harby with doubt etched all over her face.

"She's exaggerating," the cleric looked up from his lower saddle anxiously, "We found Ophelia in a petrified state a few months ago. I applied some tonics a man was kind enough to give me to reanimate her body."

"But not her sense of common courtesy," Josie grumbled before setting her horse after Ophelia and Folken.

Saya leaned down from her own black and white steed to speak to Harby, her voice soft but not quite a whisper, "Don't take Josie's words too personally. I worked with her before. She's one who would defend a friend to the death once you get to know her."

"As much as I'd love for her to be willing to do that for me, I hope she would never have to" Harby grinned back sheepishly.

Saya let out a soft laugh and the two rode to catch up to the others. The ensuing ride was filled with mostly polite conversation. Even Josie and Ophelia spoke calmly about the weather. Neither dared get more personal.

In fact, the only topic of conversation that was deeper than the polite topics one broached with a stranger was Harbenigyr.

"When did you leave the Jaded Woods?" Josie asked him.

"I was taken away when I was an infant," the cleric answered, "According to my patriarch, my village was attacked by ogres. My family hid me in a cupboard, where he found me the next day."

"Your patriarch?" Ophelia asked, slowing her horse and letting her eavesdropping be known.

Josie tried to not look insulted, though the expression on her face was only partially effective. Ophelia rode on one side of the cleric while Josie was on the other.

"Elder Gimli. He took me back to the Silver Herald Isles and raised me," Harby explained, "But he insisted that I not call him Father or Dad."

Josie shrugged, "Why not?"

"He said that I already had one," he shrugged back, "He thought it would be awkward if they turned up to be alive somehow and came for me."

Ophelia took her turn to shrug, "Do you remember anything about your parents?"

"Only images really. Feelings," the elf answered, looking back and forth from one woman to the other' "Elder Gimli told me where to find the village in the Jaded Woods and said that I should try to find some answers while I was on my pilgrimage."

"What kind of answers are you expecting to find in the ruins of your old village?" Josie's attention was so intent on Harbenigyr that her horse almost veered into the rough weeds at the edge of the road. "It sounds like a waste of time," the ranger muttered, her throat turning pink all the way up to her chin after correcting her wandering horse.

"Honestly, I don't know," Harby confessed, pretending not to hear her commentary, "But I won't find out until I go, right?"

"And if you find out that your parents were criminals or something else equally terrible?" the ranger sucked her pink lower lip between her teeth. "What if you learned that one of your parents wasn't an elf at all?"

"Or that they were the religious leaders of the town." Ophellia added another possibility, "Or even the town constable?"

Harby tried to speak up but Josie already started responding to the mercenary, "What if they were? Even if they were clerics like him, chances are it was for another god. So what difference would it make? It's not like he would convert to follow a different god just because one of his parents worshiped them. So who he is wouldn't fundamentally change," she ranted.

The cleric opened his mouth but Ophelia spoke up before he could get a word out.

"But he would know," Ophelia argued, "That alone could give a person at least some peace."

Harbenigyr gave up trying to speak and simply buried his face in the slick feathers that lined the back of Triton's neck.

"Are you talking about Harby or yourself, Ophelia?" Josie turned her whole body to face the other woman even as her horse continued forward, "It sounds like you're taking this awfully personally."

"I could say the same thing to you, Josie," Ophelia remarked, "Did your daddy not hold you enough so that means that all families are not worth knowing?"

The ranger looked as if she had been punched, "Is that why you're so tan? From sitting on the shoulders of better people than you for so long?"

Ophelia looked as if she had smelled a repellent odor that happened to have red hair and was riding beside her, "I will never have the chance that Harby has now. I lost it after I was turned to stone for years you, you... mewling clam shell."

After she finished speaking, Ophelia seemed as confused by that last insult as Josie. The mercenary glared at the handle of her bastard sword resting behind her left shoulder while the ranger, unable to decipher the taunt, couldn't maintain feeling insulted.

"I didn't realize that you had been... gone so long," Josie let out a quiet sigh before addressing both Ophelia and Harby, "I have to remember that not knowing people who could have cared for you would be as frustrating, if not more, than regretting the family you did have."

"Lady Josie?" Harbenigyr spoke up, his entire body betraying the awkwardness he was feeling. "Why do you call yourself an alphan? I was taught that it simply meant 'half-elf' yet you make it sound like a different race entirely. As if it is so... terrible."

The ranger's face flushed. The cleric expected to be chided by the woman but, instead of lashing out like she had before, Josie simply urged her horse to speed up and gallop away from the two.

"Did I say something wrong?" the cleric asked the woman still riding beside him.

This time, it was Ophelia who was interrupted, "Perhaps not in such a direct manner, young elf," Havarti spoke up, "It does appear, however, that you did strike a nerve."

"I didn't mean to. I'll make sure to apologize to her later," Harby shook his head in disappointment, speaking more to himself than Ophelia or the sword.

The journey continued as it started, with polite conversation and silences of various levels of awkwardness, particularly when they rested to eat. As the sun was starting to brush the top of the hillside on the horizon, the party finally reached the outskirts of the next town, Ash Providence.

It was a bit more run down than the previous. Most of the buildings only had straw rooftops and there wasn't even a sign to tell them what town this was. The only reason any of them knew was because Saya, Lily, Harby and Raiko had passed through on the way to the tournament in Dracoleaf.

"I vote we stay here for the night and start off fresh in the morning," Saya raised her hand to physically represent her choice for the unofficial ballot.

"The Jaded Woods are only about two hours to the north of this," Folken hesitated as he looked around, searching for the word he felt was most the most appropriate description, "hovel."

"But at least it's a hovel with an inn," Saya pointed her pale hand down the packed dirt road.

There was only one intersection of makeshift streets before the town square of Ash Providence. On the western edge of the open space was a three story stone building that had a sign that simply had "inn" written upon it hanging over the door like a wooden flag.

The largest building in Ash Providence was the library on the opposite side of the square but it didn't allow for random visitors, not that it received many. The second largest in town was the inn. Harbenigyr figured that meant it would be likely that they would have enough room to house the party for the night.

They weren't a massive crowd, being only five people, but the last inn in Dracoleaf had trouble accommodating them all because of the tournament. Hence why Harby had been doubled up with Ophelia. Not that it had been much of an issue since the woman spent much of the night drinking and the rest, typically, in a completely different room.

With such a spacious facility and, as far as the cleric could tell no special event going on at the moment, Harbenigyr had to admit that he was looking forward to the idea of having a room truly to himself, if only for a single evening. Saya had already voiced her opinion on the matter. Now the question was if Josie and Ophelia would add their voices to turn the sorcerer to the will of his cousin or not.

The ranger didn't seem interested in the discussion one way or the other. A commotion at the far end of the town square had attracted her attention. One of the men pointed in the direction of the party and Josie wandered off to assuage her curiosity.

"You're a man used to getting your own way," Ophelia slipped off the back of her horse and strode up beside Folken with a wide grin on her face, "But don't think you can argue with women when they're tired. You may win in the short term but you will come to pay for it in the long run."

The albino svartalfar leaned forward in his saddle, raising a green eyebrow at the mercenary, "Is that a threat, my lady?"

"I can assure you, sir, that I would not allow Ophelia to threaten anyone. It is certainly rude, if not outright disdainful in most circles."

Folken's eyebrow twitched at the sound of the unfamiliar voice. His violet eyes focused more intently on the woman with an unspoken question.

"My sword, Havarti, talks," the mercenary answered, "And please don't mention anything about him being named after cheese. He hates that."

"That is too obvious of an observation. Not to mention bordering on disrespectful in and of itself," the sorcerer replied. "I sensed energies transferring to and fro your sword. Speech may be a part of it but there is surely more."

Ophelia was silent for a long moment before she answered, "Nothing that your Judge friend is going to get a chance to find out."

"Now that *was* a threat." Havarti chuckled in the woman's mind.

Folken let out a soft grunt.

"You don't think that he heard that, do you?" the sword telepathically asked.

"First round's on me," Ophelia said to the sorcerer, not answering Havarti's worry as she led her horse toward the place that was to be their sleeping quarters for the evening, "That of interest to you, Folken?"

The svartalfar set his horse to a trot, "If they have a proper vintage."

Harbenigyr watched that entire exchange in silence. When the tension thankfully subsided, the cleric dismounted his griffin and guided his steed toward the inn himself.

There was surely a stable behind the building. The question would be whether they had staff at the front of the inn to take their animals or if they had to take them back themselves.

Not that it mattered to Harby. Griffins were hardly typical riding animals and, while Triton would most likely be as gentle as any horse, he couldn't guarantee that anyone else would not do anything that could make the regal animal at the very least skittish and, at worst, violent.

The elf wanted to avoid that at all costs. Triton had seen enough brutality for his lifetime.

The inn did have staff enough to accommodate all the horses as the party approached. The cleric followed the rest of the valets toward the large double doors that served as the main entrance to their pens. It wasn't a hard sale to let Harbenigyr lead Triton himself, just as he figured it wouldn't be.

The black haired elf closed the gate, arranged for a stable hand to throw a raw steak in a short time later, and then started for the front of the inn. That was when he noticed Josie finally walking toward the building.

She was being accompanied by the very men who were arguing earlier. The ranger had gone over to find out what was happening.

Josie walked with some urgency, but the men were taller and walked just a bit faster. And they were walking straight toward Harbenigyr. He even recognized one as the town's constable, although the man's name was eluding his memory.

The cleric put on his most polite smile and greeted the approaching men with a short bow, "How do you d–"

"Watch out!" the red haired ranger shouted just as a flash of pain washed through the chin of the cleric.

Harbenigyr landed flat on his back, knocking the air from his chest. He could already taste blood trailing over his teeth and into his mouth.

As much as it hurt, Harby was even more confused. He coughed, trying to get a full breath of air as he struggled to sit up on the dusty earth.

"I'm sorry, did I do somethin–?" this time a heavy boot slammed into his chest and the cleric found himself on his back again.

"You're damned right your sorry." The boot, and the thickly built human that filled it wouldn't let Harbenigyr up this time. "You have a lot of nerve to come back here, cleric."

"Come on, Hugo. You can't be sure this is the right guy," the other man, the constable, stood only a couple of steps behind the man pinning Harby down, "We'll get Magra to come down and make a positive identification."

"A positive identification?" Harby blinked to clear his vision from his watering eyes as he struggled to breathe around the weight on his chest, "What do you think I did?"

Josie knelt down beside the cleric, her face tense as her blue eyes looked him up and down. "This man, Hugo, he says that you raped his sister."

———— ◆··• •··◆ ————

CHAPTER FOUR

"That doesn't prove a damned thing," Ophelia said.

"Nor is it the main thrust of this investigation," I agreed, "However, it will need to be looked into independently."

"You claim to be thorough but you haven't read everything yet, have you?" Ophelia asked.

"There is a lot of testimony to delve through, I admit," I said, "It will take me weeks to get through it all."

"Fine," Ophelia replied, "You should start with when Apple figured out that the efreeti were involved..."

Two decades later...

"WHY DOES 'EFREETI' sound familiar, Dad?" Appelonia asked.

Harbenigyr tapped his chin thoughtfully for a long moment. He was not the first to answer, though.

"Efreeti are what people in the east call the Djinn," Jin Vega said, "Here they're called *genies*."

"You mean that old rabbit scat about a creature that can grant wishes?" Tokki Yo Bunpy scoffed, "Go fluff someone else's tail. Mine's soft enough."

The monk blinked back at the Bunny Barbarian before continuing, "In my temple, the tales of the Djinn were cautionary. They twisted their victims wishes to fit the evil desires of the monster. Like he did with Jonas."

"But I didn't make a wish!" the paladin protested. Again, "One minute, the Grand Cleric was holding him at bay and the next he was appearing, disappearing, and breathing fire."

Phinegann grunted, "After you *wished* that he wouldn't hide anymore of his tricks."

"But he did breath fire *before* that," Appelonia pointed out in defense of Jonas.

"But the teleporting and the ungodly speed came after," Jin pointed out, "Jonas didn't do it knowingly. Those things must just need to hear the 'W' word to make use of it."

"That word hardly comes up in everyday conversation," Tokki chimed in.

"Sure it does," Jin shook his bald head, "We just don't mean it as an *actual* wish."

"Maybe, maybe not, Mister Vega, but we're veering away from what I was getting at before." Appelonia shrugged, "I meant that *efreeti*, the word itself, sounded familiar. Like from someone I know in the here and now used it, not in a different country. Someone I know."

This time, Harbenigyr was the one to reply, "Ophelia. Ophelia said that the one who put those runes on her back was called Doctor Efreeti."

"And the chances of *that* being a coincidence are?" the young woman's voice dripped with sarcasm.

The Grand Cleric's eyes flickered over to Diomedes, who had busied herself by slowly spinning around in place where she stood again and again. He turned his attention back to his daughter and nodded.

"You're probably right. But, as far as I know," he couldn't help but glance over at Samson before he continued, "nobody here knows where she is."

"Then I need to go find her," Appelonia answered.

Her father immediately shook his head, stray black strands whipping around his chin, "Oh, no. You're staying in the keep until we get this all straightened out. Your pilgrimage can wait."

"You're right, Dad. It can wait," she tugged at the short front of her white tunic, "But we need to get in contact with Ophelia. Even if she doesn't know anything about this specifically, she will want to know that efreeti, doctor or not, are on the move again."

"Then your mother and I will go," the older elf insisted, "Phinegann and the Shepherd can stay here and protect you."

This time Appelonia shook her head, "They can protect me on the road as well as they can here. Besides, if I'm not here the efreeti won't come. They will be out there trying to find me."

"If I may, Harbenigyr, sir," Jonas stepped up beside the young woman, "Your daughter is right. It took all of us to take down just one of those demons. There is no way we can hold a group off if they decide to come in force."

"And what if they decide to attack from the city side next time?" Appelonia added, inching closer to the dashing paladin, "How many civilians would die in my stead?"

"That's exactly what I'm worried about!" her father protested... right after stepping between her and the paladin, "I can't just stand aside and let you march out there alone and vulnerable for any demon to pounce on!"

"But I won't be alone, Dad. You already hired Phinegann to protect me. Jonas and Tokki Yo Bunpy will come too, just as if I was on my pilgrimage," the young woman motioned from person to person as she named them.

"I'm going, too," Jin Vega stepped up beside the Grand Cleric, "It's the least I can do."

"And you will never be accused of not doing the least you can do," Phinegann grumbled as he walked up along the other side of the Grand Cleric.

Harbenigyr didn't look at all happy but he couldn't find any reasonable argument against it. Appelonia could tell. He had the same look on his face when he would get in arguments with Mom, particularly when she wanted to take Apple out into the forests overnight, and he would inevitably relent.

"When should we leave?" he finally asked his daughter.

Appelonia had a completely different response to his surrender in mind. She even started it before her father's question fully processed.

"We? You're not coming with us, Dad," she objected.

"And why not? I want to make sure you're as safe as you can be. Under the circumstances."

"First, you're the leader of the whole Order. You have work to do here," Apple said.

"Which can be delegated, as it is when I go out to the Land of the Long Toothed Rabbit," her father answered.

"And who are you going to assign to tell Mom that I left before she got back from her hunt tomorrow?" Appelonia's dark eyes narrowed as she stared her father down, "Samson? She'd rip him to pieces."

Harbenigyr was quiet for a long, long time, "You have a good point, Apple, but no one here knows Ophelia better than I do. How do you propose trying to find her without me?"

"Tokki?" the daughter of the Grand Cleric motioned to the Yo Bunpy warrior to come over, "Do you know where Lyan, er, the Child of Prophesy is at the moment?"

Even though everyone could only see his mouth behind the long teeth in his mask, Tokki Yo Bunpy looked as if he had tasted something extremely, to put it kindly, unpalatable.

"No Yo Bunpy speaks to the False One. She doesn't even have contact with Those Who Ride Outside the Tribes anymore," he shook his head, "She will be of no help to anyone. Just as she has always been."

The False One? No help? That didn't sound like the Lyan Yo Bunpy that the young cleric remembered. Appelonia took offense in Lyan's stead and readied to deliver a stern talking to at Tokki when her father stepped in between her and the Bunny Barbarian.

"Besides, the Land of the Long Toothed Rabbit is too far out of the way," he said to his daughter.

Apple had to hiss a deep breath between clenched teeth to keep from yelling at Tokki over her father's shoulder. Harbenigyr pulled her to the side, just out of hearing reach of everyone else.

"Lyan's status with her tribe may be questionable at the moment but we need to find Ophelia," he motioned over his shoulder to the warrior in black fur, "The Yo Bunpy are great trackers and even fiercer warriors. I need you protected."

Another protest started in Apple's throat only to be interrupted by the gnome woman tugging at the Grand Cleric's pant leg. Appelonia couldn't help but wonder how much of their conversation, which was intended to be private, Illyria Warflower had overheard before she made her presence known.

"I spoke with a Miss Ophelia up in Maid Gulch. She was the one who told me about the soul orbs," Illyria said, "It took a lot of honeybark ale to get her to tell me that. She may still be there sleeping it off."

"I'd say that's a lead, Dad," Appelonia cocked an eyebrow at her father, "Would you mind coming with us at least that far, Lady Warflower?"

The purple haired woman scrunched her nose at the idea, "I just want to study the orbs for a piece of tech I'm working on. I don't want to become ensconced in some kind of grudge match."

"You won't, Lady Warflower, I promise." Appelonia replied, "I just want you to come so that you can tell us if anyone still in the Drunken Dragon was there when you and Ophelia talked. They may be able to tell us where she went afterward."

"You're so sure that Ophelia has moved on?" Harby looked back up at his daughter.

"You're the one who taught me to be prepared. You and Mom," Apple grinned back, reminding him of her second point of why he had to remain behind.

The Grand Cleric sighed, "All right. I'll stay. If any efreeti do start watching, they'll think everything is normal here and that we are none the wiser. But you," Harbenigyr pointed a finger at his daughter, then to every last person accompanying her, "You had best make sure that nothing happens to her or you will have hell to pay."

The paladin's eyebrows pressed together tightly, "That's a pretty harsh threat for a cleric."

"It's not the Order of Kuan Yin we have to worry about," Appelonia said, leaning in to her father and giving him a soft kiss on the cheek.

The young woman left the meeting hall to gather supplies to leave today, rather than in two days like they had originally planned. Jonas looked up at Phinegann, who had a deep scowl on his own face.

"Surely he didn't mean..." the paladin started to say.

And Diomedes walked up from behind and rested her chin on his pauldron. The cool metal covering his shoulder seemed to soothe her after spinning around for untold minutes.

"He means Apple's mother," she said, her kaleidoscope eyes not really focusing in any direction, "She's not a cleric of the Order of Kuan Yin. She's a ranger that can turn invisible, sneak into the most secure of places and kill anyone before they even know she's there. Did you know that she assassinated the former matriarch of the Lytyl svartalfar? Josie also tracked the man who killed her husband from one end of Honua to the other and she's *even more* protective of her little girl."

The lips of the Shepherd curled into an O shape, the sound not coming out as much as simply understood to have happened.

Phinegann let out a quiet, calculating growl, "Killed her husband? She was married to someone before the Grand Cleric?"

Both men turned to look at the avatar (cleric!) of Ferekane. She wasn't there anymore. They looked around the meeting room and she was nowhere to be found.

Jonas waved Tokki over, "Diomedes was just here. Can you tell us if she teleported or if she's pulling some other kind of trick?"

The Bunny Barbarian crouched down where the paladin indicated the insane cleric had been only moments before. He bent down so low it looked almost as if he were smelling the floor like a tracking beast. Finally, he straightened up to the point that he was kneeling on both knees as he looked up.

"She's gone. Even her crazy scent has disappeared." He reported, "I guess her job here is done."

OPHELIA INTERROGATION NOTES

"It seems that Diomedes was as distracting as you are attempting to be now, Ophelia," I said.

"What are you blabbering on about now?" the subject asked.

"The criminal case against Harbenigyr," I said, "While it is not the main subject of my inquiry, we do still need to address it."

"Fine fine fine!" Ophelia yelled at me, frustration obvious in her manners, "I'll tell you what happened after he was accused..."

Two decades before...

"THAT'S HIM!" THE woman with red curls spilling down over her shoulders practically screeched before burying her head into her brother's chest, "That's the man who, who–" she lost her ability to speak as sobs rocked her body.

"I'd say that is about as positive an identification as you can get, wouldn't you?" Wyatt, the constable of this little hamlet, turned to the ranger.

"It would seem," she agreed, looking troubled.

Josie had sent word to the inn immediately after the arrest of the cleric. Folken and Ophelia both came minutes later. Saya, though, stayed in her room.

"Is there any chance that this could be true?" the ranger turned to the sorcerer.

Folken, in turn, directed his gaze at Ophelia, "This was the last (he hesitantly used this description) town before Raiko's fate was met at the tournament. Is there any chance?"

The mercenary wobbled where she stood, having already had several servings of alcohol when the message came. But while she was unsteady on her feet, a few slaps to the face and she was, mostly, focused on the problem at hand.

"Harby? Not a chance," Ophelia shook her head, then had to close her eyes in regret afterwards, "Besides, if he had, he couldn't have used Kuan Yin's blessings since then, right?"

The woman held up her bandaged hand. Already her fingertips, which poked out from the white strips of cloth wrapped around her fingertips had fresh pink skin. That would not have been possible after such severe damage without not only the healing knowledge and potions of the cleric, as well as the energies from his goddess that he would have passed on to his patient.

"Put him in the cage," The constable ordered, though he didn't seem at all pleased with this turn of events.

Two deputies wrapped their arms around the elf's shoulders. Harbenigyr didn't resist as they guided him to the small cage that sat atop the raised area right in the middle of the town square.

The elf didn't even have enough room to stand up straight in the barred enclosure. So he sat down, resting his arms on his knees.

Folken stepped up to Wyatt, leaning in close so he did not have to speak loudly, "Is this really necessary? As you can see, Harbenigyr is compliant. He is no escape risk. You could remand him into my custody and I will see to it that he remains interred in his room until a proper trial can be assembled."

"You think I'm at all happy about this?" the constable glared back at the sorcerer, "The cleric cured my son's breathing sickness when he was here last. But he's been identified as the culprit behind an antisocial criminal act. The laws of our town specify that he is to be imprisoned in a public area so that others can have a chance to see him and report if he is guilty of further illegal activity. It's out of my hands."

"How long is he to be held publicly?" Folken scanned the steadily growing crowd that was getting angrier at an even faster rate.

"Three days." the man answered.

"He *will* be killed before that time has passed," the svartalfar glared right back, "You know that."

Wyatt reluctantly nodded, "Like I said, it's out of my hands."

"I suppose investigating the crime itself is out of your hands as well?"

"Don't presume to tell me my business, elf," the constable frowned, "I did investigate. When it happened. Last week."

Folken's full attention snapped back to the other man, "Last week? When?"

"Two days before the last sabbath," he said.

The albino svartalfar, used to being mistaken for a surface dwelling elf and not prone to correcting the error, looked over the symbols that lined the edge of the raised area. Silently, he cursed the existence of such small, dirty towns and their innumerable religions. He understood the symbols but they were not being used properly for the purposes they were designed.

"What is the patron deity of your *charming* little hamlet, constable?" the sorcerer asked.

"The god of the feast, Qward."

"And what day is his to be worshiped?" the green haired man continued.

"Every seven days, the next is tomorrow," the constable answered.

Someday, Folken thought to himself (and not for the first time), that a universal calendar must be organized among the denizens of Honua. There was far too much confusion traveling from country to country, indeed, sometimes village to village as to what day was when. Particularly in isolated places such as this that took it upon themselves to create a day listing that didn't even coincide to that practiced by their countrymen.

"Then it couldn't have been Harby," Ophelia stepped up to the svartalfar and Wyatt.

Her cheeks had a fresh flush of pink. She must have just slapped herself again to refocus her mental faculties.

"Raiko was well into the tournament in Dracoleaf then," the mercenary said, "We were all there and you know that Harby had to be because of the cuffs they were wearing."

The constable's attention perked up, "What cuffs?"

"Until very recently," Folken explained, as Ophelia became distracted by something in the direction of the inn, "Harbenigyr and a man by the name of… Raiko, were forced to wear a pair of enchanted bracers. If they were separated by too great of a distance, the cuffs would drain them of their life forces."

"Magra never mentioned anything about his arm being wrapped in metal," Wyatt rubbed a couple of fingers along the edge of his smooth jaw, "How far of a distance are we talking?"

"No more than five hundred paces, at most," Folken repeated the answer given to him by his cousin when he asked it.

"When did Saya leave the inn?" Josie pointed at the three story building as Ophelia leaned on her bare shoulder.

"That's what I was wondering!" the mercenary said too loudly with her mouth too close to the ranger's pointed ear.

Josie tried to shrug Ophelia away but the other woman kept a firm grip, "She just went back in not a minute ago," the red haired alphan reported.

Folken turned his attention back to the building. His violet eyes narrowed as he considered all the information he had been given regarding the crime of which Harbenigyr had been accused, Saya sudden appearance and subsequent disappearance, and the myriad of other subjects upon which his mind had been inundated.

"Josie, go to Saya and find out where she has been," the sorcerer ordered, "And take Ophelia with you. I doubt stealth will be required and she looks as if she is ready to fall down."

OPHELIA INTERROGATION NOTES

"You and your compatriots make poor investigators," I told the subject.

"You interrupted my story just to insult me?" Ophelia glared at me.

I pointed at the testimony of Appelonia, daughter of the Grand Cleric of the Order of Kuan Yin, "The young elf girl thought to bring her troubles to light, too. Like you, she only unlocked more trouble than the truth."

The subject snatched the paper containing Appelonia's testimony away before I could stop her:

Two decades later...

WHO KNEW THAT the wings on Illyria's back could actually make her able to fly? Appelonia wondered that for the umpteenth time as she watched the small woman's waist length purple ponytails flutter behind her in the sky ahead.

Everyone else was on horseback. Phinegann's was easily the biggest, considering it had the most weight to carry in the sheer size of the rider. Jonas' horse, Andromeda, came in a close second. His mare wasn't as massive as the orc's horse on her own but, with her own armor wrapped around Andromeda in a way that was reminiscent of her owner, she at least looked larger.

Appelonia's ride was a blue haired stallion with white splatters all over his flanks. She had been given Bommer when she turned twelve. Mostly so that she could go on her first overnight hunt with her mother.

She could smile about it now but that first trip out into the wilderness with just her and Mom terrified Appelonia at the time. Especially when her mother had her set up a solo camp while she went off to do who knows what. Bommer was her only company and comfort that trip.

When Tokki's ashen gray horse bumped into her stallion, Apple was reminded of just how not alone she was this time. The Bunny Barbarian pulled his horse away from the cleric's, muttering a quiet apology before he was pulled up ahead by the helpful monk, Jin Vega.

In the time between when Appelonia arranged for everyone to have horses and supplies and when she returned to the throne room, Tokki had unpacked his weapon of choice. It was a long, black furred sleeve that stretched up the length of his left arm with an open area around his bony elbow. A couple of leather straps connected the upper and lower portions in order to keep from restricting the range of motion of his arm.

His hand was covered completely by black fur with three long, curved claws protruding from the end. As Appelonia understood it, they were one set of the claws from the hind legs of the saber-toothed rabbit he had killed as a right of passage into adulthood. It was a miracle that he could hold anything with those on his hand but he was able to keep a firm, if unseen grip on the reins of his horse. His steering ability was debatable.

Thick leather straps wrapped around his well defined chest held the sleeve up. It was a physical impossibility for the clawed sleeve to slide down his arm.

As he rode away, Appelonia could see that the acid burns she had noticed on his shoulders earlier were far more widespread on his back. It was more scar tissue than uninjured flesh at this point. A reminder of his battle with the acid spitting rabbit with which he did battle and now was now wearing, no doubt.

As for the young cleric, she now wore a chainmail vest that her father had given her. It was, of course, meant to keep her safe on her pilgrimage but was now pulling the duty a little early. The simple armor had small pauldrons on the shoulders, hooks that held the front closed where the vest folded together, and then a thick leather belt to keep it closed.

The sun was just starting to rise. The Drunken Dragon, a bar that just happened to have rooms in the back for those to rent who were unable to walk out the doors after their visit, was a day's hard ride from her home but the cleric convinced everyone to set up camp the night before. She told them it was so they could meet the upcoming challenges fresh.

In truth, it was because she had considered sneaking out during the night and continuing on without everyone else. Apple had promised her father that she would stay with them so the party could keep her safe but, the thought of anyone getting hurt in her defense... The possibility just seemed more real now than when she was planning on going out and wandering across the continent. At least before, she didn't have otherworldly monsters actively hunting her.

Ultimately, Appelonia decided against sneaking off. She was confident that she could do so without anyone even realizing she was gone until morning. After all, she was trained by the best ranger on this or, in her opinion, any continent. But she needed Illyria to come with her.

While those wings made her graceful and silent in the sky, on the ground they rattled like the windows in Dianmeyer during a windstorm. And she was the one who saw Ophelia last.

Resigning herself to having too large of an entourage for her sake, they came up to the building that rested in the shadow of a steep hill behind it. At least in was in the hill's shadow in the mornings. In the afternoon, the sunlight practically reflected off the enormous sign with a dragon holding a comically large glass of red wine painted above the door.

Appelonia thought it was comical, anyway. Especially when she first visited as a child. The bar's owner though, Mandragoria Wolvebane, assured her that it was based on a true event that she, herself had experienced during her days as a treasure hunter.

As they approached the door, a woman with olive skin and wearing a black leather coat and very form fitting leather pants stepped up to meet them. She ran her hands, that had rings on every finger, over the bandanna holding her curly black hair back to smooth out any wrinkles in the fabric.

"Welcome to the Drunken Dragon," she smiled wide with magenta lacquer painted over her lips, "Would you like me to tie your horses up for you?"

A valet had never come up to meet Appelonia on any of her previous visits. It had been some time, though. Perhaps this was some new service Mandragoria had decided to try.

The cleric shrugged at Jonas, who didn't look worried at all. Phinegann looked far less convinced than Appelonia at the woman's honesty. One by one, though, each member of the group dismounted their steeds.

Illyria gave the valet quite a jump when she came in for a landing right behind her. A dagger dropped from the lining her coat.

The woman giggled sheepishly as she quickly snatched the knife up and tucked it back into the lining, "Sorry about that. Can't be too careful these days, right?"

"Too true, Miss…?" Jin Vega nodded at the valet as he slipped off his brown steed with white fur to just above his hooves.

She looked as if she were about to say something starting with a *Fr* sound when she appeared to change her mind mid-syllable, "Brownwyn LaRue, sir," then she gave him a quick, formal curtsy.

Appelonia, then each other member of the party, each handed the reins of their horses to the woman. She seemed to smile wider and wider with each person who stepped past her.

"I doubt we will be long, Ms. LaRue," Jonas said as he guided everyone past him onto the wooden porch and the entrance beyond, "I wouldn't tarry too long around Andromeda's saddle bags. She has a tendency to bite."

As if to accentuate his point, the armored horse snorted and stamped at the ground with a heavy hoof. Brownwyn nodded back at the paladin, her smile a little flatter.

Jonas the Shepard stepped into the bar behind everyone else. The place was already bustling with business, or could it have been the previous nights business just not yet concluded?

Appelonia wrapped a hand around the arm of a passing waitress to stop and speak to her, "I don't suppose Mandragoria is still awake, is she?"

The waitress nodded and guided them to one of the few unoccupied tables before continuing to finish whatever she had set out to do before the cleric interrupted her. Everyone sat down and settled into a wooden chair. Except for Illyria, who stood where a human or elf's rear end would have rested.

"Do you recognize anyone in here, Lady Warflower?" Appelonia leaned forward and asked in as quiet of voice as possible.

If the cleric was trying to look subtle, she had just about the opposite effect. Unable to keep a quick snicker from escaping her lips, the gnome scanned around the wide open room.

"Please just call me Elly," she said as she kept looking, "My father was given that trade-name when he was working for the Queen of Knocknee Point. Personally, I want to be a Steampunch."

"That why you want to study the soul orbs?" Jin's gruff voice made his innocent question sound more ominous than was intended (at least Appelonia suspected so), "As a potential energy source?"

Illyria nodded, "With modifications, of course. Like removing the human spirit factor. Oh, he was here!" the small woman pointed at a heavily muscled orc that was only slightly smaller than Phinegann.

The one Illyria pointed at had pale green skin and hair that was braided into rows against his scalp. He plucked at a lute that was custom made for his larger-than-the-average bard size. Judging from how quickly and melodious the tune he was playing came out, he was quite talented.

The red haired cleric's thankful smile quickly turned sideways when she saw the man. She suddenly felt as if everyone at the table was staring at her. Still, she couldn't bring herself to stand up, let alone approach the green skinned half-ogre.

"Anyone else?" the question barely squeaked past Appelonia's lips.

A new someone stepped up to the table beside the cleric, "You have a problem with orcs, kid, you came to the wrong place. I use them as bouncers."

The one who arrived at the table was none other than Mandragoria Wolvebane herself. Like always, her strawberry blonde hair looked as if someone used a bowl to cut it to the specific length where it rested right around her ears, even then it still went of in different directions. Although, that could have been more due to the long nights her business tended to have.

She wore a leather vest over her thick torso. As a former treasure hunter, mercenary, bounty hunter, just about anything in her long life, Mandragoria had plenty of muscle. It had also been more years than Appelonia had been alive since she had been on those adventures so those muscles weren't quite as tight as they used to be.

But she could still wear leather pants comfortably. After pulling a chair of her own over, the older woman rested those very same pants in the seat.

"You know it doesn't have anything to do with that," Apple replied sheepishly, "I don't have any problems with ogres, half-ogres, or whatever ratio of ogres," her dark hued eyes glanced back over at the immense lute player but only for a moment. "But he's a bard," she said with a raspy whisper.

Everyone at the table looked at her with a dumbfounded expression. This time, the cleric *knew* what having every pair of eyes locked onto her did feel like.

"Does no one else find bards creepy?" the young woman self-consciously tugged at the thick leather belt wrapped around her chainmail vest.

"Creepy?" Mandragoria chuckled at the idea, "Hed? He's about the most laid back bard I ever met. And I've known my share of hyper-relaxed bards."

"That's part of the problem!" Apple energetically whispered, "They're always super relaxed or incredibly happy until... until they aren't anymore."

A waitress came and started handing out drinks, starting with placing an exceptionally large glass of burgundy in front of Mandragoria, "How would you know how they are? The most interaction just about anyone has with them is requesting to hear a specific song."

"I've never done that," Appelonia cradled her face in her hands, her shoulders rising high enough to cover up to her pointed ears, "I just can't bring myself to approach one."

"You are an odd, odd woman," Illyria shook her head, her stained glass wings shuddering behind her back.

"I'm guessing she had a run in with a bard that wasn't so happy-go-lucky as a kid," Jin said as he reached for the pewter mug, filled with some kind of ale, on the table in front of him.

"It's a minor issue at worst," Jonas pushed his chair away from the table while still in it, "I'll go talk to the bard and see if he remembers Ophelia."

"You're here for Ophelia, are you?" Mandragoria asked before taking a long drag from her large glass of wine, "What did she do this time? Would have to be pretty bad if even Harbenigyr isn't putting up with her nonsense anymore," She tugged at Appelonia's white sleeve.

The cleric reflexively pulled her arm free from the other woman's grip, "It's nothing like that. We just want to talk to her."

The short haired blonde woman let out a loud guffaw at that, "Do you know how many times I used that line when I was hunting down the 'special scumbag of the week'?"

Mandragoria didn't stop laughing for long enough that Appelonia's face matched the bright color of her hair almost perfectly. Finally, though, the bar owner wiped amused tears from her eyes with her thumb and, completely collected, resumed the conversation as if it was never interrupted.

"Does this have something to do with the attack on Dianmeyer yesterday?" she quietly gauged everyone's reactions after the question was asked.

Appelonia's eyebrows sank down low enough to drape her eyes in shadow, "How did you hear about that so fast?"

"To quote a famous character from fiction, 'I drink and I know things'," Mandragoria answered, "Maid Gulch may not be that big in and of itself but we're well centered around where a lot of action happens."

"Did you hear about *what* attacked Dianmeyer?" Apple inquired.

"That's where the reports I received vary a bit," the older woman confessed, "Some say it was a genie, others say it was a de Junamend clansman. They were difficult to tell apart even when they both still existed."

"How do you mean?" Appelonia asked.

Before Mandragoria could answer, Phinegann let out a loud belch that came out so suddenly it made everyone at the table jump. He placed his mug back on the table and leaned back in his chair again. Then he gave a small nod as if giving permission for the discussion to continue.

The bar owner had a slightly impressed look on her face before she started her answer again, "They're both related, you see. The de Junamend are born from the first mating of a genie with a human. And no matter how many centuries it has been, or how many humans have been introduced into the bloodline, everyone one of them is half-demon."

"How is that even possible?" Illyria asked, leaning on the mug that was just too large for her to pick up, "Breeding science says that the more of one species that gets introduced into a lineage, the more the traits of that species become dominant."

"Remember what Diomedes said?" Jonas slid his untouched mug to the side as he leaned forward and rested his elbows on the table, "Every efreeti demon is a direct offshoot off the first without any dilution. If just one of those demons can spawn an entire species, maybe its traits can't be watered down by adding anymore of the same its already bonded with."

Mandragoria stared at the paladin blankly, "Kid, I know I'm not stupid. You had best come to that realization, too. Because what you said made zero sense to me."

"He's saying that it's not a matter of breeding," Appelonia spoke up, "Diomedes also mentioned that time in the efreeti dimension moves slower than ours. If their, um, seed, follows the same rules as the plane of existence they call home, no other species traits could be added until much further down the bloodline by our own reckoning."

"Apparently I'm surrounded by a bunch of geniuses," Mandragoria muttered before draining the rest of her glass of wine into her mouth, "Whoever this Diomedes is, did you ask her what that, what did you call it, an efreeti? Did she tell you what this efreeti thing wanted?"

Again, all eyes fell on Appelonia, "Um, she said that the efreeti were looking for a baby that was stolen from them."

"That's impossible. Efreeti can't make other pure efreetis. You said so yourselves," The bar owner motioned around the table.

"Wait a minute," Appelonia tapped at the table, playing back a part of the conversation in her head, "You said 'They *were* difficult to tell apart even *when they both still existed*. What did you mean?"

"I meant that the de Junamend were wiped out years ago," Mandragoria said as if it were obvious, "As far as I know, they're extinct. But I'm always open to an absolute becoming not quite so when new information comes in."

"Do you know who made them," the cleric had to force herself to get the next word out, "extinct?"

The owner of the tavern shrugged, "My best guess is that demons don't typically like impure versions of themselves running around. Especially if the demons are all essentially the same person."

"So you think that the efreeti killed all of them," Jonas concluded. The older woman nodded.

"What if there were other efreeti half-breeds that weren't within the de Junamend clan?" Phinegann chimed in. "They would have the same half-demon blood as the clan but be concealed from hunting by the efreeti."

"It's possible," Mandragoria ran a hand through her strawberry blonde hair, "But if they discovered a new half-breed, it's a good bet they'd come to finish the job they started on the de Junamend."

The old adventurer's hazel eyes narrowed. If Appelonia had to guess, she would say that Mandragoria looked suspicious. About what, the cleric couldn't say.

"Who in Dianmeyer does the efreeti think is their stolen baby?" the bar owner demanded.

Each member of the party looked to and from each other uneasily. No one spoke up and none of them could bring themselves to look in the direction of Mandragoria.

"Someone here better tell me or I'll have my summoner bring an efreeti demon right here, right now to straighten all of this out!"

"Do you really have a summoner here?" Appelonia asked, even though she was afraid of the answer.

"Sure shooting, kid." The other woman nodded, "How do you think I get some of my more exotic vintages?"

"The Grand Cleric wasn't able to trace his lineage back beyond his parents," Jin Vega spoke at least a portion of the truth, "With the time fluctuations..." he shrugged.

Mandragoria used a word that made the cleric, paladin, and gnome blush to express her disbelief at that idea, "There's no way he's from an efreeti lineage. Appelonia here is proof of that."

"How do you figure?" Jonas asked.

"All de Junamend had black hair until puberty. Then it turned silver or gray, like charcoal that's been burned," the tavern owner lifted a tuft of Appelonia's bright red hair away from her shoulder to illustrate her point, "Harby's head is still as black as inside a cave and Apple's..."

The suspicions in the woman's face only became more prominent as she glared from one party member to the next. Illyria actually jumped down from her chair to avoid meeting that gaze.

"That Diomedes person made you think that she was the missing Efreeti baby," Mandragoria frowned, every line in her forehead gaining firm definition, "So, being as selfless as all Kuan Yin do-gooders, she left Dianmeyer so that the demons would follow her instead of attack the keep again. You all came along to protect her. All you really did, though, was leave her home open so that the efreeti can get whatever it is they really want to–"

A different orc hustled up beside the bar owner. He whispered something into her ear that made her let out an exasperated sigh.

"Up. All of you." she ordered, motioning for all of them to follow her.

And they did.

Mandragoria marched to a spiral staircase that rested in the back corner of the bar, on the opposite side from the entrance to the rooms that were rented out to those too drunk to leave. She climbed up until she pressed her hand against the hatch that was in the flat ceiling.

Then the owner of the bar looked down at the party, "There's only enough room for two other people besides me in here and that will be you," she pointed at Appelonia, "and you, cutie," she pointed at Jonas. "Get up here, now!"

She disappeared through the hatch. Appelonia quickly hustled up the spiral steps, followed by the paladin, who found the climb a bit awkward in his heavy armor.

With help from Mandragoria and the cleric, Jonas finally emerged from the hatchway into what looked like an observation tower, much like what guards used in forts. Mandragoria motioned to the forests to the west of the building.

Both guests of the bar owner stepped over to the waist high wall on that side of the tower, resting their hands on the top edge as they looked out in that direction. There was a thick plume of dust pouring up from between the trees.

Mandragoria pulled out a thick piece of treated leather and two pieces of rounded glass. One was a smaller than the other by about half. One end of the leather was wrapped around the larger glass, which was tied to hug around it firmly. The same thing happened to the smaller piece on the other end of the leather. Then the woman held it up to her right eye.

Letting out an annoyed sounding grunt, she passed the leather cone to Jonas, "Look," she ordered.

The paladin held the contraption in unsure hands, afraid that he'd crush it. Once he realized it wouldn't fall apart due to his gauntlets, he copied Mandragoria and held the small end up to his right eye and turned to the west.

"Blessed Commander!" he hollered at the sight of a woman rushing toward him from inside the cone.

He reflexively reached over his shoulder for his claymore but it was strapped to his horse. The young woman let out a little groan of disappointment when his hand, that had been resting on hers, pulled away.

Rolling her eyes, the bar owner snatched the leather from Jonas and handed it over to Appelonia. She did just as Mandragoria and Jonas did. When she saw the vision of the black haired woman seemingly riding the front edge of the dust cloud toward her, the cleric's eyes nearly bugged out of her head.

Apple lowered the cone from her eye and looked in the same direction. The woman appeared so much smaller. So much so that the cleric couldn't really make out that she *was* a woman at this distance. She lifted the device back up to her eye and, again, the woman looked as if she were standing only a few yards away from them.

She turned to Mandragoria, holding the leather cone toward the owner of the bar, "What kind of magic is this? And who is that?" She pointed at the approaching cloud of dust.

"This," the older woman took the leather cone back from the cleric, "is called a telescope. Their big in all the fancy scholarly towns and ship ports. It lets you see things that are far away up close, like potential threats, before they actually end up on your doorstep."

"Do you know who that is out there?" Appelonia rephrased her second question.

"Did you see her hair, black and standing straight up?" Mandragoria asked as she deconstructed the telescope and tucked the components back into the pouch on her belt.

The cleric nodded.

"She looks like how I described a de Junamend, right?" the other woman continued.

Again, Appelonia nodded, "Except she looked like an adult and her hair was black."

"Exactly," Mandragoria had a hard look on her face, "That, my friend, is what an efreeti looks like in their human guise. You may not be their baby but someone in your group has *something* they want and they're coming here for it."

"What should we do then?" Jonas looked to the woods then back at the women, "Gather up your bouncers and prepare for battle?"

"There's no *we* in this equation, cutie," The tavern owner shook her head, "You are going to take your friends, get on your horses, and leave my bar before she gets here. I figure that you have five minutes at most."

OPHELIA INTERROGATION NOTES

After I took the parchment back from the subject, I decided to show her the actual report I had intended for Ophelia to read.

"Before I ask you to continue what I'm sure is a well rehearsed story. Please read the ranger Josie's testimony into the record."

The subject loosed another vulgar outburst before turning her attention to the provided document:

Two decades before...

"DO YOU DO this a lot?" Josie looked back over her shoulder at Ophelia as they climbed up the staircase inside the inn, "Stop someplace and get slobbering drunk as fast as possible?"

The auburn haired woman glared back up at the ranger, "What do you care?"

"I care because you are on retainer like I am," the alphan said, "I care because when you're like this, you're of no use to anyone."

Ophelia held the railing at the side of the steps in a vice grip, her breath coming in rough gasps as she struggled to keep up with Josie, "The only one who was any trouble was Raiko and he's dead now. How was I supposed to know that someone would accuse Harby of something he couldn't possibly do?"

"That's the point!" the other woman snapped, "None of us saw this coming but we have to be ready for the unexpected with this job."

Ophelia cocked an eyebrow at Josie, "You're really, really serious about this, aren't you?"

She nodded back, "I can do a lot of things to survive, even be really comfortable in the wilderness. I can go months, maybe even forever, without actually having to see anyone at anytime. When I come out to civilization, I make it a point to be professional so I'll be welcome the next time and the time after that."

They turned the corner to start up the last flight of steps to the top floor. Saya insisted on having a room that would give her a view of the rising sun.

"You worry too much about what people think of you. I bet you hold everyone to your standard of popf- perf- professionalism, don't you?" Ophelia asked.

"Why shouldn't I?" Josie answered.

"You may come and visit *civilization* every few months, kiddo, but the rest of us have to live in it full time," the mercenary replied, "In case you haven't noticed, it's rough out here. The sweetest kid I've ever known is in a cage, everyone who every cared about me died decades ago, and now I'm being judged my someone I'm betting hasn't even had sex yet!"

The alphan suddenly felt her cheeks flush, "What does *that* have to do with anything?"

"Ah ha!" Ophelia pointed up at the other woman with a crooked grin on her face.

Josie's cheeks only started to burn hotter, "You keep calling me and the cleric kids and about everyone you knew being dead for decades. I'm older than you so when did everyone die so horribly? When you were two?"

"Remem-remember when I told you that Harby brought me back to life?" Ophelia asks as they finally reached the top floor.

"Of course. You did make quite the production out of it."

"Well, I was stuck that way for thirty years, okay?" the taller woman tugged at her long coat, "And before that, a monster took me from my family and erased everything I ever knew about them from me. They came for me, died right in front of me, and I had *no idea* who they were."

Ophelia's voice rose to angry, almost screaming levels by the time she finished. Nothing came to Josie that she considered to be an appropriate response, so she pointed down the hall they needed to go to reach the room Saya was thought to have been sleeping in.

After a few steps, the ranger did think of a question, "If you didn't know who they were, why are you so traumatized by it now?"

"Because they had the help of a Light Bringer. I kidnapped his little girl and he still rescued me along with her from the ones who took me. He told me their names."

"Sounds to me like he was trying to punish you for what you did to his child," Josie said.

Ophelia shook her head, "I was under mind control at the time. He understood that. He told me all this in a letter he left me be- before he died. While I was petrified. He always thought I was going to come back. Probably just not after so long."

"All this is why you're so adamant about the cleric learning about his own family?" the alphan asked.

Ophelia wrapped a hand around the other woman's shoulder and pulled her around so they were facing each other, "His name is Harbenigyr. Harby when you actually realize how sweet a guy he is."

"He's been nothing but a burden since I've been here," Josie started to turn away.

The mercenary pulled her back, "That's what I'm talking about, you judgmental harpy! You- you come out of the woods with no history, no life to touch you, and you think that's how real people live. Really real life is messy, even things that don't happen to us directly can leave a stain.

"We all deal with it differently. Harby just gets kinder and kinder, to the point that all he-he'll do is help you whether you desret- deserve it or not. I drink because I'm not so nice. If I stayed sober all the time... I- I'd have killed a lot a people by now."

Ophelia was stunned. That was the most she had rambled on in a long time. She even said some things about herself that *she* didn't even realize until just then.

"So you're protecting us by being a drunkard?" Josie rolled her sapphire eyes.

"No, I'm protecting Havarti by being a drunkard," Ophelia stepped around the ranger and started down the hall.

"I thought you said that the cler-, Harbenigyr, was called Harby to his friends," Josie started after her.

"Havarti is someone completely different," Ophelia addressed the other woman as if she were an afterthought.

The mercenary quickly glanced at each room number as she marched past, looking for Saya's room. When they finally reached it, she pressed a finger to her lips to tell the ranger to be silent.

"Saya deals with her life by embracing the attitude of being from a noble line ignoring that she lives in her cousin's shadow," Ophelia whispered, "She doesn't sneak around unless it's at his order and on Romefeller business. Folken sent us to check on her, so whatever she was doing wasn't either of those."

"So?" Josie shrugged, whispering back, "She went to do something else then."

The mercenary gently pressed her back to the door and sandwiched the hilt of her bastard sword resting there between her flat hand and the wood entrance. She looked back at the red haired woman with a questioning scowl.

"Sneaking isn't very dignified when it's not for a job," Ophelia quietly replied, "That's not how Saya does things... and there's someone in there with her!"

"What? A new boyfriend?" Despite her question, Josie still found herself pulling her short sword free of its scabbard when Ophelia started doing so with her own weapon.

Ophelia gave the other woman a stern look.

"Not how she deals with things, right," the ranger nodded.

The mercenary reached for the door's handle. When it didn't move, she didn't appear surprised but Ophelia still let out a frustrated grunt. Then her pale eyes turned to Josie's blade.

"Can I borrow that for a moment?" Ophelia wrapped her bandaged hand around Josie's right, the one that held the short sword.

The alphan was suddenly unable to let go of the weapon. Seeping liquid from sores opening up on the mercenary's hand dripped onto Josie's smooth skin. Before she could start to feel disgusted, Ophelia lowered the other woman's blade and pointed it at her own chest.

"What are you doing?" the alphan pulled back.

But not before Ophelia made the ranger stab her in the chest.

Just as Josie's sword pressed into the woman's tanned skin, Ophelia disappeared. A purple after-image that was shaped exactly like her was left behind. Even that vanished after only a second or two. The only thing that remained to show that the mercenary had been there at all was the soiled length of bandage that was draped over the red haired woman's hand and unraveling to the floor.

Ophelia found herself suddenly facing the door, from the inside of the room now. She turned around to see Saya wrestling with... herself.

Ophelia unlatched the door and then dived into the fray. Havarti's blade knocked the leather covered arm of the Saya on top away from the lower one, the short, curved blade she'd been holding flicking from her grasp to bury itself in the bedpost.

Ophelia grabbed the back of the collar of the top Saya with her formerly injured, free hand and pulled her away from the one laying with her back on the the floor. The svartalfar woman was so much lighter than the human mercenary that she couldn't resist.

After tossing the albino against the wall, Ophelia pressed the tip of her blade to the base of that Saya's throat before turning her attention to the lower one.

"I would stay still, my dear," Havarti spoke to the woman as his wielder turned her attention away, "She needn't see you for me to strike on my own accord."

Ophelia grabbed the pale hand of the other Saya and yanked her to her feet, "Explain quickly and make sense. Now," she huffed as she gripped the lower Saya's tight collar.

Josie threw the door open right then. Her short sword was reared back to strike but once the scene unfolded before her, she had no idea who to attack.

She looked just as confused as Ophelia.

"I was just sitting here when *she*," the lower Saya started her explanation, "shimmied in through the window and attacked me!"

Ophelia turned her head back in the direction of the top Saya, "No, I was on the bed when *she* prowled in and attacked me!"

The mercenary let out a heavy sigh, "Tell me you have some idea of what is happening here." Though Ophelia didn't look in her direction, the words were directed at the ranger.

Josie shook her head, "Sorry, this isn't any ability or spell or anything that I'm aware of Saya being able to do."

"It isn't," both svartalfars said at the same time.

"So how in the hell are we supposed to figure out which is which?" Ophelia asked.

"I could go retrieve Folken, I suppose," the alphan woman shrugged.

"No, don't, please!" again, they both spoke at the same time.

"Okay, this is getting really tiresome, really fast," the mercenary growled, "What do you suggest then?" The question was to Josie.

"Ask a question that only the real Saya would know?" her wavering voice made the idea not overly reassuring.

"You've worked with her before, right?" Ophelia asked the ranger, "You should know something."

"It was for a few days several years ago!" Josie protested, "I'm still trying to figure out how you got in here in the first place, let alone what's going on now."

"Fine, fine, fine," the woman in the long coat grumbled, "What does Havarti hate being called?"

"Cheese," they both answered.

Ophelia's eyes rolled so hard that she saw two (more) of everything for a split second, "You think Folken would get mad if I just killed them both?"

"I think he would frown on it, yeah," Josie answered, "From what I know of Folken, he doesn't care for much but family does appear to be one of those few things."

"Well," Ophelia cursed under her breath before she spoke up again, "Maybe you ladies could tell me why I shouldn't bring Folken in. Because leaving this up to someone else is sounding better and better."

"As a member of the Kizoku Tribe, Folken values our reputation," the lower Saya answered first, "If he hears that I let myself get ambushed by a copy, he would effectively remove me from the Romefeller Guilds as unreliable."

"Not to mention the personal embarrassment of having to bring him in to sort out something that should be so easy to figure out," top Saya added, "She was nowhere near as good as me. If you had only been a few seconds later, this would have all been sorted out!"

"You do have a point there," that gave the mercenary an idea, "Okay, Sayas, you are going to unload your arms of all their hidden cutlery. No trickery now. Havarti is very protective of my well being and Josie can cut you down if you even look in my direction sideways."

The threat of Josie was for lower Saya and Ophelia motioned to Josie to raise her blade and watch the Saya that didn't have a bastard sword at her throat.

"I already count one karambit for Lady Wallflower here, so you," her pale blue eyes moved from the curved blade in the bed post to dig into lower Saya, "are already playing catch up."

Neither woman looked pleased with Ophelia's proposed solution. They even frowned the same way. But they started pulling hidden blades of different makes and types. The small, curved blade called a karambit came out to even the blade counts first, then several daggers. Blow darts dropped to the floor, followed by the clattering of razor sharp caltrops. A couple more wicked looking blades slipped out of the long black gloves of both women.

"In blessed Juna's name, how can you fit all that in one arm and still lift the damned thing?" Ophelia honestly marveled at the idea.

Finally, after the last throwing dagger dropped to the slatted wood, both albino women announced, "That's all."

"Josie, hand me your sword," Ophelia ordered.

"Why?" the ranger looked more confused than annoyed at this point.

"So that I can cover them both while you're counting how many blades belong to each of them," Ophelia answered, "I'd do it myself but, you know, I'm so drunk and counting is *so hard.*"

The woman's voice dripped with sarcasm. When she crossed her eyes and stuck out her tongue at the ranger, annoyance quickly edged out her confusion. Still, Josie handed over the blade and started an inventory of each Saya's weaponry.

"You seem pretty spry since your disappearing act," the crimson haired woman muttered as she started sorting piles of blades.

It was a long and quiet wait. Ophelia didn't show any signs of tiring, even after holding her heavy bastard sword aloft all this time. The patience of both the svartalfar women, though, seemed much closer to being spent.

"Done," Josie announced.

"How many?" Ophelia asked.

"Thirty-three for the one against the wall," the ranger answered.

"And her?" Ophelia tapped the flat end of Josie's sword on lower Saya's pasty shoulder.

"Thirty-two," came the answer.

"You're sure?" the mercenary glanced down at the alphan who nodded back, "What kind of knife is missing?"

Josie clenched her fists as she stared back at Ophelia. Her jaw moved with curses and insults that only stayed silent because her red lips were sealed so tight they were turning white. That is, until her face suddenly turned slack. She finally understood and she held up the weapon of which the Saya that was pinned against the wall had one extra.

"A throwing dagger," she answered aloud.

"Raiko had stolen one from Saya the night he died. It was melted into slag and there's no way she could have replaced it without visiting a blacksmith. Which we didn't do yesterday," Ophelia turned all her attention to top Saya, at the same time holding Josie's short sword out to the ranger to take back, "So what should we do with her, Saya?"

The question went to the one who stood behind the mercenary. She knelt down to the organized piles of blades that the ranger made and started tucking the weapons back into the long leather glove.

"Keep her alive now, Ophelia," Saya didn't look up from her work of re-arming herself, "You hear me? No decapitations."

"That's all well and good," the mercenary answered, "Then what?"

The svartalfar identified as the 'true' Saya looked up to Josie, "Could you get Folken? Now that we've straightened out who's who, we could really use his insight on why I suddenly have an evil twin at all."

"You're one to talk about *evil*," the other Saya said, "After Middlemount, do you really think either of us could be considered *good*?"

Slipping the last blade through the black leather and into her metal arm, the true Saya raised a platinum eyebrow at her duplicate. The look on her face, it told Ophelia that the doppelganger had struck some nerve. The svartalfar woman didn't seem quite as firmly together as she did only moments ago.

"And how do you know about that?" she asked her twin.

"I remember it as well as you do," the second Saya answered, "Why does a single blade determine that you're *the real me* and I'm not?"

The noblewoman stood up to her full height. After again ordering Josie to go get Folken, the ranger ducked out of the room. Then Saya turned her attention to her doppelganger.

"It shows I was the one who has been here, faker," she declared, "The question is: where did you come from?"

"You mind taking Havarti for a sec, Saya?" Ophelia stepped aside far enough so the real Saya could reach the handle of her sword, "He can make himself light but I still can't hold him forever."

The other woman's gloved hand wrapped around the half of the handle not in the mercenary's grip, "Aren't you worried that *I'm* going to kill her?"

"You're the one who ordered to keep her alive. I can personally not care less," Ophelia shrugged, then proceeded to shake blood flow back into her left arm, "I just can't help but wonder that if there's a copy of you, does that mean there's one of me out there? Or, more importantly, Harby?"

CHAPTER FIVE

After the subject finished reading Josie's version of the events that transpired, I handed her the next report. The insignia of the Romefeller Guild was stamped along the top of the parchment.

"I already know what happened next, Ophelia," I told her, "Here is what Saya had to say..."

Several hours later...

"I CAN'T BELIEVE I let you talk me into this," *Evil* Saya said as she made her way between the trees.

The night was in full force. The moon hung directly overhead, the forest unable to block any of its cool light from hitting the party consisting of Saya with her doppelganger, Folken (who stood directly between the identical women), Ophelia, and Josie, both bringing up the rear.

"It was hardly a negotiation, Ms. Khushrenada," Folken replied, refusing to call the doppelganger by her first name, "Simply put, it was the only option given you that kept you from dying immediately by either my hand or yours, rather hers," he nodded toward the *real* Saya.

"How can you take their word for it that I'm the copy, Folken?" the doppelganger asked, "You said that even you couldn't detect any kind of difference between us."

"Within your bodies, that is true," the svartalfar man nodded, "However, while the workmanship on your prosthetic is well crafted, it is not mine. Although, I was begrudged to learn that the fruits of my workmanship were damaged due to negligence."

He looked over at the real Saya sideways. The woman looked down at her arm, fully repaired by Folken before they started this trek.

"It wasn't negligence," the albino woman insisted yet again, "Raiko sabotaged my arm the last time we were... together so I wouldn't be able to sense the missing dagger."

"A fact you tried to conceal from me, cousin," Folken said.

Come to think of it, since they left the inn, Ophelia had not heard the sorcerer refer to either of them as "Saya". Did he doubt Ophelia's findings as to who was real and the copy?

The mercenary was pulled from her reflections by Josie. The ranger leaned in close to her, as they continued walking.

"What was that teleporting trick you did to get in the room?" she whispered.

"You mean when you stabbed me in the chest?" Ophelia smirked back.

"You–!" Josie stopped herself from snapping at the other woman, "Yes, that."

"It's the same thing that saved me from that fireball Raiko dropped on me back in Dracoleaf," the mercenary answered, "It's called blinking."

The ranger waited for more detail.

"It's a defensive magick that shoots me out of the way of an oncoming attack," Ophelia explained, "One of the problems with it is that I can't predict which where it will make me reappear."

"So you didn't know that it would take you to the other side of the door," Josie guessed.

And Ophelia nodded back.

"But still, does that mean you can't be killed?" the alphan asked.

"That's the other problem," the mercenary said back, "It doesn't always work. When it does, it heals me," Ophelia held up her now pristine right hand and wiggled her fingers in front of Josie, "But a stab wound almost killed me once when it didn't go off."

"So you're saying that I could have killed you?" shock washed all over the other woman's face, "Why would you do that?"

"I was drunk," Ophelia laughed as she shrugged, "It seemed like a good idea at the time."

"So part of the healing it does," Josie pushed the hand of the mercenary down back to her side, "sobers you up, too? No wonder you don't worry about whether or not you can do this job."

"It sounds good on parchment," Ophelia sighed, "But I'd give it all back if I could know more than just the names of my parents."

Her cheek twitched after saying that. While it wasn't strictly a lie, there were other considerations to why she had to keep the runes on her back. The alphan didn't need to know those.

"We're almost there," Evil Saya announced, "He's not going to be happy to see all of you. He may attack us all on sight."

"Attacked by a cleric?" Josie scoffed, "What's he going to do, bless me to death?"

"You forget that this version of Harbenigyr does not owe his allegiance to Kuan Yin," Folken chastised the ranger, "Whatever deity he does serve could certainly have quite vicious curses available for his use."

After only a few more steps, a figure stepped out from behind a tree directly ahead of the group. The armor he wore was made of bronze and shaped to look like the muscular torso of a man. Below, he wore a kilt with black and white lines and patterns sewn into the material. The grass obscured his feet but Ophelia was pretty sure she would see sandals.

The helmet he wore had a mask that looked like the most generic face one could imagine. Silver hair spilled down his back and over his wide shoulders. It was a look they had all become familiar with recently.

"Halt!" he ordered, "Speak your business."

Folken's eyes narrowed at the man. Ophelia got the impression that the svartalfar wasn't one to take kindly to being given commands. Still, he stopped walking and both Sayas followed suit, staying beside him.

Ophelia resisted the urge to reach for Havarti as she ran out of room to keep going forward. Josie's eyes darted all around, although you had to be quick to notice that she was doing so.

"We're surrounded. Four on the right, five on the left," she whispered to the mercenary, "Whoever they are, they're good. I didn't hear them at all."

Folken spoke directly to the man in their path, "I am not seeking battle at the moment, simply a moment of Harbenigyr's time."

"Harbenigyr?" the masked man in armor lied badly.

"Yes, the man who organized this ambush. Your compatriots can come out of hiding and escort us to him under guard, if you must," the sorcerer must have caught what Josie reported as well, "We will not resist."

"Are we absolutely certain this was the best plan for this?" Havarti's worried tone seeped into Ophelia's mind.

"Relax. A search could take weeks and our Harby doesn't have that kind of time in that cage," the woman thought back, "Even after we showed the constable the other Josie, the concept of an evil Harbenigyr is a hard sell. We need to bring him back."

"But we were expecting, at worst, a duplication of our whole party. Not an army of minions with them!" the bastard sword retorted.

"Ten guys in robes hardly constitute an army, Havarti," Ophelia scoffed.

"It isn't our ability to survive the counter that worries me so, my dear," the sword replied, "Even if we do kill them all, there is no guarantee that we will be able to get this Harby doppelganger back into Ash Providence alive."

"No one said anything about bringing him back alive," the woman's hands rolled up into fists, "Just getting him back. Even just his head should do it."

"Ophelia, I only say this because I care," Havarti's delivery was that of a gentle reprimand, "But I fear you are coming to enjoy decapitations too much."

While the mercenary was having her quiet conversation, the leader of the squad of soldiers surrounding her group must have decided to escort them to the doppelganger cleric. The nine other soldiers, each looking eerily like the others down to the silver hair cascading down their backs, stepped out from behind trees or out of clumps of brush.

Every one of them had double-bladed battle axes in their hands. No matter which way they swing their weapons, they would cut something. At least that was the theory. The handles weren't as long as the ax wielded by the Cardasian back in the tournament but the blades looked much heavier. That made them more powerful, not to mention more threatening looking, but also more cumbersome. Even a bastard sword's broad blade could out maneuver them.

With a ring of soldiers wearing bronze guiding around them, Ophelia, Josie, Folken and the Sayas made their way even deeper into the woods. In the back of her mind, Ophelia was glad these weren't the Jaded Woods Harby had been so patient to come and visit. If they were, she thought it was likely they would come upon the cleric's village before reaching wherever they were going.

"Saya!" A familiar, if out of place voice called out just as they reached a small clearing, "You've either brought me the perfect gift or you made me a very unhappy man."

Harbenigyr sat on a fallen log right in the middle of the cleared out, tree free expanse of grass. Judging by how the shafts of green were toppled over beside him, the doppelganger cleric (or more likely one of his minions) must have dragged his makeshift seat to that spot.

In evil Harbenigyr's hands was a quarterstaff identical to the one the real Harbenigyr used as a walking stick. Ophelia had to remind herself that the man and weapon mere copies of the real thing. It wasn't easy, even knowing that the one true cleric of Kuan Yin was in a cage back in town.

In the back of her mind, she had a nagging question of whether he had somehow escaped and made his way here meet them like this. She knew it was absurd but she also realized that was why the constable was so reluctant to believe their evil doppelganger story.

"You are the doppelganger of the Harbenigyr with which we have traveled, I presume?" Folken gave him a polite, if brief, bow in greeting.

"I appreciate you not calling me a copy of the real Harbenigyr, Lord Kizoku," the cleric in white nodded, "I have to admit, I'm surprised to see you here. After all, Saya went into Ash Providence on a simple scouting mission. She wasn't supposed to have contact with any of you."

The hard, stern face the elf gave to Evil Saya made it easier for Ophelia to believe he was the fake. She had never seen Harby look as... threatening as that.

"Apparently, she took some initiative," Folken responded for both versions of his cousin, "She intended to kill and replace the version of Saya that came with us from Dracoleaf."

"Ah," the hard look on the cleric's face changed only just enough to add an air of disappointment, "Pity. My intent was to fulfill our objective without you ever learning that we even existed."

"Then I submit that committing a violent crime in Ash Providence was counterproductive to that goal," Folken rested his hands on his hips.

Harbenigyr pursed his lips before again nodding, in agreement this time, "True but it did ensure that you would be forced to stop here. Catching up to you would be much easier then. Not to mention, that woman's body was the stuff men dream of fondling while fondling themselves!" he whistled.

"What a pig," Josie muttered.

"Oh? Who is that?" the cleric leaned to the side on the log to look around the sorcerer, "Is that Josie?" he reflexively ran his tongue over his lips.

"Unimportant to the discussion, I'm afraid," Folken stepped between the ranger and doppelganger to block his view of the woman, "If I am correct about the company you are keeping, Harbenigyr, would I be correct in deducing at your objective revolves around the retrieval of Meteorend?"

"I haven't known you long, Lord Kizoku, but I could tell right away that you were a man of intelligence," the elf smiled, a wide, predatory smile that looked alien on his face.

"That does bring a myriad of questions to my mind, if you don't mind putting the retrieval of Meteorend on pause for a moment," the sorcerer said.

"Why not?" the cleric shrugged.

"How is it that you and Ms. Khushrenada appear to have the memories, as well as the physical attributes, of your duplicates?" Folken waved a gloved finger back and forth as he recited his question, "Not too mention that I cannot detect a whit of divergence that would come from any cloning process of which I am aware."

"The answer is simple, really," Harbenigyr lifted himself from the log, "We aren't simple copies."

Folken lifted a finger as if he were raising a point in a debate, "But for there to be no deviation between doppelgangers you would have to act exactly as the other does. As you said, I've not known Harbenigyr for long but he does not strike me as a man capable of rape."

The cleric stepped off to the side to get a clear view of Josie before he responded, "Every man is capable of taking what he wants, when he wants it."

"But the Harbenigyr of my acquaintance has, shall we say, a tight leash on such urges," Folken again stepped into the sight line of the cleric.

"If you are as smart as you think yourself to be, Lord Kizoku," a soft chuckle escaped the doppelganger elf as he spoke, "I'm willing to bet you've figured out the answer by now. But then, that would be if I thought you were smart enough."

"I'm sorry," Evil Saya whispered from directly behind Folken.

Every step Harbenigyr took was to move the svartalfar man into that position. The sorcerer prided himself on being able to think ahead. He had to applaud the cleric doppelganger on his tactical prowess. Especially when he felt Ms. Khushrenada stab a sharpened fingertip into his back.

They didn't allow Saya's doppelganger to re-equip her weapons once they were out of her arm. That didn't mean that the prosthetic limb was harmless. Claws were built into the fingertips as a last line of defense or, in this case, a last ditch weapon of assassination.

OPHELIA INTERROGATION NOTES

"Where's the rest of it?" Ophelia tossed the parchment onto the table between us.

"The rest of what?" I asked.

"Saya's testimony," the subject answered, "It stopped right in the middle of everything."

"You know what happened," I said, "You were there, weren't you?"

The subject nodded, "What does all this have to do with Apple and her friends, anyway?"

"You know," I answered, "The efreeti connect everything..."

Two decades later...

JIN VEGA BROUGHT up the rear as the party rushed out of the Drunken Dragon. Once he was outside, Illyria, Appelonia, Tokki, Phinegann, and Jonas were already searching for their horses.

"That Bronwyn was a thief, after all," the monk's voice, though he was merely stating fact, sounded as if he were growling.

"She couldn't have gotten far," Jonas looked far more displeased, "Andromeda wouldn't let her."

"You have a lot of faith in a brainless animal," Phinegann did actually growl as he kicked at the dirt.

"No animal is brainless. You just have to know where their skill lies," Tokki Yo Bunpy crouched down beside the hoof prints in the dirt where they handed their steeds to the woman, "If you judge a fish by it's ability to climb a tree, you will think they are all fools."

"That is probably the most meaningful thing I've heard you say the entire trip," Appelonia grinned at the Bunny Barbarian.

He quickly turned away from her, bending his head down so that no one could see the bottom half of his face. Jin had a suspicion that, if he could, he would see flushing cheeks at that moment.

Clearing his throat, Tokki pointed toward the hill that rested almost immediately behind the lone building, "It looks like she took them to the back of the tavern. Probably for just enough privacy to loot our saddlebags."

The entrance to the bar opened and Mandragoria stepped outside. Stomping to the edge of the porch, she frowned at the assembled, horseless people.

"Aren't you gone yet?" she shouted.

"Our horses were taken," Appelonia said back, "We're heading after them now."

"You actually bought LaRue's valet gambit? I thought you people were smart," the strawberry blonde woman snickered, "Horses or no horses, I don't want to even catch a whiff of brimstone when that genie catches up to you. You get me?"

"Like wet in a rainstorm," the cleric chewed on her lower lip, "Tokki, we need to catch up to her fast."

The black furred barbarian hopped up to his feet and sprinted for the hill. As the rest or the party rushed after him, Mandragoria hopped off the porch, waving her thick arms.

"Hey, I want you to get further away from my place, not closer!" she hollered.

"We won't be but a minute!" Appelonia held up a finger as she looked back toward the bar owner while running after the rest of her group.

A thicket of shrubbery, taller than the short barbarian, blocked the party's path. A pained grunt came from the other side, then an angry shriek. Tokki didn't even break his stride as he raised his arms in front of him and charged through the brush.

"Go around!" Jonas ordered everyone else behind him as he pressed through the dense plants as well.

Appelonia and the others did so, not even adding a dozen steps to their chase when they saw the fur covered barbarian tackle Bronwyn LaRue to the dust covered ground in the midst of all their steeds. The silver mechanism that assembled Appelonia's jade sticks into a bow and arrow tumbled out of her leather coat.

"What else do you have that's ours, eh?" a snarling Tokki Yo Bunpy slammed the curved claws of his sleeve weapon into the dirt just beside the woman's face.

She wrapped one hand around the leather strap on the barbarian's chest and tried to pull him off of her, "Nothing! The knight's stupid horse bit me before I could get anything else," she held up her other hand showing the red welts that were already blossoming on the back of her hand and palm.

The barbarian wasn't at all sympathetic. The claws of his sleeve still in the dirt, Tokki twisted them around until the sharp tips were pointed at the face of the thief.

"You are going to stay still. You are going to be searched and if we find anything else not belonging to you, I will shove these into your eyes and nose," the Bunny Barbarian made the black claws wiggle, inches in front of Bronwyn's brown eyes, "Understood?"

She nodded, releasing her grip on Tokki's leather harness, "You'll find a circle made of silver with four jewels mounted on it in my right belt pouch. It belongs to the guy in the cloak," she confessed.

Jin blinked at the unexpected admission. He didn't have anything save for food and water in his own saddlebags, so the fact that he was robbed was all the more shocking.

Pulling the charcoal cloak open, he reached inside. Jin's arm stretched much further into the folds of the garment than it really should have been able to, particularly since the outside didn't show any sign of being pushed around.

Appelonia caught a glimpse of the interior lining of the garment and gasped, "Why... why does it look like the night sky in there?"

"She *did* take my hirizi!" Despite the confirmation that that he had been stolen from, he couldn't help but be impressed.

Still, he strode over to where Tokki stayed sitting on her stomach. Kneeling down, he opened the pouch and pulled a hand sculpted circle of dulled silver. Four jewels rested at its four cardinal points. A ruby was mounted into the top, an emerald on the left, a sapphire on the right, and a diamond on the bottom. On the outside of the circle was a mounting especially made for the staff that rested between the saddlebags and the back of the horse that had been given to him at Dianmeyer.

Along the inside of the circle, projecting from the silver framework holding the jewels in place, were four curved tines that each came to a point and met in the middle, barely leaving enough room for a man to poke a finger in between the ends. There were no signs of damage. LaRue had not tried to pry the jewels loose from their mountings. Of course, she may not have had the chance yet.

"How did you get it?" Jin asked Bronwyn as he lifted himself back up to his feet.

"I picked it out of your cloak when you handed me your horse's reins," she explained, her eyes locked on the undulating claws that filled her vision.

"That can't be," the monk replied, "Only I know what's in here. That means only I can pull them out."

"What is so special about that cloak, Jin?" Jonas asked, his hand loitering on the neck of his horse as he turned to face the monk.

"There, there. There!" a completely new voice chimed in from the other side of the shrubs that the barbarian and paladin plowed through.

The plants burst into flames and a woman with black hair, standing straight up as if she were hanging upside down, stepped through the fire without any hint of discomfort. She wore a short white dress with jade patterns embroidered into the sleeves, like a mockery of Appelonia's own cleric uniform.

The dress was barely long enough to hide her modesty, leaving most of her very long legs exposed. Her feet were covered with leather poulaines that only covered up to her ankle and ended with exaggerated pointy toes.

She stood proudly with her hands on her hips as her gray eyes surveyed the people and animals before her. She fit the description that Jonas and Appelonia gave of the woman they saw from up in the tower perfectly.

"I only need one of you," the woman said, "I can't care less what the rest of you do with yourselves."

"So which of us is it then?" Tokki spoke up from where he kept Bronwyn on the ground, "We've kind of hit a blank as to who is supposed to be this baby you're looking for."

"Baby?" The stranger's eyes flared with fire that seemed to be captured behind her pupils, "Did Abernathy tell you that? That blabbermouth."

"We know it's not me now," Appelonia said, picking up the silver mechanism for her bow, "Why are you coming after us then?"

"You thought *you* were one of us?" the woman's face twisted with disgust, "Not to be too picky or anything but, lady, that shade of red means that you're just trying too hard. Besides, the baby's not my problem."

"So there is a baby mixed up in all of this?" Jonas slid his hand down the flank of his horse, slowly making his way to the handle of his claymore.

"But this is my natural hair color," the cleric self-consciously wrapped a hand around her long, crimson tresses.

"That is *definitely not* your problem, either," the woman snapped at the paladin.

"Then which of us do you want, demon?" Phinegann stepped up to the black haired woman. "I'm getting tired of this."

"*Demon* is an awfully rude way to address your better, orc." While the strange woman wasn't at all short, she nearly matched Jin in height, that only brought her even with Phinegann's wide shoulders, so she had to crane her neck to look him in the face, "Almost as rude as pretending you don't know what I'm here for."

"But we don't know what you are here for," Jin responded, "Abernathy wasn't a good source of information after he was cleaved in half."

Only a twitch of her cheek betrayed any sign of surprise when the woman noticed the monk had somehow crept within arm's reach of her, just off to her left. If he hadn't spoken, he was confident that he could have crept even closer.

"It looks like we should have a talk, rather than a fight," Jonas said, "Don't you think, Miss...?"

Though his hand rested on the hilt of his sword, the paladin did not pull it free from under the saddle or even grab the handle. The stranger turned her attention to him and gave Jonas a pleased little smile of approval.

"You may call me Genevieve. You're the one that killed Abernathy. With that big blade of yours. Aren't you?" She said, motioning to the weapon resting under his armor wrapped hand.

"He didn't give us much choice but to fight," Jonas answered, "He wouldn't listen. But you're different, aren't you?"

"You're saying that you really don't know what we want from you?" if there was one way to hold your face that said *I don't believe you, Are you people stupid*?, and *why am I wasting my time here*?, Genevieve broadcast each meaning simultaneously and perfectly, "I'd be more inclined to believe you if each and every one of you weren't positioning yourselves to try and give you the advantage in a fight. Even you, handsome human in tin plating."

"Like I said, Abernathy didn't give us a choice before," Jonas lowered his hand, as a sign of good faith if Jin had to guess, "I wish we did know what you wanted, then at least we would know if this was even worth all this drama."

Genevieve's face lit up at the words from the paladin's lips, "Well, I can see only one way of granting this to your satisfaction, master." She giggled.

Phinegann let out a terse curse, "Really, Shepherd? Again?" he roared.

Jin didn't say anything. He simply charged at the woman, intent on taking her down before she could do whatever it was she was planning.

He shot one of his knees behind hers, knocking her off balance. The woman fell onto that knee as the monk brought a fist up to meet her dropping face.

It felt as if he's struck the side of a fortress. There was no give at all. The woman didn't even seem realize that she had been punched.

No, that wasn't right. She knew she had been hit. It just didn't affect her at all.

So Jin had to change his tact. He grabbed the wrist of the woman before falling back and wrapping the rest of his body around her limb. His soft leather shoes pressed against her body as he strained to make her arm useless.

"Having fun?" the woman asked, lifting herself back up to her feet and the monk into the air with inhuman amounts of strength.

Genevieve stepped forward, spinning her body around until Jin Vega fell away, bowling the Bunny Barbarian over and off of the thief, Bronwyn LaRue. Jonas pulled his weapon free, jumped over Tokki, and charged for Genevieve as Appelonia hastily constructed her bow to attack from a distance.

That was when the ground all around every one of them started to glow. The horses reared back in fright, Illyria's colt even lost its balance and fell over.

He wasn't the only one. Jonas lost his footing before he could even reach the demon. The paladin, along with everyone else, found the light rising all around them like water with the incoming tide.

Illyria's glass wings swept downward, carrying her aloft. As they started to carry the gnome woman away, Genevieve snatched the small woman from the air with one hand. She gripped Illyria by her ankle as she hung upside down in the demon's grasp.

"He said 'we', little one. That includes you, too," Genevieve grinned as the light passed her round hips.

Phinegann rushed at the demon, slamming his metal shoulder into her midsection. Genevieve gripped one of the tufts of hair on his face and wrenched his face so that he couldn't look in any direction but at her.

"You lost your chance, baldy," she said as a matter-of-fact, "The second I reconnected with home, nothing in your realm could touch me anymore."

Appelonia loosed an arrow at the demon. It struck the human looking demon's wrist, trying to free the winged gnome, with the same effect as Jin's punch. Nothing.

Jin rolled out of the way of Appelonia's horse, Bommer, as he fell over. The monk was as helpless as everyone else to stop what was happening. As the light completely engulfed him, two things occurred to Jin Vega.

First, it was getting steadily warmer. The second, and far more disturbing thing, was that he wasn't truly sure he even had a body anymore. If he didn't have a body, though, how could he feel heat? Perhaps, he was about to learn how true the concept of hell was...

OPHELIA INTERROGATION NOTES

"Appelonia already told me all of this," Ophelia said, "And you know about Harby's evil twin so why are you treating the real one like a criminal?"

"I don't approve of how you and your band resolved the situation with the duplicate," I said, "You left too many questions open."

"Too many questions?" the subject literally scoffed at me, "What's so questionable about..."

Two decades before...

EVIL SAYA'S METAL arm fell limp at her side. A warm pair of lips brushed against her pointed ear and a voice that she knew perfectly whispered softly.

"Remember this, doppelganger?" the true Saya lifted the short, curved karambit blade into the copy's vision, "Remember what you were trying to do with it? I did. Now which of us is better?"

A fit of rage possessed the svartalfar woman's duplicate. She spun around, swinging her useless prosthetic limb like a metallic whip.

Saya stepped back, just out if it reach, with a wide grin on her black painted lips, "Did you really think I would let you hurt Folken? We think the same, remember? I knew that was the only reason you agreed to lead us here."

Ophelia was snapped out of her enjoyment of the show when the armored soldiers that surrounded the group charged. She hopped out of the way of the first blade that came her way, spinning around and slamming her elbow into the back of her assailant's head. The metal dented so deeply that the man was not going to be able to get that helmet off without help. If he lived that long.

"Are any of you the one I knew as Horta?" Ophelia asked the attacking de Junamends as she pulled the helmet of a second assailant, who was not the one she wanted, "I don't want to kill you if there's still a chance I can at least get a nightcap!"

The mercenary slammed the silver haired stranger's own helmet back into his face and he toppled to the grass. The first guard with the dented head gear turned back and started swinging at the woman with a vigor only pain can add. Vigor didn't equal skill and Ophelia was able to turn her attention back to the svartalfar cousins moments later.

"You were late," Folken chastised his cousin as he pulled his long cape wide open to inspect the damage, "You assured me that I would not need a tailor this time."

He pointed at the hole the Saya's doppelganger stabbed through the black outer fabric as well as the purple lining of the sorcerer's cape. His cousin didn't answer as she and her twin did battle. It was apparent that Folken thought that she was being rude.

He was about to involve himself when the war cry of one of the anonymous foot soldiers crossed his ears. Annoyance pulled Folken's emerald eyebrows together as one of the armored men charged at him.

"Yes, yes. I understand that you have violent duties to perform," the sorcerer lifted his gloved arm and pointed it toward the man. "But I find myself already weary of this affair."

A cylinder emerged from the forearm of svartalfar's prosthetic limb. The air distorted at the open end, pointed at the charging soldier. The deformed open space shot from the cylinder and hit the soldier right in the middle of the sculpted chest of the de Junamend's armor.

He was suddenly doing his best impression of a statue. One leg was in the air, mid-stride, while the soldier wielded his ax in both hands above his head. If he were simply frozen in that position the man would have toppled to the ground but that same distorted air that held him in that position also cradled him aloft.

Folken stepped around the neutralized soldier and strode toward the doppelganger of the cleric Harbenigyr. To his credit, the black haired elf did not make any motion to run away or join the fray. He simply leaned against the quarterstaff, waiting for the svartalfar man as he approached.

"Would it be too early for me to declare my previous worries to be for naught?" Havarti chimed into Ophelia's mind.

"Depends," the woman shrugged, "Lets see how Saya is doing."

The original Romefeller intelligence officer sidestepped the limp limb strike of her copy, "You remember the first time Folken's prosthetic failed on me?" she asked Evil Saya.

Her duplicate nodded, "It was a month after he installed it," she attacked again and the other Saya dodged again, "I had to live with it for a week before he came back to town!"

The albino woman ducked under another swipe from the powerless limb, "Remember what he told me when he did come back?" Saya asked as she stepped back, just out of reach of another attack.

The woman with the platinum hair pulled one of the armored soldiers charging toward Josie into the path of the next attack by the doppelganger. A scream of pain quickly turned into a gurgle as his throat was shredded under her still sharpened fingertips.

"Come on, the rush of anger has to be subsiding by now," the original svartalfar woman smirked, "What did he tell me?"

The 'evil' version of Saya froze mid-swing, though her arm didn't. It continued on its path until it aimlessly dangled at the woman's side, "He said I should have had it in a sling instead of letting it hang loose. But I didn't want anyone to know that it was broken."

"And what did he say I was lucky didn't happen?" the original svartalfar stepped up to her copy, wrapping her hand around the upper arm of the prosthetic to stop its swaying.

Her doppelganger's violet eyes opened wide in horror, "No. No, you wouldn't…"

Saya's grip tightened and she pulled downward with all her strength. The metal limb attached to Evil Saya's shoulder popped as if it was simply pulled out of its socket.

Then the flesh separated from the metal with a rending noise that turned the stomachs of both women. Once the blood started pouring from Evil Saya's now severed arm, Ophelia and Saya both cringed as the doppelganger wailed in a mixture of pain and… and sorrow.

And an arrow blew past Ophelia's head as Josie shot her third arrow into her third target. The mercenary hadn't noticed him sneaking up behind her.

Ophelia couldn't help but think that the armor of the de Junamend wasn't very well made. She didn't even have a chance to add to the pain of the soldier the ranger shot before he stopped breathing.

The mercenary had to remind herself that only the thickest of armors could stop a perfectly aimed arrow. Most could counter glancing blows at best and none of Josie's shots were glancing. She had to admit that the alphan ranger was good.

Ophelia noticed Josie nod back in her direction at another incoming armored soldier. The mercenary made a show of her take down her third de Junamend, matching her total to that of the ranger, and Havarti hadn't even been drawn yet. This one was a victim of his own helmet just as her first two were. Ophelia doubted that he found it tasty.

As she looked up again, Josie had to drop her bow to take on another armored goon with her short sword. The red haired woman was quicker than the other man, so she could dodge the heavy ax.

That wasn't the problem. Josie was completely on the defensive while another de Junamend was creeping up behind her. There was no way that Ophelia could reach the creeper before he would reach Josie.

"Think you can handle this one?" the woman looked down at the hilt of her bastard sword.

"Only one way to find out isn't... there?"

Before he even finished the sentence, Ophelia twisted Havarti's handle, pulling the dagger hidden within free, and threw it at the soldier about to ambush Josie. The ranger deflected the ax in front of her with her smaller blade, unaware of the coming danger. The mercenary wasn't much of a knife thrower but she could cover a long distance and, at least get it in the neighborhood of the target.

The rest was where Havarti came in. The sentience of the blade extended to the dagger, at least as far that he could sense it and feel what it could even when separated from the rest of the hilt.

The closest analogy he was able to come up with to describe the sensation was when a person was able to pick up items or do some other manual task with their hands without even looking at them.

Adjusting the aim of a mediocre throw was a lot more complicated. It wasn't like he could magically change the direction like a wizard using some telekinetic spell. To Havarti, it was more like trying to steer a panicked, runaway horse.

As the dagger flew over the distance of the clearing, the bastard sword's consciousness gave it a nudge here, a pull back there, and hoped that there wasn't a strong breeze that could push the weapon off course. Especially when someone's life counted on his accuracy.

The dagger careened off the bottom edge of the helmet with an ear grating ring. The handle spun up to hit the side of the soldier's head, knocking him off balance.

The de Junamend tripped over his own feet, his head still reeling off to the side from the impact against the dagger's hilt. Havarti did what he could, keeping the blade pointed toward the ground as best as he was able.

The armored de Junamend hit the ground hard. Then the blade sank into his neck with enough force to pierce through the other side.

Hearing the death rattle of the man behind her, Josie stepped on the shaft of the ax that just buried its head into the soil beside her feet. She had just enough time to see that she the violent fate she'd been spared before the still living soldier started fighting against her weight to free his weapon.

The ranger took a cue from Havarti's attack and drilled her short sword into the space between the pauldron and helmet of her opponent's armor. He fell immediately.

Ophelia gave Josie a nod with a wide grin as the other woman traced the path of the thrown dagger back to the mercenary. The alphan ranger freed the dagger from her would be assassin and walked it back to Ophelia.

Josie jumped in surprise as the blade started vibrating in her hands, shedding off the blood of it's target in a fog of tiny ruby droplets. As she offered the weapon to Ophelia, the red haired woman couldn't decide if she was impressed or disturbed.

"Havarti hates being messy," Ophelia explained as she returned the dagger back to its place in the handle of the sword.

"Oh," Josie blinked back.

Ophelia found herself grinning back even bigger without thinking. She still hadn't gotten around to telling the ranger any details about Havarti. Not even the basic things like he could talk. The mercenary knew that she would eventually but, for now, seeing the look of confusion of Josie's face was just so... satisfying.

"It's over, Harbenigyr," Folken's voice drifted over the air to the ears of both women.

With the duplicate of Saya laying on the ground so still that she could only be dead, the true Saya was already standing beside her cousin. As Ophelia and Josie made their way to where the sorcerer stood before the doppelganger of their cleric, the svartalfar man continued speaking.

"It was an ingenious ploy, elf," the sorcerer said, "If you had brought more foot soldiers, it may have even succeeded."

Evil Harbenigyr let out a long, dejected sigh, "I didn't expect things to devolve so quickly. All I wanted to do was get Meteorend back so that we," me motioned to the pale body of the dead Evil Saya, then the corpses of the armored de Junamend, "could take our leave of these people and live lives of our own."

"You're saying that you never wanted to kill and replace me or Harby?" The Romefeller operative crossed her arms over her chest.

"I don't know what what caused *my* Saya to attack you," the doppelganger looked thoughtful as he spoke, "But that wasn't the plan. Besides, what kind of life could I have impersonating a convicted rapist?"

The evil version of the cleric laughed at his own question. Ophelia had to stifle the urge to stab Evil Harbenigyr in the throat. Even Josie seemed to want to bludgeon him with her bow as the two women approached.

"You're the monster, not Harby," Josie declared as she stepped up beside Saya.

The doppelganger quirked an eyebrow at the ranger, "Is that a soft spot I'm detecting? For someone you said was nothing but a burden?"

The ranger couldn't hide her surprise at his comment, "How did you–?"

Evil Harbenigyr waved a finger around his face before replying to Josie's truncated question by addressing the whole of the group, "I've been around longer than you realize. Do you know what conversations you had with me and not the dull imitation in the cage back in town? I'll give you a hint. It was more than one. And none of you could tell. None of you even suspected."

"That does raise another area of concern," Folken spoke up, "Does everyone here have doppelgangers out there, waiting to pounce?"

The evil cleric shrugged, "Would you believe whatever answer I give?"

"Try me," the sorcerer said.

"Fine," Evil Harbenigyr sighed again, "The rest of the doppelgangers were killed when hers," the elf motioned to Ophelia, "came out defective and killed them all. She also chewed the head off that one you were looking for, Horta," he directed the last comment at the mercenary alone, his face apologetic.

That looked like an expression their Harby would actually have. It also made his jibe about being among the group and even holding conversations all the more convincing.

Ophelia let herself feel disappointed for a moment. Only for a moment. While the idea of seeing him again was titillating, realistically, it wouldn't have worked out. Especially with all this Meteorend nonsense still hanging over them.

"Do we believe him?" Josie asked as she turned to the sorcerer.

"We've no reason not to," the green haired man answered, "If there are more, though, they will find coming after us as fruitless an endeavor as this one has. Assuming his goal really is retrieving Meteorend to secure his freedom from the de Junamend."

"What do you mean by that?" Harby's doppelganger looked pained by Folken's comment.

"Your efforts to regain Meteorend from us are meaningless. None of us possess that particular object," the albino man explained, "Both Ophelia and I attempted to retrieve it but, as I understand it, the talisman evaporated into the ether upon the death of that... Raiko."

"You truly don't have it?" Evil Harbenigyr's shoulders slumped.

"Truly," Folken confirmed.

The cleric's eye slowly drifted from one person to the next in the short line standing before him. He rested his forehead against the smooth surface of the quarterstaff still in his hands, muttering under his breath.

If Ophelia had to guess, it was a prayer. She couldn't hear any of the specific words, let alone to who or what the prayer was directed towards, but when Evil Harbenigyr opened his eyes, that feeling of calm one saw radiating from them (a trait that was true in the real Harby but merely mimicked by this doppelganger) was gone.

"I'm not going back to the de Junamend," the cleric announced, "but I'm not going to rot in a cell in Ash Providence, either."

"You're not really leaving yourself a lot of options here," Ophelia remarked, "Especially since you are the one who *should be* in the cage instead of Harby. After all, he is innocent in all of this."

"Innocent?" the evil cleric scoffed, "Just because he didn't actually *do it* doesn't mean that he didn't think about it. He and I are literally the same, after all!"

"In looks. In memories, too, probably," Ophelia answered, "He can have all the thoughts he wants, it's his actions that make him who he is. The kindest, most selfless man I've known. Same thing goes for you. That's how I know you're a monster."

"That's rich coming from you," Harbenigyr smirked back, "I saw the *thing* that came out when they tried to copy you. What does that say about your soul?"

The evil cleric pushed his quarterstaff so that it toppled over like a tree, aiming for the mercenary. The resulting battle was brief but ferocious.

The return trip to Ash Providence was a lot shorter than the walk out. The first hints of the sun's return were just starting to tease the horizon when the party stepped into the town square.

The town constable was sitting at the edge of the raised portion in the middle of the square, only steps away from the door to the cage that still held Harbenigyr. Three more deputies sat on every other side of the cage. Wyatt was true to his word. He protected Harby from harm while they left to retrieve the true culprit responsible for attacking Magra.

Folken stood at the front of the party with Saya and Josie walking side by side just behind him. Ophelia brought up the rear, the limp body of Harbenigyr's evil duplicate draped over her right shoulder. When they were close enough, the sorcerer announced their presence to the constable.

The man, drowsy from a long night of essentially standing (and sitting) in one place all night, looked up. It took a good count of ten before he recognized what the mercenary was carrying.

The three deputies gathered around their leader as Ophelia stepped up to Wyatt. Even the true Harbenigyr lifted himself up to his knees (he couldn't stand up as the cage was too short) to try and see what was happening.

Ophelia dumped the body of the evil cleric to the ground at the constable's feet. All four law keepers jumped back in surprise when they saw the face that looked exactly like the one in the cage behind them.

"You're positive this man is the one who perpetrated the crime of which the man we have in custody is accused?" Wyatt asked, mostly for the benefit of his deputies who looked more than a little confused.

"We are," Ophelia answered.

She was closest, after all. Not to mention that she was the one who had to carry the doppelganger all this way. Why shouldn't she be the one to speak.

"I daresay that Folken looks as if he had expected to be our spokesman on this matter," Havarti mentioned in the woman's head.

"He'll get over it," Ophelia thought back.

"We were all in the town of Dracoleaf at the time Magra was attacked," Ophelia continued vocally, "One person can't be in two places at once but two people who look the same can."

"What about the one who looked like your pale elf friend?" the constable motioned back to Saya.

"Dead. In the same fight this one went down," Ophelia answered kicking Evil Harbengiyr in the side.

Nodding, Wyatt turned back to one of his deputies, "Free the prisoner," then the next, "Pick this one up and put him in when the cage is empty."

"Yes, sir," the second deputy scooped the dead body that looked just like the living cleric up onto his shoulders.

As Harbenigyr was escorted down to Ophelia and the rest of the group, the constable started addressing them all, "I'm sorry about all this. I really am. But I think it might be for the best that you all leave town. Now would be best, before anyone wakes up, sees him and thinks he's escaping," he pointed at the cleric.

Saya let out a dry huff, "All I wanted was one night in a proper bed before strolling through the Jaded Woods for gods knows how long."

"You're going to the Jaded Woods?" all the color drained from the third deputy's face as he spoke up.

Saya nodded back, as did Folken.

"Don't go in until after the sun is up completely," the deputy said, "And don't stay after dark. Those woods are haunted!"

The constable shook his head, punching the third deputy in the shoulder, "Don't try to spook them with that nonsense."

"It's not nonsense!" the man insisted, "My cousin's drinking buddy saw a woman's head floating around in there. It even tried to bite him! Or was that my brother's sister-in-law?" His confidence in his source seemed to waiver.

"We will be careful," Harbenigyr gave the deputy a kind smile, "We appreciate the warning."

OPHELIA INTERROGATION NOTES

The following is testimony from the residents of the village of Ash Providence. Neither the subject nor her party were aware of these events:

As the following night fell...

THE SUN WAS long gone. The moon was rising over the small town of Ash Providence. The residents were well settled into their homes for the night. The first patrol of the night had made its first circuit of the short array of streets, awaiting the chiming of the next hour to start their next.

In the town square, the still body of the cleric wrapped in white leaned against the bars of the cage that had been made into his itinerant tomb. In addition to the blood from the battle, dried spittle speckled his formerly white tunic and pants. The back of his slim shoulders were pressed into the cold bars while his head laid to the side, his black ponytail sticking out.

A lone shadow peeled away from the others that filled the space between the library and the other wooden buildings beside it. The figure made its way to the cage soundlessly, needing only a slight hop to continue along the raised portion.

"Oh, Harbenigyr, you look terrible," Josie whispered as she reached into the cage, gently caressing his cheek.

The smooth skin of the cleric was surprisingly warm to the woman's touch. Her hand stretched deeper between the bars, caressing down the man's chest and slipping between the tied together folds of his bloodied tunic.

It wasn't until her hand slipped into his pants that Harbenigyr's dark eyes fluttered open, "I never took you for a necrophiliac," he mumbled.

"I was just checking," Josie pressed her cheek against the back of his head, taking a deep, slow breath, "If you didn't wake up like you promised, I was going to have to try and kiss something next."

The doppelganger cleric let out a quiet chuckle, "To do that, you'd need a way in, right? That means you can get me out and I'll let you kiss wherever you like."

"After a quick bath," Josie's duplicate moved over to the door of the cage, reaching down the collar of her shirt and pulling out a brass key, "Or maybe during? I'm not picky."

The cage was opened with nary a squeak of the hinges. Harby crawled out from inside the bars and straightened up to his full height, which was just a couple of inches taller than the red haired woman.

Josie stepped up behind the man, wrapping her arms around his narrow waist. "So what good comes from the cleric and the others thinking you're dead now?"

"Saya complicated matters when she tried to kill and replace her doppelganger," Harbenigyr said, guiding one of the woman's hands back down the front of his pants, "But the goal remains the same. Ophelia and Folken were the last ones to touch Raiko before he died."

"But he already said they didn't have Meteorend before they threw you in there," Josie motioned back to the now ajar cage.

"The way the old man described how the rock works, it just may not have materialized yet," Harbenigyr let out a pleased, shuddering gasp, "So we follow and we wait. We've plenty to keep ourselves busy until then, right?"

CHAPTER SIX

"Are you aware of the full extent of involvement with the efreeti that Appelonia and her party had?" I asked Ophelia.

"They told me about what happened to Jonas, if that's what you mean," the subject answered.

"Let me enlighten you," I slid a pile of parchments over to Ophelia:

Two decades later...

WHEN JONAS OPENED his eyes, all he could see was red. His first instinct was to reach up to his forehead and check to see if he was bleeding. Perhaps some blood just got in his eyes?

While he did have a headache, it was focused primarily at the back of his head. Since he was flat on his back, it could have been from landing on it.

No, the red hue was coming from the sky. It didn't have a transitioning feel to it, like when the sunset changed the very atmosphere from blue to orange, then red to purple before finishing on the inky darkness of black with the pins of light called stars.

There wasn't any sun, as far as Jonas could tell. No moon, either. Whatever made the sky look like blood, it appeared to be permanent.

"Perhaps you should rethink your attire," the unwelcome voice of the efreeti Genevieve came to the man's ears, "You are liable to sweat to death in all that armor. I could remove it for you, if you wish it."

With a strained groan, Jonas rolled himself onto his side so that he could look straight at the woman before giving her a good chiding. What he saw made any sound he was going to make freeze in his throat.

Genevieve's human guise was shed when she came to this place. She now stood easily at seven feet tall, not including the two horns that ran up from her forehead. They weren't as random a shape as the other efreeti Jonas faced, Abernathy, but one did have a hole near the base while the other did have one short off shoot.

Her hair glowed like fire behind the horns, still standing tall and proud like her previous form. Her skin was a dark burgundy color, with orange, gold and ruby colored fur running down her upper arms to tufts of bone protruding from her elbows and knees.

What clothing Genevieve wore as a human was gone as well and her demonic form mimicked a woman's shape almost perfectly. From her chest down to her unnaturally long legs looked human.

Her hands ended in the curved black claws but otherwise looked normal. Her feet, though, They had the same curved claws, only larger, but then she had (the paladin couldn't think of a better word) a thumb protruding from the inside of her heel.

Jonas scowled as he shook his head at the monster,"What did you do?" he struggled to get his arms under his body to lift himself up at least to his knees.

It wasn't easy in heavy armor. The paladin had been wearing it for years so he had getting in and out of it down to a science. But he always felt like a turtle tipped back onto its shell when he fell down in it.

During a fight, you had the rush of wanting to survive and, at least in his case, a large, heavy sword to use as a lever to push himself back onto his feet. His hands were empty at the moment. His claymore must have slipped from his grip during... whatever it was that brought them here.

Genevieve stepped over to the paladin and slipped a hand inside the collar of his armor. Her fingers against the base of his neck felt like warm coals. With barely a grunt, the demon hoisted Jonas to his feet, then turned him to face her.

"I'm granting your wish," she looked all around as if the answer was obvious, "You wanted to know what we want."

"I guess using your words wouldn't have been dramatic enough?" the Shepherd crossed his arms over his chest.

Genevieve shook her head, "I want what the Mullah wants."

"What's a Mullah?" Jonas felt his headache getting stronger.

"A Mullah is a what they call monarchs across the ocean," Jin Vega chimed in, making his presence known, "Maybe the demons took the title from there."

The monk was rubbing at the back of his neck as if he were trying to stop a headache of his own. The blue shirt he wore under his cloak had a long tear down the front, revealing his pale skin underneath. Apparently, his landing had been a little rougher than that of the paladin.

"More like they took the name from us," Genevieve scoffed, "If you want to know what we want, you would want to hear it from the source, yes?"

Jonas and Jin looked at each other. They both had the same skeptical look on their faces.

"What's the catch?" the paladin asked.

"I couldn't just open a portal into the throne room of my Mullah," the efreeti demon grinned, "So we have to go the rest of the way on foot."

"On foot? I thought I saw our horses get dragged down with us," Jonas looked around.

"Most died. Several survived but they fled," the demon walked, no her feet didn't actually move, she floated to a pile of saddlebags and other supplies, including the paladin's immense sword, "I salvaged all I could from the fallen beasts before their meat was dragged away."

"Was my horse among the dead? She wore armor similar in style to mine," Jonas turned around in a complete circle where he stood.

"No, that animal was chased off by a burning soul," Genevieve grinned as she explained her answer, "The spirit of one who traded with us one too many times."

"So this place *is* hell," Jin Vega shook his bald head.

"No, this is home," Genevieve mirrored his reaction, "Hell is cold and darkness."

"Cold is definitely not something we'll find here," the thief, Bronwyn LaRue quipped as she stepped around a pile of black rocks that looked suspiciously like massive boulders made of charcoal.

The bandanna wrapped around the dark skinned woman's head was already soaked through with sweat. Her leather coat was draped over one arm, revealing a pink silk shirt that already had growing wet patches, as well.

Jonas could sympathize. He already felt as if he was swimming in his armor. Still, he wouldn't give the demon the satisfaction of complaining.

Instead, he pressed two fingers to his lips and let out a piercing whistle. He turned to the right and did it again. Then twice more.

"Are you crazy?" Bronwyn rushed over and slapped the paladin's damp face, "I just escaped from a *bear made of fire* and you want to call it and its friends to us?"

"We'll need Andromeda if we want to get out of here," Jonas replied, ignoring his stinging cheek.

"Speaking of we," Jin looked around, raising a hand to his brow to block the nonexistent sun, "Where is everyone else?"

This is where they are...

THE DARKNESS THAT surrounded Appelonia reeked of sulfur. The young woman felt battered, like she was lucky to have been wearing armor as she fell through... whatever that was. Not that the idea helped with the headache that was throbbing between her pointed ears at the moment.

When she finally managed to get up to her knees, Apple called out, "Anyone here?"

A groan mixed with a growl came back in reply. The cleric felt a surge of panic run through her for an instant before she recognized the growl. It was Phinegann. As relieved as she was to realize that he was alive, Appelonia wished that he would use his words more.

"Are you okay, Phinegann?" she asked.

Knowing there was at least one other person with her didn't change the fact that it was pure darkness all around them. The orc let out a heavy grunt that the cleric took to mean that he wasn't seriously injured.

"Hold on, I'm still doing a diagnostic check on my wings," Illyria's voice came from the opposite direction as the retired guard.

Another groan from a completely different direction, "What possible use could those be right now?" the annoyed voice of the Bunny Barbarian snapped.

"You'll see in a second," Illyria's sing-song response came.

There was the sound of glass scraping against glass. Some tapping and then what sounded like Illyria standing up.

Then there was a flash of light and a yelp of surprise escaped the cleric's throat. She was blind!

"Are you okay, Appelonia?" the worry in Tokki's voice was obvious.

Apple had to blink her eyes several times before things started to register. The light radiating from the gnome added a stabbing sensation to the cleric's headache but her surroundings finally came into focus.

Phinegann sat on the packed dirt floor a few paces in front of the red haired woman, cradling his forehead in his flesh and bone hand. Tokki was on his feet, his hands pressing against the wall as he faced away from everyone else. It was the first time Appelonia got a good look at the fluffy white tail with gray flecks that rested on the back of his furry pants.

The cleric turned around to see that Illyria had four streams of light pouring out of the tips of her stained glass wings, each one a different color. Blue and red radiated from the larger upper wings a bright green came from one of the smaller, lower wings while the other put out... was that cyan?

Together, they all made the interior of the cavern they found themselves in, and everything inside, roughly the correct color they would have been normally. Unless something blocked one of the streams of light and changed the color balance.

Which is what Appelonia did when she stood up and walked over to Phinegann, who was closest. When she approached him, her silhouette blocked out the red light and turned everything into varying shades of green.

"Headache?" she held out her hand as an offer to aid the man to his feet.

He stood up without her assistance. Then the orc nodded in answer to her question.

The cleric lifted her other hand, that was filled with off-white shavings of wood, "Chew on a few of these. They should help."

Phinegann's thick eyebrows sank. While it made him look angrier, Apple was coming to realize that it was mostly just his normal expression. What she did notice, though, was a hint of skepticism added to it.

"Anyone my size would only need one. That's why you should take at least three," the cleric grinned up at him.

"What is it?" the voice came from behind the woman.

Appelonia turned to see Tokki Yo Bunpy standing practically right over her shoulder. She jumped in surprise, almost dropping the wood shavings. Thankfully, she had the presence of mind to close her hand to keep that from happening.

"Willow bark shavings," she answered, "They're great for relieving headaches."

The Bunny Barbarian reached out and took a couple from her hand, "Why aren't you taking one then?" he asked.

The woman held her hand out to Phinegann again even as she kept facing Tokki, "I'm making sure everyone else is treated first."

"I was always taught that you had to treat yourself first before treating others," the short warrior slipped his hand between the saber teeth in his mask and started chewing the offered medicine. "You're no good to anyone if you pass out trying to heal another injured person, especially if there are more behind them."

"If the injury is life threatening, that's true," Appelonia nodded at Phinegann when he finally pinched some of the bark from her hand, then she moved on to Illyria. "But this is just a headache."

Illyria waved her hand at the offered medicine, "I'm fine. I don't have a headache."

Appelonia's expression mirrored Phinegann's from a moment before, with far less unconscious anger added, "Really? How were you spared while everyone else is hurting after our," she couldn't find a better word than, "trip?"

The gnome woman wiggled her wings, making the colors all around them fluctuate for the briefest of moments, "I can wrap these around me to form a protective cocoon. I haven't run into anything that's been able to hurt me through it yet."

"But you said you were doing a diagnostic," the cleric argued, "Don't you only do those when you're trying to figure out what's damaged?"

Illyria shook her head, her purple hair turning blue, red and yellow before returning to normal, "Not at all. I run diagnostics routinely. That way, all my equipment is running at peak efficiency continuously."

"So that they don't break down at an inopportune time," Appelonia nodded.

"Like falling through a portal of light to end up someplace the Great Chromatic Rabbit hasn't seen fit to reveal yet," Tokki agreed.

"Exactly!" Illyria smiled wide back at the duo.

"Standing around here won't accomplish anything," Phinegann spoke up as he marched past the cleric, Bunny Barbarian and gnome.

"I guess we're following him," Apple shrugged, smirking at the others.

Back above...

ANDROMEDA, JONAS THE Shepherd's horse, did indeed return at his whistle. She did so with a massive beast made of flame chasing after her. Fortunately, the paladin and his trusted warhorse were able to lead the monster away from the rest of the party. Upon returning to the group, he removed the heavy plates of metal from the animal.

"I'm sorry, girl," he said, giving the horse a reassuring pat on the neck, "But we have no idea how long we'll be here and I don't want you overheating on us. I'll get you some new armor when we are back topside."

"And you should explain where we are," Jin Vega addressed the efreeti demon, "As well as why our friends aren't with us."

"This is where I am from. We call it the Nova Prime," Genevieve answered, "You would call it another dimension or plane of existence."

"And why," Jonas asked as he unbuckled the last of Andromeda's armor, "are Appelonia and the others not with us?"

"You're supposed to stay still when you go through a portal," the demon huffed, "I can't help it if all of your friends got *wiggly*."

"Wiggly?" Bronwyn repeated, "I would have done more than wiggle if it would have kept me from coming here."

"You think they are still next to that tavern?" Genevieve shook her horned head, "They are here. Where the disobedient go."

"And that's where?" Jin scowled.

"Where we cannot reach," the efreeti woman replied, "The only hope your friends have is for us to get to the Mullah."

At that, they loaded Andromeda up with the saddlebags that Genevieve was able to recover from the other fleeing horses and they started in the direction that the demon indicated was the palace where her Mullah awaited. She once again assured the party that the journey to the palace would not be long.

The terrain they walked through was thankfully easy to traverse, like rolling plains. The main differences were that the soil was black like ash. The grass, which was green from where the mortals came, was red when it emerged, stopping about the height of their ankles.

Massive boulders of charcoal dotted the landscape. The group avoided those. Even from far away, they could see that was where most of the animal life, each looking in various stages of burning, seemed to gather.

The last major difference came up about an hour into their march. There was no water here. When they approached the bank of what looked like a river, they found it to be filled with flowing magma.

"Are their any bridges?" Jonas turned to the efreeti.

Genevieve shook her head, "This is the thinnest point of the river."

"That's great," Jonas shook his head, "We can't wade through it and I doubt that any of us could jump that."

"I could," Jin chimed in, "But I won't leave the rest of you behind."

"How noble," Bronwyn rolled her brown eyes.

"We wouldn't even be in this situation if you hadn't tried to steal from us," Jin said confidently, as if he was stating an obvious fact.

"You're blaming me for this?" the woman hissed, "This monster wasn't chasing me!"

"We could have avoided her if you had let our horses be." Jin rested his hands on the ropes that were wrapped around his hips to keep his baggy pants up.

"Unbelievable!" Bronwyn raised her hands, flabbergasted. "If anyone should feel wronged here, it's me, baldy!"

"Enough!" Jonas bellowed, "Recriminations won't help at this point. The only way out of here is to talk to this Mullah and get my wish fulfilled. Right?" he directed the question at Genevieve.

She nodded, "That is why we are down here."

"That's right!" Bronwyn stomped over to the paladin, shoving her finger in his face, "You're the one who wished to know their plan. You're the only one that needs to go." She turned to Genevieve, her entire countenance changing from enraged to seemingly kind hearted, "Surely you can get me back somehow?"

"Sorry," The grin, filled with sharp, pointed teeth, didn't appear at all apologetic, "He said *we*. That means everyone that was with him."

"But I'm not *with* him!" Bronwyn protested, "In case you didn't notice, I was stealing from them!"

"You're acting like she should care," Jin commented, "Djinn are notorious for abiding by their own interpretations of the wishes given to them."

"A Djinn?" the woman's jaw dropped, "She's a Djinn? They're real?"

The only response the monk gave was to motion in Genevieve's direction.

"Then I can just wish for you to get me out of here, right?" Bronwyn turned back to the demon.

"I'm strictly a one-wish-a-time girl," the efreeti shrugged.

The mortal woman let out a howl of frustration that echoed all through the plains, "I should never have let that woman talk me into the valet trick!"

Cries from several beasts in the distance came on the wind as if they were replying to the woman's scream. Another group of howls came moments later, closer than the first.

"And now you've called all the monsters down on us," Jin gripped the bridge of his nose between two fingers as he shook his head.

Bronwyn simply repeated his statement in a far more mocking tone. Regardless, she felt her entire body start to shake even as she tried to maintain her defiant expression.

Jonas let out a heavy sigh, the heat along with the sense of annoyance starting to get to him, "Okay, Genevieve. You want to grant my wish. What do you propose to make it happen?" he asked while leaning against his horse.

The demon looked thoughtful for a moment, tapping a curved claw against her pursed lower lip, "I think I have an idea," She floated over to Bronwyn.

The efreeti grabbed the woman by the collar of her shirt and the waist of her leather pants. With a quick spin, she lobbed Bronwyn across the expanse of lava.

Her scream again echoed all over the plains before Bronwyn landed in the black dirt on the other side. She rolled to a stop next to a charcoal rock about the size of her head, letting out a long, slow groan.

"Oh goodie, I can throw that far," Genevieve grinned.

"*That* was your plan?" Jonas waved a hand at the prone Bronwyn across the river of molten rock.

Genevieve shrugged back, "It worked."

The paladin noticed that the monk had a long staff in his hands that wasn't there before, not even on the back of his horse. Facing the river of magma, the bald man took several steps back.

"What are you doing, Jin?" Jonas asked.

"I won't let her throw me." he answered and then charged for the lava. "Groo-Fee!"

He stabbed his staff into the ground right at the base of a small black rock, just short of the edge of the blistering liquid. Jin's cloak billowed behind him as he was launched into the air.

His landing was much more graceful than Bronwyn's. His feet hit solid ground less than half a step from the far edge of the burning magma. It looked as if he were about to lose his balance and fall back into it when he let his knees buckle and he rolled forward.

Hopping back onto his feet, he pulled the length of his dark cloak over and behind him before it could drape over his head. Then he turned his attention back to Jonas and the demon.

"I would appreciate you throwing my staff over," he called back.

"Do you enjoy that the efreeti have such a reputation that people would rather perform suicidal stunts than actually deal with you?" the paladin asked Genevieve.

"Actually, for the most part, mortals try to milk us for anything they think they can get," She smirked, "Especially men."

Another howl from the creatures heading their way abbreviated Jonas from continuing to chide the female monster, "If you weren't sure you could get the woman across, what makes you think you could throw me?" he asked as he gathered up the staff and lobbed it over the river.

Instead of catching the length of wood with his hands, Jin pulled his charcoal cloak open. The staff hit the fabric that looked like the night sky practically dead center… and kept going until it was out of view completely. Jonas wanted to ask about it but he knew that he was running low on time.

"My surprise at throwing the girl wasn't about how *far* I threw her," Genevieve ran her tongue over her white, sharpened teeth, "It was about how far I could throw her without splattering her upon landing. That's why I tried her first instead of you."

"So you just wanted to make sure that she wouldn't land like an overripe watermelon?" the paladin's confidence was not bolstered.

"I suggest we get you across now," the efreeti said as she floated up to him, "Those burning souls will be here any moment."

"I'm easily three times as heavy as the thief, you realize," Jonas was weighing whether or not it would be worth it to stand and fight beasts made of fire rather than go through with this idea, "And what about my horse?"

"Your weight shouldn't be much of an issue," She wrapped a hand around the armor behind the paladin's neck, "And I know I can't throw the horse. I'll carry it across."

Her other hand reached down to cradle his rear end, the only part of him that didn't have any armor over it. It would impede his movement too much.

Before he could utter another word of argument, Genevieve made him airborne. Jonas didn't scream in panic, in fact, he tried to relax and keep his body limp for the inevitable crash landing.

Then he noticed that the arc he was flying in seemed to be a little shallow. His teeth grit together tightly as he realized that he was going to be short of the shoreline and land right in the lava.

Genevieve spat out a displeased curse, "I knew I should have put a little more spin into it."

As the glowing, molten rock sped toward him, the Shepherd's vision was suddenly filled with darkness. It was true that he had closed his eyes, but that was right after he was swallowed up.

When he opened his eyes back up, the paladin found himself floating in what looked like the night sky. Stars and nebulae drifted all around him. His first thought was that perhaps this was the first stage of the afterlife.

If that were the case, though, then why did he just bump into a small crate that had a half-dozen chicken eggs in it? That wasn't all, either. As the man looked around, he spotted dozens, if not hundreds of random objects just floating all around him. There didn't seem to be any form of organization at all.

"Jonas the Shepherd!" A voice echoed through the vastness all around. "Jonas the Shepherd, take my hand!"

The paladin recognized the voice as the monk, Jin Vega. This definitely wasn't the afterlife then.

A disembodied hand appeared immediately before Jonas. From the callouses and solid musculature of the arm that followed, it sure looked like that of the monk.

Taking the offered hand. Jonas found himself kneeling on the far bank of the magma river as quickly as the darkness had enveloped him before.

"Damn, I'm good." Jin let out a quick whistle, then the monk explained, "The lining of my cloak is knitted together from many bags enchanted to hold a nearly infinite amount of room. When I saw you weren't going to make it, I threw it out to catch you. I'm glad it worked."

"Me, too," Jonas nodded as he lifted himself to his feet, "It saved me from having to ask about it later, too."

The sounds of Andromeda's protesting pulled his attention back to the other side of the molten rock. Genevieve had slipped herself under the horse and hoisted the animal up onto her shoulders, wrapping one hand around a foreleg and the other around one of the rear.

"Stay still, you sub-creature!" the demon snapped.

"There has to be another way to do this," Jonas said, impotent to stop what was about to happen.

Genevieve threw herself, with Andromeda, into the air. The demon landed about two paces short of the side where Jonas, Jin, and Bronwyn stood. The efreeti woman sank into the boiling magma up to the bony protrusions at her knees. It didn't cause the demon any pain. To her, it seemed as if she had merely waded into water. The paladin should have known.

Fortunately, the horse remained suspended about a foot above the lava. But Andromeda saw the lava immediately under her and started to thrash about in a panic.

"What did I tell you, beast?" Genevieve grumbled as she took the last two steps onto the shore on this side of the river, "Stay still!"

The animal was too panicked to understand what was happening. The mare fought with all her considerable muscle to free itself from the efreeti's grip.

Genevieve fought to keep her hold on Andromeda for a couple more steps until she was well clear of the lava. Then she bent down so that the hooves of the warhorse could find the black dirt.

"Andromeda!" Jonas called as the horse reared back, several of the saddlebags tumbling off their makeshift resting place on the saddle, "It's over! You made it through!"

He reached out to snatch her bridle into his hands. He pulled her down, but did so gently, whispering to the horse tenderly as she slowly realized that she wasn't going to die. Once the mare was still enough Jin picked up the errant saddlebags and, with the paladin's permission, replaced them onto Andromeda's back.

"No need to thank me or anything," Genevieve snickered.

If Jonas' eyes had been axes, the demon would have been a very easy meal for a pack of small animals. "Just keep going," he ordered.

"As always, your wish is my command," the demon ran a sharpened claw along the polished surface of his breastplate as she stepped past.

She was walking. Up until this point, she was always floating just above the dirt. Jonas couldn't help but wonder what that meant.

Back in the catacombs...

THIS PLACE WAS a labyrinth. How did they get down here anyway? The place where they landed didn't have any way to see the sky and Appelonia could have sworn that they had fallen a long way down.

The group already had to backtrack several times as each tunnel they came across so far came to a dead end. The cleric prayed that it wouldn't become literal.

When they hit yet another dead end, this one being the last tunnel they came across, Phinegann particularly looked like he had had enough. He raised his metal fist and slammed it into the rock face.

"Why are we here?" ttone crumbled under his mechanical knuckles, "Why am *I* here?"

He slammed his steel hand against the wall again and again. Appelonia rested a hand on his shoulder. It was, admittedly, a pitiful effort to calm him but she couldn't think of anything else to do.

He jerked his flesh shoulder back as if he hoped that motion was violent enough to force the cleric away. But, several long seconds later, the orc pressed both his hands against the rock face that marked the end of their path.

Phinegann's barrel chest heaved up and down. While the man had a history of growling, the sound emanating from him at that moment seemed different. More guttural.

"Phinegann? Are you okay?" the cleric asked, her entire demeanor radiating concern.

"I don't understand it!" the man snarled over his shoulder back at the others, "If we're in here, that means there has to be a way out! Unless we're dead, are we dead?"

The orc doubled over in pain, the animalistic growling getting louder. Tokki Yo Bunpy stepped between Phinegann and Appelonia, readying his claw to strike. The orc felt it was wise, even if the Bunny Barbarian didn't know why he was doing it beyond instinct.

"We're not dead, Phinegann," Appelonia's voice was gentle despite the Yo Bunpy warrior readying for violence, "This doesn't match the descriptions on Kuan Yin's village, The Great Chromatic Rabbit's fields of glory or any of the other afterlives I have studied."

"It matches one," Tokki muttered to the cleric.

He didn't realize that Phinegann could hear him now. All of Phinegann's senses were becoming so much more sensitive as his rage grew.

"This is like the Red Hell," the barbarian whispered, "The one reserved for cowards and traitors."

The ears of the retired guard perked up, "Why would I go to your Red Hell?" he snarled.

A worried look washed over Appelonia's face when she realized Phinegann had overheard that, "He's not saying that is where we are. Are you Tokki?" She gave the small barbarian a stern look.

"No," he finally answered after the cleric punched him in the shoulder, "No, I am no traitor. I would not be in the Red Hell. Appelonia surely would not be, either. This place just looks like it."

Phinegann spun around on his heels, his eyes reflecting amber light back from the beams streaming from Illyria, "Then why am I here, Tokki Yo Bunpy? Explain it to me. I wish someone would explain it to me!"

The immense man slammed both his fists into the walls around him. The rock face that made up the dead end behind him crumbled away to reveal a rusted metal door. It was one solid piece, save for the barred window along the top.

Three sets of bars crisscrossed to leave enough space to see through to the other side but unable to reach through the open parts. Still, air could get through.

Phinegann felt the breeze over the back of his neck and he spun around even faster to face the source of this new sensation than he did to face the others, "A way out!" he chortled.

"Does this strike anyone else as awfully convenient?" Illyria fluttered up to the cleric and the Bunny Barbarian as Phinegann struggled to find a way to open the door, "Especially right after he used the 'W' word?"

The orc beat against the metal in frustration. His fingers were too big to squeeze between the network of bars in the small window and there wasn't any handle to grab. So he did the only thing he could think of: slam his shoulder against the cold metal barricade.

"Phinegann, please stop for a second. I know you want to get out of here, but we don't know what's on the other side. What if it's a trap?" Appelonia tried to reason with the massive man.

Something in what she said made him decide to not slam his shoulder into the questionable doorway, at least for a moment. The cleric turned back to the Bunny Barbarian and Illyria.

"The timing does seem suspicious," she agreed with the winged gnome, "But there aren't any efreeti around, are there?"

"Not that I can detect," Tokki pressed a finger against the pink nose of his rabbit mask. "But I'm guessing we're in their territory so they may have special ways to hide."

"We can't let our fears get the best of us," Appelonia rested a hand on both the Bunny Barbarian and Illyria's shoulders, "We can't assume there are monsters waiting for us around every corner. Besides, what if this *is* the only way out of here?"

"The Mighty Corthek has often said that sometimes the only way out is through," the man in the black fur nodded back, "Besides, I can keep anything they can send our way from harming you."

His tone was serious. Did he just promise to kill anything they came across in her name? Something about that really... she wasn't sure... was she flattered? Annoyed? The young woman settled on annoyed for the moment.

"That's why you came from your homeland to begin with, isn't it? To fight new and unknown dangers?" Appelonia scowled at Tokki, "But we have enough trouble trying to keep the giant calm without worrying about your blood lust, Mister This Looks Like the Red Hells!"

The cleric turned back to face Phinegann. She ducked under his metal arm, that was stretched out toward the side wall to aid keeping himself upright. She circled around in front of the man.

"It's not blood lust," The barbarian mumbled to himself, as Appelonia wasn't paying him anymore attention.

The orc's eyes were closed tight and his jaw was clenched, the muscles bulging in his cheeks. Appelonia wasn't sure, but she thought that his teeth seemed *sharper* somehow. Perhaps a trick of the limited light?

Normally, the cleric would think he was trying to suppress the urge to vomit but it seemed more as if he was just in a great deal of pain. This was more than a mere headache. Being in such a dark, confined meant that she wouldn't be able to give him a proper examination until...

That was it! Phinegann was claustrophobic! They were lucky he's been able to control himself, at least he hadn't hurt anyone up to this point, for this long.

"Let me have a look at the door, okay?" the red haired woman spoke with the gentlest tone she could find in her voice at the moment, "Maybe there's a way to open it without hurting yourself."

The orc didn't even open his eyes but he nodded at the cleric, making beads of sweat roll down his face and drip off the end of his nose and cleft chin. She turned her back to Phinegann and started inspecting the rusted door.

It was like the ones used in prisons. The were built to be able to withstand the kind of pounding Phinegann was unleashing upon it. As a former guard, he would have realized that if he were in his right mind. Which he was decidedly not at the moment.

It was too dark to see anything through the barred panel, though the air was at least a bit cooler than in this cramped tunnel. There wasn't enough room for Illyria to shine a wing through so the cleric moved downward.

The only way to open the door was a lock at about the middle, offset to the left side of the door. They were designed to be used with a key specifically made for it or, if one had the ability, to pick it. Appelonia was no thief but her mother taught her some basic, what she called 'locksmithing', skills. They came in handier than one would think out in the forest. Anything from unlocking a stray cabin for shelter to opening an ancient treasure chest was possible. In fact, she found a chest several years ago...

Apple forced herself to focus on the job at hand. The lock was larger than the standard ones she was trained on. That could work to her advantage. She just needed some supplies.

"Illyria, do you have a dagger I could borrow?" Appelonia called back.

The purple haired woman shuffled up beside her, holding out a knife with a straight, thin blade that was barely longer than the width of the cleric's hand. Apple took it with a thankful nod and pulled a short sliver of silver from one of the pouches on her belt.

The red haired woman looked up at Phinegann and tried to sound reassuring, "I think I can get it open."

She didn't wait for a response before she slipped the small blade into the hole that rested halfway up the rusted door. The small length of silver immediately followed.

If the lock had been the size she was used to the dagger, even one as minuscule as Illyria's, would have been too big for this task. It was lucky that they had a gnome... with them...

A quick dose of paranoia shot through Apple as she wiggled the silver around in the lock. What if the efreeti knew that she could pick a lock? That Illyria would be with them and have a dagger that could get the job done?

Appelonia shook her head. That was a far too detailed list of variables to consider. For the efreeti or anyone. She was the one who told everyone not to let their fears get the best of them. The girl forced herself to take her own advice.

This was the only way to keep moving. This was the way they had to go. She just had to hope that there was more space for Phinegann on the other side.

It was all just a matter of feeling for the change. Sure, pressing her pointed ear to the metal helped but, at this point, all she could hear was squeaking. Then the sliver of silver caught on something.

Slow and deliberate motions now, Appelonia reminded herself. The most dangerous time to get excited was just when you thought you were making progress.

With one last twist of the small dagger, the lock pulled back and the door slipped out of its frame. Appelonia was suddenly slammed against the side of the tunnel and Phinegann rushed past.

Tokki and Illyria knelt down beside the prone cleric. They each took and arm and helped Apple up to her knees.

"Very well done," the Bunny Barbarian congratulated her.

"Thanks," Appelonia smirked back, offering the little knife back to Illyria. "I don't have a giant footprint on my back, do I?" she chuckled.

"No but he's got a pretty good head start on us now," Tokki stood up and helped the woman back onto her feet.

"Illyria? Can you shine your lights up ahead?" Appelonia asked as the barbarian's hand lingered around her waist, "We need to see if there are any forks ahead. We don't want to get separated if we can help it."

The gnome nodded and fluttered a couple of steps ahead. Her glass wings curled around her, each pointing directly forward down the tunnel.

It almost immediately opened up into a wide open space. The walls were mortared gray limestone instead of the dirt that happened to be the same color as dried blood like the tunnel behind them. It looked more like the interior of a castle than a cave anymore.

There were three raised stone platforms in the middle of the spacious room. Each were rectangular, made out of the same limestone as the walls and big enough that even Phinegann could lay on any of them and not have any part of his body hanging over.

To the surprise of Appelonia and the others, the orc was only a few paces ahead of them. He was standing tall and straight, his breathing returning to normal. His broad back was to them, so they couldn't see his face, but he kept looking around from one direction to the other.

"I know this place," he revealed, "But this can't be it."

"Where are we, Phinegann?" Appelonia asked as she looked around herself.

He gave the room one last scan before turning to face the cleric, barbarian and gnome, "This looks like the processing room of the prison where I used to work."

"I'm innocent, I swear!" an unfamiliar, female voice blurted out from behind the orc, "Please, don't hurt me anymore!"

A look that Appelonia could only describe as dread overtook Phinegann's face. He must have recognized the speaker, even without looking behind him.

"You're here, prisoner. You're guilt has already been decided," another voice rang out, "That means you're here to be punished. Take it well and your clan may *just* get some degree of redemption!"

While the despaired look on the orc's face didn't change, that amber glow, the one Appelonia thought had just been a trick of the light, came back to his eyes. "Vokloss," he snarled.

Back on the plains of Nova Prime...

"HOW DID I get myself into this?" Bronwyn LaRue asked herself for the umpteenth time in the hours since she was brought into forced acquaintance with the very people she intended to deprive of their valuables.

Everything about this situation felt like a set up. The woman thought that it was for the paladin, his monk buddy, and the rest but now she was starting to wonder.

Bronwyn got the idea of pulling the valet act after talking with a woman in the Drunken Dragon. She should have realized that this woman in the weird coat with the far too long of sleeves was working some kind of angle of her own but Bronwyn let herself be blinded by the potential rewards.

Paladins and clerics didn't care about the financial worth of most anything they carried. But they, almost inevitably, carried things of great value. Like the silver contraption that the red haired girl used to make her bow and arrow. It likely could have been made of something far simpler and stronger, like steel but no, something in the hubris of the Order of Kuan Yin made it just fine to make out of such a precious metal.

And that monk was carrying jewels. Jewels! Those are practically the measurements for financial value. He wasn't going to be using them for the purpose that they were meant.

There was that gnome woman, too. Bronwyn hadn't even had a chance to get into her bags. The shorty was an inventor. They almost always had trade goods with them. Bronwyn could have made a coup off of these idiots.

Instead, she was stuck in a literal hell with them. If she ever saw that woman in the ugly green pants again, Bronwyn was going to turn her into a pin cushion with every dagger she carried.

The thief was pulled out of her unhappy reflections by the demon, Genevieve speaking up and pointing ahead, "Behold, the humble abode of our Mullah!"

The place the efreeti woman pointed out was many things. Humble surely wasn't one of them.

It was a palace! The heavy stone walls encircling it were sandstone and some kind of red rock that Bronwyn wasn't famil-iar with, alternating back and forth to form a checkered pattern. Each square stone was half as tall as the monk, Jin Vega. It stretched out so far ahead that the barrier curved out of view before it actually ended.

The wall had to reach at least fifty feet in height. The building behind the wall was even taller. The main rooftop was curved, making a structure that was already higher than the outer wall even grander at its peak. The rooftop was black, like the soil they party walked on, except it was polished to a high shine. If there had been a sun in this place, its reflection would have surely been blinding.

As they approached the main gate, Bronwyn couldn't help but notice that the portcullis was up and open wide. As they walked closer, two groups of efreeti demons, all male (tufts of fur obscured some details between their legs but not all). They stood at either end of the gate but not one of them showed any interest in Bronwyn, the paladin, the monk, or even Genevieve.

To her credit, the monster woman didn't appear surprised. Of course that dullard, Jonas, just had to broadcast his ignorance.

"Are things usually this relaxed in the home of your Mullah?" the man with the trimmed black hair asked.

Genevieve shook her head, "Not at all. Usually they kill anything that even gets near the main gate. They knew we were coming."

"How?" he continued to let himself sound stupid.

"We are all a part of the Mullah. The Mullah knows everything we do," she replied.

"Including that you brought us here?" Jonas chewed on the inside of his cheek.

"That must please him to no end," Bronwyn spouted off, rather than admit that those were actually useful bits of information to have.

"I don't know," the demon shrugged at the human woman.

"Why wouldn't you know? You said that you're a part of him, right?" the question dropped from the hirsute mouth of Jin this time.

"He knows everything we do," Genevieve explained, talking as if she were speaking to a simpleton, "We don't know everything he does. The Mullah is too great for us to house all of his immense knowledge and wisdom."

That was precisely why Bronwyn didn't like asking questions. They always made the one answering feel superior. Even if they were an underling like Genevieve.

The group strode through the gate without getting a second look. Their leader must have essentially ordered for them to stand down and all of them appeared all too eager to comply.

The palace itself was even larger than it seemed from outside. While the main portion of the building was easily the tallest, there were six other off shoots, too wide to be called towers, that stretched out from each side.

Instead of the steady checker pattern like the wall had, the sandstone and red patterns in the walls were more reminiscent of flames licking at the sides of the building. It had an... unnerving effect. Not on Bronwyn, of course, but she was sure that the others were... unnerved. Surely.

There was a moat of molten magma, much like the thin river the party vaulted over to get here, surrounding the palace. This pool was at least three times as wide. Bronwyn could see silhouettes of animals swimming around in the lava as if it were water. Some were so long and thin they reminded the woman of sea serpents that her father's ship worked so hard to avoid when they sailed on the wide open oceans.

The bridge that stretched over the moat practically beckoned them to the wide open entrance that was as grand as that in the outer wall. Once they were across the bridge, they were in a small courtyard. Considering that everything else they had seen was so large and spacious, it was surprising that the area just outside the palace was so cramped. It was also the last open area before the group would be swallowed under that polished black rooftop.

"Andromeda will be safe here," the demon declared, pointing at the dirt under their feet, "The guards would typically eat her flesh if the opportunity arose but they will not risk crossing the drawbridge to feed on her."

After giving his horse a reassuring pat, Jonas reluctantly agreed to leave his steed behind. Genevieve guided them down the halls and into the throne room of the immense building.

It didn't even have doors, just an immense archway that stretched up nearly halfway up the entire height of the palace. When they stepped through it, fire spouted to life beside the walls, climbing to well over twelve feet in height. The flames spread across the arch, cutting off any kind of exit for the group.

Bronwyn felt her stomach, which had been hiding out in her chest to begin with, drop down well below its normal place in her body. She suddenly wished that she knew if efreeti even had to go to the toilet and, if so, where one could be.

Genevieve continued walking deeper into the room and the rest of the group followed. Even with as large as the palace appeared to be, it seemed to take too long to reach anything in the room that was anything besides flat black floor or glowing flames in the distance.

Finally, set of stairs came into view ahead. They went on so far that they faded into a darkness above that Bronwyn didn't even realize was there. She thought it was just the inside of the roof she saw outside.

At the base of those steps sat another efreeti demon. This one was different than the others outside by the gate. For starters, he was bigger. Nearly twice the size of Genevieve, who was easily the largest of the party coming to visit.

Also, the demon woman's head, while she had sharpened teeth and horns, was mostly humanoid, this one hadn't even a vestige of human to it. He had a feline snout, complete with needle-like teeth. His eyes that looked more like multifaceted sapphires that gave the impression that he could look in every direction at once.

He had six ears, three on each side of his head, that became more pointed and curved the higher they were. The uppermost ears curled around a massive set of horns. Unlike Abernathy or even the guards outside, these horns did not look like frozen strikes of lightning from a thunderstorm. They reminded Bronwyn of a minotaur she saw once, those these were much bigger and had several sharpened branches, somewhat like antlers.

There were at least two more pairs of horns on his back, growing up and out of the mass of magenta fur that rested there and on his shoulders like a mink stole.

His body carried more muscle than a mortal could have dreamed. His arms were disproportionately long compared to the rest of him but they were so thick that they didn't look out of place. He had six fingers on each hand, with thumbs on either edge of his palms.

The immense demon had twelve bulges along his abdomen, that flexed tightly together as he hoisted himself to his feet. His thick legs had two sets of knees, the upper bending forward like a human's while the lower bent backward. When he stood, his arms no longer seemed too long.

"What is this that you have brought to us, Genevieve aibna Shaitajuna?"

The inhuman efreeti had a voice that could only be described as a growl. In fact, that was all the mortals actually heard but, somehow, the meaning was made clear in their minds.

Genevieve dropped onto her knees and bowed deeply, her curved horns tapping the hard, onyx floor, "It is not my intention to disturb his greatness, Alnnadhir Nikojunakalium abn Maridjuna."

"It is singly your intention, child," Tte immense demon responded, "You presumed to increase your own importance with these *things* by assuming your worthiness for a personal audience with the greatest of all, Mullah Junaperqolanijuna alab Marid Juna alnnihaya."

As they spoke, Bronwyn found herself starting to bristle as a certain word kept sweeping over her ears, "Is it just me, or do these things say 'Juna' a lot?" She whispered to the paladin.

Bronwyn didn't even have time to blink before the massive face of the monstrous demon was inches from hers, "You would *dare* speak the holiest word in the presence of his highness, the Mullah?"

His jaws snapped together and the woman realized that the creature could chomp off her head and swallow it without chewing. Such a realization was... disheartening to say the least.

"I-I'm sorry, Mister Ayatollah Niko, uh,"

"If your mind is capable of retaining it, you may call me Nikojunakalium," the demon snarled in reply, "Maester is also acceptable if your mind is as feeble as I suspect."

Before she could say anything else, the burgundy monster turned and strode away from the insulted human. She looked back and forth from Jonas to Jin Vega. All they could formulate for a response was equally clueless looks and shrugs. Some help they were.

"Great Nikojunakalium," Genevieve spoke up as if his exchange with Bronwyn had never happened, "My presence is connected to the humans, yes, but in answering of the wish of the metal encased one," dhe nodded back at the paladin, who suddenly looked worried, "He wished to know what it was I wanted, and as my desires are nothing more or less than fulfilling those of the great Mullah..." she trailed off.

"So hubris plays no part in this, aibna Shaitajuna?" Nikojunakalium scoffed at the smaller demon, "You forget that we know your heart, child. However, in this case, we may be able to take this mess and transpose it into some use."

"That is my truest hope," Genevieve returned to bowing.

The gigantic monster turned his attention to the human paladin, "You are this Jonas the Shepherd?"

"I am, Nikojunakalium, sir," he nodded in response.

"Then express whatever knowledge you seek from the mighty Mullah. Succinctly," he ordered.

The man, who had already felt as if he were roasting within the steel wrapped around him, felt streams of sweat start anew down his back and chest. Jonas took several steps forward, directing his gaze as far up the length of steps as he could see.

"Great Mullah," he motioned to Jin and Bronwyn, "we were informed that an efreeti child was taken from you and that one among my party was that child. We know this second part to be false, yet your agent," he waved a hand at Genevieve, "continued pressing her attack. I simply wish to understand why, if none of us are the one for whom you seek, do you persist in your actions against us?"

A fearsome sound, like the gnashing of inhuman teeth, came from the darkness. Unlike with the sounds from Nikojunakalium, these sounds did not receive any kind of translation.

Until the massive demon spoke, "I will speak the words of the Mullah in a way your kind can understand. Our immortal monarch asks if you insist we have no right to find the child?"

"I did not say that," Jonas shook his head, "My sect of holy warriors believes in the sanctity of families and that they should be kept whole. I seek to understand why, as your child is not among my compatriots, Genevieve continued attacking us."

More echoing snarls and spine chilling squeals came in response. The hirsute demon nodded as he considered the words that would be equivalent in the tongue Jonas recognized.

"One among you has a means of finding the child," Nikoju-nakalium finally transposed the words, "We can sense it and will take it by force if necessary."

All three mortals looked back and forth between each other before Jonas turned back to face the stairway, "What means? And who in my party is in possession of it? If you tell us what it is, per-haps we can give it to you and avoid further bloodshed."

"Avoid further bloodshed?" Nikojunakalium scratched at his chin for a long moment, "Ah, yes, you are the one who slayed poor Abernathy abn Shaitajuna with that blessed blade of yours. It is so hard to distinguish one mortal from another these days."

"I did not want that to happen, Great Mullah," Jonas spoke up to the darkness, "Abernathy refused to speak with us, as we are speak-ing now, and threatened the lives of those under my charge."

"Mortal lives are so transient, hardly worth defending," the translating demon answered, "But you, Jonas the Shepherd, you lessened the flavor of this world with the elimination of poor Abernathy. A price must be paid."

The paladin straightened his back. If he'd been someone normal, Bronwyn would have described his stance as defiant.

"I do not wish any further violence, great Mullah," he said, "And, indeed, you may be able to swat us down with little more thought than we would an annoying insect. However, even if you loose your vengeance on me, your child will remain no closer to being found after you've wasted your time on such a transient, unimportant mortal."

"Indeed, you are correct. No punishment we can heap upon a mortal can impart the lesson of the necessary respect you should show to your betters," Nikojunakalium snickered, a long prehensile tongue whipping out to drag along his lower jaw. "But, perhaps your tryst of a life could be used to teach one better than you the humility for which she stands in need. Genevieve aibna Shaitajuna, arise."

Without a moment's hesitation, the efreeti woman did as she was told. The look of confusion on her face didn't come until a moment later.

The beastly demon stepped up between her and Jonas. Nikojunakalium rested one hand on Genevieve's head, pressing her hair down, The glowing strands rebelled as best they could, curling up around and between his fingers as he wrapped both thumbs around the horns growing from her forehead.

Considering that the paladin was so much smaller, the demonic spokesperson pressed a mere fingertip to the crown of the human's head. Then one of Nikojunakalium's thumbs slipped into the hole in the horn growing out of the female demon's head.

There was a sound of crunching bone and Genevieve's knees buckled as she cried out in pain. The female demon caught herself before she completely lost her balance and whatever confusion had been there before turned to disdain. First, it was directed at the demon who was responsible for whatever was happening to her, then her amber eyes dug into Jonas.

The finger that Nikojunakalium rested on the head of the paladin twitched, the curved claw at the end slicing through the black hair that was little more than stubble. A stream of blood poured out of the wound immediately, coating the blackened tip of the offending claw. Another second passed, then Jonas flew from under the demon's hand as if he'd been struck by the kick of an invisible mule. He landed in a heap in the packed black dirt, a trail of blood drops marking the path his limp body took to end up where it did.

The almost forgotten monk rushed by Bronwyn to kneel at the side of the paladin. He pulled a rag from somewhere in his cloak and pressed it to the wound on the Shepherd's crown.

"What did you do to them?" Jin asked, his voice remarkably controlled considering how unbalanced he looked to Bronwyn.

"They are bound now," Nikojunakalium answered.

"What? No!" Genevieve objected, looking on the verge of tears as she stepped out from under the other demon's grip, "That has to be too severe a punishment! The worse you can say about me is that the pride I have in being efreeti is overwhelming. Please don't take that from me!"

"The invincible Mullah has taken nothing from you, fair Genevieve aibna Shaitajuna," the inhuman demon said back, "You've still all your beauty. But now you've a means of learning how small of a piece you are compared to the whole. You will feel a mortal's time, when his is gone, then pray that the so merciful Junaperqolanijuna alab Marid Juna alnnihaya declares that you are indeed cleansed of your impertinence."

"I... I understand," the efreeti woman was visibly shaking as she lowered herself back to her knees and again bowed.

"I don't," The monk spoke, "What happened to Jonas? What did wounding him accomplish?"

"As a mortal, a conduit was required to impart some of our daughter's," Nikojunakalium looked genuinely puzzled for a long moment as he searched for a word he felt was accurate, "essence within the meat and bone you refer to as a body."

The paladin groaned as consciousness came back to him. With Jin's help, he sat up on the ground. That put his back to the demons and the thief. Pulling the rag that was being used as a makeshift bandage off the top of his head, Jonas was surprised at how little blood there was.

"The wound is gone," Bronwyn observed.

"Of course. The ritual is complete. The rest of his blood is required to keep his limbs moving," the beastly demon shrugged, two of the horns on his immense back tapping together with the motion, as he turned to walk back toward the steps.

A thought occurred to Bronwyn and she rushed over to Genevieve, dropping to her knees in front of the demon, "Okay, he knows what your Mullah wanted. Now can you grant my wish to get out of here?"

The efreeti woman lifted her head from the ground, "No. Jonas is the only one I can serve now."

"What?" the brown skinned woman puffed, "But, his wish was granted! You said you could only do one at a time. I want mine now!"

Genevieve rose back to her feet as she spoke, "I said that I only grant one wish at a time because I choose to, not due to any kind of limitation. Yes, my Master's wish was granted but, as I am now bonded to him, Jonas is the only one who can command my power."

"Great," More sarcasm came out than even the sound of the word from Bronwyn's mouth.

The thief had to rush after Genevieve, who was already beside the paladin and helping him to his own feet. As Jin caught Jonas up on the terms of the Genevieve's punishment, another echoing roar came from on high.

"Jonas the Shepherd, Genevieve aibna Shaitanjuna, Jin Vega, Bronwyn LaRue, Appelonia of Dianmeyer, Illyria Warflower, and Phinegann," Nikojunakalium translated, "You are hereby entrusted with the finding of the child who shares of the blood of the immaculate Mullah Junaperqolanijuna alab Marid Juna alnnihaya. When you have the girl in your possession, Genevieve will provide the means to allow you to place the child within the loving arms of our

Mullah. She will also see to it that your every thought and deed is to this end for as long as necessity causes."

"I cannot speak for those not here, Mullah," Jonas objected.

"You claimed them to be part of your charge, paladin," the giant demon responded, "As such, you decide their fates. If they do not share in your responsibility, they alone will face the fates coming upon them now."

The man frowned. Even with all the flowery words, what the demon was proposing was tantamount to blackmail. Agree or your friends die.

Jonas let out a sigh of resignation, "I will need them back from wherever they are then, great Mullah."

"With Genevieve you have the means," Nikojunakalium waved a six fingered hand to dismiss them, "Begone and trouble us no more until the child is found."

"Remember, she will grant only your wishes now," Jin reminded the paladin.

"So let's get out of here then!" Bronwyn practically screamed at the men.

"You know where they are?" the paladin looked up at the demonic woman.

Genevieve nodded, though she didn't look at all happy about it, "At your word, we can join them."

CHAPTER SEVEN

"Well, that was ominous," Ophelia said after finishing the last page.

"No more so than what happened to you and your friends when you were in the Jaded Woods," I said, "Was it?"

The subject had started reaching for her drink but froze at the mention of the Jaded Woods. As I suspected, the events that occurred there have not been completely uncovered.

"What to tell me what happened?" I asked, "I mean everything that happened."

Two decades before...

THE TREES THAT made up the outer edge of the Jaded Woods didn't appear ominous. At least, no more than any other trees to any other forest. The pines stretched up to the usual height of their type of tree. Their bark was thick and brown and they had dropped a thick nest of dried needles and pine cones to the ground under their branches.

The way the man back in Ash Providence was talking, Harbenigyr half expected the sun to automatically set when they came into the mere proximity of the Jaded Woods. Seeing that it wasn't some grizzled, nightmarish span of greenery actually bolstered the cleric resolve to find the village of his birth.

The group, all still atop their respective steeds, stopped where the path slipped between its first set of trees. They formed around in a circle to face each other, though no one ordered or even requested to do so.

"Here we are, Harby." Ophelia was the first to speak, "The forest where you were born."

"Are you sure that you still want to go in?" Josie inquired, leaning forward on her horse so that she could look down at the cleric on his shorter griffin.

"I'm sure," Harbenigyr nodded as Triton idly scratched at the dirt with one of his talons, "I don't know what we'll find in there. I'm hoping, at the very least, to be able to pay my respects to my parents."

"You know that you can do that anywhere," the ranger argued with the kindest of tones.

"And *you know* that here does count as part of anywhere," Ophelia asserted, "It's not like it will kill anyone to look around a forest for a day or two, would it? Come to think of it, Josie, isn't that kind of your specialty?"

The mercenary grinned back at Josie as she started to turn her horse toward the trees. The red haired woman let out a breathy sigh before she nodded. It was quite an act of concession from Josie, which may have been why she waited until the other woman couldn't see to do it.

"I trust your patriarch provided you with a more detailed idea of where to find the village once we are inside the forest." Folken stated regally.

The black haired elf reached into one of the many pouches on the belt around his waist. He pulled out a folded piece of parchment and held it up.

"Right here," he said as he pulled it open. "This is the south-ernmost entrance into the Jaded Woods…" his voice trailed off as he studied the map, "According to this, the village is just northwest of the center."

He held the map up to display it to the others and pointed to the X marked on in the field that was colored green. There was also a network of lines that appeared to be trails drawn on the flat representation of the forest.

"Don't you find it odd that your patriarch never told you the name of the village?" Saya rested her glove wrapped elbow on the pommel of her saddle and then, in turn, her chin on the heel of her hand.

"They didn't find the village until after it was destroyed," the cleric explained, "They weren't looking for it, they just happened upon it in their wanderings. Since I was the only survivor they found…"

"And none of them spoke baby babble, I'm guessing," Josie smirked.

"Not even the midwife," Harby smiled back, "They marked it on the map they were making of their pilgrimage and, well, here we are."

"And here we are," Saya nodded.

"And there is where we want to be," Folken pointed at point indicating the village on Harbenigyr's map, "We should best move on. If we're fortunate, perhaps we can reach it before nightfall."

"I know you aren't one for camping," Josie quirked a ruby eyebrow at the sorcerer, "but you do realize that there won't be any more amenities there than in the forest itself, right? It's a ruin."

"A ruin with areas of flattened ground," Folken contended, "In our last camp, I crushed three separate stones and ripped out a tree root that all found a way under my back during the night."

The ranger rolled her eyes but kept the smirk on her face. She turned her horse toward the trees and trotted off after Ophelia.

"You really should get ahead of them, Harby," Saya leaned down toward the cleric so she wouldn't have to raise her voice, "You are supposed to be leading us through this part, remember?"

"Oh, you're right! Sorry," Harbenigyr chuckled, then set Triton to gallop after the ranger and the mercenary.

"So much trouble to keep the help happy," Saya joked at her cousin.

"My thoughts precisely," Folken said, though he appeared far more serious.

It didn't take long for the cleric to catch up to the two women who started ahead of him. It helped that they both stopped at the same point a short distance from the first fork in the trail. After all, neither of them had the map.

The cleric guided them down the left fork. The right led to a place called Silver Lake, a place up in the mountains just to the north of the Jaded Woods without any other forks for detours. That was the only path that Folken and Saya had marked down on their maps at all.

There was a lot of brush on the trail. It was apparent that this path had not been taken in some time. While the horses had no trouble stepping over some of the overgrown brush, Triton had to leap over the encroaching plants.

As they walked along, the map Harbenigyr held seemed perfectly matched with the terrain. Eventually, though, they came across a fork that wasn't marked down. It led to a small clearing and pond where the party took the opportunity to refill their canteens. Then they had to backtrack.

The variances started happening more and more. Forks that had three different paths rather than the two the map indicated, a curve to the east in the trail that was never drawn into the directions. Finally, the group came upon an intersection of packed dirt roads that didn't even resemble anything that was on the parchment that Harby had studied so thoroughly and held to so earnestly.

"Did we take a wrong turn somewhere?" Josie asked as she leaned down to take the map from the hands of the cleric.

As she stared the parchment down, the ranger recounted their trek through the woods. With an annoyed groan, Josie had to admit that Harbenigyr didn't lead them astray based on the information he had.

"It has been a few decades. I guess it only makes sense that more travelers would come and make their own trails from time to time," the cleric shrugged.

"Perhaps," Folken ventured into the middle of the intersection of the roads, "But I have noticed that every variation from Harbenigyr's information has taken us away from the area of the forest we wish to go."

"Every one?" Ophelia looked skeptical, "If the new trails were carved out by random travelers just making their way, they would be going in most every direction."

"Are you suggesting that there is some kind of organized effort here, Folken?" Saya asked her cousin.

"The only ways available to us are north, east, and south," the sorcerer motioned down each road as he mentioned them, "According to the map, Harbenigyr's village is almost due west of here."

Folken pointed at the trail they rode down to reach this place. It guided the party north for most of its length, turning to the right only a few hundred yards before the appearance of this intersection.

"If we head down the north road," Josie spoke up from the back of her brown and turquoise horse, "and there isn't any roads heading to the west within a mile, I'd say that you might just be right."

"I propose that we part ways," Folken's suggestion gave him a cacophony of shocked looks in response, forcing him to continue speaking, "Temporarily. Josie and Ophelia shall go north, just as the ranger suggested while Saya and I will continue east. I have a theory I wish to test."

Josie and Ophelia shrugged at each other then started up the road. The sorcerer and Saya started to the east. Harbenigyr sat astride Triton, not going in any direction.

Before the svartalfar got too far away, the cleric made his griffin steed rush after them. "Folken!" Harby called after the pale man.

The sorcerer and his cousin turned and waited for the elf to catch up. Once Harbengiyr was before them, uncertainty practically radiated from the cleric.

"You didn't tell me what I should do," he said.

Folken arched an angled eyebrow at the young elf, "You are still leading this group, Harbenigyr. As such, the main body is heading in the opposite direction. Saya and I will rejoin you shortly."

With that, they started again to the east. The cleric's eyebrows pressed together tightly as he considered the words from the sorcerer. If Harby were the leader, wouldn't he have been the one to order everyone to split up?

He was the only one with a map that had any kind of detail for the Jaded Woods, as inaccurate as it turned out to be. Harbenigyr turned Triton around and the muscular griffin charged back the way they came and then up the north trail. He had some catching up to do.

Fortunately for him the women, both alphan and human, were stopped at the next fork in the road. It wasn't indecision that kept them from going one way or the other but a third woman who sat on a tree stump just between the two diverging paths. She was softly plucking at the strings of a lute, playing a song that none of the party recognized.

This woman was a professionally trained bard. The crimson jacket she wore told as much. The emerald and white cuffs at her wrists were recognition for graduating from a reputable school. They served as an assurance to potential employers that the musician could, in fact, perform just about any traditional song at a professional level.

She also wore a thin scarf loosely wrapped around her neck. That wasn't part of a typical bard's look but the length of black fabric matched her form fitting pants but it also partially obscured some of the insignia the woman wore on her chest.

Harbenigyr was able to make out a crescent moon on the right side of her chest but couldn't see the other well enough to identify it. Once the woman finished playing the song, only then did she actually notice the two riding women watching her.

"Oh, hello!" she grinned a wide grin, "Did you have a particular song you'd like to hear?"

"This is kind of an out of the way place for a performance, isn't it?" Josie looked around warily as she asked.

The bard shrugged back, "Not really. My village is just down that trail aways," she motioned to the trail that led northwest, "But most everyone coming down this road are heading for Silver Lake down that way," she pointed her lute down the other path to the northeast. "So I come down here, play some music, maybe get some coin from the kinder travelers and…" she played a quick flourish on her instrument to punctuate that was the end of her explanation.

"Wait," Triton carried Harbenigyr in front of Ophelia and Josie's horses, "there's a village here? One where people are living now?"

The bard jumped in surprise at the griffin that suddenly revealed itself before her. She fell backwards into the overgrown grass so that only her legs were visible over the tree stump.

The woman scrambled to lift herself up but only high enough to crouch behind the remains of the tree that had been her seat. "That thing's not dangerous, is he?" she let out an uncomfortable chuckle.

The elf looked down at Triton before he self-consciously smiled back at the bard, "Sorry, I keep forgetting how jarring seeing him for the first time is to some people."

Harbenigyr patted the side of Triton on the side of his feathered neck. The griffin leaned his head into the cleric's attentions, letting out a happy sounding chirp.

"But he's as gentle as can be. Really!" Harby assured her.

The bard sat back down on the tree stump. The petite woman pulled her eyes away from the massive bird-headed beast and they moved up to the rider. A gleam came to her eye as an almost expectant grin spread over her lips.

"Okay then. What brings you fine people here? Looking for something specific or just exploring?"

"You were saying that your village isn't far from here?" Josie spoke up before the cleric, "To the northwest? And there are people there?"

"Of course there are people there," she laughed as she answered. "It's a village, isn't it?"

"Could you take us there?" Harbenigyr tried to keep from sounding too anxious with his request.

"Oh, sure, Mister cleric, sir. There are plenty of diversions and wares to discover in Laeradr." the bard waved a hand as if to beckon them, "Especially for a group of high rollers like you."

"High rollers? Us? I think this girl may just be blind," Ophelia repeated in a way that could be described as sardonic.

A hearty chortle came from over the mercenary's shoulder. The bard had a look of confusion all over her face when she couldn't see anything that could have made the noise.

"Actually, I was born in these woods," Harbenigyr slipped off of Triton's back and stepped toward the bard, "In a village to the west. I was told it was destroyed when I was still a newborn."

"Hmm." The bard look away from Ophelia and started plucking at the last string on her lute, adjusting the sound it made a little each time, "Laeradr hasn't been around long. But I think someone did say that it was built on the site of some broken buildings. Maybe it could be the place you're looking for."

Ophelia leaned down toward the cleric so her voice wouldn't carry, "It does seem to be in the right place," she reached over and tapped the pouch that held the folded up map.

Folken and Saya approached from the trail that stretched to the northeast on their thoroughbred horses. Once they stepped into the view of the bard, they young human looked entranced by the two of them. Then some thought snapped her out of her revelry and, clearing her throat, the bard again busied herself with tuning her lute. The startled fall at the sight of Triton earlier surely knocked something loose, after all.

"If your village was built atop the ruins of the old, are there any remnants to examine?" Folken inquired.

The woman playing the lute looked back and forth from the pale svartalfar and Harbenigyr's group with more trepidation each time than the situation called for, really, "You know each other?" she finally asked.

"Indeed," the sorcerer spoke over Harbenigyr's silent nod, "I find myself fatigued from our long trip. Perhaps we could stay in this young lady's village for the night and continue our search fresh in the morning?" Folken suggested.

"Sorry to disappoint you, sir," she looked up at the pale man directly for the first time and her jaw went slack, "I really am. But we don't even have an inn yet! Maybe you should head off to Silver Lake for the night then?" she smiled but it didn't look at all comfortable on her face.

The bard's mousy brown hair was parted down the middle, just reaching past her chin. Her blue eyes were pleasant, but hardly unique. Everything about the petite woman seemed to emit plainness. Everything except her open demeanor and brightly colored bard uniform. She seemed to be a walking contradiction.

Folken's violet eyes narrowed as he focused all his attention on the girl. She was young enough that she could barely call herself a woman yet she was out in the middle of nothing all alone.

"What is your name, child?" the sorcerer gave her a formal seeming bow while remaining mounted upon his horse, "I am Folken, Chief Adviser of the svartalfar tribe Kizoku, Great Chancellor of the Romefeller Guilds, and artisan of the studies of supernatural energies. And I am at your service."

"Oh, uh..." the young bard's face turned bright red and she was suddenly unable to look any direction but down the most coquettish manner.

Harbenigyr rode up beside the green haired, pale man. He stood up, all his weight moving down into the stirrups around his feet, to move his face level with the svartalfar sorcerer.

"Weren't you the one who said you didn't want everyone we come in contact with to know who you are?" he whispered.

"I have my reasons this time, cleric," the firmness in the voice of the sorcerer alone made the elf sit back down in his saddle.

"I'm Hero, Master Folken, sir," she finally gathered herself enough to speak again, "Humble bard of the Edge School."

The slightest smirk tugged at the edge of the mouth of the svartalfar man. "Hero, this is my cousin, Saya. If you could, would you please play Smithe Remedy's *Lullaby* for her? She likely has not heard it since she was a child."

Hero licked her lips, the lower one twitching before she nodded, "Of course, Master Folken. Consider it a gift before you head on your way to Silver Lake."

Despite the youthful woman's obvious nervousness, when she started playing the requested song, it was as if the consciousness of someone else took over. Hero's lute playing was perfect, her voice haunting as she sang the traditional svartalfar song to the albino woman.

Folken motioned for Harbenigyr to follow him several steps away and out of ear shot, "The Edge School of music is primarily attended by my people. The fact that she seemed so enthralled with us upon our arrival led me to suspect her origin. As well as why she is suddenly hesitant for us to go to Laeradr."

"What do you mean?" the cleric asked.

"Until our arrival, she was speaking of the attractions her city held," Folken explained, "When you mentioned your birthplace, she added Laeradr being built upon ruins as an another attraction."

Harby shrugged, "You don't think she was just being helpful?"

"All the trails in this portion of the forest do not match anything on your map." the sorcerer pointed to the pouch that held the parchment on the belt of the cleric, "Every new path has led away from the village of your birth until this point, right here."

"So you think this is a trap of some kind?" Harbenigyr shook his head, "It's not a very good one if the other path leads to a completely different, safe location."

Ophelia, on foot, strode up to the two men, "This is a traditional song of your people, Folken? It's kind of creepy."

"I selected it due to its length, so that Harbenigyr and I could converse," Folken said dismissively.

"Be still, be calm, be quiet now, my precious boy," Hero sang with a melody that complemented her lute playing perfectly, "Don't struggle like that or I will only love you more..."

Saya had a smile pulling at the corners of her blue lips. Her head bobbed up and down with the beat as she listened intently.

"That is precisely my point, Harbenigyr." Folken returned to the previous subject of their conversation. "There is no path to Silver Lake via the road Saya and I took."

"Then why is she so intent on sending us *that* way now instead of toward the village?" the cleric pointed out, "If the road you were on did have a trap set, why weren't you and Saya caught in it?"

"There is a stratagem at play here, Harbenigyr," Folken scowled, which looked more sinister on his pale face than a typical frown, "I don't like not knowing the motivations of those with whom I congress. But they do appear to have built their village right over the ruins of yours. If you are going to go, I doubt anytime will be more opportune than now."

The music from Hero's lute faded to silence and Saya provided appreciative applause. The two women stepped up to the small group, causing the entire conversation to grind to a halt.

"So what's the plan?" the bard smiled, "Mister cleric here seemed really anxious to see Laeradr. Should I take him and his red headed lady friend while the rest of you head on over to Silver Lake? I can give them directions and they can catch up tomorrow."

Folken hid his scowl behind an passive mask but his suspicious nature was fully realized, "As I am a student of history, perhaps I shall take advantage of this opportunity as well."

Hero shook her head more energetically than she really needed, "Oh, I doubt there would be anything interesting to the Chancellor of the Kizoku, sir. We never came upon anything that would be unusual or worthy of your attention."

"Why would I want to go then?" Josie shrugged from atop her horse.

"Oh, I thought that you were, you know, with him," the bard pointed the end of her lute at Harbenigyr while she looked up at the ranger.

"What would have given you that idea?" Josie looked as if she found the idea distasteful.

And the cleric felt his stomach turn into a heavy stone. He realized that they barely knew each other but Harby didn't realize that he had given the woman such an impression that she appeared to *loathe* him and his company.

"Are you racist or something?" the ranger snapped at the smaller woman, "Pointy ears have to stay with other pointy ears?"

"I do think that I would be more Harby's type," Ophelia chimed in with a laugh.

Again, the reaction from Josie puzzled the cleric. Her stare dug into the mercenary as if she had just been insulted. If she found Harbenigyr, at the very least useless or at worst loathsome, why would she care about Ophelia's joke?

The normally talkative bard found herself at a loss for words. Her mouth opened and closed again and again, even producing various sounds but none of them became words or even carried a melody.

"I hope you will forgive Hero," a new body stepped into the area, from the road that led to the northwest. "She is our main collector of what scant news we have from outside the forest. The last bits from the rumor mill included an elf in white and one with red hair making quite an impression on their passing through Ash Providence."

The new arrival pointed a ruddy hand back and forth between Josie and Harbenigyr. She was built very similarly to Ophelia. Although the workout to gain as much muscle as she had likely had to do with swinging a heavy metal hammer rather than the walking, fighting and drinking regimen practiced by the mercenary.

She was not dressed as a bard. In fact, her attire was much more utilitarian. The sleeves of her long, thick brown shirt were rolled up to her elbows. It was almost the same shade as the leather apron she still wore.

"I'm only half, actually," Josie muttered, turning away from the woman as she approached the rest of the group.

"I'm sorry sweetie, I didn't know that," the woman replied with a kind smile.

Josie couldn't hide her surprise that stranger had heard what she said. Still, she nodded back over her shoulder.

The blacksmith tugged at her chocolate colored hair that was already clumsily pulled back into a rough ponytail in a vain effort to neaten it up, "I'm sure that Hero was just inviting you to come see Laeradr, especially since night time is starting to creep up."

"Actually, she was trying to talk my cousin and me," the sorcerer pointed a gloved hand to Saya and then himself, "into moving on to a place called Silver Lake."

"Really?" a cold expression crossed over the woman's face as her attention shifted over to the bard, "It must be because she's embarrassed and thinks that our humble village is too plebeian for noble svartalfar types."

"That was the impression I was garnering," Folken nodded, a few strands of spiked green hair drifting in front of his violet eyes.

Hero looked ready to try and crawl into her musical instrument to escape the other woman's stare. When the blacksmith turned her attention back to the party, though, it was with a wide, welcoming smile on her face.

"Where are my manners? I just realized that I haven't even introduced myself to all of you!" she gave the group a deep bow before continuing, "My name is Miranda, the town blacksmith, historian, and mayor."

"That is quite the resume," Folken gave her a polite bow back.

"In a village as small as ours, you have to take on multiple responsibilities," Miranda nodded, "Take Hero here. She's not only a formally trained bard but also the local tour guide and one impressive cook when you can get her to stay in one place for an hour."

She planted a playful elbow into Hero's shoulder. The much smaller bard flinched but didn't physically react in any other way.

Harbenigyr then led the customary circle of introductions for the rest of the group. He couldn't help but feel that it, like everything else that had happened so far to them in the Jaded Woods, was because Folken allowed it. After Miranda and Hero was given the names of all their visitors, Folken again spoke.

"If your village doesn't have accommodations for a party as large as ours," the albino sorcerer let a hint of arrogance seep into his words as he spoke, "perhaps we *should* adjourn to Silver Lake and come visit your charming hamlet tomorrow?"

Miranda blew a raspberry in response, her lips vibrating with the noise, "Pish posh! We may not have an inn but I'm sure some of the townsfolk can take you in for a couple of nights. Wouldn't cost you any money like it would in Silver Lake, either."

Despite how... informal the woman's protest was, Folken didn't appear to be offended by her response. In fact, he acted like it was expected as he directed his gaze over to the cleric even though the words were to the woman.

"How very kind of you," he said.

"It's settled then?" the blacksmith slapped her hands together as her smile got even bigger, "We should really get going then. Don't want to be caught outside in the middle of the night."

As the group started walking, guided by the blacksmith and the bard, Ophelia stepped up to Harbenigyr. Unlike the rest of the party, who were riding, both of them were leading their steeds into town. She rested a hand on the elf's head, which had been turning this way and that as they walked down the trail.

"So are you going to ask?" she whispered.

"Ask what?" he replied just as quietly.

"If this place is haunted," Ophelia smirked, "It seems to be on your mind."

"Oh, no. No, that's not worrying me," the cleric shook his head, perhaps a little too emphatically.

"It's just me then?" the woman grinned wider, "Well, I'm worried about it so I'm going to ask."

Again, Harby tried to protest that he wasn't worried. When Ophelia ignored him and started to call out to the blacksmith, he tried to stop her but Havarti, dropped onto the cleric's hand when he started to pull on the woman's shoulder.

"Miranda, we heard back in Ash Providence that these woods are haunted," Ophelia winked back at Harby as she spoke, "Do you think that's true?"

"Haunted? I've never seen a ghost. And if you can't touch them and they can't touch you, what's to be afraid of?" Miranda turned and walked backwards as she responded to the question from the mercenary, "No, I happen to know that these woods fill up with plenty of hungry creatures in the night. That's just a fact of life that makes walls all the more inviting."

The next morning...

"WE ONLY REBUILT the old mill when we came here," Miranda pointed to a point to the north of their current location on the far more detailed map that laid on the table in between her and the cleric.

Harbenigyr, along with Folken and Saya on the other sides of the square table, looked down where the woman's finger pointed. While the place she indicated was in the middle of the map, it was actually the furthest part of the town to the northwest.

The rest of the town, not overly big, just as Hero had said, stretched out to the south and the east. But it was the left side of the map that interested the cleric.

"So most of what is left of the old village has remained undisturbed?" he asked the blacksmith/mayor.

She nodded, "I've made a few trips, found some books here and there. Most of them were copies of books you could find most anywhere, like *Peridot and the Revenant.* A couple of them were actually related to the running of the town, though."

Miranda stepped over to the short but wide bookcase that was along the wall behind her. Bending down, she waved her hand all along the lowest shelf but didn't actually touch any of the leather spines.

"Apparently, it was an important wine making town back in the day," the blacksmith said as she straightened back up, "I don't know if they'll be of any help to you but feel free to have a look through them."

"Thank you, Miranda," Harbenigyr had quickly been broken of the habit of trying to call her *Miss* or by her title after just a couple of attempts that morning.

"I don't suppose that anything you found told you the name of the village, did it?" Saya nodded at the books.

"Afraid not," Miranda shook her head in response, "Most of what I found were lists of inventory listing different vintages of wine. Some of them actually mention the names of the wine makers, could that be of any help?"

The elf stepped over to the shelves and dropped down to his knees. He pulled the first book free and flipped it open. Harby was only vaguely interested in the conversation that continued as he scanned over page after page for anything that could be useful in his search.

"The only way to find out is to go through everything," Folken didn't seem overly thrilled by the idea, "While I am hardly averse to research, perhaps my skills could be put toward some effort to improve Laeradr itself?"

"Well, we were planning on improving the heat output of my forge so that I could produce higher quality metal for our next expansion of the town," Miranda scratched at her cheek, "Coal is so plentiful around here that we can just pick it up out of some of the deeper holes around here so it hasn't been that high of a priority."

"These are above the lands of the Xaviour Tribe," Folken nodded at his own shared information, "Carbon would be plentiful."

The door to the mayor's house opened and Josie stepped inside, carrying the limp bodies of four rabbits skewered on one arrow, "Not a bad morning," she declared, handing the animals to Miranda.

The blacksmith hustled them back into her kitchen. When she was gone, the ranger stepped up to the side of the table the human just vacated and spoke in whispers to the two svartalfar.

"Have either of you seen Ophelia?" she asked.

Neither had.

"I know that there isn't much to do here but she said that she wouldn't leave Harby unprotected," Josie continued, "I'd think that she would have at least left word with him if she was going out and about."

The blacksmith stepped back into the main foyer of her house. Also serving as mayor, Miranda had set up this room so that she could have meetings with groups of other villagers about town business. It made it a perfect place for the party to meet and plan.

"Did you say something about your friend Ophelia?" the woman in the leather apron smiled as she took up the remaining open space around the square table, "I think she went out with Hero down to the fork in the trail where we met you yesterday. I got the feeling that she wasn't one for sitting around."

"So her solution was to go sit as a crossroads?" Josie contended.

"It's a nice walk?" Miranda shrugged, "Maybe she'll go visit Silver Lake and then come back with Hero around sunset."

"In the meantime," Folken interrupted, "Harbenigyr could use some assistance going over papers scavenged from the ruins to the west."

Josie started to protest but stopped the words before they slipped by her lips, "I'm not big into paperwork but okay," she said instead.

The red haired alphan sat down beside the cleric and pulled out another book from the bottom shelf. Her blue eyes glanced in Harbenigyr's direction for a brief moment before she looked down and started reading.

Elsewhere...

OPHELIA AWOKE WITH a headache. Everything was blurry as she looked around. This wasn't like any hangover she had before. This pain was more *piercing*.

The last thing she remembered, it was arranged that she was going to sleep in the house of a woman by the name of Bianca. She was a nice enough woman, even if her answer to if there were any eligible men in the village was to invite other women to come have a little drinking party.

Now that she thought about it, Ophelia hadn't seen one man in town. Admittedly, she had only been in Laeradr for one night but you would think at least one man would have been curious about this random group of strangers coming to visit their home.

As Ophelia's head started to clear, the piercing pain wasn't just in her head but in her hands, as well. Her arms were stretched out as far as the woman could reach to her sides. The pain she felt were long metal stakes literally impaled through her palms and pinning her to the floor.

It wasn't until then that she realized her back was cold. Her red trench coat was missing and she was lying on packed dirt. Light came in only from a thin, horizontal window up along the ceiling. Ophelia thought it was very likely that she was in a basement, likely the one under Bianca's house.

The woman's pale blue eyes shot open in a panic, "Havarti! Havarti, are you okay?" her thought practically screamed for her bastard sword.

"Oh, my dear, I'm sorry I didn't see this coming," Havarti's voice sounded remorseful in her head.

"What is *this*?" she asked.

"As far as I can tell, they slipped some kind of sleeping agent into one of your drinks," the sword explained, "Once you fell unconscious, the women dragged you down here and, and..."

"Stuck me in a way I never would have approved of," Ophelia finished for him, a surge of pain coming from her hands as she flexed her fingers.

"I am so sorry," Havarti said again.

"Any idea what they're planning for me?" she mentally asked, "Or at least where my coat is?"

"As for their plans, I'm afraid I have no idea," the sword answered, "As for your coat, it is crumpled up with me in this... wherever I am."

"I don't suppose screaming for help would accomplish anything?" Ophelia sighed.

"I've been doing so for hours," Havarti admitted, "I even redoubled my efforts when I heard Folken and Harbenigyr walk past the window shortly after sunrise."

"They're bound to start worrying about me at some point, right?" she sucked in a lungful of air as she tried to pull one of her hands up along the length of cold pole that protruded above her palm.

The stakes only became thicker the higher up she went. She wasn't getting loose that way.

"We've barely hit midday," the sword said in answer to her question, "I am willing to wager that these *ladies* (he used the term loosely) can keep them distracted and lie about your whereabouts until at least nightfall. At least."

From a direction that Ophelia couldn't see, she heard a door open. Then a progression of footfalls as someone made their way down a set of wooden stairs.

"You're awake already?" the voice belonged to Bianca.

The woman stepped into view. Her blonde hair hung loosely around her face as it hovered over the mercenary. Unlike Ophelia, Bianca had changed into new clothes since the impromptu drinking party. Or set up. Whichever made her feel better, Ophelia supposed.

The white shirt Bianca wore had strips of brown up and down the sleeves where soil had rubbed into the fabric and she smelled faintly of sweat. But she had mastered the technique of crouching without getting her billowing pink skirt underfoot. That thing still looked immaculate.

She was one of the women who tended to the village gardens. Most of the work was in the mornings, when it was cooler, so she must have finished her responsibilities for the day.

"I would have expected you to be screaming your head off like your friend in the box over there," She nodded in the direction of Ophelia's feet.

The mercenary looked down to see a wooden box with a heavy lock shaking on top of a workbench that was attached to the wall by several lengths of chain. Havarti spat some colorful language that he must have learned from Ophelia at Bianca.

It was the least gentlemanly Ophelia had ever heard him act. She couldn't help but love him more for it.

"It wouldn't do any good, would it?" she returned to attention to the gardener, "What are you doing all this for? In fact, what are you doing?" the mercenary demanded.

"Oh, that's right," Bianca pouted, "You fell asleep before we could even ask you to join us."

"Fell asleep?" Ophelia repeated bitterly, "More like passed out because of some drug you laced my drinks with."

"Just one drink," the other woman held up a single finger to visually confirm her word, "I didn't expect you to down three more after that."

"Still waiting for the explanation for why I am STAKED TO THE FLOOR!" Ophelia bellowed.

"Oh, the changing process is quite, how should I say this?" Bianca ran her fingers back and forth over her plump lower lip for a moment, "It's quite energetic."

"Changing process?" both Havarti and Ophelia asked at the same time.

"Of course. You can't join us if you aren't one of us, silly!" the blonde woman laughed.

"One of you. You said that before," Ophelia stared back up at the gardener, "What are you that you think STAKING MY HANDS INTO THE DIRT will make me want to join you?"

"Oh, it's not a question of want, Ophelia," Bianca replied, the smile quickly dropping into a look of worry, "Asking is just kind of a formality. You'll be joining us for the same reason we're all here. Survival."

"Survival," Ophelia scowled, "Then you definitely don't want me in your little band. When I get free I am going to kill every last one of you!"

The mercenary rolled her knees to her chest and then launched her boot covered feet straight up into Bianca's chin. The woman tumbled back out of Ophelia's sight, landing with a crash. She must have knocked something over.

That unseen door opened again. Another set of steps walked down and another familiar voice spoke.

"That's what you get for coming down where you know you're not supposed to be, Bianca," that was Hero's voice!

"What are you doing here?" the gardener sounded different, like her voice was vibrating or something, "Aren't you supposed to be at the split in the trail?"

"Miranda ordered me to stay hidden," the bard answered, "She doesn't want me to come back out until after the new," Hero had the briefest pause in her voice before she was able to get the next word out, "livestock is taken care of."

"She really thinks they're going to be that much trouble?" even through the odd sound added to her voice, the tone in Bianca's sounded doubtful.

"From the svartalfar, yes." Hero replied, "That's why I was trying to get rid of them in the first place."

"I know you have a soft spot for the leaf ears, Hero," Bianca's face just slipped into the edge of Ophelia's field of vision, "But from underground or no, they're just food. Just like the rest."

It wasn't just the gardener's voice that was off. Her face, from what Ophelia could see as it bobbed in and out of view, looked as if she had a cut that stretched from the corner of her mouth to the back of her jaw. The jagged gash looked fresh but it didn't bleed. If that wound came from the mercenary's kick, there was no way she could have cauterized it so fast.

"But why did Miranda have to choose this one?" Hero's hand appeared, pointing toward Ophelia, "She was friendly with the rapist, you know."

"Doesn't matter. She was the only human among them," Bianca responded, "You know how Miranda doesn't share your affinity for pointy ears. She won't let any join us after what happened to change her."

"But there's no reason to make another one of… of us," the bard protested, although it sounded more like pleading to Ophelia's ears, "You said yourself that what we really need is more meat for the coming cold."

"There's strength in numbers, Hero," Bianca looked down at the mercenary as if she were appreciating a new pet. "Just look at her. Any perverts we meet will flock to her and she'll be able to take down any bandit and make a meal out of them. No more hiding!"

The gardener hovering over Ophelia had the same cut on the other side of her face. The mercenary doubted that she had caused the wound with her attack after all. While Ophelia was curious about what did injure the woman like that, her more pressing concern was reminding Bianca that…

"You keep forgetting the little detail that I'm going to kill ALL OF YOU. You're not going to need any meat for the winter because your carcasses will be feeding the," as Ophelia spoke, she was appreciative that Havarti didn't even try to make her censor the curse from her mouth here, "-ing wolves."

"See? She doesn't want to join us anyway!" Hero stepped into view, shrugging in Bianca's diection.

"None of us wanted to at first," Bianca's voice fluttered back, "But she'll come around. Everyone does."

Before Ophelia could say anything else, the door to the basement opened once again, "Hero, you were right about those leaf ears being inquisitive. I need you to tell them that Ophelia ran off and then guide them out to the ruins to the west," It was the voice of the blacksmith, their mayor, Miranda.

"You promised that I could be here for the transformation this time!" the bard whined.

"You will be, little one," the blacksmith promised, "No one said that we were going to perform the ceremony right this instant. I just need you to make sure the criminals are gone long enough that we can make the preparations uninterrupted."

"They aren't criminals," Ophelia butted in.

"What are you talking about?" Hero turned to look down at the mercenary, "The cleric attacked Magra back in Ash Providence."

Ophelia shook her head, "That was a different elf that looked like him, I killed the bastard myself."

"Really?" Miranda stepped into view with a *please smack me because I'm so condescending* look on her face, "Then why did the red haired one break him out of his cell?"

The pinned down woman quirked an eyebrow at the three others. "Not possible. We've all been on the road to here since we straightened out that mess."

The blacksmith shook her head in disappointment, "It's a shame that our new sister is a liar, too."

"Then why make her into one of us?" Hero again sounded more like she was begging rather than just asking a question.

"Aren't you supposed to be taking all those pointy ears out to the ruins, girl?" was Miranda's only answer.

The bard started to argue again, only to be hushed by the older woman once more. Finally, Hero nodded and stomped up the stairs.

"Yes, Ma'am," she sulked.

Once the door to the basement closed behind her, the mayor turned back to Bianca, "Be a dear and grab the sacrificial wafers, would you?"

"I thought you said that we were going to wait for Hero to come back to do the ceremony," Despite the gardener's protest she stepped around Ophelia, well out of reach of the mercenary's legs to pick up a box that rested just beside the one holding Havarti.

"She's been letting more and more prey slip by lately," Miranda replied, "Once Ophelia is reborn, all of our hungers will be triggered. Hero ripping into the pointy ears will be good for her. Remind her of her real place in the pecking order."

Wait a minute. Ophelia just saw Bianca retrieve a box across the room, yet the mayor was speaking to the woman as if she were still right beside her. Ophelia caught a glimpse of Bianca's blonde hair, mere steps from the town's leader but her body was still across the room.

Up in the village proper...

"MIRANDA SAID THAT you wanted to see me?" Hero said as she stepped into the mayor's house.

"Not precisely," Folken answered, "We were inquiring after Ophelia's whereabouts."

The petite human shrugged, "She went with me out on the trail but she got bored at the fork and wandered off. She's a big girl. She can take care of herself, right?"

The svartalfar sorcerer let out a quiet grunt and then returned his attention to the map on the table. Saya waved the bard over to her side.

"You're right about Ophelia, of course," the albino woman began, "so would you be able to guide us into the ruins? Miranda mentioned that you accompanied her on several of her outings."

Hero stepped up beside the svartalfar noble, focusing the entirety of her attention of the parchment representation of the area instead of looking at Saya directly, "Did you have a specific place in the ruins you wanted to check first?"

Harbenigyr approached the table from the other side, cradling and open book to his chest. "According to everything I've gathered so far, right here," he pressed a finger to one of the remains of one of the largest structures, "is the best place to start."

Hero's face hardened as the cleric spoke, though she tried not to show it, "What's so special about that building?"

"Your mayor mentioned that the old village's main source of income was wine making," Harbenigyr said, "That means that this building was likely one of three things. It was either the house of whatever town elder they had, it was one of the main facilities for supplies, or this was were the law enforcers and/or the prison were."

"And what do any of those things gain you?" the bard asked.

"Two out of the three options give us any surviving records of the townsfolk," the cleric placed the open book on the table, pointing to a specific passage as he continued speaking, "Even if it is just the place where they kept empty casks for distribution, this says that every house had to order a specific quantity or opt out. That could give us anything from names to the locations of any of other places they could have kept records."

The elf was excited, Hero could tell that much. If she didn't miss her guess, she figured that Harbenigyr was doing everything in his power to not jump up and down and act all giddy. The woman had to admit that he sure didn't act like the monster he'd been made out to be. But then, she personally knew how deceiving someone's looks could actually be.

Josie appeared to be the opposite of Harbenigyr when it came to excitement level. She continued thumbing through the book on her lap as she sat cross legged on the floor. The ranger didn't even look up as the rest of the group conversed. In Hero's view, she didn't exactly fit the description of being an enthusiastic minion to the cleric that broke him out of prison.

The bard curled her forefinger and pressed her knuckle to the destroyed building that was to be their destination. Spinning her hand around, Hero rested the smaller knuckle just below her folded fingertip to the paper. Then she turned her hand again, her lower knuckle coming to rest right beside the house of the blacksmith.

"It will take us about an hour to get out there, maybe a little less," she asserted, "That will leave you around two hours to look around. That would make it right around sundown when we get back."

"You people really don't like being out at night," Saya proclaimed.

"No," Hero still couldn't bring herself to look over at the woman, "We don't."

"Then I'd say we shouldn't waste anymore time and get going!" Harbenigyr marched around the table for the front door.

While everyone agreed and started for the door, the ranger didn't share the rest of the group's enthusiasm. As she shoved the book she'd been reading back on to the shelf, Josie even found herself grumbling under her breath.

Josie's mood did lighten, however, once they were actually outside. She even offered to take the bard along with them on her horse, since Hero didn't have one of her own.

The walk wasn't quite as long as Hero figured it would take. The sun only moved about three finger widths, meaning that it took only about forty-five minutes to reach the ruined structure.

The roof was completely gone. That made it like every other building that made up this long abandoned village. Two of the outer walls remained, the back and the east. Half of the north wall still stood, right up to where what looked like at least part of the doorjamb of the main entrance was.

All the rubble had collapsed into the building. Very little was actually outside among the overgrown grass and roads that were barely able to be differentiated from just dirt.

Just the idea of the sheer amount of heavy stone that needed to be moved to even do a cursory search made Hero's back ache. Harbenigyr, though, looked determined as he slid off the back of his wingless griffin.

"Go see if you can find yourself some nice rats or voles, boy," he patted Triton's feather covered head, "We may be here for awhile."

With that, he stepped through the partial doorway. The cleric hoisted a rock about twice the size of his own head from a pile that were all roughly around the same size. He turned around hauled the stone to the outer edge of the crumbled building and tossed it just beyond where the wall would have been.

"Harby," Saya called to the elf as she swung herself off of her horse, "That way will take forever. Perhaps there's a way Folken and I can expedite matters?"

She glanced over at her cousin who was still astride his obsidian black steed. He didn't look pleased by Saya's suggestion but he didn't say anything in protest as his stallion strode over to the outer wall.

"Do your part first, my dear," he said, "then I will do mine. You know how I so hate dust and rubbish."

"Oh, alright," Saya sounded put out but the smirk on her face told everyone watching that she was enjoying the feeling of being in charge, if only for a moment.

The svartalfar woman stepped past the bard, who was still sitting behind Josie on the ranger's horse. "I don't suppose you know any good songs to play while we're working?" she grinned.

With some help from the ranger, Hero awkwardly clamored down the side of the brown and turquoise colored steed. Pulling her lute from where it rested on her back, she plucked at a few strings to make sure it was still in tune before starting into a lively, but not too ruckus tune.

Saya stepped through the incomplete doorway and straight for the pile that Harbenigyr had already taken a stone from. Reaching out with her gloved hand, she spread her fingers as wide as she could and pressed her palm against the cold rock.

With a flex of her fingers, the head sized piece of wall shattered into innumerable tiny pieces. Hero jumped in surprise at the sudden cracking noise but didn't miss a beat of the song she was playing.

Saya repeated her rock crushing feat again and again until that waist high pile was little more than pebbles that spread over more than double the area the bigger stones covered, "I'd say it's your turn, Folken," She blew gray dust off the the black leather wrapped around her hand.

Only then did the sorcerer dismount his horse. He stepped up beside his cousin, raising his own glove wrapped arm and pointing it at the demolished pile of rubble.

The same cylinder he used in battle only days before again slipped free of his metallic arm. The air contorted and bent at the open end toward the man's hand before spurting toward the rock pile.

The stones shimmered in place, as if they were under water reflecting sunlight, but they didn't move, "Harbenigyr, please pick up one edge of the pile. Josie, you may need to pick up the other side. It will not be heavy but the load may be a touch cumbersome for one set of hands."

"Saya already made the stones smaller and lighter," Harbenigyr looked befuddled as he addressed the sorcerer, "Picking them up now won't be that easy. Maybe we should find something to sweep them out?"

Hero didn't understand what Folken was talking about, either. He may have made the individual rocks shiny but Saya appeared to have already done all the hard work in lightening the load, as well as increasing the amount of trips to clearing such a large pile.

Josie slid from the top of her horse and strode over to the side of the pile opposite the cleric. "Just do it, Harbenigyr. It will make sense in a moment," she patted the cleric's shoulder as she passed him.

The full-blooded elf shrugged and bent down beside the rocks. Josie did the same on the other side.

As Harbenigyr slipped his hands under the two closest stones, he noticed that they didn't feel how they looked. Somehow they felt *flatter*. His brow furrowed as he looked up at the ranger, who simply started counting.

Once they reached three, both elves stood up and the entirety of the pile that Saya demolished rose with them until it was waist high to both Harby and Josie. The floor underneath was completely cleared of rubble, revealing the worn, scratched and warped wood underneath.

"Amazing!" Hero announced from where she stood just outside.

"No argument from me," Harbenigyr grinned back at Josie and then the sorcerer.

The two elves walked the pile to the outer wall and dumped it on top of the stone the cleric had already hauled out. Folken took three steps away from the pile just before the shimmering stopped and a cloud of white dust erupted from the pile as if it had fallen from a great height.

"Physical laws can be delayed but they must still be fulfilled," the svartalfar man stated as he waved his flesh hand in front of his face the way one would to fan away an unpleasant odor.

Laws must be fulfilled. Hero felt her stomach tighten at Folken's words, even though they were about a completely different subject.

The system of Saya demolishing, Folken enchanting entire piles to be nearly weightless, and the elves clearing it out went on until they found a wooden hatch that led down into a cellar. Harbenigyr almost jumped down the passageway first, followed by Josie and then the svartalfar cousins.

Hero, licking her dry lips, followed them down. She had to be careful not to hit the neck of her lute against the edge of the hatch as she climbed. While the party looked around at the toppled and collapsed shelves, the bard hopped down and skipped the last rung of the ladder, accidentally kicking a bottle that was just laying on the packed dirt that served as the floor.

The opaque bottle spun around until it hit a rock and cracked open. Instead of the the rich smell of wine that should have come from a bottle like that, the room was suddenly filled with an acidic scent.

Folken's green hair fell in front of his eyes as the sniffed at the air, "Vinegar. What a shame, some air must have seeped in while that wine was fermenting."

"I didn't know that vinegar was spoiled wine," Saya said as she picked up another bottle by its long, narrow neck without looking up at her cousin.

"As with most things, it is simply the order of steps that determine the outcome," the sorcerer scooped the bottle from Saya's hands and inspected it, "Still, a vinegar from an ill-prepared wine is not necessarily good for consumption, either. In this case," He stabbed the pointed fingertip of his gloved forefinger into the cork and pulled it free from the bottle. "It appears the corks themselves may have had some undetected fault."

Folken showed his disappointment on his face as he dumped the contents of the wine bottle in the far corner of the room. He dropped the bottle into the puddle and turned back toward the group.

"So the residents of this village were going to have a bad year regardless of whether they were attacked or not?" Saya suggested.

"Not according to this," Harby emerged from another corner thumbing through a thick ledger in his hand, "Someone caught the defect in the stoppers so they were trying to figure out a way to turn these into a store of palatable vinegar to try and lessen the financial impact, just like Folken suggested. These people were clever," the cleric said admiringly.

"Surely they set aside a portion of each successful vintage in the event of lean years, as well," Folken added.

"If we can figure out what kind of wine they made here, we may just be able to find out the name of this place," Saya suggested, "Then maybe we can piece together who Harby's parents were."

"You think so?" the cleric looked at the pale woman hopefully.

Hero knew that they said they were looking for information about the elf's family before but, seeing the innocent look in Harbenigyr's face made it seem more, well, real somehow. What Folken said about laws and the doubt that was already scrambling all around the mind of the bard finally made her find her voice. She had to know for sure.

"Harbenigyr, did you really do what you were accused of back in Ash Providence?" she blurted out the question, fidgeting uneasily.

The unexpected question made the cleric freeze mid-step. Josie had to catch him before he fell over.

"You heard about that out here?" Harby didn't even try to hide his shock, "How?"

"One of my... sisters in the village makes regular trips back and forth almost everyday," Hero explained, "She told us about what you di–"

"It wasn't me," Harbenigyr interrupted, pulling himself free from the grip of the ranger, "It was an evil duplicate that looked like me."

"An evil duplicate?" the bard scowled.

"It is true," Folken spoke up from behind the bard, "A group thought that we were in possession of an artifact they wanted. In order to take it from us, they created doppelgangers of various members of our troupe to do so surreptitiously."

"Huh?" Hero's face was blank.

"To steal it without anyone knowing," Saya interjected, "I personally killed the doppelganger that tried to replace me."

"So all of you have evil twins? That explains how she," Hero pointed at Josie, "was able to break him out of that cell then."

"I *do* have an evil doppelganger?" Josie fumed, "That bastard lied to us!"

"My evil twin is still alive?" Harbenigyr yelped at the same time, "How is that even possible?"

Folken raised both his hands as he approach the the ranger and the cleric, "While those are subjects are truly unsettling, we can address them later. We should keep to the task at hand. Perhaps the information we find here will aid us in being able to differentiate your from your doppelgangers if they do end up resurfacing."

"You think so?" Josie rested her hands on her bare, round hips, "The evil Saya and Harby both shared their memories. How do we know they don't somehow get them now?"

"Because Saya's doppelganger didn't wait to try and replace her. Knowing our plans would have made that all too easy," Folken commented, "She attacked at her earliest opportunity. It stands to reason that the memories they share end roughly around the time of their initial creation. Which, if Harbenigyr's duplicate is to be believed in this particular case, could be no more than two weeks ago."

"Around the time we were in Dracoleaf." Saya nodded. "That was where we first encountered the de Junamend."

Folken nodded in agreement.

Hero cupped her face in her hands letting out a long, heavy sigh into her palms before letting them drop down to her sides again, "We need to get back to Laeradr," she announced.

"Were you not just listening?" Folken countered, "In addition to finding anything about Harbenigyr's past, we could also use what we find here to protect ourselves from infiltration from his and Josie's doppelgangers."

"I heard you," Hero wanted to snatch the violet flaps of the sorcerer's collar and shake everything she had to say into him, "But we have to save Ophelia now!"

"What's happened to Ophelia?" Saya's purple eyes narrowed with suspicion.

"I- I lied to you," Hero wrapped her hands around one of the rungs of the ladder that connected the hatch to the cellar, "Miranda drugged her and is going to turn her into one of us. We-we were also going to kill all of you and store your bodies as food for the winter."

"What?" Harbenigyr's black colored eyes couldn't help but stare at the petite woman, "What are you talking about? What are you that you think eating people isn't a *terrible* thing?"

"It is terrible. I hate having to do it!" Hero wailed, clutching at her midsection, "I didn't ask to me made into a monster! If we don't hurry, Ophelia's going to be one, too!"

"What kind of monster, Hero?" Folken's voice was calm, methodical, "We need to know what we are facing."

"I talked the sisters into only killing criminals," the bard sobbed, scratching at her neck through her long black scarf, "I thought Harby and Josie were bad guys but then Folken and Saya showed up and Miranda is racist against elves and she forced me to bring all of your back to town–"

"What kind of monster, Hero." Folken repeated, his tone firm as he interrupted her rambling.

Hero sniffled, wiping at her button nose with the back of her hand, "I'm a, I'm a penanggalan."

Josie, Harbenigyr, and Saya stared back at her blankly. Folken, however, groaned and shook his head.

Hero turned away from them, resting her forehead on the smooth steel rung of the ladder. Her eyes closed tight, she cleared her throat and her hand reflexively reached up to scratch at her neck.

"Ow!" the bard pulled her hand away from her scarf.

Her fingers were burnt, as if she had just touched some kind of acid. She turned back to look at the elves in horror.

"You have to get out of here. Now. Leave me behind, close the hatch and bury it. Now!" she hollered.

"What's happening?" Josie asked as she started toward the ladder and Hero.

The bard would only shake her head as she stepped back, away from the rest of the group. She pulled the scarf off of her shoulders, thin wisps of smoke rising from the portion that was actually touching the bare skin of her neck.

For the first time, the party could see the long scar that stretched all around Hero's neck and throat. And it was opening. Instead of blood, a viscous, puss-like yellow liquid was oozing out of the pink tissue as it continued to pull apart.

"Get away!" Hero pleaded, pressing herself tightly against the wall, "I'll kill you all!"

The basement...

BIANCA'S BODY MADE its way back from across the room. Ophelia didn't see it before since she wasn't watching closely but now she saw that woman in the pink skirt was walking backwards. Not in the sense that she was walking over the same path she had taken around the mercenary before (which she was) but that her back was leading the way.

Then the smell hit Ophelia. That copper mixed with brimstone stench that usually came with someone's death.

"What in the world is this woman? No, this *thing*?" Havarti voiced the very same question in Ophelia's mind that she had.

The mercenary finally noticed one last detail. One that the limited light from the thin window had obscured until Bianca's body was again walking past her with its jerky, awkward backwards gait. It was the source of the stench.

Bianca's head was still attached to her body! Ophelia's pale eyes stretched open wider and wider despite her revulsion. The other woman's neck wasn't simply extending to an unnatural length. No, the torn flesh at the bottom of her throat was easily seen, with puss oozing along the ragged flesh.

The woman's innards stretched out from the opening in her neck. Bianca's intestines ran from her body and up beyond where Ophelia could see like some stinking, horrific rope as thick around as the woman's actual neck.

The mercenary strained to look up toward the women standing over her, a fresh rush of pain coming from the metal spikes in her hands as her entire body shifted. Miranda looked completely normal, even wearing the same clothes she had on when she met the party on the trail yesterday.

Bianca's guts floated in the air, somehow able to support their own weight, and run up into the bottom of the woman's head. When the gardener noticed Ophelia's disgusted look on her face, her floating head turned upside down as it closed the distance between the two women.

"I'm sorry you're seeing me like this early," the reason her voice was vibrating was that her tongue has split into two separate, prehensile tentacle looking muscles, "But you do kick awfully hard."

The reason Ophelia was able to see her revolting tongues was because of those cuts on Bianca's cheeks. The spread open like extensions of her mouth, revealing not only her tongue but the sharpened, monstrous teeth her face had been hiding.

Some of that acrid puss dripped from the torn flesh just under the chin of the gardener, landing on the dirt just beside Ophelia's head. A squeaking hiss, along with a thin trail of smoke told the woman that the puss was acidic.

"Want another?" the mercenary lifted her boots into the air, wiggling her feet mockingly.

Bianca snapped her head back and out of Ophelia's view, not wanting a repeat of what caused her to change into her monstrous shape already.

"What kind of monsters are you, anyway?" dhe asked her two captors, "I've never seen anything like you and I've seen beasts that literally came from hell."

"We will explain everything to you, child," Miranda smiled in a way that Ophelia was sure was supposed to be comforting but she only found it sanctimonious, "Once you are one of us."

"I like my neck the length it is already, thank you," Ophelia growled back rolling her body up just like she did to attack Bianca before.

Both female monsters rushed back out of her reach, just like the mercenary hoped they would. Ophelia twisted her body to the side and slammed her feet into the metal stake that was pinning her left hand down.

Something snapped in her right shoulder. Ophelia's fingers shuddered around the length of metal as her right arm suddenly went numb even as she wrenched her left hand free of the ground.

Miranda screamed with rage as she charged back at the human. Ophelia reared back with her left arm, dropping the metal stake down on the foot of the blacksmith like an improvised club.

The mercenary tugged her hand free of the cold metal with a sickening slurping noise coming from her palm before it was free. Ophelia rolled onto her right side. Her bloody hand was already reaching for the stake in her right palm when Bianca's hands wrapped around Ophelia's face, slamming it into the packed her and her nails scratching into the human's cheeks.

"No! You're got getting away so easily!" Bianca's head protested from well outside of Ophelia's reach.

Ophelia slammed her palm into the stake, causing a rush of pain and nausea to rush through her entire body. The vision of her head tethered to her body by her own entrails was enough to force the woman to keep her consciousness and hit the metal still impaled through her other hand again.

Bianca pulled Ophelia's shoulders back down into the dirt, forcing her to look up. Her jaw snapped open and closed unnaturally wide and fast as she chattered back at her leader.

"I think the labor pains are severe enough that we'll have to dispense with the niceties, Miranda!" she struggled to keep Ophelia down.

The blacksmith agreed, fumbling with the lock on the small wood box in her hands. After a few moments, she dropped the key and simply ripped the lock from the gold mounting on the lip of the box.

She pulled a thin disk, about the size of a coin, that looked like a dried scab of blood from inside and set the box on the lowest step of the stairs behind her. Miranda started toward Bianca and Ophelia, chanting something the human couldn't understand.

What neither monster noticed was that Ophelia's right hand was free. The metal stake that had held it down was in Ophelia's left hand. With what strength she could muster, the woman shoved the stake down Bianca's neck hole, piercing her intestines as it entered her torso.

The creature gardener reared back, shrieking in pain. Ophelia rolled away, struggling to her feet as Miranda continued to close the distance.

"My dear, can you get me out of this casket so that I can assist you?" Havarti's voice popped into Ophelia's head.

"Not yet," the woman shook her head as she tried to figure out a way to fight the coming monster with what she called a sacrificial wafer, "Right arm's dislocated and useless. Left hand is shredded. Need to blink at least once to stand a chance."

"Come on, Miranda," Ophelia said to the other woman between pants, "Do you really want me to join you? After all the trouble I've caused? One of you is dead already. Do you really think she'll be alone by the end of this?"

"Whose dead?" the blacksmith asked, almost within arm's reach, if the mercenary's arms could have moved, that is.

"Bianca. She's lying right back th–"

Ophelia motioned to wear she stabbed the gardener only to see the ghastly body, covered in ichor and puss, lift itself up. It still moved backwards, with her chest pointing up in the air as her arms contorted to get her back onto her feet.

Her neck wasn't able to stretch out with that stake planted in her torso through the neck. Ophelia couldn't help involuntarily retching when she saw Bianca gnaw through her own entrails with her monstrous teeth, followed by her now disembodied head take to the air on its own.

"I wonder if this is how the people I fight feel when they see me blink," the mercenary groaned to Havarti.

——— ◆··• •··◆ ———

CHAPTER EIGHT

"You know that all these difficulties could have been avoided if you and your compatriots simply spoke to each other openly," I said.

"It's easy to pass judgment when you aren't there," the subject responded.

"Who said I wasn't there?" I asked.

"You did," the subject pointed at me, "At the start of your little inquisition here."

I looked back over the dictation I have been keeping during our interview, "Ah, yes, I can see how you got that impression. You missed a very important word in my description, however."

"And what was that?" the subject asked.

"I believe it is me who is supposed to be asking the questions here," I responded.

"Now who's being evasive?" Ophelia sneered.

I answered, "Perhaps Phinegann's revisit of his days as a prison guard will provide you with the insight you desire... "

Two decades later...

A MASSIVE ORC in the same style of black armor as Phinegann turned to the man in red. His skin was a soft green, reminding Appelonia of pond scum, but that was the only thing soft about this man.

He had two tusks that seemed overgrown for his face, reaching up to the bottom of his repeatedly broken nose and reaching out about a hand's width ahead. Phinegann was easily the largest of the party including the cleric of Kuan Yin, the Bunny Barbarian, and the gnomish inventor whose wings wouldn't stop shaking, but this mammoth of a orc towered over their half-orge by at least a head in height.

"This is the most annoying part of our jobs, Phinegann," the green man began, "It happens every time we process a new inmate. They come in whining about how they're innocent, the trial wasn't fair or some other story about how they aren't to blame for what we've been hired to punish them for."

Hatred twisted every feature of Phinegann's face as he stared at the other man in black armor. Despite this obvious vitriol stewing within the orc, he didn't scream at the other man, didn't throw a punch, didn't do anything to hurt him or show the even bigger man his true feelings.

Phinegann only forced himself to choke out a simple, "Yes, Vokloss."

The green man, apparently named Vokloss (Appelonia thought that when Phin said it before that it was some kind of orc cuss word.), turned and strode to the far side of the stone tables that lined the middle of the room. Every muscle in Phinegann's body tensed but, finally, he followed after the other orc, albeit not completely willing.

The cleric and the others followed as well, confused as to what was happening. None of them dared to interrupt it, either. Something about this place was doing to the retired guard exactly what Abernathy and Genevieve did to Jonas: granting his wish.

Just like with the paladin, it wasn't being done in a straightforward way. For some reason, Phinegann was being forced to relive, as far as Appelonia could tell, one of the earliest days of his career in Obsidian Fjord Prison. Back when he was still in training. What this was going to do to tell the orc why he was in some hell-like caves in the here and now was anyone's guess.

"Take this prisoner here," Vokloss pointed at an orc woman with a skin tone similar to his. "She was found guilty of inciting a coup against the chieftain of the Rite of the Boulder. Made his own son challenge for leadership."

The orc woman wore a leather tunic with shoulders that came to a point just beyond where her actual, firm shoulders ended. Her belt had already been removed as a potential weapon when she first arrived at the fortress.

Her pants were made of the same treated leather as her tunic. The legs would have usually slipped inside her boots but those were taken from the woman for the same reason as her belt.

She was laid out on the cold, stone ground, running a hand over her bald head to see if she was bleeding. She would surely bruise, but when her palm came back clear, she lifted herself up onto her hands and knees. If Appelonia had met this woman anywhere else at any time, she would have easily been intimidated. As it was, the cleric felt her heart going out to the orc.

"No I didn't!" the woman wailed, "Treamor did it all on his own. He wanted to take the chief-seat and me as a wife. When he lost and Tungsta didn't kill him, he told his father that I put him up to it! But I didn't! I swear!"

"You mustn't let your will be swayed, particularly when the convict is an attractive one like this," Vokloss warned Phinegann, "They are skilled in using their wiles to get their way from men. We must be stronger than that. When a prisoner comes here, they are guilty. Those who are wiser and smarter than either of us say so. We do not question their decisions. Understood, guard?"

Phinigann's hands curled up into fists so tightly that both of his hands, flesh and metal, shook. "Yes, Vokloss," was all he said.

"Very good," the green guard nodded, "The first order of business is getting her into proper prisoner garb."

Phinegann growled through clenched teeth, "Yes, Vokloss." and he strode over to the second table, picking up a folded pile of burlap.

Vokloss stopped the shorter orc before he could walked past the higher ranked guard, "Remember procedure, new blood. Give her instructions well before you are within the convict's reach."

Phinegann nodded again, his leathery face darkening with a mix of embarrassment and shame, "Prisoner Delilah, you will remove your clothing and change into the garb provided you. Do you understand?"

The face of the orc woman was a mask of shock, "You want me to strip down in front of you? Can't I get some privacy at least?"

Phinigann glared back at Vokloss for a long moment before he addressed the woman again. "Procedure demands you change in full view of your escorts in order to assure no smuggling of weapons or other contraband into Obsidian Fjord Prison."

"Are there no women guards here?" she scowled.

Delilah let out a soft groan as she found her feet. Apparently, the trip hadn't been without a beating or two. Whether that was due to her own defiance or the cruelty of the guards that brought her to the fortress, Phinegann couldn't say.

"No," Vokloss answered for the lower ranked guard, "You are the first female inmate to see the inside of these walls. A mercy considering that attempted usurpation is usually punished by execution."

"Execution may have been more merciful in the long run," Delilah muttered to herself but sound carried better than she would have liked in the wide open chamber.

"What was that, convict?" Vokloss leaned a curved, pointed ear in her direction.

"Nothing," the woman shook her head as she started to pulled her pants down the length of her thick legs.

The leather tunic protected at least a portion of her modesty as she, with great care, folded the leather she just removed and laid the pants on the corner of the stone slab closest to her. The tunic didn't have sides to speak of. The leather was just enough to cover her chest and stomach, stretch out to make her shoulders look broader and then thin down again as it stretched down her back. Without the belt that usually came with it, the leather didn't hide much and what it did keep the guards from seeing was only because she took great care not to move too suddenly.

Swallowing hard, her honey colored eyes turned in the direction of Phinegann, "May I have the uniform now, please?" she requested, her voice soft to avoid appearing confrontational.

The hand of Vokloss dropped down over the wrist of the other guard to keep him from tossing the clothing at Delilah's feet, "Finish stripping first, convict," he ordered.

The scorn in Phinegann's face told Appelonia and the others that he wanted to kill Vokloss so badly at that moment. The ranking guard didn't appear to notice. That wouldn't have been something a high ranking guard would tolerate from a trainee, especially when he was teaching procedures and sowing discipline. The cleric couldn't help but wonder why Phin didn't lash out.

The best explanation for it was that Vokloss wasn't reacting to the Phinegann of now, but how he acted back then. If this was indeed a reenactment of what orc guards did before, Phinegann's body was going through the actions but his emotions were from the hindsight of having lived through this previously. Whatever was causing Phin's cooperation couldn't control him completely. Just enough to torture him.

"Our orders are to be followed immediately, convict!" Vokloss stomped over to the woman.

The orc slipped a hand into the collar of of Delilah's tunic and ripped the leather off from around her neck. Red welts started to billow up on her green skin almost immediately.

Delilah lifted her muscular arms to obscure the view of her breasts and the rest of her body from the men as best she could. That only seemed to enrage the guard.

"Who told you to cover up, convict?" he reared back a hand and swatted the woman across the face.

Appelonia felt her stomach shudder as she watched the other woman fall to the ground limp. Tension built faster than the silence in the hall during the visit from Diomedes. Until Phinegann spoke up.

"What are you doing, Vokloss? That is not procedure!" for the first time since this scenario began, the words left his mouth without resistance.

"You don't know if she is hiding a weapon, new blood," the higher ranking guard turned to Phinegann and snatched the burlap clothing from his hand, "We need to see everything!

"Where could she hide anything?" Illyria whispered from beside the cleric, "In her cleavage?"

"The man is a pervert," Tokki shared his observations, "A sadistic pervert on a power trip. This will not end well for her."

"Surely Phinegann wouldn't allow..." Illyria frowned back at the Bunny Barbarian, who only shook his head.

"Go and ready her cell." Vokloss ordered, "I will finish processing her myself, new blood."

The larger orc shoved Phinegann, who stumbled back several steps as uncertainty racked his body. His expression, though, was very sure of what he wanted to do. But he did what the new blood Phinegann mast have done, he turned around and started to leave.

"No." Illyria gasped.

Appelonia shared the gnome's horror. Surely, this wasn't the kind of man that had been entrusted with her safety? What Phinegann was doing could only be described as, there was no avoiding it, as cowardly.

"Not this time," the orc in red kept walking away.

That amber color returned to his eyes and a snarl came from Phinegann that was more that of a beast than a person. Even an enraged one.

His steps started to stutter. Phinegann fought to keep from walking away. Whatever force that was making him relive this failure from his past, was losing its grip on him.

Phinegann came to a stop. He slowly turned back in the direction of Vokloss and the woman the senior guard was beating, "Not this time."

As his face came back into view, it wasn't Phinegann anymore. He looked like a wolf! The only reason they could even tell it was still him was that the canine head had the same black and red striped jowls.

He was growing, too. The armor that was wrapped around his body spread apart as if it was designed to do so, with straps of leather holding the plates of black steel against his torso.

While he was a hairy man to begin with, Phinegann's arms now looked covered with fur. Even the metal one. It looked as if each strand of fur was crafted from thin shafts of metal polished to a high shine.

Except for the claws. They were black and lethally sharp on each hand.

With a howl of rage, Phinegann flexed every muscle in his body that was now with twice as much as it had before. He lunged for Vokloss, who was still going through the motions of what happened before.

"Not this time!" a voice that only vaguely resembled the original Phin came from the mouth of the monster.

Phinegann stretched his maw open wide as he charged. Just as he snapped his jaws shut, he found the curved blade that had been resting on the hip of Vokloss between his peaked teeth.

"Now now, new blood," the green guard's demeanor was of a disappointed teacher, "You can't change history. You know I had her. At will. Whenever I wanted. Starting here," he smirked, thin lines of saliva dribbling from the base of his tusks.

Phinegann released the blade from between his teeth and lunged again, "Not this time!"

Sparks flew from the sword of Vokloss where his blade connected with the shined metal of the other orc's forged claw. Despite now being smaller than Phinegann and fighting two hands full of claws and a jaw full of snapping teeth, the guard from the past kept the beast at bay.

"I think whatever rules there were about what's happening have been broken," Illyria observed, "What should we do now?"

Appelonia chewed on her plump lower lip as she decided, "Help Phinegann. Whatever he did then, he's trying to make amends, at least to himself, now."

Tokki Yo Bunpy didn't need to hear anything more. He charged toward the melee, loosing a proud battle cry as he closed the distance.

"You keep your lights pointed at them, Illyria," Appelonia ordered as she pulled her jade bow off of her shoulder, "If we can't see Vokloss, we can't fight him. You are the key."

The cleric pulled an arrow from the thin quiver that hung off the back of her belt and nocked it onto the string. Pulling back, the bow string stretched and the jade bent much further than the gnome was aware that the stone could bend. All thanks to Yo Bunpy construction techniques.

"Just keep your distance," the red haired elf said as her black eyes stared down the length of the arrow with the dulled head, "I promised you wouldn't have to fight and I'll do my best to keep my word."

The Bunny Barbarian leaped at Vokloss just as he slashed at Phinegann's metal arm with his curved blade. Despite not even looking in the furred warrior's direction, the free hand of the green orc snapped out to smash Tokki in his bare chest.

The barbarian fell to the ground flat on his back. He rolled out of the way of the guard's boot as it shot down to stomp him.

"You weren't there," Vokloss said before looking back at Phinegann, "Playing with forest animals now, new blood?"

Again, the half-ogres clashed as Tokki struggled to get air back into his lungs. Phinegann's wolfish shape was faster than Vokloss and his attacks. The green man wasn't able cut him.

But Appelonia could tell that he was an experienced fighter with a scimitar. He was able to position himself to keep the transformed orc from getting too close to bite or grab him. All he had to worry about were the claws.

All Phinegann needed was an edge, a small advantage to be able to beat this opponent. Appelonia loosed her arrow. It sailed through the darkness, unnoticed by the green orc until the rounded head struck him in the eye, sending him stumbling off balance.

Phinegann howled a lupine howl, seeing an opening for attack. But so did Tokki.

Both men lunged at the green orc, one with two claws courtesy of some kind of transformation, the other with a sleeve of claws that once belonged to a giant rabbit.

Vokloss lobbed his scimitar at both men in a last ditch effort to keep them away long enough for him to get his bearings. Phinegann dropped under the spinning blade, dropping onto all fours, a natural looking position for him in his current shape.

Tokki threw himself to the side to try and avoid the flying sword. Its sharpened edge slashed across his chest, chopping the leather strap that held his clawed sleeve in place, as well as spilling blood from the lengthy gash left in the weapons wake.

Phinegann pounced on Vokloss, pinning the man on his back by the shoulders. The green orc spat at the other man defiantly as his wolf-like jaws wrapped around his throat and snapped together.

Vokloss gurgled away the last breath of his life. Phin returned the defiant spat by returning the other man's trachea to its owner, albeit crushed and on his cheek. Not exactly where it was supposed to go.

With her bow back on her shoulder, Appelonia rushed over to Tokki Yo Bunpy, who laid still on the cold floor, "Don't move. Let me check you," she ordered.

The barbarian's rabbit faced helmet bobbed, "As you command," he said with a wide smile on his face.

The grin only diminished slightly at the stinging sensation as the cleric dabbed at the wound on his chest with a rag from one of the many pouches on her belt. Apple ended up having to sit on top of him, resting her arms over the wide cloth on his toned chest to put pressure on it and stop the bleeding.

The gnome woman, her glass wings still pouring out light, stepped up beside them, "Is he going to be okay?" she asked.

Appelonia nodded back, "It's only a flesh wound."

"What about him?" Illyria pointed in the direction of Phinegann.

The other woman looked that way, as well. The massive man was hunched over on the ground, heaving for breath. His black armor seemed to be back in one piece.

Oddly, there didn't appear to be any sign of Vokloss. Looking over toward the far side of the stone tables, Apple couldn't see any sign of where the female prisoner, Delilah, had been either.

"Are you okay, Phin?" the cleric called.

Phinegann looked back in their direction, his face back to normal, if somewhat more surly than before, "Uninjured."

He looked down at the ground where Vokloss' dead body had been only moments before. He looked where Delilah was huddled, naked and scared. She was gone, too. All of this had been for nothing. In his rage, he'd only managed to waste his time and put those in his charge in danger.

When Appelonia walked over and placed a hand on his flesh shoulder, he jumped at his fuming being interrupted. He turned to look up at the elf, who had a look of worry on her face.

"Did what happen here, you know, really happen?" she asked.

Phinegann nodded, "Up until I unleashed my rage pointlessly."

"Unleashed your rage?" Apple frowned, "Is that was you call it when you transform into that wolf thing?"

The orc quirked an eyebrow, "A wolf? I didn't know that. I'd never left anyone alive to describe it afterwards."

"How does it work?" the woman asked, "You can control it?"

Again Phinegann nodded, this time as he straightened up and stood back on his feet. "It is the effect of an experimental potion that was being tested within Obsidian Fjord. In the riot where I–," he glanced down at his metal arm, "I was captured by the prisoners, who injected me with it. It ended up being the very thing that saved me."

"There were experiments being performed on prisoners?" A torrent of ethical conflicts came to Appelonia.

"On volunteers." the man answered, "In return for reduced sentences. Folken felt that forcing such matters would have skewed the results."

The cleric's stomach sank at the mention of the sorcerer's name, "I should have realized. That's why he made you your new arm," Appelonia tapped on the back of his metal hand, "In appreciation for aiding his research."

"He allowed me to continue a normal life," Phinegann scowled back, "Even though I had to leave Obsidian Fjord."

"You actually *liked it* there?" Illyria chimed in as she and Tokki stepped up to them.

The bleeding on the barbarian's chest had stopped. Appelonia dipped into her pouches again and turned her attention to Tokki's wound.

Phinegann let out a soft grunt, "Despite Vokloss, I was able to do good. Until the riot, the convicts and I had an understanding, some even respect."

"Until they had the advantage of you," Tokki commented.

Which was followed by a pained hiss when Appelonia packed healing herbs into his wound very, very tightly. Then she wrapped a fresh bandage around his chest and started muttering a quick, quiet prayer.

"I can't argue," Phinegann shrugged, "So I'm not there anymore."

"But you can control that transformation in the wolf thing, right?" Appelonia again asked as she clapped her hands together after finishing up Tokki's treatment.

"I can," Phinigann assured her.

"Even if we find ourselves in tight tunnels again?" the cleric gave him the same look Apple's mother always gave her when she was making her daughter promise to do something.

He turned and started for the far wall of the chamber. "If this is still like Obsidian Fjord Prison, there should be an exit this way."

"Do you realize that is the most he has said," Illyria tapped her lower lip, looking as if she were counting, "this entire trip?"

Apple agreed, "You should help him find the way out," She patted the gnome's shoulder.

"Do you have needle and thread so I can repair my harness?" Tokki held up the severed ends of the leather strap that used to stretch across his chest.

"I'll see what I can do for you once we're on the move," she poked a thumb toward the rest of the party in a silent order for him to follow them.

He did so. Once Appelonia was standing alone, she took a slow, deep breath as she looked around the darkness. She wasn't really looking for anything, just reflecting on all that she had witnessed.

Despite his words, Apple couldn't help but wonder if reliving a past mistake and changing it, even if it wasn't real, was cathartic for Phinigann. She wondered what she would do differently, given the chance to do some event from her past over again?

Shaking her head, she silently prayed that the orc had at least found some kind of peace after going through… whatever it was that had just happened. She started after Illyria's light that was starting to shrink into the distance. She didn't want to be left behind.

That was when she heard a new voice, "I am sorry that you had to go through that again, dearie."

Appelonia turned back to see as strange, thin man wearing a tweed cloak and a top hat. He was facing the furthest slab.

Delilah rose from behind the stone. She was dressed, although not in the same clothing she had not when she initially appeared.

Her feet were bare like before, apparently she liked it that way now? The green woman was wearing a white linen loincloth around her hips. The same white material was wrapped around her chest and her left shoulder.

She carried a round wooden shield in that arm. On her back was a scimitar with a wide blade. A brass hand guard wrapped around the handle, covered with spikes, that peeked over her right shoulder.

Delilah was facing the thin man, too, but the cleric could see a familiar violet glow coming from the muscular woman's back. It was just like the glow from the runes on Ophelia's runes! From this far away, though, Appelonia couldn't really see any detail.

"It's alright, Doctor," Delilah said, "The hard part was not reacting to how much he'd changed."

"I did promise he would survive the riot, child," Efreeti pushed two frames of round glass higher up along the bridge of his angular nose, "I could not guarantee that he would get out unscathed."

"Still, it was nice to see Vokloss die," Delilah looked at the floor where Phinigann had ripped out the other guard's throat, "Again."

"I did hope you would find that enjoyable," This 'Doctor' tipped his tall hat at the woman, "When that oaf- I mean gentleman made that wish in my presence, I couldn't help but indulge in a little role play. Since you were the one to kill him the first time, of course."

"How were you able to find him? Vokloss, I mean," Klymidja asked the thin man with long white hair.

"I simply went to your pantheon's version of hell," he shrugged, as if it was a easy thing, "That was the simple part."

"That was the easy part?" The woman smirked, if only to camouflage her doubt, "What was the hard part, then?"

"This part, right here, child," the thin man pointed at the floor beneath his feet before turning to face Appelonia, "Your friend rushed off before I was able to fully complete his wish, child of Harbenigyr."

The thin man's mouth spread into such a wide grin that it looked as if the top part of his head might separate from the lower.

The cleric couldn't help gasping and stepping back in a mixture of surprise and fright.

"You are a part of his little troupe, yes?" the 'Doctor' tilted his head in the opposite direction, "This should sufficiently fulfill his request, then. Do be sure to tell him?"

Appelonia started walked backwards, away from the thin man and woman orc but not willing to turn her back on them. Her mouth opened and closed, letting out only partially formed words of excuse. Or agreement? Both? Neither?

When she felt she was far enough away, Apple sprinted down the tunnel after her friends. She didn't even give herself time to breathe. She just wanted to put as much distance between her and that man as possible.

As she chased after the four colors of light, Appelonia realized why that woman had reminded her of Ophelia. It was because of that man. He fit Ophelia's description of Doctor Efreeti perfectly!

He must have done the same thing to Delilah that he did to Ophelia. What was his part in all of this?

OPHELIA INTERROGATION NOTES:

"Doctor Efreeti visited Apple directly?" the subject asked, "I didn't know that."

"Yes you did," I said, "You have read every word I have written."

"It's not like you're making any real effort to hide it," the subject said.

Then Ophelia snatched the next sheet of parchment from my hand, "Romefeller Guild again, eh? So you want to go back to the Jaded Woods. Who are we reading this time? Saya? Folken?"

Decades before...

UNNATURALLY SHARP TEETH bit into the black leather wrapped around Saya's metal arm. Even though Hero's disgustingly large mouth didn't contact any flesh, the svartalfar woman couldn't stop herself from being pulled off the ladder and back down into the packed dirt at the bottom of the cellar.

The body of the bard was still pressed against the wall, in the same position from which she was begging them to leave. Her face, though, was still attached to the other woman who was now half a room away.

Hero's own entrails connected her head to her body, the stomach churning stench of blood and offal filling the enclosed space of the underground room, carrying it like a disgusting, flesh stripped neck. One that could stretch to any length.

The body of the bard, its back to the party, started shuffling toward Saya. The exposed entrails constricted back down the woman's neck with a sickening slurping noise. Despite the awkward gait, the monstrous woman's body bent over backward with her arms stretching out toward the pale woman fighting off her gnawing, inhuman head.

Harbenigyr started chanting something that mentioned something about "mockeries of true life". The shelves made space tight so his quarterstaff would be next to useless against the... thing that Hero had become so there was little else he could do.

Josie shot an arrow over Harbenigyr's shoulder, striking Hero in her shoulder blade. The body of the bard straightened up, her head releasing its grip on Saya's arm enough to let out a surprised gasp.

Another arrow flew over the shoulder of the cleric to strike the monster right in the middle of her back, which should have severed her spine. Hero's body stumbled back (or forward if she'd been normal) against the wall but remained standing.

Josie loosed a third shot into the exposed intestines spouting from the bard's body. Hero didn't seem to even notice as the razor sharp heads slashed through her entrails, only to embed itself in the wall just above the short woman's shoulders.

"She is not a revenant, cleric," Folken admonished the young elf as he snatched the lunging head of Hero by her unremarkable brown hair before she could snap her jaws around Saya again, "An ill-humoured force possesses her body. You cannot turn it away with your mutterings."

The monster's head preferred being upside down, making it awkward to handle as it lunged upward at the sorcerer, who held it at arm's length. Two tendrils tumbled from the formerly kind bard's mouth and whipped at the green haired man, forcing him to extend his artificial arm out even farther than would have been possible for his natural flesh and bone limb.

Harbenigyr and Josie both aided Saya up to her feet. With Folken holding Hero at bay, there was no room for them to get by and climb the steel ladder to safety.

"The most tragic thing is this," Folken pushed the woman's head up so that his companions could see the feral thing chomping and spitting voraciously, "While she cannot control her actions, Hero is still within. A silent, horrified witness to her body's actions."

Looking at Hero's eyes revealed the truth to the words of the svartalfar man. Tears spilled from her brown eyes as they darted around, helpless to do anything to stop herself.

"When I move, we will not have much time," Folken forced their attention back onto him by pulling Hero's beastly head into both of his hands, "Once I am out of the way, get up the ladder as quickly as you are able!"

"What about you?" Saya demanded.

"I will be right behind you, cousin," the sorcerer assured her as he started pushing Hero's head toward the far corner, "You know I am not one to sacrifice myself."

And Folken dropped to his knees, pressing Hero's face into the puddle of vinegar he had dumped from the bottle of spoiled wine earlier. The inhuman woman screeched in pain as smoke and steam suddenly billowed around her.

"Now!" Saya snapped as she lunged for the ladder.

Skipping every third rung, the pale woman was out in the cooling air as the afternoon transitioned into evening. Harby tried to push Josie past him to go up next but she shoved him into the metal rungs first.

She was was right under the cleric, grunting with effort as she pushed on his backside to make him climb faster and over the wooden lip of the hatch. Josie jumped from the top of the ladder and into the ruined building, landing right on top of Harby. She breathed a quick apology and quickly rolled off him, making sure he couldn't see her flushed face.

True to his word, Folken was up almost immediately after. He more ascended than climbed out of the cellar. Josie wasn't sure that he even touched the ladder at all.

"What just happened?" Saya asked her cousin as his feet met the planks of the floor, "How did you know that vinegar would hurt her?"

Instead of answering, Folken gestured at the door to the hatch and it fell to again seal the contents of the cellar away from above ground. That cylinder again revealed itself from his forearm.

As he busied himself burying the hatch under every rock and stone they had moved before, Harbenigyr answered the woman's question for the sorcerer.

"Vinegar is a cleansing agent," he explained, "A creature like that, with some form of spiritual possession or corruption in the body would react to it like we would to acid. I wish I had thought of that."

"Is it dead, then?" Saya turned for the partially collapsed doorway.

"It is not," Folken took his turn to answer, "That was not nearly enough for a creature of even Hero's diminutive stature."

"Which is why he barricaded her down there," Josie finished the thought for the green haired man as she pulled Harby up onto his slipper covered feet.

"We need to return to Laeradr." Folken followed his sister out of the demolished building, "You do remember Hero mentioning that her *sisters* intended to turn Ophelia into another of their brood?"

"But surely, with her blinking ability she would be immune to–" Saya started to say.

"We cannot count on an ability we do not fully understand," her cousin interrupted, "As this curse is of a demonic origin, it is more powerful than most every mortal incantation or enchantment."

"Then we don't have any time to lose," Harbenigyr said as he stepped past the svartalfar before suddenly stopping, "Where is Triton?"

"And our horses," Josie added, her sapphire eyes scanning around the area.

"How many women do you figure live in Laeradr, Folken?" Harbenigyr's face tightened into a mask of worry and fear.

"Several dozen," the svartalfar man answered, "All women. And all surely penanggalan like Hero."

"There's no way the bodies of five people would be able to feed that many over an entire winter," Josie ran her tongue over her suddenly dry lips.

Saya felt a shiver run along her spine, "That man who said the Jaded Woods were haunted. Didn't he say that he saw a woman's head floating around?"

The ranger didn't look back at the other woman as she nodded, "With the way Hero looked, I'd say that her head could have been described as floating."

"But he wouldn't have been any deeper than the south end of the forest," Harbenigyr added, "We're well into the northern part."

"That means that the penanggalans have been hunting throughout the forest for animal and person alike," Folken concluded.

Josie stepped onto the worn out road, kneeling down to examine the indentations in the dirt. There had been a lot of activity up here since they climbed underground. She looked up and down the road, her crimson hair spilling over her shoulders more and more with each motion, as she tried to make sense of all the signs she was reading. Finally, she stood up and pointed toward where the road bent south.

"The horses went that way," she shared her conclusions with the party, "In a hurry. There are some boot prints, too, but I can't tell which way they were going."

"We'd best hope our steeds are still alive," Folken started down the road along with the rest of the party, "Otherwise there will be little chance of us getting back into Laeradr in time to prevent Ophelia from being changed."

With that added motivation, Saya and Josie ran ahead of Harby and Folken only to skid to a halt in the middle of the road less than a minute later. Four women were hunched over or kneeling just outside of the ruins of what, if the ranger recalled from the notes she read, was the home of the town elder. The women swarmed around the prone body of Josie's chocolate and turquoise colored horse.

The ranger's breath caught in her throat, "I'm so sorry, Noesis."

She felt her eyes start to sting but Josie had to remember that this wasn't the time to mourn. Even if she had known her horse longer than all the people around her combined.

On the opposite side of the road (Josie had no idea what building the stones there had once been) five more gathered around the black form of another horse. From this angle, the ranger couldn't tell if it was Saya or Folken's steed.

The men caught up to the Saya and Josie in short order. When they saw what the women had stumbled upon, the pale sorcerer let loose a quiet curse.

"All my liquor was packed away in those saddlebags," he shook his head.

Josie had a thought that having the alcohol on Folken's horse was to hide it from Ophelia, who the alphan saw first hand very much enjoyed getting drunk. It should have brought a smile, smirk, or something to her face but it didn't. Not with one of her oldest friends lying dead only a short walk away.

"Now what do we do?" Harbenigyr whispered, "Weren't we Ophelia's only hope of not becoming a monster?"

Even though he was quiet, all nine women looked up from the two dead horses. They all did so at the mention of Ophelia.

Every one of their faces were smeared with blood. From this distance, Josie and the others could see all of them open their mouths wider than they should have been able, with blood and half-chewed pieces of raw meat tumbling out.

As they rose to their feet, the ranger noticed something else. The women were all backwards. The ones straightening up had their chests pointing toward the dark sky. Three were faster than the rest, rushing toward the party, stepping toe to heel as they ran in reverse.

"Run!" Folken commanded.

No one argued. After Hero barely noticing getting hit by three arrows, it was a safe bet that these penanggalans were just as resilient.

The group went back the way they came. When they reached the half-demolished building where they entrapped Hero, the pile of stones still laid undisturbed. So at least one threat was still contained.

Folken stepped in front of Harbenigyr, stopping him in his tracks mid-step, "Cleric, that list stated that the main stowage for the town's stock was two blocks east of here, yes?"

"Y-yeah. I think so," the elf nodded, "I think it's still standing, too."

He pointed to the worn corner of a building that looked, at least from here, to be mostly intact. It was only about fifty yards away. But the monsters giving chase were closing the distance while they were just standing there.

Josie pointed that out to them as she stepped behind everyone and loosed a barrage of arrows at the penanggalan.

"What use is that?" Saya snapped as she started after her cousin, "You know it doesn't hurt them."

"I'm aiming for their feet," Josie said as she let another arrow fly, "They can't walk if they're pinned to the ground. It may give us a little time."

While impaling an Achilles tendon didn't appear to hurt them, one monster woman fell when she couldn't lift her foot from the ground and lost her balance. Another was already reaching down to break the thin length of wood stopping her when Josie simply shot her other foot.

Then Josie hit one more penanggalan with an arrow that drove through the woman's knee and down into the foot of her other leg. She tumbled to the ground and took one other down into the dirt with her.

"Good thinking," Harbenigyr said to the ranger after one last shot, "But we'll need every second to get there now!"

He wrapped his hands around the ranger's bare shoulders and pulled her after the svartalfar. The run was short but both Harby and Josie were out of breath when they ran through the door and into the building. Folken slammed the door shut, dropping the heavy board of wood that would have served that duty back in the village's heyday back in place on the black iron struts. The door was locked.

"Josie, Saya, make sure any other possible points of entry are sealed," the sorcerer ordered, "Harbenigyr, come with me."

The women nodded, rushing off to opposite sides of their makeshift fortress. Folken, with the cleric in tow, started for the back. The svartalfar man let out a pleased sounding grunt upon finding another hatch much like the one that held the spoiled wine where they left Hero.

Against the back wall was a line of large cupboards, each big enough to hold a member of the party inside with room to spare. Most were collapsed but the four closest to the men were still intact. Folken stepped away from the hatch and straight toward those.

"Those wouldn't be very good hiding places," Harby objected, pointing at the closed hatch, "Wouldn't we have a better chance barricading ourselves down there? None of the other cellars are connected to this one according to the maps."

"Indeed, cleric, these are poor places to hide," Folken said as he pulled one cupboard open to find it empty.

He moved on to the next. Before he opened it, both Josie and Saya returned.

"The windows are barely wide enough for me to shoot through," the ranger reported, "Unless they can make themselves flat, they aren't getting in that way."

"Same on my side," Saya said, "It's as if they wanted to make this a defensible position."

"They did," The green haired svartalfar answered as he opened the next cupboard. "Most villages that depend on a single commodity often store their wares where they can be defended from raiders to ensure survival of the community."

"It worked wonders for them here," Saya asserted with an unamused sigh.

"Whatever caused this town's demise, it was not some raid by a rival hamlet," Folken replied, "I would wager that it had something to do with our long necked friends outside."

The sorcerer opened the third cupboard to reveal an old suit of armor. Considering how long it had been in there, it was in remarkably good shape with only some tarnish along the where the right pauldron connected to the top of the breastplate.

"Here we go," Folken said at the sight of the steel, "Harbenigyr, I need you to put that on."

"What? Me?" the cleric stared at the other man in shock.

"I've no time to explain, cleric," the sorcerer turned to the ranger, "Help him with this or force him," he ordered.

A confused Josie pulled the suit of armor off the rack it sat upon, a beastly shriek echoed from above. Looking up, the entire party took in the vision of all nine penanggalan crawling over the top edge of the wall, which was over thirty feet high.

Then the first monster over the edge dropped down to the floor in front of Josie, Saya, Folken, and Harbenigyr. She rose to her feet unscathed, her head unsheathing from her neck until her head hung upside down in the air like a horrific lantern.

"You never said they could that," Saya gasped as the other monsters followed her down inside the walls.

"I didn't know they could do that," Folken scowled back.

OPHELIA INTERROGATION NOTES:

I took the paper back. As I straightened out the growing stack, I spoke again.

"You're trying to distract me again, Ophelia."

"Why would I do that?" the subject asked.

"Perhaps because of the little secret you kept from Harbenigyr and the others?" I said.

"I don't know what you mean," the subject was unconvincing in her protest.

"Allow me to refresh your memory then," I said, "Let's see. We were still in the basement..."

Back in Laeradr...

"YOUR SCENT HAS already awakened our sisters' hunger, Ophelia," Miranda said as she closed the distance between herself and the mercenary.

Ophelia felt her left hand throb as blood spilled down her fingers. The slightest shift of her weight caused a rush of dizzying pain from her dislocated right shoulder, that arm was useless.

"My scent? You do realize that smelling people isn't exactly a nice way to greet someone, right?" Ophelia grunted... and something the blacksmith said finally processed, "Wait, sisters? More than just you and big floating head?"

Bianca's disembodied face snarled back at the mercenary in response. Ramming that stake down her torso may not have hurt her but it sure did put her floating skull into a surly mood.

Miranda nodded, still inching closer to Ophelia, "All of us awoke when the ritual started."

"The ritual?" the tattooed human shuffled along the back wall until she was in front of the box that contained Havarti and her leather coat, "What ritual? All that's happened is Bianca literally falling to pieces in front of us."

"Not all, Ophelia," the town's mayor held up the reddish brown disk between her thumb and forefinger, "I've blessed this to ready it for you. Now the rest of the pack is hunting for nourishment as we speak."

"Nourishment?" Ophelia didn't like the sound of that.

"Your compatriots," Bianca's buzzing voice clarified the human's suspicions for her.

Great. Not only was she being threatened with turning into just about the ugliest kind of monster she could imagine, but Ophelia had to figure out a way to kill an entire village full of monsters that found decapitation to be a minor irritant at worst. That was practically the mercenary's specialty so that was a problem.

"Okay, so you're going to eat my friends," the lone human nodded at the wafer in Miranda's hand, "So how is that supposed to make me one of... what do you call yourselves again?"

Neither Ophelia nor Havarti had any ideas of how to get out of this situation. All the woman could do was try and stall, hoping some inspiration would strike.

"I call this a sacrificial wafer," the blacksmith answered, "I made it from the blood of my daughter."

"Your daughter? I never saw any kids around here," Ophelia forced herself to breath slowly through another surge of pain from her shoulder.

"I killed her years ago," Miranda shrugged, "To make myself into a penanggalan."

"That has to be the stupidest name I've ever heard. Penanggalan." the sword woman scoffed.

"Madam Oyotsu showed me how to do it," the mayor continued as if Ophelia had never spoken, "The town elders found out that I had tampered with the shipment of stoppers for the last year's batch of wine. They were going to send me to some penal colony in the mountains. Can you imagine that? Me picking rocks out of some random mine?"

"What town elders?" Ophelia asked, blinking hard, "Your *the* town elder."

Ophelia was starting to feel the main problem behind her stalling tactic. She was beginning to feel lethargic, standing was becoming a tremendous effort, and the room was starting to spin. If she was going to do anything to save herself, it had to be very, very soon.

"Not this town, silly," Miranda snickered, "No, the last town, Odoshift. The ruins your friends are wandering in now."

"I take it back, *that* is the stupidest name I've ever heard," Ophelia groaned.

"Anyway, Madam Oyotsu felt that the punishment was disproportionate to the crime and wanted to help me right the wrong," Miranda kept talking, "My daughter was going to be ostracized by the other villagers with me gone anyway, so I thought it better to send her off on my terms rather than theirs."

"So you killed her because she would have been mocked?" Ophelia felt her knees waver.

"My dear," the voice of Havarti popped into her mind, "I think they have been stalling as well. Waiting for you to bleed out to the point that you can no longer resist."

"I noticed that, too," the fading mercenary muttered.

"A daughter needs her mother!" Miranda snapped, "Without me, who knows what kind of shrew she would turn out to be!"

"Yeah, you're a pinnacle of maternal grace," Ophelia felt her eyelids start to drop by their own will and she directed her next words to Havarti telepathically, "This is it, lover. We'll just have to improvise."

When her eyes closed, Miranda took that as the opening for which she was waiting. She lunged toward the mercenary, reaching out with the wafer of dried blood.

Ophelia dropped her left elbow into the top of the box imprisoning her sword with all her weight behind it. It wasn't difficult. She was having trouble staying upright anyway.

The wooden boards shattered and the box tumbled to the floor with the woman. The mercenary struck the packed dirt hard, her dislocated arm feeling as if it was being wrenched off her body.

The narrow end of Havarti's cross guard fell into Ophelia's side, feeling like a cold finger pressed between her ribs. The box followed, smashing into the bastard sword.

Havarti cried out in horror as he realized that he was being driven into Ophelia like a nail by a hammer. The woman's eyes shot wide open as the new pain washed through her.

She saw Miranda's approaching hand, the dried blood of her murdered daughter coming right for Ophelia's face. Then the mercenary was suddenly sitting on Bianca's prone body. The town's mayor tumbled to the ground right on top of the pile of splintered wood where the other woman had been moments before.

Still getting her bearings, Ophelia looked around. Miranda still had her back to the mercenary. Ophelia looked behind herself and there were the stairs up and out of the house.

"Go, my dear," Havarti said telepathically, "Find the others and run away! There is nothing they can do to me."

Before Ophelia could even think of a reply, the formerly still body of Bianca reached up and started blindly grabbing at the sword woman. In reflex, Ophelia's right hand shot down to punch the headless body in the chest. Blood and other fluids squirted out of the base of her neck to coat the entrails that still hung loose from her body.

She smiled. Her arm was back in its joint. Her blinking had healed that as if it never happened. Ophelia grabbed one of Bianca's wrists with her left hand and wrenched the monster's hand away from getting a grip on her.

Her main hand hurt but the wound that split her palm in tween was clotted over and she had use of her fingers. Ophelia could fight again.

"No," the voice of her bastard sword came again, "Get away from here! We've do idea how to kill them!"

Miranda noticed wrestling match between Bianca's body and Ophelia. She stood up, taking a moment to observe the scene, before making her way toward the lone human.

"Don't you dare, you fustilarian!" Havarti yelled out loud.

Miranda would have ignored him if the sword hadn't started violently shaking, sending shards of wood underfoot. Just as she turned to order the blade to calm itself, Havarti had built up enough momentum to bounce over and slam himself across her knee. The blacksmith howled in pain as she dropped, clutching at her freshly bruised leg.

Slamming her own knee into Bianca's side, Ophelia felt the satisfying snap of several ribs. As the monster woman's body froze in shock, the mercenary took her chance to roll off and grab the bastard sword.

Leaping to her feet, she charged straight for the stairs, "We'll go find Folken and Harby. Between the two of them, we should be able to figure out how to get out of this," She jabbered as she started up.

Ophelia's body abruptly froze. She was barely halfway of the steps but couldn't move.

A new pain made itself known. In her neck. The back of her neck. It felt as if all the vertebrae were being squeezed in a vice.

Not only that. There was a ripping pain, like she was being bitten hard enough to draw blood. Ophelia let out a quiet apology to her sword but nothing crossed her lips.

"Very good, Bia," Miranda still sounded pained but she was back on her feet.

Ophelia could hear the monster woman limping up the wooden steps behind her. One of the calloused hands of the blacksmith wrapped around the mercenary's bare shoulder.

Bianca's disembodied head kept gnawing on the back of Ophelia's neck, keeping her from being able to move somehow. She let out little moans of pleasure as her teeth dug into the woman's flesh, just a little deeper, with each nibble.

Miranda turned Ophelia around to face her, "I didn't realize that you would be so much trouble," Despite her words, the monster woman was smiling, "This means that, someday, you may just be able to start a coven of your own."

The penanggalan pressed the dried blood waver to Ophelia's forehead. After the initial scratchiness of the hard scab pushing against her skin, what felt like tendrils or plant roots dug into her, through the bone of her skull as if it was barely any obstacle. Then her vision started to blur as the pressure wrapped around her brain. It felt like she was being crushed.

"No, my dear, fight it!" Havarti hollered in her mind. "I can feel things changing. Don't let them. You're strong, Ophelia! You can resis–" And the voice of her sword was gone.

Ophelia couldn't hear him anymore. Tears rolled out of her eyes as she felt even his presence fall away from her. Havarti was nothing but a lump of steel in her hand now.

"I sacrificed my flesh and blood daughter for revenge," Miranda started speaking again, "As a result, I have a bigger family than I could have ever dreamed. You are my newest, beautiful baby daughter, Ophelia."

Miranda leaned in and kissed the mercenary's cheek tenderly. Then the pain in Ophelia's neck stopped. Bianca's upside down, floating head circled around in front of Ophelia, licking at the sword woman's blood that dribbled out of her mouth, up her nose and down between her eyes.

That was the first time Ophelia noticed that, while the prehensile tongue and the unnaturally wide mouth seemed so pleased with themselves that the blonde woman's eyes, they looked confused. About what, the mercenary couldn't even pretend to guess.

"You'll need some time to adjust, of course," Miranda continued, "You'll blossom within the hour. Whatever remains of your friends, we will reintroduce you to them and you can have your first proper meal."

OPHELIA INTERROGATION NOTES:

"No!" Ophelia interrupted my review, "That's old news!"

"Of course, but it did lead to the events that snowballed into the catastrophe we're here to discuss," I said.

"That catastrophe involved Apple and Phinegann's group," the subject replied, "No one in Laeradr was there."

"True," I agreed, "Shall we review the gnome's testimony on how they came to escape the tunnels?"

"Illyria," the subject said.

"Excuse me?" I asked.

"The gnome has a name," the subject said. "It's Illyria."

Decades later...

THANKFULLY, THE TUNNEL they found and decided to continue their trek through was nowhere near as narrow as the first ones the group traversed through. That didn't mean that they were spacious by any stretch but the light from Illyria's wings couldn't reach the other side of the tunnel. The opposite wall could have been yards away or mere inches but at least it was enough of a comfort to Phinegann that he didn't appear to be bordering on going berserk like earlier.

The vision of him taking such a big bite out of that other orc's neck, almost taking the head completely off his shoulders, still haunted Illyria. She did her best to ignore it, of course. Phinegann was their protector and while what happened was horrible, it also ultimately led to the four of them being able to progress.

"Are we there yet?" the gnome groaned.

She may have been the main source of light for the group but she was third in line of the procession that had settled into Phinegann in the lead. He kept his flesh hand pressed against the wall just to their left. He must have been taught, like most people, that if you stick close to one wall you would eventually solve whatever labyrinth you would find yourself in.

Tokki was right on his heels. Illyria, keeping her wings pointed ahead, made sure to aim them just above the shoulders of the two in front of her. That was much easier with the Bunny Barbarian, who was quite a bit shorter than the orc (although he was still much taller than the gnome.) This was decided after Phinegann mentioned that he didn't want to have his night vision reduced by having Illyria's lights waving around in front of him. Tokki immediately agreed with him, which wasn't much of a shock.

Appelonia stayed back with the smaller woman, actually liking being able to see what was in front of her. If she did become needed in a fight, her bow and arrow was better from a distance anyway. Mostly, it was because neither she nor Illyria enjoyed the endless prattling of the barbarian about battle history, battle strategy, battle this, or battle that. Phinegann, at least, seemed to tolerate it best of the rest of them.

"Do you think this will actually lead us anywhere?" the cleric, her voice just above a whisper asked, "It feels like we've been walking around in a big circle."

"I noticed that myself," Illyria looked back and up at the taller woman, "That's why I started dropping beads along the path."

"You did? When?" Apple blinked in surprise.

"About twenty minutes ago, according to my chronometer," the winged woman held up her left arm, with a strap of leather wrapped around the wrist that had a round piece of glass embedded in it that looked like it was about to slip out and tumble to the ground.

"What's a chronometer?" the red haired elf scratched at her cheek.

"It's like a clepsydra, only it doesn't need water and I can carry it," Illyria smiled proudly.

"So it tells time," It may have came out as a statement but it felt as if Apple wanted confirmation.

"Yup," the inventor gnome provided it.

"Then can you tell me how long we've been stuck down here?" the young elf blew an errant strand of crimson hair out of her face.

"I didn't think to look until we were in this," Illyria motioned to the tunnel they were in as they turned yet another hard left, "But, if I'm right, we should be coming up on the first bead I dropped right... about..." she moved one of her lower lights to the dusty floor, "now."

And the woman who was barely half as tall as the elf stopped just short of kicking a polished black rock on the ground. Beside it, though, was a bead that was made of swirled together green and purple glass. Illyria's toes wiggled with excitement in her sandals, even though the meaning of this realization was far from happy.

"Guys, hold up!" Appelonia called after the two men still walking ahead, "We've been walking in a big circle all this time!"

"What?" Phinegann's gruff voice echoed in the tunnel as he and Tokki walked back toward the women, "What are you talking about?"

Appelonia pointed at the bead at the feet of the gnome, "Illyria dropped this about twenty minutes ago, right?" she looked back at the winged woman.

Illyria nodded, her short violet hair bobbing with the motion.

"Twenty minutes?" Tokki wrapped his bare hand around the hooks the cleric had given him to repair the harness of his claw sleeve, at least temporarily. "But we've been walking for at least two hours."

"More like three," Phinegann interjected.

The Bunny Barbarian continued, "But we have made right turns as well as lefts. If we are going in circles, should we not have seen the tunnel that dumped us in here then?"

"Not if it's on the other side of the cave," Appelonia pointed at the shadows to the right.

Phinegann let out a long, slow grunt as he tugged at the black and red hair on his jaw, "Your solution?" he finally asked.

Apple opened her mouth to answer when she suddenly realized that she didn't have one. She turned to look at Illyria, who had bent down to pick up her bead.

She didn't even notice everyone staring at her until she was standing back up and had tucked the little glass sphere into her pocket, rather than trying to thread it onto the thin tuft of hair she pulled all the beads she used from earlier. When Illyria did see everyone, it took her a moment to remember the subject at hand.

After all, she had already figured out they were going in circle. She already started trying to figure out how to offset the growing heat from her wings. They weren't designed to do this for so such an extended time. The glass could crack if this went on much longer.

A long silence hang over the group. Illyria could practically watch Phinegann's patience physically shrink as his eyes (for the first time she noticed that his right appeared to be permanently bloodshot) stayed on her. It was Appelonia, though, who finally spoke first.

"You figured out our problem, Illy." she said, "Do you have any ideas on how to get us out?"

"There are two ways I can think of," the gnome answered, "We can switch what wall we follow and see what new information that gives us."

"If Appelonia's right, that should at least show us the tunnel we came from," Tokki nodded at the cleric.

Illyria caught herself grinning, as if she learned a secret no one else knew (that was completely unrelated to the job at hand so was filed away for later), and continued, "Or we can turn around."

"What would that do?" Phinegann scowled.

The tiny woman fluttered her wings so that she was roughly at the same eye level as the rest of the tall people, "You see these striations on the wall?"

She ran her hand into a long horizontally carved line that stretched as far back and forward along the the wall as far as the party could see in their limited light. It wasn't the only one.

Lines like it covered the wall from the dusty floor up to the ceiling. They stretched up and down and far ahead and back as the light could made visible for the party. The grooves were far too shallow to use as hand holds or footholds to climb, not that there was anywhere to go (at least in this part of the tunnel) anyway.

"What about them?" the orc idly scratched at the wall.

"They aren't here naturally," Illyria said, "If someone took the time to carve them, that means that they are here for a purpose."

Tokki Yo Bunpy shrugged at the gnome, "And what would that be?"

Illyria fluttered back down to the ground, "Think like a puzzle maker, bunny-man. You don't want people to be able to get through your maze but everyone knows how to beat one now. That's what Phinegann's been doing almost the whole time we've been here."

The retired prison guard was trying to decide if the small winged woman had just insulted him. He still hadn't made up his mind (admittedly, it wasn't much time) when she continued.

"So they didn't make a maze," she proudly declared.

Again, there was only silence. This time, it was the Bunny Barbarian to break it.

"What did 'they' make, then?"

"What did I tell you to think like?" Illyria grinned wide, "They made a puzzle!"

"Making me remember something specific you told me earlier to figure out your question," Tokki waved a finger in the air as if he were writing on some unseen parchment, "Wouldn't that have been more of a riddle?"

Everyone groaned at that. Whether it was from annoyance or impatience depended on the person.

"Anyway, you people have your heads too close to the roof," the violet haired short woman said, "All these lines look right to you. From down here, everything has seemed a bit... off. Now that I know what to look for, I think I can get us out of here!"

"Then should we switch walls or go backwards?" Appelonia repeated Illyria's previous options to the gnome.

"Why, both, of course," the tiny woman strode over to the opposite wall.

Placing her left hand on the cold stone, she waited for the others to join her as she faced the opposite direction. Surprisingly, Phinigann was the first to step over. He pressed his hand to the wall where he stood right behind Illyria.

"What if some kind of beast appears?" Tokki motioned to the gnome as he spoke to Phinegann, "Would she not be in danger?"

Appelonia rested a hand on the Bunny Barbarian's bare shoulder as she stepped past him to the other wall, "Just because you can fight doesn't mean you always have to take the lead, Tokki."

The orc nodded, "She has the plan, she takes point."

Tokki stepped into line, next to the wall right behind Appelonia. When she looked back over her shoulder at him, he smiled awkwardly before resting his hand on a carved line about shoulder high.

They started back in the direction they had come from. Unlike the limited view of light they had before due to Illyria having to point around two muscular warriors, particularly the massive Phinegann, much more light filled the tunnel ahead. Especially since Illy let the wings change direction as the group walked.

After a few minutes, the gnome stopped, "This is kind of giving me a headache," she muttered.

"Are you declaring defeat then?" Tokki chimed in from the back.

"Phin, could you hand this to her, please?" Apple handed the orc a shaving of willow bark... and then elbowed the barbarian in the stomach.

It wasn't hard enough to do any real damage but it did elicit a pleasing "oof!" out of him. Illyria giggled as she slipped the offered medicine between her lips.

"Not defeat, bunny-man," the gnome said as she chewed, "Just taking a break. You would, too, if everything didn't look right."

"I'm still not sure what you mean by things not looking right," he replied.

"All these lines were made to make it look like all the walls are solid and line up perfectly." Appelonia explained for the shorter woman as they started walking again, "But they were carved by someone around our height, so it's to our perspective. Illy's quite a bit shorter so the lines don't quite match up for her."

"How would that cause a headache?" Tokki sounded genuinely curious now.

"Because the lines are made to trick the eyes," Appelonia explained, "Her brain knows something's off with the perspective but her eyes are instinctively trying to force them to make sense."

"So she's getting conflicting information," the barbarian nodded, "Like a feint in battle. You want the enemy think the wrong thing and react one way so that you can take the advantage."

The cleric sighed. They had actually gone a few minutes without him relating something being said to fighting up till then. Still, he wasn't completely wrong so Appelonia nodded back.

"Devious," Tokki commented.

They only had to go for another minute or so before Illyria flapped her wings and hopped into the air. She only stayed up for a moment before dropping back to the ground. Then she shuffled from one side of the tunnel, to the other, and back.

"I think I found the way out," she announced, "It's easier to see coming from this way then the way we came by before."

"Meaning that these lines were likely made for coming from that direction," Appelonia added.

"Yup," Illyria confirmed.

"How could they know which way people would go in their circle?" Phinegann asked.

"Remember how we could never find the way we came in?" the winged gnome recalled, "It was hidden by the lines. We could probably find it easily if we kept going this way."

"How do you know this isn't it?" Tokki pointed at the now visible gap in the wall.

"Based on where my first bead dropped, I figure we on the far side of where the entrance is," Illyria answered, "I think."

"You think?" Both Appelonia and the Bunny Barbarian quipped at the same time.

"Only one way to know for sure!" the winged woman grinned back and started for the gap.

It definitely didn't lead back to the room they encountered Doctor Efreeti. It was just another tunnel and it was small. As small as the first ones they had come across after they awoke in this subterranean place.

Phinegann paused where the larger cave and the smaller tunnel met. His face looked as if it was molded out of iron. Even the furry chops on his cheeks didn't move.

"You can do this, Phin," Appelonia assured him, "It's small but it has to lead somewhere. Maybe even back to the surface. No walls or ceilings up there."

Appelonia looked back at Tokki, the confidence in her voice not reflected in her face. Tokki nodded, taking his turn to be reassuring.

Phinegann's breath came in short, growl filled burst before he finally hunched as stepped into the tightly spaced tunnel. They didn't walk far, maybe one hundred paces. Then the space opened up into an antechamber that even Phinegann couldn't feel cramped in.

Torches ran all around the circular room making the room as bright as midday. Illyria turned off the lights in her wings, thin wisps of steam escaping from the tips where the metal frame and the kaleidoscopic colored glass met.

They weren't alone anymore. There was a man sitting on the far side, in front of a large door, like the ones that led into the keep of Dianmeyer.

There were also doors to the left and right in the walls, but each of them had thick black bars stretched across them in random patterns. Even if they weren't laid out with any kind of system, they still effectively blocked those doors from being able to open.

As they walked closer, it became more apparent that the man was not exactly that. While he was roughly human sized, his fingers looked more like the paws of a massive striped cat, albeit with fingers that still ended with claws. His head was the same, much like the striped cinsing tigers that Illyria once saw in a traveling circus.

He was wearing the finest pearl necklace with a gold medallion hanging of it, resting on top of a fine silk shirt that was tucked into an equally fine pair of maroon satin pants. He didn't even look up as the four people approached. He was far too enveloped in what he was doing with his hands which, as far as any of them could tell, was finding new and interesting ways to interlace his fuzzy fingers.

They all looked at each other as they realized they were being summarily ignored. They silently argued over who should try to speak to the feline person. Phinegann refused, he was one to send when the situation either needed to prevent violence or, as more likely happened, required it. Tokki was just a smaller version of the second reason why the orc shouldn't be their initial introduction. Illyria, she barely came up to the being's knees while he was sitting, leaning back in his lashed together wood chair.

Finally, both Phinegann and Illyria pushed Appelonia forward to be their spokesperson. Her boots scraped against the sand that made up the floor in this room as she tried to resist by standing firm. Once she was alone in front of the cat-like man, she realized her opposition was all for naught. But not until then.

The cleric bit down on her lower lip, having no idea of what to say, "Um, pardon me?" she finally said.

Looking back at the others, they were hardly impressed at her initial introduction. Still, they waved her on to keep trying.

"Excuse me, sir, is this the way out?" Appelonia started again, "Could you please allow us to pass?"

"Have you the right to pass?" the cat-man replied, not looking up from his hands.

His accent was thick, from a land that Illyria wasn't familiar with. Still, at least he was understandable. Unlike those miners she met from the Griffin Mountains. They claimed to speak her language but it was like they were doing so through a mouthful of gruel.

At least kitty-guy's voice had a charming lilt where it seemed like he was about to roll his tongue with every other syllable and his inflection at the end of every word was almost like he was asking a question. Making the fact that he actually asked a question all the more convenient.

The cleric shrugged back at the others. She had no idea how to answer. Illyria shrugged back, Phinegann didn't say or do anything, but Tokki Yo Bunpy nodded.

"We aren't sure how we came to be here in the first place, sir," Apple said after she turned back to face the feline man, "We are only seeking a way to return home."

Only after she said that did the yellow eyes of the man look up, "To return home, eh? Aren't sure how you came to be here, eh?" he turned his head and spat into the dirt, "No one comes here by accident, child. You are simply here for one reason, to make recompense."

"Recompense?" Appelonia's brow furrowed, "To whom? Who are we supposed to have wronged?"

"To be here you must have disobeyed the will of the great Mullah Junaperqollanijuna or that of one of his vassals. It is the same," he returned his attention to his interweaving digits.

Each of the party members frowned as they envisioned Genevieve in their mind's eye. Appelonia sighed, running her hands up and down her face a couple of times before speaking again.

"I think that all we have here is a misunderstanding," she said, "The efreeti woman we were talking to made this portal that we fell through. I don't understand how you can disobey someone's will when we obviously went through the portal she made."

"You did not wish to go?" the feline guard dropped his paws to his lap.

"No, no we didn't," Appelonia answered, "A friend of mine said something that she misconstrued as a wish and we were separated."

"Unfortunate," the kitty-guy replied, "As you are in the Nova Omega, the end of all things. There is no appeal when you come here."

Appelonia thought for a long moment, "Then how do we make recompense? What do we do to obtain forgiveness for our slight and gain the right to pass, as you put it?"

"There are three ways of righting your wrongs, child," Kitty-guy leaned forward in his seat, dropping the front legs down into the sand, "The first is the easiest. Simply remove an offending limb as a sacrifice to show your repentance," For the first time, he looked back at the rest of the party, his predatory eyes falling onto Phinegann, "He will not be eligible, as he already knows that pain."

Appelonia looked back to Phinegann, who merely grunted, and back to the cat man, "What's the second option?"

"Spill all the blood from one as your as champion for the others," he explained, "One must stay for the others to leave."

"That's not going to happen," Appelonia declared.

Illyria agreed, as did Phinegann. Tokki Yo Bunpy became very quiet.

"That leaves you with the third option then," the feline guard sighed, "Ritual combat. If you defeat one of our champions, you show the pride of your convictions and may leave."

"I'll take that option," Tokki interjected.

Illyria rolled her eyes, so did the cleric. Of course that would be the option he'd pick.

Appelonia spun on her heels and dug a finger into the Bunny Barbarian's chest, "Are you crazy? You don't even know what kind of monsters they have here! Do you just have to pick a fight wherever you go?"

"You heard the beast," Tokki argued, "This is the only viable option. I can take on whatever they send. I best it, we are free. If I die, you can use my blood for the second option. See? Either way you can leave."

"Don't you dare make this about helping me, Tokki Yo Bunpy!" Appelonia fumed, "You've been itching for a fight since you missed the one with Abernathy the day you came to Dianmeyer."

"I seek glory for my people and my family, cleric of Kuan Yin," he wrapped his hands around her wrist, pressing her hand to his chest, right over the hooks she usually used to suture wounds closed. "You seek it by serving others through medicines and prayer. I can do so by allowing you to return to your duty. By doing standing against their champion."

"You are certain that you wish to take this option?" Kitty-guy picked at something between his fangs with a curved claw.

"Yes, I wish it," Tokki stepped away from Appelonia and toward the cat man, "I with to do battle with your champion!"

"Very well," Kitty-guy pointed at the left door with the same finger he picked his teeth, "You and your friends will face an efreeti of strength proportionate to your slight."

"Wait, I said that I would face your champion," Tokki objected, "I meant to do it alone."

"To get out via combat, all who wish to leave must fight," the cat man shrugged.

The black bars that were strewn in front of the door each fell away, tumbling into the sand in little clouds of dust. The immense doors opened and in slithered a twenty foot tall woman.

At least her head and torso were human. She had six arms that ended with six-fingered hands that held curved scimitars easily as tall as Phinegann. From her hips down was the body of a snake with amethyst colored scales.

As she made her way to the middle of the antechamber, Illyria realized that this wasn't some random room in a system of caves. This was an arena. That meant that there were likely other efreeti demons looking down on the proceedings like it was a game, only they were out of reach of the torchlight.

A rattling sound filled the air and the gnome noticed it coming from the back of the massive tail of the she-demon. As the thing loosed a heavy breath of fire up into the air, Illyria and Appelonia looked at each other.

"If this is proportionate to whatever slight we pulled, what do they give someone who really wronged whoever this Mullah is?" Appelonia wondered.

"Do you wish to find out?" Kitty-guy inquired.

"NO!" Both Appelonia and Illyria screamed.

"Then say hello to Marilith!" the feline man announced.

OPHELIA INTERROGATION NOTES

"But, of course, you are not the only one who held back, shall we say, important part of the truth," I said.

"So who are you bad mouthing this time?" the subject asked.

"As one of the highest ranking members of the Romefeller Guild, Folken is not one to face accountability for his actions often," I answered.

Ophelia reluctantly nodded, "Did you have a specific omitted detail in mind?"

"We need only look to how he planned to escape the penanggalans that surrounded him, Saya, and Harbenigyr," I held up his marked testimony.

Decades before...

FOLKEN BENT DOWN, pulling the trap door open without taking his violet eyes off the monsters in front of him and Saya. Josie held the armor for Harbenigyr in her hands for... some reason, yet neither moved. The door that had been intended to hold them out now served to keep the party trapped inside with them.

"Josie, continue helping the cleric into that cuirass. It is imperative to my plan," the sorcerer barked at the alphan ranger.

Both Harby and Josie looked at the man in confusion but only for a moment. The woman pulled the breastplate from the cupboard and turned to the cleric.

"Take off your tunic," she said, letting the interior shirt made of linked chainmail slip out of the steel cuirass. "and lift your arms."

The elf felt his cheeks turn bright pink as he did just as the woman ordered. She had already seen him in little more than a loincloth before so he wasn't sure why this was so embarrassing to him. Likely because he didn't have a choice before when he was barely conscious and injured.

Harbenigyr wasn't one to parade around half-clothed usually. Despite the dangers, he had to fight that self-consciousness back just to take his shirt off in front of Josie.

The woman had a moment of pause when Harby straightened up in front of her with his tunic removed. Josie hadn't notice when she helped him limp out to the tournament grounds back in Dracoleaf, but, while he was thin, the muscles of the cleric were well formed. She shook her head clear. This was hardly the time to get distracted.

The chainmail draped onto the cleric easily enough, just like a heavy shirt. Pulling the bent steel of the cuirass apart, Josie slipped it over Harbenigyr's head, accidentally raking one edge of the split collar over one of his pointed ears. He stayed quiet but couldn't help flinching at the painful sensation.

"Sorry," Josie's cheeks flushed as she stepped up close to the cleric, her chest pressing against the cold metal of the breastplate as she hurriedly tightened the buckles on either side, "We'll get this properly fitted for you later."

As the surface elves were playing dress up, the svartalfar noblewoman turned to the Great Chancellor of the Romefeller Guild. In too short of a time, all nine that had been pursuing them outside landed inside the building.

"Whatever your plan is, cousin, now is a good time to unleash it," Saya commented.

None of the party even thought to see if the rooftop was intact when they first entered. Nor had they considered that the penanggalan would be capable of scaling a thirty foot wall, especially one worn to the point that the there was no edging to differentiate one brick from another, let alone get a hand or foothold.

Add to that the fact that the monstrous women waited until they were all together again before attacking. They were unnatural creatures, but thinking monsters, not operating solely on instinct as Folken had supposed. That was troublesome, especially to make the next phase of his plan work.

The nine penanggalan women started toward the party but not in one tightly formed group. No, they spread out just as slowly as they advanced, making sure that there was no direction any of the party could run without coming within reach of either their backwards, distorted hands or spread out maws on sickeningly elongated necks.

Saya had throwing knives in each hand, with the grip of each blade left in the arsenal of her metal arm poking out of the torn black material covering her limb. Neither she nor Folken were sure how much good they would do but neither were willing to die without putting up a fight.

"Toward the hatch," Folken simply stated as he straightened up, pulling his rapier free of the sheathe on his belt with his flesh hand.

The platinum haired woman nodded just as something heavy slammed against the barred door that led outside. She and her equally pale cousin shared wary glances.

The penanggalan paused, too. Whatever was happening, Folken surmised, was not their doing. Something hit the door again and the piece of wood holding it shut splintered. Whatever was making its way inside, it was powerful.

Another hit and the beam of timber fell to the floor in two pieces. While the rest of the monsters couldn't stop staring at the buckling door, two of the penanggalans regained enough of their senses to charge at Folken and Saya.

Two throwing knives immediately buried themselves into the eyes of one female creature. While one was unscathed, the other should have been blinded. Neither even slowed down as each snapped their jaws at the two svartalfar, who ducked out of the way.

The door finally crumpled and the room was suddenly filled with a pastel blue blur. One monster, and then another fell to the ground. When the party could finally focus on who or what the new arrival was they saw the Bunny Barbarian, Lyan Yo Bunpy. Sje held a penanggalan in the air impaled on the blade of her long spear.

"Throw that down into the hole, Yo Bunpy!" Folken pointed at the wide open hatch in the floor as he pressed his metal hand, suddenly engulfed in flame, against the snapping face of the penanggalan who dared attack him.

The barbarian didn't argue. She stepped over to the trapdoor and stabbed at the hole. The body of the woman on the end of the blade folded in half as the head on the elongated neck shrieked with rage.

It tried to lunge at the barbarian, but the penanggalan's body slid of the end of the rabbit head shaped blade and, when it fell, the cranium couldn't extend its intestine constructed neck fast enough. It couldn't help but follow.

Another of the woman creatures tried sneaking up behind the barbarian, only to double over on the blunt end of Lyan's spear. The seemingly autonomous head, though, lunged at the heavily muscled woman, sinking its sharp teeth into her already scarred and blackened arm.

The other penanggalan started piling on Lyan Yo Bunpy, sure at their sheer number would overwhelm her. Saya was busy stabbing another beast's jaw shut as Folken dumped the charred head of the woman he battled down the hatch, with the body sliding down after it. With Josie struggling with the last buckle on the armor she was putting on the cleric, no one was in a position to come to the rescue of Lyan.

A familiar falcon cry pierced the cold air and Triton came barreling through the door. He charged straight into the pile of monstrous women, scattering them all over the debris ridden floor.

Lyan was revealed, lying on the floor, repeatedly pummeling the head that had latched onto her arm with her sharpened gauntlet. By the time she was finished swinging her arm, the lump of flesh that had been the head of the penanggalan was less than half the size it was before and there was nothing left attached that could have hinted as to what part of the body it had been before.

The body of that penanggalan laid deathly still on the cold floor as Lyan lifted herself to her knees, fresh cuts and bite marks from the mass attack each dribbling blood. Still, the Bunny Barbarian looked undeterred, in fact, she appeared to be enjoying herself as she made it back to her feet.

"Apparently, these things cannot live without their heads," Lyan smirked as she slashed at the entrails holding another monster's head to its body.

At the same time, the massive griffin snapped its beak around the intestines of another penangalan that was acting as an unwanted rider on his back. The head was severed from the body like scissors cutting parchment.

The body mounted atop Triton slipped from its perch and onto the ground sure enough. As did the torso of the penanggalan Lyan slashed apart. But their heads stayed in the air.

The one attacking the griffin sank its teeth into his feathered neck while the other dived straight for the Bunny Barbarian. Lyan swatted the head away with her spear. It flew into the shadows. Then the barbarian threw the spear in Triton's direction. The stylized rabbit head stabbed right through the ear of the monster without a body.

"Simple decapitation will not kill them but my stratagem will!" Then Folken ordered again, "Throw the bodies down the hole!"

Lyan grabbed the body at her feet and lobbed it in the direction of the svartalfar sorcerer. It landed just short of the trapdoor. The penanggalan that was attacking Saya, though, tripped over it and the pale woman guided its fall down into the hatch.

"Done!" Josie yelled to the Romefeller Guilds Grand Chancellor as she stepped away from Harbenigyr.

"It's a little tight," the cleric muttered, pulling at the collar.

"Get the rest of these monsters down into the cellar and then complain," Folken barked.

Harbenigyr used his quarterstaff to keep the monsters at a distance while Josie pinned their feet to the floor with arrows. Saya followed suit with her throwing knives.

Unable to get out of the way of Lyan or Triton's massive bodies, it wasn't hard for the party to drive the remaining penanggalan down the trapdoor. Folken made sure they did not climb back up into the fray with blasts of flame from his palm that spilled down the length of the metal ladder.

As the Bunny Barbarian hoisted the final female creature over her head, Harby keeping the thing's head at bay with his staff, Folken wrapped his flesh hand around the handle of the trapdoor to close it.

A pearlescent sphere formed in his metal hand, with swirls of pale bluish green sweeping around the surface as it started to glow with a white light. Lyan threw the last body down, its head immediately following, and the sorcerer tossed the small globe of light down into the cellar.

Screams of pain and fear erupted from the room below, yet the svartalfar man held the door open. Then the sounds of shattering glass bottles and rending earth started to overpower the hollering.

"Ultima is a hurricane force of kinetic energy," Folken started explaining, "It is destroying the bottles of spoiled wine, turning the vinegar into an aerosol, and ripping the carbon rich walls of earth into clouds of dust."

"Not to mention the damage it is doing to those things," Lyan added.

"But we cannot count on that alone to destroy them," Folken scowled, "That is where the next phase of my plan comes in."

The sorcerer stuck his hand down the hole and unleashed another blast of flame. Slamming the trapdoor shut, he reached up and grabbed the cleric by his collar.

"Harbenigyr, I need you to lay here right now!" Folken slammed the elf down on top of the closed trapdoor, flat on his back.

Snatching Harby's quarterstaff from the elf's hands, the albino man pushed the end down on the chest of the cleric so that he could not get up. Seconds later, the wooden hatch under Harbenigyr started to bow out as the sound of muffled explosions came from underground.

"What are you doing?" Josie yelled even as Lyan started to stomp past her toward the svartalfar man.

"Saving all our lives," Folken responded.

He kept all his weight on the staff, keeping Harbenigyr pinned to the top of the hatch that was shattering under the metal encased torso of the cleric. Folken raised his metal arm toward the two protesting women. That familiar cylinder rolled out of his forearm and unleashed a blast of distorted air that froze both Lyan and Josie in place.

The wooden trapdoor couldn't take any more of the stress from the blasts below and finally crumbled. Spurts of flame licked all around Harbenigyr's body, quickly heating up the steel armor to the point that it was glowing red against the elf's back.

Harby couldn't help screaming as his skin started to blister under the metal. Disgust was painted all over Lyan Yo Bunpy's face like a mask while Josie's flushed the same shade of crimson as her hair in rage.

Saya refused to even look in their direction. That was why she was able to spot the disembodied head before it could lunge for the exposed backs of the still barbarian and ranger.

The svartalfar noblewoman rushed at the penanggalan head that had hidden in the shadows, wrapping her metal fingers around its dirty brown hair. The creature snapped its jaws in desperation at the albino woman, who held it at arm's length.

Then it fell limp, rolling in Saya's grip until it was again right side up. Blood spilled from the ripped gash that had been where its body would have been attached. The svartalfar woman looked back at her cousin questioningly.

"Just as the body cannot live without the head, the head cannot live without the body," Folken explained, only half of the quarterstaff that belonged to the cleric still in his hand.

The other half was on the ground next to the still elf. The explosions stopped as quickly as they had started. Harbenigyr was lucky that the armor he was wearing was barely longer than the hatch was wide so that he didn't fall down inside.

"What just happened here, Folken?" Saya asked.

"Vinegar has trace amounts of phosphorus in the form of a chemical called niter" he explained. "When it is mixed with coal, which Miranda said was abundant in the soil of this area, it creates a highly flammable black powder. When mixed in the proper proportions."

Then the woman realized that luck hadn't been involved at all, "That was why you used Utima. To rip everything down there into the smallest bits possible. When you threw the flame down there you knew that at least some of the niter and the coal would be in those proportions."

"I figured that rendering most of the vinegar and soil into airborne particulates would make the conditions as close to ideal as possible," her cousin agreed.

"You knew the explosions would rip the trapdoor open," Saya continued, "You were worried that the penanggalan would be able to escape so you made Harby into a human shield."

"Elfin, but your point is valid," Folken nodded, "He is still alive."

With a wave of his hand, Josie and Lyan tumbled forward. They found their balance just in time to keep from falling to the floor beside the still smoldering cleric.

"You bastard," Josie growled at the sorcerer as she dropped down beside the elf. "Harby? Harby, can you hear me?"

He let out a quiet groan and the ranger get out a relieved laugh. His black eyes slowly opened and he tried to smile at the red haired woman but found himself wincing instead.

"Can you... get me out... of this?" his breath came out in small gasps, "Can't breathe."

Josie nodded and pulled him away from the hole his body covered. As she fumbled with the buckles that, miraculously, didn't get destroyed in the flames, Lyan completed her short march over to the sorcerer.

Grabbing him by the collar, Lyan rested the sharpened teeth of her other gauntlet at the base of his pale neck, "Tell me why I should not kill you for attempting to sacrifice one of your comrades to save your own skin?"

"First, I am the only one that can treat his burns since he will not be able to maintain consciousness for long," Folken answered in the most matter-of-fact way, "Second, you will need to ride Triton into town to rescue Ophelia."

"Rescue Ophelia?" the barbarian turned to Saya questioningly.

"She was captured by the leader of these monsters," the noblewoman answered, "They are going to try and make her one of them."

Dropping Folken back onto his feet, Lyan Yo Bunpy started marching for the door, "You will take the griffin. I can keep up." She declared to Saya before returning her attention to the sorcerer, "If Ophelia is dead or a monster when I find her, your life will be forfeit."

——— ◆··• •··◆ ———

CHAPTER NINE

"You said yourself that not telling the whole truth was part and parcel of being a leader in the Romefeller Guild," the subject said.

"That hardly excuses the behavior," I replied.

"If you don't like it," the subject said, "then take comfort that there are Yo Bunpy barbarians out there. They're big on honor and honesty."

"Like this Tokki Yo Bunpy?" I asked.

Ophelia nodded.

"He is hardly one that should wield that banner," I said.

Ophelia groaned, "What in the hell could he have been hiding?"

"Besides his predilection for battle," I started to say.

"That was hardly a secret," the subject interrupted me.

"He had his own secrets," I held up an excerpt of his testimony regarding his escape from the tunnels..."

Decades later...

TOKKI YO BUNPY had heard songs of great warriors being struck so hard that they flew through the air and landed in the dirt only to rise and take the fight back to their enemy. As the young Bunny Barbarian sailed through the air himself, he was surprised at how little pain there was.

Sure, there was the ache in his chest and stomach from the actual strike that threw him off his feet but tightening the muscles just when the impact came minimized that. No, the real pain happened when his back struck the red rock wall. There was literally no way he could see it coming and prepare.

He was pretty sure a crater was left in his wake but, even then, Tokki immediately tumbled to the dust covered ground. Every part of his body screamed in protest as he tried to move. The warrior couldn't even get his hands under him to start to lift himself up before the rattle at the end of the massive snake tail slammed down on top of him again.

"Phin, we have to get her away from him!" he heard Appelonia scream.

Tokki thought she had such a nice voice. Even if most of the time he was hearing it lecture him about being blood thirsty or battle hungry.

And she was a good shot with a bow and arrow. Three of them hit the monster's tail, just under where the rattle met the scale covered flesh. Too bad the heads of the arrows weren't sharpened. They would have done some real damage.

As it was, where they did strike must have been sensitive because the tail of the massive snake woman jerked away from the barbarian. That brought Phinegann into Tokki's field of vision.

The orc was already swinging the spiked ball at the end of the brass chain around in a circle over his bald head. His flesh hand let go of the metal links in its grip and the sharpened sphere launched at the snake woman.

The creature ducked under the projectile with the ease of a normal human laying down. The monster woman, called Marilith by the cat man who introduced her, had long violet hair that moved almost like it was underwater while the rest of her body moved with whip-like efficiency.

Until this moment, the six-armed beast had not used the swords she held in each hand. Up to that point, Tokki wasn't enough of a challenge to warrant even having to raise them, considering he couldn't even get around her tail to even get within reach.

Even with their size difference, Marilith was still over twice the height of the not at all diminutive orc. That was just counting her humanoid torso, the chain of Phinegann's weapon gave him the reach advantage and the snake woman saw that she needed to negate that quickly.

Curved blade after blade slashed at the bronze-skinned man. Any attack he couldn't dodge, the chain was pulled taut to block.

Despite his thick limbs, Phinegann was quite graceful with that chain and ball weapon of his. Tokki was jealous.

Then he felt a pair of hands wrap around the back of his neck. He tried to shrug them off, to pull himself away, but they only pushed him back down onto his stomach.

"Stay still!" Appelonia's jingling voice played over the ears of the Bunny Barbarian. "I'm checking to make sure you don't have any broken bones!"

"What would you be able to do about it now if I–" his question was interrupted when he felt her arms slide under his abdomen and chest to flip Tokki onto his back, "– did?" he groaned.

"I was just making sure I could roll you over without making things worse," the cleric said as her hands glided over his sides, "You are definitely going to be sore in the morning."

She added a pained hiss as she got a good look at Tokki's skin, which was now more newborn bruises than flesh at the moment. She pulled out a vial of something and poured it onto his chest. Throwing the bottle to the ground, she started rubbing the solvent into his chest and stomach.

"Purple and pink are not good colors on you, Tokki." Appelonia commented, "But, like you said, there's nothing I can do about it now. What I'm doing is rubbing you down with a numbing agent. It's isn't going to heal anything but you can move without feeling the pain that would normally come with it. Understand?"

The warrior nodded, "Thank you."

"You should be thankful," Appelonia scoffed, "My hands are going to be numb for hours after this, too. My arrow shooting is going to be worthless after this."

"I'll keep her away from you," Tokki was surprised that he didn't have to groan as he pulled himself up to a sitting position.

The cleric huffed, "My feet work just fine. I can keep away from her on my own. You just remember that this isn't a cure all and figure a way out of this with Phin!"

It was the barbarian's turn to scoff, "Phinegann does not need me to be able to stand against that–"

And the massive man dressed in red with black armor slammed into the wall in almost the exact same place Tokki had hit. He slid to the dusty ground with his back to the cleric and the Bunny Barbarian.

"Phinegann!" Appelonia spun around on her knees, pressing her hand against the back of the dark skinned man's neck, "Are you okay? What happened?"

"Good and bad," the orc growled as the woman helped him roll onto his back.

He held up his metal arm, one of the blades wielded by the snake woman impaled through it just below the elbow. The fingers were stuck in positions that, if they had been flesh, the Bunny Barbarian would have thought them to be broken.

"I disarmed her of one sword," Phinegann chuckled without a hint of mirth, "She still has five more."

"Speaking of which, why hasn't she pounced on us yet?" Tokki's question was rhetorical as he lifted himself to his padded feet and turned around.

He saw the tiny woman, Illyria Warflower, flying just out of reach of the half-snake. She fluttered in the air around the height of Marilith's face, the spotlights on the tips of her glass wings flickering blinding lights into the slit pupils of the feminine monster.

Just because she was keeping her distance didn't mean that the snake demon wasn't trying to cut the little woman in half. Finally, Marilith feinted a slash with two swords that drove Illyria one way... right into the waiting remaining three blades the creature swung with all the strength it could muster.

Illyria's wings closed around her at just the last moment before the razor sharp metal connected. The colorful cocoon struck the wall, stuck for a moment, then slid out of the shallow gash it had made in the blood colored stone, and toppled into the dust and dirt across from the remaining three members of the party.

"Tell me you have Phinegann back on his feet," Tokki's voice was barely above a mumble while he kept his eyes locked on Marilith as she turned her attention back in their direction.

"Working on it," Appelonia grunted as she pulled the sword that was taller than her out of the metallic arm of the retired guard.

The blade immediately dropped into the dirt, too heavy for the cleric to hold on her own. She let the handle follow and the sword laid on the ground at her boots.

Phinegann groaned with a mixture of effort and pain as he lifted himself back up, "We must disarm her to make the fight more even."

"I will see what I can do about that," Tokki flexed his hand in the black furred sleeve, making the curved claws wiggle with the motion, "Be ready to jump in if I get lucky and knock one out."

And the Bunny Barbarian charged the slithering snake woman, who was already rearing back to strike. He couldn't be sure but Tokki thought he heard calls of "idiot!" coming from Appelonia. He was touched that she actually did care.

The warrior in the black fur was able to dodge the first sword that buried itself in the dirt beside him. He ducked under the second, pleasantly surprised that neither of the floppy ears attached to his helmet were chopped off.

He threw himself forward, somersaulting in the dust to avoid the next strike. As he regained his feet, Tokki saw the next sword coming. There was no way he could dodge this one. This would all come down to technique.

The Bunny Barbarian jumped straight up, throwing his clawed arm out as he spun around. The curved rabbit claws met the broad side of the blade as it came to chop him down with a deafening clash that reminded Tokki of the gong that signaled the curfew to return to camp back in the Land of the Long Toothed Rabbit.

The momentum of his weight as he dropped and the rotation of his body drove the blade under the warrior. The sudden impact made Marilith lose her grip on the weapon and it clattered across the dusty surface of the arena to rest against the far wall.

Tokki was tempted to take a moment to appreciate his successful maneuver but the knew there was one more blade coming for him. As he turned in search of it, the flash of steel was inches from his face. He didn't even have time to raise his hands in a futile defense.

The sword came to a sudden stop. Marilith let out a grunt of frustration before the weapon flung off the opposite direction to land several paces away from the one Tokki had knocked loose. Then he saw the chain from Phinegann's weapon uncurl itself from around the sword just before the spike sphere whistled just over the barbarian's head to strike the snake woman square in the face.

Tokki let out a soundless chuckle before he collapsed to his knees. Why did he do that?

Looking down at himself, the Bunny Barbarian saw that the entire front of his body was painted ruby red with blood. Was it his blood? That would explain why he was suddenly feeling weak...

He fell back first into the dust covered ground, watching the almost poetic motion of Phinegann's chained sphere whip all around Marilith as she dodged and blocked, moving away from the Bunny Barbarian.

Then his vision was filled with the worried face of Appelonia. She pulled his helmet off his face before pressing both hands to one side of his neck.

"Don't move, Tokki." she said hurriedly, "Phin didn't quite stop that last attack in time. It nicked your carotid artery. I have to keep pressure on it or you'll bleed out!"

She started muttering a prayer under her breath and the Bunny Barbarian could see a soft green glow at the edge of his vision but he didn't feel any better. He didn't feel any worse, either. Was this because of the numbing agent Apple applied to him earlier? He didn't remember her massaging it into his neck.

"You are all dead!" Marilith seethed with rage, swinging her swords without any hint of technique or strategy at the orc.

"To be honest, we've done better than I thought we would already," A bruised up Illyria commented as she crawled up beside Appelonia, who was in turn beside Tokki Yo Bunpy, "What can I do to help?"

The cleric wrapped her blood coated hands around the gnome's and pressed them to the warrior's throat. "Press down as hard as you can! I have to prepare a cauterizing agent."

The face of the little woman went white as a sheet as she was thrust into an unexpected, and wholly unpleasant, responsibility. Appelonia was rummaging through the pouches on her belt, no easy task when she couldn't feel her fingers. Tokki was sorry about that. If it hadn't been for him, she would still have full use of her hands. Then Phinegann let out an echoing howl.

"Oh, merciful Kuan Yin!" the cleric gasped, her expression one of horror that relief.

Tokki risked moving his head just enough to see what had happened. He saw Phinegann, reverting from that wolfish state that had made him so powerful against Vokloss, back into his normal visage. A sword the same height as him ran through his body and into the ground behind him, with the black breastplate of his armor torn in half. One side was already half buried in the dirt as his feet. As he shrank back to his normal size, the wound the sword caused only became bigger.

"One down," Marilith hissed.

She didn't bother to pull her sword free of Phinegann's body. She let it go, leaving him standing and dying in the middle of the arena as she started toward the two women kneeling beside the Bunny Barbarian.

It was over. Phinegann was the strongest of them all. If Appelonia had not sacrificed her ability to fight so that Tokki could, she may have at least been able to escape with Illyria somehow.

Apple was right. This was all his fault. If he hadn't been so headstrong and eager to jump into a fight, they may have been able to all get out of this together. All he accomplished was all of them dying together.

The wall behind Appelonia and Illyria suddenly exploded, raining bits of red rock and dirt all over three huddled together party members. Coughing, not from the cleric, gnome, or warrior, came almost immediately after.

"What was that, Genevieve?" the voice of Jonas the Shepherd came between bouts of trying to breathe in the remaining cloud of dust.

"You wished for the quickest route here, *Master*," the efreeti woman answered, not seeming to have any difficulty with the dust filled air, "This was it. The doors are sealed shut and require special, time consuming rituals to open from the outside."

Appelonia was lying on top of Tokki. She shielded him from the shower of rock from the blast as best she could. The fact that she hadn't lifted herself up yet told the barbarian that she was either knocked unconscious or found him very comfortable. Personally, he hoped for the latter.

He tried to stifle a jump when Jonas and Genevieve came into view. He'd known that Genevieve was a demon, much like the one that the paladin had slain just before he arrived at Dianmeyer, but seeing one still living *felt* entirely different.

Fear had been forged out of Tokki Yo Bunpy years ago, replaced with what the cleric described as a thirst for battle. But the burgundy colored woman who floated toward him beside Jonas, her very presence almost demanded strategic withdrawal be the strategy used against her.

Appelonia felt Tokki stiffen at the sight of the demon and straightened up to turn and look back herself. Her hand slapped over her mouth to muffle the gasp of shock.

Genevieve stood taller than all of them, even without floating. She had horns growing from her forehead, one with a hole near the base while the other with another short, sharp branch poking from it.

Her hair glowed like fire, rising from her head like true flame. Orange, gold and ruby colored fur ran down her upper arms to tufts of bone protruding from her elbows.

The efreeti woman didn't even bother with clothes in this guise. Her naked body still looked almost completely human, save for the unnatural hue of her skin. Tokki couldn't help but notice that Appelonia seemed more self-conscious about Genevieve's state of undress than the demon herself.

Jin Vega then emerged from the newly formed hole in the wall, followed by that thief. The bald monk waved billowing dust out of his face as best he could while the brown skinned woman radiated irritation in everything from her posture to facial expression.

When the paladin and the monk were finally able to take in the scene in front of them, both rushed to the side of Tokki. They knelt down on either side of the cleric while Genevieve remained standing behind Appelonia, looming over the entire group.

"What happened here?" Jonas asked the cleric.

Appelonia pulled her eyes away from the efreeti woman, her cheeks still flushed with a mix of fear and embarrassment, to answer the paladin, "We woke up in a cave. We made our way up here and this cat man said that the only way out was to fight that thing."

The red haired woman motioned to Marilith, who was watching the proceedings with a confused look on her face. She didn't press her attack even as the dust cleared. Tokki had a feeling that Genevieve being there had something to do with that.

The paladin's eyes fell wide open at the sight of the snake monster. That was when he noticed Phinegann impaled on one of the curved swords that Marilith wielded.

"Is he?" Jonas nodded at orc who stood motionless.

He didn't say the word 'dead' but Appelonia caught the inference. Tears started streaming down her face before she could even find words to speak.

"I don't know. Tokki's throat was cut. I have to treat him before– "

The woman jumped and frantically started rifling through one of the pouches on her belt again. Pulling out a pouch that was so small she could have hidden it in her palm and still looked empty handed, Appelonia tried to grip the string that held it closed but her fingers wouldn't cooperate.

"Open that please!" She pushed the mouth of the leather pouch toward Jonas.

He did so easily. Apple pulled Elly's hands away from Tokki's neck and the cleric immediately dumped the powder the pouch held onto the wound. Then she again pressed her hands over the blood and powder coated wound.

Jin jumped to his feet and ran over to Phinegann to check if he was still alive. Marilith started to move to intercept him but Genevieve cleared her throat. That made the snake woman stop on the spot.

"What's wrong with your hands?" the paladin asked the cleric.

Appelonia explained about the numbing agent she had used to make Tokki able to continue fighting. Then she told him and Jin about everything that had happened in more detail, all the way back to Phinegann reliving one of his earliest days as a prison guard.

"And Doctor Efreeti is involved in all of this somehow," the woman finished.

"Who is Doctor Efreeti?" Bronwyn asked.

Jonas answered for Appelonia, who had bent down to check to see if the bleeding from Tokki's neck had stopped, "He's a demon like Genevieve. He's been trouble back home for years now."

"He is nothing like me... Master," the efreeti woman added the title as an afterthought, "*That one* is the part of us that we do not speak of."

"A demon afraid of another demon?" Bronwyn groaned, "That doesn't bode well."

"Not afraid," Genevieve corrected, "Ashamed."

"One that's depraved by another demon's standards," the thief shook her head, "That's even worse."

"Phinegann is still alive!" Jin called back to the others, "He won't be for long without your help!" That last part was directed at Appelonia.

Inspecting Tokki's wound one last time, she was only moderately sure that the bleeding had completely stopped, "Do not let him move," she commanded Jonas before she forced herself onto her feet and toward the orc.

"They're both goners anyway," Bronwyn shrugged, "Why can't we just leave them here and go home?"

"Pillar of empathy you are," Illyria snapped up at the other woman as she tried to wipe some of the barbarian's dried blood from her hands.

"I'm just being realistic here!" Bronwyn griped as she pointed at the Bunny Barbarian, "His neck's been slashed and he's been run through," she pointed at Phinegann, "Do you know anyone whose survived those kinds of wounds? I don't!"

"I can heal them," Genevieve said without any air of enthusiasm, "If you wish it."

Tokki coughed, a false start for the words that came out a few moments after, "Then the battle with Marilith will just start anew. We cannot leave unless one of us finishes her."

His voice was weak, wavering. That alone seemed to support Bronwyn's argument.

"Is that all?" Genevieve guffawed, "I can kill the marilith and we can all be underway."

"Not with Tokki and Phinegann so badly injured," Jonas warned the demon woman.

"I told you that I can heal them if you wish it," Genevieve asserted, "I can even use Chagrin's life force to do it. Better than deforming by beautiful horns," the woman's amber eyes glanced up, "anymore than they have been, anyway."

"Efreeti's horns deform when they grant wishes?" Illyria tapped at her lower lip thoughtfully. "That does explain why Abernathy's looked so different. Genevieve's a stingy wish giver!" she laughed.

"It isn't being stingy," Genevieve argued, "It is being... mindful. The more strain an efreeti puts on themselves, the more their horns contort. I can assure you that it is an unpleasant sensation."

"Then why keep offering to grant wishes at all?" Jonas had a suspicious look on his face.

"Why do you accompany helpless and buxom she-clerics on their treks of self discovery?" Genevieve retorted, "Or he jump into a fight without thought? It is our natures. It may be malicious and harmful to oneself but it must be done."

"Except when it's something I want," Bronwyn muttered.

The demon ignored her, "I suppose this is the part where you find out how your ogre friend is faring?" she turned to face in the direction of Appelonia, Jin, and Phinegann.

"Okay, Genevieve, fine. I'll bite," Jonas stood up, cupping his gloved hands around his mouth, "What's his condition, Apple?"

The bald, bearded monk frowned at the cleric, "What *is* his condition?"

Even with her back to Tokki (a view he didn't mind), the slump in her shoulders told the dying barbarian that Appelonia wasn't hopeful. Jin Vega reached up to touch the sword handle that was as long as his arm, only to have the cleric swat it down.

"Don't touch it!" she insisted, "The reason he's still alive at all is because the wound is so tight around the blade that his blood doesn't have enough room to escape. If it gets jostled, he'll bleed out faster than Tokki."

"What can we do?" Jin looked the long sword up and down, awestruck. "How do we get this out without killing him then?"

Appelonia bit down on her lower lip to try and stop its trembling, "I don't know," the admission seemed to cause the young woman more pain than any wound could have.

"It seems to me that your options run thin, Master." Genevieve turned back to face the paladin.

Jonas looked from the embittered face of Bronwyn LaRue, to the unsure expression of Illyria Warflower, to finally rest on the pale, sweating face of Tokki Yo Bunpy. The barbarian and the paladin locked their gazes.

Tokki tried to lift himself from the ground. The full body-weight of the tiny gnome dropped onto his chest to stop him. He didn't have the strength to throw her off so he dropped back into the dust but his eyes never left the paladin.

"This is my fault, Jonas," Tokki's voice was still weak but it found conviction, "Do not allow her to suffer for my failure," he raised a shaky hand to point at Appelonia.

"No tricks, Genevieve," the paladin stepped up to the demon, "I wish for Phinegann and Tokki Yo Bunpy to be restored to the same physical state they were in just before their fight with the snake monster over there. No *improvements*, no changing their ages, no manipulation of their minds or spirits. Just restoration of their bodies to how they were immediately before the fight."

"And what about Chagrin?" Genevieve's amber eyes flicked in the direction of the giant, six-armed snake woman, "The party is still required to defeat her before being allowed to leave. The contract has already been made."

"Tokki agreed to this fight and the cat man decided that his agreement included the party. I agree with that point whole-heartedly. The battle with Chagrin includes the *whole* party," Jonas motioned to all the mortals in the arena, "That includes not only Appelonia, Illyria, and Tokki, but also Bronwyn, Jin, and you and me, Genevieve. You defeat her, the contract is fulfilled and we can all leave. Add to that, you said you could use the life force of the marilith as fuel. Do it."

It was only then that Tokki realized that the monster was not *named* Marilith but rather that was the type of creature it was. It's name was, apparently, Chagrin. Why wasn't just dying enough? Now he felt stupid, too.

Jonas never used the 'W' word during his entire diatribe about killing the snake monster. What he did do was make sure to name every mortal, as well as Genevieve herself, as members of the party that were now a part of the contract. Now the efreeti woman was bound by its outcome, too.

Genevieve grinned wide, exposing a row of sharp, shining teeth, "My clever Master."

The efreeti woman's feet sank to the dusty floor. Genevieve started making her way to the massive snake she-monster. She made a show of it, too, swaying her hips with each step, tilting her head back and smiling so sanctimoniously at her prey.

Tokki instinctively wanted her to lose but, intellectually, realized that he needed her to win. With the condition half the party was in, he only hoped that none of them were caught in the inevitable crossfire.

"You can't do this, Genevieve aibna Shaitanjuna," the snake woman, Chagrin, lifted the two swords she still held in her two highest arms as she protested, "I was winning! They are merely mortals, little more than meat for the rack! Why are you doing this?"

The efreeti woman strode closer and closer to the marilith, not bothering to answer. When Chagrin started swinging her weapons to keep the other demon at bay, Genevieve grabbed the massive blade slashing for her neck in one hand, stopping it as effectively as if it hit a wall.

Genevieve's other hand grabbed the other sword swinging in from the opposite side. Perhaps Chagrin thought that, with her hands full, the efreeti woman wouldn't be able to defend herself as she snatched one of her lost blades from the ground and it flashed up between Genevieve's legs to chop the demon in half (Tokki remembered that the corpse of Abernathy was laid out in a similar fashion).

The demon bonded to Jonas simply lifted a foot and caught the blade between her foot and that extra toe that grew out from the inside of her heel, "This tantrum is meaningless, Chagrin. I am the superior, my word is law to you. I have declared that you are to die. Face that death with some dignity," the smaller, humanoid demon sighed as he pulled all three swords free of the snake monster's grip and threw them to the far ends of the arena.

"But why?" Chagrin pleaded, "I am of you! They are mere blinks of time!"

"You heard the one the great Mullah Junaperqolanijuna alab Marid Juna alnnihaya has seen fit to place me into bondage," Genevieve stepped over to Phinegann, Appelonia and Jin as she waved a clawed hand at the paladin, "I am a member of this party. This party must continue on to find the child for which our Greatness seeks. That path lies over your corpse."

The efreeti snatched the curved blade still impaled through Phinegann's body and blood immediately sprayed from the wounds in the man's chest and back. Appelonia wailed as she and Jin caught the body of the orc before he fell to the ground.

The movements of Genevieve were so fast that they were a blur to Tokki as he watched. Chagrin wasn't even able to lift one of her many hands before her head was separated from her shoulders. Then each arm followed, landing in grotesque piles to either side of the snake's body.

The efreeti woman chopped down the front of the torso of the marilith before tossing the sword away. Then Genevieve slipped both of her hands into the vertical gash in Chagrin's chest and proceeded to pull her ribcage open.

She pulled the no longer pumping but still steaming hot heart from the monster's chest, "She-cleric Appelonia, I need you to press this to the ogre's chest while I tend to the one who thinks himself a rabbit."

Genevieve dumped the heart into the mortal woman's arms without bothering to see if she was ready for it. The fresh organ was big enough that the cleric needed both arms to support it. There wasn't anything else she could do for Phinegann, he was going to bleed out in a matter of moments anyway, so she did as the demon asked and pressed the heart to the front of his chest.

Genevieve then snatched the marilith's head from the ground by her amethyst-colored hair. She held it, blood still spilling from its neck, over the Bunny Barbarian and chanted something in what must have been her native tongue. Then she dropped Chagrin's head onto Tokki's body.

It disappeared the moment it made contact and the barbarian suddenly found that, not only was his strength restored but there wasn't even a drop of blood on him anymore! Tokki pulled Illyria off of his chest with little effort and sat up in the dirt, astonishment written all over his face. His elfin face.

The heart in Appelonia's hands disappeared at the same time. She had to jump out of the way as the shred of black armor that had fallen from Phinegann's breastplate jumped from the dirt to reattach itself to the rest of the black metal. There wasn't even a seam where it came back together.

The eyes of the orc snapped open where he was laid out prone on the ground with his head resting on Jin Vega's lap. The first expression on his newly revived face was confusion.

Then he hurriedly lifted himself off of the other man and onto his feet. The busied himself by patting away dust that covered his armor and red pants but there was no sign of any injury or blood from his wounds on any part of him.

The same could not be said for Appelonia. The chainmail wrapped over her chest, as well as the white sleeves of her tunic were still drenched in blood.

The same with Illyria. Bruises still covered her body from her tumble down the wall when she was wrapped in her glass cocoon. Who knew glass could be so sturdy that it could stand such punishment without shattering? Her hands were also still covered with Tokki's blood, which she was struggling to wipe off even as the rest of the party was trying to wrap their minds around what had just happened.

"Wish granted," Genevieve bowed, "Now we should head back to the surface and reacquire as many of your horses as we are able."

OPHELIA INTERROGATION NOTES:

"He was a boy with a crush!" the subject protested.
"It was still a secret," I insisted.
Ophelia rolled her eyes, "What about Lyan?"
"What about her?" I asked.
"She was the Child of Prophesy," Ophelia pulled a page of testimony from the barbarian free from the pile we had not yet read, "She surely could be considered a standard bearer."

Decades before...

LYAN YO BUNPY was as good as her word. Even though Saya pushed Triton to run as fast has he could carry himself, the woman in the blue fur pushed herself to that pace. By the time they reached the outer edge of Laeradr the moon was sinking behind the trees but there was still a hefty chunk of night to go.

"Do you know where they are holding Ophelia?" the barbarian asked.

She was out of breath, but nowhere near as badly as Saya figured she should have been. The svartalfar woman took a deep breath as she scanned the buildings, mostly houses, of the small township.

"Hero said that the town's leader, Miranda, was the one that was going to change her into one of those long necked things," Saya let the words escape with her breath, "I guess her place is as good as any other to check first."

"That doesn't sound reassuring," Lyan muttered.

"Just be ready for trouble," Saya responded with a shrug, "As far as we know, every woman in town can be one of those things."

Lyan gripped her spear, the blue fur on the head still covered in a thick layer of dried blood, tighter, "I will be cautious."

Saya slipped off of the back of the griffin. As much as speed was important to get them here, the now had to be ready to fight anyone who would try to stop them. Having the sharpened beak and talons of a griffin ready to pounce would be a great aid to them.

As they turned a corner to start down the street where the house of the mayor awaited, one of the many women Saya had seen around town stood in their path, as if she was guarding the road. Lyan reared back with her spear and the woman with brown hair started running away just at the sight of the warrior. She dashed up the small set of stairs that led up to the front door of the building that Saya presumed to be her home and practically dived inside.

Not that either the Bunny Barbarian or svartalfar woman heard it, but that door was surely locked as securely as it was able immediately after it closed so that neither woman could follow. Not exactly the gauntlet of inhuman creatures Saya was expecting.

"If she were a monster, would she not have attacked?" Lyan scowled at the platinum haired woman in black.

"I would think so," Saya rested her hands on her hips, "This doesn't make any sense. Wouldn't they want to protect a ritual that was meant to increase their number?"

They continued in the direction of the mayor's house. The road was nearly deserted. Anyone who was outside disappeared back into their homes at the first sight of Saya, who they had intended to be food, and the massive barbarian in the brightly colored fur.

As they crossed the last road before the Miranda's house, only one figure stayed outside in the dark, crouched in front of the door two buildings down from where Saya stood. From this distance, the noblewoman couldn't tell if the person was listening at the keyhole or trying to pick the lock The silhouette didn't even seem to notice Lyan and Saya. As every other woman ran and hid before they even shared the block with them, that was unusual to say the least.

"I wonder what she is so focused on," Saya nodded down the road.

"Are we worried about strangers now?" Lyan shrugged, "Should we not be focusing on finding Ophelia?"

Saya pointed a gloved finger at the Bunny Barbarian, "I am, I mean, we are. I think that is the house that Ophelia slept in last night. Maybe she barricaded Miranda outside so she couldn't perform the ritual."

"We had best find out then," Lyan sprinted at the figure without another moment wasted.

Saya actually had to grab Triton's saddle to get his help to catch up. When they came up on the unknown woman, it ended up being the last person the albino woman would have expected.

"Hero?" Saya couldn't decide if she was more confused or surprised.

The bard's plain hair went off in every direction and her face from her left cheek to down the front of her chin was covered is blisters from where Folken burned her. But she did appear to be human again.

Her neck had a long scar that ran all around. The flesh was lumped and pink with patches of red irritation from where the yellow acid attached her head back onto her body.

Her brown eyes were sunken with dark circles under them. Her cheeks were sunken, as if she hadn't eaten for a week rather than simply failing to eat Saya or any other member of her party earlier that night.

The sight of the svartalfar woman and the massive barbarian beside her caused the bard to topple over. Landing on her rear end, Hero's green boots scraped against the dirt, searching for purchase so that she could lift herself up and run away.

Hero froze in place when Lyan's spear flashed past her shoulder, just missing her face, and embedding itself in the dirt behind her. The petite woman stared at Lyan. The bard was sure that she was about to die.

Lyan nodded at Saya, who focused all her attention on Hero, "What are you doing here? How did you get out of that cellar?" she asked the disheveled woman.

"I'm... I'm trying to save Ophelia," Hero answered, pointing at the door she had been crouched before.

Saya pointed her gloved hand at the door, "She is in here? You're sure?"

The smaller woman nodded, "Miranda and Bianca have her down in the basement."

"Then why are you hanging out up here?" Lyan added her own question.

"I was failing at picking the lock. They don't want to be interrupted," Hero's voice came out as a croak but she straightened up as she focused her attention of Saya, "You can pick it though, right?"

"Of course I can. But that would take to long," Saya tapped Lyan's shoulder and motioned to the slab of wood that was their newest obstacle, "You still need to tell me how you got out of that cellar."

Lyan pulled her spear free of the floor, then backed several paces away from the house. Her face contorted into a tight grimace as she charged. The barbarian's blackened shoulder slammed into the door and reduced it to splinters.

Saya pulled Hero to her feet as Lyan kicked the last standing parts of wood out of their way. Hero couldn't bring herself to look at the albino woman directly as she answered her question.

"I'm, I'm really strong when I'm the... thing," she said, hoping it would be enough.

"We should move," Lyan snapped at the other women, "They surely heard that!

Saya waved a hand at the barbarian as a silent order to wait, "Why aren't you a penanggalan now, Hero? Why haven't any of the women in town tried to stop us?"

"I can't say for sure." Hero's chapped lips pursed, "The start of the ritual forced me to change, to make me feed. The hunger stopped a short while ago."

The Bunny Barbarian wasn't fully aware of what was happening in this town. All she knew was what Saya had been able to explain during their rush into town, that Ophelia was a captive and that their leader was trying to change her into a monster like the ones they just destroyed back in the ruins. She had accepted that the rest could be explained later but Hero's words caused her to have a moment of pause.

"Is that a good thing or a bad thing for Ophelia?" Lyan inquired.

"I don't know," Hero looked as if she was about to weep.

"Then I suggest we go find out," Lyan frowned and stepped into the house.

Saya nodded, pulling a knife out of her gloved arm, "After you, Hero. I'm not quite ready to trust you at my back yet.

The bard nodded and followed the barbarian into the house. Saya was the last in.

Lantern's filled the interior with faint light. They were set just bright enough for one to be able to find their way without burning through the fuel too quickly.

There wasn't anything that would have screamed to the Saya that a monster lived in the place. Just about everything in the house screamed 'typical' to the pale woman. There wasn't anything that seemed representative of home's owner, Bianca, individually. Perhaps that, in and of itself, should have been a warning sign.

"The basement is that way, past the bedroom," Hero pointed off to the left.

And that was the way that Lyan went. The bard followed with Saya bringing up the rear.

As they neared the door, muffled voices could be heard. The barbarian shrugged back at Saya, who shook her head. Neither of them could understand what was being said.

Hero cocked her head to the side, her eyes narrowing, "That doesn't sound like Miranda or Bianca," she said.

"How can you tell?" the svartalfar woman asked, "What are they saying?"

"I can't hear the specific words," the bard admitted, "But the tone is too deep for either of them. Wait, there are two voices!" she was still for a long moment, "The new one is definitely a man.

The other is a woman. Maybe Ophelia. I don't know her voice well enough to be sure."

"Only one way to find out." Saya looked up at the barbarian.

Lyan grabbed the handle of the door, more for leverage for when she slammed her shoulder into the wood to break it down. She almost tumbled down the stairs immediately on the other side when the door actually opened.

The three women looked at each other apprehensively. All of them were surprised that it wasn't locked.

"Come on down! What's left of your bosses could use the company!" the threatening tone of Ophelia's voice was only slightly muffled as it made its way around the walls and up the stairs, "Unless you're squeamish. Then you may want to stay up there. It does smell kind of funny down here."

"Ophelia?" Saya leaned over the bard to call down into the cellar. "Are you okay? Do you need any medical attention?"

"Saya?" the mercenary replied hesitantly.

"Yes, I'm here," the pale woman answered, "Along with Lyan Yo Bunpy."

"Lyan? How in the name of Quagmire's frozen tit did you end up here?"

The Bunny Barbarian spoke up for herself as she started down the stairs, "After we parted ways, the tournament was canceled. I started on my way and found myself– oh."

Lyan stopped speaking the moment she reached the bottom of the steps and saw the state the cellar was in. Saya couldn't and, judging from the expression on the barbarian's face, she wasn't sure she wanted to do so.

Ophelia noticed Lyan's sudden hesitation, "Oh, sorry about that. I don't suppose you or Saya have a spare pair of pants?"

"Hero, go and see if Bianca had anything that Ophelia would wear," the svartalfar woman ordered.

The smaller woman nodded and started back down the hall. She slipped into the bedroom and started rifling through the drawers just barely visible from Saya's vantage point.

Despite the svartalfar's better judgment, she started down the stairs. Once she could see the entirety of the room, Saya was able to understand Lyan's sudden pause.

Almost the whole packed dirt floor was red with soaked in blood. The still, headless body of a woman in a long pink skirt was laying on one side of the cellar while the decapitated body of Miranda, still wearing her leather apron, was prone at Ophelia's feet.

Speaking of the mercenary, Ophelia was sitting on a wooden box that, if the skid marks of dirt that interrupted the ichor coating on the floor were any indication, she moved to sit in that precise location.

Her long red coat was wrapped around her shoulders, though her arms were not in the sleeves. Her sword, Havarti, was in his usual resting place on her back. As the box was at the far edge of the horrific display, the leather of the trench coat didn't touch any of the blood. It seemed to avoid most, if not all of the mess completely.

Since no one else appeared to be alive down there, Saya guessed that it was the voice of the sword that Hero heard through the door. That was odd, considering that Havarti only really spoke vocally for the benefit of the mercenary's companions. Usually, he communicated with Ophelia telepathically.

The mercenary leaned forward, resting her elbows on her knees while she held a bottle of wine in both hands. Ophelia rolled it back and forth between her palms before lifting it to take a long, slow sip.

Her boots were ruined. The blood and viscera covering them would never come out and, once it was dried completely, would shrink and distort the leather so that they wouldn't fit properly again. In fact, she would probably have to cut them to get them off her feet.

Ophelia's pants were in shreds. Her leather belt was still around her waist but the fabric was torn from her hips and legs. All that was left was some stiff gray fabric that was sticking to her knees and shins thanks to all the dried blood.

"What happened down here?" Saya couldn't take her eyes off the scene as she spoke.

"Bianca drugged me last night and, next I knew, I was staked down to the floor by my palms," Ophelia held up her scabbed over hands as a visual aid.

She proceeded to describe everything that happened between Bianca, Miranda, and her up to the point that the gardener bit down on her neck. Ophelia skipped to the part where she stomped the heads of both women into the floor until they were barely distinguishable from the clotted up soil that was stirred up from her pulling the stakes loose from the floor.

"That means that you destroyed Miranda's lineage," Hero spoke up as she came down the stairs herself.

Ophelia shot up to her feet, pulling her bastard sword free of his scabbard, "What is she doing here?" the mercenary demanded.

"I brought you some clothes?" the bard held up the bundle of clothing in her arms, her worried eyes darting back and forth from the enraged Ophelia to the far more still Saya.

"She told us about what was happening here," the svartalfar woman answered Ophelia's question before turning to face Hero, "What do you mean by that she destroyed Miranda's lineage?"

The smaller woman didn't dare move any closer to Ophelia, so she kept a hold of the clothes as she spoke, "Miranda made a blood pact by killing her daughter to become a penanggalan. She used the the dried blood from her to make what she called sacrificial wafers that she forced upon every woman in town to make everyone monsters. When Miranda died, her blood lost its power over everyone, every penanggalan that she created reverted back to their human selves."

"Which is why none of the women even tried to fight us when we came into town," Lyan commented.

"Most of us have been trying to figure a way out of this for years," a look of sheer awe crossed over Hero's face as she turned toward Ophelia, "You freed the whole town all by yourself! You're amazi– erp!"

Forgetting herself, Hero started prancing toward the mercenary only to be stopped by Havarti suddenly whipping in her path. The tip of the blade hovered only inches from the nose of the bard.

"You wanted to be here when they changed me," Ophelia growled, "Don't think that I forgot that."

"No, I just said that to try and buy some time," Hero's entire body shook, sweat dripping between the blisters on her cheek as she stared at the mirror sheen of the blade before her, "I didn't want you to be made into another one of us."

"She was willing to have us become fodder for the village's pantry until she learned that Harby was actually innocent, Ophelia," Saya rested the forefinger of her metal hand on Havarti's tip, "When she learned the truth, she tried to warn us about what was planned for you. They only wanted her out of the way so that they could turn you without her interference."

The dusty black bottle that the mercenary had been nursing rolled around on the floor. It was empty. She must have finished it off with that last sip.

Ophelia's blue eyes narrowed at the small woman. If she wanted, she could have easily chopped the bard down. Saya knew that too, the gesture of pressing her hand to the blade of the mercenary's sword was just that, a gesture. She didn't have any real way of stopping Ophelia.

Without lowering Havarti, Ophelia turned her attention to Lyan, "So how did you end up here again?"

The Bunny Barbarian cleared her throat as she took in the scene, trying to decide if any action was necessary. She decided that the best course, for the moment, was to speak.

She restarted her story where she left off, "After I left Dracoleaf, I made camp in a field to the west. When I awoke the next morning, I found a black rock resting on the ground beside the base of my spear."

"Meteorend." Saya pursed her azure lips.

"It looked like the same artifact that Raiko used to attack us," Lyan agreed, "As I have no use for it, no desire to keep it, and no way of contacting those de Junamend people, I figured my best course of action was finding you. I saw your party leave on the trail to Ash Providence. I picked up your trail from there."

"And you just happened to find us tonight?" Ophelia's tone wasn't accusatory as much as befuddled, "We had over a day's head start on you plus you went a day in the opposite direction."

"That was due to the griffin," Lyan continued her explanation, "He was being chased by one of these pentecostals or whatever they are called when I happened upon him in the woods. He led me back to the cleric and the others."

"She saved us from nine more of the penanggalans," Saya added, "When we were finally able to come for you, we happened upon Hero trying to get into the house. Folken and Josie are treating Harbenigyr's injuries as we speak."

"What happened to Harby?" Ophelia asked as she snatched the folded clothes from Hero's arms as she slipped her sword back into its scabbard.

"The magician used him as a shield," Lyan said, the words rolling from her lips with nothing short of disgust.

Saya was right, Ophelia did have to cut the boots off her feet just to even try and slip into a pair of Bianca's pants. She tossed the remnants of her footwear to the side before slipping her arms into the sleeves of her coat.

Tossing the rest of the clothes onto the box she was sitting on before, Ophelia slipped one leg into the black cloth and then the other. She couldn't even get the black cloth around her hips.

"Sounds like Folken and I need to have a talk," the mercenary muttered before pulling her legs free of the ill-fitting garb.

She had to settle on one of the gardener's floral print skirts. Even then, Ophelia could barely lace the side up enough to tie it well enough to stay on. Red from the floor already started soaking in to the hem of the skirt.

Ophelia motioned for everyone else to start up the stairs while she turned back to that wooden box. Tossing the unwearable clothing to the floor, the woman tugged the top off the crate and reached inside. She pulled out two more bottles of wine.

Stuffing one into one of the pocket of the coat, Ophelia pulled the cork free of the other and took a long sip. She started toward the stairs but stopped and turned back to the crate and pulled out another bottle.

She couldn't help but scowl as she found herself glancing toward a closet tucked into dark corner. Tucking the bottle into another pocket, she started up after the others.

OPHELIA INTERROGATION NOTES

"Indeed, Lyan was a trustworthy witness," I observed, "Her story even pointed out that you were hiding something."

"Really?" the subject said, "You're just going to insult me again?"

"The truth is only insulting to the guilty," I said.

"I never said I was innocent in all of this," the subject replied.

I nodded in agreement, "Very well. Would you hold Appelonia to such a judgment?"

"I would," the subject said.

"Perhaps you should read this," I held out her next page of testimony.

Decades later...

IT WASN'T UNTIL the group was back on the surface of Nova Prime and Appelonia saw Andromeda, stamping at the ground that Genevieve explained that all their horses were dragged through the portal with them. That started the cleric worrying about Bommer. And she felt like a terrible person it not occurring to her earlier.

She saw that the horses were caught in the light. It was logical to assume they came with the rest of them to this hellish place. Bommer could be dead already and it never even occurred to her to think of him. Was she really that selfish?

"Genevieve, go see if you can find any of the other horses," Jonas ordered the demon but then added, "Please."

"Am I to be your manual labor, Master?" Genevieve pouted, crossing her arms over her chest.

"I can make it a wish," the paladin shrugged, "If you want your horns to be bent out of shape more."

The efreeti woman sighed, "Very well. I will endeavor to retrieve your remaining beasts of burden. However, I can make no guarantees of how many remain living without a wish."

"I understand," Jonas nodded, closing his eyes after the motion to fight of a wave of nausea, "Find as many as you can and we'll make due."

With that, the demon floated away from the party in search of the remaining horses. She already mentioned that at least one other was dead already but she couldn't identify which ones they were. Appelonia could only hope.

Once Genevieve was out of view (it didn't take long as the pace she was moving) Jonas herded everyone to stand in a circle. Appelonia was just to the right of the paladin. Tokki was just to his left.

He didn't put his rabbit head back on after he was healed by Genevieve's magicks. At least, mostly healed. The condition of the Bunny Barbarian was restored to how he was just before the battle with the marilith. That meant that he still had the slash across his chest from the fight with Vokloss.

The bandage that the cleric had used to, along with the healing herbs under, were also restored to the clean state they were in before, as well. Deciding it was too hot to wear for the time being, Tokki slipped the long, floppy ears of his helmet under the leather belt around his waist and let it bounce on his furred covered hip as he walked.

What surprised Appelonia more than anything else was the fact that Tokki was an elf. He had pointed ears and angled eyebrows, the classic signs of her race. Also, while he was well muscled, he wasn't bulky like most of the warriors from the Land of the Long Toothed Rabbit that Apple had come to know over the years.

Just about every other Bunny Barbarian was human and pretty much related to each other to some distant degree. There was no way he was related to anyone else among the Yo Bunpy, lineage-wise, anyway.

Tokki had short black hair, similar to Jonas and blue eyes of a slightly darker shade. Despite all the scars all over his torso (with a new one coming when that cut across his chest healed), his face was remarkably clear. There wasn't even a sign that he'd ever broken his nose.

Phinegann was on the other side of the barbarian. He looked as stern as ever, although Applelonia had become familiar enough with his expressions now that she could tell he was relieved to be outdoors again.

Jin stood on the other side of him. During the trip back up to the surface, he had replaced the blue shirt that that been rendered little more than scraps with one that was a dust hued shade of brown that he pulled out of that bottomless area inside his cloak. It was also of a thinner material so it helped keep him cooler in this warm climate. That had to be at least some help, considering he put the cloak back on immediately after he replaced his shirt.

Illyria was beside him. She was performing yet another diagnostic of her wings. This time, she was actually replacing some slivers of metal that looked melted at the tips. Keeping those lights on underground must have taken its toll on the technology.

Bronwyn completed the circle to Appelonia's right. She carried her black coat draped over one arm, her pink silk shirt was soaked and untucked to allow what little air that moved around better access to her dark skin. She'd even threatened to start marching around naked if they didn't get back to their plane soon.

"We need to decide where we are going to go," Jonas spoke quietly, almost as if they were conspiring against the absent demon woman.

"What do you mean?" Bronwyn scoffed, "Just wish us back to the human world so we can part ways already!"

"Let's say I do that," the paladin's tongue flicking over his chapped lips, "She could drop us off in the Akshar desert, some far off country on a different continent or, even worse, in the middle of the ocean. I'm not exactly dressed for swimming, you realize."

"But then she wouldn't find the Mullah's baby," Jin wrapped a hand around his thick beard thoughtfully.

"Genevieve doesn't have any more leads to finding it than we do at the moment," Appelonia said, "That's why she was chasing us in the first place."

"I'm open to suggestions," Jonas announced, wiping a few lingering beads of sweat from his brow.

Illyria knocked on the hard metal of the layered cuisse that covered the paladin's thigh, "You have noticed that none of us appear to have met by chance, right? Diomedes made sure we all were together for this."

Bronwyn noticeably stiffened at the sound of the cleric's name. Her already dour demeanor further darkened.

"What's your point?" Jonas knelt down beside the tiny woman as he asked.

"You, Phin, and Tokki were brought to Dianmeyer to protect Apple during her pilgrimage," Illyria lifted three fingers as she spoke, then another as she continued, "I *just happened* to be the last of us to speak to Ophelia before Abernathy attacked..."

Again, the thief's expression only got more troubled. She actually physically turned away from the rest of the group to loose a silent tirade of cursing to herself.

"Jin *just happened* to be revealed during that fight," the gnome raised every finger on one hand, "And Diomedes insisted that he come along, despite not having anything to do with any of this."

"Diomedes did leave us all with the impression that Appelonia was the missing efreeti baby," Tokki added, "That ensured that she would not be left behind for all of this to occur."

"That accounts for everyone here except for..." Illyria looked up at Bronwyn, her small hands resting on her hips, "Did you talk to anyone unusual before you met us?"

The olive skinned woman turned back to face them again, "With this group really needs to define unusual."

"A woman who wore a jacket with really long sleeves," the gnome waved her short arms around.

"With crazy looking eyes that couldn't settle on being one color?" Appelonia added, unable to suppress a shiver at the memory.

"She wore bright green pants," Jin took a turn to add to the description of the avatar (cleric!) of Ferekane.

Bronwyn LaRue groaned, cradling her forehead in one hand, "Yeah. Yeah, I saw her. She was the one who talked me into pulling the stupid valet job."

"What a coincidence," Jonas said with a groan as he stood back up.

"That means that Diomedes probably thought that you had something to add to this little endeavor," Illyria concluded.

"The lady was crazy!" Bronwyn snapped, "Who knows what she was thinking?"

Everyone else had to agree that she had a point there. Almost everyone didn't notice Jonas have to take a step back to right himself as they tried to figure out their next move.

Accepting that Diomedes was merely crazy meant that they were stuck with nowhere to go next. While everyone looked to the paladin to decide what to do next, it was Phinegann who spoke up next.

"Besides thievery, what do you do topside?" his rough voice made his question sound accusatory.

And Bronwyn took it precisely as if she was being accused of some wrongdoing, "None of your business, orc! I just want to get back to the real world, find my father and, most importantly, get away from all of you!"

The brow of the paladin jerked up, "What does your father do?"

Brownwyn cursed, "He is a businessman of Craigh Na Troon," she admitted.

"And what does he have to do with Ophelia?" Appelonia asked. Then she preemptively answering the the question she knew was going to come from other woman, "I saw your reaction when Illyria mentioned her name."

Another curse, "Father didn't want me to know but I overheard that a woman named Ophelia was going to be a passenger on his next consignment. He actually kicked me off the crew for this job, dropping me off at Maid Gulch and telling me to go to the Drunken Dragon."

"That must be where he picked Ophelia up," Appelonia looked at Jonas expectantly, then her expression changed because of what she saw.

Jonas nodded and had to take a moment before he could speak, "Makes sense. But I'm still not sure what Ophelia has to do with any of this."

"Doctor Efreeti is involved somehow," the cleric of Kuan Yin said, starting to dig into one of the many bloodstained pouches on her belt, "She's made it her business to ruin his."

The paladin had to clear his throat before he could ask, "Do you know where your father was going?"

Bronwyn shook her head, "He'd be pissed if he knew I had heard that much."

"You're usually a member of his crew," Jin spoke up, his arms folded across his chest, "You must have at least some idea."

"And why would that be, baldy?" the woman snapped.

"You're also his daughter," the monk stated the obvious, "You must have an idea of how he thinks."

Bronwyn merely shrugged back.

"He probably had a feeling that whatever Ophelia was mixed up in was dangerous," Appelonia said, "So he wanted you off the ship and safe. It's what my father would have done with me. Which way was your ship readying to go when you debarked?"

The olive skinned woman wanted to argue but the cleric was just putting into actual words the very worries Bronwyn had since she was kicked off the ship, "North, toward Loch Aeris. But I'm pretty sure that was meant to throw me and anyone else watching off. I'd bet that he was going to turn and head south after launching."

"Why?" Phinegann grunted.

"That's what he usually does when we're carrying," Bronwyn caught herself getting overexcited and wondering why she was telling these people all of this, "Questionable cargo," she couldn't figure any other way to finish the sentence without it being an obvious lie.

"Would Ophelia be considered questionable?" Illyria asked, looking from one tall person to the next.

"It depends on who you ask, Elly," Apple couldn't help but chuckle as some of the stories her father told her about the woman (most of the time with Lyan) came to mind, "But I'd say if she's trying to find or avoid Doctor Efreeti, she's flirting with trouble either way."

"So misdirection would be the best course of action," Tokki nodded, scratching at the bandage still under the leather strap wrapped around his chest.

"So where should we go then?" Jonas reiterated the question that started this whole conversation.

"Her father is a businessman," Jin said, "Businessmen work out of Craigh Na Troon."

"If the *Galleon* did go south, it is the most likely place," Bronwyn looked resigned as she spoke, "If she made port, Ophelia could have boarded any number of ships that go just about anywhere in the world. We can ask around at the bar there."

"You really think it will be that easy?" Jonas chimed in, blinking hard, "I mean, if she's on some kind of clandestine mission would she really stop off for a drink?"

"Even if she didn't," Tokki answered, "The men on the ship would and businessmen aren't exactly known to be the best keepers of secrets."

"Especially with alcohol involved," Phinegann agreed.

"Does that mean that we have a plan?" Illyria's wings fluttered behind her back.

"I think it does," Appelonia nodded.

While the cleric agreed, the vast majority of her attention was on the paladin. He wasn't able to stand still. He wavered from side to side as he tried to lead the discussion.

After he wiped at the last bit of sweat, no more came out to replace it. Outside in Nova Prime wasn't any cooler than down in Nova Omega and wearing armor was surely uncomfortable to say the least.

"Tokki?" Appelonia addressed the Bunny Barbarian even as she looked toward the paladin, "Can you catch Jonas?"

"What?" Tokki's head tilted to the side, "Why?"

"Because he's about to pass out," she threw her arms out around Jonas as his eyes suddenly rolled back.

Tokki did the same thing and both he and the cleric caught the paladin as he collapsed. Appelonia expected him to be heavy with all the armor but she was still shocked at the sheer weight that dropped into her grasp.

If Tokki hadn't been there, there was a very real possibility that she would have been crushed. As it was, they laid him on the black ground flat on his back.

"What's wrong with him?" the Bunny Barbarian asked, sweat dripping down his pale nose and tanned chin.

"He's severely dehydrated," Appelonia answered before looking up at those who accompanied him before they were reunited, "When was the last time he drank some water?"

"We all ran out of water shortly before our audience with the Mullah," Jin said, "He gave the last of it to Andromeda."

"Of course he did," Apple muttered before uttering a quiet prayer over the empty leather bladder that Jonas used to carry water, "And people wonder what use clerics are on long excursions."

With quiet sloshing, the bladder filled with water. The metal of Jonas' armor even started to fog, showing that the water was much cooler than their surroundings.

Once the bladder was stretched full, the cleric pulled the stopper from the mouth and dumped two different packets of powder into the water. Replacing the stopper, she shook and squeezed the leather to mix the ingredients together.

"How did you do that?" Bronwyn asked.

"What did you put in the water?" Jin asked simultaneously with the woman.

"A blessing of Kuan Yin," Appelonia opened the bladder again and lifted it to the mouth of the paladin, "When we are in true need, we can ask for a necessity to be provided to us like water. It falls under the idea that we have to keep ourselves going to be able to be of service to others," A little half-smile pulled at her mouth as she glanced over at Tokki.

The red haired woman slowly fed water to the unconscious man. If she simply dumped it into his mouth, his body would instinctively choke and spit it out. That wouldn't help anyone.

Apple continued, "I did it once while we were wondering around in the caves below, too. But once we're back on our plane, I doubt she could give so much."

"As water is more plentiful there," Illyria looked quite impressed as she slipped the tools she was using to repair her wings back into her pockets.

"But what did you add to it?" Jin asked again.

"Just a little salt and some sugar," Appelonia slipped another sip into the mouth of the paladin, "It helps the water get absorbed more efficiently."

Something in the distance caught Phinegann's attention and he pointed to the west (at least that was the direction the cleric arbitrarily decided to be west) with his metal arm, "Our horses."

Jin looked off in that direction, "Some of them at least."

The paladin smacked his lips together, his eyes fluttering as he returned to the realm of the conscious, "What happened?" he asked, groggy as if he'd just awoken from a nap.

"I could ask the same thing," Genevieve said as she walked up to the group, "If I were paranoid, I would think you were trying to damage he to whom I am bonded."

"He's just dehydrated," Appelonia lifted the water to his lips again as she gave the demon a flat look, "He'll be fine in a few hours."

Jonas gulped down another mouthful of water before, with the help of Tokki and the cleric, he sat up. He was just in time to witness Genevieve dumping the heavy metal pieces of Andromeda's armor to the red grass covered ground.

"If you had taken me up on my offer, Master, you would not have fainted," the demon laughed under her breath.

Appelonia quirked an eyebrow at Jonas, "Offer?"

All the paladin did in answer was shake his head and take another sip of water. Genevieve was only too happy to aid him in explaining.

"He stripped his horse of her armor to drive away the heat," she said, "I offered to do the same for him but I fear he is too shy," Again she laughed, dragging her pink tongue over her sharp white teeth.

"My reasons are my own, Genevieve. Although shyness isn't one of them," Jonas gave the demon a defiant smirk before starting to stand, "How many horses were you able to find?"

"Two more, Master," the efreeti woman answered, "A large one that I presume was meant to carry the ogre..."

With that, Phinegann marched over and snatched the reins from the hands of Genevieve. It was indeed the horse he'd been entrusted with back in Dianmeyer. It was just about the same size as Andromeda, the paladin's horse, with rich brown coat and long white fur hanging just above its hooves.

The efreeti continued, "And this blue one."

"Bommer!" Handing the leather bladder to the paladin, Appelonia jumped to her feet and rushed to her horse, wrapping her arms around the base of his neck, "I'm so sorry I left you alone for so long," Her voice was muffled by his shining coat.

"There should be three more," Phinegann said as he moved his saddlebags from Andromeda back to his own horse.

"Two and a half, if you count Illyria's horse by size," Jin grinned down at the gnome.

"Oh ha ha," Illyria chortled back sarcastically at the taller man with the bushy beard.

"The midget one was was devoured by a burning soul," Genevieve reported, "As was the one that carried this pack."

The efreeti woman tossed Tokki's tightly packed bag to the ground. There was a bow draped across the top of the pack, held in place by the flap that sealed the contents inside.

It was wrapped in black fur but polished wood peeked out at several points along the arch of the bow. Arrows poked out from the right side of the flap, each with different colors of fur just above the nock, where the fletching that was usually made of feathers would be.

"Let's get back to our plane," Jona said after he was finally again upright (thanks to help from Tokki and Jin), "Get our horses and supplies straightened out, and get to work finding that child."

"Oh?" the demon stepped up beside her Master, "Where shall we go then?"

"We were figuring that out while you were gone," the Shepherd said, "I wish for all of us to go to Craigh Na Troon."

OPHELIA INTERROGATION NOTES:

"I don't see the problem here," Ophelia handed the parchment back to me.

"That's because you're limiting the scope of your own vision," I replied.

"And what's that supposed to mean?" the subject asked.

"Do you realize that you haven't actually looked directly at me the entire time we have been speaking?" I asked.

"No, I hadn't," the subject answered.

"Do so now, please," I said.

Ophelia slowly turned her head. It seemed to take her a tremendous amount of effort but finally she faced my direction precisely.

"What do you see?" I asked.

"You're in the uniform of a Light Bringer," the subject said.

I nodded, "And this is an organization you trust?"

Ophelia nodded back.

"But not so much the Romefeller Guild?" I inquired.

No response from the subject.

"Would you like to read more of Saya's statement before you decide?" I offered.

Decades before...

SAYA STEPPED THROUGH the doorway of the building she, Folken, Lyan, Josie, and Harby had their last stand against the penanggalan. "Folken? Josie? Are you still here? Is Harbenigyr alright?" It took a moment for her violet eyes to adjust to the darkness of the shadows that still clung to the interior of the structure. Particularly since the sun had just started to come up outside.

"We are well," the sorcerer's deep voice answered his cousin.

Folken rose from his kneeling position beside the cleric, who was laying face down on the flat boards of the floor. Josie was applying the last of some ointment that Saya was sure her cousin had given the ranger. He would have been loathe to do it himself. Folken surely did abhor being messy.

The armor Harbenigyr had be pressed into had, of course, been removed so that they could treat the burns that the explosion from the cellar caused. Thankfully, there didn't appear to be any blackened, charred flesh, so there was a good chance that the elf's back would not even scar permanently.

Lyan Yo Bunpy stepped into the building shortly after the svartalfar woman, followed by Hero, who looked at ill-ease, and then Ophelia, who took another long sip from the bottle of wine in her hand. The sorcerer stepped toward all four women.

While he was not one to usually report results of his actions, he felt it appropriate here. Especially when he saw the looks on the faces of Lyan and Ophelia.

"I have drained the blisters on the cleric's back and Josie is administering a healing salve of my own design to his skin," he said, "It will be as if the unpleasantness never occurred in less than a day."

"Except for our dead horses, a dozen dead women, and a town we've left open to ransacking by the next band of thieves that decide to come through," Ophelia said as she wiped a stray bead of liquid from her lower lip.

"They did attack us," Folken responded to the mercenary, "I take it that you've come to some sort of arrangement with the rest of the penanggalan women in the village? Otherwise, surely Hero here would be leading a charge against us."

The bard shook her head even as she could only bring herself to look at his boots, "We're no threat to you anymore, Lord Folken. I never wanted to be."

"What does she mean by 'anymore'?" Folken returned his attention to Saya.

"The women in the village are no longer penanggalan," she answered, "Ophelia killed Miranda. Apparently if you kill the source of the bloodline, anyone created by her return to being mere mortals."

"So you did not need rescuing after all," the green haired man turned his attention to the mercenary.

"It would have been appreciated if it had been earlier," Ophelia took another long sip from the bottle, "But it all worked out, I suppose," the woman shrugged.

Folken arched an emerald eyebrow at the mercenary, "Is that a vintage from this ruined hamlet?"

Again Ophelia shrugged, "I... found it in the cellar after I stomped Miranda and Bianca's heads in."

The sorcerer let out a quiet grunt, "I do hope you've brought a stretcher of some sort to transport Harbenigyr back to your little hamlet," he directed his words to the bard.

She nodded, "Along with horses for the rest of you. We can't really make up for what we tried to do to you, but we hoped that you'd find that at least a little bit of recompense, my Lord."

"You don't have your lute," Josie noticed even from where she remained kneeling beside Harbenigyr.

"It's still, um, down there," Hero motioned in the direction of the cellar they had trapped her last night, "I'll get it back today."

"We really should get the cleric loaded up and out of here," Lyan interrupted, stepping around Saya with the rolled up litter under her arm, "The sooner he is healed, the sooner we can move on."

"We, Lyan?" Saya rested her hands on her hips, "I thought you didn't want to join our little party."

"You also said if I changed my mind that I should look for you," Lyan didn't look up as she flattened the stretcher on the floor beside the cleric, "I still have that Meteorend rock that we need to sort out, as well."

"She has Meteorend?" Folken looked back and forth from his cousin to the barbarian.

"She said it appeared beside her spear the day after the tournament," Saya answered.

Josie started pulling Harby up by his shoulder. Lyan slipped the flattened stretcher under the elf and shuffled sideways. She pushed on the man's hip to lift his legs and slid the bottom half under the cleric. Gently, they laid him face down again.

"What did you give Harby to knock him out like that?" Ophelia asked as she stepped around Hero.

"It was a simple sleeping draught. We needed him to stay still for treatment," the svartalfar man responded.

"How did he get so badly burned, anyway?" Ophelia's question was met with a lot of quiet stares.

Those from Josie and Lyan turned to lock on Folken, their faces harder than the stone that made up the stubbornly standing walls of the ruin. Saya looked anywhere but in his direction while Hero kept a sharp eye on the floor.

"Looks like I hit a tender subject," Ophelia took another sip from the bottle.

"Or perhaps, your attire has caused some distraction," the sorcerer quipped.

"That is a lot of pink," Josie commented before tidying up the cleric's black ponytail.

"It's not by choice," the mercenary said, "Miranda ripped my pants to shreds begging for her life while I slammed her head against the wall."

"And Bianca's style isn't much like hers," Hero chimed in, "I'm sure Betsy, our tailor, will be able to provide you with something a little more, um, battle ready."

"You don't have to do me any favors," Ophelia practically hissed back at the diminutive bard.

"More like penance," Hero returned her gaze to the floor, "We've been forced to be monsters for so long that I think it's only fair that we try to at least start making up for it."

"Pretty words," the mercenary said before wrapping her lips around the bottle again.

"Has anyone seen Harby's tunic?" Josie suddenly spoke up.

Ophelia suddenly choked on her wine. She wiped several streams of dribble from her chin as she coughed up what liquid when down her throat wrong.

The ranger was looking back and forth at the ground, all around where she had been kneeling. While the armor that Harby had been wearing was haphazardly tossed off to the side, his white robes were nowhere to be seen.

"They must have gotten lost in the shuffle while we were fighting the pentagons," Lyan conjectured, "Perhaps the shirt fell into the cellar with them?"

"I guess it's possible," Josie shrugged, "It wasn't like I was keeping track of it when Harby was turned into a human shield."

"Elfin," Folken corrected, "But your point stands. It was not a popular decision. Nevertheless, we all survived the encounter."

"We will take the chainmail and breastplate with us," Lyan motioned to the pieces of armor. "At the very least, he can have the option of wearing the chainmail until Hero's tailor friend can provide him with something more appropriate."

The Bunny Barbarian hopped up to her feet and picked up the two pieces of armor. She gently rested them on the back of Harbenigyr's legs for transport along with him into town.

"Is there anything else anyone needs here?" Lyan asked the whole group.

Everyone agreed it was time to get back to Laeradr. With the aid of the horses, and two women who could carry Harby's stretcher and keep up with the rest of the group (Lyan and Ophelia), the trip didn't take long at all.

Some of the women in the village were already starting to board up Bianca's house, to bar anyone else from entering. Whether this was going to be permanent or temporary, Saya had to admit to herself that she just didn't care.

They ended up taking Harbenigyr to the only building in the small village that was not only unoccupied but didn't have the stink of death coming up from the basement: Miranda's house. Josie and Lyan put Harbenigyr into the woman's bed as carefully as possible.

The cleric muttered something about something burning confusion from a cold heart, making it pliable again. Saya figured it was some verse from whatever scriptures a cleric of Kuan Yin studied.

Josie was closer, perhaps she heard the whole phrase? Whatever it was she did hear, her cheeks flushed a soft pink.

One by one, everyone filed out of the room. Ophelia finished off the bottle she'd been nursing. She opened this one when they entered the town limits. It was just after her hands started bleeding again and the ranger took her side of the litter to carry the rest of the way.

Saya stepped out, followed by the mercenary, leaving only the ranger in the room with the cleric. She said something quietly enough that even someone with as sharp of ears as the Romefeller Intelligence Officer couldn't catch it before she stepped out to join the rest of the party in the front room.

"What is wrong with everyone in town?" Ophelia asked, pulling yet another bottle from her long coat, "They aren't monsters anymore. You'd think that they'd be happy."

"They are," Hero said, "but the strength being a penanggalan gave us is how we were able to stand up to the wandering bands of thieves and marauders. Now, Laeradr essentially defenseless."

"You make it sound like women are incapable of defending themselves," Lyan stamped the sharp teeth of her gauntlet into the table beside the map of the town, "Ophelia alone has shown that to be more than untrue."

"You are a good argument against that idea yourself, Lyan," Saya said.

"I speak of women I've seen in battle," the Bunny Barbarian nodded, "Even if I were female, I would not speak of myself in such a braggadocios manner."

Everyone in the room froze when they heard that. The first sound that finally filled the room was a chuckle from Ophelia. Words came shortly after a quick drag from her opaque bottle.

"If you aren't a woman, then what are you, Lyan?" the mercenary just had to ask.

"I am the Child of Prophecy for my tribes," the barbarian answered in all seriousness, "Born on the night of the Shooting Rabbit Eclipse, I am the warrior foretold to rid the all the lands of Honua of the Great Evil."

"And what is the Great Evil?" Ophelia asked.

"That is what I must search for," Lyan replied, "I must find and destroy it by my own hand. Only then, will my destiny be fulfilled."

Folken arose from the chair he'd been sitting in, listening intently, "Tell me, Child of Prophesy, are women allowed to be warriors among the Yo Bunpy?"

Lyan scoffed, "While Ophelia, and perhaps even your sister here, could handle themselves with with troubles you may stumble upon in these lands, there is no way they could withstand the grueling, tempering fires that is the training of a Yo Bunpy warrior. No woman could!" she declared.

"Cousin," Folken simply corrected her.

"What is that?" Lyan's pride was derailed by confusion.

"Saya is my cousin, not my sister," Folken said, "While I understand the confusion, I cannot let it stand."

"My apologies," Lyan gave the man a polite bow.

Ophelia slipped around the Bunny Barbarian and up to the sorcerer, pressing herself close enough that almost any prying ears couldn't hear. Almost.

"Folken, how could she think she's a man with boobs like that?" Saya heard the mercenary whisper to her cousin.

"She was the only child born under that astronomical event that occurred that night," Folken whispered back, "As women cannot be warriors in their culture, she was raised as a boy. How they maintained the ruse? That is anyone's guess."

"Puberty had to be fun," Ophelia smirked as she made her way back to her side of the table.

The sorcerer nodded in agreement before changing the subject completely, "Are there any reports of suspicious bands wandering within the Jaded Woods at the moment?" he asked Hero.

"Not that I'm aware of," the bard answered, "The last group to attack Laeradr came last month. Then there was one six weeks before that."

"That is unusually high activity for this region," Folken said, mostly to himself.

Saya spoke up, "The Jaded Woods would be a perfect short cut for the bands if most of them were simply passing through to other destinations like Silver Lake or Ash Providence. Judging from the conditions of the roads, it's doubtful that the Light Bringers patrol with any regularity. And with the rumors of the forest being haunted, the brigands would avoid detection as they moved their entire operations."

"And coming upon Laeradr would be considered a target of opportunity too tempting to pass up," Folken agreed, "Very well, I have a solution."

"I'm going to check on Harby," Josie interrupted before stepping around the sorcerer and back down the hall to the room where the cleric slept.

The pale man continued, looking slightly annoyed at the disruption, "As Emerald City is closer than Valen Court, Saya will send for a detachment from the Soldier Guild of Romefeller to watch over Laeradr until the Light Bringers can bring a regular presence into this forest."

"I will?" she blinked at the man who outranked her within organization, "Wouldn't your word carry more weight?"

Folken waved the idea off dismissively with his clawed hand, "Yours carries almost as much weight as mine, cousin. Particularly when you are traveling with me. Treize would expect me to delegate such a task."

Not even Saya dared used her father's first name in such a conversational manner. But she couldn't argue. So she simply nodded to the Romefeller Guilds Grand Chancellor and he continued.

"That leaves us with the task of what to do with the artifact we know as Meteorend," Folken said, "Lyan, could you please produce this rock for inspection?"

Instead of bending down to reach into any kind of bag or anything else like a pocket (not that there was any place for one in her revealing armor), the heavily muscled woman simply raised the butt of her spear over the table. She tapped it against the flat surface of the wood and the very same black rock that Raiko had protected so vehemently suddenly appeared.

"I tried leaving the thing on the side of the road when I first discovered it," she explained, "After several hours, it reappeared when I pressed my spear into the ground while I walked. I finally placed it in one of my bags, but it still reappears this way after several hours."

"Fascinating," the fingers of Folken's metal hand rhythmically opened and closed one after another absently as he stood in silent thought, "The de Junamend mentioned that Meteorend must be recovered by the victor of battle before the loser breathes his last. Since Lyan's spear is what killed this... Raiko, Meteorend must have judged Lyan to be who bested him."

"It's true, for all intents and purposes," Ophelia shrugged. "The question is, how do we get it back to the de Junamend? We left our only contact with them dead in a cage back in Ash Providence. At least, we thought he was dead."

"Harbenigyr's evil doppelganger is still alive," Folken ran a finger over the map on the table from the building they were occupying at the moment to the abandoned building where their fracas with the penanggalan occurred, "We also know that there is a second Josie about, as well."

"Wait a moment," Lyan held up a hand to physically repeat her request, "Evil doppelgangers?"

"Yes," the sorcerer nodded, "As we already had this conversation with the constable of Ash Providence, may I suggest you simply take our word for it for the time being?"

"Speaking of Josie, where is she?" Ophelia spoke up.

Hero answered, "She went back into Miranda's room to check in on Harbenigyr."

"And he's still asleep," Josie said as she stepped back into the room, "Whatever Folken gave him has him out colder than a week old campfire."

"If I am correct, he will not regain consciousness until tomorrow morning," Folken said, "By then his burns should be completely healed."

"I don't know, those burns seemed awfully severe to me," the ranger frowned.

"Nonsense," Folken again waved his metal hand dismissively, "You underestimate the recuperative power of sleep, not to mention the synergistic effects such a state has with the healing salve."

"Boy, you really do think of everything. Don't you?" Ophelia chimed in flatly before sipping at the bottle in her hand.

"As much as possible," the svartalfar man agreed.

"If we can get back on the subject at hand," Ophelia plopped the wine bottle on the table then leaned forward, resting both of her hands on the table. "What do we do with Meteorend? Put it on a pedestal in the town square for Evil Harby to find with a sign asking nicely for him to leave us alone?"

"I'm afraid it isn't that simple," Folken replied, "Miranda does indeed have a tremendous library. Particularly when it comes to the Clan Wars."

"What does this have to do with that?" Lyan asked, pointing down at the black rock.

"In my studies, I have learned that it was the de Junamend who started that very conflict," the sorcerer said, "They used the destructive power of Meteorend to attack the Grissom Clan and decimated it in a matter of days. Then they moved on to the Palancias, and so on."

"In your studies?" Ophelia narrowed her pale blue eyes at the even paler man, "Just when did you have the time to go through her library?"

"I require little sleep and can be quite silent when I wish to be," he answered.

"So you snooped through Miranda's house while she and Saya were sleeping," the mercenary clarified.

"To leave such bounties of knowledge untapped for want of several hours of unnecessary rest sounds just this side of foolhardy to me," Folken waved a hand toward the many shelves full of various sized books.

"The point is, he had the time and motivation to read up on the Clan Wars, Ophelia," Saya stepped in, "This is all connected to Meteorend and puts us in a real predicament."

Lyan tapped the table with a fingertip, her brown eyes locked on the rock, "I remember when I was a child, I heard whispers that the de Junamend would come to the Land of the Long Toothed Rabbit. That they would burn it before we could even throw a spear at one of them. Do you believe that if they get Meteorend back, they'll start the war again?"

"I do," the sorcerer said, "The Clan War only ended when the de Junamend finally came to the table to negotiate with the remaining clans. The Light Bringers arbitrated the truce but none of that was possible until the de Junamend lost their offensive edge."

"You think that was when Raiko took Meteorend and left their lands," Saya figured that was where Folken's train of thought was leading.

"Indeed," He nodded back at his cousin, looking pleased with her, "Horta mentioned that with Meteorend out of their control, the de Junamend went from being the hunters to the hunted. Whatever reason Raiko had for taking the artifact, he felt it was worth his people losing most, if not all of their gains from that conflict. The Gryphton Point Treaty distributed the lands taken by the de Junamend to the surviving clans as penance for the de Junamend's wanton destruction during the conflict."

"So what do you think we should do with it, Folken?" Ophelia placed her palm on the mouth of the wine bottle and started making it roll lazy circles along the top of the table, "I'm guessing that your solution involves the oh so safe hands of the Romefeller Guilds."

The sorcerer cocked an eyebrow, "You have some objection to this?"

"You're not the only one who has done research," Ophelia replied, "The Romefeller Guilds are an army for hire. Sure, you have a dozen different divisions with a dozen different areas of expertise but, bottom line, each one fights for whichever side has the most gold."

"Your point?" Oddly, Folken looked amused by the mercenary's comments.

"What happens when your Guild takes up a contract that's more trouble than you anticipated?" Ophelia then shook her head, "Scratch that, what if your Guild takes up a contract you just want to have over and done with quickly?"

"I agree with Ophelia," Lyan stated before the sorcerer could answer.

Folken's violet eyes drifted back and forth between the Bunny Barbarian and Ophelia. The fingers of his metal hand flexed and relaxed one after the other as he considered his next words.

"Ophelia, as you are under the employ of this very *army for hire*. I do not see how you can feel morally superior to myself or Saya," he finally said, then turned his attention to the barbarian, "As you are from an isolated tribe, Lyan Yo Bunpy, what dealings with the Romefeller have you had to come to such a disingenuous opinion of us?"

The Bunny Barbarian let out a heavy sigh as she shook her head, "You used Harbenigyr as a human shield without any consideration of his willingness to do it."

"Elfin," Folken corrected, and then let out a sigh of his own, "As you are but one warrior, I doubt that you could keep Meteorend from the hands of the de Junamend for long. Especially when they learn that it is in your possession. What makes you think that the Yo Bunpy Tribe has any better chance against them now than when you were a child? Perhaps you plan to use it on them pre-emptively yourself?"

Lyan ground the sharpened tips of her gauntlet deeper into the wood of the table. She couldn't think of anything to say.

"We can take it to the Light Bringers," Ophelia chimed in.

"You would trust them and not the Romefeller?" Any hint of amusement that the pale man had earlier was gone, "Please tell me how they have garnered such fealty when we have come to your aid and they did not?"

"It's not a question of fealty, Folken," Ophelia said, "They're the ones that negotiated the Gryphton Point Treaty. They would want to keep Meteorend out of de Junamend hands and they would have an army of support to keep it from happening."

"And then what happens when they come across a force that's *more trouble than they anticipated*?" Saya argued for her cousin, "You would trust them to not use the artifact's power to save their own skins?"

"I have not witnessed them use dishonorable tactics in battle," Lyan answered for Ophelia.

"And to which Light Bringer will you take it?" Folken asked, "Do you plan to walk up to the first foot soldier you see and ask them to take Meteorend to his superiors in Valen Court?"

Ophelia shook her head. "I know one of their Colonels back in Riverbelt. I trust her to get it where it can be protected."

"That sounds noble but Riverbelt is on the coast," Saya raised her long gloved arm, pointing to the southwest, "It would take you weeks to get back there. Emerald City is only a couple of days away."

"The de Junamend would have to find us first," Lyan straightened up to her full height, which was just a shade taller than the sorcerer. "We could avoid the roads. Go cross country."

"Bold talk for one who has only a map to guide her," Folken replied, "You do not know the terrain. The de Junamend have been searching for Meteorend for years. They must be familiar with the entire continent by now."

"I'll guide them," Josie spoke up, stepping next to the table between Ophelia and Lyan, "I know routes that could cut down travel time to Riverbelt dramatically. Not to mention that I know ways to hide our tracks."

"As do I," Lyan added

"You are revolting as well , Josie?" Folken's face was as still as stone.

"I'm not a member of the Romefeller Guilds, Folken," the ranger stated, "I work for who I want, when I want."

It had been some time since Saya had seen her cousin that angry. Surely, as the other women didn't know Folken as well, it was unlikely that they could tell thanks to his well practiced mask of indifference.

If he hadn't already loosed his charge of Ultima earlier that evening, the svartalfar woman thought that he would have likely unleashed it on the three standing across from them right there. Still, Folken didn't act rashly.

His entire body mimicked his face and became as stiff as stone. The only part of him that moved were his eyes. He was calculating. Always calculating.

But Saya was almost out of every bladed weapon she usually carried. Most of her blades were blown away in the cellar along with the rest of the penanggalan that died down there.

Add to that the prospect of fighting for something that belonged to Raiko. It was important to him, true, but he had not been important to her for weeks now. What he thought was love didn't go further than his pants.

"As I am out voted four to one, I relent," Folken declared.

Saya had to blink a few times before it actually registered that he'd spoken. Even then, it took her a few seconds longer to realize the meaning of what he'd said.

"Four?" Saya glanced around the table, "But neither Hero nor I have said anything."

"It is true that young Hero hasn't said anything in some time," the sorcerer nodded at the short woman, who couldn't suppress a smile even as she dropped her head to stare at the table, "You are the fourth vote against to which I was referring."

The svartalfar woman's platinum eyebrows pressed together, "Me? I didn't object to taking Meteorend back to Emerald City."

"You forget that I know you, cousin," Folken motioned toward the black rock as he spoke, "While Meteorend was important to this... Raiko, you haven't the desire to fight over it. After all, he had not endeared himself to any of your for some time before his demise."

"True," Ophelia nodded in agreement.

"As such, in our newly formed band of six, four is a decided majority," the green haired man continued, "Once Harbenigyr is sufficiently recovered, Josie will guide us to Riverbelt where Meteorend can be turned over to a trusted body of influence for protection."

"Would you mind if your band numbered seven, Lord Folken?" Hero unexpectedly spoke up, "I can't stay in Laeradr anymore."

"You were already counted in his six, Hero," Saya answered for her cousin, "I have to stay behind to organize the guard that the Soldier Guild sends from Emerald City."

CHAPTER TEN

OPHELIA INTERROGATION NOTES

"Did you not find it strange that Folken dismissed Saya so suddenly?" I asked.

"She took orders from him," Ophelia shrugged, "It's not my place to say if they were righteous or not."

"That's an interesting word," I said, "Righteous. It seems to me that you do not think that this Folken is a trustworthy individual."

"He's not exactly in the trust business," the subject said.

"Nor is Saya," I replied, "Yet you appear to trust her."

"I never said that," the subject said, "I thought you said that you only dealt in facts."

"I do. However, the places where you place your trust intrigue me," I said, "Take that paladin, Jonas, for instance. Would you say that he has your trust?"

"Just hand me his statement about what happened in Craigh Na Troon," Ophelia motioned to me in a beckoning manner.

Decades later...

LIGHT SURROUNDED THE group as Genevieve started the process of granting the wish Jonas made to return the party to the mortal realm. The cleric had not been to Craigh Na Troon since she'd hit puberty. While she hadn't thought of it before, Appelonia suspected that her father had something to do with that decision.

Craigh Na Troon didn't exactly have the, for lack of a better term, cleanest reputation. Not in regards to the tidiness of the city itself but more along the lines of the various less than above board things you could get or do there. Surely Dad didn't want to her see or somehow get involved in any of that.

This trip through the portal was far more pleasant than the first. Firstly because they were expecting it this time. Also, it was getting steadily cooler as the light enveloped more and more of the group. That was a relief after being stuck in chainmail in the oppressive heat of Nova Prime and Omega.

The light faded away to reveal the party on the bank of a wide river, long grass curling around their feet as a cool breeze washed over all of them. Illyria and Jin Vega both let out long sighs of delight at the sensation. In fact, the monk fell flat on his back and just enjoyed the cool air and sunshine.

Appelonia looked around to make sure everyone else was there. After all, their first time through one of Genevieve's portals ended up with half of them trapped underground.

Not this time. In addition to Elly and Jin, Phinegann looked so much more at ease than he did before, although that air of discipline he carried was still all around him. He didn't even smile.

Tokki had already loaded his heavy pack onto his back, despite Apple's invitation to stow it with her belongings on Bommer. He put his black rabbit helmet back on just before the portal swallowed them all up. While he would have denied it, Appelonia was well aware that the Yo Bunpy were not big fans of magic. She found herself giggling at the thought of Tokki putting his helmet on to hide the worried look on his face. just to make sure that the women weren't disheartened, of course.

Speaking of women, Bronwyn LaRue made it through the portal with everyone. No unfortunate detour for her.

Once the portal had faded and she was sure they were all firmly back in the mortal realm, Bronwyn pulled her bandanna off her head to expose her wavy black hair to the cool air. Then she slipped her coat back over her shoulders as she looked around to get her bearings.

And there was Jonas. He was a little pale after passing out from heat exhaustion but he was already kneeling beside the water and splashing his face with the cool liquid, then splashing some down inside his steel armor as best he could one handed. His other hand was holding the leather bladder from which he was still drinking.

Cooling himself down was just what she would have recommended. That and taking off all that armor. Admittedly, part of that prescription may have been a bit self serving but... Appelonia to herself and turned away rather than finish the thought.

The cleric found herself frowning when she saw Genevieve walk up to the paladin. She was back in her human guise. Appelonia couldn't be sure but she thought that the other woman's short white dress, a mockery of the robes worn by clerics of the Order of Kuan Yin, was even shorter than it was before (if it was at all possible).

She reached into the water with both hands and splashed Jonas, as well. In short order he was soaked and, physically looking much stronger. Genevieve was drenched as well and none of the white clothing hid that fact. It had become practically translucent.

Appelonia turned to her horse, checking to make sure his saddle and the bags were securely fastened. Again. She led him to the river so that he could drink. He had to be thirsty after being chased around by monsters in a hell dimension for who knows how long.

Phinegann took Apple's lead and pulled his horse to the water. Along with Bommer and Andromeda, the orc's horse had not only his gear but a portion of some belonging to everyone else whose horse had died down in Nova Prime.

Again, the cleric gave a silent prayer of thanks to Kuan Yin for protecting Bommer. Apple didn't know if she could have lived with herself if he'd been hurt because she let herself get dragged away from him.

"Are you okay, Appelonia?" Jonas was right behind her when he spoke.

The young woman jumped at the at the unexpected attention. Especially from him. Her cheeks only turned a deeper shade of pink and she started patting Bommer's shoulder at a pace that seemed a bit too... energetic.

"Oh, I'm just fine. Thanks for asking," she glanced back at the paladin before looking down at herself, "Why? Do I look like there's something wrong with me?"

Jonas shook his head, "Nothing like that. You just seemed a little, well, distracted." His dark eyebrows furrowed together as he did look down at her tunic, "Although you do look like you could use a change of clothes."

Appelonia couldn't help but agree. She looked as if she had just finished slaughtering an animal or even killing someone and practically bathing in their blood. Sure, the entire mess was from holding the giant heart of a monster so that Phinegann could be healed but that would be hard to explain to random passers by.

The cleric opened the saddlebag closest to her and reached in, only to pull black rocks and ash from inside. Letting them tumble from her hand to the ground, Appelonia found herself glaring at Genevieve.

"Apparently, I don't have any," she said flatly.

She wiped the ash covering her hand on the leg of her white pants, leaving a gray streak on her thigh. All the demon woman did in reply was give a "who, me?" expression by pursing her red lips at the cleric. Appelonia was pretty sure it was to keep from laughing in front of Jonas.

"Genevieve, could you come here please?" Jonas waved the efreeti over to join him and the cleric.

Apple found herself standing a little taller, trying not to take pleasure in the berating that the demon woman was about to receive. Genevieve, for her part, maintained her "I don't know what's happening" composure as she walked up to the other two.

"What can I do for you, Master?" she grinned at the paladin before her gray eyes moved to focus on the other woman.

"Not for me, Genevieve," Jonas said, "About Appelonia."

The cleric found her lips starting to stretch into a thin smirk. Surely, the demon would think twice before messing with Appelonia or her things again.

"Is there anything you can do to help Appelonia clean her tunic?" he asked the efreeti.

"What was that?" Both women asked at the same time, with similar expressions on their faces.

"We need to try and not stand out when we actually go into Craigh Na Troon," Jonas motioned to the cleric, specifically her stained sleeves, "Being covered in blood only makes people want to ask questions."

"Are you wishing I," the efreeti woman's eyes dragged up and down Appelonia's frame before returning to the paladin, "cleanse her, Master?"

"If it has to be, Genevieve," Jonas nodded.

Appelonia found herself glancing up at the other woman's standing hair. It was where her horns would have been if she'd still been in her true form. The cleric found herself wishing they became so deformed from the portal and this *wish* that they ended up poking Genevieve every time she moved her head.

"Very well," the black haired woman nodded back, "Give me a moment."

Just up the river, only about fifty paces, was a pier that had a group of merchants and fruit stands and other regalia for sale. Genevieve merged into the traffic of customers making their way from seller to seller.

After a few minutes, the demon woman returned with a small net filled with six lemons in one hand and a pouch filled with some kind of powder in the other, "One freshly laundered cleric, coming right up!" she announced.

Genevieve stepped up to Appelonia, who seriously thought about grabbing one of her sticks to keep her away. The other woman stopped less than a step in front of her before dropping the net of lemons and the pouch to the ground.

The efreeti woman reached for the belt that held the cleric's chainmail vest closed and unfastened it before Appelonia even thought to slap her hands away. Genevieve moved her attention to the hook that connected the top portion of the linked armor closed, where it slipped into a loop just under the right pauldron.

Once that was unfastened, Genevieve slipped the chainmail off Appelonia's shoulders, letting it fall to the ground behind her. Then the woman with standing black hair reached down for the lemons.

Appelonia leaned to the side to get the attention of the paladin, "What is she doing, Jonas?"

The man looked as if he was enjoying the show, though he tried to hide it, "Cleaning your tunic first, I suppose."

"These are an odd style of pants," Genevieve commented.

Apple looked down at herself. She wore the same style of pants as her mother and Ophelia. The hips of the garment were cut open with only the leather of the belt around her waist touching her sides. They were made of the same white material of her tunic, which had long tails but the front was cut just high enough to expose her navel.

The swirling jade pattern that ran up and down her sleeves were obscured by the blood but, as Genevieve took Appelonia's hand, the efreeti pulled the arm of the cleric out to the side. With the net hanging off the wrist of the hand holding Apple's, Genevieve lifted one of the yellow fruits over the other woman's arm and squeezed.

Juice rained down on Appelonia's arm as the efreeti moved her hand up and down the length of the cleric's sleeve, as if she were seasoning it. Once the lemon was squeezed dry, Genevieve bit into one side and spat the thick skin off to the side.

She then rubbed the rind in the middle of the lemon along her sleeve, specifically where the bloodstains were thickest. She did this again with another lemon, and then one more before switching to Apple's other arm.

The process repeated itself and the cleric kept going back and forth from staring at Genevieve and then over to Jonas. She looked at both with equal amounts of disbelief, "Jonas, is she cleaning my tunic or readying me to be dinner?" the tone in Apple's voice was almost pleading.

"She does raise a good question," Jonas finally acknowledged the cleric, "Genevieve, what do lemons have to do with laundry?"

"Lemon and mineral infused water are both effective at removing blood from cloth, Master," The efreeti answered as she tossed the last lemon to the grass and picked up the pouch, "Along with the assistance of cleansing agents, of course."

"That doesn't mean that you have to do that with the tunic still on–"

The paladin's comment was cut short when Genevieve dumped all the powder over Appelonia's head, all at once. A chalky cloud suddenly surrounded the women and when Jonas was able to see them again, Genevieve had hoisted Appelonia over her shoulder and was marching straight for the river.

"As we are at the mouth of the river where it meets the sea, the two waters mix and have an eclectic mix of minerals with which to aid the cleaning," Genevieve continued explaining to Jonas, ignoring Appelonia as she struggled to free herself from the grip of the efreeti.

When they reached the edge of the water, Genevieve simply bent over and dropped the red haired woman in. After the resulting splash, everywhere that the water hit the still standing demon woman's dress was again transparent.

Genevieve had already turned and started back toward Appelonia's chainmail when the cleric rose out of the water. Apple sputtered at the cold liquid matted her crimson hair to her face. Holding her arms out to her sides, she flicked them several times to loose several streams of water just to lighten her limbs.

As she huffed for breath, Appelonia slogged out of the river. With a flip of her head, her hair was out of her eyes and she was able to see again. The sight that greeted her was a staring Jonas and Tokki Yo Bunpy.

"What?" she asked.

Looking down at herself, Apple saw that all of her clothing was reacting to the water just as Genevieve's did. She might as well have been naked!

With a loud squeak of embarrassment, Appelonia's arms shot up to cover as much of her body as she could. She couldn't see, but she was sure that steam must have been rising from her soaked head as her entire body flushed pink.

"I would get that water out of your boots before they are ruined, girl," Genevieve said as if she were trying to be helpful.

She stepped up beside Jonas and Tokki, carrying the cleric's chainmail armor draped over one arm. It was still more red than steel colored.

Sliding her free hand under the bottom edge of the armored vest, fire spurt to life in Genevieve's hand. The flames quickly engulfed the chainmail and the smell of burning copper was suddenly on the breeze.

It only lasted a moment before it was replaced with the scent of heated steel. Again, Genevieve stepped to the river. This time, she dunked the vest into the water and pulled it out to the sound of hissing as the metal cooled.

Giving the garment a few shakes, droplets of water sprayed all around. Genevieve looked the vest over and didn't look satisfied.

She pursed her lips as if she were about to whistle. Instead, warm air jetted from her mouth and over the links of metal, forcing any remaining water to fly off the now polished looking surface.

Then the efreeti held the vest out to Appelonia, "You may want to put this on while its still warm," she smiled wide.

Appelonia stomped over to Genevieve and snatched her armor from the grasp of the other woman. Then, after turning her back on the two men still watching, she slipped the vest on and fastened it closed. Now, at least a portion of her modesty could be maintained.

Jin stood up behind Jonas and Tokki, looking amused himself, "Even if you don't like her methods, Appelonia, you have to admit that your tunic is clean now."

Lifting her sleeves again, the cleric did indeed have to agree that here wasn't a hint of red, or even pink left behind. That didn't stop her from grumbling as Appelonia pulled one of her boots off to dump water out.

"So that truly is your natural hair color," the efreeti woman let out a surprised grunt, "That powder would have rendered anything non-animal based to be invisible."

"Is that why my clothes became see through?" Appelonia snapped, "Because they're cotton?"

"As well as remove any other stains that were not blood," Genevieve nodded, a smirk still spread all over her face, "After all, my Master wished you to be completely clean."

"Will they return to normal soon?" the cleric asked, still glaring at the other woman.

"As soon as they are dry," the demon answered.

"Great," Appelonia pouted as she slipped her boot back on.

"Actually, that lemon really did do a good job getting Tokki's blood off my hands," Illyria chimed in from the behind the black fur covered barbarian.

She tossed one of the lemons discarded by Genevieve away herself before rinsing her hands off in the river, followed by splashing her face. Some of the powder must have found its way into Illyria's hair when it was a cloud because half of her scalp was suddenly visible where hair had been just moments before.

Illyria jumped when she saw her reflection in the water. Then she started laughing.

"It's a good thing I have a well shaped head!" she snickered.

"So where to now?" Appelonia looked down at the portion of her bare looking legs that her armor didn't cover and at the half-bald looking gnome (she couldn't help but grin at the little woman's reaction). "Where are we going after we've dried off?"

"While I was on the pier," Genevieve spoke up as she pointed, "I did notice a tavern that went by the name of the Flustered Mermaid. Perhaps that could serve as our next destination?"

OPHELIA INTERROGATION NOTES:

"And what was the point of this?" the subject asked.

"Were you aware of what he was hiding?" I asked in response.

Ophelia's brow furrowed. She placed the parchment back on the table, taking a long moment before answering.

"Not at that time, no," the subject finally answered.

"Yet you still consider him trustable?" I inquired.

"As much as any man is, I suppose," the subject replied.

"So is it a gender thing for you then?" I asked, "Do you trust women more easily than men?"

"You know that isn't true," the subject said.

I honestly did not expect that response. I looked Ophelia over for any signs of duplicity before speaking again. I found none.

"What makes you say that?" I inquired.

"You're about to take me through my little chat with Hero back in Laeradr, aren't you?" the subject responded.

"I am," I said.

"Let's do it then," the subject demanded.

Decades earlier...

HERO TUCKED HER spare bard uniform into her leather backpack. Another pair of pants in. Some other odds and ends into the bag and the bard realized she was finished packing.

Her hand drifted up to the bandages on her chin and cheek, idly running over the white cloth. The reality that she was leaving hit her just then. She'd been a virtual prisoner of this town for so long that Hero had started to doubt that she'd ever be out from under Miranda's control.

"What's going through that head of yours?" the voice of Ophelia came from behind the smaller woman.

The mercenary stepped into Hero's room, taking a heavy sip from the bottle in her hand. Her steps were slow and steady, not showing any sign that she was at all inebriated. Despite the bottle after bottle of wine she had downed in the days since she killed Miranda and freed the rest of the town from the awful curse of being cannibalistic monsters.

"Nothing specific," Hero busied herself by fastening the buckles of her backpack, "Just getting ready for the trip."

"It's a long slog to Riverbelt from here," Ophelia said, "Are you sure to want to take it with us? I mean, you are free to go wherever you like."

"You mean wherever I like away from you," the bard turned to face the other woman.

Ophelia raised an eyebrow, "You realize that this is the first time you've looked me in the face since the basement?" a thin smile pulled at the corners of her mouth.

"Really," Hero's voice was monotone, "Is it a big worry to you, where and what I look at?"

"Not at all," the taller woman shook her head, "It's just a way of telling what kind of a person someone is."

"And what do you think you know about me?" Hero asked.

"You feel guilty," Ophelia answered.

"Of course I do," Hero felt the urge to look away but forced herself to keep looking at the mercenary, "I personally led more people than I can count to their deaths just so I wouldn't... hurt anymore."

The woman in the long red coat took another sip from her bottle, "Hurt? How do you mean?"

It took Hero a long, quiet moment to figure out how to answer, "You do realize that I never wanted to hurt anyone, right?"

Ophelia nodded, "But Miranda made you."

"Yes and no," the bard sighed, "Miranda was the one who decided who could feed and who had to wait. Anyone who resisted her was starved until the p-penanggalan took over her body. Then I was forced to watch as my own body ate another human being."

"Folken mentioned something like that when I tried to talk him into leaving you behind," Ophelia interjected, "That it was like you were a passenger when the monster came out. I got that impression from Bianca, too."

"The worst part," Hero swallowed hard as she continued, "Was you not only felt the pain go away as you fed but it actually started to feel, " the woman had to stop a dry heave before she could finish, "good. It felt good to be that creature, even just for that moment."

"Then why didn't you just embrace it?" the mercenary wondered, "You said that you've been irritating Miranda, forcing her to accept that you would only eat criminals and other compromises. Why do all that?"

"Some did embrace that rush of euphoria. Some actually came to enjoy the power of the creature. I couldn't. Whenever I think about it, I keep seeing the looks of terror in the eyes of the people as I took that first bite," Hero closed her eyes tight and wrapped a hand around her mouth.

Ophelia rested a hand around the bard's shoulder, "If anyone can understand being forced to do terrible things you don't want to do, it's me. Believe me."

The bard's eyes fluttered open and focused on the mercenary, "What do you mean?"

"It's a long story," Ophelia said, "Best told over drinks."

She held of the wine bottle to Hero, silently offering the other woman a sip. Hero took the opaque bottle from the mercenary with unsure fingers.

She raised the mouth of the bottle to her lips and took a quick sip... followed immediately by burning pain that drove Hero to her knees. The bard rasped, trying to cough but it was as if her throat had blistered closed.

"I knew it!" Ophelia hollered, "You're still a penanggalan! You didn't change back into a human like the rest of the town. Why?"

It took several long, agonizing seconds but air slowly found its way back into Hero's lungs. She gasped for breath as Ophelia kicked the wine bottle away and stepped over the bard.

Ophelia lowered her sword, pressing the tip of the blade into the carpet just beside the bard's eyes, "Vinegar. Another thing that Folken mentioned is that the demon part of you hates it. Because it's a cleansing agent, right?"

Ophelia sat down on Hero's chest, pinning the smaller woman to the floor. The bard wanted to hate the other woman but she couldn't do it. She knew that, if their positions had been reversed, Hero would have tried to keep a monster away from her friends when they were about to travel in the wilds.

Hero nodded in answer to the mercenary's question.

"Why didn't you change back with the rest of Laeradr?" Ophelia asked, her blade still looming at the edge of the bard's vision.

"I'm from a different coven," Hero's voice sounded like a series of croaks.

"Then what were you doing here?" the other woman continued her interrogation.

"Do you know what needs to happen to make someone into a monster like me?" the bard asked back.

"I know that Miranda killed her daughter for it," Ophelia answered.

"There's more to it," Hero replied, "Especially if you want to become the progenitor of your own line."

"I'm all ears" The woman in red said.

"Miranda was already studying black magicks before my progenitor came to her," the bard said, "She was arrested before Hosun finally found her."

"Who's Hosun?" Ophelia interrupted.

"A powerful penanggalan. A progenitor of her own line," Hero answered, then continued, "She freed Miranda and Hosun offered to make her one of her children but Miranda wanted more."

"She wanted to make a coven of her own," Ophelia said.

The bard nodded. "Hosun didn't like it but she agreed to teach Miranda the rituals."

"That included killing her daughter," the mercenary said.

"That was only part of it," Hero said, "That was just part of the spell to summon the demons that would give Miranda the power she sought. To finish the call, she had to eat her daughter's heart to show her devotion. All of it."

Ophelia had to stifle a gag, "And?" she reluctantly urged the other woman to continue.

"When the demons arrive, they are literally starving," the bard explained, "They eat the rest of the body, bones and all. Then Miranda had to live with them until they digested her daughter and... loosed her remains. Those are the sacrificial wafers."

"Those things are *literally* demon crap?" Ophelia stared down at Hero.

"Made of Miranda's daughter," she nodded, "But demons don't digest like mortals do. It takes days for them. Miranda had to keep them... entertained the whole time they were on this plane of existence."

"By ransacking Odoshift," Ophelia came to the conclusion.

Hero nodded again, "But destroying Odoshift didn't take them long. Afterward she had to let them ... use her for their entertainment. "

"Why would she agree to that?" Ophelia scowled down at the bard, "Feeling powerless was why she called for them in the first place!"

"Is that what Miranda told you?" Hero asked but didn't wait for an answer, "Miranda wanted to run the town but the man she married was passed over for another when it came time to choose the new Elder. Her husband killed himself, not realizing that she was pregnant. She blamed Odoshift's patriarchy for his death."

"So she wanted revenge." Ophelia sighed, chewing on her lower lip. "But why let demons have their way with her for days on end?"

"To know true power, you have to know how it feels to be truly powerless first," Hero recited the oft heard line, "At least, that is what Hosun told her. Once Miranda had the power of the penanggalan to build her new coven, Hosun gave her the idea of spreading out. Of running her own fiefdom in the Jaded Woods and beyond."

"And how do you know all this, Hero?" Ophelia brought her sword down so that it filled the bard's entire field of vision, "If all this happened before Odoshift was destroyed?"

"I was there!" Hero blurted out, "Hosun was the one who sired me!"

"Miranda said that she learned all this from someone called Lady Oyotsu," the blade touched the bridge of Hero's nose.

"Hosun is Lady Oyotsu!" the bard yelled, "Oyotsu is her family name. She only allowed those of her lineage to call her by her given name of Hosun!"

"I hate to interrupt, Ophelia," a voice from someone Hero couldn't see came into the room, "But it sound's to me like you have the whole story now."

"Almost," the mercenary responded, "I just have one more question. Any objections?"

The newcomer must have just nodded because Hero didn't hear any reply but Ophelia's weight found its way back onto the chest of the bard before she spoke again.

"So why are you here if you're from a different lineage?" she asked.

"Miranda pledged her fealty to Hosun," the bard answered, the blade slowly pulling away as she continued, "Hosun always leaves one of her own with every nest she creates, just to make sure the newborn penanggalan mother doesn't get too ambitious."

"Which is why she never killed you, even with all your insubordination," Ophelia concluded.

Hero agreed, "Hosun would sense my death and come destroy her,"

The mercenary stood up, allowing the bard to take in the view of the whole room again. Saya stood in the doorway, leaning against the doorjamb as she waited. Ophelia slipped her sword back into the scabbard hidden within her long coat, and Hero lifted herself to a sitting position.

"So what do you want to do now that you don't have to play watchdog for your sire?" It was Saya who asked the question this time.

"I want to find a way to cure myself," Hero said, "I want to be human again, too."

Ophelia bent down and picked up the black wine bottle. Stepping back over to the bard, she offered it to the smaller woman.

"Harbenigyr says that if you take a sip of this every few hours, it will suppress the monster from being able to come out," she ordered before adding, "You will need to find more in the cellars below Odoshift before we leave."

"But it nearly killed me before," Hero protested weakly even as she took the bottle with both hands.

"You'll get used to it," Ophelia replied before stepping out of the room.

Hero looked as Saya questioningly. The pale svartalfar woman gave the bard a quick shrug before actually speaking.

"We had to make sure that you weren't trying to entrap my cousin or my friends," she explained, "We've had a bad run of that lately."

"With only the latest coming from us here in Laeradr?" Hero commented before forcing herself to take another sip from the bottle half full of vinegar.

Saya nodded, "While Folken is able to read people pretty well the others, particularly Ophelia, wanted to know for sure that you weren't going to be a threat."

After the mouthful of bitterness finally made its way down her throat, it took a long time for the grimace to fade from Hero's face, "Why is Ophelia so suspicious of me? You're the one I actually attacked, why weren't you the one to wanted to question me?"

"Let's just say that I'm related to our little band's particular trust issues at the moment," Saya smirked without a hint of amusement, "As for Ophelia, she's protective of all of us, particularly Harbenigyr. Now that he's only just regained consciousness, it was miracle to get her out of the same room."

The idea of keeping herself from changing brought a broad smile to the bard's face. Just by drinking a simple, if bitter, concoction. If the solution was just that simple, Hero found a sense of hope that she thought had been gone for so long now.

"It's amazing that he was able to come up with a remedy to keep the monster in me at bay so quickly," Hero said as she stood back up.

Saya's green lips pursed tight, "It is."

"He must be a genius," the bard added.

Hero picked up her backpack and slung it over her shoulders. She started out of the room but the abino woman didn't step out of the doorway.

"There's no way that any of Miranda's lineage could have survived, is there Hero?" she inquired of the bard, her voice barely above a whisper.

"No way," Hero said, "The demon part of the monster needs demonic energy to anchor it into a human body. Without Miranda's living blood that connected her to the ritual, there's nothing demonic in a person to latch onto."

Saya turned aside to let the bard pass. Hero had a new found bounce to her step as she passed the room that had formerly belonged to the mayor of Laeradr but now held the recovering cleric, Harbenigyr.

"It is amazing," She muttered to herself.

OPHELIA INTERROGATION NOTES:

"So you're a hypocrite," I concluded after reading the subject the report.

"That was direct." the subject replied.

"And accurate," I said, "Wouldn't you agree?"

"I'm still trying to figure out why a Light Bringer is so interested in what happened so long ago," the subject did not answer my query.

"Shall we cover a more recent time then?" I gave the subject another article of testimony, "The monk. What was his name? Jin?"

"Jin Vega," the subject clarified further.

"He was among Appelonia's party," I said, "and they were searching for you. Cleaning up your mess, in a way."

"I've always had respect for the Light Bringers," the subject responded, "but you are really starting to try my patience."

"And you mine," I said, tapping the parchment, "Read."

Decades later...

"WHERE'S BRONWYN?" JIN asked as he looked around the group.

"Apparently, she fled from us," Genevieve gave a cursory glance around but didn't seem concerned, "Why should we care?"

Jonas couldn't help sounding annoyed, "Because she was the one lead we had to finding the efreeti child. We need to know where she went," he focused his attention on the demon woman.

When everyone else in the party followed the paladin's lead, Genevieve let out a sigh to signal her surrender, "Very well, Master."

Closing her gray eyes, Genevieve spun around in place. Her left hand slowly rose from her side, finally settling in the direction of the pier a short distance away that marked the northern edge of Craigh Na Troon.

"How convenient," a smirk tugged at the corner of the demon's mouth, "She has gone to the Flustered Mermaid."

"Why go there before us, though?" Appelonia wondered, "She knew that was where we were going, didn't she?"

"I don't know how long she has been gone," Illyria shrugged up at the other woman, "Any of you notice when she left?"

No one did.

"There's nothing for it," Jonas grabbed Andromeda's reins and started marching for the pier and the city beyond, "We need to catch up to her and find out if her father's ship's here."

"That's why she left," Jin fell into step behind the armored paladin leading his steed, "She wants to protect her father."

"From us?" Illyria fluttered her wings and launched herself into the air, hovering only a foot or so above the others.

Appelonia made a clicking noise with her lips and Bommer started trotting behind her as she walked. Tokki moved after the cleric faster than he really had to in order to catch up. The mask may have hidden it but it was likely he was still enjoying the view of the cleric's transparent clothing. Although they were mostly dry and solid again.

Phinegann gripped the bridle of his horse and guided it after the others, rolling his eyes at the smaller warrior in black fur. The orc marched at the rear of the line the party had instinctively decided upon. All the better to maneuver through the pockets of people meandering along the wooden streets of Craigh No Troon.

It wasn't crowded yet, being not quite midday (how long had they been down in Nova Omega?), but the citizens of the city were starting to fill up the elevated streets. Once they reached the pier, Appelonia waved at Illyria to land on top of her azure horse. The retired guard had to agree that the little woman would have stood out too much if she had stayed in the air.

Genevieve led Jonas and the others to the entrance of The Flustered Mermaid. The wooden sign was faded from years of exposure to the sun and the humid air but the painting of a topless mermaid with bright red hair was still able to be made out.

As Phinegann tied his horse beside Bommer at the wooden poles provided in front of the bar, he glanced over at the cleric of Kuan Yin. His brow furrowed as the random thought that Appelonia bore a striking resemblance to the painting occurred to him.

The paint had flaked off some of the more *interesting* parts of the mermaid's anatomy but there was still plenty left to appreciate. After what he'd witnessed by the river, Phinegann wondered if Appelonia had somehow posed for the artist. Everything looked just about right from the waist up.

The guard glanced over at Tokki, wondering if he'd noticed the sign. Judging by the fact that he was still able to function as he put his leather pack onto Bommer's back and was actually conversing with the red haired cleric, he'd guess that he hadn't. At least not yet.

Jonas had but he was enough of a gentleman that he almost immediately let it go and focused on tying Andromeda beside another mare that was much smaller than her. Then Genevieve looked up.

As the grin on her face grew to painfully wide proportions, the orc stomped in the direction of the efreeti. Just as her mouth started to open and something that was surely going to be acerbic was about to be loosed from it, Phinegann was pressing his armored torso to the demon woman's chest.

"Focus on the job," he growled under his breath, just loud enough for the efreeti to hear.

She started to protest, trying to lean around Phinegann's wide frame to look for the Shepherd and, maybe, ask for his help. But she thought better of it after only a couple of seconds. She shrugged up at the man who was taller than her in her current shape.

"Very well," she sighed, "But I'll not be held responsible for how popular she will be inside."

With that she stepped around the orc and followed Jonas to the door. Appelonia and Tokki (who never looked up) walked side by side after them, followed by Illyria and Jin. Phinegann allowed himself a brief, amused grunt at yet another unspoken formation being agreed upon with the group. Again, he brought up the rear.

Inside, the bar was only about half full but the crowd that was inside was raucous. Glass and pewter cups flew across the room at almost regular intervals. Not like they were being used as weapons but more like exclamation points to a particularly passionate statement from the men scattered throughout the room.

"Does anyone see her?" Jonas didn't yell but he had to raise his voice above its usual volume to be heard.

One by one, each member of the party shook their head. Except for Illyria, she flapped her wings and hopped into the air, just until her feet were level with Phinegann's shoulders and, even then, for just a moment. She landed back on the worn wood floor as if she had simply jumped.

But she looked to Jonas and pointed to the back left of the bar, "She's at the largest table in here, surrounded by at least a dozen men, probably more," she reported, then her shoulder's slumped, "I didn't have enough time to do a proper head count."

"Don't worry about it Elly." Appelonia smiled down at the smaller woman, "It's more than me had a moment ago."

"I wonder why she's so popular so fast," Jin scowled as he ran a hand through his thick beard.

"Only one way to find out," Jonas said, "Let's go reintroduce ourselves."

The group weaved its way through the crowd. One would think it would be easiest for Elly but, with her wings, she took up a lot more horizontal space. Her solution was to wrap the glass around her body. It blocked her view but she grabbed Appelonia's pant leg to keep her going in the right direction.

Finally they found the table. It stretched out wide enough that eight people could sit on each side and it was indeed full. Bronwyn sat on the middle of the opposite side. When the party walked up, she had been leaning in close to the, if Phinegann had to guess, "businessman" to her left to whisper something she didn't want anyone else at the table to hear.

"Hello again, Bronwyn," Jonas made their presence known, "Who are your new friends?"

The color drained from the olive skinned woman's face when she saw the paladin and the others, "You have got to be kidding me. Did you really miss me that much? Couldn't you have given me an hour to myself?"

"Charming to the last," Jin quipped, "You forgot that we need your help. That a child still needs your help."

"I've never liked kids," Bronwyn shook her head, "And they've never liked me. So we came to an understanding that we'd stay out of each other's ways for the foreseeable future. It seems to have worked so far so, please, get lost," Despite her protests, she motioned to the bar. Subtly, trying to keep the men around her from noticing.

Jonas stood still, like a statue made of the very same material as his armor, for a long moment. Everything seemed to go quieter as he stayed motionless, to the point that the other men at the table looked in his direction to figure out what was happening.

"No, really, get lost." Bronwyn's tone wasn't matching her more and more desperate hand signals, "We can talk after I've had plenty of alcohol."

"We don't have time for this," Phinegann had had enough. He stepped around Jonas and leaned between two businessmen to close the distance between himself and the thief, "Where is your father's ship?"

Bronwyn let out a heavy groan as her face dropped into her hands. "You're all idiots, aren't you?" She muttered.

The largest man at the table, just two places down from the woman in the bandanna, rose from the table and strode around it toward Phinegann. He was almost as tall as the orc and, even though he appeared to be completely human, was even wider at the shoulders. His skin was a lighter shade of brown than Phinegann but both men were bald.

Neither had sleeves on their shirts, either. It was almost like the two men could be related.

"I think the lady told you to get lost, friend," the business-man huffed.

"What's the problem?" Jonas stepped up to the side of both massive men, "We are all just talking here."

"Conversation's over," the bald pirate said, "Leave. Now."

Behind the businessman, Phinegann caught a glimpse of Tokki and Appelonia. The woman had both of her hands on his shoulders. Surely, she was trying to keep him from turning this, the guard didn't want to call it a stand off but another term wouldn't come to him.

The pirate sitting beside Bronwyn patted his hip, "Hey! She took my keys!"

Bronwyn was immediately on her feet, her empty hands up, "I didn't take anything. I was just feeling you up, I swear!" she grinned the most insincere grin that Phinegann had seen outside of Obsidian Fjord Prison.

After that, the businessman who rivaled Phinegann in size punched the orc. Phinegann punched him back with his metal fist and he crumpled to the floor. After that was a blur of violence.

It spread through the Flustered Mermaid quickly until the entire bar was one big brawl. Illyria had curled up inside her wings completely, cocooning herself just like she did against the marilith.

Jonas was blocking more punches than throwing them. But those he was fighting were breaking their knuckles against steel, so he wasn't in immediate danger.

Jin was avoiding being hit so expertly, it looked almost as if it was choreographed. He even made one businessman strike another so that they focused on each other and let him move on... right into another angry pirate.

Genevieve was upside down, standing on the ceiling and watching the proceedings well out of reach of anyone. In fact, she looked amused as she watched the fighting ebb and flow like currents through the wide room.

Appelonia had long since lost her grip on Tokki and he was cutting a swath of blunt force through the crowd. He was so much shorter than all the 'businessmen' around him that it was hard to keep track of the Bunny Barbarian.

One of those men stumbled into Appelonia, his rough hands finding her soft chest even through the chainmail wrapped around her, "Hey, look! It's the mermaid herself! Let's say you and me find a quiet corner, eh sweetness?" he laughed so boisterously he had to be drunk to do it without straining something.

As he went for another squeeze, a black fur covered hand wrapped around his throat. Tokki pressed his acid scarred back to the other man and leaned forward, throwing the man away from the cleric and flipping him into another pirate.

Then Tokki turned back to Appelonia and shrugged, "What is he talking about?"

Appelonia shrugged back before pulling one of her jade sticks free from the thin quiver on her belt and smashing it across the face of a man charging at Tokki from his blind side.

"Thank you," he grinned at the cleric, then was almost immediately swallowed up in the sea of fighting bodies again.

"We need to get out of here before someone gets killed!" Jonas yelled at Phinegann as he finally found his way to the orc.

Phinegann grunted in agreement as he broke the arm of another pirate foolish enough to try and grab him. He started looking around for another member of their party. What he spotted was Bronwyn getting close to the doors leading outside.

"She's getting away!" he pointed.

"Appelonia's getting swarmed by men who recognize her from the sign!" Jin pointed as well.

"Where's Tokki? Wasn't he watching her?" Jonas slammed an elbow into a man who just tried to tackle him to the ground. He slumped to the worn wood without the paladin.

Jin climbed another heavily muscled man like a tree and stood on his broad shoulders, "He's busy with three men wielding daggers!" the monk slammed his heel to the side of his mount's head and leaped back into the crowd.

The paladin did something that surprised Phinegann. He cursed.

"Genevieve!" Jonas called, "Clear a path for us to get out of here!"

"Aww!" the efreeti whined from where she sat on the ceiling, "It was just starting to get interesting!"

"Rescue Appelonia first!" Jonas glared at the demon as he barked his orders, "Phin and I will make our way to her and then you clear a path out for us. Got it?"

"Yes, Master." The efreeti woman rose her her feet and started meandering toward where the cleric was pushed down to the floor.

"Now!" the paladin screamed.

In a burst of flame, Genevieve disappeared and reappeared standing immediately over Appelonia, with her long legs on either side of the young cleric. All the men that had been on top of the red haired woman were scattered in every direction, only just finding their feet again.

Genevieve opened her mouth and belched a plume of flame that businessmen dived out of the way to avoid. The demon grabbed Appelonia by her linked metal collar and hauled her up to her feet.

The right sleeve of the cleric's tunic had been ripped off. The leather belt holding her chainmail vest closed was ripped and the lower half hung open awkwardly. Appelonia herself, though, didn't appear to be seriously injured.

"You'd best run!" the efreeti ordered the mortal woman before shoving her in the direction she just cleared with her flames.

Jonas, Phinegann, and Jin stomped on the men that made up the edge of the newly cleared area that Genevieve made. None of those businessmen tried to get up again.

"Where's Tokki?" Jonas snapped.

"Apple's helping him up," Jin answered, looking toward the main doors.

It was more accurate to say that the cleric was patting the smoldering parts of Tokki's helmet to extinguish the flames from Genevieve's outburst. But he was getting up at the same time so it wasn't wholly inaccurate.

Bronwyn shoved one of the doors open with her shoulder and rushed out of the bar. Phinegann ran through the closing path that the demon woman made, knocking men out of the way to open it up again for the monk, paladin, and his monster.

Phinegann reflexively squinted at the light of day as he made it outside. Bronwyn was already running towards the docks, as were many of the other men who had been at her table. Pretty much all of them were ahead of her.

The orc was so much faster than the olive skinned thief that he had her pinned to the ground in half a dozen paces. Jin (who had somehow snatched his claymore from the back of his mare), Genevieve, the monk, and Tokki, along with the cleric were around them seconds later.

"Let me go, you idiot!" Bronwyn snarled, "They're getting away!"

"What are you talking about?" Jonas asked, "Fast."

"The crew of the *Spotted Dick* just transferred some cargo onto my father's ship last night!" she wriggled pointlessly under Phinegann, who was trained to hold unruly murderers twice his size down, "I stole a message to be delivered to their Captain from my father! I need to get a look at her records!"

With his flesh hand, the orc patted the woman down and pulled a sealed parchment from the lining of her leather coat. The wax that held it closed was marked '*H.R.S. Galleon*'. That supported at least a portion of her story.

"Let her up, Phin," Jonas made the order sound more like a favor.

The retired prison guard stood up, then pulled Bronwyn up to her feet. He still held her arms behind her back in his metal hand.

"Which one is the *Spotted Dick*?" he asked the thief.

"The one everyone is running onto!" she motioned further down the wooden road where a line of ships were docked.

"Which one?" Jin asked, "They're splitting up and getting on two separate ships."

"What?" Bronwyn squinted past the men she had been chasing, "That's the *Galleon*. That's my father's ship!"

"There goes our answers," Tokki shook his head, the floppy ears of his helmet slapping against his shoulders.

"Not if we get moving," Jonas snapped back, "Run!"

No one argued as they sprinted down the length of the dock. Before they were even halfway to the *Galleon*, the crew hurriedly tossed the plank they used to get aboard off the side and the ship was already starting to make way.

"We're not getting on that ship," Jonas stopped, huffing for breath.

He looked toward the *Spotted Dick*. They weren't as organized as the crew of the *Galleon* and were only just getting their last man aboard.

"We'll have to get their help," The Shepherd ran to the closer ship.

Bronwyn cursed, sharing the sentiment that Phinegann surely felt and suspected the others did, too. The paladin and the others were up the plank before the crew could toss it overboard. Swords and daggers were already starting to be drawn when Jonas dropped his massive blade to the deck and raised his hands.

"I'm very sorry about this but we need to follow that ship," he pointed toward the launching *Galleon*, "Could I speak with your captain? Maybe negotiate a fare after we're underway?"

Unexpectedly, Appelonia's voice drifted from the back of the group, "Where's Elly?"

Phinegann glanced around the group, even sparing a quick glance up to the sky. The cleric was right, the little woman was nowhere to be found.

"She must still be in the Flustered Mermaid," Jin said.

"Genevieve, go get her and bring her here," Jonas ordered the woman with standing black hair, "Fast, I'm hoping to be underway in minutes at the most."

Groaning, the efreeti woman galloped down the gangplank and rushed back the way they had come. She was already out of view by the time the Captain of the *Spotted Dick* came up to the paladin, which was only seconds later.

The Captain was a middle-aged woman, about the same height as Appelonia but about twice as wide. A good portion of that was likely muscle, with the way she carried herself.

Running a ship like hers must have been good business, as she was wearing a emerald colored silk shirt. Her pants, though, were made of thick cotton to be able to stand up to the wear and tear of the work that came with sailing on the high seas.

The Captain easily had the largest hat, tallest and with the widest brim among any of the other crew on the deck. That must have been how they kept track of rank on this ship.

"Why would I welcome a group of thieves onto my boat?" she asked, her curved sword lightly bouncing against her thick hip.

"Actually, she's the only thief," Jin interjected, motioning to Bronwyn.

"Hey! Kidnapping is frowned on around here, too, you know!" the olive skinned woman snapped.

"I am a paladin of the Order of Stewart. She is a cleric of the Order of Kuan Yin," Jonas said ignoring Jin's exchange with Bronwyn. "We are searching for a child that was taken from her family. The *Galleon* is our only lead to finding the child and getting her back. Will you help us, please?"

"Since when did clerics pose for nudie pictures for bar signs?" the Captain snickered, looking back at Appelonia.

"I didn't! Really!" the red haired woman wrapped her arms around her chest, "That was just an... awkward coincidence."

"Uh huh," the Captain didn't believe her, "According to my boys you started the brawl at the bar. I was just launching to get away from you hooligans. I don't think I'm going to let your trouble come with us down river." She lifted her blade and pointed it straight at the paladin. "Get off my ship," she ordered.

A loud, inhuman scream came from the docks behind the group. Phinegann turned (as Jonas didn't have the liberty with the threat from the Captain) and saw Genevieve fleeing from what appeared to be every other person who had been brawling inside the Flustered Mermaid.

Under her arm was the stained glass cocoon that surely contained Illyria Warflower. The efreeti woman was already halfway up the plank and onto the *Spotted Dick* before Phinegann was able to turn and report.

"We should launch before they come to lynch you!" Genevieve announced as she ran on deck.

"That's not our fight," the Captain declared, changing the target of her blade to the woman in the short white dress, "You get back down there and face them on your own!"

"Really?" Genevieve smirked as she straightened up, still carrying Illyria under her arm. "You think I would be taking my chances with them? They are only chasing me because he ordered me to return quickly," she motioned to Jonas before continuing, "I would say that you are the one taking a terrible chance. Are you more afraid of that mob coming aboard to pillage and rob your ship?"

The efreeti lifted Illyria's cocoon in one hand, then spiked it into the deck without even a grunt of effort. The stained glass buried itself halfway into the wooden deck. Panicked screams from crewmen echoed from below.

"Or me? Who can do that to your hull just as easily?" Genevieve's teeth turned to their true, sharpened shape, "I've not even exerted myself yet."

"Launch! Now!" the Captain found herself barking the orders immediately as she awkwardly stepped away from the demon woman, "Follow the *Galleon*! Ready for full speed to overtake her!"

The glass cocoon unfurled itself and a confused looking Illyria found herself wedged into the deck up to her waist. "Okay, I've obviously missed something," she commented.

OPHELIA INTERROGATION NOTES:

"Everyone has been totally forthcoming up to this point except for yourself," I said to the subject, "I want the truth, Ophelia."

"No, what you want is for me to say that everything was my fault so that you can write up a nice, tidy report to take back to Valen Court!" Ophelia slammed her fist down on the table.

"You know this is all your fault!" I yelled back (admittedly, I strained the guidelines of procedure regarding interviews in this exchange).

"I did not cause everyone's troubles!" the subject protested.

"Oh?" I slapped the parchment that the subject herself signed into the record as the truth, "You kept what happened from everyone. When you finally realized you were caught in your lies, what did you do? What did you do, eh?"

Decades before…

OPHELIA WAS THE only one who had her horse from the time they left Ash Providence. Lyan didn't have a steed at all, and Harby did still have Triton as well, but he was a griffin. So they didn't count.

Everyone else had new horses provided by the penitent women of Laeradr. How was it that Folken always ended up with one that was not only massive but completely black?

They also provided the group with enough supplies for two weeks of traveling. Not an insubstantial amount. It was spread out among the horses as evenly as possible (even Lyan carried her share) and had more than one nonessential treat that several of the women from town added to further apologize for attempting to cannibalize them.

They didn't have enough material to create a new white tunic for Harbenigyr. For the interim, They took what white cloth they did have (several bedsheets) and fashioned a short doublet over the chainmail that he wore under the cuirass. The linked metal could still be seen in some spaces where the sheets tended to bunch but one woman stitched green thread (not quite the same shade as jade) along the seams of his new jacket/shirt, to at least make it feel more like cleric robes.

The first of troupe of mercenaries from the Soldier Guild of Romefeller Guilds arrived mere hours before Folken, Ophelia, Harbenigyr, Josie, Lyan, and Hero left to deliver Meteorend to Riverbelt. Saya stayed behind to organize their patrols of the Jaded Woods until Folken passed the responsibility on to the Light Bringers. Surely around the same time they did the same with Raiko's troublesome rock.

The trip was far from easy. Josie was true to her word in keeping the party off the roads. Ophelia was sure they weren't moving nearly as fast as they could have been. Of course, stealth was an utmost priority, perhaps even more so than speed.

When it came time to camp after the first day of the trek, no one argued. As everyone else started putting up tents, another luxury provided by the residents of Laeradr, Lyan, Ophelia and Josie decided to go without. Lyan volunteered to patrol the perimeter and left almost immediately. The remaining two unoccupied women decided to build a fire.

Josie gathered tinder and wood while Ophelia volunteered to start on the fire pit. The mercenary pulled a shovel off the back of her horse and found a patch of dirt wide enough for her to dig in without a risk of setting the tall grass around them on fire.

She dug down deep enough that the flames couldn't be seen in the distance. It was deep enough, though, that getting enough air to the wood may be an issue so Ophelia dug another, thinner hole just upwind of the one she decided would serve as the fire pit. That made a little wind tunnel to feed the fire once they started it going.

"You've dug concealed fire pits before," Josie observed as she walked up with an armload of sticks and dried moss, "Who taught you?"

Ophelia chewed on her lower lip for a long moment, "No one. Just another thing in a long line other things that I just know."

"What does that mean?" the ranger asked as she started setting up the moss and some smaller sticks as kindling.

"Remember those tattoos that make me blink?" Ophelia patted the small of her back as she sat across the pit from the alphan woman, "The one who put them on me, he also included all this knowledge that I'm never really sure I have until something comes up. I've never been taught how to sneak, how to use a sword or anything. I just... do it," she shrugged.

"That sounds convenient," Josie smirked before spinning a foot long stick of wood against another, flatter piece.

"You'd think," Ophelia pulled a wine bottle from one of the pockets of her coat, "He had to erase a lot of other things to do it."

After only about a minute, a glowing ember rolled out from the bottom piece of wood, a thin wisp of smoke betraying the heat it held. Josie gently placed the glowing seed of fire into the little construct of moss and sticks and gently started to blow. Once the flames caught, it was an easy matter of feeding it steadily larger sticks and branches to keep them all warm.

Once it didn't need continuous attention, the red haired woman looked back up at Ophelia, "You mean memories of your family?" she said, then positioned herself to sit cross legged from the other woman, "He erased your memories of your family?"

The mercenary nodded, "Everything. I don't know who taught me to count or read, who assured me I wasn't going to bleed to death when I started through puberty, who took my virginity, nothing."

"Except what your Light Bringer friend told you about them," Josie said.

"Her father but, yeah. Their first names, they were farmers. My father liked to brew beer and my mother was a chemist. That's pretty much it," Ophelia took a sip from the bottle.

"I know we had this debate before," the red haired woman said, "but what if your family life was so terrible that you *didn't* want to remember?"

"You alluded to that before," the woman in the long coat pointed the mouth of the bottle at Josie, "I can only guess you're talking about your own family."

The other woman sighed, "Mostly my father, I guess. He was a full blooded elf that married my mother. From what I understand, though, it was only because she became pregnant with me."

"What happened?" Ophelia worked to keep anything that could be construed as mocking out of her tone.

"My father was the one who taught me the basics of living outdoors," Josie started her story, "Some of my earliest memories were him taking me out into the woods to teach me how to track animals. I remembered it being so fun then. As I got older, he added trapping, then finally outright hunting."

The other woman waited for the ranger to continue.

"He was strict when he taught. He always called it the *elfin* way," Josie said, her tone mocking his words, "If I guessed which way a vole or something went wrong, he would beat me with his bow. Always across my stomach. A mistake like that would make me starve in a real situation and he wanted me to know what that felt like."

Josie's hand, only now did Ophelia notice it was shaking, rose to cradle her flat stomach, She was quiet for a long moment before the alphan woman found her voice again.

"As I got older, the punishments got more severe," her eyes closed as the memories washed over her, "Once I started becoming a woman, they started involving having to strip and sleep outside naked, like the senseless prey I was. Then he started to make me do it even when I hadn't done anything wrong during training.

"I did anything I could to please him. If I brought extra food, he'd call me wasteful. If I came back earlier than he wanted, he accused me of being lazy. Later was the same thing. Every time, I slept outside with nothing to keep me warm."

Ophelia felt her stomach sink. She couldn't think of anything to say but, as her mouth suddenly went dry, she wouldn't have been able to talk anyway. So she took another sip from her bottle.

"After I turned," Josie's blue eyes flicked back and forth for a moment, "the human equivalent of sixteen, I was sleeping outside our cabin, enduring my father's latest punishment even though I'd successfully caught dinner. I heard a sound that was kind of like when a reigndeer dies. Have you ever heard that sound? That honking yelp when an arrow takes one down?"

Ophelia nodded.

"When I went to investigate, I saw that my father had murdered my mother," the red haired woman kept speaking, "His big plan was to take me into town and sell me to some traders. He'd thought that I would fetch a good enough price that he could travel west and start over. Without my dull eared mother and me, an alphan, a half-elf mockery of his elfin heritage."

Ophelia wrapped her hand around her mouth, not sure if she really did want to know. But Josie was coming to trust her, "What-what happened then?" Seeing the anxiety all over the other woman's face made Ophelia decide that Josie needed to finish the tale, whether or not she wanted to hear it.

"I ran into the woods," the alphan woman forced her voice to work again, "He followed. I used everything he taught me about evasion. We had been dealing with a pack of gray wolves who were making their way through our part of the woods. I had set some traps for them near the herds of reigndeer that we preferred to hunt from.

"I put the traps up on my own. He never saw where I set them," A tear rolled from the corner of Josie's eye as she took a slow, deep breath, "He stepped into one of my spike traps, it ripped his leg to shreds."

"And you left him there?" Ophelia asked before taking a long sip from her wine bottle.

That's what the mercenary would have done. Ophelia thought to herself, and only herself.

Josie shook her head, "Believe it or not, I tried to help him."

When Ophelia stared at her in disbelief, the other woman raised her hands defensively, "I didn't know what he was doing wasn't normal at the time! I did all the first aid he had taught me. Looking back, it wasn't much compared to what I know now. Even though I stopped the bleeding. He still couldn't walk.

"The graywolf pack still must have caught his scent because they started howling and howling as they ran for us. When I saw the first flash of yellow eyes reflected in the darkness, I ran away from my father and left him on his own."

"Good," Ophelia said without thinking.

Josie didn't look appeased, "I went back to the same spot in the morning. Every fleshy bit of him had been eaten by the pack. I went back home, took everything I could carry and started for town right after that. I joined the first ranger school I found and never looked back."

Silence hung between them for a long time after that. Long enough that Hero and Folken each stopped by the flame pit long enough to warm up. Then Harbenigyr came.

He'd noticed that Josie had been crying. To his credit, the cleric didn't ask why. He simply gave her a clean rag, a quick blessing of his goddess, and adjourned back to his tent.

"I can understand not wanting to remember that. I don't know if its worth anything but I even think that you did right by your old man," Ophelia said once everyone else had settled in to their makeshift sleeping quarters, "But why are you telling me all this? We haven't really been on the closest terms up to this point."

"True," Josie, surprisingly didn't seem upset by the other woman's statement, "But I saw that basement. Then I saw how close you watched over Harby while he was recovering. I decided that you are the kind of friend I'd like watching my back. I wanted you to know that I trust you."

Ophelia's lips pressed so tightly together that they practically disappeared. It was at times like this that she needed Havarti the most. He was always able to tell her what the most appropriate thing to do would be. She really, really wished she had that at this moment.

"Thank you, Josie," it sounded so hollow to the mercenary's own ears, "I'll try to be worthy of that trust."

"Does that mean that you'll finally introduce me to your sword now?" Josie grinned.

Ophelia barely kept herself from jumping physically, "Oh... you mean Havarti?" She looked back over her left shoulder at the handle of her long bastard sword.

What kind of excuse could you give someone who had just told you one of her closest guarded secrets? Especially without insulting, practically destroying that new found trust?

Ophelia couldn't hear Havarti anymore. Not since the basement. Should she tell Josie? The secret the mercenary was more... immediate than the ranger's. Was there a third option?

There was, and Ophelia felt as if her heart wanted to stop beating. She could let Havarti go.

He wasn't anything more than a normal sword to Ophelia thanks to whatever it was that Miranda and that sacrificial wafer did. Ophelia hoped that her connection would be reestablished after killing the blacksmith but it didn't.

Instead, she became the savior of a town, turning the population from monsters back into normal humans again. All Ophelia truly wanted was to have her other half back.

But it wasn't going to happen. Havarti was a prisoner as long as Ophelia had him, unable to communicate with her or anyone. Perhaps this was the best choice. Was Josie the best person? She wasn't the heavy blade type.

But she could help Ophelia and, more importantly Havarti, find a new wielder that could appreciate him. Especially if Havarti could talk again.

"I'll tell you what," Ophelia pulled the sword out of the scabbard on her back, flipped the blade around and held the long handle out to the ranger, "Shake hands and see if he'll make his own introduction."

She tried to make the moment seem light even though she felt as if she was giving up anything and everything that was good inside of her. Without Havarti, there would be nothing left but the monster that Doctor Efreeti created.

No! She had to be strong. Ophelia had to let Havarti go so that he could actually *be* Havarti instead of a lump of metal in her hands.

Josie wrapped her hand around the grip of the bastard sword. She almost immediately had to bring her other hand up to support the weight.

The sword suddenly started screaming as if it was in agony, making both women almost jump out of their skins. While Josie's blue eyes were wide open in shock, thankfully she didn't drop Havarti into the fire.

"I'll tear you both apart!" Havarti bellowed, "I will carve out your brains and have my lady use your skulls as goblets!"

"What was that?" Lyan ran into the camp from a small clump of trees just at the edge, "Havarti's voice echoed all the way to the river!"

Folken, Hero, and Harbenigyr rushed out of their tents to the fire pit, all of them wondering the same as the Bunny Barbarian. Both Ophelia and Josie looked from one person to the next with no idea of what to say.

It was Havarti himself who spoke next, "Where am I? This isn't the basement. Where are Miranda and Bianca? They both must die for this atrocity!"

"They're already dead, Havarti," Ophelia choked the words out, "You helped me kill them."

"They are?" the sword wavered in Josie's hands, though not from her lack of a firm grip, "What happened? How long has it been since that happened?"

"Only a couple of days," the mercenary answered, "I was wondering why you haven't been answering me."

"You've not been able to communicate with your sword?" Folken spoke up, "For days now?"

The woman shook her head, her view instinctively locking on Hero, "Not since Miranda put that sacrificial wafer on my head."

"But once you killed her," Harbenigyr spoke up, tugging some bunched up cloth back into place on his doublet, "Shouldn't anything having to do with her penanggalan bloodline have ceased to exist?"

"If she's human, it would have," Hero looked as confused as everyone else, "It should have."

The cleric turned his attention to the sorcerer, who stood beside him silently, "Folken? Do you have any ideas?"

The green haired man stayed quiet for another long count of time before finally speaking, "Are you changing, Ophelia?"

The bard let out a sudden gasp as she realized, "She is! She's the one who told me to drink vinegar to keep from changing!" Hero pointed at Harbenigyr, "He told her about drinking the spoiled wine from Odoshift to stop it. She said the information was for me but she's drinking it, too!"

Folken stepped around the fire pit. He knelt down beside Ophelia, who didn't move at all. He reached for the wine bottle between her legs and pulled it out of her hands.

Lifting the bottle to his lips he tilted it back just enough for a thin stream of liquid to trickle down. He immediately turned his head to the side and spat the acrid taste from his mouth.

"It is vinegar," he handed the bottle back to Ophelia and straightened back up.

"But, I never told her to start drinking it," Harbenigyr looked so confused, so lost.

Ophelia sighed, "It was Harbenigyr but not this Harbenigyr," she confessed.

Josie's entire face tightened, "You mean you spoke to his doppelganger?"

The mercenary nodded, "He found me in that basement shortly before you did...

Several days ago...

MIRANDA LEANED IN and kissed the mercenary's cheek tenderly. Then the pain in the other woman's neck stopped. Bianca's upside down, floating head circled around in front of Ophelia, licking at the mercenary's blood that dribbled out of her mouth, up her nose and down between her eyes.

That was the first time Ophelia noticed that, while the prehensile tongue and the unnaturally wide mouth seemed so pleased with themselves that the blonde woman's eyes, they looked confused.

"You'll need some time to adjust, of course," Miranda continued, "You'll blossom within the hour. Whatever remains of your friends, we will reintroduce you to them and you can have your first proper meal."

Ophelia tumbled down the stairs and back to the floor of the basement and out of reach of the town's mayor. Control of her muscles was slow in coming back. Opehlia forced herself up to her hands and knees, her entire body feeling as if it was being stuck with thousands of little needles.

It made it hard to plan, hard to think. Even opening and closing her eyes took a couple of tries to get right.

Ophelia finally arched her head enough to finally look straight at Miranda, "You should have looked a little more thoroughly into my background, bitch," the mercenary croaked, "I've already got demons claiming my hide."

"You mean these lovely tattoos on your back?" Miranda giggled, "They're already starting to fade. Can't you feel it?"

Ophelia stretched back to slap at the small of her back with her knuckles. The usual hypersensitivity was gone. In fact, it was the opposite. While the rest of her body was painfully tingling, everywhere a rune was etched on her back was numb.

"No one can serve two masters, child," the blacksmith lectured, "And I just laid a fresh claim."

The mercenary crawled over to the workbench. Wrapping her hands around the edge, Ophelia pulled herself up onto her feet.

"Really? Already?" Miranda sounded impressed, "It usually takes a newborn hours to learn to walk again."

"You'll find I'm quick at a lot of things, lady," Ophelia snarled, "I'm a quick learner, quick healer, quick to anger..."

The mercenary took an unsteady step toward the mayor of Laeradr. Miranda slapped her hands together for a quick round of applause, only to be interrupted by the sensation of an unusually large sword blade slicing through her stomach. All the way through until the crossbar at the top of the hilt pressed into the leather of her blacksmith apron.

"And a quick sword draw, too," Ophelia grinned but her pale eyes were full of nothing but malice.

"You- you know this can't kill me," Miranda found it hard to catch her breath but her voice still had an edge of laughter to it.

"I know, but Bianca's body and head were enough of a pain to fight all at once," Ophelia pushed Havarti to the side with all her strength, slicing though the spine of the penanggalan.

Miranda immediately buckled to her knees as she lost control of her legs. Ophelia lifted a foot and pressed it to the blacksmith's chest. She shoved Miranda off of Havarti's blade with her boot and stumbled back into the workbench. But Ophelia didn't fall down.

Slipping Havarti's scabbard into the belt of her pants on her right hip. The sword woman caught a flutter of motion at the edge of her vision.

Bianca's disembodied head lunged for Ophelia, snarling its rage. This time, the mercenary expected it. Curling her fingers to pantomime curved claws, the mercenary jabbed them into the monster's panicked eyes (before they were gone).

Ophelia's fingers slid through the gelatinous orbs. Bianca's head impaled itself on her hand.

Taking a firm grip, the mercenary felt the hard surface of the interior of the monster's skull. The penanggalan couldn't pull itself free. It was now at Ophelia's mercy.

And, at that moment, she had none, "Bite me once," she slammed Bianca's head into the stone wall, leaving a splash of blood and offal that erupted from her throat on the wall, "Shame on you. Bite me twice..."

The woman's decapitated head met the wall again with a sickening crack. Then it met the workbench, blood and viscous jelly spilling out around Ophelia's fingers. Then Bianca's head met the hard, packed soil of the ground. Again and again.

Ophelia kept slamming it down until the pieces that had once been it's skull and internal soft tissue sloughed off her hand into a lumpy puddle in the dirt. As her anger finally let her see what she had done, along with the smell ... the woman felt herself retch.

She almost raised her free hand, the one not still holding Havarti, to her mouth to try and stifle it, only to see all the blood and ichor coating it. Instead, Ophelia looked away and held her breath as she stood back up.

When she was sure that she could open her mouth without vomiting, Ophelia turned her attention back to Miranda. She had flipped herself onto her stomach and started crawling the mercenary's way just in time to see the fate that befell Bianca.

"Let's see her come back from that one," Ophelia demanded before pain shot through her stomach.

Ophelia tumbled back down to her knees. The scent that had make her sick just moments ago suddenly smelled... pleasant. It reminded the woman of the honeybark ale that she'd been introduced to shortly after becoming free from Doctor Efreeti's machinations.

A rush of fury washed through Ophelia as she looked back at Miranda, "What's happening to me?"

"It's the hunger I mentioned before," a hint of pleasure came back to the thickly built woman's voice, "I'm the one who decides who eats and when, my child. If you curry my favor, you can feed on a whim. If you displease me," her brown eyes scanned over the remains of Bianca, oozing blood and offal all over the floor in a widening puddle, "You get to feel it become stronger and stronger until the monster starts literally eating your body to sustain itself."

"You were expecting this to kick in sooner, weren't you?" Ophelia cradled her midsection with both arms as Havarti tumbled to the floor.

Miranda nodded, "You are a special girl," the mayor chortled as she started to again crawl toward the mercenary. "Now you know your place, yes?"

Ophelia's stomach growled loud enough for both women to hear, betraying the infernal hunger that was growing inside her. Her slate blue eyes flicked over to Bianca's corpse, her body reacting as if it was seeing a roasted beast on a spit instead of the corpse of a felled enemy.

Sweating so much that it looked as if she had just stepped out of a lake, it took Ophelia everything she had lift her blood soaked right hand to the workbench and start pulling herself back up, "I-I've never been good at knowing my place. Miranda."

Ophelia picked Havarti back up with her. The corner of her mouth twitched, hoping to hear his voice snap back into her head. It didn't.

She found her feet and glared down at the crawling blacksmith, "Being told what I can and can't do just makes me angry. It makes me just want to crush something!" A lilting cackle escaped the woman's mouth as she glanced at the mound of flesh that had been Bianca's head.

The paralyzed blacksmith visibly shivered at the sound of Ophelia's humorless laugh, "Forget that then. Please. You're a strong woman, Ophelia. You could even have a coven of your own. I can make that happen," Miranda reached up, gripping the gray cloth of the pants that covered the standing woman's thighs.

Ophelia didn't move to swat her away. In fact, she was enjoying watching the penanggalan beg.

Havarti still didn't raise a protest to the mercenary's actions. Maybe he was as curious as Ophelia was.

"Something just occurred to me, Miranda," Ophelia wrapped her bloodstained hand in the hair of the town mayor, "You haven't let your head separate from your body. Even though you can't use your legs, you haven't changed to attack me. I thought being the monster made you powerful."

Ophelia pulled. She tugged on the blacksmith's hair and pulled her face up to meet hers. Miranda's body didn't follow as the sucking sound of flesh tearing away from itself filled the room.

Miranda's face was a mixture of surprise and nerve twitching pain. Just seeing it made Ophelia feel more euphoric than a barrel of honeybark ale.

"Or is it something else?" Ophelia hissed at the other woman whose eyes were only inches from hers now, "Is it vanity? Do you find the form of a penanggalan as disgusting as I do?"

The shame that washed over the other woman's face elicited a squeaking giggle from the mercenary. Ophelia knew she was right.

"Please, Ophelia," Miranda's voice now had that same buzzing undertone that Bianca's had after her transformation, "You can have this nest. I'll follow you! Imagine it, your own private town. A town full of loyal Penanggalan can destroy anyone, any *thing* that would come and do you any harm!"

The front of the mercenary's pants started ripping as Laeradr's mayor clawed at her thighs so desperately. Ophelia wrenched Miranda's head to the side, still staring into her eyes as she gave her answer.

"Have you noticed that whenever someone offers up their leadership position, they always list the benefits?" Ophelia licked her lips before continuing, "They never warn about the responsibilities. Like feeding your minions, the bands of brigands that regularly attack, or even the troubles of finding a shirt to fit your neck size."

The mercenary slipped Havarti's blade between herself and the line of intestines that made up Miranda's monstrous throat. With a flick of her wrist, the blacksmith's head was severed from her body.

Miranda's body stiffened at that moment then fell to the floor like a sack of flour. Her hands tore the legs from her pants, exposing her thighs and calves to the cool air of the cellar.

"Fortunately, that's not your problem anymore," Ophelia said.

"Then you'll take my offer?"

There it was. That last glint of hope in her eye. Even though the mercenary had been taking Miranda down a piece at a time, the woman still thought she could win Ophelia over. That would make this part all the more satisfying.

"I think I'd rather make the world a little more beautiful by scrubbing your penanggalan face off of it."

And that last spark was extinguished from Miranda's eyes. The mayor screamed in a panic as Ophelia slammed her nose first into the wall.

The mercenary scraped Miranda's face back and forth across the stone and soil, leaving bits of flesh and blood in a grisly trail. The woman stopped when she heard the blacksmith's nose, along with several teeth, snap loose.

"Maybe I should have said making the world more beautiful by scrubbing your face *onto* it?" Ophelia laughed as she pulled the mayor's unrecognizable head away from the stone so that they could again look at each other.

With that, Ophelia slammed Miranda's head back into the wall. Putting that piece of steel that used to be the mercenary's better half back into his scabbard, the woman took her now free hand and started crushing it into the flesh and bone she held onto so tightly.

While the rage burned, and Ophelia just kept hitting and hitting, the hunger faded. By the time the woman dropped the lumps of red goo to the floor, the smell of the results of her handiwork were again sickening.

Once the head was truly dead, blood and ichor from the torso of the mayor spilled all over the other woman's boots. The puddle under the feet of the mercenary quickly expanded to meet with the gummy blood that flooded from Bianca.

The smell made Ophelia's eyes water. She grabbed a rag from the workbench and wiped her hands off as best she could. Then she looked around.

It was truly a horror show. One of her making, to be sure, but the sight again turned her stomach. As much as it was disgust, part of it was the sudden worry of what the one closest to her would think.

"Havarti?" his name tumbled from her lips.

With Miranda dead, whatever she did to Ophelia should have been undone. Her heart fluttered at the very idea.

"Havarti," She said again, "Tell me you can hear me now. Please."
Silence.

"Please, Havarti," Her eyes blurred with tears as she looked at his hilt resting on her hip, "Even if you're disgusted by what I did, I just need to know you're okay!"

"Are you okay, Ophelia?" a familiar voice came.

But it wasn't from the sword. It came from the stairs where Harbenigyr stood in his long white tunic and a look of worry on his face.

"Harby?" Ophelia tossed the now pink rag rag onto the workbench, "How did you find me?"

"It wasn't hard, once we realized Miranda, Hero and the others were lying," the cleric shrugged, "You were invited to sleep here last night, remember?"

The woman nodded, "Havarti said that he heard you and Folken this morning. That he yelled and you couldn't hear him."

"I am so sorry about that," the elf stepped down into the cellar proper, avoiding the chunks in the shallow lake of blood that had been the dirt floor, "This would have turned out a lot different if their... wicked plans had been figured out earlier."

The rage the mercenary had been overwhelmed by was all but forgotten now. She gave the elf a smile to let him know he was forgiven.

"Is everyone else okay?" she asked. "Where are they?"

"Josie's upstairs," Harbenigyr motioned to the steps, "Everyone else is in the outskirts of town. Hero took all of them out there."

Ophelia felt her face tighten at the mention of the bard, "She's one of them, Harby! She was told to take all of you away so that they could make me a monster like them."

The elf nodded, "And she did. Everyone fell for it hook, line, and sinker."

"Except you," the woman quirked a thick eyebrow at the shorter man.

"Oh, no," Harbenigyr chuckled lightly, "Clerics of Kuan Yin are far too trusting. But I'm here now."

He rested a comforting hand on her shoulder. Then he stepped around her to bend down and pick something up.

"We wouldn't want this to get ruined, would we?" he held up the woman's long red leather coat.

Holding the garment by the sleeves, he slipped it around Ophelia's shoulders. She moved Havarti from her belt and into his usual resting place on her back.

It was then that she noticed that more than just the legs of her pants were gone. All but immediately under her belt had been torn away by Miranda, leaving only shreds of gray cloth hanging. She glanced back over at Harby, who didn't seem at all embarrassed at her state of being only half-dressed.

"Is Harvarti okay?" the cleric asked as he stepped back in front of her, "You looked worried about him when I first came down."

"Miranda pressed this chip of blood to my head," Ophelia replied, turning to look back over her shoulder, "Since then, I haven't been able to hear him. Or even feel him."

"Then Miranda did start the ritual to change you?" the cleric scowled, "I was afraid of that."

Ophelia's eyes narrowed as she looked back at Harbenigyr, "What do you mean?"

"Your tattoos, Ophelia. Are they acting like they did before?" the elf patted the lower portion of his own back.

The woman did the same and felt the familiar rush that came when someone touched the overly sensitive flesh, "They seem to be now."

"But you can't talk to your sword?" Harbenigyr questioned her again.

Ophelia shook her head.

"With Miranda dead, everyone in town became human again," the cleric started to explain, "Killing her made the take over of your body by the penanggalan stop but the power of the monster is using Doctor Efreeti's runes to keep a hold of you. You can still become one of them."

"What? How?" Ophelia's hands curled into tight fists.

"It's going to keep eating away at you," the cleric's black eyebrows pressed together, "Much slower than it could before. It was trying to take over Doctor Efreeti's runes before, now it is going to use them as a power source to transform you. It will make you host to two demons."

"Host to two demons?" Ophelia stepped closer to the elf, "How do you know all this, Harby? I've never heard of penanggalans before this and I only suspected that Efreeti was a demon. I never mentioned that to you before."

Harbenigyr sighed, "Well, Kuan Yin doesn't exactly answer the prayers of doppelgangers without souls of their own, now does she?"

"You're supposed to be dead," Ophelia poked a heavy finger into the narrow chest of the elf, "How can you be here?"

"I got better," he shrugged back.

Ophelia's hand rose to Havarti's handle, "I'll make it worse again."

Harbenigyr raised both hands, "You kill me, you'll never know how to cure yourself of the curse that Miranda slapped on you."

The mercenary froze in place, "Talk. Quickly."

"Josie! Bring it down!" the false cleric called.

The door leading into the basement creaked open. The red haired ranger became visible moments later, carrying a wooden box in both hands. It was heavy, too, judging by the huffing and puffing the alphan was doing as she methodically stepped down one stair at a time.

The cleric took the opposite side of the box in his hands once Josie's doppelganger made it to the bottom. The two soulless copies of Ophelia's compatriots set the crate down at the far edge of the pool of blood. Once both of them were free of the load, the cleric slapped his hands together and let out a quiet sigh of satisfaction.

"These bottles are the key to keeping the penanggalan at bay," he lifted the top off and pulled an opaque wine bottle out from inside, "A couple of sips every few hours and you will stay you."

Ophelia snatched the bottle from the cleric doppelganger and worked the cork free, "You're telling me that wine is the cure to becoming a penanggalan?" she scoffed.

With a hollow pop, the cork tumbled down the back of the sword woman's hand and into the crimson mess at her feet. She lifted the mouth of the bottle to her lips. The possibility of the drink being poisoned crossed her mind.

It didn't really matter if it was. If it was truly dangerous to her, Ophelia would blink and the effects would be gone. So she shrugged and took a big gulp of the liquid.

Immediately, her throat burned. The wet flesh blistered, sealing her airway shut.

As Ophelia choked, she wondered why she hadn't blinked. She thought about pulling Havarti's dagger free to stab herself, to try and force the magick to work. But after a few seconds, the pain stopped and air again filled her chest.

Ophelia found herself bent over the workbench, the wine bottle miraculously resting upright on the slab of wood just by her hand. She quickly straightened up and turned to again face the cleric and ranger. Ophelia had to admit that she was surprised they didn't try to attack her or anything while she was convulsing.

"What was that?" her voice was barely above a squeaking whisper, "That was not any kind of wine I've tasted before."

"It's spoiled wine," Harbenigyr answered, "The town where I- I mean the other Harbenigyr was born used to make wine. Their last batch went sour and turned to vinegar."

"You made me drink vinegar?" again, the mercenary reached for the handle of Havarti.

"Demons, by definition, are unclean beings, Ophelia," Evil Harbenigyr continued his explanation, the words coming out a little faster now, "Vinegar is a cleansing agent. You will get used to the taste. You will keep drinking it until you find Meteorend."

"You already know we don't have that rock!" Ophelia snarled, Havarti slipping free of his scabbard.

Again, the cleric raised his hands up in front of him, "Not yet but it will materialize soon. It's a living thing. That's why it's so unpredictable, you see. But it always becomes physical for the one who defeated its previous owner."

"I didn't kill Raiko," Ophelia stepped toward the elf, "But I'm willing to give you a second try."

"Just shut up and let him finish," the doppelganger of Josie spoke up, an arrow loaded in her bow and ready to shoot it at the mercenary.

Ophelia stopped at the sight of the arrow, not so much due to the threat but that she sounded so much like the real Josie when she spoke up, "You know that won't kill me," She pointed the bastard sword at the red haired ranger.

Evil Josie mockingly lipped the words back at the other woman. She didn't lower her bow.

"I know you didn't kill him," Evil Harbenigyr started speaking again. "But you fought him, bested him even. Folken also countered all of Meteorend's attacks that he unleashed. I think Meteorend is still trying to decide which of you are the most worthy to wield it. That's why it's is taking so long to become physical again."

"Great theory," the mercenary said flatly, "What does the rock have to do with me not becoming a penanggalan?"

"Meteorend is the petrified heart of an efreeti demon," Evil Harbenigyr said, "The problem right now is that the penanggalan energy and efreeti energy are too even. If you had Meteorend, that would shift the efreeti energy in your body to become dominant and burn out the other demon."

It made sense. If everything that the evil cleric doppelganger said was true, that is. It did beg another question, though.

"How do you know all this?" Ophelia stopped herself from using the cleric's name, "My Harby wouldn't. We never found any information about Doctor Efreeti outside of the genie folk tales."

"Ah," the doppelganger grinned wide, "The explanation to that is simple. Do you know what spiritual being I serve? You and I both know that it couldn't possibly be Kuan Yin."

Ophelia groaned, "You're not saying that Doctor Efreeti..."

"Is my patron deity," Evil Harbenigyr finished proudly, "Did you really think you were beyond his sight? Beyond his reach? That you were free? You're his masterpiece, Ophelia," he glanced down between her legs and only smiled wider. "Why would he let you go?"

"Is that why you're still alive? Did he tattoo runes into you, too?" Ophelia fumed.

Harbenigyr shook his head, "If he marked me, I wouldn't be able to pass myself as your favorite cleric, would I? You had no idea I wasn't him when I first came down, did you?"

Doctor Efreeti did something to keep him from dying. There was no way the doppelganger could have survived what she, Saya, and Folken did to him when they killed him the first time otherwise.

The mercenary dropped the bastard sword back into his scabbard on her back. It would be pointless to try and kill him again if he served Doctor Efreeti. At least while he was still of use to the demon.

Evil Josie lowered her weapon, slipping the arrow back into the quiver hanging on her belt. The red haired woman stepped away from the shallow sea of red and explored the far side of the cellar.

Pulling open the doors of an armoire that rested against the wall, the doppelganger revealed gardening tools with long handles. There were at least a dozen rakes, hoes, and other things that Ophelia couldn't recognize. Mostly because it was incredibly boring.

"So Efreeti doesn't want me to be a penanggalan," the mercenary reviewed, "Suddenly, I have a desire to have a neck extension."

"Oh, you don't want that entails," Evil Harbenigyr motioned to the carnage around them, "First, they smell bad, even when they're alive. Then they have uncontrollable urges to eat the ones they care about most. Not exactly a selling point for a bodyguard, is it? It will also keep you from ever hearing Havarti again."

That caught Ophelia's attention, "How would Meteorend give me Havarti back?"

"A penanggalan is the jealous type. They only like their influence in their host's mind," Evil Harbenigyr said, "Doctor Efreeti doesn't care what's in your mind. He owns everything else already."

The sound of crashing came from upstairs. All three of the people in the basement reflexively looked up even though there was no way they could see the source.

"It looks like the penanggalans don't like that we locked them out. Or maybe one of your friends finally made it back?" the cleric smirked, "Either way our time is suddenly short."

Ophelia forced another sip of the spoiled wine down her throat. She didn't say anything.

"Get Meteorend. We'll know when you have it," Evil Harbenigyr stepped toward the armoire next to Josie's doppelganger, "But I still need to tell you *how to* use it to cure yourself. If you tell your friends we're here, you'll never find out and Havarti will stay dead to you. You understand?"

Evil Josie and the cleric cleared the tools from the inside of the closet. It didn't take long. Then the ranger stepped inside, followed by Evil Harbenigyr. As the woman pulled the doors closed, Harbenigyr wrapped his hands around the woman's rear end.

Ophelia tugged the crate full of wine bottles filled with vinegar closer and sat down on it. Everything revolved around that blasted rock.

She wouldn't do it. She may not be able to wield Havarti anymore, but Ophelia was no traitor. That's what she would be if she took Meteorend for the doppelganger cleric.

Pointing them out hiding in the closet to the penanggalan coming down could give her a chance to escape. Then, at the very least, she could find anyone who is still alive in her group.

If it was her friends coming down, admittedly far less likely, she couldn't let the evil cleric know that she wasn't going to play along. If he really couldn't be killed, he killed one of Ophelia's would be rescuers. Or worse, even if they somehow imprisoned him, he would just come back and trouble them again. So she wouldn't tell them that he was in the armoire.

She could hear whispering through the door upstairs. Ophelia wouldn't let herself be afraid of the monsters coming.

"Come on down! What's left of your bosses could use the company!" the threatening tone of Ophelia's voice was only slightly muffled as it made its way around the walls and up the stairs, "Unless you're squeamish. Then you may want to stay up there. It does smell kind of funny down here."

"Ophelia?" Saya called down into the cellar.

CHAPTER ELEVEN

"You aided and abetted a known criminal," I said.

Ophelia shook her head, "I didn't aid Harby's evil twin."

"You could have ended him then and there," I pointed out the simple fact.

The subject nodded in agreement, "But I didn't. I regret that, but that doesn't make me the cause of all the ills in the world."

"I didn't say that you were," I replied, "Just those of your friends and anyone close to you."

"How can you say that?" the subject screamed, "You weren't there! You don't know how hard it was to decide what to say, what to do, what would protect the others, and what would put them in harm's way."

"I told you that I was there," I said, "Just not in body."

"What the hell is that supposed to mean, anyway?" the subject snapped at me, "You think reading some reports makes you an expert on me? Some statements tell you what I was thinking then?"

"No," I said, "I am simply telling you that if you had been forthright with your compatriots from the beginning, what happened to Appelonia, Illyria and the others could have been avoided altogether."

"But I didn't," the subject said, "I can't go back and change it now."

"No, but you do have to relive it," I gave her the next report, "If you want to see justice truly done, you must."

Decades later...

'Overtake' the Galleon? It was a good idea. The only problem is that it was faster than their ship, the *Spotted Dick*.

By the time the ship carrying Jonas, Genevieve, Appelonia, Tokki, Phinegann, Jin, Bronwyn, and Illyria was underway and streaming along at its top speed, the *Galleon* was already almost out of sight.

At least to everyone on deck. The spotter up in the crow's nest reported that their quarry was still sailing north, deeper inland. He called updates down every few minutes. The *Galleon* showed no signs of slowing down, let alone stopping.

After an hour of giving chase, the initial excitement had worn off. Especially for Illyria Warflower. She was already on the prowl for something new to focus her attention on.

That brought her to Mister Renthrow, the First Mate. As second-in-command of the *Spotted Dick*, surely he had an idea of something that needed doing.

"But I have extensive knowledge of mechanical engineering!" Illyria pouted at the man who was twice her height, "Is your compass in working order? Your clepsydra? I could increase the angle of the arc on your octant to 120 degrees to make it more accurate for you."

The man with overly loose jowls looked down his crooked nose at the gnome, "Little pimple, your party may have forced their way on this ship. You may have forced the Captain's hand into granting you our service. That does not mean that I must allow you access to our most essential and necessary gear. So go count reeds on the river's bank or something."

"I was just trying to help," Illyria turned and stomped away from the First Mate.

Another sailor rushed past her and down the stairs toward the stern to get below deck. A lot of them have been doing that, one every few minutes. In fact, up top had to be running short of enough hands to keep everything running smoothly. What could be so important down inside the ship?

Illyria came across Appelonia, who was chatting with Jonas and Genevieve as she was treating some scrapes on the arm that had the sleeve of her tunic ripped away. Both she and the paladin sat on a couple of barrels that the gnome guessed had water for the crew to drink as they went about their duties. Genevieve, on the other hand, paced along the deck nearby. I guess it was presumptuous to count her in Jonas and Apple's conversation.

"I'm pretty sure your father will fire me after he hears about what happened in the Flustered Mermaid," the paladin had a thin smile on his face even as he shook his head.

"Why? You weren't the one who looked like the sign," Appelonia giggled back, "I think it was a little exaggerated in the chest area, personally."

"Not as much as you might think," Jonas muttered under his breath.

Appelonia leaned in closer to the armor wearing man, "What was that?"

An elf's hearing was more sensitive than that of a human, so Illyria doubted that the cleric didn't catch Jonas' little comment. She started to point that out to the two giants and only got to the word "sensitive" before Appelonia's boot popped her in the rear.

It didn't hurt but it did garner a stern look from the gnome. Apple merely shrugged back with a self-conscious smile on her lips.

Jonas looked as if he were about to ask a question, if Illyria had to guess it was about the random violence a cleric just performed on her backside. Before he could get a word out, the jowly First Mate strode over and interrupted everything.

"Paladin, I do hate to impose but the Captain was wondering if she could ask a favor of you," The man gave the small group a quick bow before clicking the heels of his boots together and straightening up.

"Whatever we can do to make up for the inconvenience we've caused, Mr. Renthrow," Jonas nodded back at the man, as bowing while sitting was most inconvenient.

"It turns out, sir, in our haste to depart some of the crates containing our new shipment shifted out of place in a most inconvenient matter," the First Mate said, "I'm afraid they are too heavy for my men to manage on their own."

"We'd be glad to add our arms to the effort," Jonas shrugged. "But if they're so heavy that your crew can't move them, I'm not sure how a half dozen more hands will help."

Mr. Renthrow cleared his throat, making his cheeks vibrate, "That's just the thing, sir. It isn't your arm, as mighty as I'm sure it is, we were asking assistance of."

"Of which we were asking for assistance," Illyria corrected the First Mate.

"Excuse me?" the sailor again stared down his nose at the gnome.

"Your grammar was off in that last sentence," the small woman with glass wings said, "I just want to make sure you don't have any misunderstandings."

Mister Renthrow again cleared his throat, looking severely annoyed at Illyria. She couldn't understand why. She was just trying to help.

"Elly," Jonas chimed in before the First Mate could say something snarky (again), "Could you fly up to the lookout and get an update on our distance from the *Galleon*? They're a bit overdue on their latest report."

The gnome could recognize when she was being shooed away, "Fine. I'll will go and get an update on the ship about which you are asking."

She gave Mister Renthrow a curtsy and a smiled sharpened at the edges before fluttering into the air. The crow's nest, or lookout as the paladin just called it (maybe he had a thing against crows?), was where the spotter called out distant contacts. It wasn't hard to get to when you had wings. Climbing was far more troublesome with all the ropes and cloth flopping all around.

"Genevieve!" Jonas called to the efreeti in her human guise, "Please accompany this man below decks and move some crates for him. We've already caused enough trouble for them, it's only fair we help them a bit."

Even as she neared the top of the main mast, Illyria could hear the annoyed sigh that came from Genevieve, "Yes, Master," She didn't really say it as much a groan? Growl? Snarl? Whatever way you would describe it, none of them would be *happy*.

The small woman landed on the rounded edge of the crow's nest, her wings stretching out beside her to help maintain her balance. The lookout wasn't big, even by Illyria's compact standards. Strangely, it was empty.

Where had Taimak gone? Illyria had made several visits during the trip and was getting pretty friendly with the svartalfar spotter. But he wasn't up here.

The gnome remembered all the crewmembers who had been running below decks. Now she wondered if the spotter was among them.

Regardless, she had to get a report on the *Galleon*. If they lost her (Illyria did like that boats were referred to as the fairer sex), all the trouble they went through would have been for nothing.

Illyria turned to look toward the bow, again wondering why sailors needed another word for 'the front', of the *Spotted Dick*. The trees on the shore that had started as little posts here and there had quickly built up into a full fledged forest to the west. The river had enough curve ahead that their target was out of view.

"Oh, that just will not do," the small woman declared to herself.

She launched herself into the air. Her wings pumped hard to drive her upward. She had to almost double the height of the *Spotted*

Dick to get high enough to be able to finally spot the *Galleon*. It had sped further ahead in the last half hour than Taimak had reported.

It was so far ahead, in fact, that their crew felt safe enough pull in and stop at a small pier. It didn't look big enough to accommodate a ship that size. It must have had to have something to do with the dark figure standing there. It looked as if it were waiting for them. Illyria couldn't make out any details from this distance.

Then the sudden pop of an explosion came to the gnome's ears. Spinning around, she quickly searched for the source. It wasn't the *Galleon,* they were much too far away. Finally, the woman looked almost straight down.

Smoke billowed out of the right side of the *Spotted Dick*. It was white instead black, meaning that the ship wasn't on fire. It was more likely that they had fired a cannon but there didn't appear to be quite enough smoke to account for that. Not to mention that nothing was hit by any projectiles from the ship.

Illyria swooped down to the ship as fast as she dared. It took her approximately thirty four seconds, according to her chronometer, to reach the deserted deck. She heard screaming coming from the back of the ship and ran in that direction.

"You have no right to hold Genevieve!" Jonas stared down the Captain.

The paladin, along with Appelonia, Tokki, Phinegann, and the monk, Jin Vega, stood nearly toe to toe with the woman who commanded the *Spotted Dick*, who was flanked by six of her largest crewmen. They were blocking Illyria's friends from the door that led below deck, from where the explosion came.

The small woman tugged on the length of chainmail hanging behind Appelonia. "What is going on here?" she asked the elf.

"Either she stays below or you can jump off and swim right now," the Captain replied to Jonas, "A genie can fetch a handsome price down south."

"They have Genevieve downstairs," Appelonia hurriedly whispered, "They want to keep her as payment for us commandeering their boat."

Jonas' eyes narrowed, "Who said she was a genie?"

"Who's the only one of us not here at the moment?" Tokki waved his clawed sleeve at the rest of the party.

"Bronwyn," the paladin groaned, "Captain, the efre- I mean, genie and I have our disagreements but I cannot condone trading another living being as payment for anything. You know that."

"You seem to only fall back on the code of a paladin only when it's convenient," the stocky Captain sneered back, "You do realize that you effectively hijacked my ship, don't you? Last time I checked, and I check every morning, that was still a crime."

"I know the circumstances are less than ideal," Jonas replied, keeping the tip of his massive sword blade on the deck and the handle of the claymore in the crook of his arm, "But I fully intend to compensate you for your inconvenience. Properly, with coin of the realm, as soon as I can send a message back to my Order to explain the situation to them."

"And I'm simply supposed to take your word for it?" the woman scoffed, "You haven't exactly endeared yourselves to me or my crew."

Appelonia turned from the gnome to address the Captain, "Madam, I understand that you must be frustrated at the situation. But this truly is an emergency."

"First, I haven't been a *Madam* since I came out west, girl," the Captain snapped at the cleric, "And you and I have very different definitions of *emergency*, missie. Now shut up and let the adults talk!"

Appelonia's jaw jutted out and she looked like she was about to say something that, as a cleric to a benevolent deity, she may regret. Instead, Illyria tugged on her leg again.

"Would it really be so bad to be rid of Genevieve?" she asked.

"What was that?" the cleric couldn't hide her shock at the question.

"What was that?" Jin turned to look at the gnome.

The monk looked far more amused by the little woman's question than Appelonia. Admittedly, she could only see half a smile but there could have been a full one under all that bushy black hair on his face.

"The baby is one of Genevieve's people, Elly," the cleric crouched down close to the gnome to keep the Captain from hearing their argument, "The whole reason we're here is because of her."

"That is exactly my point!" Ilyria literally pointed at Appelonia, "With Genevieve gone, we can all go back about our respective businesses. You can keep wandering with Jonas, Tokki, and Phinegann. Jin can do… whatever it is he does. And I can go back to Dianmeyer and study those soul orbs."

"That's a valid argument," Jin knelt down beside the cleric, resting his arms on his knees. "Without Genevieve, the efreeti have no leverage over any of us anymore."

"I can't believe I'm hearing this," the words came from Appelonia's mouth very slowly, methodically, "Genevieve is a b- very unpleasant person, yes, but she is looking for her people's child. That motivation isn't evil. Even if we think they are," Her black eyes shifted back and forth from Jin, to Tokki, and back to Illyria before she continued, "We promised to see this through. Jonas gave his word to the Mullah and we all agreed to be held by it."

"But we never foresaw a situation like this coming up," Jin countered, "This could be the last chance we have to be free of this demonic extortion."

Jonas continued arguing with the Captain. He made sure not to make any movements that could be considered threatening as they spoke. She had no such worry. The six crewmen behind her all unsheathed their scimitars, resting them on their broad shoulders. Illyria found herself wondering why pirates seemed to prefer that style of weapon.

"But two wrongs don't make a right, Jin. Yes, we're in a bad situation but that doesn't mean…"

The monk was not going to be moved by that argument. Realizing that, Appelonia let out a lingering sigh before looking him straight in the eye.

"Do you really want Bronwyn to win like this?" she asked the man, "You want her to beat us? To beat you?"

Now he definitely had a full smile behind his bushy beard. Illyria could see the white of his teeth. As did Tokki.

"Now that is a motive I can support," the Bunny Barbarian chuckled.

Jin Vega grinned as he straightened up, "I wanted to make sure that you were willing to fight for this. Because a fight always costs."

"Before fists and swords fly, can I try something?" Illyria offered, "Or is this the wrong crowd?"

Apple looked over to the gnome, "What do you have in mind?"

"We all heard that explosion that came from below, right?" the winged woman said, "Let me sneak down there. I can check to see if they have anymore traps like that waiting for us. If they do, maybe I'll be able to repurpose them to aid us!"

"That does sound like a plan," Tokki threw in his support.

"All we have to do is keep Captain Silky busy," Appelonia looked back over her shoulder at the stocky woman who was losing her patience with the paladin, "So you better get going."

With that, Appelonia straightened up and strode up beside Jonas, "Listen, I know I'm not as... mature as you, Captain," the female pirate visibly bristled at that but the cleric kept talking, "But it seems to me that Bronwyn wouldn't have told you about Genevieve if she didn't get something in return. What, pray tell, did you give her? Money? Did you know she was the one who took the message written by another captain to you from your crewman? Also, did you leave her alone at any point?"

"Don't try to fester distrust, child," the Captain snarled, "We had a deal that was firm and well versed."

"Well versed?" the cleric raised a crimson eyebrow, "You mean you let her talk her way into your stores and all she gave you in return was information that Genevieve was a genie? A fire breathing one at that?" Appelonia shook her head, "Doesn't that strike anyone as a bad idea to try and capture on a ship made entirely of wood?"

"She wanted away from you! It was a request with which I could sympathize. So I allowed her use of my skiff to take her to shore," the pirate Captain retorted, "And taking mythical beasts is my business, child. It would take more than a little flame to burn out the finest Algonquin oak in all of Honua. It's withstood more than..."

Illyria missed the rest of the bragging and subsequent arguing. While Jin and Phinegann used their bodies to block the shorter Bunny Barbarian and the small woman from the view of the Captain and her men, Tokki hoisted Illyria over the railing.

Hanging off the side of the *Spotted Dick* with nothing but the barbarian's grip on her hands to support her, Illyria kept shifting her wings one way and then another. When her glass wings caught the breeze, her hands were pulled from Tokki's and she started gliding down the length of the ship to find an open porthole.

It did not take long. One of the little windows that was meant for shooting the cannon was open along the starboard side of the ship.

Illyria crawled in to see that all of the heavy iron weapons had been turned to point toward the *inside* of the boat. That did not make any sense.

At least not until she saw at what they were aiming or, more accurately, at whom. Genevieve wasn't even in her human disguise anymore. She had a length of chain wrapped around her with halves of iron spheres attached to either end and pinning her to the floor.

The efreeti was still full of vim and vigor, kicking at any man or woman who dared to try and get within her reach. It was, as far as Illyria could tell, a stalemate.

Genevieve, being a demon, was unnaturally strong, though. Why didn't see just rip her way out of the chains and tear her would-be captors to pieces?

That answer came after only a few minutes of Illyria's silent observation.

"She's not reacting to the Thokcha the way that the Captain said she would, sir!" the crewman closest to (but thankfully with is back toward) the cannon that the gnome was perched upon shouted.

"Nonsense, lad!" First Mate Renthrow scowled at the lower ranked pirate, "The fact that she's not killed us means that them chains are holding. We just need to get another set on her!"

Illyria looked closer at the links of metal wrapped around Genevieve. The chain was wrapped around her middle pinned her arms down to her hips. The iron looked like the typical black of the metal, although it had a wavy pattern along the surface that was unusual.

There wasn't any kind of glow but the sheen of the iron made it look like it was wet against the skin of the demon. That impression was only reinforced by the steam rising from where the metal touched her burgundy skin.

"Load the other Thokcha shell!" the First Mate hollered the order.

As the sailor in front of the cannon turned in Illyria's direction, she realized that she had overstayed her welcome. He immediately started reaching for the curved sword on his hip.

"Intruder!" he yelped.

Ilyria spread her wings open wide, "Yup! Take a good, long look at the intruder!"

The gnome burned the bright lights at the tips of her wings at full brightness, turning them on and off again like a strobe. The pirate immediately in front of her fell back as if he had been physically struck. Another sailor rushed for Illyria from the side.

The little woman slipped off the top of the cannon, the would-be attacker tumbling over the heavy weapon, and rushed over to the demon. Illyria was surprised at how easy it was to lift the half-sphere that made up one end of the chain. Even then, it still took both hands.

"She's trying to free the genie!" the First Mate yelled, "Stop her!"

Illyria turned the four beams of light on steadily, aiming them right in the faces of whatever pirates crept closest. All the while, the gnome carried one end of the chain over Genevieve's torso. She stretched her legs out as far as she could reach to keep from stepping directly on the efreeti.

Illyria dropped the half of the cannonball and Genevieve shot to sit up on the floor. In her rage, the efreeti screamed so powerfully that black smoke bellowed out of her mouth and nose.

"You impudent insects!" the wood under her body started to smolder even as she adjusted herself to stand, "You dare to think that you could contain me?"

The door leading up to the deck suddenly sounded as if someone was knocking on it in a panic. Genevieve spewed flame at the men, forcing them to back away as Illyria rushed for the stairs.

One sailor was unlucky enough for his shirt to catch flame. He flailed over to one of the ports the cannons usually pointed out and crawled outside.

Before Illyria was halfway up the stairs, the door shattered into splinters. The woman's glass wings wrapped around her, protecting her from the barrage of splinters.

When she peeked out between the panes of glass, it was to the sight of Phinegann stepping over her and deeper into the ship. Jonas was immediately behind, although he stopped in front of Illyria instead passing her.

"Genevieve! After Phin and Tokki took out her men, the Captain became more agreeable!" the paladin called down, "Don't kill anyone... unless you absolutely have to! We need them to sail the ship. I'm sure we're way behind the *Galleon* by now."

"Actually, it docked next to a small pier on the far side of the bend in the river," Illyria reported. "I never got a chance to tell you with all this happening."

Jonas tilted his head to the side as he stared at the gnome, "So we've almost caught up?"

"Depending on how long they stay stopped," she shrugged back, "I think Bronwyn was waiting for them."

"How could she have gotten a signal to them?" Jonas said, shaking his head, "No, it doesn't matter. Everyone get ready for a fight!"

OPHELIA INTERROGATION NOTES

*"It seems you have associated yourself with a nest of traitors,"
I observed.*

"Everybody does what they think is right at the time," the subject said.

"You say that, yet you knew hiding Evil Harbenigyr's involvement was wrong from the beginning," I said.

Ophelia nodded, albeit reluctantly, "So did everyone else."

Decades before...

AFTER OPHELIA'S REVELATION, the party briefly reconsidered going to Riverbelt since it had been Ophelia's idea. Harbenigyr, of course, voted to give her the benefit of the doubt. It wasn't until Folken declared that he believed that Ophelia's motive to thwart the plan of the doppelgangers was genuine that the rest of the party agreed to continue.

Ophelia found that ironic.

Nevertheless, the trek continued for another two days. Nothing happened as they rode. A whole lot of nothing.

They made camp, again with Josie, Ophelia, and Lyan goint to sleep without tents. Just as the sun started to tease coming over the horizon, Ophelia felt a heavy handed poke at her shoulder.

Even through the blurry vision of caked sleep trying to keep her eyes closed, the mercenary could see the bright blue of Lyan Yo Bunpy's armor laying on the ground beside her.

"What? What is it?" she groggily said to the barbarian.

"I apologize for awakening you," the Bunny Barbarian whispered, "But I felt that we needed to talk."

Ophelia lifted herself onto her elbows, "It isn't like you haven't had ample opportunity. You have a specific reason why it had to be now, Lyan?"

The other woman nodded, "I have tried to put my concerns aside but I cannot do so any longer. If I am to travel with you, I must know that you can be trusted."

Ophelia rubbed the lingering bits of sleep from her eyes with her left hand, some lingering scabs on the back of her palm the only sign that it had ever been impaled, "Ask your questions."

"How many evil duplicates are we facing?" she started, "Of whom?"

"As far as I know, two," the mercenary answered, "Of Harby and Josie. If he's to be believed, my doppelganger killed all the others, including herself. Except for Saya. She killed her own."

"Do you believe him?" Lyan stifled a yawn.

Ophelia shrugged, "He said he was the last. Then Evil Josie popped up. Since then, they're the only two I've seen. I don't believe Evil Harby's words but I do believe my eyes."

"How do you know none of you had been replaced with your doppelgangers before?" the Bunny Barbarian's brown eyes narrowed as she watched Ophelia.

"We've all had plenty of chances to betray each other," the woman using her long coat as a blanket responded, "I find it hard to believe that, if any of us were the doppelgangers, they haven't found an opportunity to strike."

A disturbing thought suddenly ran through Ophelia's mind. She sat up straight, looking at the leather satchel that Lyan always kept on her since the start of their journey across the continent.

"No one has found an opportunity, have they?" she pointed at the bag.

Lyan pulled the flap open and pulled the black rock out. Leaving it exposed to the cool, dim predawn air for a moment, "It has not left since I put it in for this trek," then she tucked Meteorend back inside.

"Why is this stone so important to the evil cleric?" the Bunny Barbarian asked as she tied the flap shut again.

"The doppelgangers were created by the de Junamend. The ones who claim that rock. Evil Harbenigyr has some kind of deal with them. If he gets them the Meteorend, he and Evil Josie get their freedom or something. Maybe some kind of bounty, too," Ophelia shared what she knew, "But if the de Junamend get it back, Folken says there's a good chance they will start the Clan Wars again."

"I remember," Lyan nodded, "I wanted to make sure that you remembered what was at stake, as well."

"I understand your concern. Really," the other woman sighed, "But I do want to keep the de Junamend from getting the rock. If the Clan Wars started again, that would put the last person who actually gives two craps about me in danger."

Lyan looked at the mercenary questioningly, "I was under the impression that you have no one outside of this band."

Ophelia glanced back at the tents, "That's mostly true. I haven't told anyone about–" her mouth shut and wouldn't open again.

"About whom?" Lyan leaned toward the other woman.

"You swear not to mention this to any of them?" Ophelia still hadn't decided whether or not to answer truthfully yet.

"I do," the barbarian said.

"On what?" the mercenary asked.

"What do you mean?"

"I don't have much I'm attached to," Ophelia replied, "If someone asked me to swear my word of honor on the seal of Kuan Yin or some other god, I'd laugh in their face. I'm asking you, Lyan Yo Bunpy, what would you swear your honor upon?"

The Bunny Barbarian was quiet for a long moment. She pulled her knees up high enough to perch her forearms, then in turn rest her chin on them. Finally, Lyan answered Ophelia.

"The life of my father," she said, "I have seen the fervor with which Kilfcoyme, his childhood friend, defends him. My father can fight for himself but has not had to in all the days Kilfcoyme has been at his side. Anything worth fighting for so diligently is worth taking an oath upon."

Ophelia thought that her words sounded so... honest, so she could accept that, "Then swear that you won't repeat anything about this person to anyone else in the group."

"I swear," Lyan held up her right hand, "On the life of my father."

Ophelia took a deep breath before she could bring herself to speak, "The Light Bringer we're going to see. She's the only person still alive who knew me from before Harby brought me back to life."

"I was told about the gorgon," Lyan mentioned.

"She was only a kid when I knew her," Ophelia continued, "I was under mind control when we first met. I killed her mother and kidnapped her. Her father, a member of a group within the Light Bringers called the Night Shield came after her."

"This does not sound like a foundation for trust," Lyan observed.

The mercenary ignored the comment from the barbarian, "After the mind control on me was broken, he and the girl took me into hiding with them. We traveled around for months. In that time, we grew into something somewhat resembling a family. In a highly disorganized manner, at least.

"After Harby brought me back, the first thing I did was look for her and her father," Ophelia shivered as echoes of the dread she felt back then washed over her, "He'd died while I was a statue. Once she grew up, she joined the Light Bringers and fought in the Clan Wars that the de Junamend started. That's who we are going to see now."

Lyan listened. When the mercenary finished, the Bunny Barbarian took a moment to digest her words.

"What is her name?" she asked, "This woman warrior you trust."

"Tillyria Mitchell. She's a Colonel with the Light Bringers, stationed in Riverbelt," Ophelia answered, resisting the urge to use the girl's maiden name as one final, if flimsy layer of protection.

"Which is why we did not go to Valen Court even though it was closer," Lyan said.

"Exactly," Ophelia nodded, "Just because you're a Light Bringer doesn't make you automatically trustworthy. At least to me."

"Nor to... me," the other woman was distracted as she finished her short sentence.

The mercenary turned to see why. It was a good reason, too. The red haired ranger, Josie, was slipping out of Harbenigyr's tent.

Under normal circumstances Opheila and Lyan would still be asleep. Everyone would be.

"Why do you suppose she was in there with the cleric?" the barbarian whispered, "Perhaps she is not feeling well?"

"I don't think so," Ophelia shook her head, "I think she's finally gotten over whatever hang up has been keeping her from enjoying Harby's company."

"Enjoying his company?" Lyan looked confused for a moment, "You mean sex."

"If they're lucky," Ophelia couldn't stifle her laugh.

And Josie noticed them watching her. The alphan woman's cheeks radiated bright pink as she self-consciously walked toward the horses in the opposite direction that the two other women were in. Pure coincidence, surely.

Less than an hour later, the tents were packed and everyone was ready to continue their walk. Ophelia strode over to the ranger with a wide smirk on her face.

"I never got a chance to see how far we made it yesterday," she said to Josie, "Care to pull out the map and show us where we are?"

The red haired woman's face almost matched her hair when she first saw the mercenary approaching her. Relief washed over her when Ophelia asked such a neutral, professional question.

She pulled a piece of parchment from the pocket on the leg of her baggy pants. Josie noticed that Ophelia's pants now mimicked hers with the hips being cut out, although the mercenary's were much tighter that what the ranger wore.

Unfolding the map, Josie pointed near the middle, "We're here."

She was pointing just south of the city-state of Wildevale. Well, it looked just south on a small map but, in reality, the city was at least a day's ride away at a full gallop.

Ophelia whistled, "We're almost halfway there already? It doesn't feel like we've gone that far."

"People don't realize how much time you can save by not actually following the curve of a road," Josie smirked back.

Ophelia gripped the top of the map with one hand and ran a fingertip from her other hand along the path they had taken so far, "So how far along your curves did you let Harby go last night?"

The other woman's hands fell from the map and her jaw dropped open. Not only her face, but Josie's neck, chest and shoulders flushed firepepper red at Ophelia's question.

"Relax, Josie. You don't have to tell me if you don't want to," the human woman laughed, "Harby's a sweet kid. You could do a lot worse."

Ophelia folded the map back up and handed it to the ranger. Josie cleared her throat but still couldn't bring herself to say anything to the other woman so she busied herself by tucking the map back into her pocket.

They were off again on another long ride in the middle of nowhere. The only difference between this day and the last was Ophelia decided to walk, letting her horse haul some of the extra supplies. This made splitting her time between making Josie blush and walking beside Harbenigyr easier.

"So what were you up to last night?" the mercenary wiggled her thick eyebrows at the cleric atop his griffin, Triton.

"What do you mean?" he bit down on his lower lip as he tried to hide his sudden nervousness.

"Lyan and I saw Josie sneaking out of your tent this morning," Ophelia whispered so that neither Folken nor Hero could overhear.

"You saw that?" the elf sucked more of his lip in between his teeth, "She really didn't want anyone to..."

"It's alright, Harby," Ophelia reached up to playfully hit his shoulder, making the chainmail around his chest jingle lightly, "It is natural, you know."

"If you say so," he gulped, turning his head to look in any direction than back at the mercenary.

Ophelia's brow furrowed, "Maybe Josie should stay in a little longer tonight. You still seem tense."

The ranger just happened to look back at the cleric and the taller woman then. Harbenigyr gave the ranger a quick, awkward wave before returning his attention back to Ophelia.

"Oh, no, it's not that," Harby smiled uneasily, "It's just that, you know, she didn't want to tell anyone but now almost everyone knows where she was…"

"Don't worry. As long as the bard doesn't know," the mercenary glanced back at Hero, who was playing a song that she was sure Folken would enjoy, before leaning in close to the cleric, "no songs about your conquest will be written between here and the next tavern."

"C-conquest?" Harby practically shriveled up at the word.

"Sorry," Ophelia laughed, helping him straighten back up, "I keep forgetting that you're not a typical guy. You'd think I'd be used to the idea by now."

After a few more minutes of chit-chat, Opheila drifted back to walk beside Folken. His horse walked along the path with no real need of the pale svartalfar to even hold the reins.

Once Ophelia's inability to hear Havarti was revealed, the sorcerer took possession of the bastard sword. The jeweled scabbard bounced against the cape draped over his back, the strap running over his right shoulder to wrap around one of the svartalfar's metal fingers.

He could have just stored Havarti on the saddle, like most people would a weapon of his size. Instead, he carried it as if he were walking. Or at least out of reach of Ophelia while she was on foot.

"Transmutation is not as simple a process as you seem to represent it, Folken," the snooty voice of the sword said to the sorcerer, "To change something on its most fundamental level, while keeping an element of consciousness– oh, hello my dear."

Havarti stopped mid-sentence when he noticed Ophelia walk up. She was practically touching Folken's knee by then. She didn't know why, but the fact that Havarti had taken so long to notice that she was there, it… it hurt.

"Hello, Havarti," she smiled at the hilt, though the gesture didn't fully reach her eyes, "Have you been talking Folken's ear off about magic theory again?"

"We have had a spirited debate, I would say," the sword replied, "What say you, sir?"

Folken nodded, "He and I have born witness to some remarkable feats that were similar in outcome but far different in the challenges presented and overcome. It has been fascinating to compare our experiences."

"I've only understood every third word or so," Hero smirked, switching to an instrumental song to rest her voice, if not her lute plucking hand.

Ophelia all but ignored her as she spoke again, "I'm glad you found someone who can keep up with you," she sighed to the bastard sword.

"Oh, it is nothing like that, my dear," Havarti said back, "In fact, my motives for sharing my experiences with our sorcerer friend here have been to, perhaps, find a way to restore my means of being able to communicate with you directly."

"We know a way," Ophelia shrugged, "But we can't trust Evil Harbenigyr's word."

"Oh, I wholeheartedly agree about that," the sword replied, "But there is, as they say, more than one way to skin a griffin."

Ophelia wished she shared Havarti's optimism. The fact that he didn't know that she was so unsure just made her stomach sink more.

"There's no reason to be so upset, Ophelia," the sword said.

Air rushed into the woman, "How did you—?" she wanted to jump up, grab Havarti and give his hilt a great big kiss.

"I may not feel your presence anymore, my dear," Havarti said, "But I still know you. We will get through this."

He wasn't able to sense her after all. She had to remind herself that nothing had changed from before. She needed to change that disappointment into something else.

"I know you will, Havarti," And Ophelia marched away, "I know it."

Later that night…

OPHELIA COULDN'T SLEEP for most of the night. Sure, she was lying down beside the fire, her long coat on top of her like a blanket, but sleep was elusive. It was hard to sleep alone after having someone with you for so long

When the moon was at it zenith, mostly full and coating everything its light touched with a silvery gloss, the mercenary just counted the two hundred sixty-third cricket chirp when Harby's tent opened. The muffled whip of the flap that separated the inside from the cold night was easy to miss. Even for someone wide awake.

Josie stepped out, like she had just before dawn. This time, though, Harbenigyr followed closely after. Neither one, but particularly the cleric, looked as if he were enjoying any kind of afterglow. If Ophelia had to describe it in any way, Harbenigyr actually looked scared.

Josie didn't look much happier. She pointed in the direction of Lyan and Ophelia beside the fire pit and Harbenigyr nodded. They both started toward the two women who didn't bother with tents.

As they closed the distance, Lyan started to stir. While the ranger was silent, the cleric, with his new chainmail shirt, wasn't exactly built for stealth.

Harbenigyr slapped his hands together and muttered words that Ophelia couldn't hear from this far away. The jade green glow that came from the spiritual energies of the goddess Kuan Yin engulfed the Bunny Barbarian's head all the way down to the tips of her thick black braids.

Lyan went still again, back into a deep sleep.

Ophelia had a feeling that she knew what they were after. Could Evil Harbenigyr had taken the true one's place? He'd alluded to doing so before. But Evil Harbenigyr didn't have the same clothes as the real one anymore. He had to steal his previous tunic to replace the bloodstained, shredded one from when Ophelia and the others had killed him the first time.

That was just a one time thing. Harby's new shirt was one of a kind, an improvised design that wasn't widely available. With Ophelia sleeping so poorly, she would have heard if the doppelganger would have tried to make an attempt to replace the cleric, or even just steal his shirt again.

Ophelia realized that they had no outward way to differentiate their Josie from the doppelganger. They really should have thought of something earlier.

While she was (mostly) sure that was the real Harbenigyr, Ophelia wasn't so sure about Josie. But then, why would Harby help the doppelganger?

Harbenigyr hesitantly continued toward the barbarian. His hand was shaking as he reached for the leather satchel that Lyan kept right next to her.

Under normal circumstances, the Bunny Barbarian would have awoken and, on instinct alone, pummeled whoever was within reach of the bag. But Harbenigyr had used some kind of power to keep the other woman asleep.

Ophelia thought that the abilities of a Kuan Yin cleric couldn't be used for nefarious means. She was under the impression that such an act would cut the cleric off from the grace of his goddess.

They must have figured that Ophelia was fast asleep. Now was as good of time as any to disappoint them.

"What are you doing?" Ophelia said, her tone conversational.

She quickly sat up, her long coat still draped over her legs. The look of surprise from the ranger was just the side of precious to the mercenary.

The look of horror on the elf's face only confirmed that he was the real one to Ophelia. While that did relieve her worry in one way, it just reinforced the other. Why would he help the doppelganger get Meteorend?

"I know I encouraged you two to play together," Ophelia continued speaking, "but I meant under some blankets. Don't you think this is taking things a little far?"

"I'm sorry," Harbenigyr's voice was barely a whisper, even as he slipped the strap of the satchel over his shoulder, "I don't have any choice."

Ophelia kicked her coat away and turned to face Josie, who was about five paces behind the cleric, "Now why would he think something like that?"

"Because, unlike you, he knows my word is good?" the ranger shrugged.

The mercenary thought it odd that the comment came out as if she were asking a question. She also considered herself lucky that Josie didn't have an arrow ready to fire. Mostly for Lyan's benefit. Ophelia had a chance of her blinking saving her, the barbarian was utterly defenseless in her mystically enforced unconsciousness.

"When did you switch with our Josie?" Ophelia asked as she rose to her feet, not bothering with her coat that rested in a pile on the dirt.

"Does it matter?" the fingers of Josie's right hand rubbed together.

If Ophelia's guess was right, the ranger was getting ready to snatch an arrow from the quiver on her hip. She would still have to raise her left arm, that held her bow, and aim it but Josie had shown herself to be adept and doing so at speeds that the mercenary didn't think possible.

And Ophelia didn't have any way to close that much distance. If she still had her connection with Havarti, she could have told him to awaken Folken and warn him. She didn't, of course, so she went with the only real option she had. Stall.

"I'd really like to know," Ophelia said to the ranger, "Was it before or after we caught you coming out of his tent yesterday?" she motioned to Lyan and then to Harby as she spoke.

"Before," Josie confessed.

"Is our ranger still alive?" Ophelia asked.

Harby looked at the red haired doppelganger anxiously. The mercenary suddenly had an idea of how Evil Josie obtained his help.

"She is," the ruby haired woman stepped up to the cleric and grabbed his shoulder, "As long as we get where we need to be in time. Otherwise, there won't be a surplus of me's in Honua anymore."

Pulling Harbenigyr away, Josie stayed in one place as he stepped by her, heading south. Josie kept her sapphire colored eyes locked on Ophelia.

"I know you're hoping Folken or Hero will wake up and come to the rescue," Josie said, "But if you raise your voice, the other Josie won't be the only one dead. I'll put arrows in both Harby and Lyan's necks before Folken even stirs. Then I'll shoot you a couple of times, just in case that blinking helps you dodge a shot."

"So you're playing errand girl for Evil Harby?" Ophelia slowly edged her way around the fire pit as she spoke, "I thought the idea was for me to get Meteorend and then bring it to you. That was what the cleric told me. What did he tell you?"

"That you were taking too long," before Josie had even finished her sentence and Ophelia even noticed her move, an arrow pierced the ground just beyond the toe of Ophelia's boot, "The next one goes in Lyan," the ranger warned.

"Okay, okay," Ophelia raised her hands to gesture her surrender, "Why don't you take me instead? You don't need a second Harby. Besides, maybe I could still salvage my deal with Evil Harbenigyr."

"Just because we don't act like the one you know doesn't make us *evil*, you know. I don't want to hurt Harby," Josie snapped, "And, just like the other me, I'm not that gullible, Ophelia. You never intended to fulfill your end of the bargain and still won't even now."

Josie nocked another arrow before pushing Harbenigyr to get him to start walking again. The cleric mouthed the words "it will be okay" before he turned away from the mercenary.

"Don't follow us or I will kill him," Evil Josie motioned to Harbenigyr, "I don't want to but I will. You know I will."

"How long will Lyan stay asleep?" Ophelia asked, although she made no move toward the Bunny Barbarian.

After Josie nodded her consent, Harby answered, "A couple of hours. I couldn't harm any innocent with Kuan Yin's power. You know that."

"Yeah, I know that," Ophelia muttered.

Evil Josie pushed the cleric to walk faster, "By then we'll be long gone and this will all be over."

The mercenary glared at the alphan as she and Harbenigyr made their way to their steeds. Ophelia didn't say anything as they rode away. Vocally anyway.

"They have until Lyan wakes up. Then we're going to kill them all," She thought to Hava– to no one. There was no one there to listen.

OPHELIA INTERROGATION NOTES:

"You're idiots. All of you," I said.

"You're sounding less and less like a Light Bringer every passing minute," the subject responded.

"Who said that I was a Light Bringer?" I asked.

"But, your uniform..." Ophelia pointed at me.

"You put me in it," I responded.

"Me?" the subject asked, "Who are you?"

"Were Bronwyn's friends as forgiving?" I hurriedly changed the subject.

Decades later...

"SHE WAS HERE," Tokki called back to the ship from the small pier Illyria told them about.

"Of course she was here," the green skinned orc loomed behind the much smaller barbarian in black furs, "I rowed her here."

"Fine," the Captain scowled at the Shepherd, who leaned against the railing on the port side of the deck, "You have confirmation. Now get off my ship."

"How can we do that?" Appelonia asked as she walked up behind the woman who commanded the *Spotted Dick*. "Your men tossed the gangplank right after we launched."

"To keep a rioting mob from swarming all of us!" the Captain grumbled back, "You can jump off and swim or... no, that seems to be your only choice. Now leave!"

"Forgive me if I take a moment to see if I can find another option," Jonas pushed himself away from the railing and stepped up to the Captain, "Steel plate is a little heavy to swim in."

"You can always take it off," the stout woman smirked, "That way I can enjoy watching you go while celebrating seeing you leave."

"Need I remind you that time is a factor?" the short barbarian called up to the deck.

"Give us a minute, Tokki," Apple leaned over the railing and called back, "None of us feel up to swimming like you did!"

"I'm not looking forward to smelling him with all that wet fur," Jin Vega shook his head.

"I heard that!" the Bunny Barbarian yelled.

"He is right, you know," the orc standing beside Tokki scowled down at the little man, "You do smell bad."

"A small price for victory," Tokki replied, "No one said you had to stay here," He waved a dismissive claw covered hand at the green skinned man.

A growl started growing in the back of the throat of the orc that was interrupted by the voice of the Captain ringing down, shrill and clear as a bell, "Don't antagonize him, Smeegonizetain ringing down, shi! He's... scrappy."

"Scrappy?" the orc called Smee glared at the Bunny Barbarian.

"Your crewmen thought so," Tokki stood proudly, "Six of them. They tried to keep us away from going below deck to retrieve our genie. They did not get their way."

Smee turned to walk to the hard packed dirt where the pier met just inland of the shore of the river. The skiff that Bronwyn had bartered travel upon was resting to the side of the wood structure. As it was too tall to simply jump down into the boat without causing considerable damage, especially with his heft, Smee took the more time consuming route.

He boarded the small boat and almost immediately started rowing toward the back of the *Spotted Dick*. Smee wasn't going to be any help in getting the party off the ship.

Jin Vega stepped up beside Appelonia at the railing and bumped her bare shoulder with his, "I have the solution."

Appelonia waited, looking at him without saying anything. It became pretty awkward in short order.

"Shall I take that as an order to get to it?" the monk smirked.

"Since when have you taken orders from me?" the cleric grinned at him.

"Since you used the *Mom Voice* to get us to rescue Genevieve," Jin answered with a chuckle. "All mortals fear and respect the *Mom Voice*."

Thinking back to all the times she did as her mother said just because she sounded upset or disappointed, Apple had a pretty good idea of what the bald man meant. And Appelonia didn't know whether to take that as a compliment or an insult.

Before she could ask him which way he intended his comment, Jin already pulled his cloak open with one hand and reached into the starry abyss inside with the other. More and more of arm sank into the darkness, all the way up to his shoulder.

"Would you mind holding this, please?" his voice echoed as he flapped the open side of his cloak with the hand that was holding it.

Appelonia took a hold of the charcoal gray cloth with both hands. As soon as she did so, Jin's arm slipped out of that sleeve and joined his other limb in the enchanted space within his cloak.

He ended up having to reach so far in that Jin had to duck his head in. Finally, a distorted noise that Appelonia could only guess was a satisfied grunt came from the cloak.

Jin emerged, followed by flat board that was as wide as the monk was tall. His cloak shifted around his body to make room for the platform. After about a yard, chains that were attached to the outer edges of the board came into view.

As soon as Jin had enough to stretch the platform over the railing, he hopped on top of it. Motioning for Jonas to come over, the monk slipped the garment off his shoulders and handed it to the paladin. Both he and Appelonia held it on either side.

Jin started walking as if he wanted to reach the cloak. Instead of him moving, though, the board was pulled out further behind him. The chain stretched higher and higher away from the wood, pulling the shoulders of the gray cloth up out of Jonas and Appelonia's reach.

Looking back over his shoulder, Jin nodded to himself, "That should be enough,"

The monk dropped back onto the deck. Crouching, he slipped under the yard of wood that was still over the deck on the ship's side of the railing and pushed up.

It was slow going, but the end of the long ramp that protruded from Jin's enchanted cloak finally touched the pier, only about three paces away from Tokki (and that was only because he had enough sense to scramble out of the way).

"What is that?" Jonas finally asked as the monk stepped out from under the ramp to stand beside him.

"It's the bridge to an old siege tower," the bald man answered nonchalantly.

"What happened to the rest of the tower?" Jonas replied.

"Nothing," Jin shrugged back, "It's still in one piece."

"How could you get a tower as tall as the walls of a castle in there?" the eyebrows of the paladin pressed together as he looked at the ramp, inside the cloak that he now held by the bottom hem, and back.

"It's a long story. To be honest, even I don't know most of it," Jin turned toward Phinegann and Illyria and whistled, "All ashore that's going ashore!"

The orc and gnome both looked confused as they approached the monk's thirty foot long solution to how they were getting off the ship. The bulky man and diminutive woman looked at each other then simultaneously shook their heads at Jin Vega.

"There's no way that's going to work," Illyria protested, "One end can't just hang in the air! The second any of us put any weight on it, we'll be flung off into the water!"

Jin maneuvered himself between the cleric and paladin before he grabbed the bottom of his cloak, "Nonsense! The top part is resting on the railing..." he pulled the gray cloth down until the wood of the siege tower bridge and the rail met with a dull clack, "And the bottom is already resting on the dock. Solid support all around. Show them, Apple."

Appelonia stiffened at the mention of her name. Suddenly everyone was staring at her. She was sure that even Tokki was from the pier below, though she didn't look. Her eyes were locked on the bridge emerging from thin air.

She could feel her eyes twitching as she tried to hide her worry and doubt, "You're sure it will work?" she whispered to the monk as she hesitantly moved toward the rail.

"Positive," he nodded, bunching more of the fabric between his fingers.

"If I don't fall and die," Appelonia muttered at him as she started climbing up onto the slanted surface of the bridge, "remind me to hit you for your *Mom Voice* crack."

"It was supposed to be a compliment," Jin responded.

"I know," Apple said back, "But I really feel like I'll need an excuse to hit you anyway."

With that, both of her boots met the angled surface meant to carry them all off the ship. She let out a little squeak as the bobbing motion of the floating ship was amplified where she stood now.

Licking her desert dry lips, Appelonia turned toward the pier. Holding her arms out to her sides, some of the cool breeze found its way into her tunic through hole where the sleeve on her right side had been. It did help with the sweat forming on her skin. A little.

Once she was halfway down, the bridge felt much steadier. It must have been thanks to the motionless pier taking up most of the load on this side. Still, Appelonia was thankful when her hands found Tokki's and, in turn, her feet were off the siege tower bridge. They were on solid earth seconds later.

"See?" Jin's voice carried on the breeze, "She's just fine!"

Jonas made his way down the ramp a few moments later. His claymore was so bulky that it almost pulled him into the water, eliciting an anxious gasp from the cleric. Finally, he held it out in front of him, one hand on the handle and the other grasping along the top half of the blade. It actually made his balance better and he was on the pier in seconds.

The human looking Genevieve made the walk look easy. In fact, Appelonia wasn't sure that her feet even touched the wood. The cleric had to admit that she was a little disappointed that the efreeti didn't fall in. After all, she did toss Apple into the river.

Phinegann took more convincing. Everyone on the pier could hear Jin trying to talk him down the bridge. It wasn't until the Captain offered to have Smee help him that the retired guard decided to step onto the ramp.

His first steps were heavy with annoyance but that made the boards bounce under him. The orc immediately dropped to his knees and clutched each side of the bridge in his hands.

Come to think of it, Appelonia never even thought to ask if Phinegann could swim. Even if he could before his arm was replaced with one of solid metal, she had no idea how much it weighed. Would he sink like Jonas in his full armor if he tumbled into the water?

It was slower going that the first two, but Phinegann made his way down the siege tower bridge one sliding knee at a time. When he finally reached the pier, he jumped up to his feet and pointed a steel finger at Jin Vega.

"Never again!" he bellowed.

"Agreed!" the monk called back, although he did mutter something afterward. Appelonia couldn't be sure but she thought it was something along the lines of, "You caterwauling, saber-toothed fluff baby."

Illyria skipped the bridge altogether and merely flew down. She was likely going to do that the whole time. She just didn't want to make the orc feel bad.

Appelonia found herself wondering how Jin was going to come down. If he simply walked down the plank, he would be leaving his cloak up with the pirates. Who knows if they could figure out how it worked but, if they did, what other strange things would they find inside?

If he pulled the bridge back, Jin would be left with the option that Tokki took: swimming. That was the more likely option. But would river water rush into his robes? The cleric suddenly found herself very curious but not at the expense of risking the life of the man who just, if in an unorthodox way, helped them to shore.

The monk ended up not choosing neither of those options. He leaped from the side of the ship, clutching his cloak tightly. The bridge upended, becoming almost completely vertical as it sank back inside his cloak.

As the last of the siege tower bridge was swallowed up back into the gray garment, Jin rolled onto the pier. He almost bowled over Illyria and Appelonia but stopped himself by spreading his arms and legs so that he came to a stop on his back right in front of the women.

"See?" he grinned up at them, "No trouble at all."

Tokki stepped up to the space between some brush that could only loosely be called a trail, "She has at least two men with her," he reported.

"Why didn't Bronwyn just get on the *Galleon* with her father and leave us all behind?" Illyria asked, "They had plenty of time."

The Bunny Barbarian waved a thumb at the bushes, "All I know is that she went this way."

"I don't like it," Genevieve chimed in, "It feels like a trap."

"For all Bronwyn knows, you were captured on the *Spotted Dick*. Leaving us dead or marooned somewhere else on the river," Appelonia stepped up to the efreeti woman, "Who could she possibly need to set a trap for?"

"Perhaps she thinks more of your friends than you do, little girl," Genevieve replied.

"We should be ready for trouble, traps or not," Jonas stepped between the two women, "Bronwyn isn't going to be happy to see us, either way."

As soon as Appelonia and the efreeti turned their backs to each other, the paladin let out a quiet sigh of relief before marching for the Bunny Barbarian.

"Lead the way, Tokki," Jonas ordered, "This is still our best lead to finding the child."

After sunset...

ONCE IT WAS too dark to follow the trail left by Bronwyn and the mystery men accompanying her, everyone started to miss the supplies that were carried by the horses they were forced to leave behind in Craigh No Troon.

Still, it wasn't too rough for the party. After digging a hole with her bare hands deep enough that the flames couldn't be seen, Genevieve burned the caked on dirt off her hands and started a fire with ease.

Jin had some food in his cloak, including some eggs. As Illyria and Tokki busied themselves cooking, Appelonia excused herself to find a quiet spot to pray. Judging by Phinegann's reaction to her words, he probably thought she meant to go relieve herself.

Not that she probably wouldn't before returning to the group. But she needed guidance from Kuan Yin. Now more than ever.

Finding a small, isolated area, the cleric lowered herself to her knees and bowed her head.

This was all supposed to be a simple right of passage from neophyte to become a fully testimony-born cleric. Assuming that was what she wanted by the end of her pilgrimage. This was the time she was supposed to figure it out.

Appelonia was still sure it was. Her father made it a point for Josie to teach her daughter about life outside of the Order so that she could make an informed choice.

She had hunted with Mom quite a few times. She had killed some animals for meat. Admittedly, Apple felt a little guilty with the first animal she shot. A black and white rabbit.

But she did learn that it was a natural part of life. Animals hunted others to eat and survive. Mom explained that people should be thankful for the animals they hunted, not think less of them simply because they couldn't talk. That made sense to Apple and she always said a prayer of thanks after a successful hunt. Her conscience was clear because she did not waste what she had been given.

One day, when she was twelve, Appelonia and her mother were attacked by some brigands. Mom, of course, fought fiercely but they were outnumbered five to two.

One of the villains had pinned Mom down, leaving Appelonia alone to fight the others off. The young girl shot two men with her bow before one grabbed her from behind.

Apple used to carry a dagger with her in those days. She pulled it out to stab the man... but she couldn't. It didn't feel like killing for food did.

He laughed at her hesitation. Then he broke her arm, just so she couldn't change her mind about being a coward.

The brigand didn't realize that Apple's mother taught her to fight with both hands. With his back to her, the girl picked her knife back up. She sliced the back of the man's legs, taking his ability to walk.

The rest of the bandits must have been shocked that the girl fought back like that. It gave Mom the opening she needed to take the rest of them down.

But Appelonia watched the man she crippled. With sweat pouring down her brow as she cradled her arm to her chest, the girl who looked very much like her mother, pressed the dagger to this throat.

He didn't resist. In fact, he begged her to let him live. The man who had just broken her arm and laughed.

Appelonia knew that the throat was the easiest place to cut. It was the quickest way to kill an animal to keep it from suffering.

It would only take a little pressure. Her blade was sharp. She could see the fear in his face. It wasn't like an animal's. Animals didn't have regret in their eyes. He did.

She could take him back to Dianmeyer. He could face charges there. People could change, right? Repent of past misdeeds to become better?

He wouldn't have that chance if she just leaned forward a little. The major arteries didn't have a thick hide to protect them.

He had made his choice, right? He was a criminal. The villain tried to take Mom's coin purse.

Mom had killed the others, She didn't hesitate. Everything she did was to protect Appelonia.

But the girl was fine now. It was her decision whether or not to send this man back to whatever god or goddess he worshiped. Or not. He could still face punishment and repent back in town.

He wasn't an animal. Animals were set in their ways. They couldn't change their nature. A person could. Surely, that was the best course of action. Yes, she and Mom would take him back to Dianmeyer to face punishment for his crime.

That was when Mom pulled Appelonia away and stabbed the man in the chest with her short sword. The girl knew that it was to protect her, but for some reason Appelonia had never been so upset with her mother than she was at that moment.

That was when she decided never to kill again. Not even animals. But she knew that she still had to defend herself.

Appelonia begged her father to teach her how to fight with sticks rather than blades, as she had learned from her mother. She didn't speak to Mom for weeks. Not until after her arm had healed.

The anger that Apple had felt toward her mother did not last long after that. The girl would not allow herself to forget the skills Mom had taught her but Appelonia had made a promise to herself.

That was when she designed the blunt heads for the arrows. For them to be effective at all, though, she had to be a better archer than average. So, as she learned the long staff and short sticks for self defense, she also trained to attune her eye for better aim.

She didn't realize it then, but Appelonia had decided to become a cleric of Kuan Yin. One that could hunt like a ranger. What an odd combination.

The cleric's eyes fluttered open. What brought that flush of memory on?

When she actually focused on what was ahead of her, Appelonia saw Bronwyn. She was sitting cross legged in front of the red haired woman, patiently waiting.

"Please don't scream for help," the olive skinned woman said softly, "I'm not here to hurt you or anyone."

"Why did you leave then?" Appelonia shrugged though she found herself speaking quietly, too.

"My father got wind that we were looking for him," Bronwyn held up a folded piece of parchment as she started to explain, "He told me exactly why the efreeti are hunting down the kid."

She held out the missive to the cleric. Appelonia took the parchment and pulled it open. Scanning over the message for a moment, Apple found herself glaring back at the thief.

"It's in some kind of code," the cleric scowled, "You know there's no way I can read this."

"I didn't give it to you to read," Bronwyn responded, "I gave it to show you that it's the same parchment from back in Craigh Na Troon."

Appelonia handed the message back, "Tell me what the efreeti want with the child then. If it's not to simply reunify family."

"It's not," Bronwyn heaved a heavy sigh, "That's why my father and Ophelia have been hiding the kid all this time."

"Your father?" Appelonia's black eyes narrowed, "And Opheila? Don't you think that's a little convenient?"

"I know you have no reason to believe me," Bronwyn said, "Especially after I ran off but I had to hear it from my father's own mouth to be sure."

"You know we're on your trail," Appelonia motioned back in the direction of their camp, "How do I know this isn't some kind of trick? That you're not just running off with stuff you've stolen from us and the crew of the *Spotted Dick*?"

"You can talk to my father and Ophelia yourself in the morning," Bronwyn said, "But you can't bring Genevieve along. If one efreeti knows where the baby is, they will all know where the baby is."

"Because the Mullah will know and commands them all," Appelonia nodded, remembering Jonas' retelling of what happened in Omega Prime, "Okay, Bronwyn, but I'll talk to Ophelia and your father. Give them a chance to explain everything. But I'll need your help if you don't want Genevieve there."

"She's too crafty for me to kill her in her sleep," Bronwyn shook her head, "Besides, I'm not an assassin."

"What?" Appelonia's face curled into a mix of disgust and confusion, "I'm a cleric of Kuan Yin, a healer. I wasn't going to ask anything like that!"

"Oh yeah. Sorry," Bronwyn slumped her shoulders, "I keep forgetting that, with the company you keep."

"None of us are–" the red haired woman started to protest then stopped herself, "What I need from you is to create a second trail that forks off of the one we're following now. We'll split up the group and I'll make sure that Genevieve goes down that new, wrong trail."

"That is actually," Bronwyn pursed her lips appreciatively, "smart."

"I'm so glad you approve," Appelonia said flatly, "I should get back. They'll start worrying if I don't return soon."

Bronwyn nodded and stood up, "Thanks. I appreciate the faith. That's why I came to you."

"Just remember that faith isn't the same as gullibility," the cleric reminded the other woman, "If you try to double cross us (she forced herself not to say *again*), we'll come after you all together and not listen to another word you have to say. Clear?"

"As Dwakar crystal," the other woman said, "See you in the morning."

As Appelonia made her way back to camp she wondered who, if anyone, she should tell about Bronwyn's visit. Jonas would be the one she'd want to tell first but Genevieve was always looming around him since they returned to the mortal plane. The cleric couldn't risk her overhearing.

Illyria might be a good choice. She's open minded. But she's also not one for subterfuge. Would she be able to sell the idea of splitting up without making it obvious that the cleric wanted to get rid of Genevieve?

Jin seemed to be a man who could keep a secret. But, of everyone in the group, he was the one who butted heads with Bronwyn the most. Would he be able to put his personal feelings aside to her, well her father's, side of the story?

Phinegann would likely not care that the efreeti might have an ulterior motive to finding the child. His job was to protect Appelonia, right? Would that make him care? More likely, he would reveal Appelonia's little gambit just so they can all confront Bronwyn once and for all and, if her father does have the child, give it to Genevieve so that they can all just get on with their lives.

That left Tokki. If he was anything like Lyan Yo Bunpy, his honor was as important to him as his life. He wouldn't reveal Appelonia's plan if she made him promise not to do so. But when Apple mentioned Lyan before, he practically took it as an insult. What if he wasn't like how Appelonia remembered the Child of Prophesy? What if his thirst for a fight outweighed getting to the truth?

She would have to think on this. But she only had until they decided to break camp in the morning.

Speaking of camp, it was more lively than Appelonia expected it to be when she returned. When she stepped into the faint firelight, Tokki hopped to his feet and rushed over to her.

"Appelonia, you won't believe it," he grinned wide behind the saber-teeth of his mask. "But Bommer and Andromeda followed us all the way from Craigh Na Troon!"

"What? Bommer's here?" her head whipped around until she saw the familiar blue fur of her horse, "How did that happen?"

She rushed over to her stallion and wrapped her arms around his neck tightly. The horse neighed back, lightly patting his chin against her back.

"Andromeda is trained to find me if we get separated," Jonas said, "I'd like to say that Bommer just tagged along but, from the looks of things, it looks like they worked together to find us."

CHAPTER TWELVE

OPHELIA INTERROGATION NOTES:

"You lead everyone into danger like farm beasts to the slaughterhouse," I said.

"How can you say that?" the subject asked, then continued, "I wasn't even with Appelonia's party at this point."

"But it was because of you that they were there in the first place," I answered.

"You can't put all of this on me!" the subject could not control her outburst.

"I can do just that!" I retorted.

"You weren't there!" the subject yelled.

"I told you that I was." I replied, "That's your problem. You don't listen!"

"What are you talking about?" the subject asked, visibly agitated.

"Look at me, Ophelia," I ordered.

"I did already. You're wearing a Light Bringer uniform but you say that you aren't one of them!" Ophelia was obviously agitated at this point.

"Look at me!" I repeated the order.

It is difficult to describe the look on the subject's face when she finally looked me in the eye. I hadn't seen such a look of shock and shame on her face since back in the time before...

Decades before...

OPHELIA, FOLKEN, AND Hero gave chase to Lyan as she followed the trail of the doppelganger ranger and Harby. Even though the Bunny Barbarian was on foot while everyone else was on horseback, Lyan was fast enough that the horses had to keep to a solid gallop to keep up.

The mercenary had to admit that Evil Josie was clever. Ophelia saw them ride off to the south but then she turned to head north after they were out of view.

"I don't like this," Hero said, shielding her eyes from the morning sun, "Josie and her doppelganger are both rangers. They have training to keep from being tracked. That was what we were counting on our Josie for, wasn't it?"

"What's your point?" Ophelia kept her pale eyes locked on Lyan's back as she made her way through the field of tall grass.

"How is it that we can tell where they're going so easily?" Hero's worry had a genuine point.

But Ophelia's patience was also genuinely strained, "Because Harby isn't doing this willingly. He's subverting every trick Josie knows so we can follow and rescue them."

"Them?" Hero's brow scrunched up.

"Him *and* the real Josie," Ophelia said, "The only reason he's doing this is because they're keeping her alive as bait."

"Bait?" the eyebrows of the bard further sank, "You mean we're heading into a trap."

"It is hardly a trap if the targets are aware of its existence," Folken slipped between the two women as he followed Lyan's movements, "This is more of a negotiation for the release of our compatriots and the return of Meteorend. The chosen currency appears to be blood."

"How poetic," Havarti chimed in from the sorcerer's shoulder.

Ophelia thought the same thing. Realizing that she was still in sync with her sword should have pleased her, but it only made that silent place in her mind all the more foreboding.

They skirted around the eastern edge of Wildevale, avoiding the city altogether. So Josie wasn't going to try and hide among the throngs of people. That meant that the ranger had a particular destination in mind.

"It's a long way back to the lands controlled by the de Junamend, isn't it?" Ophelia nodded to the north.

"It is," Folken said, "They lay a short distance to the east of the Griffin Mountains."

"She couldn't hope to avoid us for that long," Ophelia said.

"It is more likely that she has a more convenient destination in mind," Folken scanned the rolling hills around them, "If we keep going in this direction, we will reach the road to Dracoleaf." he observed.

"So we're going in one really, really big circle," Ophelia huffed.

"Not necessarily," Folken disagreed, "Roads have more than one destination along their lengths. Not to mention the countless forks and intersections. Horta was not alone when we encountered him in Dracoleaf, but his kin did not appear until the day they attempted to retrieve Meteorend."

"So you think that the de Junamend have some kind of a base camp between here and there," Ophelia concluded.

"It's a logical conclusion," he nodded.

"I need a weapon," Ophelia stated the simple fact.

"If you wield Havarti, whatever restrained him before will make him unable to speak again," Folken's voice was a tone of stern warning, "He may not escape its grip a second time."

"I know," Ophelia cursed to herself, "The last thing I want to do is risk him. That's why you have him in the first place."

The svartalfar regarded Ophelia silently. Then his horse snorted, noticing Lyan Yo Bunpy change directions toward the northeast.

"Now we are starting to form a circle..." the bastard sword muttered.

"Don't these people ever need to rest?" the mercenary sighed before returning her attention to the sorcerer. "But I can't go into a fight empty handed. My blinking is purely defensive."

Folken looked thoughtful. "Are you versed in the use of a rapier?"

The woman shrugged, "I used one to cut the snake hair off of a gorgon once."

"I will go with her," Havarti interrupted the man as he started to reach for the thin blade hanging on his hip, "As it is my life that appears to be the issue, it my decision whether it is worth the risk, is it not?"

Ophelia started to argue, "But Havarti, you know I won't be able–"

"Oh, pish posh!" the sword cut off her comment as surely as if his blade could sever a bundle of sticks, "We may not be able to converse but I will be with you, my dear. I will not give up over such a trivial detail as wordplay."

They were all silent after that. Finally, Folken lifted the sword in his scabbard and held Havarti out to Ophelia.

"No, not yet," the woman shook her head, "I want him to be able to speak as long as possible before we drop into a fight."

"Very well," Folken said, then turned and held the sword out to Hero, "Take this so that she may converse with the weapon. I am not one for idle chatter."

The bard took Havarti in unsure hands and the green haired man rode ahead to check in with the Bunny Barbarian. Hero had a look on her face that reminded Ophelia of a clueless carbuncle staring at a collector's net before getting snatched up in it.

"Relax," Ophelia gave her a smile that only partially hid churning of emotions inside her, "You look like you need a drink. I know I need a drink."

"Hey!"

Hero protested as the mercenary pulled the flap of the bard's saddlebag open and reached inside. Ophelia pulled a wine bottle free and pulled the cork.

After taking a long sip, she held the bottle out to the other woman, "Do it," she ordered.

Balancing the sword on her thin thighs, Hero took the offered bottle. She took a small, self-conscious sip of the vinegar.

After seeing the mercenary's displeased face she took another, larger gulp of the spoiled wine. Hero's entire body tensed, her face cringing to the point that she lost sight of everything around her for a long moment.

"I don't want any unpleasant surprises," Ophelia grabbed the bottle back, took another swig, then tucked the cork back into the neck of the bottle, "From either of us."

Hero motioned down to the sword, "I thought you wanted to spend the rest of your time talking to it."

"Him," Ophelia corrected, "Havarti is a *he*."

Hero squinted as she looked up and down the length of the scabbard and hilt, "How can you tell?"

"By asking, child," the sword spoke for himself.

The smaller woman jumped in surprise when Havarti came to life in her hands. Afterward, Hero blushed hard, making her face look sunburned.

"Sorry. I guess I'm not used to, um, things being able to talk," the bard apologized.

"As I am not accustomed to women who can transform into monsters being so..." it took the bastard sword a couple of seconds to find the word he was looking for, "ingenuous."

"I don't know what that means," Hero confessed, her blush spreading to her ears.

"You look innocent," Ophelia translated, "It was how you were able to sucker us all in when we met in the Jaded Woods."

"Oh," A cloud of shame washed over the young woman's entire countenance.

"Hey. Hey!" the mercenary had to resort to punching the other woman in the shoulder to get her attention back, "If you help us get Harby and Josie back, you'll be well on the road to redemption."

"Indeed," Havarti agreed, "One must be judged by their actions when their wills are their own. Yours is so now, child. Make it worthwhile."

The conversation varied greatly from there. As they followed the woman in the pastel blue fur, Ophelia not only spoke to Havarti but listened intently. She wasn't sure she was going to get the chance again. Even if they won the day and his voice returned when Ophelia again relinquished him from her grasp.

That was the part no one else knew. The part that Opheila hadn't told anyone.

Assuming they retrieved Meteorend, they would again head for Riverbelt. Once the rock was given to Tillyria, Ophelia was going to ask the Colonel to lock her up.

The mercenary was too much of a danger to just about everyone now. Especially now that Ophelia was... infected with some kind of monster that could take over her body if she forgot to drink a foul tasting, acidic concoction.

Sure, Hero was a penanggalan, as well. That, of course, worried the mercenary but the bard was in search of a cure for her condition. All she had to do was kill the one that made her. Not easy but it was simple.

Ophelia had already killed the monster that made her into one. Something in the manipulations to her body that Doctor Efreeti made gave the penanggalan some kind of a foothold inside her. Ophelia was the start of her own cursed bloodline. She had no progenitor to kill.

But since Doctor Efreeti's runes were especially made to protect her from harm, killing Ophelia would be difficult. Too much so for the outside world if she went on a rampage.

No, the only way to keep everyone safe was for her to be locked up. Then Ophelia could keep trying to end her own life until the blinking missed its chance to save her or ran out of energy to do it.

Ophelia was pretty sure that not even Havarti realized that this was what had to happen. As night fell and they continued talking, he gave no indication of such.

The party finally reached an outcropping of rocks that amounted to almost a small mountain. Beyond that was a growing stretch of rolling hills. It was too dark to see how far they went.

"That must be where they went," Lyan's voice drifted back to Ophelia, Havarti, and Hero.

The mercenary and bard slipped off their horses to join the barbarian and sorcerer at the edge of a small cliff. Taking a knee, Ophelia positioned herself immediately behind Lyan, her jaw just short of resting on the mocha skinned woman's broad shoulder. She looked down into the shallow gully that Lyan pointed into.

There was a large tent with a fire burning inside if the glow was any indication. It was made of fine cloth, though the different walls and top were slightly different shades of tan.

It was big enough to be able to hold about a dozen people. That told Ophelia that it probably only housed one: the leader of this band that left the de Junamend lands to give chase to Raiko.

A short walk past that was a cave in the rock face. Both entrances faced each other, meaning that Ophelia and the others were behind the fancy, if temporary, shelter.

"You think they're in the tent?" Ophelia whispered.

"In my lands, we would call that a house," Lyan commented, "And the Chief would be the only one to have a home of that size."

"That sounds like a 'yes' to me," Hero whispered from beside Folken.

"Correct me if I'm wrong," Havarti chimed in, "but is that not Harbenigyr emerging from that cave a short way beyond?"

Everyone turned their attention in that direction. Inwardly, Ophelia thanked Havarti for his sharp eyes (wherever they were). Her stomach sank when she remembered that he couldn't hear her thoughts but there wasn't time for thanks vocally.

The thin elf indeed looked exactly like the Cleric of Kuan Yin. He was wearing the same long white tunic that Harbenigyr had on until the party was attacked in Laeradr.

"It's Harby's doppelganger," Ophelia said, "He stole our Harby's tunic so that he could pass for him when he spoke to me in the basement."

"He's stopping," Lyan sounded surprised as she spoke, "He is not going into the tent."

"Can anyone hear what he's calling for?" Ophelia strained to listen but she just couldn't make out the words Evil Harby was spouting toward the tent.

"He is demanding additional guards to watch their new arrival," Folken said, "It would appear that they are within the tunnel, rather than the tent."

"That complicates things," Ophelia muttered, dropping her chin onto Lyan's shoulder, "What are our chances with a frontal assault?"

The Bunny Barbarian chewed on her lower lip for a moment, "Narrow corridors inside the cave would nullify any number advantage they may have. If there are few to no soldiers in the tent, our chances would be fair. If they have troops able to meet us on open ground. Our odds of success dwindle."

"Any brilliance coming from you, Folken?" the mercenary moved her eyes, but not any other part of her body, to look in the direction of the svartalfar sorcerer.

The fingers of Folken's metal hand rhythmically opened and closed again and again before he finally spoke, "Their leader is not in the tent. It has, at most four beings inside."

"And how do you know that?" Ophelia straightened up.

"If they were not short of personnel, Harbenigyr's doppelganger would not be coming to demand additional support himself," the man explained, "Nor would the demand be so slow in being followed. They are arguing over who must leave the warmth of the tent."

"But how, pray tell, do you deduce the total of four soldiers remaining in the tent?" Havarti inquired, wiggling ever so slightly in the hands of the bard.

"There is a great deal of motion. All of it has centered around the brightest area, where the fire itself rests," Folken answered, "But the silhouettes projected against the cloth by the fire inside have not numbered more than four the entire time we have been observing."

"And two are leaving to follow the evil cleric back into the cave," Lyan observed.

"That leaves only two for us to deal with," Ophelia said.

"Or avoid," Havarti voiced the alternative, "If they are indeed more interested in staying warm than patrolling, we could reach the mouth of the tunnel without our presence being discovered."

"That would be our best advantage," Lyan agreed.

"Then, my dear, I suppose that means it is time," the sword directed his words to Ophelia.

The woman stiffened. Without even thinking, her left hand shot out for Havarti's hilt but the mercenary stopped it just short of touching him.

It took Ophelia a few tries to get her mouth wet enough so that words could get out, "You're sure about this, Havarti?"

"I am, Ophelia," the sword replied, "Truly."

Her hand didn't move.

"We will be properly together again, my dear," Havarti assured her.

Ophelia's stomach sank. She knew it wasn't true. But she wanted him back so much...

"Okay, Havarti. We'll talk again at the end of this," she lied.

She took the bastard sword from Hero's grip as if she were cradling a baby. Slipping the scabbard back into the hidden pocket in the back of her coat, everything just felt *right*. Well, not everything.

Ophelia took a moment to enjoy the familiar feel of Havarti's weight on her back before focusing her pale eyes on the others, "Okay, Lyan, you take point. Folken, you and Hero stick close to her and I'll cover the rear."

OPHELIA INTERROGATION NOTES

"That's it," Ophelia reached for her weapon, a bastard sword, only to find him absent, "What?"

"You will not find Havarti here to come to your aid," I informed the subject.

"What did you do?" the subject asked.

"Me? Nothing," I answered, "You don't get what's happening yet, do you?"

"This is some kind of trick," the subject said, "You're some kind of figment made up by Doctor Efreeti."

I shook my head, "Sorry to disappoint. This is all you, Ophelia. That's why I look exactly like you."

"You and I both know that the evil twin thing is impossible," the subject said.

"I'm not a twin, evil or otherwise," I replied.

"What are you then?" the subject asked.

"Everything, all of this, is in your head, Ophelia," I informed her, "I'm your conscience. The you that you could have been if you had taken Tilly up on her offer to join the Light Bringers. We haven't spoken in a while."

"This is crazy," the subject commented.

"Maybe," I agreed for the most part, "but nothing compared to what awaits Appelonia and the others..."

Decades later...

DESPITE HAVING BOMMER back, Apple didn't ride her horse as the party followed Bronwyn's trail. She led her horse along by his bridle, wanting to stay close to him. The woman had already lost him twice, she didn't want there to be a third chance for them to be separated.

Tokki had again taken point but Appelonia was keeping as sharp of an eye on the signs of the woman's passing (another reason for not riding) as the Bunny Barbarian. She couldn't risk letting the split Bronwyn promised to create in the trail slip by unnoticed.

It didn't. The barbarian in the black furs stopped, staying crouched low to the ground. He let out a surprised grunt as he turned back to face Appelonia, Illyria and Jin. Phinegann, Jonas, and Genevieve were just behind them.

Andromeda was just too large to allow the group to stay completely bunched up. At least, that's what the cleric told the paladin. But he did agree.

"Bronwyn's boot prints go off in two directions," Tokki reported.

"How is that possible?" Jin Vega quickly opened and closed his dark cloak several times to force cool air to wash around his body.

The short barbarian shrugged, "One trail goes off that way..." he motioned to the left, "and the other trail goes that way," he pointed ahead, his finger just veering off to the right.

Jonas stepped through some of the brush, a hand resting on the trunk of a nearby tree as he had to muscle one of his metal wrapped legs through the entwined branches of underbrush. He stepped up beside Appelonia, then looked down at the Bunny Barbarian, which is just was the cleric was doing.

"So what do we do now?" Illyria asked, "We already nixed the idea of me flying around because we'd lose the element of surprise. Do we want to re-vote on that?"

"We may have lost that anyway," Jonas said, "This is the kind of thing you do when you think you're being followed."

"But not necessarily," Appelonia pointed out, "One trail could just go off far enough for Bronwyn to take a toilet break. Then she could have returned to the other path."

"What a charming idea," Jin let a disgusted look cross over his face.

"That was just a 'for instance'," the cleric shrugged, "She could have needed privacy to do dozens of other things."

"Without making another trail to get back to the first?" Jonas scratched at his chin thoughtfully, "That means she walked back over her own footprints to obscure the real path from the other, which could lead to some kind of trap."

"It could," Appelonia agreed, "So which is which?"

"Tokki, is there any way to tell which path is older?" the paladin relied on the tracking abilities of the Bunny Barbarian.

Tokki shook his head, the floppy ears slapping his shoulders with faint popping sounds, "They were made within a few minutes of each other. I can't tell which was first."

"Maybe we should split up?" Appelonia suggested.

"Do you think that's wise?" Jona frowned.

"I don't know about 'wise'," the woman responded, "But we have to do something. The longer we stay here, Bronwyn and whoever she is with are potentially getting further and further away."

Jin spoke up again, "That will effectively split our fighting strength in half."

"Not necessarily," Appelonia rested a hand on Elly's shoulder, "I could take Illyria with my group. She can fly back and find you if we come across Bronwyn's camp. Knowing where they are, she could do so without having to worry about being spotted then."

"How would the other group signal if they are the ones to find Bronwyn's camp?" Jin's eyebrows practically had a canyon between them.

"Genevieve," Appelonia turned her black colored eyes to Jonas, "She can move faster than any of us. She could find my group and we can all gather together before actually confronting Bronwyn."

"Good idea," the paladin nodded, "Now the question is who goes with whom?"

"We're already practically separated into groups because of our horses anyway," the cleric said, "Tokki, Illyria, Jin and I can take one way while you, Genevieve and Phin take the other."

The face Jonas told anyone looking that he didn't like that, "I don't know how to track. I don't believe Phinegann or Genevieve does, either."

Appelonia let out a fast, heavy sigh. He was supposed to just agree to everything! Stifling the urge to channel Phinegann and growl, the cleric thought fast.

"Tokki?" she rested a hand on the barbarian's bare shoulder, "Would you mind accompanying Jonas and his group down the left trail?"

With most of his face covered by the rabbit head, it was hard to read Tokki's expressions. Still, the lower part of his face didn't look happy with the idea.

"That would leave you less combat ready than my group," Jonas frowned, "I mean, in this wooded terrain your archery skills aren't going to be at their most effective. And you're a decent fighter up close, but you need someone with cutting and rending capabilities."

Appelonia turned and smirked at Jin, "I think he just insulted us stick fighters."

The monk grunted back.

Some help he was. Apple returned her attention to Jonas.

"Then we'll trade Tokki for Phinegann." Appelonia said.

Again, Jonas shook his head, "I'm already here, it would be easier if we just separated now, as is."

"But Genevieve won't—" the cleric started to protest.

The paladin held up a hand to stop her mid-sentence, "Genevieve will do what I tell her."

After brief moments of reorganization, the party of seven rearranged themselves into two parties of three and four. And Appelonia couldn't think of a single way make it go the way she'd wanted it.

This. This was why she was a cleric. Subterfuge was definitely not a skill she wielded.

Tokki would guide Phinegann and Genevieve (with Andromeda) down Bronwyn's false trail to the left. Appelonia, using the ranger skills her mother taught her, would guide Jonas, Jin (minding Bommer), and Illyria down the true path to Bronwyn. Where Jonas will figure out Appelonia's little deception.

The cleric could only hope that the Shepherd would understand why she did it and let Bronwyn speak her peace, as she requested and Apple agreed. Hopefully, Jonas wouldn't hate her afterwards.

As the groups parted, the cleric gave the Bunny Barbarian an apologetic shrug before the trees blocked their views. Then she started following Bronwyn's trail.

If Apple had to guess, one of the other two men were her father. He would have had to disembark from the *Galleon* like the cleric and her compatriots did. Since he was the Captain of the vessel, perhaps the other man was a guard?

While they were, essentially, following Bronwyn, it was actually the footprints of the other two men that were easier to find. They had not had the same training in being a thief like Bronwyn had, although, she was hardly stealth personified.

Appelonia was impressed that she was able to make the second trail without being so obvious about it. Sure, Apple had let Tokki in on her plan (he reluctantly agreed) but neither he nor the cleric had found any other tracks before they split. He only fibbed about which trail was fresher.

So Appelonia, with Jonas as an unplanned tag along, was surely on the true path. The group of four plus the azure-furred horse weaved between the trees.

She could tell that Bommer was not enjoying the cramped (for a horse) space of the woods. Fortunately for him, they didn't have to stay in them any longer than about forty-five minutes. The time being announced by Illyria as they came to the edge of a clearing.

Fortunately, she didn't just yell it out. Otherwise, Bronwyn and the two men sitting beside their campfire would have noticed Appelonia and her group.

The olive skinned woman was poking at the embers with a stick while a man who at least looked old enough to be her father sat on a rock just to her left. They were talking. Not even Appelonia could hear what they were saying.

"Illyria should fly back and find the others," Jonas said.

Appelonia took a deep breath before responding, "No. I'm going to go talk to her."

"What?" Jonas was incredulous, almost forgetting to keep his voice down.

"She came to me last night, after I was prayed," the cleric motioned to Bronwyn, "She said that the efreeti weren't seeking out the child for any altruistic reason. She asked me to come so that she could explain herself."

"And you believed her?" Jin looked as if he's smelled something unpleasant, "With her track record?"

"I'm fully aware that this could be some kind of trick," Appelonia responded, "But she obviously knew we were coming so why not just set traps, like we were worried about? Why tell us this story about the efreeti?"

"To foster distrust between us," the paladin's face was as hard as the metal of his armor, "You set up the two separate trails just so Genevieve wouldn't be here, didn't you?"

The elf nodded back. "Everything she knows, the Mullah knows, remember? If they are up to no good, we need to know what their plan is in order to stop it."

"I don't like this," Jonas grumbled, "I never would have thought you the deceptive type."

"I'm not very good at it," Apple found herself admitting, "I just want to avoid bloodshed. Maybe we can get to the truth, too."

The paladin fumed silently but he finally nodded, "Fine. You and Jin can go talk to her. She knows you're not alone so she'd be suspicious if you showed up that way. Illyria and I will watch from here. If they attack, I'll come to your aid while Illyria goes and finds the others. Agreed?"

The cleric looked to the monk to see if he had any objections. He gave her a quick nod.

"Agreed," Appelonia nodded and then stood up, "Here we go, I guess."

OPHELIA'S SELF-INTERROGATION:

"Everything is connected, Ophelia," I said, "Everything that is happening to Appelonia and her friends now, along with what happened back twenty-some years ago."

"Fine," the subject now couldn't look away from me as she spoke, "So why have you been such a bitch to me if you are me?"

"Because it's what you think of yourself," I explained, "Remember the cave..."

Decades before...

INSIDE THE CAVE, Harbenigyr held the bag containing the black rock, Meteorend, tightly to his chest. His doppelganger had not returned yet. The brightly lit antechamber was filled with at least twenty guards.

Six were in front of the door that led to the tunnel he and Evil Josie entered through and the remaining surrounded a bed in the corner furthest from the cleric and ranger. It was also the one closest to those doors. There was no way out except through all of them.

Being in such an open space meant that Harby was always in view of each guard. The cleric was sure that it was prescribed by his doppelganger so that the original wouldn't have even a chance to try and pass as his evil copy and attempt escape.

Regardless, Harbenigyr still hadn't seen the true Josie yet. That was the only condition that he had to agree to relinquish Meteorend. They could kill him and take it but, at least at this point, Evil Harbenigyr was at least trying to appear honorable.

To keep them from being able to pull some kind of switch like the cleric's doppelganger wished to avoid, Harby insisted the Josie's duplicate stay with him. Evil Harbenigyr looked amused at the idea.

Both the elf and the alphan sat on opposite sides of a simple bed, the furthest away from the one surrounded by twelve guards. As tightly as Harbenigyr held the bag to his chest, Evil Josie was loose, leaning back until her shoulders touched the cool rock of the wall. One leg was bent, her boot pressed into the thin mattress and the other one stretched out in front of her.

She was tapping the rhythm so some song with which Harbenigyr wasn't familiar, just like the true Josie did when she was simply sitting and waiting. It was odd that even the little habits they had carried over to their doppelgangers but not their fundamental personalities.

"Did you know that this was the first thing I was given when I was born out of the crystal?" Evil Josie pushed a finger into the mattress, "The first thing I remember thinking after laying down was that it would be nice to share it with someone."

Harbenigyr thought about trying to play the strong and silent type. To try and make it seem like he saw and knew more than his adversary thought. But the evil version of him was likely to see right through it, so he figured that the best course of action was to simply be true to himself.

"I must be a bit of a disappointment in that regard," he gave her a self-conscious chuckle.

"Actually, you're not," the ranger's smile looked sweet, "After I met you, you became the prime candidate."

"Me or *me*?" Harby motioned toward the door beyond which his doppelganger was wandering.

The woman's smile flattened slightly, "You do know that, while he looks like you, Harbenigyr isn't you. Right, Harby?"

"My doppelganger is evil," the cleric of Kuan Yin responded, "He's hurt people. Maybe even killed. I couldn't do anything like that!"

"I hope you realize that just because we were all created by the de Junamend doesn't make us all automatically evil," Josie answered.

"Then why are you working with him?" Harby again motioned to the door, "He's the worst nightmare version of myself."

"Maybe," the woman sighed, "But he's enough like you that I can live with it."

"You make it sound like you're in love with me," the elf brushed the idea aside, "As far as I know, we've never even talked before you kidnapped my friend and forced me to steal this," he bounced the leather satchel in his arms.

"I watched you with the other me a lot," Josie's doppelganger said, "I heard the gentleness in your voice when you spoke to her. That little nervous squeak you get when you tried to bring up something personal," she chuckled, "I thought it was cute. So did she."

Harby's black eyebrows pressed together, "What do you mean?"

The woman was quiet for a long time, her teeth clacking together behind her closed lips as she considered how to answer, "The reason I feel like I can talk to you like this is because the other Josie responded to you the way I would have pretty much every time. Every time you spoke to her, it was like you were talking to me, too," she leaned her head in his direction, "So we had very similar reactions to your words. I felt what she felt and vice versa."

"But, you two are so different," he replied.

"Only because our situations are different," the red haired woman responded, "Survival requires an ability to adapt. Being less... frigid made staying with your, what term did you use, doppelganger? I'm a bit looser than the Josie you've been traveling with. That is what has been keeping me on *your doppelganger's* good side."

"That's only one of a myriad of differences I've noticed," Harby said.

"True," Evil Josie fiddled with the bow still in her hands, "I think Laeradr was kind of a fork for us. She and I started becoming more different there."

"How so?" he asked.

She ran her hand up and down the end of the smooth wooden bow several times before she answered, "Did you know that she told Ophelia about how we grew up? About our father?"

The cleric shook his head.

"If it had been me, I would have told you first," she continued, "I'm sure Josie wanted it to be, too. Before."

"Then why didn't she?" Harbenigyr asked.

"Because of what happened when you were burned. She and I had the same feeling when we saw our parents die. I ran to my Harbenigyr. His reaction was... cold. But I didn't have anyone else to go to," the other Josie answered, her face turning more and more dour as she continued, "The other Josie took it upon herself to watch over you. So did Ophelia. It gave them a chance to talk, mostly about you and your kindness. The way she described you was so unlike just about every other elf we have ever met. She thought that telling Ophelia about our father would repair the rifts she'd let fester up to that point."

"That makes sense, I suppose," Harby replied, "But why wouldn't you have done the same?"

"She still trying to protect herself. To keep a buffer between you and her so that if you don't turn out to be the way that Ophelia portrays you, she can cut ties cleanly," Josie's doppelganger said. "That's something I've had to drop around the other you."

"What do you mean?" the cleric leaned forward, resting his elbows on his bent knees.

"He can... sense when I'm holding back on him," her cheek twitched at some flash of memory before she continued, "I betting that you can, too. You just let people protect themselves until they feel comfortable enough to open up to you. He doesn't. Your doppelganger wants honesty around him at all times. Thankfully, when he's calm, he is easy to talk to."

"But he has hurt you for holding back on him before?" was the worry in the cleric's voice for her or himself?

Again, it took some time for Josie's duplicate to answer, "That's... one of the ways he *isn't* like you. It's also why I've stayed so close to him until I traded places with your Josie. That way I couldn't have any new secrets from him.

"I don't want to tell him about our conversations on the way here," her throat moved so heavily as she gulped that it looked like it hurt, "You've made me feel so... at ease. Like I'm not just some *thing* created to some dubious end for some silver haired miscreants. But, he knows everything you know about people's bodies. He *really* knows how to cause pain if I don't... give up these feelings to him."

This time, it was Harbenigyr who had trouble figuring what to say next, "Why are you telling me all this?" it seemed like such a stupid question to ask.

"Because I like the way you make me and *the other me* feel. In her heart of hearts, your Josie and I want the same thing," the woman said.

"And what is that?" Harby couldn't stop the question from rushing out of his mouth.

Before Josie's doppelganger could answer, the doors leading to the tunnel opened and the cleric's doppelganger stepped into the antechamber. Behind him were two guards on either side of the original Josie, each holding one of her arms.

Judging from what the true Harby and the second Josie saw when they rode in, pretty much every guard stationed to his camp was now in the room. The cleric and ranger were outnumbered twenty-four to two.

"It's time to make the exchange, brother," Evil Harbenigyr strode over to the bed where Harby and Josie's doppelganger were sitting.

The cleric of Kuan Yin and the ranger stood up as the other black haired elf closed the distance. Harby kept the leather satchel clutched tightly to his chest.

"My Josie doesn't look free to me, neophyte," Harby replied, his entire demeanor had transformed to the same sternness that Elder Gimli had when he taught the cleric back on the Silver Herald Islands, "You've not held up your end of the agreement yet."

"The armored shirt making you feeling authoritative, is it?" the doppelganger smirked, "You forget that I know how you think. I want to confirm that what you have is the true Meteorend before I let you two lovers off on your merry way."

The true Josie's mouth shot open, surely to correct the elf's assessment of her and the true Harbenigyr's relationship, but shut just as quickly. Instead, her blue eyes turned to lock on the cleric of Kuan Yin. With disapproval was the only way Harby could describe how she looked at him but, apparently, she figured that chastising him was as much of a waste as correcting his duplicate.

"And how do you propose to do this?" Harby didn't loosen his grip on the bag.

Evil Harbenigyr motioned to the bed surrounded by over a dozen guards, "The one who created us is laying just over there. He knows Meteorend. He'll know the real from a fake."

"Fine," the true Harbenigyr nodded, though still didn't relinquish the satchel, "Where are Josie's things? Her bow, arrows, sword, and horse?"

"Am I really this untrusting?" the evil cleric of some demonic force chuckled, "Her weapons and saddlebags are waiting at the mouth of the cave. Triton and her horse are right next to the tent, ready to go."

The true Harby's black eyes flicked back and forth along the room, first to the true Josie, then her duplicate, to the bed surrounded by guards, to the leather bag in his arms, and then finally on his twin. Letting out a breath he didn't realize he'd been holding, the cleric let the satchel slip from his arms until it was hanging by its strap in one hand.

"Then we should complete our business so that Josie and I can be on our way," he held the satchel out to Evil Harbenigyr.

The doppelganger turned his attention to his twin, the bag, Josie's twin, then to the real one before focusing on the bed surrounded by guards, "How about it, Vulcan? Do we continue with the exchange?"

"Yes, yes!" a gruff voice, sounding like it belonged to an old man, came from behind the guards in the sculpted armor that made them all look as if they had the same, average looking face, "Bring Meteorend to me!"

Evil Harbenigyr stepped toward his counterpart and lifted the strap of the bag from the other cleric's grip, "*My* Josie, please aim your bow at your twin. If my copy moves at all, please shoot her in the throat so he can hear her choke to death on her own blood."

The woman beside the real Harby nodded and pulled an arrow from the quiver on her hip. Slipping the projectile onto the string, the alphan pulled back and aimed straight for the woman who looked exactly like her.

"She does have a way with long shafts," the evil cleric smirked as he stepped toward the bed where this Vulcan lay.

The guards at the side of the bed parted to make way for the elf copy. Vulcan was indeed old. His silver hair was twice the length as what Raiko wore and Harby was under the impression that the duelist had never cut it. Ever.

Still, he had an air of regal bearing that even being laid up with, as far as Harby could tell a broken hip, couldn't take from him. He scowled at Evil Harbenigyr as the elf sat the leather bag on the edge of the thin mattress.

"Let's be done with this, cleric," Vulcan's voice was just barely on the civil side of a growl, "I wish to see Raiko's folly corrected."

"Of course," the doppelganger cleric said with as kind of a tone as the true Harby had ever heard.

Evil Harbenigyr untied the flap holding the bag shut and pulled it open to reveal the inside of the satchel. The black rock was the only thing being held in the bag, glinting back the light from the numerous torches hanging off the walls.

The doppelganger reached for Meteorend. Just as his fingers brushed over the smooth surface, jade light suddenly erupted from the stone.

The room was rocked with the explosion of green energy. The light ceased as quickly as it started, leaving everyone lying on the hard ground. With the exception of Josie and her doppelganger. Harbenigyr landed on the second Josie's bed and was already scrambling to his feet. The evil cleric had been launched into the dirt but was still conscious.

Evil Harby blinked hard to try and restore his vision. "What was that?" he asked breathlessly.

"A ward," the true Harby said as he stepped toward his twin, "I blessed Meteorend to be protected from my touch."

Meaning that his doppelganger couldn't touch it, either. Evil Harbenigyr laughed to himself, pulling himself up to a standing position as the real Harby closed the distance between them.

"That sounds like something I would have done," the doppelganger cleric said, "Not me dealing in good faith."

"Well, Josie did say that we weren't polar opposites," Harby slipped his hands under the back of his chainmail shirt.

Pulling the two short sticks that were the repurposed remnants of his quarterstaff, Harbenigyr slammed one into the side of Evil Harbenigyr's neck, then the other upside his head at the temple. The evil doppelganger was knocked out before he dropped back to the ground.

Then Harby rushed over to the original Josie, "Are you okay?"

"I have to admit that I didn't see that coming," the ranger smiled sweetly at the full-blooded elf.

She bent down to steal a short sword off the unconscious bodies of the guard laying at her feet. The rest were scattered all around them.

Harbenigyr turned to look at Josie's twin, "You don't have to stay with him anymore."

"What was that?" the true Josie looked up, not realizing that he wasn't addressing her yet.

The duplicate ranger still had the arrow ready to fire in her hands. Though the shocked look on her face betrayed that she wasn't quite ready to shoot it.

That surprise passed quickly and the doppelganger focused her attention down past the cleric. The bow aimed and fired, aimed well below Harby's waist.

"No!" the cleric yelled.

He thought to move in the path of the arrow but he was nowhere near fast enough. It flew right by the elf with unerring aim. The real Josie had just enough time to gasp as the arrow shot through her hair and impaled a guard who had just found his way up to his hands and knees behind her. He fell back to the floor.

The ranger's doppelganger pulled another arrow from her quiver as she stepped up to the cleric and the woman who looked just like her.

"Are you okay?" she asked the original Josie.

"I-I thought you were aiming at me," Josie said before motioning to the unconscious cleric,"like he told you to."

The second Josie offered a hand to the first and help her back up to her feet, "I know this is hard to believe but I'm not bloodthirsty. I just want to be able to live my life. Just like you."

"What kind of arrangement do you have in mind?" the first Josie wondered, "We aren't going to be able to travel together for long. We would drive each other crazy."

The other ranger nodded and shrugged at the same time. Apparently, she had come to the same conclusion, "We should probably discuss that later, don't you think? We still need to get out of here."

Josie silently agreed this time, turning for the door to the tunnel, "There were two guards on the other side. I'm surprised that the blast didn't make them rush in to investigate."

"I guess it's really good wood?" Harbenigyr chuckled.

"Just be ready for a fight, Harby," Josie rolled her eyes at the cleric, even though there was a smirk pulling at one corner of her mouth, "You, too, er... What should I call you? Calling us both by our name can be confusing at the wrong time and kill us."

"We can go with Swythchild for now," her doppelganger clicked her tongue behind her teeth, "We can argue about everything else later."

Swythchild drew back her bow, ready to shoot at anyone who came though the door when Josie opened it. Josie held up a hand, silently counting down as her other hand wrapped around the handle.

She had just reached 'two' when Harby called out, "Wait! We can't leave Meteorend behind and I can't touch it. Swythchild, could you...?"

Outside…

HERO FELT NAKED with only a knife as a weapon. Lyan Yo Bunpy had a spear that could stab, slash and bend in the oddest ways. Ophelia had a sentient sword. Even if it couldn't talk at the moment, that blade was huge!

Even Lord Folken had an entire arm made of metal with claws. Not to mention that it also had magic stored inside of it somehow. Why did he even carry a rapier at all?

The bard had a knife. She usually used it to cut cheese.

She also felt kind of silly with her lute hanging on her back but she just couldn't bring herself to leave it behind. It wasn't like she was planning on playing a set for Evil Harbenigyr to suddenly make them all friends. Why bring it then? Quite possibly because it was the only friend she really had now.

Not that the musical instrument was intelligent, like Ophelia's sword. But the bard had it since before her days of being a monster. Even before her days of training with the Edge School. It was the only thing she had left from when she was completely human.

The woman thought it odd that there weren't guards just outside or inside the mouth of the cave. There was a table with a couple of stools to one side of the tunnel entrance. It was likely where guards would have been, plus any kind of supplies. Although they didn't leave anything behind, whoever had been here.

Lord Folken and Lyan slipped into the darkness. Following, Hero found herself wondering what was taking Ophelia so long. As the shadows that engulfed them, making Hero wonder what kind of horrors were awaiting them.

The darkness didn't last long. After the first bend in the path, torches lined the walls and made the cave seem not quite as scary. It was almost like standing outside in the sunlight. Flickering sunlight that casts randomly shaped shadows on the walls, giving anyone just enough cover to spy on them or lay in wait to attack.

Maybe the cave was still scary after all.

"Does anyone else think it's weird that we haven't run into any other guards yet?" Hero whispered.

The Bunny Barbarian looked back over her broad shoulder at the bard, "Folken did conjecture that they are short handed."

"Meaning that the vast majority of their force is protecting the most vital area, in turn containing the highest ranking individual, to their efforts here," the sorcerer added.

"So, instead of a bunch of little fights that could kill us, we have one big fight that will almost definitely kill us waiting?" Hero felt her stomach threaten to release the bread and cheese that made up her last meal.

"You can still turn back," Lyan pointed out.

The bard shook her head, "Don't mind me. I'm just rambling because I'm... well, rambling could be considered normal in a situation like this, you know. Right?"

Lord Folken turned and rested his flesh hand on Hero's shoulder, "Try to focus on the goal, not the dangers. Then your fear will not find a threshold upon which to focus."

The petite woman nodded and they continued deeper into the cave. Only a minute or two later, Lyan signaled for them to stop with a closed fist.

"A door. Two guards just ahead," she whispered before looking back in the direction they had come from, "Do you think Ophelia has deserted us?"

"But all of this was her idea!" the bard hissed back.

Before anything else could be said, everything around them shook. Dirt and dust scattered from ceiling immediately after. It was more confusing than damaging, leaving the bard and barbarian to wonder what just happened.

"An explosion," Folken declared, directing his attention to the wooden door.

The guards were already reaching for the handles when a flash of red leaped from a shadow draped crevasse. The arm of the guard reaching for the handle fell to the ground, followed by his head.

The second guard already had his sword drawn and slashed at the red shape that turned out to be Ophelia. As quickly as Hero was able to identify her, she was gone. Her purple silhouette was all that remained.

Again, the mercenary jumped out of the thin space in the rock wall, impaling Havarti through the back of the soldier's bronze armor, his flesh and bone torso, and out the front of the armor pounded into the shape a musclebound chest and stomach (right through the right nipple).

Pushing the still gasping man off the length of her blade, Ophelia turned in the direction of Hero, Lyan, and Lord Folken. They stopped there just so they couldn't be seen so she surely couldn't see them either.

"You can come out now guys," the woman reported, staring at her blood drenched sword with a blank expression on her face, "There's no one else on this side to bug us."

Lord Folken stepped out first, marching straight for the mercenary, "From where did you come?"

"There was a secret passage from the tent that came out here," Ophelia pointed to the thin gap in the rock face that was just barely wide enough for her to squeeze through.

"You went to the tent?" the sorcerer's words didn't sound like a question to Hero.

The woman in the long red coat nodded as she pulled a rag from the belt of one of the dead guards. She started using it for what they surely did, wiping the blood of her weapon. Although it was apparent that it wasn't something she had done often.

"The way out is clear," Ophelia locked gazes with the svartalfar man, "We have multiple escape routes available to us. I'm not seeing the problem here."

"We agreed to avoid the guards in the tent," Lyan said as she stepped up beside Folken.

"No. You agreed to that. I decided I didn't like a potential threat waiting for us on the way out. Especially if we're leaving in a hurry. And we will be unless we kill everyone on the other side," Ophelia jutted a thumb at the double doors behind her.

Hero felt a familiar sensation as she watched the mercenary speak. The monster was influencing the mercenary's mind, trying to make her want to change into the penanggalan.

Folken wrapped his metal hand around her sword wielding arm to stop her from turning away from them, "The lives of your friends are the priority, are they not? Control your blood lust, woman!" Lord Folken commanded.

Ophelia shrugged her arm out of the man's grip, her slate blue eyes glaring at the sorcerer, "Harby and Josie are my priority," Despite the sternness of her face and how she carried herself, the mercenary sounded ashamed that she had to be reminded of that.

"Then we had best get a move on," Lyan stepped to the door opposite Ophelia.

"I doubt our friends are priorities of yours," the mercenary's eyes narrowed as she remained focused on Folken, "You just focus of finding Meteorend."

"On the count of three," the Bunny Barbarian whispered.

"One."

That was as far as the count got before the doors burst open. The wood whipped out, wrenching its hinges, and slammed into the face of Lyan Yo Bunpy. When the door finally came to a stop, the barbarian was wedged between the door and the wood wall that had been built to hold it.

Ophelia avoided most of the door lashing out for her. Although the edge did slap her knee, making her spin around as she tumbled to the dirt.

Josie stumbled out, flashing streaks of molten metal flying through the air and her midsection faster than arrows. As the barrage of orange light ceased, the ranger dropped to her knees.

Ophelia crawled over as fast as she could, the red haired woman's head finding the mercenary's arms before it could fall and hit the ground, "Don't be dead, don't be dead, don't be dead, don't be dead..." Ophelia kept chanting as she cradled the other woman's head to a gentle meeting with the dust strewn floor.

When the mercenary looked to inspect her wounds, she found them all cauterized. Whatever it was that attacked the ranger burned so hot that she didn't even bleed.

Hero took that as a stroke of luck. Whatever weapon had just been used wasn't as effective as the enemy surely thought it would be. The bard was about to say as much when she saw the look of dread on the mercenary's face as she looked over Josie.

Even if she couldn't bleed outwardly, the alphan woman coughed up a stream as she doubled over. Her sapphire colored eyes looked up at the mercenary, unable to completely focus.

"He has Meteorend," she rasped, "Run!"

Even as Ophelia looked up to see who this 'he' was, Harbenigyr jumped through the doorway, just avoiding another barrage of molten metal shooting over their heads. Landing just beside Ophelia and the ranger, the cleric's black eyes opened wide in horror when he saw the red haired woman.

"You need to stop him!" Harby pointed into the room the streaks of light were coming from as he scrambled to his knees beside Josie, "I'll do what I can for her."

An old man with long silver hair was floating in the middle of the room. Guards, who had been laying on the ground, were rising and gathering around the man. Each and every one of them had eyes that looked like burning coals.

"This is like what happened with Raiko." Lord Folken observed, stepping over the threshold where the doors used to be and into the wide antechamber, "I take it you are the man who sent Horta to retrieve Meteorend?" he called to the old man.

"I am," the floating, wrinkled man's voice echoed from his throat, "I am Vulcan, Elder of the de Junamend, keeper of the sacred heart of my forefather. I am the wielder of the flames of virtue. I am the shield of the true people. Perdition's sword, I am–"

"Blah, blah, blah," Ophelia, her entire body flush with rage, scooped her bastard sword from the ground and strode into the room, "He's Raiko's daddy. That's all I need to know to hate him."

"You daren't speak of my son!" the old man seethed, smoke spilling from his mouth, "That failure, that half-wit, that–"

"I get it!" Ophelia held up a hand to stop his ramblings as she turned to address Lord Folken, "He wasn't popular at home, either."

The sorcerer scowled at the woman, "Perhaps we shan't antagonize him while he's holding a relic imbuing him with demonic power?" he suggested.

At the sound of splintering wood, the bard ducked to avoid shards of the door as Lyan freed herself from behind the broken barrier. The barbarian's face went slack when she saw the ranger laying on the ground with the cleric and kneeling over her.

"What happened?" the Bunny Barbarian ground her teeth.

"The old man in there shot her with Meteorend." Hero answered for Harby was far too busy trying to save Josie's life.

"It would be best if you could aid Harbenigyr to get her someplace safe," Lyan said to the bard.

"I tried already," the smaller woman said, "He said she won't survive being moved at all in her current condition."

"Then we must eliminate the threat so the cleric can work without interruption," the barbarian declared, "Choose now, Hero. Join the fight to defend them or flee. I will not think less of you if you run. You are no warrior."

Without waiting for Hero's answer, Lyan turned and found her way into the antechamber. She was already rolling her massive shoulders, loosening up for what seemed to be the inevitable coming fight.

"If it makes you feel any better, she's the one who killed him," Ophelia motioned to the Bunny Barbarian, as Lyan stepped up beside her and the sorcerer.

Lord Folken shook his head as he realized that his words had fallen on deaf ears. He turned his attention to his metal arm and it started twisting into a shape that would have surely shattered a normal limb.

"And what good does it do us to tell him such things?" Lyan whispered to the other woman, mirroring the thoughts of the svartalfar.

"Keeps him focused on us," the mercenary answered, "That will give Harby a chance to do his work rather than be a target."

The old de Junamend bellowed with rage. White light suddenly poured from him, flooding the wide room and blinding everyone inside.

The white light didn't fade as much as everyone's eyes slowly adjusted. At least well enough that Hero, who was standing and shaking behind the Bunny Barbarian and mercenary, could finally see again. Each and every guard that had gathered around the old man looked different. They each had the head of cats.

All of them had sharp, pointed teeth. They also still had their dual-sided battle axes.

The old man didn't look as decrepit as he did just moments ago, either. His chest, which looked as muscular as his son had been in life, glowed with the orange light of... the silhouette of the dark rock was in his chest. Only it was no longer a rock. It beat like a massive, demonic heart, feeding power into the Elder of the de Junamend.

Vulcan's long hair floated behind him, as if being carried on the wind. Two thin horns protruded from his forehead and his skin had taken on the color of a boiled lobster, a shining scarlet.

Wherever they were, it wasn't the cave anymore, although everything that had been inside was there was still around. The torches, without walls to cling on, fell to the floor. Even if the bard couldn't see where it separated from the walls and ceilings, which were equally washed out in white, she and the others were still able to stand so it had to be there.

The beds that were laid out to the left. They made the trip with the group. As did... was that a bow? With a quiver of half spilled arrows laying beside it, unused. The bard recognized it as belonging to the ranger. She must have dropped it when she was attacked.

A familiar stinging sensation started scratching at Hero's neck. She reached up, only for her fingertips to again feel the burn of acid.

"No ... not now!" she muttered as terror completely overwhelmed her.

Then Hero saw a shape dash from between one overthrown bed to another. Another of Vulcan's minions? Soon the bard and her friends would be surrounded. How could this get any worse?

Decades later...

APPELONIA HELD HER hands away from her sides to make it immediately apparent that she wasn't armed. Even though he didn't like it, Jin did the same as he walked beside the young woman.

The two men with Bronwyn immediately jumped to their feet and drew their curved swords. This was going to be the moment that showed if the thief's word was good or if this was indeed a trap.

"Here I am, Bronwyn, just like I promised," the cleric said, still walking forward.

"Dad! Bob!" the olive skinned woman stepped between the two men and Appelonia with Jin, "I asked her to come. Don't attack!"

The older pirate looked at the young woman in black in a befuddled way, "You said they would be coming to kill you, darling," he pointed the tip of his blade at the cleric and monk.

Now able to get a closer look, the man and Bronwyn did have similar tastes in fashion. Both seemed to be big fans of black. Where she wore leather, he wore well crafted cloth with plenty of buckles and gold edging.

When his coat pulled away from his body, Appelonia caught a glimpse of a row of throwing knives tucked into the lining. He also shared a taste in weaponry.

"That was a *tiny bit* of an exaggeration, Dad." Bronwyn confessed.

"Getting tinier as we go along," Jin muttered to the cleric.

Appelonia would have smiled or giggled or something if not for the other man. He still looked intent on attacking the cleric and bald monk.

"Trevir, stand down," the older man waved his sword like a fan at his crewman, "Let's hear what they have to say."

When Trevir sheathed his sword, Appelonia turned to walk toward the fire, "Actually, it's more along the lines of hearing what your daughter has to say. We've been... commissioned to find a child and return it to the family from which it was taken. She says we're being deceived."

"And she'd be right," the old pirate said as he retook his seat beside the flames his daughter had been tending.

Appelonia sat on a rock that just happened to be across the fire pit from Bronwyn. Jin sat cross legged in the dirt between the cleric and the pirate crewman, Trevir. He was staring at them and just waiting for an excuse to jump up and attack again.

"I'm listening, Bronwyn," Appelonia announced once everyone settled in.

"You remember that I told you that my father kicked me off the *Galleon* just before he brought Ophelia aboard?" the woman in black said.

The cleric nodded.

"Well, Dad got wind of what happened in Maid Gulch," she motioned to the old pirate who simply nodded to confirm this detail, "So he sent a note to the *Spotted Dick*. He wanted them to find me and keep me away from Craigh Na Troon."

"Some good that did. You intercepted his letter *in* Craigh Na Troon," Jin spoke up, "That was the first time you tried to ditch us."

The woman nodded, her shoulders slumping in her leather coat, "I was going to find you some information, then ditch for good. I just barely got the message off of that crewman before Phinegann started that brawl in the Flustered Mermaid."

"Is your entire recollection going to be this... understated?" Appelonia interrupted, "It's not helping you seem at all honest about why we're here."

"Okay, fine," Bronwyn huffed, "Before Clemson started that brawl by hitting Phinegann. Better?"

"At least truthful." Jin said.

"The point is, I didn't get a chance to read the message until we were already underway and chasing Dad's ship," The woman continued, "I showed it to Appelonia, so she already knows that Dad sends his correspondences in the code of the businessmen. Otherwise, I'd just let you read it."

"And have to take your word for it that it told the story you said it did," Jin added.

Suddenly, Trevir launched from his perch beside the fire and charged for the edge of the woods. "They've got spies on us!" he called out.

"No, don't!" Bronwyn reached out to try and grab the crewman, "I already know that–!"

She missed. Trevir continued his charge that ended with the sound of metal scraping against metal.

The sword of the pirate flew back halfway between the treeline and the fire pit. It was followed shortly after by Illyria, flapping her wings to hover about shoulder level, and Jonas the Shepard.

The paladin had his massive claymore resting on one shoulder with the handle in one hand. In the other was the unconscious, but still alive, Trevir. He simply dragged him back to his compatriots by his collar.

Dumping him just beside Bronwyn, Jonas let out a heavy sigh as he made his way beside Appelonia, "We really need to get to the 'we're being deceived' part. Because all I'm hearing so far is everything we already know," He glared back and forth from Bronwyn to her father.

"Genevieve isn't here, is she?" the thief asked, "I know I specifically asked you not to let her come."

"She isn't. She's with Tokki and Phinegann following your false trail," Appelonia assured her, "So you know better than we do how long you have before they catch back up to us."

"How can we believe them?" the pirate Captain griped to his daughter, "They already proved themselves to be untrustworthy."

Jonas visibly bristled at that, "*We're* untrustworthy? Your daughter tried to steal from us, run away after agreeing to help us, and sell one of us into slavery! Can you blame us for not wanting to expose ourselves to whatever she may have planned next?"

"Okay. Fine," the old pirate gave his daughter a sideways look that she took as an order to continue her story.

"The letter told me that the efreeti that attacked Dianmeyer wasn't looking for the child, but some kind of rock that would lead them to it," Bronwyn said, "From what intel he's been able to gather, Genevieve was heading for Dianmeyer but changed to follow you. Apparently, one of you took whatever they were looking for from the vault."

"That's ludicrous!" the cleric stamped her foot, "Abernathy died before he could get his hands on anything! I wouldn't take anything out, all those relics are dangerous! Who would be so stupid as to..."

Appelonia stopped. Her black eyes slowly turned to focus on the woman who was literally half her size sitting on the ground just beside her. Elly pulled at her two long purple braids when she realized that everyone had turned all their attention to her, as well.

"It wasn't me!" she said defensively, "I'm only interested in the soul orbs! I only picked one up and put it back down again! I didn't take anything!"

"Which orb did you pick up?" a voice echoed out of the tunnel just a few step away.

"And you were getting all uppity when you learned that we were hiding?" Jonas lifted his weapon away from his shoulder, both hands on the handle and ready to strike at whatever emerged from the cave.

A tall woman in a long red coat stepped out of the shadows. The entire right sleeve was wrapped in armor. In her left arm rested... a baby. The child was only a few of months old at the most but it already had black hair standing straight up as it wiggled against the woman's shoulder.

"Ophelia?" Appelonia didn't, couldn't hide the shock in her voice.

Two braids framing either side of her face. Eyes that were such a pale blue they almost looked gray. Pants that mimicked the style that Appelonia and her mother wore, with the hips cut open.

She looked exactly as the red haired cleric remembered her from when she was seven. Only now, after having not seen her for several years again, did Apple think it strange. In over a decade, Ophelia didn't have any gray in her hair, no wrinkles, nothing that betrayed how much time had past.

Except for her coat. It had been patched and repaired many times but she still refused to get rid of it.

"Miss Ophelia!" Illyria jumped to her feet when she saw the woman, as well, "I wasn't expecting to see you again."

"I figured not," the woman holding the baby smirked, "Which color of soul orb did you pick up, Illyria?"

"Oh, uh," the gnome twisted her long braids around each other as she thought, almost to the point that everyone thought that she might try to strangle herself with them, "Violet, I think."

Ophelia nodded, "And have you seen a black rock just kind of popping up when you least expect it?"

"A... couple of times?" Illyria answered hesitantly, as if she knew she was giving a wrong answer.

"They do have Meteorend. They just didn't realize it," Ophelia turned to the pirates, "We need to get out of here, now. Before it decides to make its presence felt!"

Bronwyn and her father jumped to their feet, the elder pirate slapping Trevir back to life and ordering him to prepare to leave. The crewman ran into the cave while the young woman and pirate Captain huddled around Ophelia. As they were talking, though, the baby started to fuss and the mercenary started to bounce her shoulder up and down to try and quiet the newborn.

"What's so scary about a rock?" a confused Illyria asked Appelonia.

Not having an answer for the question from from the gnome, the cleric rushed over to the pirates and Ophelia. All their arguing overlapped to the point that neither Jin nor Jonas could understand what anyone was saying.

So Jonas slammed his blade into the fire, spreading ash and sparks around the clearing to get everyone's attention, "What are you talking about?" he demanded.

Even the baby was shocked into silence as everyone stared at the paladin. It was Ophelia who finally answered the man.

"Meteorend is the fossilized heart of the efreeti demon that spawned the entire de Junamend race. The efreeti can use it to track down any beings from that lineage. They were able to obtain it for a while several years ago and use it to hunt down and kill every last de Junamend. All but one.

"Juna's mother married into the de Junamend. She wasn't one by birth so Meteorend couldn't track her. She died giving birth because I couldn't get her to Dianmeyer in time," Ophelia looked at Appelonia, her pale eyes full of regret, "This little girl is the last of the de Junamend. If the efreeti get their hands on her..."

"They'll kill her," Jin interjected, "We get the idea."

"Worse," the mercenary cradled the baby in both arms, "The de Junamend share the power of the first demon that spawned them. The fewer of them there are, the more demonic energy the remaining can wield. At least until they come of age."

"What do you mean?" Jonas asked at the same time.

"They can't actually wield the power until they reach adulthood," Ophelia explained, "But then, they can only use it once. After that, their black hair turns silver or gray, like charcoal becoming ash. From then on, they are only conduits to pass the power onto the next generation."

The baby started to fuss again, trying to wiggle out of Ophelia's grip. Appelonia stepped up beside the woman, pulling a soft rag from one of her pouches and draping it over her chainmail covered shoulder. Lifting little Juna from the deteriorating grip of the mercenary, the cleric rested the infant on her shoulder.

"What does that have to do with this little girl?" she asked when little Juna was finally quiet. In pretty short order.

Ophelia just stared at Appelonia for a moment, as if she were trying to figure out what she just did to the child to make her calm so quickly, "She is, literally, the last de Junamend. She has the full power of an efreeti demon in a mortal shell. Unspent demonic power."

The mercenary reached over to the little girl and ran her fingers through the standing tuft of black hair as if to illustrate her point. Jin stepped up beside the cleric, his eyes falling onto the baby.

"So?" he said, "The baby has a much power as an efreeti demon. They're legion back in Nova Prime."

"Exactly!" Ophelia responded, "But they are all from Nova Prime. They can make their way to our dimension in small numbers but, what if they had something with their power to gain a foothold here? They can make this little girl open a portal to allow every demon to come to this plane and destroy everything. Conquer everyone!"

"But they would have to wait until she matured, right?" Appelonia's face was a mask of worry, "You said the de Junamend couldn't use their power as children."

Ophelia answered, albeit reluctantly, "*They* can tap into her power now, create a portal for their leader to come through, then he could bring the rest across."

Jin looked from from making a cross-eyed face with his tongue hanging out at little Juna, "What would happen to her?" he lifted her little hand that was wrapped around his finger.

Ophelia was even less eager to answer now, "She would burn."

"We *do* need to go then," Appelonia turned to Jonas, "You need to get Genevieve as far from us as possible. Whatever way you go, we'll head the opposite."

"What about me?" Illyria tugged on the leg of the cleric's pants.

"Go back to Dianmeyer," Appelonia reflexively stepped away from the little woman, "Get in the vault, study the soul orbs all you want. When Meteorend appears, lock it up!"

"Wouldn't the efreeti just start sending demons to your castle again?" Jonas frowned.

"It may be too late for that," Jin spoke up before the cleric could answer.

He pointed at the fire pit. Just beside the smoldering pile of ash was a smooth rock that had a sheen like black glass. Except for the orange glow throbbing in the middle. It became brighter and brighter with each beat until, finally, Genevieve burst from the trees and into the clearing.

She had fully shed her human guise, landing on her hands and feet, the dirt smoldered as her curved claws dug into the ground, "Where is the child?!" she bellowed.

CHAPTER THIRTEEN

"All of this over a rock," Ophelia shook her head.

"It's not your typical rock," I said, "It's part of something bigger. Something sinister."

"You mean something that's a part of me," Ophelia replied.

I did not argue.

Decades before...

THE TWENTY-FOUR SOLDIERS that surrounded Vulcan were now something... more. Their helmets had been replaced by the genuine head of big cats. Ophelia recognized several as rumble tigers. A couple more as lions with manes of different thicknesses. There may have even been a stray panther or two.

Vulcan himself looked even more like Raiko than he did before. That in and of itself just made Ophelia more angry. He had that same condescending grin his son did. The mercenary wanted to slice it off.

But first, she and Lyan would have to get through the cat men. So many jokes started going through her head as she took a step forward… only to double over in pain. Ophelia's stomach felt as if it was literally ripping itself to pieces!

She had only felt this kind of pain once before and Ophelia's face went white when she remembered where. That basement. It was the unnatural hunger she felt after Miranda cursed her with that sacrifice wafer.

But why was it happening? She had been drinking that awful vinegar… but then she blinked. Blinking made her sober when she was drunk. It must have undone whatever effect the spoiled wine had built up to keep her from becoming a penanggalan.

Hero rushed to the mercenary's side. Lyan turned, her confusion obvious as she saw Ophelia already on her knees.

"You're starting to change, aren't you?" Hero's fingers traced along the side of Ophelia's throat, "You feel the monster starting to come loose."

"Now?" the Bunny Barbarian looked conflicted, "Can you make it wait somehow?"

"Fascinating," Folken was the first to directly address Vulcan in these new surroundings, "Is this a pocket dimension of your own creation or is it somehow linked to the energy signature of the efreeti demon blood in your veins?"

The svartalfar wizard strode away from the women, pulling the rejuvenated, silver haired man's attention toward him rather than the three women. Ophelia was finally thankful that he was as perceptive as he was.

"I have a little more wine here," Hero pulled a small leather bladder from the pocket of her green coat.

Ophela waved it away, "It took almost two bottles to make me feel under control before. Besides, it looks like you need a little nip, yourself."

Hero self-consciously raised a hand to her own throat, just short of touching the acidic blister forming on the scar that ran around her neck.

"Lyan," Ophelia forced herself to stand as she addressed the barbarian, "I'm going to change, there's no stopping it at this point."

"What can I do?" the barbarian shrugged, her spear wobbling in her hands, "I cannot kill you and fight two dozen soldiers at the same time."

"You won't have to," Ophelia cringed as another surge of pain washed through her, "Clear a path for me to Vulcan. I'll take everything I have left to him. When I become the monster, hopefully I'll kill him just before he kills me. That way, I won't be your problem anymore."

"I can fight Vulcan as the monster," Hero volunteered, again offering the bladder to the mercenary.

"Drink that. Now," Ophelia stared down the bard.

"To clear a path for you, I will leave Harbenigyr and Josie open for attack," Lyan protested.

"I'll hold them off as best I can," Hero said, just after downing the entire contents of the bladder at the sight of Ophelia's displeased glare.

"You are still no warrior, bard," Lyan responded, "You will be lucky to stop one when they come."

"Leave that to me," a voice from behind the women said.

The barbarian and Ophelia turned with battle-honed reflexes to spot the source of the voice. Hero was just a bit slower but still in time to see Josie step out from behind the tipped beds with a sword like those carried by the guards in one hand. She bent down to pick up the bow, slinging it over her shoulder, and the spilled quiver of arrows off the white ground as she closed the distance.

"I'll watch your backs. protect Harby and," she hesitated for the briefest moment, "his patient, from any of your overflow. Sound like a plan?"

"I do not understand," Lyan said, "If you are Josie's twin, why help us? Unless you are the true Josie, then why is Harbenigyr aiding the enemy?"

"We'll talk later," the ranger set the quiver of arrows at her feet and pulled the bow taut, the sword hanging from her hand holding the bowstring, "Didn't Ophelia say that she wouldn't last much longer?"

"She right, Lyan," Ophelia cradled her stomach against another rush of pain, "Go. Now!"

The Bunny Barbarian aimed the tip of her rabbit shaped blade directly for the silver haired man whose sole focus was on the svartalfar magician. The cat-guards clogged the ground immediately under him, protecting him from weapons even with the reach of Lyan's tall spear.

That would not be the case for long.

Lunging at the feline soldiers, Lyan launched the spear at her target. As it sailed through the air, the barbarian lowered her blackened shoulder and barreled for the cat men.

The woman's charge was so fast that her spear and she hit the crowd almost at the same time. Cat-guards roared as they were bowled over, one mewling in pain as the barbarian broke his jaw and threw him to the floor. Many axes toppled to the floor, the unexpected barrage disarming many of the beasts.

Vulcan swatted the spear out of the air, the unusual bending of the shaft of the weapon making it spin in place more than fling away until it landed less than a step from the Bunny Barbarian.

Lyan snatched the weapon up before it could topple flat to the ground and started bludgeoning her enemies. Arrows whipped past the muscular woman, striking ax wielding cat men in their slit eyes.

Vulcan turned in the direction of this challenge, forgetting Folken as Ophelia used a crouching Lyan as a springboard to leap at the rejuvenated man. The mercenary loosed an inhuman roar as their bodies collided.

"Do you want to know how your son died?" Ophelia growled her face cheek to cheek with Vulcan, "He took Lyan's spear right... about... here!"

She buried Havarti's blade into his gut all the way to the hilt.

The man's eyes opened wide in surprise but, once that moment passed, he wrapped a hand around Ophelia's face and shoved her away. She dropped onto the dead bodies of two cat-guards, face down.

Vulcan then turned his attention to the bastard sword in his stomach, "I cannot be killed any longer, child. I possess the strength of my father's father. The de Junamend line cannot be severed by a mere whore like you."

Ophelia did little more than twitch as yellow puss poured from her mouth and coated the bodies that broke her fall. Josie ran through her meager supply of arrows and Lyan was taking hit after hit from fist and claw. She was getting overwhelmed.

Throwing down the now useless bow, the ranger ran for the barbarian. As she started to raise her stolen sword, Folken raised a hand in her path to stop her.

"I think you have missed one quite important detail in your bloviating, Vulcan." the sorcerer said. "I do not believe that your father's father would approve of what you just let happen."

Vulcan rolled his eyes. It was a few moments later that he noticed that something felt... off. Looking down, the silver haired man saw his chest and only his chest. The beating, enchanted rock was no longer within him.

"I believe the *whore*, as you eloquently put it, took her thirty silver from the nightstand for services rendered," Folken's violet lips stretched into a half-smirk.

"The penanggalan..." Ophelia hugged herself as she slowly rolled to her side. There was no wound visible on her her neck or anywhere on her body, "The penanggalan... the monster... the parasite... is... is BURNING!"

The woman shrugged out of her red coat, tossing it away as she whimpered in pain. Lifting herself to her knees, the bones of the dead guards under her crunched as she pulled her shirt over her head and threw it away. Meteorend was beating in her chest, the view unobstructed.

"Too hot!" the mercenary yelled, "I– I can't!"

With her back to Folken and Josie, they were able to see that Ophelia's tattoos were glowing brighter than either had seen before. Hero let out a gasp as she noticed that Ophelia's skin seemed to *crack*, with more violet light pouring from the wound instead of blood.

Vulcan laughed as the mercenary desperately removed her boots, then unbuckled the belt of her pants, "Once the show of this peasant's punishment is concluded, I will move on to you, Folken." he promised.

"That's not a wound," Folken said just loud enough for Josie and Hero to hear, but not the old man, "Look closer. More light is piercing through her skin. In patterns. They are tattooed runes that must lay hidden until they are given the energy to reveal themselves."

"Then Ophelia isn't dying?" Hero looked at the sorcerer hopefully.

"No," he answered, "But *we* may not survive this, after all."

Decades later...

GENEVIEVE BELLOWED SMOKE as she paced the clearing. She walked like an animal, on her hands and feet, grunting and growling as her amber eyes shot to look one way and then the other.

"Get her out of sight," Jonas whispered.

He slowly pushed Appelonia, who was holding little Juna, behind Ophelia and Bronwyn. He didn't want to draw the efreeti's attention. Not yet, anyway.

His looked down at the glowing rock called Meteorend. It was glowing like it sitting in the fire of a blacksmith's forge now. The light was steady now, not fading in and out like before Genevieve's arrival. So it was some kind of tracking device, after all. Bronwyn was honest about that.

The paladin stepped away from the group that was a serving as a makeshift hiding spot for the baby. He stepped toward stomping demon cautiously, with his blade pointed down toward the dirt.

"What is the meaning of this, Genevieve?" his voice was firm with the demon bonded to him, "You're supposed to be with Tokki and Phinegann. Where did you leave them?"

The efreeti woman's face snapped in the direction of Jonas. She crawled over to him, the look of rage only softening slightly as she neared the human.

"Master," her voice rumbled, "You have the baby."

The man bent down so that his face was level with Genevieve's, "Where are Tokki and Phinegann?" he repeated.

The efreeti made a dismissive noise before turning away from Jonas, away from all the humans. Shaking her head, she spat to the side, the ground steaming where the spittle hit. Then she turned back to face the paladin.

"They are at the edge of the river, Master," Her long tongue ran over her sharpened teeth, "I get the baby now?"

"Why do the efreeti want the baby, Genevieve?" Jonas straightened up to his full height, forcing himself to keep his breathing steady, "Was it to reclaim family who was taken from you? I wish to know the truth."

The demon huffed smoke and again paced away from the paladin. She was struggling with two instincts, the one to find the child, fulfilling the desire of her Mullah, and the instinct to fulfill the wish of the man to whom she had been bonded to assure loyalty. It had been done for the benefit demons, true, but true loyalty cut both ways.

"You haven't denied me a wish yet, Genevieve." the Shepherd pressed the efreeti, "Why do you hesitate now?"

"The child is here!" Genevieve slammed a clawed fist into the dirt, "I am to find it for Mullah Junaperqolanijuna alab Marid Juna alnnihaya, the greatest of all. He seeks new lands to conquer and desires these to rend in his glory."

"How does the child accomplish this?" Jonas demanded, "I still wish for the truth!"

Genevieve rushed straight at the man, stopping when her face was just inches from his and roared loudly. Spittle flying from the woman's mouth left little burns the cheeks of the paladin but he stood his ground.

"Fulfill my wish," he ordered once she stopped to breathe.

Genevieve muttered what must have been a curse in her native tongue, "You wish for information only the Mullah has! I cannot cast him here to answer, his countenance is too great for my strength to bring."

"Okay then, Genevieve," Jonas said, "Answer this for me, then. Why do you want to help him?"

The efreeti woman dropped to sit beside the smoldering fire pit, "We are all part of Junaperqolanijuna alab Marid Juna alnnihaya but can never be complete in him again. It is a pain you cannot understand, being permanently... fractured like this. He seeks to spread pain in the meticulous ways eons of torture and ingenuity have taught him to give. To give you at least the barest taste of what he feels."

"Do you support this plan of his?" the paladin tightened his grip on his blade.

"Do you ask your knee if it supports your choice to accompany buxom elves?" the demon loosed a sad chuckle.

Jonas took a long moment before he spoke again, "You aren't just a part of the Mullah anymore, Genevieve. You are a part of me now, remember? That means you have a choice."

"You are merely a blink in the eye of eternity, Master," Genevieve responded, "The Mullah is forever."

"Maybe," the man shrugged, "But he's not here right now. You don't have to kill a child just so he can have a new hobby."

"The babe *is* here," Genevieve glanced up at him as she picked up Meteorend from the ground. "I had begun to hope that this was not with you. That we could have just kept wandering aimlessly, like you wished to do with Appelonia."

"We didn't actually know it was here until just before you arrived," Jonas chuckled sardonically, chancing sitting beside the efreeti woman on the ground, "It seems to have a habit of appearing and disappearing."

"It is the heart of the one who bred the de Junamend. It can find his children but will not do so willingly. It is... resistant," the demon inspected the rock as she replied.

"You mean it wants to protect the de Junamend from the efreeti?" the man asked.

"As any parent want to protect their child," she nodded, "But he is still part of the Mullah and the Mullah does not tolerate impurities for long."

"I was going to say that the de Junamend have been around for over a century," Jonas shook his head, "But that isn't long for an efreeti, is it?"

"No," Genevieve ran a hand along her horn that had only become more deformed since meeting the paladin and his group.

The brush along the tree line started to rustle, pulling the attention of the paladin away from the efreeti woman. After a few seconds, Andromeda, Jona's horse burst into the clearing. She galloped straight to the man, coming to a stop right beside him with a loud snort.

"What a pleasant surprise," he reached up to pet the nose of his horse before he turned his attention back to Genevieve, "You think that Phinegann and Tokki are right behind–?"

The all too familiar battle cry of the Yo Bunpy barbarian rang in the air as the warrior in black fur rushed out of the trees, "Get away from her, Jonas! She has gone rabid!"

To the surprise of the paladin, Tokki didn't charge straight at her but lifted his bow. Up until this point, it had remained tied to his pack that rested on Andromeda's back.

He launched an arrow at the demon and Jonas as shocked that the Bunny Barbarian was so accurate with a weapon he used so rarely. The barbed shaft flew through the air, the powder blue tuft of fur on the back making it easy to follow.

Genevieve grabbed it before it the bladed tip could touch her face. A rush of electrical energy tensed one shoulder, made a shiver run down her spine and, finally, make her empty hand clench so tightly that her claws drew blood from her palm.

Jonas launched himself to his feet, "Stand down!" he ordered.

Tokki had already loaded another arrow into his bow. A quiver full of arrows, with different pastel shaded colors of fur on the butt of each arrow shaft, rested on his back. But he didn't fire.

His face snapped from the direction of Genevieve and over to the paladin. He took some time to take in the scene. Then he shook his head in disbelief.

"Phinegann and I were almost killed," he said, "We were following the trail when she suddenly turned into her demon shape. She slashed at us with her claws and then she leaped away."

"How were you able to find us?" Jonas stepped over to the Bunny Barbarian, "Andromeda wouldn't have been able to track me down this fast."

"Because of this," Phinegann spoke as he stepped out of the trees, pulling Bommer along.

He must have found where the paladin tied him up beyond the treeline. But it wasn't to the horse that he was referring. It was what was in his other, metal hand.

It was the piece of Abernathy's antler-like horn that the orc gave the paladin as a trophy after he slayed the efreeti at Dianmeyer. He held the base of the yellow mass of twisted bone in his palm but the tip was pointing at the rock that Genevieve dropped on the ground beside her hip.

"Even dead pieces of you are attracted to that rock?" Jonas turned to look at the efreeti woman.

Genevieve stood up, finally able to toss the arrow away but again picking up Meteorend, "We are all a piece of the Mullah. We want to be one again, even though we know we cannot."

Even though she wasn't capable of becoming pale in her demonic shape, the burgundy color of the woman's face faded to a just too dark to be pink hue, "He is coming."

"What? Who?" the Shepherd vocalized the question but all three men started looking around for some new arrival, "The Mullah can't come without sacrificing the baby, right?"

"Not the Mullah," Genevieve started toward the mouth of the cave, "He knows I decided not to take the child! The Wisest Mullah is sending Alnnadhir Nikojunakalium abn Maridjuna!"

"You mean that monster that translated for him in the palace?" Jonas tightened his grip on the handle of his sword, "I thought you couldn't sense their thoughts."

"No, but I can sense his presence drawing near!" Genevieve looked on the verge of panic, her limbs practically flailing as she rushed for the cave.

"Okay, Phinegann, Tokki, maybe we should take cover in the cave," Jonas started toward the mouth of the tunnel even as he continued scanning all around for any sign of the massive beast that had suddenly hammered so much fear into the efreeti woman.

He couldn't see anyone. Or anything.

Tokki and the orc, pulling the blue horse along, hurried past the paladin, who grabbed Andromeda's reins and was right behind them. Even though it was only nearing midday, Jonas had the impression that it was starting to get darker. He couldn't explain how, though. The sun was still visible in the sky and there weren't any clouds of any real consequence in the sky.

As Genevieve reached the cave entrance, she had to jump aside as Bronwyn and her father sprinted out. Ophelia and Appelonia, cradling the baby to her chest, were right behind them.

"Run!" the woman in the long red coat bellowed, "We can't let that thing get Juna!"

"What thing?" Jonas turned to look into the cave.

And his stomach dropped.

A massive six-fingered hand wrapped around the edge of the rockface that fed into the cave, followed by another on the opposite side. With an echoing grunt, the creature known as Nikojunakalium pulled himself out of the tunnel and into the fading daylight.

His massive, cat-like maw chopped down on the remains of the pirate that had served as Bronwyn's guard, Trevir. As the legs of the man slid down the monstrous efreeti's throat, his faceted sapphire eyes flickered as the rotated around until they settled upon

Genevieve. The only way the paladin was able to tell was because the demon spoke to her directly.

"I am so disappointed in you, Genevieve aibna Shaitajuna," his growling voice rumbled through the clearing, "Your sentence was intended to teach you that the fleeting nature of these things was precisely *why* it was our holiest Mullah's right to come and annihilate them."

Nikojunakalium freed himself of the rock face. Taking a moment to straighten up, to almost three times Phinegann's height. Then he stretched and rolled his gigantic shoulders.

"As it is," he sighed, "The responsibility of fulfilling our great Mullah Junaperqolanijuna alab Marid Juna alnnihaya's truly appropriate wish falls upon me."

Dozens of men with feline heads like the one who sicced the marilith on Appelonia and her party in Nova Omega started spilling out of the cave. Immediately, Phinegann, Tokki and Ophelia were swarmed. Jonas and Genevieve slashed at any of the beasts that got too close. He couldn't see what became of Andromeda or Bommer.

"And you know how seriously we efreeti take our wishes," Nikojunakalium grinned, licking his razor sharp teeth.

Decades before...

FOLKEN WAS, OF course, right. More and more purple light poured from Ophelia's skin, each revealing a new pattern and rune that imbued some new ability on the woman. Ophelia screamed, flames spewing from her mouth, as splitting pain poured through her.

Ophelia desperately pulled at her auburn hair, "No, no, NO! Get out, Doctor! Get out of my head!" she shrieked as she again rolled onto her hands and knees.

This time, Vulcan took in an unobstructed view of Ophelia's naked back. He could clearly see the same runes that had been on the back of the doppelganger that had injured him so grievously. He also remembered who wrote those runes into the woman's skin.

"No! Doctor! I did not realize she was yours!" He yelled into the empty air around him, his arrogance instantly dropping to begging, "I never sought to undo your work! My only wish is to protect my people! We are nothing compared to you! Nothing! Please, oh please be merciful, fire-god! We will leave your sight, never to return, I swear!"

Violet lightning erupted from Ophelia's back. Whatever unseen wall or ceiling there was in that whiteness was ripped red where the bolts struck to immediately melt the rock that had been hidden. Instead of dissipating, though, the purple lightning stayed in place until the woman looked as if she had wings made of the celestial violence.

Ophelia straightened up. The pain, it seemed, had passed. She looked around, as if she'd never been able to see before. When her eyes turned toward Folken, he could see that her eyes were literally made of ice. The crystals moved about in her sockets and she didn't appear to recognize him. She didn't even acknowledge the women beside the sorcerer.

"You are clean again. Pure," a voice that felt like an orchestra playing a melodic symphony crossed the ears of every living being in Vulcan's little pocket universe, and licks of flame spilled from her mouth with every word, "You tried to keep this one from fulfilling her purpose."

Ophelia (?) did not look up at the silver haired man until after she had made her declaration. Even though her expression was perfectly blank, the runes tattooed all along her face surged with violet energy.

"No! Please! I repent! I see the error of my ways! Please allow me to serve you!" he dropped back to the ground, immediately sinking to his knees in front of the woman who appeared to no longer be human.

"Even now, you would seek to conjure some schema to manipulate my prize to somehow fulfill your piddling goals," Ophelia's body said, though to Folken they did not feel to be her words any longer, "You still see yourself a ruler, though you have been bested by just the presence of your betters."

With Meteorend out of his grasp, Vulcan's rejuvenated form could not be maintained. He aged before the cold eyes of the being that was no longer Ophelia as she paced around the cowering man. The lightning scraping the edges of this reality followed with her, digging liquid gold from the super-heated rock face.

The metal flew to the woman who had been Ophelia as if her body were a magnet, swirling around her head until she raised her right hand. The gold flew to her fingertips, a shapeless glob of metal.

"A true monarch shares the pain of those he rules," she who had been Ophelia spoke, "Shall this one demonstrate?"

The molten gold pulled to her fingertips. Wicked looking barbs rose up about a foot before the base slid together into a circle that matched the size of her outstretched hand. It looked like a crown but she surely didn't handle it as such.

As she lowered the tip of her newly artifact to Vulcan's chest, the woman froze. The glowing tattoos from the crown of her head to the heel of her feet stopped pulsing with light. Even the remaining, unneeded gold that orbited her stopped in place.

The old man looked around uneasily, making sure to move only his eyes. If he moved his head, Vulcan may draw the no longer Ophelia's attention again and pull her from whatever trance she was suddenly imprisoned within.

"You are right," the symphony again spilled from the woman's mouth, addressing no one, "These fodder beasts have not earned the honor to be here for such a coronation."

Ophelia's body did not move but the violet glow resumed throbbing within her. The bolts of lightning pulled away from the gaps they made in the white edges of Vulcan's dimensional space. Then they lunged into the bodies of the cat-guards that swarmed all over Lyan.

Each was burned to ash in seconds around the barbarian. Lyan was suddenly coated in the powdered remains of those who were formerly ripping her skin to shreds. The two men impaled on the spear of the Bunny Barbarian evaporated into nothingness. They were also what was keeping Lyan on her feet. When they were gone, she fell to the floor, unable to support her own weight.

Once every body that had been guarding Vulcan was little more than flakes of carbon floating in the air, Ophelia's body... twitched. The golden crown launched from her fingers like a spear and plunged into the old man's chest. He took one last shuddering breath as the five barbs started spinning, drilling into his heart.

"Now you truly know the pain of your subjects," she who had been Ophelia declared, "Or, at least, the pain they will all feel soon. You are merely ahead of the curve."

Vulcan's body straightened and the five barbs of the no longer Ophelia's crown erupted up from his weathered skin all around his neck. Then continued up. One barb impaled his chin while the rest sliced into the sides of his head as they rose. Long strands of silver hair fell around the man's knees and onto the floor, followed by streams of blood.

The crown came to its final resting place wrapped around the top of Vulcan's head. Blood poured from where the front most barb protruded from his forehead. Folken half expected his face to fall from his severely damaged skull.

Air rattled out of Vulcan's chest with no force behind it. He had finally given up any visage of hope and died, his hands falling from the long handle of Havarti, the bastard sword still impaled through his abdomen.

"The king is dead," she who had been Ophelia laughed, the sound like reverberating bells, "Long live the king."

Ophelia's body had just started to turn to face Folken and the others when she froze again. She didn't struggle to move or anything. The naked woman just stood in place like a statue. It would have been a commission, an entrancing piece of art that Folken would be proud to own.

Then she spoke, again addressing no one, "Indeed. He is no longer using it."

The gold melted around the head of the old man and sank back into his body. Vulcan's torso distorted, the skin stretching one place and then another. Muffled ripping sounds could be heard inside the meat that made up Vulcan's body. Then the areas immediately around the blade of the bastard sword burned to ash.

He was being dissected. Each part was methodically cut away and burned to free Havarti from the cooling flesh of the dead man.

When his body fell back to the ground, the gold had reshaped itself around the sword, protecting it. A wiry metal cage wrapped around Havarti, no part actually touching the blade as it was somehow held suspended in the middle of the exquisitely shaped shell.

Three legs formed on the sword's tip end of the gilded cage. The floating shell rotated until the legs touched the floor and Havarti stood hilt side up inside his new cell.

Ophelia's body simply stared at the sword. While she again didn't move, the light from the runes covering her entire body were again throbbing, unlike the previous times when she froze.

This was the first time Folken was able to get an unobstructed view of her back since the woman's transformation had completed. There actually was one spot on her back, beside the crown that marked the apex of her normal tattooed runes, that was still a small patch of bare flesh.

Doctor Efreeti had so thoroughly, so meticulously covered the rest of her body with runes that the small patch of darkness stood out against the violet light. He was not sure what it meant but it could be useful later.

The sorcerer had been lost in his thoughts but none of the others observing even saw the no longer Ophelia move before she was standing before Folken. He did well to contain his surprise when he finally looked up, his purple eyes suddenly locking with her crystallized ones.

The woman's head tilted to the side as she looked the pale man over, as if she were inspecting him. His fine raiment seemed little more than rags compared to the glory and light that poured from she that had been Ophelia. It was the first time the sorcerer had ever felt... flustered by another. Well, *maybe* the second.

"You understand what this one is," she observed, "At least partially."

His head bobbed once, "I cannot presume to comprehend the endgame that you have in mind for *this one* but, yes, I understand the functions with which she has been gifted."

"It is a pity," she responded, "You know that if you answered this way, this one would have no choice but to destroy you. All of you."

Again, Folken nodded, "But if I had attempted to lie, you would have detected it. The result would have been the same."

Hero and Josie both looked at the albino man quizzically. Neither of them understood what was happening. That their chances of living beyond this moment depended on one, small detail.

It was probably for the best. They would have likely called attention to it and spoiled the one chance the party had to get out of this alive.

Molten gold again poured from the rock face that the violet wings of lightning ripped asunder. And again, the metal migrated back into the no longer Ophelia's right hand.

"You do realize that Ophelia was left handed?" Folken said.

"It will be a shame to watch you die, Lord Kizoku." the ringing bells of the woman's laughter again filled the air, "It is a rare thing to find another who can appreciate the small details of another's work. With such in mind, one such as you should know the honor of meeting their end at the hand of perfection."

She who had been Ophelia's hand lunged for the sorcerer's face. It stopped short, just only just. The svartalfar could feel the heat from the metal on his pasty skin.

Unlike the times she froze before, Ophelia's body struggled to move, every soft part of her body jiggling with the effort. Her iced eyes darted around in confusion, but only for the briefest scant of time. They quickly found the source of what had just happened.

The cylinder in Folken's metal arm, the one that suspended an attacking soldier and made piles of unmanageable rubble able to be lifted in one hand, was extended. He had fired the spell at the woman just in time. A microsecond later, he would have been blind. Half a second later, deceased.

The compartment in his palm opened as the sorcerer raised his hand, "Run!" he ordered as he shoved an opalescent orb of energy into the face of the no longer Ophelia.

Folken, Josie, and Hero sprinted in the direction of the doorway to the antechamber even though it was nowhere to be seen. As Ultima's signature whine started, Lyan bolted past all three of them, carrying the still encased Havarti under her arm.

Another compartment opened in Folken's artificial arm and a black disk, about the size of the sorcerer's spread out hand, unfolded from the interior. Just as the kinetic force of Ultima spread, shredding all matter around them, a flash of emerald green light burst from the disk.

"Stay close to me!" Folken barked, "This field only negates the damage from my spell a few yards beyond myself!"

Lyan didn't even pretend to understand anything beyond 'stay close'. It must have felt unnatural to her to slow her pace while trying to escape some kind of magical explosion.

The sorcerer noticed the still unconscious form of Harbenigyr's doppelganger. The energies of Folken's spell had already reached him and were just starting the process of tearing the elf apart. He was already too far away to benefit from Folken's shield. But the svartalfar could find no sympathy for the soon to be dead evil cleric.

The strength of Ultima was such that, just as the lightning wings that emerged from she who had been Ophelia ripped through the edges of the pocket dimension, the opalescent glow did so as well. It was not as... clean a severing as the lightning, however. Even as shreds of Vulcan's pocket reality were ripped away, to reveal the true cave and the doors that lead to the tunnel and the way out, strips were also left behind.

That meant that they were still trapped inside the white space. If they tried to run through the strips as if they were the finish line of a race, they would slice the would be escapee into ribbons.

"A futile gesture, Chancellor," the melodic voice echoed from behind them, "I am disappointed in you."

They would have to wait until Ultima had ripped an opening large enough for them to pass through. It was taking longer than the svartalfar sorcerer had calculated and the no longer Ophelia was getting closer.

"'*I*'? Not '*this one*'?" Folken had stalled it before with conversation, here's hoping the stratagem would work again, "What has caused this inconsistency?"

She who had been Ophelia walked through the whipping razors of light that made up Folken's most destructive spell. They didn't appear to even touch her.

"No inconsistency," she replied, "*This one* could care less what you do. I, on the other hand, thought better of you. I thought that you understood the situation as it truly was."

"I am sorry to disappoint," the sorcerer said, "However, I must forward the hypothesis that you are looking at this situation from a limited perspective, Doctor Efreeti."

Folken could see the lips of Ophelia's face spread into a wide smile. Her teeth looked as if they were made of cooling magma as the bells of her laughter rang through the air again.

"I am limited by nothing. I haven't the limitations of your meager senses in that of one being to narrow my vision," the no longer Ophelia answered, "Do not expect that knowing the name of the one who holds the strings will keep the puppet from playing her part, Chancellor."

"I do not," the svartalfar said back, "But puppets have no will of their own, Efreeti."

"Your point?" she who had been Ophelia asked as she just stepped within arm's reach.

"My point is, that while I have compatriots that are lesser than you and I," Folken said, "they can still show an initiative that is surprising and timely."

Jade green light spilled in the space around the sorcerer, Josie, Hero, and Lyan. The shredded wall of the white reality was slashed wide open to reveal the cleric Harbenigyr just on the other side, in the cave.

His hands were clasped together as he chanted his prayer. Again, the party ran for the exit to the tunnel. Josie had to grab Harby by the shoulder to get him to stop praying and come with them.

"Where's the other me?" the ranger asked.

"I couldn't save her," the cleric confessed as he focused on the way ahead.

The cave started to rumble around them, stones and rock getting steadily bigger as the shaking became steadily more and more violent. Josie's bow was knocked from her hands. As she bent down to pick it up, Harbenigyr tackled her out of the path of a boulder that fell right at that moment.

"Are you okay?" the cleric ran a hand along her cheek.

Her entire face turned pink as she looked up at the cleric as he laid on top of her, "Did we make her angry enough to drop a mountain on us?" she asked with an unsure chuckle.

Lyan pulled Harby off the red haired alphan. Then she pulled Josie up to her feet next, followed by shoving her bow into her arms.

"No, we cannot outrun Ophelia, nor can we fight her, so she has no cause to be angry. This is the effect of Ultima." Folken explained as they started moving again, "The spell has been loosed from the pocket dimension and is making its way through every open space in this outcropping of rock." Then he added as an afterthought, "Hardly a mountain."

"I feel so much better," Josie scoffed as they all ran.

"If we cannot fight her," Lyan decided to bring up the rear, to herd everyone else forward as they fled, "How do we stop her?"

"A fair question," Folken responded, "I have no idea."

"I do," Havarti spoke up from under Lyan's blackened arm, "But I need to be freed from this contraption first."

Decades later...

APPELONIA RAN FOR the trees. She held little Juna tight in her arms as she fled from the man-beasts.

But they were faster. One reached out with a clawed hand and grabbed the cleric by her long crimson hair. When he pulled back, Apple lost her footing and she started falling backward.

Closing her eyes, the young woman huddled herself around the baby as best she could to protect her. When she landed, it was a lot softer than Appelonia anticipated.

She opened her eyes to find Tokki under her. He had dived under her as she fell to keep little Juna from getting hurt. Still, the shock of the sudden stop caused the little girl to start crying.

Appelonia tried to hush her as she pulled herself off of Tokki's back. She noticed that all the arrows that had been in the quiver spilled out all over the ground because of his last minute heroics.

"Are you okay?" the Bunny Barbarian groaned as he pulled himself up to his hands and knees.

"Yeah," Appelonia hurriedly answered as she bounced the baby in her arms, "We're okay. Thank you, Tokki, She could have been really hurt."

"You really need to be more careful," Ophelia snapped as she slashed throat of the cat man who had lunged for the cleric in the first place, "Kids are fragile, you know."

"This from the woman who let me jump off the roof of the stables?" Apple breathed a silent sigh of relief as Juna finally calmed down.

"There was hay underneath!" Ophelia protested before she suddenly blinked out of view.

Another monster man charged through the violet silhouette. The blade of his sword splitting the afterimage of the woman and now charging straight for Appelonia.

Tokki reached out and grabbed the cat man's ankle, tripping him. They wrestled until the barbarian was able to climb on top of the feline headed man. Tokki ran his clawed sleeved across the man's throat and he gurgled his last in seconds.

"We have to get her out of here," the cleric pressed her cheek into Juna's black hair.

"You're right," Ophelia said from behind Apple.

The red haired woman jumped, making the baby giggle at her reaction.

"Give her to me," the mercenary slipped her sword into its scabbard on her back and held out her arms, "My blinking at least has a chance of keeping her a little safer."

"Can you blink another person with you?" Appelonia asked even as she carefully passed little Juna to the other woman.

"Not another adult," Ophelia admitted, "But I blink with Havarti and he's an even bigger baby than her."

The sword responded with mocking laughter, "Very droll, my dear."

"You have longer legs, that means you can run faster than me anyway," Appelonia said as she pulled the silver centerpiece of her disassembled bow from it's pouch, "Tokki and I will cover you as best we can while you get out of here."

The Bunny Barbarian tackled another cat man that dared get too close as Appelonia pulled her jade sticks out of her quiver and started putting her bow together. Ophelia just grinned at her until the ranger trained cleric nocked one of her bludgeoning arrows.

"You are your father's daughter," the mercenary chuckled.

Apple pulled and released the arrow, "You'd better get moving."

The arrow struck a cat man right in between his slit eyes. Unconscious, he toppled to the ground, taking two other monster men to the dirt with him.

"With your mother's aim," Ophelia laughed again.

Then she started for the trees. With three bursts of flame, the mercenary's escape route was cut off by three efreeti demons. They looked like the ones that outside the palace of the Mullah in Nova Prime. They were at least as powerful as Genevieve.

Ophelia let out a curse so loudly that it made little Juna cry, "Now look what you did!" she snapped at the demons.

One of the monsters slashed at the mercenary. She bent down and turned away, putting her body between the efreeti and the baby. Ophelia threw her boot up and slammed it into the chest of her attacker.

He stumbled back with a puff of smoke from his mouth but the other two attacked in unison. One slashed high with his claws while the other dived low to take out the woman's legs. All they managed to touch was purple fog.

Ophelia reappeared behind the one that was now laying on his stomach. She pulled Havarti free with her right hand and dropped the blade on the back of the efreeti demon's neck. The mercenary's strike didn't cut through his neck completely, but it was enough to keep the beast from rising. Ever again.

"These things have tough hides," the woman observed.

"Don't be too hard on yourself, dear," Havarti chimed in, "You are using your off hand, after all."

The second demon turned to face Ophelia just in time to take a dulled arrow to the throat. As the beast gagged, Ophelia finally took a moment to look at the bundle cradled in her left arm.

"Oh good, I can blink with her," she said.

"You mean you really weren't sure?" Appelonia was flabbergasted as she kept shooting arrows at the demon to drive it back, "I thought you were just making a joke!"

"I was," Ophelia shrugged, the bouncing motion making little Juna burp, "I also didn't want to worry you."

"Well, too late for that now." the cleric frowned, even as Genevieve leaped atop the beast she had been driving back.

"Listen, Apple," Ophelia's voice was stern. "If it were up to me, I'd let you carry the kid. I'm a lot better at the fighting part. But we've already seen that my blinking makes me the better choice to keep her safe."

"We may need your fighting more than the blinking for the baby," Tokki spoke up, "They're cutting off every avenue of escape with efreeti like Genevieve."

The Bunny Barbarian strode back from the direction of the demon that Ophelia had kicked. Blood dripped not only from his clawed sleeve but his exposed arm as well.

Ophelia let out another curse as she looked around the battlefield. Juna started crying again.

"Let me have her back," Appelonia slung her bow over her shoulder and held out her arms.

Another pack of cat men suddenly charged for the trio. Ophelia wrapped her armored sleeve around the baby as Appelonia was tackled off her feet. Tokki spun around one cat-headed man while slashing at another with his clawed sleeve.

The feline jaws of the man-beast on top of the cleric snapped shut inches from her face. Apple suddenly regretted taking her hands off her bow. She could have collapsed it back into her two fighting sticks with a press of a button.

As it was, she did everything she could to hold the monster at arm's length. The cat man's grip ripped into the one remaining sleeve of her tunic, not finding it much of a barrier to reach the skin below.

She could feel blood dripping over her elbow and along her bicep on the way up to her shoulder. If she let him keep scratching at her arm like this, she wasn't going to have use of it much longer.

Looking down, Appelonia just hoped that having a tiger head was the only major difference these things had from normal mortal men. The woman shot her knee up between the man-beast's legs, right into his groin.

His slit pupils dilated into full circles as a pained squeak escaped his throat. Appelonia shoved him off to the side and started to pick herself up off the ground.

"I am glad I am not fighting you," Tokki chuckled, huffing for breath.

He'd been rushing to the cleric's rescue, only to not be needed at the last moment. Appelonia noticed that the barbarian's bare arm was not only covered with blood but hanging limply.

"We need to get that treated," She started reaching for his wounded limb.

Tokki lunged forward, slamming his blood soaked shoulder into Apple's chest ank knocking her to the ground. He tried to duck under the efreeti demon's slash but the attack caught the top of his helmet, knocking the bunny skull off his head and dazing the barbarian.

The beast charged in with his other arm. Tokki barely brought his furred sleeve up in time to keep from getting his head ripped off.

Instead, he tumbled back. Off balance, he bumped into the back of another cat man. The creature spun around and slashed his claws across Tokki's chest.

When the feline-headed monster pressed his advantage and charged, the Bunny Barbarian bent over, his shoulder crushing into the creature's midsection, and straightened up. Spilling the cat man to the ground behind him. Tokki slammed his foot down onto his opponent's neck with a heavy snap.

But he couldn't take a moment to enjoy his victory, or even get his bearings because the efreeti demon was again right on top of him. The beast's fist slammed into the elf's jaw, sending him flying over the corpse of the cat man he had just killed.

His breath was knocked out of his body when he finally landed. Hard. Blood poured from his mouth. He must have bit his tongue when he was struck. Hopefully, it wasn't in two pieces.

The efreeti stomped over the small man. Smoke billowed from his nose as he gave the Bunny Barbarian an inhuman grin.

Just as he raised his arm for the finishing blow on the barbarian, an arrow struck him in the eye. Blood spurted around the shaft that had a pastel pink tuft of fur hanging from the back.

The efreeti reared back, roaring in pain, when another arrow hit him in the throat. This arrow had a white puff of fur. The black smoke stopped pouring out of his nose, replaced by the white vapor one exhales in the cold of winter, but his focus never left the Bunny Barbarian.

He stepped forward, intent to finish Tokki before he fell in battle himself. Two more arrows struck the monster in the chest, both had blue fur on the butts. A burst of lightning suddenly arced between the two shafts, up through the white and into the pink furred shaft, frying the demons entire top half. The efreeti fell back into the dirt, dead.

Wheezing for breath, Tokki looked back in the direction from which the arrows came. There stood Appelonia her bow already nocked with another arrow ready to fire.

After it was clear that the efreeti wasn't going to rise again, the cleric tossed her bow to the ground and rushed to Tokki's side. The barbarian looked around, trying to spot any incoming threats but the tide of battle was turning away from them for some reason. Not that he was complaining.

"Don't move," Appelonia ordered, "I need to check you for a broken neck, back, and any internal injuries."

He didn't raise a word of protest.

"I think you're going to have quite the story to tell when you get back home," the cleric smiled sweetly as her hands lightly ran down the back of his neck.

If he got home alive. If by some miracle they did, Appelonia was right. He would have quite a glorious tale to weave. That should have pleased him but, if he'd been physically capable of it, Tokki would have jumped when a disturbing thought disrupted his thoughts of glory.

"Where's Ophelia?" he asked, "Where's the baby?"

Decades earlier...

AS THE PARTY reached the mouth of the cave, Harbenigyr realized something he didn't bother to notice when he first arrived. They were in a canyon. Even though they could see the sky, the cleric still felt trapped.

Lyan busied herself by ripping the gold cage that was wrapped around the bastard sword apart with her bare hands. When the restraints are only thin lengths of gold, it may not be physically difficult but, judging by the Bunny Barbarian's reaction when the sword came loose, it was cathartic.

"What is your plan, Havarti?" Folken took the sword from Lyan with his flesh hand.

"I know Ophelia is still in there," the sword said to the man, "When Meteorend burned out the last remnants of the penanggalan inside her, our connection returned."

Lyan tapped the hilt of the bastard sword like one who was tapping another person's shoulder to get their attention, "How does that help us? The angel of destruction is in complete physical control."

Havarti cleared his nonexistent throat, "Eerily accurate but that great evil's control is hardly complete."

"Great evil?" Lyan suddenly looked troubled as the sword continued.

"I was able to get through to Ophelia several times down there," Havarti said, "The first time, I convinced her to destroy the guards that were swarming around Lyan."

Hero stepped up to the sword, "But it said that it destroyed them because they weren't worthy to be there."

"That was how the *angel of destruction* justified the action to itself," Havarti answered.

Folken spoke, "It was your voice that caused Ophelia's body to freeze, wasn't it? Every time she became like a statue, it was you trying to talk to her."

"Indeed," the sword agreed, "That is why I know it does not have absolute control."

As the group was speaking, the outcropping of rock that formed one side of the canyon was collapsing in on itself. No rubble threatened Harby or the others, which is why no one noticed until...

"Folken, is that the effect of Ultima?" Josie pointed at the sinking rock.

The sorcerer shook his head, "I'm afraid not. It appears Lyan's *angel* does not enjoy navigating caves and prefers a more direct route."

As the rocks continued to disappear, Havarti shook in Folken's hand to get his attention, "Please hand me to Harbenigyr. He is the only one she may hesitate to strike down."

"May?" Folken quirked an emerald eyebrow, "Hardly reassuring."

But he did as the bastard sword asked and Harby, to his credit, didn't argue. His unease at holding the weapon, however, could not be more obvious.

"I will also need Lady Josie's assistance," Havarti said once he was in the hands of the cleric.

The ranger stepped up beside Harbenigyr. She had no idea how she could be of help. That much was obvious just looking at her face.

"The rest of you," Havarti said as the last of the rocks crumbled away, "I would recommend concealing yourselves."

"Hiding?" Lyan Yo Bunpy scoffed.

Hero wrapped both of her hands around the barbarian's elbow and started dragging her toward the tent, "If it makes you feel better, you can think of it as laying in wait."

Folken followed the bard and Bunny Barbarian into the tent. Not that he thought it was adequate cover, but because he knew that running from this Angel of Destruction would be pointless.

Once the dust settled, there was the no longer Ophelia standing in the middle of the crater had been something that took nature millennia to create. She destroyed it in seconds.

The precious metals that had been in the stone of that outcropping now swirled over the woman. One loop was made of pure gold, still glowing from the heat of its forceful extraction. It was large enough to encircle Ophelia's body if she decided to let it descend from just above her head.

The other loop was of silver. It wasn't quite as big as that of the gold and actually floated within the larger ring, though its orbit was slightly offset from the other metal.

There was a third swirl of metal within the silver, not quite enough to make a complete ring. If Harbenigyr had to guess, he would say that it was copper.

The violet lightning erupting from the back of the transformed woman dropped from the sky, where it had annihilated all the rock surrounding her, to sink into the soil around her. But, the dirt didn't melt at its touch. Instead, Harbenigyr could feel the ground… vibrating under his feet. And he was yards away.

Josie was nowhere to be seen as the no longer Ophelia took her first step toward the cleric. Plant roots shot up around her bare foot, swirling around her leg. When they finally made contact with her rune covered skin, they immediately wilted away. Every step was like this as she climbed the slope of the crater she had made.

Havarti waited patiently for the Angel of Destruction to come. Harbenigyr, on the other hand, had trouble keeping himself from shaking.

The teachings of Kuan Yin taught him not to fear death. To be honest, the elf was curious as to the kind of paradise his goddess had awaiting those who served her faithfully. It was that transitional period, the one involving pain and violence that delivered fear to his body.

Harbenigyr held the bastard sword with both hands, it was awkward with such a short handle. Despite the vibrating under his feet and the instinctive shaking of his body, the sword stayed cool and still in the elf's grip. The cleric hoped at least some of that would transfer to him.

Then he wondered: was this why Ophelia never seemed to be scared? Was Havarti some kind of calming influence on her? Was this why he thought his plan would work?

"You are willing to sacrifice your oaths to your goddess to save your own life, cleric?" the symphony of the angel's voice pulled Harby out of his thoughts as she finally reached where the entrance to the cave had been.

To the outside observer, it could indeed seem that Harbenigyr was standing ready to fight. The cleric took a deep breath and, he may have been imagining it, but some of the swords calm seemed to fill him, too.

"Ophelia knows me better than that," he responded, "I'm only holding Havarti so that they can talk."

"Talk?" the Angel of Destruction repeated, "This one finds it more likely that your sorcerer is lying in wait, using you as a diversion while he attempts to conjure some esoteric energy into some form that he feels may at least damage, if not destroy, this one. Where could he be?"

The vibrations under the feet of the cleric surged in strength. The no longer Ophelia turned to face the broad tent.

"As hiding places go, that is the least creative one could be in this terrain," the transformed woman observed, "He will be given no more time to loiter in his ignorance."

The halos of metal shattered into more pieces than could be counted. Then they rained onto the tent like a unholy hailstorm.

The canvas was quickly ripped away to reveal a webbing made of black metal. It stood between the deluge of golden shards and the svartalfar man.

It was made by the sorcerer's prosthetic limb. Spreading out from his hand (in fact, his hand was merged seamlessly into the shield), the structure was completely solid immediately around the man with green hair. As it moved further away from Folken, the gaps in the spiderweb-like patterns grew bigger.

While the svartalfar was completely unscathed by the attack from the Angel of Destruction, Lyan's shield was embedded with gold and silver all along the left side, making it appear as if the saber-toothed rabbit painted on its surface was headless. Some shards found their way into her scorched arm, though she acted as if she didn't notice.

Hero was spared the barrage of metal but the main post that held up the middle of the tent was felled like a tree and dropped on top of her. From what Harbenigyr could see, she was knocked out, perhaps even severely injured.

"Stand your ground, cleric!" Havarti barked at the cleric.

"She could be dying!" Harbenigyr protested.

"We will all be dead if we don't succeed here!" the sword shouted back.

"That was a purely reactive tactic," the Angel of Destruction sighed, "Perhaps he is resigned to his fate, after all."

"If there is one thing I know, Efreeti," Havarti physically turned the elf so that the sword could address the transformed woman directly, "It is that Ophelia will fight against whatever it is you want to happen."

"Until this one realized that the only choice she did have was what kind of monster she was to become," the no longer Ophelia said, "You were the one to made her realize that, sword. You were the last edge of leverage to keep this one under control until the time came. That knowledge that she had something to lose if she proved disobedient. Without you, she would have resigned herself to being a blood sucking fiend."

"That may have been your purpose for me, Doctor Efreeti," Havarti finally spoke up, "But Ophelia and I aren't leverage against each other. We watch out for each other. If need be, we bring the other back home."

The angel scoffed, the sound like a fork scraping the bottom of a scorched pan. It was the first unpleasant noise, if not words, to come from she who had been Ophelia.

"If you speak of the saccharine sentiment of *love*, that is a force reserved for the telling of fairy tales," the Angel of Destruction said, "In reality, it is merely a chemical reaction within a two mortals bodies that causes their intelligence quotient to either temporarily or permanently lower and teach each victim to accept abuse."

"But I have no body to have 'chemical reactions'," Havarti countered.

"Exactly," the no longer Ophelia replied. "So you counted on this one's reactions toward the elf holding you to give you time to what? Talk sense into this one? I can assure you that you are merely wasting effort."

The wings made of lighting started sweeping toward the cleric. He was surrounded by the violet light before he could even think to dodge. The vibrating bolts sank towards him like fingers wrapping around to grasp him.

"Throw me!" Havarti commanded.

"What good could that do?" Harbenigyr had never been claustrophobic until now. Now, as the very light he witnessed destroy so much careened towards him, he was having trouble breathing.

"Just do it!" the sword snapped.

Chanting a quiet prayer, the cleric whipped the sword over his head and then forward. Letting the weapon go, the elf knew that he wasn't in danger of breaking his vow not to kill but he was worried that he had just condemned the life held in the blade to death by the purple violence surrounding them both.

"Ophelia!" Havarti bellowed as he spun through the air, "You must take control back! You mustn't let this bobolyne enact his will upon you any further!"

"Bobolyne?" a confused look crossed Ophelia's face.

The lightning around the cleric stuttered and came to a stop mere inches from the crouching elf. Havarti skidded to the ground at the feet of the Angel of Destruction.

Ophelia's body, seemingly on instinct, reached down to pick up the weapon, "I've not heard that term in some–"

The lightning disappeared completely. Steam wafted from the back of the transformed woman, between her shoulder blades and where her original runes rested, as her face turned to look back over her shoulder.

There was Josie, her hand still on the handle of the dagger that was usually hidden in the hilt of the bastard sword. The blade sank into the one small patch of skin that was not covered with Doctor Efreeti's runes.

"That cannot kill this one, sword," the voice of the angel sounded as if part of the symphony was suddenly playing out of tune.

"It isn't meant to," Havarti replied, wiggling contentedly in the woman's left hand, "I figured that I might need bypass your interference and gain a more, shall we say, direct conduit to reach my lover. Have I found it, my dear?"

The Angel of Destruction's icy eyes slowly closed. When they opened, the pale blue, almost gray, eyes of Ophelia took their place, "Why does everything involving Doctor Efreeti involve me being naked?"

Despite the mirth in her now normal sounding voice, Ophelia sounded exhausted. Flames no longer slipped from her mouth with every word, either.

In fact, all the newly formed runes quickly faded from the skin of the woman. As she dropped to her knees, Harbenigyr was there to catch her before she was completely laid out.

"Why didn't she blink?" Josie looked over Ophelia's shoulder at the cleric.

Harby eased the woman down to the ground and onto her side, "I don't know. Maybe the monster who changed her thought she didn't need it anymore."

Josie still had her hand around the handle of the dagger. She was as afraid to let it go as she was to keep the blade in the woman's back, "Should I pull it out?"

"No!" Harby's hand wrapped around hers, "The blade is in her aorta, if we pull it out, she'll bleed to death in a couple minutes," the elf gently, carefully pulled Josie's fingers open and lifted her hand away from the dagger, "But you don't have to hold it anymore."

Neither pulled their hands away for a long moment. That is, until Folken walked up beside them.

His arm was back in its normal shape. The leather of the lower part of the glove, though, was shredded.

"What is her condition?" he inquired of the cleric.

"I think the dagger is in her abdominal aorta," Harbenigyr reported, "If I'm careful, I may be able to repair the damage, but we won't be able to move her for a few days, maybe even a week, at minimum."

Folken let out a thoughtful grunt as he turned his attention to the ranger, "Josie, Ophelia will need her clothing when she is recovered. Could you check to see if anything survived the destruction of the cave?"

The woman stopped looking up at the sorcerer to glance over at Harby, who nodded back. Only then did she get up and start back down into the crater.

The sorcerer knelt down beside the cleric, his attention was again focused on Ophelia's back, "The only runes that remain are the ones that were already visible."

"But where's Meteorend?" Harbenigyr ran a hand over the woman's chest, just below her collarbone, "If she absorbed it like Vulcan did, the heart should still be visible. Or on the ground next to her."

"I don't have an answer for that, cleric," Folken said, "And you and I both know that the kind of surgery you are planning for Ophelia is difficult under ideal circumstances. Which these are not."

The elf shrugged back, the metal links of his chainmail rattling together lightly, "What else could I do? Kuan Yin will only imbue her healing energies once the source of the injury is gone. Who knows how much blood she would lose as I pray for the wound to close after the blade is removed? That's why I have to operate."

"You forget that, with her runes being restored to their original condition, it is likely that her abilities are as they were before, as well," Folken said.

"Maybe," Harbenigyr's lips pursed.

"More probable," the svartalfar insisted, "Considering how easily Doctor Efreeti relinquished control over Ophelia, I'd say he would want her to survive for whatever he truly has planned for her."

"Easy?" Harby waved a hand at the crater beside them, "You call that easy?"

"Ophelia is a part of some bigger ploy that demon has in mind," Folken said, "While some of the circumstances involved in activating her latent power were met, many were not. Otherwise, we would truly have been destroyed."

"Perhaps we should let her die then," Lyan let her presence be known. "If she is to be a part of the Great Evil, perhaps it is better to let her die as a human instead."

She stood just behind Folken, looking down at the unconscious form of Ophelia. She leaned against her spear, using it to keep herself upright.

"I won't let her die over something that may or may not happen," the cleric shook his head.

"I do not like the idea any more than you do," the Bunny Barbarian sighed, "Ophelia and I are kindred spirits. She would not want to play the part of a pawn in a monster's game."

"I understand your meaning, Lyan Yo Bunpy," Havarti spoke up from where he rested on the ground beside the naked tattooed woman, "But you forget. While Ophelia did indeed abhor being controlled, she would not take a cowardly way out and die now. She would fight Doctor Efreeti, stop whatever he has planned, and make herself truly free once and for all."

Lyan grunted, "You are right, Havarti. As a warrior, she should have a chance to fight whatever comes her way."

"That still leaves us with the question on what to do for Ophelia now," Harbenigyr said.

"Is she in immediate danger?" the barbarian asked.

"Not as long as we keep the dagger in place," the cleric answered.

"Then perhaps we should deal with the reason I came over in the first place," Lyan said before turning back in the direction of the collapsed tent, "The monster took advantage of the bard's unconsciousness to emerge. It is trying to chew its way through the post pinning her down at the moment."

"Go get the bottles of vinegar from her horse, Harbenigyr," Folken said, "Splash her with enough, and then force feed her more, she should return to normal."

"What about Ophelia?" the cleric didn't want to leave her alone. Not with him.

"I will watch over her," the svartalfar man responded.

"Okay," Harbenigyr lifted himself to his feet, "As long as you promise to not pull the dagger out to try and make her blink."

Folken nodded. The barbarian and the cleric, though hesitant, started in the direction of the tent.

"Perhaps you should mind Lyan's wounds after you have neutralized Hero, as well?" the svartalfar suggested.

CHAPTER FOURTEEN

OPHELIA'S SELF-INTERROGATION:

"No! I refuse to accept that!" Ophelia protested.
"What is so hard to accept?" I asked.
"I am not evil. I'm not." Ophelia growled.
"Who are you trying to convince? Me? Or yourself?" I inquired.
"Didn't you say that there's no difference?" the subject surprisingly grinned, "But I'm not the one I need to convince."

Decades later...

OPHELIA'S ARMORED RIGHT sleeve kept the cat men from being able to get a grip on the baby. But the scraping sound of their claws raking across the steel only made little Juna cry harder.

Unfortunately, having both her arms around the baby to protect her from harm did hamper the ability to fight. Not that she was defenseless.

She felt ribs snap under her foot when she kicked one of the feline-headed fighters that made the mistake of assuming that. Her other foot cracked his jaw and he landed on the dirt in a heap.

"And people thought that dance lessons were a waste of time," Ophelia snickered.

"I think people only considered it such because you insisted on me as your partner and I have no feet, my dear," Havarti chimed in, "Regardless, I still cannot find a clear path out of here."

That wasn't what the woman wanted to hear. She felt bad enough leaving Appelonia and the Bunny Barbarian behind against those higher tier of demons but the mercenary just couldn't get clear of all the rabble.

Another cat man jumped out at Ophelia. This one wasn't going to be having any children in the near future, thanks to the woman's boot striking between his legs with vicious precision.

It was still conscious, even if it was on his knees. In between meowing rasps of breath, he muttered some quiet chant as his slit pupils stayed locked on the woman and child.

Ophelia turned away from the man and started into what looked like a quarter of forest that was clear of the demonic foot soldiers. A loud, echoing roar suddenly filled the woman's ears and made the ground under her feet quake.

She had to stop to maintain her balance. That was only the start of her problems, though.

The earth stilled but the sound of toppling trees came almost immediately after. And it only got louder and closer. Ophelia started running again.

And was blocked by a wall of flame. It rushed from her left and stopped right in front of her.

Then the monstrous head of the one called Nikojunakalium emerged from the burning light. The rest of his immense body followed as he stomped toward Ophelia.

She walked backwards, Havarti guiding her telepathically to keep from hitting any trees. They wanted little Juna alive, at least until *they* killed her for whatever ritual they needed to summon their Mullah, so Ophelia was at least partially sure the demon wouldn't do anything too rash.

"That child is the blood of the holiest Mullah Junaperqolanijuna alab Marid Juna alnnihaya," All that came from his monstrous mouth were growls but Ophelia could understand them just the same, "Turn it over now, and you will only die. Resist and taste the eternal torment of being a burning soul upon the plains of Nova Prime."

"That is a lovely offer but I'm afraid I'll have to decline either option," Ophelia kept on walking, "You see, my eternal torment has already been promised to another demon. Perhaps you've heard of him? Goes by Doctor Efreeti?"

"Doctor Efreeti?" Nikojunakalium reared back at the mention of the name of the other demon. "You are a part of that louse's machinations? You?"

"'Fraid so," Ophelia smirked, "I don't suppose that convinces you to back away, preferably enough that I can leave to parts unknown with the tyke?"

The demon looked away from the woman. Even though his face wasn't human, it was a look with which the mercenary was familiar. It was the same look Ophelia had when she listened to Havarti speaking in her head. Someone, likely this 'Mullah', was giving him instructions from on high.

"If you are destroyed, the schema of Gydytojas Ebibi Rahasia Rewera dies with you," the monster's tongue turning the color of burning embers as he continued speaking, "The Udokotela will finally be brought to his knees!"

Nikojunakalium belched a fireball that would have easily enveloped Ophelia. If she had still been standing where it struck.

But she had blinked, thankfully just out of his sight behind two intertwined trees. But the hiding place wouldn't last long. Juna started wailing at the wash of heat, the sudden disorientation, or even the woman holding her too tight, Ophelia wasn't sure why.

"Was that Gydytojas phrase that thing spouted Doctor Efreeti's true name?" Havarti conjectured as Ophelia started running away from the beast as fast as her feet could carry her.

At this point, she didn't care where she was going. She'd figured that mentioning the demon who marked her would have either filled Nikojunakalium with fear or anger. With fear, she could have just left as he ran off or simply cowered.

He just had to choose anger. Blinking away from an attack was part of that plan but not that he would become so violent that he would be willing to sacrifice the Mullah's big scheme of conquering this world to do it. At the Mullah's instruction, no less!

"I think Efreeti might just be a bastardized version of that part of the Doctor's name, Ebibi, He's probably been around long enough for that to happen," Ophelia thought back to her sword as she hopped over a felled tree trunk, "But what could Ebibi want to do that would make the Mullah just give up on his plan for Juna?"

"Give up may be a strong choice of words, my dear," Havarti replied.

Before Ophelia could even ask what he meant, the mercenary found herself back in the clearing. When the baby's crying reached the ears of the cat men still swarming around, Ophelia let out a resigned sigh.

Her foot crushed the nose of the first creature to charge at her. She ducked under the slashing claws of another before blinking away from another slash at her back.

"Look, kid, I'm sorry," Ophelia muttered as she stepped around another feline-headed fighter, "I know you don't like the blinking but it's keeping us both alive."

Nikojunakalium burst back into the clearing. Stretching to his full height, he opened his maw wide.

"The one in red serves the Udokotela!" he roared, "If you can take the child, do so, but the half-breed is now secondary. Destroy the pawn of the Udokotela without fail!"

"Half-breed? Josie would not appreciate such a label-ohmykuan watch out!" Havarti's tone went from snide to panicked in the space of a word.

The monsters leaped for Ophelia with renewed vigor. Too many were attacking her at once now for her blinking to avoid every slash, tear, and hit. Every time she did blink, though, the wounds stopped bleeding, if not aching.

Leaving a trail of violet outlines behind, Ophelia concentrated her efforts on keeping her armored arm over little Juna and getting as far away from the massive Nikojunakalium as humanly possible.

She had to hand the baby off to someone else. She was too much of a target now. Ophelia hadn't anticipated this.

Another blink and Ophelia tumbled immediately after landing a few feet away. Falling to one knee, there was no way she could avoid the claws streaking straight for her eyes.

A suit of steel slammed into the side of the cat man, sprawling him out on the ground. A massive blade, almost as tall as the man wielding it, slammed down on the monster and killed it instantly.

It was that paladin, Jonas the Shepherd. Ophelia breathed a sigh of relief.

"We need to get Juna to someone else," the mercenary said before letting out a groan as she regained her footing.

She could feel cold air against her back. Her coat must be in shreds by now. No matter, Ophelia could always get it repaired.

"Where's Appelonia?" the paladin had to chop down two more feline-headed fighters before he could return his attention to the woman for an answer.

Ophelia looked around to get her bearings. The first time she really had a chance before she painted a target on her own back.

The mercenary pointed to the other side of the clearing, almost straight across from the cave entrance, "Over there! Near your lady demon friend."

"You mean Genevieve?" Jonas squinted in the direction Ophelia indicated, "Okay, I can get us there."

Lifting two fingers to his lips, the paladin loosed a piercing whistle onto the winds. A neighing in the distance was timed so perfectly that it had to be an answer.

A short time later, a horse armored in a very similar way to Jonas bowled through the herd of cats and stopped just beside the young paladin. He gave his steed an appreciative scratch behind the ears as she came to a stop.

"Hop on," he ordered.

"You'll need to hold Juna," Ophelia replied.

The baby started wiggling in the grip of the woman when she moved her armored sleeve away. It was an awkward trade, to say the least. Particularly with the worry of another cat man charging along any second.

"Come on, kid," Ophelia ran a hand through the crying girl's black hair, "We get through this, you're back in Apple's arms. You know the elf with the red hair and big boobs you liked?"

Ophelia slipped a foot into the metal stirrup to pull herself up onto the back of the mare. Another cat monster decided to leap from behind the horse right at that moment.

Havarti was free of the confining scabbard on the mercenary's back and already swinging at the tiger-headed fiend keeping her from getting on the armored steed. Unfortunately, this one was smarter than the rest Ophelia had taken down. It leaned back to avoid her slashes, jumping just out of her reach.

The woman heard "Blessed commander!" come out of the mouth of the paladin like a curse. She had to hop awkwardly to be able to turn around enough to see him but, when she did, her choice of words were not as sanitary as the those from the man in the armor.

Two feline-headed men jumped him while the Ophelia was distracted by the first. Jonas cradled the baby to his chest, using his gauntlets as shields to protect her. He raised his shoulders and drooped his head down as far as he could so that the high collar of steel attached to his breastplate would protect as much of his head as possible from their claws. Without a helmet, it was the most vulnerable part of his body and definitely what they were targeting.

The bald man in the black cloak, Jin Vega, crept up behind one, reached out with his bare hands and snapped its neck in one deft motion, "R'stinpices!" he grunted, the words drowning out the sound of cracking bones.

The cat man facing Ophelia roared with rage, knocking the off balance woman aside as he lunged at the paladin with the baby still in his arms. Jin elbowed the other cat man in the head, knocking him out, so that he could step around the Shepherd and then quickly whipped his gray cloak between the charging beast and Jonas.

The lion-headed man-beast disappeared into the folds of the garment. Ophelia would have taken a moment to be impressed but her foot was stuck in Andromeda's stirrup. The woman's legs were stretched out wide into awkward splits. The fact that the other foot was on her long leather coat rather than the ground made finding a purchase so she could stand up that much more difficult.

"I will have to be careful the next time I reach in to for a piece of meat," Jin said as he continued around Jonas.

Helping Ophelia straighten up, he stopped short of aiding her onto the horse before he again faced the paladin. Juna was crying up a storm until the monk leaned in close to her. When her little hands got a grip on his bushy beard, she started giggling happily. After a couple of failed attempts to pull away, Jin resigned himself to his fate and took the baby from the other man's arms.

"We need to get her to safety," Jonas said to the bald man.

"And as far away from me as possible," Ophelia added, tugging her foot free from the stirrup.

"What does 'Udokotela' mean, anyway?" the monk asked.

The woman shrugged, "It's a pet name for Doctor Efreeti. That's all I know," Ophelia pointed at over her shoulder, toward her back with her thumb.

The large red demon woman, Genevieve landed on the ground beside the armored man, leaving small craters in the dirt around her feet. She straightened up beside him, well taller than any of the mortals immediately around her. Strings of flesh, skin and internal, hung from the curved claws in her fingertips.

"It means '*he who is of us but seeks to make us suffer*'," she informed them as she raised her hands to eye level. "Unlike these rakshasa, mariliths, and myself, he does not share a tier in our hierarchy."

"That's... detailed," Ophelia sighed.

After loosing a quick gasp of fire from her mouth, she burned the ichor from her hands. "The efreeti language is far more nuanced and detailed than any mortal tongue," she said proudly before turning to face Jonas directly, "Those of my rank who attempted to slay the cleric have been slain themselves, Master."

"Should we expect more powerful efreeti like them to show soon, Genevieve?" the paladin asked.

The demon nodded, "Surely. The longer the Maester of the efreeti is on this plane, more of my rank will be pulled to his presence. Particularly because of her," Genevieve motioned to Ophelia. "If this woman is indeed a party to the schemas of Doctor Efreeti, it would be best for all of us to strike her down now."

"Why?" Jin interjected, "Sure, she's tough in a fight because of that teleporting she does but why does that worry Niko so much?"

Before Genevieve could even open her mouth to answer, Nikojunakalium slammed into the ground beside them. Andromeda reared back, the only barrier between the humans and the massive efreeti demon.

He did exactly what Genevieve had done moments before; jumped from one end of the battlefield to the other. All the pomposity, all the confidence the female demon had just seconds before instantly wilted at the sight of him. If Ophelia didn't know better, she'd have sworn that Genevieve's skin tone turned almost human there for a moment.

"How considerate of you, keeping both things I want within convenient reach of each other," the massive demon growled, "The bald human will give me the child. Now."

"I thought killing me was higher on the priority list," Ophelia smirked back up at him, trying to sound insulted, "After all I'm the one who was Udokotela's plaything, right?"

"Thanks to you, I can have both," the demon replied, "I will kill you with these other sacks of meat once the child's purpose is fulfilled."

Nikojunakalium swept Andromeda aside with one massive paw. The mare slid along for the first few yards but lost her balance and fell to her side after only a few seconds. The horse cried out in pain as one of its legs cracked at the forces being pushed against it.

"You bastard!" Jonas yelled as he rushed to the side of his steed, "She was no threat to you!"

It was pure instinct. His claymore was on the ground, forgotten, beside Ophelia's feet. He had totally given up on any kind of tactical thought. As he knelt beside his injured horse, his friend.

"You mean after you've killed the baby and created whatever portal you need to bring your boss up here?" Ophelia scowled up at the beastly demon.

"Precisely," Nikojunakalium answered.

He dropped his six-fingered hand to the ground immediately in front of Jin Vega, palm side up. The bald man wrapped both arms around the child, the loose sleeves of his cloak completely obscuring the child from view. The monk made no motion to put the child down.

"And all of us are dead regardless, right?" Ophelia's pale eyes stayed locked looking up.

"The longer you delay giving me the 'she', the more painful it will be," the Maester efreeti snarled.

Ophelia raised her unarmed hand and gave a beckoning gesture, "You are immeasurably bad at this whole *negotiation* thing, you know that?"

"There is no negotiation," the demon replied, "There are no terms of surrender. Even if you kill the child before the ritual, I will still devour your carcass. No blinking, shading, transformation or any other toy your father has provided you can withstand the heat of my belly."

"Okay, one," Ophelia held up three fingers, "Ebibi is *not* my father. Second," she curled one up so that one two fingers were still straight, "I'm very selective about who I let eat me. Third," Only one finger stayed up, "You are absolutely right that we aren't willing to kill little Juna."

"Then you are admitting defeat," Nikojunakalium barked.

The mercenary shook her head as she pointed straight at the demon, "That doesn't mean we aren't willing to sacrifice ourselves. Now!" Ophelia screamed into the air.

Nikojunakalium turned to look up into the sky, where Ophelia had actually been looking the whole time. That winged little mortal was fluttering around, well out of reach. But she was carrying two spheres made of iron.

The gnome dropped them. They fell straight onto the efreeti Maester, hitting him square on the head.

Nikojunakalium started to laugh, the bouncing motion causing the ball to split in half. One half slid down one side of his neck, the other half down the other, with a length of chain connecting them.

The amusement in the feline face of the demon was replaced with confusion when he suddenly found himself unable to stand. He fell forward, slamming into the dirt and covering everyone in a cloud of dust.

"Get out of there!" the voice of the flying little woman echoed down, "The *Galleon* is firing explosive rounds!"

"What... is... this?" the massive demon struggled against what should have been no effort to lift kept him pinned to the earth.

"Thokcha, Maester Alnnadhir Nikojunakalium abn Maridjuna. Iron from the heavens. The humans attempted to capture me with it yesterday," Genevieve answered before dashing toward Jonas and the whimpering Andromeda.

As the first telltale whistle of incoming fire came on the breeze, Ophelia and Jin started running in the direction of the cave.

Ophelia was knocked off her feet by the force of the blast when that first cannonball hit.

The dust up that the demon caused when he fell was nothing to the cloud surrounding the mercenary when she finally opened her eyes. Another explosion went of only yards away from her.

She threw her arms up to protect her head from flying debris. That was when she realized that her sword was missing.

"Havarti!" she called.

"Just to your left, dearest," the bastard sword hollered back.

Unable to see more than a few inches in front of her, Ophelia slid her hands through the dirt in search of her weapon. The biting pain of the sharpened edge of his blade sliced into her knuckles.

"Ooh, my apologies, my dear," Havarti mumbled in embarrassment.

Another explosion hit right about where the immense demon was lying. Ophelia dove on top of the sword as if she were protecting it with her body.

As clumps of dirt pummeled her back and shoulders, she found herself laughing back at the blade that had been her constant companions for decades, "How many shots do you think they're going to take?"

One more, it would seem. The cannonball struck the ground just in front of Ophelia, the fuse still hissing inside.

"Mothe–" she muttered just as the surface of the sphere shattered.

"-Ucker!" Ophelia found herself standing next to a tree that had the entire top, from the height of her shoulders splintered away. Looking around, the cloud of dust that had been where Niko-junakalium was pelted with the heavy weapons was only a short distance away.

That was the longest distance she ever recalled blinking, "Those balls must pack a real punch," she commented.

Havarti was in her hand. That was a load off her mind. Now she had to see what kind of damage the pirate ship had done.

It was a lucky break that Illyria Warflower was able to find the ship. Or, more likely, Bronwyn had told them to come back today to pick up Ophelia, her father, and herself. The mercenary did have to admit that the crew of the *Galleon* was efficient, particularly for a crew of pirates.

Without any major breeze, the cloud of dust from the cannon barrage was taking its time to clear. Whatever cat men had been left were surely killed or fled from the explosions. Judging from the half-human bodies with feline tails that the woman came across as she walked.

Finally, she was able to spot the silhouette of a massive lump that was roughly about the right shape to be Nikojunakalium's body. As she walked closer, it was indeed the Maester of the efreeti.

What was surprising, though, was when he let out a breath of air from his nose, causing pebbles to scatter. He was still alive.

"How are you doing there, Niko?" Ophelia asked, Havarti ready to strike.

"Petulant," he huffed, "mortals."

"You can always go home," Ophelia shrugged as she stepped closer, "I can guarantee no one wants you to stay."

"You have given me but a... moment's pause," Nikojunakalium responded with a growl.

Ophelia crouched down beside his head. There were the half sphere's on either side of his head, so he still could not rise from the ground.

They looked at each other directly, without any obstructions, "But it was one hell of a moment, wasn't it?" she smirked.

The demon lunged at her! As he rose off the dirt, Ophelia could see the chain still stretched between the halves of the can-nonballs. It must have slipped off his neck during the barrage and he just laid in wait!

Ophelia had no chance to dodge. He was too close and too fast. Usually, she could count on her blinking to save her but the woman had to wonder, did Nikojunakalium have some way to counter the abilities of her runes like the demon inferred?

The demon's head slammed back down into the earth. Ophelia let out a surprised gasp as the reality that she wouldn't be putting her blinking to the test, after all.

A spiked bronze ball rested at the crown of Nikojunakalium's head, right in between his wide horns. Thin streams of red blood trickled out from under that orb. On either side of it were two half-spheres like the ones that held him down before.

The chain that linked these together, though, were tied to a bronze chain that was much, much longer. Ophelia's eyes followed the length back to the steel arm of Phinegann, the orc in black armor.

He started marching toward her, the chain not losing tension as he closed the distance. In fact, while the heavily muscled man did indeed grip the chain in his hand, that wasn't where it ended.

It wound around his thick arm, blood from the cuts on his bronze skin smearing on the links, and into a compartment in his shoulder. Every step he took, that much chain reeled back into his arm.

Ophelia straightened up as the ball lifted away from the demon, "Thanks."

When chained cannonball reached Phinegann's hands, he unwound the thokcha chain to free the bronze. Then the spiked ball shot back into his shoulder of his artificial arm and the steel 'skin' closed around it.

Once the bronze weapon was stowed away, the half-ogre guided the iron chain back into the hollow center of the spheres and then slapped them together into one sphere again. It wasn't until then that Ophelia was able to see the unusual wavy pattern in the black metal.

Reaching down for the one that had restrained the demon, the mercenary saw the same pattern. It must have been made of whatever 'thokcha' was. Genevieve referred to it as 'iron from the heavens'. Did she mean meteorites?

To Ophelia it just looked like iron. Pulling it out from under the massive demon (being able to kick him during the process was pleasing, to say the least), she draped it back over the monster.

"He must be dead," Phinegann's baritone voice surprised Ophelia a little.

"He is not," Genevieve said as she stepped up behind the former prison guard.

It appeared to Ophelia that the efreeti woman had come from the same direction Phinegann had. Looking around, there was no sign of Jonas and his horse, Andromeda. No twisted metal, no stray limbs, nothing to show that they had been there only minutes ago.

"Are the knight and his horse okay?" Ophelia inquired.

"Paladin of the Order of Stewart," Genevieve corrected, "I carried him and his steed, Andromeda to the cave. They are recovering there."

The human woman nodded, "So why can't big boy here be dead after taking a thokcha ball to the head?"

"Because he is efreeti," the demon woman shrugged as if it were obvious.

Phinegann stared back at Genevieve. He didn't ask for an explanation.

Neither did Ophelia. She was curious to see what kind of dynamic this monster had with the rest of the newly arrived group. Phinegann, on the other hand, merely waited until she felt she had to share her reasons.

Genevieve sighed and relented, "The rakshasas are the lowest of our kind. Many were killed this day. Congratulations."

"But my rank of demon is different," she continued, "We do not *die* as you do. Our meat may be spoiled on this plane, but *we* are returned to Nova Prime. Of the three efreeti met on the battlefield, I banished two back to our home, but thanks to an... eclectic mixture of enchantments in her arrows, the cleric elf successfully slayed the last."

"Appelonia?" the skepticism Phinegann's voice was obvious.

Ophelia turned to the orc, "Doesn't she still use those dulled arrows?"

Phinegann nodded.

"Then how did she–?" Ophelia held up her hands to stop herself mid-sentence, "You know what? I'll just ask her. Is she back at the cave with Jonas?"

"No," Genevieve answered, "Illyria had just landed when I left after him," she motioned to the orc, "That left Jonas, Bronwyn, and her father with the gnome."

"Jin's missing, too?" Ophelia cursed, "Okay, Phinegann, why don't you two go find Appelonia. Last time I saw her she was with the Bunny Barbarian," she pointed in the direction she last saw the duo, "I'll look around for the monk."

"I don't need her," Phinegann pointed at the efreeti woman, who merely stared back.

Ophelia groaned, "Fine. Genevieve, I believe Appelonia had her horse here. Would you kindly go and find Bommer. And bring him back if he's alive."

"You are not my Master," the demon objected.

"Do you really think he'd not want you to do this?" the mercenary scowled at the efreeti.

"Very well." Genevieve pouted and marched off.

"I'm willing to bet that Apple's going to need help getting the Yo Bunpy back into the cave," Ophelia said to Phinegann, "They do have a history of taking as much damage as they hand out."

The orc nodded in agreement at that. Then he started in the direction Ophelia pointed.

"Now, if I were a monk with a baby, where would I be?" she asked.

Havarti answered, "If I failed to protect the child, perhaps running as far and as fast as I can to avoid your wrath?"

"I doubt he failed," Opheila responded, "You saw what he did with that cloak of his."

Havarti harumphed, "Perhaps he did something along those lines to avoid the shrapnel from the cannon fire?"

"You're probably onto something there," Ophelia spun around where she stood, "He was standing over there. The cannonballs hit over there," she pointed at the still body of Nikojunakalium, "so he probably ran this way."

She walked in that direction. The mercenary didn't have to go far before she saw a pair of wiggling feet sticking out of a pile of gray cloth.

The pile was only about as big around as the trees still standing nearby. It should not have been able to hide the entire body of a fully grown man. Add to that there wasn't any noise coming from the baby, and Ophelia suddenly found herself worrying.

"Could he have actually stuffed himself into his own robes?" she wrapped a hand around one of the ankles of the monk.

"He did manage to make an entire rakshasa disappear," Havarti conjectured, "I worry what would happen if he put himself in the same place as the cat creature."

"Good point," Ophelia said as she pulled.

The legs of the man slid across the dirt, then his hips, then the brown shirt wrapped around his torso. Although the dust colored cloth started bunching up, exposing his chiseled abs.

Then little Juna slipped out from under the gray fabric, blowing a loud raspberry with a bubble of snot growing out of her nose. Jin's left arm was wrapped around the child's chest to keep her pressed against his torso.

Then the monk's head emerged, "I was starting to worry," the man chuckled, his right arm was still under his bundled up cloak, "Could you take her for me, please?"

Jin motioned to the baby. Ophelia lifted Juna, who took a deep breath as if she were about to cry. But she didn't.

"I told you that I would have to be careful," the man said as he slipped his other hand back under the cloak.

With a groan of effort, Jin Vega pulled and the dead form of the rakshasa slid out. The monk dumped the body on the dirt then grabbed his cloak. Giving it a quick whip to rid it of stray dust and twigs, he slipped the gray garment back over his shoulders.

"We should meet back up with everyone," the man suggested.

"We should," Ophelia nodded with a look of disgust on her face, "and we should also get someone to change this kid's diaper. I thought she looked like she was concentrating too hard."

Decades before…

THE DARKNESS DIDN'T hide much from Josie as she made her way through the crater. Sharp eyes. One of the few things she considered a benefit of being born part elf.

Josie scraped the tip of her bow along the small chunks of rock that filled the crater that had been a cave surrounded by rock less than an hour ago. As she figured it, she was roughly standing where Ophelia took off all her clothes. Right before she became that, as Lyan put it, Angel of Destruction.

A splash of red caught the ranger's eye. She pulled back the bow to get a clear view and crouched down where she'd been scraping at stray pebbles. Gripping the patch of color among the dull dust and rock, Josie pulled and that long leather coat that belonged to Ophelia emerged.

Giving it a few whips to clean the worst of the dust off, the woman gave it a quick inspection. The scabbard of the sword belonging to the mercenary was still inside. There were a few stray tears along the length of the coat but, it hung so loose on her that just getting it sized for the mercenary could simultaneously get it repaired. The right sleeve, though, was shredded. That was going to be a harder fix.

Next, she found Ophelia's boots and pants, again damaged but at least salvageable. Folken's spell, Ultima, must not have reached all the way back to the antechamber when the cave was still standing, otherwise Josie would have only found shredded strips of crimson leather and cloth rather than mostly intact garments.

If these were intact, what else could have survived the destruction of the cave? Or more to the point, who?

Josie's heart started pounding in her chest as the thought of 'Evil' Harbenigyr surviving occurred to her. The ranger draped the long coat and pants over her shoulder and turned for the area she roughly figured the original Harby had knocked his doppelganger unconscious.

It was much closer to the front of the antechamber, very near where the svartalfar sorcerer unleashed the spells. It wasn't surprising that there was no body, no bulge in the debris to hint where one could be buried. The way that Folken described how Ultima worked meant that he could very well have been shredded to pieces. Still, she was a tracker, a damn good one if she said so herself. She bent down to search for any sign of the elf, at least any of his remains.

There was a faint scent of copper in the air. Someone had been bleeding. Josie had to squint to look hard but she caught the sight of little droplets of blood, drying to the greenish brown tint common to elf scabs.

She bit down on her lower lip when she realized that the drops didn't stay in this one spot. At first, there was a spread in all directions. That must have been when he was initially struck by Ultima. Even the blood flowing out of him was struck and turned into little, easy to miss droplets when they hit the ground.

Josie followed the trail up to the edge of the crater. There were a pair of bloody hand prints where he pulled himself up and out. Peeking out to the landscape beyond, the trail headed toward the forest about a quarter mile away.

Up to the treeline was clear and there wasn't any unconscious or dead cleric laying on the ground. How could he have survived such a... thorough shredding? There was no mistaking it, Harbenigyr's doppelganger lived.

Not only lived but escaped. 'Evil' Harbenigyr was surely going to come back into their lives someday. Josie felt the dread of such an idea, truly, but why did she also feel a trace, a hint of... was it excitement?

The doppelganger elf wasn't one to let betrayal go unpunished, which led Josie to her next search. Where was the body of the Josie that Vulcan had killed?

Harby mentioned that he couldn't save her. Things were so chaotic when the ranger and the cleric were reunited that she didn't get a chance to see her twin. It was only right that she somehow pay her respects.

Unlike 'Evil' Harbenigyr's trail of blood, the ranger couldn't find anything like that in the area where she last saw the other Josie. That was even closer to where Ultima was activated. And, as Harby swore, she was dead, unlike the doppelganger of the cleric. Perhaps she and any trace of her body had been simply eradicated?

Josie swore to herself that she wouldn't be forgotten. Anyone who had lived, no matter for how long or short of a time, deserved some remembrance for being here. Josie promised herself to be that remembrance. Her life would start completely anew. Here and now.

The first change? She would no longer call herself 'alphan'. It literally meant 'half-elf' but the way many full-blooded ones used it was meant to make those like Josie feel inferior. She wasn't and never would be again.

The red haired ranger marched out of the crater. The destroyed tent wasn't far. It appeared that everyone had gathered around there in the time she took to search the remains of the cave.

The group sat around the fire pit that had been in the middle of the tent when it stood. Someone had restarted the fire. Folken sat on a dented, welded metal chair beside Ophelia sat on the ground closest to where Josie approached. Their backs were to the ranger.

She had not actually seen the other woman's runes before then. Not counting when they were surrounded by the new ones worn by that transformed form of hers. In her normal shape, they covered a large portion of her back, all the way from between her shoulder blades to the small of her back. Josie couldn't help but wonder if getting them had hurt.

Ophelia jumped in surprise when the ranger draped her long coat over her bare shoulders. Then Josie dropped her torn pants and boots of the ground beside her.

"Sweet Juna, you are a quiet!" the mercenary gasped, "Even Harvarti didn't notice you coming."

Ophelia motioned to the sword standing between her spread legs with its tip in the ground. Not a very lady-like position for Ophelia to sit in, even on a felled log (part of the posts that held the tent up?). But she never claimed to be one, did she?

Across from them sat Harbenigyr, who glared at Folken until he saw Josie. Then he turned sheepish.

Ophelia was sitting upright. That meant that Folken must have broken his word and made the mercenary blink. While the cleric was upset, and reasonably so, with the sorcerer, Folken would undoubtedly have responded with 'it worked'.

Next to the cleric was the Bunny Barbarian. Both her arms and legs were completely wrapped in bandages, surely from the stores of the Harby's pouches. The wounds on her torso had ointments of various colors applied on top of them. Apparently Harby ran out of clean cloth.

Lyan stared at the ranger, "Which one are you?" she asked.

"Come again?" Josie's eyebrows pressed together.

"Which Josie are you?" the heavily muscled woman said, "The original or the doppelganger?"

"I'm the only Josie Swythchild, Lyan." the ranger shrugged.

"Because one died in front of us," the barbarian nodded back, "One was our ally, the other our enemy. Which are you?"

"Josie's doppelganger wasn't our enemy," Harby interrupted, "in fact, she was helping the real Josie and me escape when Vulcan got his hands on Meteorend."

"And which one were you?" Lyan pointed the stiff piece of pemmican in her hand at the ranger.

"Would you believe me if I told you I was the original?" Josie chuckled, "Or would you think I was the doppelganger trying to take her place?"

The fur wrapped warrior sat silently after that, her mouth wide open for a long moment. Then she let out a heavy grunt and bit into the piece of dried meat.

"Is Hero okay?" Josie turned her attention to Harbenigyr as she stepped around the fire pit.

The cleric looked behind him as the bard was sleeping only a couple of yards away. She was human again. Lyan had lifted the post that pinned her down off of the petite woman.

She had also wrapped a blanket of think pink fur around Hero. If the fire wasn't enough to keep the bard warm, that surely would be.

The Bunny Barbarian had made a trip to their steeds to retrieve some supplies. Josie didn't realize that Lyan had a blanket in her pack at all.

"After we got her head and entrails…" he struggled to find the best way to describe what happened, "back in, she was so upset, begging all of us to forgive her. She was worrying that she had killed one of us, particularly when she didn't see you. She became so distraught and started crying. So I dosed a kerchief in sleeping powder and gave it to her under the pretense of comforting her."

"That's pretty conniving for a cleric," Josie giggled as she finally sat on the ground beside the elf.

"It is," Lyan agreed, eyeing them both out of the corner of her eye.

"Relax," Josie smirked, "I know for a fact that this is the real Harby."

"How can you?" the barbarian frowned.

The smile on the face of the ranger faded as she told them of the blood trail she found and how it led into the woods to the northeast.

"We should hunt him down and be done with him," Lyan spat.

"None of us are in any condition for another battle, Yo Bunpy," Folken finally spoke up, "Nor is the cleric's doppelganger in a position to trouble us at the moment. Our time would best be spent recuperating before we start back for Emerald City."

"We are not going to Riverbelt?" Lyan's head tilted.

"There is no need," the sorcerer replied, "Meteorend is gone. With the weapon of the de Junamend out of play, it would be best for us to return to our plans from before the unpleasantness overtook us."

"Does that mean that you'll be leaving us, Lyan?" Ophelia looked up from Havarti to the barbarian, "Going back to whatever mission you had before Meteorend brought to us?"

Lyan's brown eyes narrowed as she considered the mercenary's question. All was quiet in the makeshift camp until the massive woman nodded, coming to some kind of decision within herself.

"Among my people, I am called the Child of Prophecy," she said, "As such, I am expected to find and destroy the Great Evil before it can unmake Honua. That is why I have been traveling outside of the Land of the Long Toothed Rabbit. I am hunting."

"So why have you been doing it alone?" Ophelia responded, her fingers lightly dancing up and down the length of her sword's handle, "Don't the Yo Bunpy have hunting parties?"

Lyan chewed on the inside of her cheek before answering, "I thought, being the sole warrior foretold to destroy the Great Evil, I should do so alone. It would keep anyone else from coming under danger from the fiend when the confrontation comes."

"Or get you killed *before* it even comes," Ophelia said.

"After my experiences with you, I am inclined to agree," the Bunny Barbarian nodded, "So, if you will have me, I formally request an alliance with you and your party, Ophelia."

"Her party?" Folken arched a emerald eyebrow.

"She is surely the strongest fighter of your band," Lyan said, pointing her now empty hand from Harby, to Folken, then Josie and finally Hero, "Healers, magicians, rangers, and bards surely have their roles but, when battle comes, surely it is she that you turn to, yes?"

"Barbarian logic," Folken muttered.

Ophelia couldn't help but smile wide, "You're pretty strong yourself, Lyan. Are you going to be challenging me for leadership then? I presume the Yo Bunpy way is some kind of fight?"

"If we were to use the traditions of my people, yes." Lyan grinned, "But I do not wish to lead you. You will not have to worry about usurpation from me."

"That's a relief," Ophelia laughed, "Any objections from *my* party?"

Everyone shook their heads. All of them had amused smiles on their faces of various sizes, save for Folken. He didn't object or argue. He simply changed the subject.

"What do you know of this Great Evil, Yo Bunpy?" he asked, "How are you to recognize it when it rears its villainous head?"

"I'm not sure," Lyan confessed, her face turning in Ophelia's direction, "I was told I would know it when I saw it. Until that day, I am to be continuously diligent."

Decades later...

Appelonia wrapped her arms around the base of Bommer's neck, leaning into the horse and burying her face into his blue fur. It was a miracle that he got through the battle without a scratch. Again, it had nothing to do with anything the cleric did.

The stallion trotted into the cave just after Phinegann helped the cleric carry Tokki in. Bommer was still tied to a massive branch. He snapped it off the tree and dragged it with him to find Appelonia. The young woman kept apologizing to the horse again and again as she unwrapped the reins from the branch.

One by one, everyone else gathered around a fire that Jin Vega stoked to life. Bronwyn and her father tickled and teased the baby, little Juna, who kept trying to grab their fingers or the ends of their bandages. Phinegann aided Tokki, his helmet still somewhere on the field of battle, to a sitting position. Illyria was getting frustrated as she tried to find a 'glitch' that had developed in her wings.

Jonas, with help from Appelonia, had successfully splinted Andromeda's broken leg. Although, it took Genevieve's strength to remove the armor from the mare before the cleric could even treat the animal's injuries. While she wouldn't be running any races for awhile, the horse would recover.

"Is there anything to eat?" Ophelia, sitting next to the reflecting paladin, asked, "I don't know about anyone else but I'm starved."

Bronwyn's father was the first to answer. "The bags in the back of the cave should still be there, assuming the demons didn't incinerate them with whatever portal they used to sneak in here."

The mercenary hopped to her feet and walked back. The leather sacks weren't even singed, each still tied closed. They were large, too, coming up to the woman's thigh. The Captain of the *Galleon* had prepared to stay here for a long time.

As she started to open one of the bags, Ophelia called back to the others, "Anyone else want anything? We have some jerky, some apples, a couple of carrot– blessed Juna!"

The woman jumped away from the bag. Everyone looked up from their own reflections that caused Ophelia to have an outburst like that.

A hand emerged from inside the now opened mouth of the bag Ophelia untied. It was followed by an unkempt brush of crimson hair. The person then stood up, the brown leather bag falling into empty folds around her feet.

She was wearing a magenta coat, the long sleeves falling to conceal her hands once they dropped to her sides, and lime green pants. It was Diomedes, the avatar (cleric!) of Ferekene.

"Hi!" she giggled.

"What is *she* doing here?" Phinegann snapped, jumping to his feet.

"She wasn't here!" Ophelia responded, "I was just looking for a blasted apple."

"I didn't want to miss my cue this time," Diomedes waddled past the mercenary toward the rest of the group, "It's time to get little Juna to safety."

"She *was* safe until you sent them after us," Ophelia insisted as she pointed at Appelonia and the others, "The only reason the efreeti got this close was because they had Meteorend!"

Illyria's face sank down between her thin shoulders as she tried to make herself even smaller. That only drew the avatar (cleric!) right to her. Diomedes proceeded to pinch the gnome's cheeks through the material of her long sleeves.

"Well, I forgot where I had hidden you," the insane woman said, "I do my job too well sometimes."

"No, because of you we almost had a literal hell overtake us all!" Phinegann growled.

Diomedes straightened up and stepped over to the orc. "Where's hell? I mean, I see a demon but she's one of the nice ones now, right?" she blew a kiss at Genevieve.

The efreeti woman, back in her human guise, looked confused by what was happening. Jonas started whispering a hurried explanation of the party's earlier encounter with the cleric of Ferekene.

Diomedes interrupted by running her fingers through Genevieve's tall black hair. No one even saw her move behind the demon.

"So shiny," the crazy cleric commented.

Genevieve turned and whipped a suddenly clawed hand back at Diomedes. But she was already not there anymore. She was again standing in front of Phinegann without having to walk back over.

"So, I'd say that everything ended just fine. Wouldn't you, Phin-phin?" she resumed her previous conversation with the orc.

Ophelia stepped up to the insane cleric, "Not exactly. The efreeti are going to need some time to regroup but Meteorend is still a threat," she pulled the black rock from the pocket of her shredded coat, "And now I can't stay and protect Juna because they would be willing to kill her to get to me regardless of the Mullah's plans."

"Yeah, I knew that was going to be a problem," Diomedes let her lower lip poke out into a pout... but only for about a second. Then she grinned again, "But that's why I'm here now. I'm the problem solver!"

There was a collective groan from everyone in the cave. Except from Appelonia. She pulled herself away from Bommer and addressed the oddly dressed woman.

"Why go about that ruse to make try and make me think I was the efreeti child?" she asked, "If you just wanted us to find Ophelia, why didn't you just ask us to do that in the first place? We're an Order that is devoted to helping and serving others."

Diomedes looked confused, "What Order?"

Appelonia's expression mirrored the other cleric's, "The Order of Kuan Yin."

"You're not a cleric of the Order of Kuan Yin," Diomedes said as if it was obvious.

"Yes I am," Appelonia looked around at the others in bewilderment, "I was supposed to be on my pilgrimage when you sprang all this on us."

The insane avatar (cleric!) shook her head, "But you have to be a part of her Order to go on a pilgrimage. You're not a cleric of Kuan Yin."

"I am!" Appelonia didn't mean to yell but it just … came out.

"Clerics of Kuan Yin don't kill things," Diomedes again spoke in a matter-of-fact way.

A vision of the demon Appelonia shot flashed across the mind's eye of the cleric. She didn't have an answer to what Diomedes said.

Tokki Yo Bunpy, though, rose to his feet and marched (with a pronounced limp) directly at the insane woman, "She only did so to save my life. Apple was out of the special arrows she usually used and only had access to mine. It isn't her fault! They were my arrows, my weapons. The responsibility for that monster's death his mine."

"Did you shoot them from your bow?" Diomedes asked the Bunny Barbarian.

The (former?) cleric of Kuan Yin knew that Tokki's code of honor, that of his people, demanded that he be honest. But doing so would be to admit Appelonia's guilt. So he did not answer.

"But, I was able to treat everyone's wounds," the words came weakly from the mouth of the young woman.

Diomedes bent forward, resting her head on Tokki's shoulder as her kaleidoscope colored eyes stared at Appelonia, "Most if it was your knowledge of medicine. Kuan Yin can't take that from you. The blessings you did give, they were for the sake of those who fought to keep hell from encroaching on this plane. Not yours."

Appelonia turned away from the avatar (cleric!) of Ferekene, not wanting to look into those eyes any longer. She had to be sure. This could have just been another lie from Diomedes.

So Appelonia silently prayed. There was a... blankness that had never been there before. Not since she took the oaths to become a neophyte within the Order of Kuan Yin. The goddess was truly not with her anymore.

She let out gasp of shock, falling to her knees at the revelation. No matter who asked her if she was okay or what was wrong, Apple didn't answer. Her black eyes only stared straight ahead.

Ophelia snatched Diomedes up by the collar and pulled the crazy woman close, "What did you do to her?" she growled.

"Nothing!" Diomedes insisted, "And she's not being punished. The young lady's still perfectly healthy. She's just not allowed to use the powers bestowed by the goddess because she broke one of the promises to be able to do it. She's just a normal person now."

Appelonia blinked.

"But being a cleric is all she's ever wanted to be!" the free hand of the mercenary reached for the handle of her bastard sword, "If you hadn't sent her on this pointless venture, she wouldn't be in this predicament now!"

Apple's hand wrapped around Ophelia's, keeping her from drawing Havarti, "Don't, Ophelia. As much as it hurts to say, she's right. She's not to blame. I am."

"What kind of goddess would banish one of her own for not letting someone else die?" Tokki demanded.

Diomedes was again leaning on the shoulder of the Bunny Barbarian. If he wasn't on the verge of falling over already, he would have shrugged her off, or punched her, or something.

"She's hardly banished," she answered, "Dianmeyer is still her home and she is still welcome there, just like her mommy."

"Tokki, it's okay," Appelonia shooed Diomedes away so that the former cleric could wrap her hands around his bandaged shoulders, "Really. Lyan Yo Bunpy said something that I didn't really get until now. She said: 'Sometimes, we have to give up what we want to do in order to do what's right'."

"But you cannot trust the word of the False One–" the Bunny Barbarian started to protest.

"Is that what you all are calling her now?" Ophelia looked even more unhappy, "I've known Lyan for a long time and I can tell you one thing as absolute truth. Lyan Yo Bunpy is the most honorable of any warrior I've ever met. Not even any Light Bringer comes close."

"But–" his protest had lost much of its former force.

"Later, Tokki," Appelonia kissed his forehead softly, "We still have to hear why Diomedes is really here now."

Phinegann made his presence felt again. He stomped up to Diomedes, blocking her view of the baby.

"Explain. Now," he commanded.

"I told you," Diomedes smiled wide again, "It's time to take little Juna to safety!"

"Where can you take her? As long as this exists," Ophelia held up Meteorend, "Efreeti will be able to track her down eventually."

"If we kept her here, that's true," the crazy woman nodded, and kept nodding, and nodded some more before speaking again, "That's why I'm not keeping her here."

"They can find her in *all of* Honua," Phinegann grumbled, "Nowhere is truly safe."

"Nowhere is absolutely not safe!" Diomedes frowned up at the orc, "There's not even air in nowhere! She'd suffocate! I'm not taking her to nowhere, I'm taking her to there."

The insane cleric didn't point in any direction. Everyone looked all around and couldn't see anything that would indicate any kind of destination.

Diomedes skipped over to Bronwyn and held out her arms, "Gimme, please?"

Bronwyn looked over at her father apprehensively. He looked from the baby in his daughter's arms and up to the avatar (cleric!) of Ferekene.

"I think you have to," he said, "There's no way we can really stop her anyway."

Phinegann growled, the memory of her arm becoming a tree branch when he tried to attack Diomedes coming to mind. Unfortunately, the pirate's words rang true.

So Bronwyn carefully handed little Juna to the insane cleric. Diomedes made little kissing noises at the baby and Juna immediately started to giggle in her arms.

The avatar (cleric!) of Ferekene walked back over to Ophelia, as attentive to the little girl as a mother making her way through a crowd, "I'll take Meteorend, too," she said without looking up at the mercenary.

"What? No! Keeping her and the rock in the same place is fool–" Ophelia held her hand up to find it already empty.

Diomedes rested the black rock on top of the baby. Little Juna wrapped her arms around Meteorend and it started to glow faint... pink. Not orange.

Genevieve gasped at the sight. When Jonas looked at her, the efreeti woman shook her head and stared straight at the ground.

"So where are you taking her then?" Ophelia inquired of the cleric, "Where could you possibly go that the efreeti can't track you? Where's *there*?"

"Did I say there?" Diomedes cocked an eyebrow, "I meant I'm taking her to Heaven."

"What?" Appelonia gasped in horror, "You're going to kill her?"

"Huh?" the insane cleric said, "You don't have to be dead to go to Heaven. Just good. And who's gooder than a baby?"

Diomedes started making a a bunch of silly sounding noises as she tickled the little girl. Juna laughed and giggled as she played with the colorful cleric.

"But, can she have a life of her own in heaven?" Appelonia asked, "I thought that it was supposed to be where you go to rest *after* your life here? Juna hasn't even had time to have one yet."

"Oh, Juna's has such a life ahead of her," Diomedes replied, "I'm only taking her to Heaven until I can get her to then."

Phinegann groaned, rubbing his at his temples with his flesh hand.

"I told you that time works differently in other planes, right?" the insane cleric said, "Time in Nova Prime goes faster than here. In Heaven, time goes backwards."

"Huh?" Appelonia was with Phin on this one.

"Why do you think divine interventions always seem to happen only in the nick of time? It's the earliest *they* can get involved!" Diomedes giggled, "Or when the gods don't do anything at all and things end up working out well afterwards? It's because they already know what happens!"

"I... never thought of that," the former cleric of Kuan Yin said.

A portal of golden light opened behind the colorful cleric, "I'll take her to Heaven for a while, then give her a good home before the efreeti know to even be looking for her," Diomedes explained as she stepped back.

Looking into the portal, Appelonia couldn't see anything on the other side but a feeling warmth, of calm washed through the whole cave when the portal opened. Wherever the child was going, it was peaceful.

"And I never lied to you, Appelonia," the cleric of Ferekene said, "You are of a line of the efreeti, just as your father is. But don't think that makes any part of you evil. As with any other bloodline, it is only the smallest part of who you are."

The red haired elf looked from Tokki, to Phinegann, then to Ophelia. All of them looked as confused as she did.

Diomedes suddenly looked a little anxious, "You know, efreeti do have awfully long memories. I may have to go back centuries, maybe even over a millennium to get Juna where she needs to go."

The colorful cleric muttered other things but they were more and more muffled as the portal closed. When the light was gone, that feeling of peace lingered over everyone.

Until Genevieve spat a vile curse, "We brought this on ourselves?"

"What are you talking about?" Jonas shrugged at the demon in human disguise.

"The plan of the Mullah," Genevieve said, "He wanted to use the blood of an impure offspring, his words not mine, to open a portal to Honua and share the pain we feel with mortals."

"What does that have to do with the baby?" Jin Vega blinked and looked away from where the portal had been.

"The one who took the child. Diomedes? She also gave Juna the heart of the efreeti," the demon started to explain, "When that child embraced Meteorend, I felt as if I was... reassembled for a moment. That baby is the Juna of yore who turned the Mullah from one to many, into our severed parts. She was the one for whom our mostly holy word came, so we would never forget who brought us our shame."

"Wait a minute," Jonas looked from Genevieve over to Appelonia, "The savior of Honua. Her name was Juna, right? Wasn't one of the feats she performed dispersing a demon that sought to enslave all species of humanity?"

Appelonia nodded, "The story never actually named the demon, though. Just described it as red, horned and... Oh."

"We just saved the person who turned Honua into a bastion against the darkness for all mortals?" Shock washed over the face of Jonas the Shepherd.

The feeling spread quickly to Appelonia, Tokki, Jin Vega, and Illyria, as well. Phinegann may have shared the feeling with the rest of the party, but he did not show it outwardly.

"But what was that cockatrice droppings about Appelonia being of an efreeti line?" Genevieve again interrupted the party's reflections, "The de Junamend only birthed half-demons. She is not half-breed," the efreeti woman motioned to the former cleric.

"Time works slower for efreeti but it still moves forward," Jin tugged at his beard thoughtfully. "You said it back in Maid Gulch, Appelonia. What if an efreeti's seed needed more time to dilute into the mortal bloodline?"

"Are you saying that I'm somehow related to Savior of Honua?" Apple didn't realize that she almost fainted until Tokki's arm was around her waist, holding her upright.

"Truly, my dear, you have nothing to feel guilt over now," the poncy voice of Havarti piped up from Ophelia's shoulder.

"What is he talking about?" Appelonia patted the barbarian's shoulder thankfully as she pulled herself away.

"You couldn't have just said that to me telepathically?" the woman in the shredded red coat scoffed at the sword, "It happened back when you were only five or six, Apple. It was also the reason Diomedes recruited me to protect Juna in the first place..."

WHEN OPHELIA WAS CAPTURED
BY THE XAVIOUR TRIBE OF SVARTALFAR...

THERE WAS A bright light. Ophelia was sure that, this time, she would know what it was like to die. That didn't last long and, when the light faded away, all that was left was a vision that Ophelia thought she would never see again. Or was it hoped she'd never see again?

Doctor Efreeti stood still, waiting. He was like a statue save for the tweed cloak he always wore. It billowed and waved despite there being no breeze to cause it to do so.

Ophelia found herself once again in his 'lair'. It was a seemingly endless room of darkness. There were no walls or a ceiling. That made the window that just... hanged in the air a short distance from the skeleton thin man all the more odd. On top of that, the window did not appear to show the passage of time. Whether it was light or day, sunny or storming, was all dependent on the mood of Doctor Efreeti.

The only piece of actual furniture was a marble table just big enough for a person to lay on. Technically, it was where Ophelia was born.

At least, it was the first thing she remembered seeing after Doctor Efreeti tattooed the violet runes into her back and erased her memories of her entire life before. Despite the growing dread rushing through her entire body, Ophelia continued walking toward it. Toward him.

That was because of the one who brought her to this place. The obsidian skinned svartalfar woman marching half a pace behind Ophelia. Ophelia hadn't even seen her yet, just flashes of a dark-skinned hand holding a purple sphere out of the corner of her eye.

"Mistress Stohbease," Doctor Efreeti's first acknowledgment of either woman's presence came with a shallow bow, "I see the soul orb performed its function admirably."

"It brought her to me just as you said it would, Efreeti." a gravelly voice that sounded more sultry than regal, at least to the mercenary, came from the svartalfar woman, "But you and I do need to discuss an interesting side effect."

Doctor Efreeti did not have any eyebrows, otherwise, one would have lifted behind the thick round lenses he wore on his face, "Please, do tell."

This Stohbease stepped around Ophelia and the mercenary felt her legs come to a stop under her. She hadn't told them to do so. All Ophelia could do was stand and watch the two other beings converse.

"I pulled Ophelia away from the blast at the last moment as you recommended. All of her friends believe she died," the svartalfar flipped her long silver hair back behind her shoulders, "When she appeared before me, however, this odd rock appeared in my other hand."

Stohbease held up the purple orb in her right hand, and then the black stone known as Meteorend in her left. Ophelia felt surprise run through her like a stampede but her body didn't react in any way.

Efreeti bent down to take a closer look at Meteorend, his face only inches from the black rock. Not to mention the hand of the subterranean elf and she did not look happy to have him so close.

"You said that I would only need Ophelia's soul orb to control her, Efreeti." the woman who was the same color as unburned coal scowled, "I do not appreciate unexpected variables appearing without notice."

"In order to be unexpected, dearie, by definition they must appear without notice," Doctor Efreeti chuckled as he straightened up, "But this is not unexpected. Rather it is a boon which works to our mutual advantage."

Stohbease wrapped her fingers around Meteorend and pulled it in close to her chest, "And how is that? Beyond your giving me Ophelia, body and soul, as a slave to my will?"

"That petrified relic is the most treasured of a mutual irritant of ours. As well as their most feared," the thin man answered, "The de Junamend wielded it for centuries to keep their foes at bay."

"This?" the dark-skinned woman looked down at the rock skeptically, "They lost it years ago."

Doctor Efreeti nodded, "When Ophelia killed their Elder. You see, Meteorend relinquishes ownership to whomever defeats the previous owner, appearing in the grasp of the mortal at its earliest convenience."

"Then why had Ophelia not used it in all that time?" Stohbease turned to look back at the still mercenary, "Surely a woman such as her would have used such power at the appearance of the earliest inconvenience."

The unnaturally thin man smiled so wide it looked as if he head would split in two halves, "That is due to one key word in what I just said. *Mortal*."

The dark-skinned woman stared back blankly.

The thin man sighed, "The reason Meteorend hasn't appeared before now is because it needed a complete soul to wield it. So it laid within the energy of the soul orb, awaiting the touch of a being that lives a normal life span."

"Are you saying that Ophelia isn't mortal?" Stohbease scoffed.

"The proof is in your very hand," Doctor Efreeti reached out and tapped the violet soul orb, "As long as you possess this, a fragment of Ophelia's very soul, her will is your will. She cannot die by the hand of any assassin or magick your rivals could wield against you as long as this exists and, I can assure you, it is indestructible.

As I told you earlier, Ophelia is your key to your ascension to the throne of the Xaviour Tribe."

"Which is of no advantage to your master in the Al Razheem," the silver haired woman replied with sarcasm thick in her voice.

"General Kitanah approved of our union, Stohbease," he nodded in response, "You have known from the start that there was to be a debt to my, what did you call her? My liege? When you have renewed the... strained relationship between your people and those under the thrall of Kitanah, it will be repaid."

"And what is to keep me from sending my unkillable assassin after your precious General, or you for that matter?" Stohbease rolled the perfectly round orb between her fingers.

A crack of thunder came from the curtain of gray that suddenly filled the space outside the window. Rain pelted the panes of a window that only moments ago, let in glowing sunlight.

Efreeti looked amused as he leaned back against the edge of the marble table, "While you may hold a piece of Ophelia's very soul in your hand, I am Ophelia's very creator. And it would not do to have a creation that could turn on the one who made it. Would it?"

Ophelia crept up behind the obsidian woman. With a quick lunge, she wrapped her bare arm around the svartalfar's neck.

Stohbease sputtered and clawed at Ophelia's arm as air was suddenly denied her. The mercenary pulled the other woman off her feet so she could not find any leverage to try and escape.

Doctor Efreeti pushed himself away from the table and strode toward the formerly arrogant svartalfar woman. He crouched down in front of her, the wide smile still threatening to split his face expose his skull to the open air.

"Remember that you came to us for aid, child," he said, "Which we are more than willing to provide. As loyal as Ophelia is to me, she will be to you. Not just in matters of violence, either. She can serve you in whatever manner you deem fit."

To demonstrate, the mercenary immediately let Stohbease have use of her throat again. As the svartalfar woman was catching her breath, Ophelia leaned into her and gave the other woman a deep, passionate kiss.

Stohbease instinctively enjoyed the sensation for a moment before she fully realized what was happening. Then she shoved Ophelia away and scrambled back up to her feet.

"That was... presumptuous of you, Doctor," she muttered as she worked to straighten up her robes that denoted her rank as a wizard within the Xaviour Tribe.

The sun once again poured into the room. The panes that hung in the middle of the air, unattached to anything, showed no sign that they had held back a storm only seconds ago.

"Hardly," the thin man giggled, "I saw how you were watching Ophelia as you marched in here with her. Without that obstructive red coat, she is... easy to watch."

"You did mention that she would have a coat," the silver haired woman said as if she were confirming an earlier reminder, "along with a sword. But she came to me like this. She had neither."

"Unimportant," Doctor Efreeti waved a dismissive hand, "It simply means that your control will be that much more complete since you will not have to contend with another voice in your servant's ear coming from her previous weapon of choice."

"I like the sound of complete control," Stohbease smirked, then turned and ran the cold surface of Ophelia's soul orb along the edge of her slave's jaw, "I will return to my lands and start my ascension immediately."

"Before you depart, Stohbease," the still crouched thin man pointed at the black rock that the svartalfar dropped while she was struggling to breathe, "May I make use of this? While your disagreements with the de Junamend are political, mine are more of a... personal nature. With this, I can eliminate them all from either of our concerns."

Stohbease nodded, "One less thing for me to take care of. It will make this go all the quicker."

The svartalfar swatted Ophelia on the backside and the mercenary turned and started for the lone door. Again, Stohbease took a moment to appreciate the view before returning her attention to the thin man in the tweed cloak.

"But I would like it back when you are done," she said, "I would very much enjoy a trophy to remember those I had a part in vanquishing."

"Of course, dearie." Doctor Efreeti scooped the rock up from the floor and it started to crackle with a malevolent orange light, "Of course."

CHAPTER FIFTEEN

OPHELIA'S SELF-INTERROGATION:

*"Who do you need to convince that you're a decent person?"
I asked.*

"Hmm? You're still here?" Ophelia responded.

"Answer, please," I said.

*"I can't prove something like that," Ophelia answered, "What I
can do, though, is right the wrongs that I've let fester for far too long..."*

Years before...

LYAN YO BUNPY, unlike the rest of the party, did not ride a steed.
Still, she did not fall behind as they made their way to Emerald City.

Again they followed Josie cross country rather than take
the roads. Not out of any need to stay hidden but at the insistence of the magician, Folken. He wanted to be back 'home' as
quickly as possible.

But the Bunny Barbarian was uneasy. Through their travels,
she had found herself drawn more and more to Ophelia's company.

The woman was a kindred spirit. A warrior despite her disadvantage in gender.

Now, though, that could prove to be a liability. Throughout the trek back to Emerald City, Ophelia kept to herself, mostly speaking to her sword. That is, until they made camp. Then she always came to speak with Lyan, both Ophelia and Havarti appeared to enjoy the company of the barbarian.

Lyan Yo Bunpy could not help forgetting her troubles when they were together. While they were both warriors, both Lyan and Ophelia lived their lives so differently. From outside the group, one would assume that Ophelia lived carelessly. She drank to well more than her fill. The mercenary would often pick fights and, even more often, lay with any man who caught her eye. The Bunny Barbarian had to admit to favoring some of the woman's tales of those particular conquests.

But, once the night was done and they adjourned to their separate sleeping arrangements, Lyan's worry would again return to gnaw at her. Every night, before sleep claimed her, the barbarian would decide to distance herself from Ophelia.

Then the next day, she would almost immediately fall back into the habits of conversing and fellow-shipping with the woman again. It came down to the point that Lyan knew she needed to speak with with magician. She needed his help, as loathed as the warrior of the Yo Bunpy Tribe to admit it.

She couldn't do it when they stopped for the evening. That was Lyan's time to spend with Ophelia. Undoing the previous night's choice every time. The Bunny Barbarian knew it would happen again so she had to have a word with the magician during the day.

Lyan finally decided to act on the day before reaching the city Folken called home. It was early in the afternoon. They still had hours of walking before they laid out camp one last night. Ophelia would be busy conversing with Havarti.

The healer, Harbenigyr could barely pull himself away from the side of the ranger. Josie, to her credit, seemed to truly enjoy his company now. The barbarian couldn't decide if it was proof that she was the doppelganger or not, so she had to accept that, since she was truly the only Josie left, she was the true one.

Hero continuously played songs to keep the party's energy up. Lyan had to admit that she was a talented musician and a quick study. The barbarian taught her several songs of her people. Of course, Lyan only knew the vocals but Hero was able to play serviceable chords with the words almost immediately.

She was involved with a long arrangement at the moment. If Lyan was going to pull the magician aside to have words, now would be the best opportunity to do so without drawing much attention.

The one last piece that worked in the favor of the Bunny Barbarian was that Folken had taken to riding at the back of the group, keeping to himself. Until today, Lyan kept a respectful distance.

Until the Yo Bunpy stopped marching and waited. When the green haired man was beside Lyan, the barbarian kept pace beside the magician.

"Folken," the Yo Bunpy warrior announced up to him, "we will have words. Now."

The pale man rolled his violet eyes as he sighed. He did, however, relent to her wishes.

Lyan pointed to a patch of rocks a short distance away. They could speak there for a few minutes and, if all went well, gallop to catch up with the group before they even noticed they were gone.

Once they reached the area Lyan indicated, Folken leaned forward in his saddle to make it so his head was only about a foot or so above the barbarian, "What is it you want, Yo Bunpy?"

It was harder to get started than the Bunny Barbarian thought it would be. Still, it had to be done so Lyan finally found the words.

"You asked me before about the Great Evil. How I would recognize it."

The albino man nodded.

"I believe I have," Lyan continued, "I believe that Ophelia is that Great Evil."

Folken raised an angled eyebrow, "You are awfully friendly with the very thing you believe is meant to destroy all of Honua."

"I do not believe it is of her own will," the barbarian retorted, "I know that the healer will not accept the real danger that the woman represents. And none of the others could kill Ophelia even if they wished to do so."

"But you believe you can," the man interjected, "and, in fact, should."

"I must accept that it is very real possibility," Lyan admitted, "And I also admit, as she has the aid of some magician called Doctor Efreeti, I must conscript assistance from a magic user of my own."

"I am hardly *one of your own*, Yo Bunpy," Folken refused the label, "And you've hardly convinced me that Ophelia is any threat beyond anyone else whose been enchanted to do battle for some incorporeal force, malevolent or benign."

"Did you not see what she did back in the camp of the de Juanmend?" the barbarian frowned.

"I am capable of destroying a small mountain, Lyan Yo Bunpy," the magician replied, "Am I an aspect of your Great Evil as well?"

"It is not just *what* she did, but how she did so," Lyan sighed, "You saw the color of her magicks?"

Folken nodded.

"Of all the colors the Great Chromatic Rabbit bathed this world, there is only one that is forbidden from us. It is the hue of the Great Evil. It is to wield the very light of that spectrum as its weapon," the Bunny Barbarian felt that dread well up within her again, "Ophelia wielded that very color as the Angel of Destruction. Her light was pure purple."

"I wear purple," the man said, "My eyes are also purple. Again, how am I not an aspect of this Great Evil, too?"

"I've not seen you wield the purple light as she did," Lyan answered, "And while I find your choice of attire… ill-advised, there is more than purple in it. Nor is any of your purple upon you or about you made of light.

Ophelia's power was only that purple," the Bunny Barbarian shook her head, "I must be prepared to kill her if she is overtaken by that destructive force again. At the very least to save her soul."

"So your ultimate act of altruism is to be murder?" the fingers of Folken's gloved hand opened and closed one after another, back and forth as he thought quietly, "What is it you would have me do for you?"

"The magician controlling Ophelia undoubtedly has enchantments and magicks to protect her," Lyan answered, "Like her blinking even in her current state. What I need from you are countermeasures to any kind of defensive measures so that I may strike the lethal blow."

"With all the magicks and energies involved, you still insist on performing the killing strike yourself?" the man straightened up in his saddle, "Commendable, Yo Bunpy. Very well, I will study Ophelia's powers and devise counter agents. If and when the time comes to use them, we will destroy the physical form of what you have deemed the Angel of Destruction."

"The Great Evil," the barbarian corrected.

"The Great Evil," Folken repeated.

Decades later...

AS THE PARTY waited for the *Galleon* to finally place its new gangplank onto the small pier, Appelonia was shocked to see the white robes and red hair of her parents standing on deck and leaning against the rails.

The moment the board allowing people to move to and from the ship touched, Harbenigyr and Josie sprinted off of the ship. The ranger was the first to reach their daughter, her bare arms wrapping tight around Appelonia.

The young woman almost wished that she had kept the chainmail on, her mother squeezed her so tightly. Almost.

"Oh, sweetie, we were so worried about you!" Josie's voice was muffled as she spoke into her daughter's shoulder.

Apple felt her insides tighten up and start to quake, "It's okay, Mom. I'm okay," she finally choked out.

"You don't have to lie to us," her father wrapped an arm around his daughter's shoulders as he softly kissed Appelonia's temple, "Kuan Yin already told me what happened."

And Appelonia collapsed. She couldn't see. She sobbed so hard, she couldn't talk.

Harby and Josie both held their little girl up. Apple should have realized that she couldn't keep her shame a secret, even for just a short while.

Even as the former cleric of Kuan Yin descended into a blubbering mess, work progressed to load supplies, people, and even Andromeda and Bommer onto the ship. Apple's parents simply held her, stroking her hair and lightly kissing her face until she finally calmed down enough to pull herself away.

She took a clean rag offered by her father, wiped her eyes dry, and blew her nose, "I'm sorry."

"For what?" Harbenigyr asked.

"I can't be a cleric of Kuan Yin now," Apple's lower lip trembled, "I failed at everything."

"You've always been too hard on yourself, sweetie," Josie caressed her daughter's cheek, "You get that from your father."

Harby took a split second to look insulted but then almost immediately shrugged and nodded, "Not being a cleric doesn't mean you failed, Apple. You didn't do anything wrong, you just haven't found the code to live your own life by yet."

The young woman blinked as she looked at her father, "You mean you're not disappointed?"

"In you?" he looked genuinely shocked at the idea, "Never!"

A fresh bout of tears spilled from the girl as she pulled her parents in tight. After holding them for a long, long time, Appelonia finally let them loose.

"Thank you," she sniffled, then a thought occurred to her, "How did you get here so fast? I didn't become disfellowshipped until this morning."

"We've been looking for you since you disappeared from Maid Gulch," Josie answered.

"That was only two days ago," Appelonia frowned, "You can't get word from there to Dianmeyer and then get here in that amount of time."

"Two days?" the girl's mother looked at Harby in genuine confusion before turning back to Apple, "Sweetie, that was over three months ago."

"What?" Appelonia jumped.

"It was," her father assured her, "We've been searching for you all that time. Then Diomedes came us about a week ago. She acted as if we never met before. We had the argument about whether she could be called a cleric and everything, just as she said. But the important thing she ended up telling us was about the *Galleon*. When she said it would take us to you, we rushed to Loch Aeris, jumped on board to came to find you!"

"Then you saw the fight?" Apple asked.

Both Josie and Harbenigyr nodded.

"It was the hardest thing not jump off the ship and swim ashore," her mother confessed.

"I had to keep telling her that we couldn't reach you any faster on foot," Harby added, "Still, we felt so... powerless not being able to get to you before now."

Jonas stepped up behind Appelonia's parents, flanked by Genevieve in her human guise, "We have loaded up the horses. We're ready to get underway when you are."

"Thank you," Josie answered barely looking at the Shepherd before waving a hand dismissively.

Apple couldn't help but scowl at her mother, "Mom, Dad, could you excuse me and Jonas for a second?"

"What?" Both her parents asked.

"I just want to talk for a minute, if that's okay," the words were directed to the paladin as much as the cleric and ranger.

Jonas nodded, "Genevieve, could you please escort Apple's parents onto the *Galleon* and make sure their comfortable?"

The woman in the short white dress looked back and forth from the man still wearing his armor, to the former cleric, and back before reluctantly nodding, "Yes, Master."

"Master?" Josie cocked an eyebrow.

Jonas' cheeks flushed bright pink, "It's a long story."

Appelonia's parents were taken back to the ship by the efreeti woman, a wary Josie staring down Jonas the entire way. A very self-conscious paladin waved back at them when they reached the deck. Only then did he turn to face the young woman.

"What did you need, Apple?" Jonas asked, clearing his throat.

She quickly gave her cheeks a quick slap, rubbing at her eyes to try and make them look at least a little less puffy. The woman knew she wasn't really going to have a chance to be alone with the man after they boarded the ship so this was their last real chance to talk.

Appelonia's pink tongue flicked over her suddenly dry lips. "I... was wondering what you were going to do once we got back to Dianmeyer."

The man tapped on his chin several times, "I can't really go anywhere until Andromeda's leg has healed," he shrugged.

The red haired woman felt herself jump but tried to keep it inside, "So you're going to be staying awhile?"

"Looks like," he nodded.

"Would you like to, um, do something when we're back in Dianmeyer?" she folded her arms behind her back just to keep them from fidgeting, "I know the town really well. I can show you some of the best things tourists never get around to finding."

The eyes of the paladin lingered on the woman long enough that Apple's mother wouldn't approve. Apple herself, however... Jonas rubbed at the back of his neck uneasily.

"I, I would love to," the man said, "you are a beautiful woman, Appelonia."

The butterflies in the former cleric's stomach took wing. She felt a wide smile start stretching her lips.

"But I can't," he gulped, "I mean, I shouldn't. It wouldn't be... proper."

The butterflies crashed and the corners of Appelonia's mouth dropped. "Proper? What do you mean? You don't take oaths of celibacy in the Order of Stewart, do you?"

"What?" his black eyebrows shot straight up at the question, "No, nothing like that."

"Then why?" the woman shrugged, "You just said that you find me attractive. I think you're handsome, too. Inside and out."

"I feel the same way about you, Apple," the paladin responded, "Inside and out. That's exactly why I can't right now."

The confusion on her face was exceptionally, tremendously obvious.

"You do remember that I'm literally bonded with a demon right now, right?" Jonas pointed back to the ship, "You've seen how jealous she's gotten when we just look in each other's direction. How do you think she would react if we tried to do... more?"

"You're worried about how Genevieve would react?" some of that jealously percolated inside of Appelonia at that moment.

"What she would do. At least partially," Jonas took a slow, deep breath. It came out in a shuddering gasp before he breathed in again to speak, "The rest of it has to do with whatever this... bond is doing to me."

"What are you talking about?" the woman's eyebrows pressed together.

"I'm worried," his gaze locked on the boards of the pier under his feet, "Ever since Genevieve and I were forced together. Every time I've made a wish I've been feeling like something inside me becomes... lessened."

"Lessened?" that jealously Appelonia felt was quickly turning to worry.

"It's like my, my control is becoming less, I don't know the best way to describe it, less solid?" he said, "As we've been going along I've been indulging more and more thoughts of a less *noble* nature."

"How do you mean *less noble*?" the red haired woman asked, wrapping a reassuring hand around his arm. "Like violent?"

He nodded, a look of shame crossing over his face, "It started with the idea of strangling Genevieve. I thought it was okay because of all the trouble she caused us. But then, I started thinking about the *indulgences* I could have with her. Then I started thinking about being with you."

"Thoughts aren't reality, Jonas," Appelonia said, "And it doesn't sound like all of them are bad. Just *ill-timed*."

"You don't understand," the man shook his head, "like when I walked up to you with your parents. I saw you crying, right?"

The woman nodded.

"I started thinking about whether your would cry like that if I *forced* myself on you, Appelonia," Jonas had a look of horror on his face as he confessed, "And I didn't dislike the idea outright. It took real concentration to get it out of my head."

A shiver ran down the former cleric's spine. For the first time, she felt a tinge of fear being alone with the paladin. But she forced herself to stay calm. He was being honest and he was worried about his behavior.

She may not be a cleric of Kuan Yin anymore but that didn't mean that she couldn't help. Or, at the very least, she could be supportive.

"They were still just thoughts, Jonas," Appelonia's words started hesitantly, "They aren't actions. Not yet. When we get to Dianmeyer, we can figure out how to separate you from Genevieve and you can find your true center again."

"But thoughts are what eventually become actions!" the man protested, "I can become a real danger to everyone if I'm not careful!"

"You're right," Appelonia nodded, her face looking stern, "You could. That's why you have to exercise diligence, right? Until we can free you of the demonic influence, you have to diligently work to control yourself and your thoughts. When you feel yourself starting to stray, focus on some basic, fundamental teaching of the Order of Stewart."

The paladin finally forced himself to look directly at the red haired woman. For a moment, Jonas looked as worried as when he looked at the suspicious face of Josie, because her daughter wore the exact same stern expression.

But then he realized that he wasn't going to have to go about freeing himself from Genevieve's influence alone. That must have been comforting to him, because his shoulder pauldron's dropped several inches.

"Go ahead and board the ship, Jonas," Appelonia said, "I'll be up in a second. I just want a chance to gather myself. So I don't cry at the sight of my parents again."

She gave him a self-conscious wave as he turned toward the ship. That conversation definitely didn't go the way she thought it would.

Appelonia turned to look out over the river. The sun was transitioning to afternoon. They were going to have to stay a full night on the *Galleon* before they finally reached Loch Aeris again. From there they would head for Maid Gulch, then back to Dianmeyer.

The trip was going to take awhile, particularly with Andromeda's broken leg. With her father there, though, it was likely Kuan Yin would be able to bestow some healing power to aid in the mare's recovery.

Appelonia herself was looking forward to being able to sleep in her own bed again. Sure, to her it only felt as if a few days had passed but her parents insisted that it had been three months! No wonder she was tired.

"Appelonia?" the voice of Ophelia drifted over the woman's pointed ears. "Are you okay?"

The red haired woman turned to face the mercenary, who was several inches taller. All while she was growing up, she always thought Ophelia was just so much... bigger. Bigger than her, bigger than the rules, maybe even bigger than life itself. That just made the fact that they looked to be about the same age all the more strange.

Appelonia remembered Ophelia being the first 'tree' she ever climbed. And like a tree, she looked almost exactly the same. That meant, of course, that Lyan Yo Bunpy her first mountain.

As the memories washed over her, Appelonia couldn't help but grin, "I'm fine. My parents still love me, I'm going home, and no one is going to have to die for me now. I can't get much better."

"That's good to hear," Ophelia draped an arm over the shoulders of the shorter woman, "I saw Harby and Josie. They must have been relieved to see you."

"They were," Apple nodded, "I thought I'd only been gone a couple of days. But time moves faster in Nova Prime so, to them, its been three months."

"I'm surprised they let you out of their sight at all then," the mercenary looked back toward the ship.

"I asked them to get back on board," the red haired woman replied.

"So you could talk to that Jonas guy," Ophelia grinned.

"Spying on me?" Apple eyed her suspiciously.

"More like on him," the other woman laughed, "He's nice to look at, after all."

"Did you hear what we talked about?"

Ophelia nodded, "Poor paladin. He's having to think like a normal person for a little while. What a tragedy."

"How sardonic of you, my dear," Havarti chimed in.

"That's how normal people think?" Apple scowled at the other woman.

"Maybe 'normal' was the wrong word," Ophelia sighed. "How about 'typical'? You've been raised by clerics. Not everyone has religion from day one."

"I guess." Appelonia shrugged. "But my problem is I don't have it anymore."

The mercenary nodded as she guided the young woman toward the ship, "That was something I wanted to talk to you about."

"What?" the elf felt her curiosity pique.

"You heard what Tokki called Lyan, right?" Ophelia said.

Appelonia nodded, "The False One."

"It's my fault they think of her that way," the other woman admitted.

"I suppose explaining why would be a–" Apple started.

And Havarti finished for her, "A long story."

"So what do you need from me?" the red haired woman shrugged.

"I think it's high time to redeem Lyan Yo Bunpy," Ophelia said, "Don't you?"

Appelonia nodded, though she did look uncertain, "What can I do about that? I don't have my spirtual powers anymore. And the Yo Bunpy don't think much of clerics anyway."

"Then it's a good think you're not a cleric anymore," the other woman answered, "No, what I need is your help tracking her down. You have a nose for tracking as good as your Mom's. Not to mention that you have an in with everyone else I want to get to help me."

"You mean Phinegann and the others?" Appelonia sighed, "I don't have a pilgrimage anymore. There's nothing to keep them from leaving Dianmeyer after they all get paid off."

"You'll see, Apple," Ophelia smirked, "You'd be surprised at how far loyalty can get you."

"You really think I can convince them all to go to the Land of the Long Toothed Rabbit?" the elf asked.

"Some will be harder sells than others," Ophelia admitted, "Like Tokki. I say it's high time we educate him on the *real* Lyan Yo Bunpy. Don't you?"

Appelonia agreed wholeheartedly.

"Then let's go have a conversation with a bunny about a mountain," the mercenary slapped her hands together.

Decades before...

THE DAWN HADN'T even had a chance to spill its light through the window yet. Lyan Yo Bunpy, however, was already up. The unsealed, unfolded parchment rested on the bed. She had read it several times to make sure there were no mistakes, no room for misinterpretation.

The Bunny Barbarian tucked the pink blanket, that she had loaned to Hero before, back into her heavy pack. She looked around the room that Folken had seen fit to provide her for her visit in Emerald City. It was easily the most luxurious space she had ever slept in. Everyone in the group had rooms of similar opulence.

Admittedly, the warrior had not expected to be leaving so soon. Lyan had been keeping an eye on Ophelia, awaiting any sign, any hint of her reverting back into what the barbarian had called the Angel of Destruction. That was, of course, before Lyan suspected the mercenary of being the Great Evil that the Bunny Barbarian was prophesied to destroy.

But Lyan could put that aside. For this, the warrior could.

Slinging the pack over the barbarian's broad shoulders, Lyan stepped out the door. The Bunny Barbarian would have to be silent as Lyan marched down to the lower floor of the building. The whole reason Lyan was leaving so early was to keep from disturbing everyone else. This was a matter for the Yo Bunpy people alone.

Lyan strode down the stairs. All that was left was the foyer and then the front door. After a short march to the city gates, it was merely a matter of turning north for the mountains.

Three long couches, able to hold up to five (normal sized) people surrounded a fireplace that was on the opposite wall as the oak doors that led outside. The first wasn't burning at the moment. No one else in the household was awake yet to light it.

The stairs ended just behind the couches. It gave the barbarian a good view of almost the entirety of the ground floor. The only wall that separated any of the rooms from the others was on the opposite side of the building, concealing the kitchen.

The Bunny Barbarian considered going in and taking some food for the trip but it felt improper without explicit permission. Besides, a warrior of the Yo Bunpy was more than capable of hunting and gathering their own sustenance.

So Lyan headed straight for the exit. As she reached for the handle...

"What's the hurry?" the voice of Ophelia came from behind the barbarian.

Lyan froze. She had not expected anyone else to be up, obviously, least of all the mercenary. Last the Bunny Barbarian had heard, she was in the room of one of the men from the Forge Guild of the Romefeller Guilds.

"It is time I moved on," Lyan's answer was vague, but hardly a lie.

Ophelia sat up and leaned over the backrest of the couch she had been lying on, "This have something to do with that letter you got from home?"

"And how do you know of this?" the Bunny Barbarian turned her back on the door.

"The messenger wasn't overly subtle," the woman mercenary answered, "The rabbit shaped wax seal was kind of a giveaway."

"I told you that I am meant to travel alone," the barbarian shrugged back, "So I am doing so."

"What's the trouble, Lyan?" Ophelia asked, "Your people wouldn't call you back from a mission to fulfill a world saving prophecy if it wasn't something monumental."

"They simply... call for aid," the warrior again answered vaguely, again turning and reaching for the handle of the door.

"And you jump straight into action for family," Ophelia commented.

"It is not something I expect you to understand," Lyan started pulling the door open.

The mercenary's hand wrapped around one of the barbarian's massive shoulders, stopping her movement. Lyan had not even realized that Ophelia had risen from the couch.

"I wasn't criticizing you," Ophelia said, "It was volunteering."

"Volunteering?" the massive warrior scowled, "For what?"

"To go to the Land of the Long Toothed Rabbit and help you," the woman answered.

"I cannot ask you–" Lyan's protest started.

And the mercenary interrupted, "You didn't. That's the problem with you honorable types. Your friends want to help when you find yourselves in need."

Shame bit at the Yo Bunpy's stomach as the memory of what she asked of Folken's flashed across her mind, "It is a private matter."

"You cannot expect those who care for your well being to not come to your assistance, my warrior friend," Havarti chimed in from Ophelia's back, "To do so would be like you refusing to aid your countrymen. It would dishonor all of us."

"All of us?" Lyan's brow furrowed under her furry helmet.

Ophelia stepped around the Bunny Barbarian and pulled the door open herself. Just outside the building, Saya, Folken, Hero, Harbenigyr, and Josie stood beside their respective steeds.

Saya, wearing black cloak with a collar lined with dark red fur to hold off the morning chill, smiled when the mercenary and Lyan emerged from the bed and breakfast. Steam escaped from between her painted scarlet lips as she gave the two a kind greeting.

Folken gave Lyan a formal bow simultaneously with the greeting from his cousin. Long, thin green feathers blossomed from the collar of his long black coat. Of course, with the man being among the highest ranks of the Romefeller Guilds, gold patterns where threaded into the dark material.

If Lyan wasn't mistaken, the barbarian thought she could see the outline of a polished black breastplate wrapped around the torso of the magician. He was surely prepared for trouble.

The short bard was beside the albino svartalfar man. Her uniform had been cleaned and pressed. The lute on her back polished and it was a sure thing that it had been tuned to a perfect pitch. She waved at Lyan sheepishly as she turned to her horse to pull something out of one of the saddlebags.

Harbenigyr was back into a long white tunic that looked more like the one he had when the Bunny Barbarian first met him. His shoulders, however, seemed wider. That vest of chainmail, complete with the thin pauldrons, must have been sewn in under the fabric.

Those sticks that had been his quarterstaff before it was snapped in half were sanded, polished and hanging off a new belt. The leather around his waist also held more pouches than seemed possible. His healing supplies had been replenished.

Josie looked almost exactly the same as she always did, with the exception of the gray cloak she wore around her shoulders to counter the cool predawn air. When any light, which only came from the lanterns that lit the streets of Emerald City at the moment, hit it just right the cloak reflected a rich green color.

Beside her was a new steed as well. It was a massive dire wolf with white fur. It was easily as tall as the griffin, Triton, that Harby rode. Lyan was hardly an expert but, judging from how the red haired ranger was looking over at the cleric as she gently stroked the canine's fluffy neck, the full-blooded elf may have had a hand in finding this new, exotic steed for her.

Triton loosed a trumpeting call, eliciting a bid for silence from the healer. It was immediately followed up with petting of the beast's feathers and apologies for being 'harsh'.

Saya and Folken's horses were again coal black. The sorcerer's stallion, of course, was several hands taller than that of his cousin.

Hero had the same horse that had been given to her back in Laeradr. It looked fat, happy and somewhat reluctant to leave the surely luxurious treatment it had been given over the last several days.

Two unmanned horses, one caramel brown and the other a shining blue, awaited their riders. Ophelia stepped down onto the street and immediately strode over to the caramel mare.

Slipping up onto the back of the horse, Ophelia motioned to the blue one, "For you."

Lyan walked down the steps and onto the cobblestone road, "You know I do not need an animal to ride."

"It's not for riding," Ophelia smirked, "He can haul your bags for you while you can march to your heart's content on your furry pads."

When the Bunny Barbarian looked at the horse again, she noticed that there indeed was no saddle. It was also even larger than Folken's steed. Lyan did not need a pack animal, either, but it would be nice to at least walk without all the extra weight slowing down the pace.

The warrior stepped over to the blue horse, taking his reins from the mercenary, "Does he have a name?" the barbarian asked, running a hand along the bridge of his long nose.

"Torj'ohnsyn," Ophelia answered.

"Torj'ohnsyn," Lyan repeated, "A good, strong name. Are you willing to haul my supplies for me, Torj'ohnsyn?" she asked the horse.

The stallion nickered, bobbing his head up and down. The Bunny Barbarian nodded back and stepped to the side of the animal, after securing her pack on his back, Lyan started leading Tor'johnsyn to the city gates.

"That has to be the first time I've seen someone actually ask a horse if they wanted to do their job," Ophelia snickered as she rode up beside the barbarian.

"No living thing should be forced into service for another," Lyan responded.

"Dammit, now I'm going to have to have a talk with Vicomte, here," the mercenary patted the neck of her horse, "Because you just said something that I completely agree with."

Ophelia hopped off her saddle and draped an arm over the horse's mane. She leaned in close and started having a conversation with the beast that Lyan couldn't quite hear.

Folken came up beside the Bunny Barbarian, on the side opposite where the mercenary was speaking to her horse, "Slavery, as a practice, is one to be frowned upon. Although, I find it interesting that you wish to slay the servant, rather than the one who seeks to force her to do his will."

Lyan stopped walking right then and there. He was right. While Ophelia did wield the forbidden color in her magicks, it was not by her hand that she was given these cursed gifts.

But she was still a danger to everyone around her, should this Doctor Efreeti somehow regain his control over her. Lyan still had to be prepared but she could not delude herself into believing that Ophelia, herself, was the Great Evil.

Josie had to pull her dire wolf to a stop with a rough tug to keep from running into Lyan after the barbarian stopped so suddenly. The canine let out an annoyed bark but otherwise didn't make a fuss.

"What gives, Lyan?" the ranger asked, "Did you forget something?"

The Bunny Barbarian looked back at the red haired woman, "My apologies. No, I did not forget anything. I merely came to a realization."

"Anything you care to share?" Josie asked.

"Not at the moment," Lyan gave Ophelia one quick glance before starting to march again, "If I am lucky, perhaps I will never have to."

"Okay," the woman looked confused as she trotted her immense wolf around the barbarian and her horse.

As soon as Josie was a few paces ahead, Lyan started marching again. The sun was threatening its arrival over the tops of the nearby mountains to the east. The massive rock formations curved around the city and continued northward, separating the Land of the Long Toothed Rabbit from the rest of the continent.

Now leading her horse, much like Lyan was, Ophelia stepped up beside the Bunny Barbarian, "How does it feel to be heading home again?" she inquired.

"It has only been a few months so I am sure they do not expect me to have fulfilled my purpose yet," the barbarian replied, "However, I feel as if I should be, I do not know, more by now?"

"How do you mean *more*?" Ophelia said.

"While my mission is to destroy the Great Evil, I always believed that I had to become more aware of me," Lyan sighed, "Does that make sense?"

"I think so," the woman nodded, "That's one of the most common reasons I hear from people go on pilgrimages. To find themselves."

"Harby certainly seems to have made some progress on that front," Lyan chuckled.

The Bunny Barbarian watched as the cleric and ranger spoke. The expression on Harbenigyr's face, to anyone not involved in the conversation at least, was silly and he didn't care. Josie, for her part, seemed to find it charming as well. Perhaps defeating a being that was literally the worst parts of him made him realize that he was not as weak as he feared himself to be?

"But you feel that you haven't," Ophelia pulled the other warrior out of her reflections.

Lyan nodded, "All my life, I feel as if I have not been… complete. All through training as a child, the other warriors treated me different. I always believed that it was because of my status as the Child of Prophesy."

Havarti spoke up, "But, as you traveled, you believe that you have come to another conclusion?"

"I have only become more confused," the Bunny Barbarian grunted, "I have tested my strength against any comer, and even upon victory, been called a woman for my effort. In these lands, it is as if mastery of battle is of no value."

"Lyan," Ophelia turned to face the barbarian, walking backwards as she continued to talk, "You do realize that you *are* a woman, right? It's not an insult, it's a biological fact."

"Don't be ridiculous!" The Bunny Barbarian scoffed, her voice just this side of a shriek, "Women aren't allowed to be warriors within the Yo Bunpy! My father wouldn't allow it!"

Ophelia quirked an eyebrow, "There's no reason to get so defensive, Lyan."

"I am not defensive!" the barbarian snapped, "I am stating the truths of my people!"

"Who is your father to the Yo Bunpy, Lyan?" Ophelia acted as if she already knew the answer to the question.

"He is our Chief. Our leader into battle," she answered, "He would not perpetrate such a dishonorable deception. Not to me!"

"Were there any other warriors born on the night that the conditions for being the Child of Prophesy occurred?" the mercenary asked.

"No," Lyan shook her head, "Otherwise I would have been challenged for the mantle before leaving on my hunt."

"Did you ever bathe with the other warriors?" Ophelia smirked as the question crossed her lips, "Ever bedded any of them? Or any woman within the tribe?"

"No, I always trained longer than the other warriors," Lyan's brow started to ache, it furrowed so tightly, "I always bathed alone."

"What about bedding someone?" the other woman asked again.

Lyan shook her head, "I always thought chasing after the women was a distraction from my mission. The other men would not... even speak to me about such things."

"And you don't *any* of this unusual?" Ophelia said, "None of the other warriors bragged to you about which wench they had their way with the night before? Never heard a woman talk to her friends about how this warrior performed in bed compared to that warrior? Like I have with you?"

Again, Lyan shook her head. Her face was a mask of shock and doubt. She leaned into Torj'onhsyn for support to be able to keep walking.

"But my father, he would never pull such a cruel deception on his own blood. Would he?" the Bunny Barbarian looked back at Ophelia, her brown eyes practically pleading with her.

"I don't think he was trying to be cruel, Lyan." Ophelia responded, "I think he just didn't know what to do. Everything about the Child of Prophesy sounds connected to the warrior caste of your people. He must have thought that some kind of a mistake had been made. So he just did his best and raised you the way he would have raised a warrior."

"You are saying that I am some kind of mistake?" the woman could not have wounded Lyan any more effectively without actually pulling her sword from its scabbard.

"Not at all, child," speaking of the sword, Havarti spoke up again, "When one is given a situation they do not expect, they fall back on what they do know to get through. While you being female was not mentioned in the prophecy, your being a warrior was. So he raised a warrior in the only way he knew."

"And it's pretty obvious that he trusts you," Ophelia added, "He must believe in you, too. To call you back home for help. We'll just have to make him understand that women can be warriors, too."

"If I am a woman," Lyan scratched at an itch that wasn't really there on her cheek, "Of which I am still not convinced. Nor about their abilities as warriors."

"Tell you what," Ophelia grinned wide at the Bunny Barbarian, "when we stop for camp tonight, you and I can have a sparring match. If I win we'll both get undressed and compare body parts. If yours match mine, you have to accept that you're a woman. Agreed?"

The fact that the mercenary seemed to enjoy the idea so much was a touch disconcerting to the warrior. But, Ophelia had always treated her fairly. Besides, what if she was right? What if Lyan was, in fact, a woman? Her father should acknowledge this fact.

"My only caveat is that if you use your blinking during our match, you automatically forfeit," Lyan responded.

"Agreed," Ophelia spit in her right hand and held it out to the Bunny Barbarian.

"Are you sure you wish to commit that thoroughly?" Lyan eyed the mercenary's offered hand, "Spittle-vows are hardly to be taken lightly."

"Spittle-vow?" Ophelia laughed, "Do the Yo Bunpy take everything like this so seriously?"

"We do." Lyan spit into her hand and shook the other woman's. "We also do not lose."

"We'll see who's the winner when our pants are off," Ophelia winked.

It would almost be a shame if she did turn out to be a woman. Lyan thought that it would not have been the worst fate to be among Ophelia's stories of conquest.

ABOUT THE AUTHOR

Spencer Stoner lives in Reno, Nevada. He is the third of four children, the other three being sisters. In addition to writing, he is also a black belt in American Kenpo Karate and draws as a hobby. (He draws a lot of his characters to make sure they don't get, what he calls, "wandering mole syndrome".)

Spencer also an avid gamer, appreciating a good, digital story. It doesn't matter if they are role playing games, fighting games (which have been improving their story presentations lately!) or side-scrolling Metroidvanias. If you're one to play online, you may spot him by his player ID: sjcloudxiii.

www.ingramcontent.com/pod-product-compliance
Lightning Source LLC
Chambersburg PA
CBHW050559170726
48283CB00001B/32